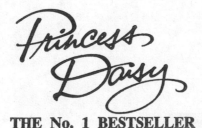

THE No. 1 BESTSELLER

"With unfailing panache and a style
that swoops from crisply cynical
to downright voluptuous, Princess Daisy
is a guaranteed winner."
—*Cosmopolitan*

"THOROUGHLY ENTERTAINING."
—*Over 21*

"In true saga style,
this blockbuster weaves its spell across
an international landscape.
A breathless spin of a romance."
—Kitty Kelley, *Hollywood Reporter*

"THIS PAGE-TURNER IS A CHAMPION."
—*People*

Also by Judith Krantz

MISTRAL'S DAUGHTER

and published by Corgi Books

JUDITH KRANTZ

Princess Daisy

CORGI BOOKS

PRINCESS DAISY

A CORGI BOOK 0 552 11660 2

Originally published in Great Britain by
Sidgwick & Jackson Ltd.

PRINTING HISTORY
Sidgwick & Jackson edition published 1980
Corgi edition published 1981
Corgi edition reprinted 1981 (twice)
Corgi edition reprinted 1983
Corgi edition reprinted 1984 (twice)

Copyright © 1980 by Steve Krantz Productions

Corgi Books are published by Transworld Publishers Ltd.,
Century House, 61-63 Uxbridge Road,
Ealing, London W5 5SA.
Printed and bound in Great Britain by
Hunt Barnard Printing Ltd., Aylesbury, Bucks.

For Steve—
my husband, my love, my best friend—always.

Special thanks go to these good friends who answered questions with the gift of their experience:

Bernie Owett

Steve Elliot

Dan Dorman

Aaron Shikler

and, particularly, to Rosemary de Courcy and her lurcher, Jake.

Princess Daisy

1

$\mathcal{W}$e could always shoot this on top of the RCA Building," Daisy said, walking past the parapet, above which rose a high, metal railing designed to forestall would-be suicides. "They're not nearly as paranoid as you Empire State people." She gestured scornfully at the ledge behind her. "But, Mr. Jones, if it's not the view from precisely here, the message just won't be New York."

The man in uniform watched, motionless in surprise, as Daisy suddenly leapt high and held on to a rung of the railing with one strong hand. With her other hand she took off the sailor hat under which she had tucked her hair and let it blow free. The silver-gilt tumble was caught by the breeze that separated it into a million brave and dazzling threads.

"Come down, Miss," the man in charge of the Observation Deck begged. "I told you it's just not allowed."

"Look, I'm trying to show you what we're after," Daisy persisted. "It's a hairspray commercial, and artistically, what's a hairspray commercial without wind blowing in the hair—can you tell me that? Just hanks of hair, all chunky and boring—wind is *essential*, Mr. Jones."

The uniformed official looked up at Daisy with perplexed admiration and dismay. He didn't understand anything about her. She was young and more beautiful than anyone he'd ever seen but she wore a man's moldy baseball jacket which bore the now mournful legend BROOKLYN DODGERS on its back, a pair of United States Navy sailor pants and dirty tennis shoes. He was far from a romantic man, but everything about her stung his imagination with an unaccustomed fascination. He found himself curiously unable to look away from her. She was as tall as he, at least five feet, seven inches, and something about the way she walked had suggested the balance of the trained athlete even before she had jumped up to the perch from which she now gestured, intrepid, high-hearted, as if she were trying to catch a beam of the sun itself. The roof supervisor was aware of a particular clarity and cadence in her speech that made him think that perhaps she wasn't American, yet who but an American would dress like that? When she'd first appeared all she'd asked was for permission to film a commercial on his roof and now she was hanging up there like a goddamned angel on a Christmas tree. Thank heaven the place was closed for the day.

"You can't go up there. You didn't tell me you wanted to the last time you came," he reproached her, circling cautiously closer. "It's never permitted. It could be dangerous."

"But all great art has to break rules," Daisy called down to him gaily, remembering that when she had first checked out this location, a week ago, two twenty-dollar bills had ensured Mr. Jones's cooperation. She had many more twenties in her pocket. Several years as a producer of commercials had taught her to travel strictly on folding money.

Daisy scrambled a little higher and took a deep breath. It was a fresh, glinting spring day in 1975 and the wind had blown all the soot away from the city; the rivers that circled the island were as blue and as lively as the ocean itself, and Central Park was a great Oriental rug flung at the feet of the gray apartment buildings of Fifth Avenue.

She smiled down at the worried man looking up at her. "Listen, Mr. Jones, I know all three models we're going to use; one of them lives on raw veggies and is working on her black belt in Karate, the second has just been signed for her first movie and the third is an est trainer who's engaged to marry a man with oil wells—now, would three wholesome American girls like that have any intention of jumping? We're going to build a strong, absolutely safe platform for them to stand on. I guarantee it personally."

"A platform! You never said . . ."

Daisy jumped down and stood close to him. Her dark eyes, not quite black, but the color of the innermost heart of a giant purple pansy, caught the late afternoon light and held it fast, as she deftly pressed two folded bills into his hand. "Mr. Jones, I'm sorry if I alarmed you. Honestly, it's safe as houses up there—you ought to try it."

"I just don't know, Miss."

"Ah, come on," Daisy cajoled him. "Didn't you promise me you'd be all ready for us on Monday? Didn't you promise me a special freight elevator open for business at six A.M.?"

"But you never said anything about going *above* the roof level," he grumbled.

"Roof level!" Daisy said indignantly. "If all we wanted was a simple high view there must be a dozen buildings in this city we could use—but we want yours, Mr. Jones, no one else's." The story board for the commercial had specifically stated the Empire State Building. Leave it to Revlon to complicate her life. As Daisy reached into her reserve pocket for an additional twenty, she remembered that, three years before, when she had started working as a production assistant, she had first seen a taxi-cab driver cheerfully accept forty dollars to turn off his meter to allow his taxi to be used for six hours in the background of a street scene. "But that's bribing people," Daisy had objected. "Think of it as rent, if you want to stay in the business." She'd been warned, and she'd taken the advice. Now, as the experienced producer of many of the best commercials ever filmed—if you like commercials—Daisy was hardened to the objections of civilians, and if Mr. Jones was more difficult than many, he was easier than some. Her next gambit was the one that usually clinched matters.

"Oh, I forgot to tell you," she said, coming closer to him. "The director wanted to know if you'd be in the commercial, standing there in the background, like the keeper of the keys to the kingdom. We only pay Screen Actors' Guild minimum, so you don't have to do it if you don't want to—we could hire an actor to play you, but it wouldn't be nearly as authentic."

"Well . . ."

"And, of course, you'd have to have make-up," she said, playing her best card.

"Oh. I guess it'll be all right. Yeah, without wind in the hair why would you need hairspray? I see your point. Make-up, huh? And would I have to wear a costume?"

"Your uniform will be perfect, just as it is. Goodbye,

Mr. Jones—I'll see you first thing Monday morning." Daisy waved cheerfully at him as she walked toward the covered center core of the building. As she waited for the elevator to reach the eighty-sixth floor, the blonde girl in the baseball jacket, born Princess Marguerite Alexandrovna Valensky, reflected that it was truly fortunate that there was one thing you could count on in this world: *everybody* wanted to be in show biz.

Mr. Jones was only one in a long line of men who had been fascinated by something in Daisy Valensky. Among the first of them had been the famed photographer, Philippe Halsman, the man who would take more *Life* cover photographs than any other in the history of the magazine. In the late summer of 1952 he had been assigned to take Daisy's first official photographs for a *Life* cover, since absolutely everyone, or so it seemed to the editors of the magazine, wanted to know what the child of Prince Stash Valensky and Francesca Vernon looked like. The sudden marriage of the great war hero and incomparable polo player to the matchless romantic American movie star had intrigued the world and inspired rumors which were only expanded and exaggerated by the seclusion in which Prince and Princess Valensky had lived with their first child since her birth in April.

Now, in August, Francesca Vernon Valensky sat in a field of long grass, in a Swiss meadow, with Daisy in her arms. Halsman found the actress faintly pensive, even remote, although he had photographed her twice before, the second time after she had won an Oscar for her Juliet. But it was the laughing child who interested him even more than the mystery of her mother's mood. The tiny girl was like a new hybrid rose in the inconsistency of her coloring. By rights, he thought, only generations of selective breeding should have produced a child who had the classically Italian dark eyes of her mother, and skin that had a Tuscan warmth to it, like the particular part of a peach into which you bite first, knowing that it will be the ripest spot on the fruit. Yet her little head was covered with Saxon-white curls that blew around her vivid face like the corolla of a flower.

Stash Valensky's old wet nurse, Masha, who still formed part of his household, had, with her characteristic self-importance, informed the photographer that Princess Daisy's hair was exactly like that of her father when he was a child. It was true blonde hair, she explained proudly, which may become gold in time but never changes to ash brown with age. She boasted of this Valensky hair, which was found somewhere in each generation as far back as the family could be traced, yes, back to the days of the earliest hereditary Russian nobility, the *boyars,* who were the companions of the Tsars for almost a thousand years before Peter the Great. After all, she asked, almost indignantly, was not her master a direct descendant of Rurik, the Scandinavian Prince who had founded the Russian monarchy in the 800s? Halsman quickly agreed with her that little Daisy's hair would always remain blonde. Remembering Masha's imperious ways, and realizing that she would soon be coming to take the infant back for her supper, he worked quickly to make the most of the time left to him.

Tactfully, he decided not to ask Francesca to jump in the air for a picture, his favorite ploy after a sitting, and a trick he had practiced with success on many celebrities and dignitaries of the highest order. Instead, the photographer used his charm to cajole Stash Valensky, who had been standing behind him, observing the scene, into posing with his wife and daughter.

But for all his poise and pulsing authority, Valensky was not at ease in front of a camera. He had lived for much of his forty-one years with two phrases somewhere in the back of his mind. One of them came from Tolstoy: ". . . living like a nobleman is a nobleman's business, only the nobility can do it." The other phrase came from a tattered text on the beliefs of Hinduism which had fallen into his hands during a brief period of hospital convalescence after he had bailed out of his first Hurricane fighter plane during the Battle of Britain. "Be like the eagle when it soars above the abyss. The eagle does not think about flying, it simply feels that it flies."

Neither of these two guiding principles permitted him to feel comfortable while holding still for a photograph. He was so stiff that Halsman, in a flash of inspiration, suggested that they go to the stables where the Prince's nine polo ponies were kept in loose-boxes, attended to by three grooms.

Francesca cradled Daisy in her arms while Valensky indicated the fine points of the animals. Carried away by his enthusiasm, Valensky had just invited the photographer to inspect the mouth of his favorite pony, Merlin, when

Halsman wondered out loud if the pony would allow the Prince to lift Daisy on his back.

"Why not? Merlin has a contented mind."

"But he isn't saddled," Francesca objected.

"So much the better. Daisy will have to learn to ride bareback some day."

"She still can't sit up by herself," Francesca said nervously.

"I don't intend to let go of her." The Prince laughed, firmly taking the baby and setting her astride the low curve of the pony's back between loins and withers. Francesca reached up to steady her child and Halsman finally got his cover picture; the magnificent man and the magnificent woman, their hands clasped around the little body, faces uplifted eagerly toward the sprite in a flowered lawn dress whose hands fluttered the air in jubilation.

"She has no fear, Francesca," Stash exclaimed proudly. "I knew she wouldn't have. Valensky women have ridden hard for hundreds of years—haven't I told you?"

"More than once, darling," Francesca answered with a laugh that held a wisp of sadness in its loving mockery, a laugh that only sounded for a brief moment. It was at that instant Halsman decided that the timing was right to get a jumping picture of the Prince. When he proposed the idea Valensky barely hesitated. Then, lifting Daisy from Merlin's back, he grasped her under her arms, held her high above his head, and jumped straight up into the air, with a wild and ferocious leap. The child screamed with delight and Francesca Valensky shuddered, she who had once been so dangerously reckless. What had this marriage done to her, Halsman wondered?

2

$\mathscr{N}$ormally the *Queen Mary* makes the New York to Southampton crossing without a stop. On this particular trip, in June of 1951, the great engines came to a full halt as the ship arrived at Cherbourg. It lay just outside the harbor while a barge approached the ocean liner and tied up at a baggage port. A dozen sailors wheeled large carts piled with luggage down the gangplank and deposited it in two heaps, one mountainous and one relatively modest. By the time all the trunks and suitcases were arranged, thousands of curious passengers crowded the railings to discover the reason for the unexplained delay. After a brief wait, three people walked down the gangplank, a slender man, arm in arm with a trim woman, preceded by four small excitable dogs, and finally another woman whom the college students in third class immediately recognized and greeted with cheers and applause. While Francesca Vernon sat on one of her suitcases and waved merrily at her admirers, the Duke and Duchess of Windsor, standing with dignity near the dozens of steamer trunks which held their summer wardrobes, saw no reason to respond to the democratic hullabaloo, nor did they deign to even nod to the actress whose face was as famous as theirs. Since they never set foot in England, yet always traveled by Cunard, their yearly arrival on the Continent was made in this unfortunately public fashion. While on board the *Queen* they invariably ate in their suite and only emerged to walk their band of cairns. Inured by habit, resolutely they paid no attention to the spectators, but to Francesca the audience only increased the swelling thrill she felt as the barge approached the customs shed where her agent, Matty Firestone, and his wife, Margo, were waiting for her.

The Firestones had been in Europe for several weeks before her arrival. They had rented a huge, prewar Delahaye touring car and engaged an English-speaking chauffeur. Francesca sat mute with expectation as the car sped along the poplar-lined roads leading to Paris. Her dark beauty, which spoke of fifteenth-century Italy in its uncontemporary cut and fashion, was lit by most unclassic anticipation as she leaned forward on the cushions of the car. She possessed a combination of tranquility and pure sensuality in the composition of the essential triangle of eyes and mouth. Her black eyes were long and widely spaced, her mouth, even in repose, was made meaningful by the grace of its shape: the gentle arc of her upper lip dipped in the center to meet the lovely pillow of her lower lip in a line that had the power of an embrace. Margo watched her with maternal emotion. She thought that Francesca had never been quite as touching in any of her roles as she was now, her whole being ignited with the excitement of her first hours on European soil. Few people besides Margo, who had been her friend, confidante and protector for six years, knew just how influenced by the stuff of fairy tales and stories of high romance the twenty-four-year-old movie star still was.

"We'll do Paris for a week, honey," Matty told his client, "and then the grand tour. Straight down France to the Riviera, then along the coast until we get to Italy. We'll hit Florence, Rome and Venice and go back to Paris through Switzerland. Two months of it. Sound good to you?"

Francesca was too moved to answer.

By late August the Firestones and Francesca returned to Paris, where Margo had serious shopping to finish before their ship sailed at the end of the month. They stayed at the George V, then and now the hotel for rich tourists who don't care that the hotel is full of other rich tourists, but who do care about good beds, room service and efficient plumbing.

In the hotel bar, on the first evening of their return, Matty was greeted by David Fox, a studio vice-president he lunched with at least once a month back in Hollywood.

"You all have to come to Deauville for the polo match

next week," David insisted. "It's the first important one since the war."

"Polo?" asked Matty indignantly. "A bunch of fancy no-goods on nervous little ponies? Who needs it?"

"But they've reached the finals—everyone will be there," David persisted.

"How do they dress in Deauville?" Margo interrupted curiously.

"Exactly the same way you'd dress for a cruise on the largest yacht in the world," the man replied knowingly. "And, of course, everyone changes three times a day."

Margo barely prevented herself from licking her lips. The semi-marine mode had always been particularly kind to her.

"Matty, darling, I *need* to go to Deauville," she announced, with an inflection that told Matty there was no use in further discussion.

Deauville, that timelessly chic resort, was established on the coast of Normandy by the Duc de Morny in 1866. From its inception it was intended to be a paradise for moneyed aristocrats, deeply involved in racing, gambling and golf. Because the grass of Normandy is the richest in France, its cows produce the best cheese, cream and butter. This same grass inevitably attracts Horse People, and the breeding and raising of horses takes place on the great stud farms of the surrounding countryside. The city of Deauville itself consists almost entirely of hotels, shops, cafés and restaurants, but the fresh sea air provides the illusion that enables the briskly strolling crowd on the boardwalk, the Edwardian *Promenade des Planches,* to imagine that the previous night, spent at the casino, must have been, in some way, good for their health.

The Hotel Normandy, in which Matty had been able to secure last-minute accommodations, is built in the English half-timbered style, rather as if someone had taken a normal country manor house and turned it into a seaside giant. In August, the Normandy, the Royal and the Hotel du Golf shelter a large portion of the people who will, inevitably, be in Paris in October, in St. Moritz in February and in London in June.

In 1951 these people were called the International Set. For lack of an engine the term "Jet Set" didn't exist, but even then newspapers and magazines, although less preoccupied than they are now, were fascinated by the comings and goings of this gilded mob who had, somehow, escaped the mundane, workaday world.

It was all fueled by money, although money alone didn't guarantee entry. Charm, beauty, talent—none of these attributes, even added to money, could make a person part of the International Set. What was essential was the willingness, the wholehearted intention to spend a life of a certain *kind;* a life in which the pursuit of pleasure and leisure could go on and on for years on end without causing any guilt, a life in which work had little meaning, and accomplishment, except in sports and gambling, had no place of honor. It was a life in which one's best efforts were expended on the exteriors and décors of life; grooming, fashion, luxurious and exotic interiors, constant travel, entertainment and wide acquaintance, rather than deep friendships.

Integral to the life of the International Set was the man then called a playboy. The true playboy did not usually have a great deal of money himself, but he was only to be found where the money was. He had good humor, reliable charm, the capacity to acquit himself well at almost any game, the tact to drink like a gentleman, to avoid gambling debts and to give women so much pleasure that they inevitably told their friends about him.

Prince Alexander Vassilivitch Valensky was not a playboy. But since he could so often be found where playboys clustered, the press had dubbed Stash Valensky a playboy as a careless point of reference.

Stash Valensky's vast personal fortune separated him completely from the playboy ranks. It was a fortune he had never had to question, even in his periods of wildest extravagance. Indeed, he never had to consider himself extravagant since he could afford to spend whatever he chose. The easeful relationship to wealth had been common to his ancestors, right down to his father, the late Prince Vasily Alexandrovitch Valensky. Nevertheless, Stash Valensky could never have been called a businessman. Until 1939, when polo stopped for the duration of World War II, he had devoted most of his adult life to the game. He had carried a nine-goal handicap since 1935, which made him one of the top ten players in a sport in which it was so expensive to participate that only nine thousand men in the world ever played it at any one time.

Valensky had the physical presence of a great athlete who has punished his body without pity throughout his life and the watchful, fighting eyes of a natural predator. His glance was bold and his thick brows were many shades darker than his blond hair, cropped short and as coarse as the coat of a hastily brushed dog. Valensky had never had to ask for anything. Either it had been given to him or he had taken it. His nose, broken many times, gave him the air of a roughneck. He had well-weathered, outdoorsman's skin and strong, blunt, almost brutal features, but he walked with the gait, rapid and graceful, of a man who was in control wherever he found himself. He was considered to have the best "hands" in the world of international polo. Not only did Valensky never employ unnecessary force on the bit and reins but he had been born, as some men are, with an instinct for establishing a communication between himself and his pony which made it seem as if the animal was merely an extension of his mind, rather than a beast with a will of its own.

Nevertheless, Prince Valensky owned nine ponies, rather than the more usual five or six, because he rode like a barbarian. It is not safe to ride a polo pony, galloping and turning at top speed, for more than two chukkers in any single game. Stash rode so aggressively that he preferred to have a fresh pony for each of the six chukkers and he chose never to have fewer than three animals in reserve. According to the rules of the Hurlingham Polo Association, under which he played, no man is allowed to "Ride at an opponent in such a manner as to intimidate and cause him to pull out." Stash stopped just short of that ambiguous distinction, but he never rode at an adversary without the clear mental intention of unhorsing him. There were many players who thought that the HPA Field Rules should have contained some special penalty which would disqualify Valensky, although no umpire had ever yet ordered him off the field.

It was a gala day in Deauville as the crowds pressed politely into the stands for the polo finals. When the Mayor of the city had been informed by the management of the Hotel Normandy that Francesca Vernon was their guest, he had called at the hotel in person and, with great formality, asked if she would present the cup to the winner of the day's match.

"The honor was to have been mine, Mademoiselle," he

told her, "but it would be a great day for Deauville if you would consent." The Mayor understood perfectly that with the participation of a film star the outcome of the play would be covered more prominently than if it were a mere sporting event.

"Well. . .," Francesca said, hesitating for form's sake, but already she saw herself clearly at the center of the competition.

"She'd love to," Margo assured the Mayor. She owned a white silk suit trimmed with touches of navy that she hadn't worn yet on this trip. She had suspected that it might be too formal for polo, but if Francesca had a place in the proceedings it would look entirely suitable. Margo was a great fan of pictures of royal personages presenting things to natives, something she would never have admitted, even to Matty. Sometimes Margo saw herself standing, gracious, smiling and about five inches taller than she was, being handed a huge bouquet of roses by a small curtsying child. It would never happen to her, but why shouldn't it happen to Francesca?

The Firestones and Francesca watched the match with interest which soon turned into confusion. The play was really too fast to follow without some familiarity with its intricate rules. However, the atmosphere of the match was electric. Polo spectators are elegantly dressed, superbly perfumed and given to a kind of upper-class hysteria which balances the intense knowledgeability of the bullring crowd in Madrid with the polite, dandified excitement of Ascot. All three of them soon gave up trying to figure out what had triggered the moments of applause or groans and gave themselves up to the spectacle of eight great athletes riding fast horses. What ballet is to dance, what chess is to board games, polo is to sport.

A burst of cheering signaled the end of the match. The Mayor of Deauville approached their seats and held out his hand to Francesca. "Quickly, Mademoiselle Vernon," he said. "The ponies are hot—we must not keep them out on the field."

Francesca, holding the Mayor's arm, picked her way across the polo grounds, now marred by divots which had been kicked up by the ponies' hooves. The full skirt of her green silk dress, printed with tiny blue and white flowers, snapped like a sail in the stiff breeze. She wore a large white straw hat with an undulating brim, banded and ribboned in the silk of her dress. As she used one hand to keep it on her head, Francesca realized that at some time during the match she must have lost her hatpins. The actress and the Mayor approached the spot where the eight players, all still mounted, were waiting for her. The Mayor spoke briefly, first in French and then in English. Abruptly he handed Francesca a heavy silver trophy. Automatically, in order to receive the trophy, she took her hand off her hat. It blew off at once, and went skimming along the ground, bounding from one tuft of turf to another.

"Oh no!" she exclaimed in dismay, but as she spoke, Stash Valensky leaned down from his pony and scooped her up in one arm. Holding her easily, across his chest, he urged his mount after the wayward hat. It had come to rest two hundred yards away, and Valensky, still holding Francesca to him, bent down from his saddle, picked the hat up by its ribbons and carefully replaced it on her head. The stands rang with laughter and applause.

Francesca heard nothing of the noise the spectators made. Time, as she knew it, had stopped. By instinct, she remained silent and waiting, passive against Stash's soaking-wet polo shirt. She could smell his sweat and it confounded her with desire. Her mouth filled with saliva. She wanted to sink her teeth into his tan neck, to bite him until she could taste his blood, to lick up the rivulets of sweat which ran down to his open collar. She wanted him to fall to the ground with her in his arms, just as he was, flushed, steaming, still breathing heavily from the game, and grind himself into her.

Collecting himself, Stash trotted his pony back to the other horsemen. He slid to the ground, Francesca still in his arms, and placed her gently on her feet. Somehow she was still holding the trophy and she tottered in her high heels. He took the cup from her, let it drop to the turf and grabbed both of her hands to steady her. For an instant they stood facing each other, linked. Then he bent from the waist and kissed one of the hands he was holding. Not the formal kiss that barely brushes the air above the hand, but a hard, hot imprint of his mouth.

"Now," he said, looking right into her astonished eyes, "you're supposed to give me the cup." He reached down for it and handed it to her. She gave it back to him, silently. The crowd applauded again, and under that sound, she said, in a barely audible voice, "Hold me again."

"Later."

"When?" Francesca was shocked at her abrupt, naked voice.

"Tonight. Where are you staying?"

"The Normandy."

'Come on. I'll take you back to your seat." He offered her his arm. They didn't speak again until she had been restored to Matty and Margo. Everything essential had been said. Anything else was impossible to say.

"Eight?" he asked.

She nodded agreement. He didn't kiss her hand again, but just bowed slightly and strode out to the field.

"Jesus Christ, what was all that about?" Matty demanded. Francesca didn't answer him. Margo said nothing, because on Francesca's lovely and familiar face she saw a dazed expression which, to Margo, was instantly apparent as a *new* expression, one that had been created by something outside the borders of Francesca's previous experience.

"Come on, darling," she said to the actress, "everybody's leaving." Francesca merely stood where she was, not hearing. "What are you going to *wear?*" Margo said in her ear. This time Francesca heard her.

"It doesn't matter what I wear," she answered.

"What!" Margo was shocked, genuinely shocked, for the first time in twenty years. "Come on, Matty. We've got to get back to the hotel," she ordered, and, leaving him to escort Francesca, she led the way, muttering incredulously to herself. "Doesn't matter! Doesn't *matter?* Has she gone mad?"

Francesca Vernon was the only child of Professor Ricardo della Orso and his wife, Claudia. Her father was head of the Foreign Language Department at the University of California in Berkeley, to which he had immigrated from Florence in the 1920s. Both of Francesca's parents had origins, centuries old, in the many-towered, once noble hill town of San Gimignano, near Florence. In each of their families there had been strikingly lovely women, too many of whom had come to dishonor or disgrace, according to the strict values of their times. For hundreds of years, many a noble Tuscan gentleman had ridden to San Gimignano, attracted by the legend of the glorious daughters of the della Orso and Veronese families. Often, too often, they had not been disappointed.

As soon as Ricardo and Claudia della Orso saw the hereditary features appear in their daughter they realized that she would, inevitably, be beautiful, perhaps unsuitably beautiful. They hoarded their one precious child, keeping her to themselves as much as possible, although Francesca needed the companionship of children her own age. Years in the battlefield of a playground sandbox, and more years in the rough and tumble of kindergarten, throwing things, building things, and playing with all manner of boys and girls, would have been far more healthy for this girl, who had inherited the wild blood of all those dark and captivating women of San Gimignano, than the hundreds of hours that were spent nourishing her fantasy life as, endlessly, her mother read fairy tales out loud.

In their effort to keep Francesca safe, her parents fed her growing mind on old stories of gallant deeds performed for love, of heroes and heroines whose lives were filled with risk and honor. They were a willing audience for the dozens of plays she soon began to perform for them with plots borrowed from the tales on which she had grown up. Her parents, innocent and proud, never understood that they had encouraged Francesca to view herself from the outside, to watch herself *being someone she was not* and take deep pleasure in it, to find role playing more real than anything else life had to offer.

When Francesca was six and went to school, she found her first wider audience. In the part of the crafty Morgiana in a first-grade production of *Ali Baba and the Forty Thieves*, the same "Open Sesame!" that revealed the treasure cave gave her a sure knowledge of her future. She would be an actress. From that moment on, although she seemed, to the outward eye, to be following a normal course through school, she acted in her head. When she wasn't actually involved in the yearly class play, she would come to school in the character of the heroine of the book she was currently reading, and such was her cleverness that she was able to go through an entire school day without betraying herself to her classmates. They found her full of unexpected responses and unexplained moods, but that was just Francesca, who had, by reason of her inaccessibility, come to occupy a high position in the pecking order of school, Everyone wanted to be her friend because so few were granted the privilege.

Year after year, Francesca was given the lead in the school plays, and no one, not even other mothers, ever complained that it was unfair, since she was so clearly better than anyone else. A production in which she played a lesser role than the central one would have been lopsided. She had only to walk out onto a stage to project an inescapable flash of aroused expectation. There was an inevitable quality in her smallest gestures. Francesca didn't learn how to act: she merely turned her roving fancy toward the character she was playing and became that person with such naturalness that it appeared as if all she had done was to unwrap her emotions and let them appear on her face.

"Of all the occupational hazards of an agent's life, high-school plays are my least favorite," complained Matty Firestone.

"What about actresses' love affairs?" asked his wife Margo. "Last week you said they were even worse than negotiating with Harry Cohn."

"Point well taken. At least a play is over quickly," Matty agreed, although he still felt deeply aggrieved at being condemned to seeing a Berkeley High presentation of *Milestones* by Arnold Bennett; a warhorse of a production much favored by graduating classes.

"Don't you dare fall asleep with your eyes open again," Margo warned him affectionately. "It makes me nervous ... and anyway, the Hellmans are your old friends, not mine."

"But you're the one who had to let them know we were in San Francisco. You should have remembered that it's June—graduation month," Matty grumbled. He always expected Margo to have his private life as perfectly organized as her enormous wardrobe. She was the ideal agent's wife; cynical, but never without harmless illusions, warmhearted, unsurprisable and totally kind, just as Matty was the ideal agent; a man of audacity and loyalty, gifted with a keen sense of exactly how far to go in a negotiation; of how much was too much and how little was too little; added to a scrupulous disinclination ever to tell an actual lie, yet not cursed with a dangerous compulsion always to reveal the truth. Neither he nor Margo could ever become the victims of flattery, but they were incapable of resisting the seduction of talent.

In the first act of *Milestones*, Francesca della Orso appeared as a young woman about to be wed; the woman who would, in the last act, be seen celebrating her fiftieth wedding anniversary.

"That brunette!" Matty said in Margo's ear in a tone whose meaning she knew well. It heralded good tidings. It was a voice loaded with solid gold. They looked at Francesca together, exploring the exquisite oval of her face, the small, rounded slightly cleft chin, the straight nose, the eyebrows set high so that her eyelids were of a strange and touching importance. Matty had only seen one woman as beautiful as this girl before and she had started his career and made his fortune. Listening to Francesca speak her lines, he felt sweat suddenly beading his upper lip. The hairs on the back of his neck rose; he felt his sinuses constrict. Margo, for her part, was keenly aware of the dark promise in the girl's wide, calm, imperious eyes, of the passionate spirit that was evident in spite of her smooth forehead and long, docile neck. Neither of them yet could understand the force of Francesca's fantasy life, the intensity of her moods, the fury of uncompromising emotions into which she could fling herself.

As soon as it was decently possible after the curtain rang down, Matty and Margo deserted their friends' lackluster daughter and went in search of Francesca della Orso. They found her backstage, still in the make-up of a woman of almost seventy, surrounded by an admiring crowd. Matty didn't bother to introduce himself to her. It was her parents who were his target.

His siege of Claudia and Ricardo della Orso lasted for weeks. Although they had always been filled with quiet joy and wonder by their daughter's performances in school plays, they were bewildered and outraged at the agent's proposal that he sign Francesca to an exclusive personal contract and that she come to live in Los Angeles under his wife's strict supervision. But eventually, to their own astonishment, they overcame their deep mistrust of Hollywood, vanquished by their perception of Matty Firestone's excellent intentions and the satisfactory protective qualities they saw in Margo.

Although the events that followed the production of *Milestones* startled Ricardo and Claudia, Francesca was not surprised. She had long lived in the world of dreams in which wondrous happenings took place predictably, and her ranging imagination had always whispered to her that she was not destined to lead the life her friends would lead. Nothing could have prevented her from reaching out for everything life offered.

Francesca Vernon, née della Orso, became a star in her first picture. Her reputation grew with astonishing speed in those lush days when studios could use the same actress in three or four major pictures a year. From the age of eighteen to the age of twenty-four Francesca went directly from one film to another, for she had been born to play the great romantic roles. More than ten years younger than Ingrid Bergman, Bette Davis, Ava Gardner or Rita Hayworth, she reigned alongside them, capturing parts which might normally have gone to English actresses, because there was no one in Hollywood who could match her as a heroine on the grand scale; the noble, the star-crossed, the stuff of tragic legend.

Francesca lived with the Firestones for a year before she bought herself a small house next door to them. Although she went to San Francisco to visit her parents on her rare, brief vacations, by 1949 they both died. Since Francesca didn't plunge into the Hollywood social scene she was soon typed by movie magazines as a mystery woman, an approach which wily Matty encouraged, knowing how tantalizing it is to the press. The studio's publicity department cooperated completely in the screen of secrecy which surrounded Francesca, for they realized, as well as Matty, that the truth about her would have been totally unacceptable to the prudish public of the 1950s. Francesca fell dangerously in love with almost every one of her leading men, and her discreet but full-blown affairs only ended when the final scene of each picture was shot. This amorous habit of hers might have killed Matty from sheer weight of aggravation if he hadn't learned that each affair had a finite end. She had never loved a man, a real person. She had loved the Prince of Denmark and Romeo and Heathcliff and Marc Antony and Lord Nelson and a dozen others, but once the ordinary mortal actor stood before her, she grew cold. It was wild, theatrical passion or cold porridge when Francesca's emotions were involved.

Margo Firestone, concerned with Francesca's succession of intense affairs, often with married men, asked her finally why she didn't try to have more *fun*, like other young actresses of her age.

Francesca turned on her indignantly. "My God, Margo, what the hell do you think I am—a Janet Leigh, or a

Debbie Reynolds, with their cute little movie-magazine romances? And who the hell wants to have *fun*—what a silly word that is. I insist on *more*—and I know perfectly well how corny that sounds, so you don't have to bother to lecture me. Oh, I'm fed up with actors! But they're all I ever meet."

She had just turned twenty-four when she said this, and that evening Margo Firestone decided that Francesca needed a change of scenery. She was too caught up in the artificial world of the sound stage, too restless, too vulnerable. And the deaths of her parents during the last few years had left her depressed.

"If she were my daughter," Margo said reflectively, "I'd be damn worried."

"Still, last year she won the Oscar," Matty mused.

"I'd worry even more. Remember Luise Rainer?"

"Please! Don't even say it." Matty knocked on wood to fend off the memory of what he considered the mishandled career of the fragile Austrian actress who had won two Oscars in a row and then virtually disappeared from film importance in the late 1930s. God forbid such a thing should happen to Francesca. Or to him.

"Let's ask her to go with us to Europe next month," Margo suggested.

"But I thought you wanted a second honeymoon," Matty objected.

"I don't really believe in honeymoons, first or second," Margo said firmly. "As soon as Francesca finishes *Anna Karenina* have your office arrange to put her on the next boat—we can meet her there."

By seven-thirty of the evening after the polo match, under Margo's feverish direction, Francesca was ready. She wore a floor-length rosy-white chiffon evening gown designed by Jean Louis. The strapless bodice was held up by tiny bones and draped softly over her bosom. The first layer of chiffon was a dark pink, the next a lighter shade of pink, until the fifth and final layer, which was pure white. Around her bare shoulders she flung a chiffon stole of five layers like the skirt. Yards long, it was ornamented here and there by delicate sprays of palest pink silk flowers. The entire effect was eighteenth century and as fanciful as if she had stepped from a portrait by Gainsborough. Francesca's long hair, which she had refused to sacrifice for the new poodle cut, was caught up in a huge chignon at the back of her neck, and tiny curls of hair escaped just in front of her ears and lay on her smooth forehead.

Margo surveyed her with admiration and envy. Matty had wandered into the sitting room of Francesca's suite to inspect his client. "I hope that guy's dressed up too, hon."

"Matty, in Deauville they won't even let you in the gambling rooms at the Casino unless you're in evening clothes," Margo said, dismissively. She knew what was proper for a first date with a prince. She'd been planning one for herself since she was fifteen.

"Listen, hon," Matty continued, undeterred, "this fellow is a genuine prince. I've checked up on that. But he's got quite a reputation as a ladies' man. He's been divorced once. So keep that in mind. You're a big girl now—I know, I know, so don't tell me again."

As they sat waiting, there was a knock on the door Matty opened it to find the hotel bell captain standing with a stiff white pasteboard box in his hands.

"Flowers for Miss Vernon," he announced. Matty took the box and tipped the man. "At least he knows all the gimmicks," he observed sourly. Francesca opened the box and found that it contained a triple circle of white rose-buds that she could twine around her wrist. Then, sharp-eyed Margo spied another smaller, black velvet box, tied in blue ribbon, which had been tucked under the roses. Francesca opened it quickly and drew in her breath in amazement. Fitted precisely into the velvet interior of the box lay a crystal pot, three-quarters filled with water. In the pot were three sprigs of thickly clustered flowers on stems of gold. Each flower was made of five round petals of turquoise with rose-cut diamond centers and leaves of jade. She took it out and set it on the table. The entire magical object was three inches high and the illusion of water was due to the clarity of the rock crystal.

"What. . . ? What is it?" she asked.

"Artificial flowers," said Matty.

"Fabergé . . . that's Fabergé . . . it couldn't be anything else," Margo breathed. "Read the card!"

Only then did Francesca tear open the card concealed in the old velvet box which bore the double-headed eagle, mark of the Royal Warrant.

These forget-me-nots belonged to my mother. Until this afternoon I had lost hope of finding someone to whom they should belong.

Stash Valensky

"He knows gimmicks they haven't even invented yet," Matty said, his face dour. But even to his unsentimental eyes the little vase was an extraordinarily precious object. Whatever else this bozo was, he certainly wasn't handing those out by the gross.

As Francesca finished twining the rosebuds around her wrist, the front desk rang announcing Prince Valensky. "Listen, hon, just remember that pumpkin can turn into a coach," Matty said hastily, but Francesca had left the room so quickly that she didn't hear him. He turned to Margo with an expression of dismay. "Hell, I meant the coach into a pumpkin—do you think she got it?"

"You might as well have been speaking Chinese," said Margo.

Valensky and Francesca Vernon, by unspoken accord, moved quickly through the crowded lobby of the Normandy where people had stopped to look at them the minute she stepped out of the lift, her beauty unfurled above the great float of chiffon. His open, white Rolls-Royce convertible was waiting at the door, and within seconds they were driving through the almost deserted streets of a city in which most people were either drinking or still dressing for the evening.

"Do you realize that this is unfashionably early?" he asked.

"But you did say eight."

"I don't think my nerves could last till nine."

"So you suffer from nerves?" Her famous voice, deep and gentle, came with difficulty, through lips that were suddenly dry.

"Since this afternoon, yes." Her tone of badinage had evaporated. He took one hand off the wheel and laid it over hers. The sudden, simple contact left her incapable of responding. None of her many lovers had, even in their most intimate moments, touched her in such a way. There was ownership in his fingers.

After a minute he continued. "I had planned to take you to the Casino for dinner . . . there's the polo ball tonight

... it's the peak of the Season. Would you mind missing it? We could go to a restaurant I know on the way to Honfleur—Chez Mahu. It's good and it's quiet, or at least it will be tonight with everyone in Deauville."

"Oh, yes—please."

They drove in renewed silence through the lambent evening of Normandy, an evening of vast gray-blue skies covering a landscape cosily patterned by fields, orchards and farmhouses, seen in that last light of day, which for ten minutes makes everything look greener than it really is.

At Chez Mahu they found that they were able only to talk of unimportant things. Stash tried to explain polo to Francesca but she scarcely listened, mesmerized as she was with the abrupt movements of his tanned hands on which light blond hair grew, the hands of a great male animal. For his part, Stash hardly knew what he was saying. Francesca played straight into the heart of his deepest, most thoroughly concealed dream. For years he had had as many women as he chose to reach out for, sophisticated, clever, practiced and decorative women of great beauty, women of the International Set. He was a hardened man of the world who was, at last, experiencing the *coup de foudre,* the thunderclap of unreasoning, instant infatuation.

She was so young, he thought, and luminous in her majesty. Her dark and blushing beauty could have been as Russian as it was Italian. She reminded him of the miniatures of young princesses, framed in jewels and gold, the princesses of St. Petersburg that he had seen, when he was a child, in dozens of frames set in a nostalgic profusion on the tables around his mother's fireplace. The flesh of her shoulders, when she threw back her stole, had an almost impossible polish and freshness. The curve of her jaw where it approached her ear was of such a heart-breaking purity that he knew it would remain in his memory forever.

Francesca listened to Valensky's low voice, which had traces of an English accent, a brutal man's voice which seemed to vibrate with an underlying tenderness, as if he were talking to a newborn foal, and thought that this man was as far from the sort of man she knew as if he had sprung from another species. Every time she dared to look directly into the fighting gleam of his gray eyes she felt as if she had taken another step into a foreign land. He told her that he was forty but about him there clung an air of strength and purpose which made youth seem an awkward dream. Matty was forty-five. Stash made him seem seventy-five.

As they finished their coffee he asked her if she would go with him to visit his horses.

"I never turn in without checking the stables," he explained. "They expect to see me."

"And do they like female visitors?"

"They have never seen any before."

"Ah!" She shivered at the stern simplicity of the compliment. "Yes, I'll come."

They drove back toward Deauville, and, just outside of Trouville, took a road which branched off into a country lane which wandered through half a mile of ancient apple trees until it stopped at a gate set into a wall of irregular stones. At the sound of the horn a man appeared quickly and opened the gate so that they could drive through. Inside the courtyard was a substantial stone farmhouse and a number of farm buildings.

"My manager, Jean, lives here with his family," Valensky said. "The stableboys live in the village and ride their bikes over every morning."

He took Francesca's arm and led her toward the stables which were at some distance from the farmhouse. At the sound of their footsteps some of the ponies immediately whinnied and started to move around in their boxes.

"They don't get much to look at, poor beasts," Valensky laughed. "I'm their nightly floor show." He walked slowly from box to box, stopping to name each pony to Francesca, to tell her something of the animal's peculiarities while he observed, with a quick, keen eye, the health and mental condition of each one of them.

"Tiger Moth here is spending the week out to grass. He has a cut mouth—nothing serious, but I won't ride him until it's completely healed. Gloster Gladiator has a bad habit of eating his bed so I've had it changed from straw to peat moss. Good; Bristol Beaufighter is sleeping. He had a hard afternoon."

"Bristol Beaufighter, Gloster Gladiator?"

"I know they're odd names for horses. They're the names of planes ... great planes. Some day I'll tell you more about them."

"Tell me now," she demanded, not really caring. His

careless phrase, "some day I'll tell you" was all she'd heard.

"The Tiger Moth was a trainer ... de Havilland. The Gladiator was a fighter, the Bristol a night fighter ... there were many, now forgotten, unless you've flown one. Then you can never forget."

His voice trailed off as he saw she wasn't listening. The moonlight on her ball gown turned it into a sculptural mass of white marble.

"Come," he said reluctantly, "I should take you back. The gala isn't over yet and we can be at the Casino in less than fifteen minutes."

"The Casino? Certainly not. I want to hear more about the Tiger Moth."

"No, you don't."

"Oh, but I do." Francesca entered an empty box in which blankets and tack were stored and sat down on a bale of clean straw that stood against one wall. She tilted her head back against the wall and let her wrap fall carelessly away from her shoulders, knowing exactly how the promise of the movement would affect him. He saw immediately that she was not playing the coquette or the tease. The look she gave him was so profound that it gathered together her entire ardent nature and offered it to him with artful purpose. In one stride, Valensky followed her, put his arm around her waist and turned her to him. He whispered into her ear, "The Tiger Moth was a basic training plane for the RAF."

"Basic ..." Francesca breathed.

"Very, very basic ..." Valensky kissed the curve of her jaw, near her ear, moving his mouth softly until their lips found each other. At that instant something changed forever in both of them. They had crossed an invisible barrier and discovered themselves firmly planted on the other side of their lives. They knew almost nothing of each other but they were already beyond questions, reassurances or preconditions. It was as if they, two separate beings, had, in coming together, formed a third, quite different entity, that would never, now, be resolved back into the originals.

Francesca pulled away from his lips and, reaching up with both arms, unpinned her chignon so that all her dark hair fell down over her shoulders. She shook it loose impatiently and then, looking full into his eyes, she adroitly managed to unfasten her strapless dress and her crinolines, throwing them as hastily aside as if they were made of hopsacking. Recklessly she flung herself out of her clouds of chiffon plumage only to appear in her resplendent flesh, lying totally naked on a pile of horse blankets, laughing softly as she watched Stash Valensky, momentarily bewildered and taken by surprise, struggle out of his dinner jacket. Soon, very soon, he was as naked as she. He savaged her abandoned flesh with an urgency, almost a cannibalism, he hadn't known in years. This creature of roses and pearls had become, in a flash of magic, a demanding mortal who begged him, in hungry, hoarse tones, to take her as quickly as possible. She would not let him linger at any point; considerations of her own pleasure melted before her craving to have him inside her; deeply, fully, to possess him. When he mounted her and she opened for him, a queen joyfully squandering all her treasures, it was a primeval act. As he gave himself, shatteringly, to his climax, Francesca looked up at his face in the moonlight, his eyes tightly closed, an expression of intense concentration, almost of agony, furrowing his features, and smiled in a way she had never smiled before. Afterward they clung together under the horse blankets, their bodies radiating a triumphant heat, able now to touch each other with tenderness, to explore rather than plunder, to caress rather than raven. Again they made love and this time Stash would not permit Francesca to set the pace, but brought her with infinite skill to an orgasm so stabbing, so victorious, that it frightened her. They slept awhile and awoke to see the change of light, the unmistakable signs of approaching dawn in that fraction of the sky visible from their corner of the horse box.

"Your friends—my God, what will they think?" said Stash, suddenly remembering the Firestones.

"Matty will be making noises like an outraged father in a Victorian melodrama and Margo will be excited and curious and pleased with herself. Or they went to bed early and don't even know I'm still out . . . which would be most unlikely. In two hours Matty will start to think about going to the police, but he won't because he doesn't want publicity."

"I'd better let them know you're safe."

"But, it's too early to phone . . . look, the sun is just rising."

"I'll just go and tell Jean to ring up the hotel and say you're fine and will be back soon. Don't move."

He was back in minutes. "That's done. Now we'll make our plans and then we'll find some breakfast."

"Plans?"

"The wedding. As soon as possible and no fuss ... or all kinds of fuss, if that's what you'd like. Just so it's soon."

Francesca rose halfway out of the pile of blankets in astonishment, her nipples still tender and sore from the assault of his lips and teeth, bits of straw in her wildly disordered hair. She gaped in astonishment at this man who was looking down at her with utter conviction.

"Married?"

"Is there any alternative?" He sat down and took her in his arms, pressing her forehead to the place where the tan of his neck turned into the rosy-white skin of his chest. She lifted her head and asked again, "Married?"

Stash pulled a blanket over her shoulders against the morning damp. His strong hands, accustomed to obedience, grasped the top of her arms and when he spoke his voice, though low, had the ring of a cavalry charge.

"I'm old enough to know that this sort of thing doesn't happen twice in a lifetime. At my age there's no such thing as infatuation. It's love and, damn it, I'm *no good* at love—I don't know the right words, I can't tell you what I feel because I've never done it before. I haven't used the real words, just other words, play-love words, seduction words—"

"But I have used *all* the real words, the most beautiful ever written—and *never* been good at love either—so we're equal," Francesca replied slowly, realizing a truth she had not said out loud before.

"Have you ever felt like this? Can you imagine feeling like this again?" Stash demanded.

Francesca shook her head. It was easier to turn her back on everything that had made up her life until yesterday than it was to think of life apart from Stash in any way.

"But ... shouldn't we get to know each other?" she said, and then laughed deeply at the conventionality of the question.

"Know each other? Oh, God—we'd just end up in the same place. No, we will tell them we've decided to get married and that's that. Francesca, say yes!"

All of Francesca's romantic nature rose up within her. She didn't say yes but she inclined her queen's head and passionately kissed his hands in a fury of submission and possession. She wept and he kissed her wet eyes.

The sun was up and all the noises of the farm suddenly burst into their consciousness.

"You'd better dress," Stash grinned like a boy.

"Dress? Have you any idea. . . ?" Francesca pointed to a heap of crumpled chiffon and silk flowers lying on the dirt floor of the stable. "To say nothing of this!" She flourished a white lace undergarment which had worked its way under the horse blankets. It was called a Merry Widow, a corselette which started at a strapless bra, continued to form a fashionably tiny waist and reached halfway down the hips where garters were attached to hold up her stockings.

"I'll help you—but you got out of it so quickly."

"There are ways and ways—but getting back in is another story. No, Stash, I just can't put this all back on," she implored. "Look, my fingers are shaking."

They both froze, startled by the whistle of an approaching stable hand.

"I'll head him off," Stash whispered, trying not to laugh. "Get back in there." Francesca dove into the blankets giggling. The transition from high romance to farce was complete, as, with one eye, she could see the pony in the next box stretch his head in her direction and snort as if in shocked indignation, no doubt she thought wildly, trying to alert the entire stable to their carryings on. Before long Stash was back, holding a pile of clothes.

"I made a deal with that boy," he said, handing her a pair of well-polished old riding boots, a frayed blue shirt, and a pair of shabby riding breeches. "He's about your size and I think he had a bath this morning—but I don't guarantee it."

While Francesca managed to dress in the boy's clothes, mercifully clean and only two sizes too big for her, Stash brought her evening bag from the car. She peered into the mirror of her compact and saw that no trace of make-up remained on her face. She decided not to bother with repairs. Francesca loved her scraped and reddened skin, her bruised lips, her unfamiliar, excited eyes.

"I need a belt," she discovered.

Stash inspected the variety of tack hanging on the wall. "Martingale's too long. The bridle? No, it won't work, nor the curb chain. I'd give you my bow tie if I could find it, but it'd be too short. Here, this should do." He handed her a long length of material, doubled over.

"What's that?"

"Tail bandage—keeps the pony's tail from catching on the polo stick."

"Who said romance was dead?" she asked.

"Tell them it was an Act of God." Francesca laughed at a stupefied Matty.

"You'd have to be pregnant for that!" the agent exploded. "You don't even have a decent excuse! You're throwing away a great career to marry some Russian polo player out of nowhere and you're as fucking light-hearted as ten thousand goddamned angels dancing on the head of a pin."

Francesca flung clean defiance in the teeth of his logic.

"Matty, how many years does a person have to live at the peak? The sky-rocket years, Matty? The firework years? I'm in love with a real man for the first time, so be happy for me!" She made her demands with an infuriatingly carefree smile. "We want everything, Matty—all—all there is, and we want it now. Why shouldn't we have it? Can you give me a single reason that will mean anything —even in ten years?" she challenged him.

"All right, I'm happy, I'm thrilled, I'm overjoyed—my best client, like a daughter to me, is getting married to some bozo she met yesterday—who could ask for a better reason for feeling happy? And what does she say when I ask her why it has to be so sudden, why she can't go home and just do *Robin Hood* first and then get married? What does she say when I tell her that nobody wants to stop her from marrying her prince, but maybe she should get to know him better?"

"I said," Francesca answered dreamily, "that it *felt right*. I said I'd never been really sure of anything before —that I'd been waiting for him all my life and now that I'd found him I'll never leave him."

Margo heard a note in Francesca's voice that told her that whatever the girl was doing, it could not be delayed nor denied.

Matty threw up his hands. "I give up. I never had a chance anyway. All right, you're going to do it, so that's that and I'll cable the studio. So they'll sue—they have every right. And they'll win, too. I knew we shouldn't have come to Europe. It makes people *crazy!*"

3

$\mathscr{F}$rancesca had lapsed from Catholicism years before, but, like all Catholics she remained familiar with the rites of the church. In contrast to her Berkeley Sunday-school days, the marriage service in the Russian Orthodox Cathedral in Paris seemed like a phantasmagoric Hollywood production, Byzantine and bizarre. She almost expected to hear the director's voice calling "Cut" as, after an interminable service, she and Stash drank three times from a cup of red wine and were led by the priest three times around the lectern. Clouds of incense billowed around them in the light of hundreds of candles, and the unreality was underscored by the majestic, deep bass notes of the male choir singing without instruments, their only counterpoint the celestial sound of a choir of children. Two of Stash's friends held golden crowns over their heads as they walked and it seemed to Francesca that the circle of fascinated spectators was a crowd of dress extras.

Although they had tried to keep the date of the service secret and had invited only a small group of friends, word of their intentions had spread and the entire cathedral was jammed with the curious, standing, as was the custom, throughout the wedding and barely keeping order, so great was their desire to catch a glimpse of the ceremony.

Stash, for all his early talk of no fuss, had wanted this service, in all its grandeur and lengthy ritual, remembering the hasty insignificance of his first marriage in wartime London, at a Registry Office. He wanted to see Francesca doubly crowned, first with flowers in her hair, then with the heavy nuptial crown, held in the air over her head. He, who had only spent the first forgotten year of his life in Russia, wanted all the rich symbolism of the noble public service, atavistic, but still fully alive. He had even asked the superbly bearded and solemn priest wearing a silver chasuble and a sacerdotal head dress to link his hand with Francesca's in a silk handkerchief as he led them around the altar, rather than merely taking their hands in his.

Francesca consented to everything. No detail seemed of the slightest importance to her from the time she had made her decision in the stable. She existed on a plane of sublime indifference to everything but her concentration on Stash and her inner vision of the two of them together forever.

Margo was in her element, making arrangements which no one else could have managed. She gloried in Francesca's triumphant marriage and she made the most of the occasion, admitting to herself that at heart she thoroughly detested and mistrusted tasteful simplicity.

The wedding reception at the Ritz was certainly the greatest Margo Firestone production ever recorded. Afterward, Prince Stash Valensky and his new princess disappeared. Not even the Firestones knew that they were staying in Stash's large villa in the countryside outside of Lausanne where, at last, they could begin the never-to-end, not-to-be-rushed exploration of each other. As they rode or walked or lay together they told each other long tales of their childhoods and marveled that, but for the chance remark of a man neither of them knew, in the bar of a Paris hotel, they might never have met.

Francesca often stayed awake at night, although her body, bathed in the halcyon weather of satisfied passion, told her to sleep. She preferred to watch over Stash, brooding over his features in the flickering light of the tiny lamp lit beneath an icon that hung on the far wall of their bedroom. He was the hero, she told herself, of all the stories she had ever read. Bold, gallant, fearless . . . he was all that and something more. She searched for the word and finally found it. Imperishable.

Had he lived long enough for her to know him, Francesca might have used the same word to describe Stash's father, Prince Vasily Alexandrovitch Valensky. That man of dauntless presence, high rank and great physical strength had been the veteran of half a hundred affairs with the exquisite ballerinas of the Marinsky Theater, when, at the age of forty, he decided that it was time to take a wife. Quite dispassionately, he had chosen to propose to Princess Titiana Nikolaevna Stargardova because, of all the debutantes of 1909, she was most suited by birth to his own position. Now, incredulously, in the winter of 1910, he realized that in the most unexpected, undignified and irreversible way he had fallen totally in love with his own wife.

Before their engagement, Titiana was alluringly pretty though she had always kept her large blue eyes downcast whenever they met at a party or the opera. She had worn demure, rather high-necked ball gowns and she spoke in the softest voice which nothing more seductive than a pure gaiety was allowed to animate. From her simply dressed blonde hair and her habit of blushing when she spoke to him, Vasily Valensky had expected a wife who would be placid, correct, certainly conservative. And almost surely as boring as the wives of most of his acquaintances. But before their honeymoon was over, Titiana, who was as hot-blooded as she was clever, had utterly captivated her husband and he discovered that he had married an imperious and demanding mistress.

Today, less than a year after his marriage, as Prince Valensky left his marble-columned palace on the Moika Canal, he noted with amusement, barely touched with resignation, that once again everything and everyone in the palace was being turned upside down and inside out as Titiana prepared for another of her balls. She was reveling in her new position as one of the leading hostesses of St. Petersburg. Freed by marriage from the splendid, but chaperoned, decorum of the *bals Blanc*, at which young girls danced a sedate cotillion, the newly vivacious nineteen-year-old princess lost no time in placing herself near the center of the sumptuous society of the Imperial city.

"To Denisov-Uralski's," Prince Vasily commanded the bemedaled and uniformed doorman who guarded the entrance to the seething palace. Two footmen closed the heavy doors behind him and he stepped lightly into the back seat of the magnificent sledge, carved from ebony and lined with quilted glove leather.

Boris, the coachman, was wearing his winter uniform, a dark ruby-red velvet coat, completely doubled inside with thick fur and belted in gold, with a matching three-cornered hat. In common with all the coachmen of the nobility, he was an immense bearded man who enjoyed nothing more than driving his team of four huge black horses as fast as if there were no one else on the crowded streets of St. Petersburg. Indeed, Boris, who discounted the Grand Dukes as merely decorative, was convinced that his master, who wore the decorations of the Alexander Nevsky, the Vladimir and the St. Andrew, was next in importance only to the Tsar himself. He prided himself that he had traversed the distance between the palace and the shop of Denisov-Uralski without stopping or even slowing for another sledge. To have done so would have insulted the Prince.

On that December day Vasily Valensky's errand was to purchase a veritable menagerie. His wife still had a childish love of animal figurines and he had determined to overwhelm her this Christmas—if, he thought to himself with an inward smile of memory, she could ever be satisfied. Within a half-hour he had selected a number of precious animals, two of each so that Titiana would have a Noah's ark to play with. There were elephants carved from imperial jade with Ceylon sapphire eyes, lions of topaz with ruby eyes and tails of diamonds threaded on gold and giraffes made of amethyst whose eyes were cabochon emeralds with diamond pupils. Next the Prince went on foot to Fabergé and added smaller animals to the collection: turtles fashioned of pink agate with heads, feet and tails of silver and gold, their backs studded with pearls; parrots of white coral; and an entire school of goldfish carved in green, pink, mauve and brown jade, all with eyes of rose-cut diamonds.

This pleasant business done, he directed Boris to drive him to his offices. In the eleven hundred years his family had been noble, their estates had spread over the vastness of Russia and it was only with the aid of a corps of managers, many of them German and Swiss, that Prince Vasily was able to keep his affairs in order. In the Urals his estates produced one quarter of the world's output of platinum. In Kursk he owned the hundreds of miles of sugar plantations and dozens of sawmills, fed by still another hundred miles of forests. In the Ukraine he was the proprietor of immense tobacco plantations. But it was in the fertile province of Kashin that he had his favorite estate. There, on land blooming with orchards and dotted by dairy farms, he raised his winning race horses and invited parties of a hundred noblemen to shoot his fat deer, his wild boar and his thousands of game birds.

There, too, he and his wife rode together through the forest pathways and, as Prince Vasily was still astonished to remember, there they had made love often last summer, hiding in secret places deep in the woods, just like the peasants. It was hard to reconcile the tumbled, eager girl he took so urgently in the nest they had made of moss and leaves, with the great lady, crowned with his mother's diamond-and-emerald tiara, who would receive eight hundred guests tonight, all of them noble and all of them dressed to her command in cloth of gold or silver. They would dance to the music of six orchestras and be served a midnight supper from gold and silver dishes presented by a hundred uniformed footmen while they were serenaded by both Colombo's and Goulesko's gypsy bands. As he had left the palace, Valensky had seen the heated carts arriving with the flowers Titiana had ordered from the Riviera. Their private train had been dispatched to Nice to be loaded with flowers still in bud. They were sped through the winter of Europe, unloaded at the station in St. Petersburg as they were beginning to flower. Half the blossoms of France, lilacs, roses, hyacinths, daffodils and Parma violets, opened for just one night in this city on the Gulf of Finland where the winters were endless and the winds were damp and freezing.

In November of the following year, 1911, Vasily and Titiana's son was born. They named him Alexander after his paternal grandfather, and the young mother who had missed so many entertainments while she was pregnant was more determined than ever to dance every night. Valensky did nothing to dissuade his wife from her pursuit of pleasure as she graced the balls given by the Sheremen-tevs and the Yousoupovs, the Saltykovs and the Vasil-chikovs. She led all the other ladies of St. Petersburg in the élan of her waltzing, and she astonished them with her inventiveness at the costume balls of Countess Marie Kleinmichel.

The approach of Lent, which began on the Sunday before Ash Wednesday, signaled the end of dancing. During Lent, concerts and dinner parties replaced balls and, in the private opinion of Masha, Alexander's wet nurse, it was a good thing that her mistress was going to be forced to go to bed earlier. Although the Princess only flitted in from time to time to watch Masha as she nursed the baby, the peasant girl, stout, plain and sensible, thought to herself that in spite of her prettiness the Princess looked tired and too thin. Masha was only seventeen. She had spent all her life on the Valenskys' Kashin estate where she had been unlucky enough to bear an illegitimate child the day before Alexander's birth. However, Masha's baby had not lived and the estate manager immediately sent her to St. Petersburg to nourish the newborn heir. Her homesickness had disappeared as soon as little Prince Alexander had claimed her milk.

On that last Sunday the Valenskys went to a lunch party on a country estate. Afterward they joined in a parade of galloping troikas and finished the afternoon with an especially boisterous snowball fight. When the last dance of the season stopped at the sound of the great clock in the hall striking midnight, Vasily found Titiana strangely willing to drive home. He had expected her to be in despair at the prospect of a temporary end to merrymaking, but instead she felt so tired that she went to sleep in his arms in their heated carriage and the next morning she slept late and woke up no more rested than she had been the night before. She complained, in petulant tones, that she must be getting old.

Vasily immediately sent for the doctor. He had never seen Titiana listless and fretful before, and he was frightened. The doctor spent an endless amount of time in Titiana's pink and silver damask bedroom. When at length he emerged, he spoke of a minor congestion of the bronchi, of a tendency to overstrain the nerves, of a febrile condition.

"What is the treatment?" Vasily demanded impatiently, interrupting the man's interminable medical obfuscation.

"Why, Prince, I thought you understood at once. It may be an inflammation of the lungs, in effect, although I am not a specialist, you must understand, in effect, it may be tuberculosis."

Valensky stood as if he had been shot and was waiting to fall. Titiana and *tuberculosis*? Titiana, who galloped in breeches as in the time of Catherine the Great; Titiana, who only laughed when she was thrown into a snowbank from an overturned troika during a race; Titiana, who tobogganed fearlessly down the dangerous twisting slopes of the ice hills; who had given birth to their son in six hours without a whimper; Titiana, who would let him take her even in a field where the harvesters might have found them?

"Impossible!" he cried.

"Prince, I am not an expert. You must call Dr. Zevgod and Dr. Kouskof. I cannot be responsible." The doctor edged toward the door, anxious to escape before the Prince realized that he had pronounced what, at that time, often amounted to a death sentence.

Zevgod and Kouskof agreed on the necessary steps to be taken. Princess Valensky had admitted to them that, for the last months, she had been troubled by night sweats and a loss of appetite, but she had refused, foolishly, to worry about them. Her lack of caution and her strenuous life had aggravated the condition and now no time could be lost. The Princess must go directly to Davos, in Switzerland, where the treatment of the disease was clearly superior to that found elsewhere.

"For how long?" Vasily asked sternly.

The two doctors hesitated, neither one willing to commit himself. Finally Zevgod spoke.

"There is no way of knowing. If the Princess responds to the treatment, she may be back within a year . . . or two. Perhaps a little more. But she must not return to this damp city until she is perfectly well. As you know, it is built on marsh and swamp. To come back would be suicide for anyone with a weakness of the chest."

"A year!"

"That would be a miracle," Kouskof said gravely.

"Then you really mean that it could be for many years— is that not what you are trying to tell me, gentlemen?"

"Unfortunately, Prince, yes. But the Princess is young and strong. . . . We must hope for an early recovery."

Valensky dismissed the doctors and went to his study and closed the door. He could not possibly tell his sparkling, brave, treasured wife that she had to go away for even as long as three months or three weeks. There was nothing on earth which would make him sentence her to live in a sanatorium. The very word filled him with horror. No! She would go to Davos, that was essential, but they would take Russia with them.

Prince Vasily dispatched his chief male secretary to Davos to rent the largest available chalet. Three French lady's maids were immediately put to work filling Titiana's trunks. There was one which contained nothing but gloves and fans, three which held only narrow embroidered satin slippers, twelve for her dresses, four for her furs and five for her underclothes. Pouting enchantingly over the clothes she had to leave behind, she told Vasily that it was a good thing that she was not overfond of her wardrobe, like the Empress Elizabeth who had owned fifteen thousand dresses.

Meanwhile, the other servants were packing the finest furnishings of the palace, under the direction of another of the Prince's private secretaries, who chose only the best French pieces from the period of Louis XV and XVI. Valensky himself made the decisions about which works of art to take. He was an avid collector but since he didn't know the dimensions of the chalet they were to inhabit, he took only easel paintings by Rembrandt, Boucher, Watteau, Greuze and Fragonard, leaving behind the vast canvases by Raphael, Rubens, Delacroix and Van Eyck.

In spite of the modern way in which they lived, the Valenskys, like all Russians, had never stopped venerating icons and the Prince stripped the separate rooms which had been kept as an oratory. There, rows and rows of icons, many of them so adorned with gold and jewels that they were literally priceless, stood with lamps burning before them day and night. Their protective curtains were drawn, they were laid in their own velvet-covered boxes, after which they were carefully placed in special crates. Certain icons, particularly personal, that were considered to be protectors of the household, would travel in the train with the family in their own compartments.

Nothing that was needed to reproduce the palace on the Moika was left behind, from kitchen pots and pans to three rock-crystal chandeliers that had once belonged to Madame de Pompadour.

Ten days later, forty servants, an adequate if skeleton staff in Vasily's opinion, gathered at the station in St. Petersburg. Additional sleeping cars had been added to the Prince's train to accommodate them all. All the baggage cars were fully loaded, and the two kitchen cars were so packed with food that the chefs had difficulty going about their tasks.

Prince and Princess Valensky, with Masha carrying little Alexander, drove to the station in a closed carriage accompanied by a most important servant, Zachary, the chasseur, in his dark blue uniform with gold epaulets and his formal cocked hat trimmed with white feathers. Zachary was in charge of the actual logistics of the journey; he was responsible for making sure that there would be no frontier delays, no lack of fresh provisions, no lost baggage or any other problem that might disturb the smooth progress of the train on its long southwest journey.

At Landquart, in Switzerland, the private train had to be abandoned since it could not run on the narrow-gauge Alpine tracks. The Valenskys remained in it for several days until all their servants and possessions had been laboriously transported by a smaller Alpine train up to the heights of Davos-Dorf. Then they, too, made the steep, winding, upward journey among frozen waterfalls and snow-smothered fir trees. Titiana shivered although the compartment was warm and she was covered with furs. Her glance recoiled from the vast drop into the abyss on one side of the train but could find no comfortable resting place on the peaks toward which they climbed. Her small, gloved hand clutched her husband's arm as they climbed higher and night began to fall. It was dark outside before they reached the point at which the valley began and the roadbed became level.

"We're almost there, my darling," Vasily said. "Boris will be waiting at the station with the Rolls-Royce."

"What?" Titiana asked, her strange terror momentarily canceled by surprise.

"Certainly. Did you think we were going to drive in some hired cabriolet like a good bourgeois couple on their way to a christening? I ordered the new Silver Ghost last year as a present for you. It was ready two weeks ago so I merely telegraphed Mr. Royce in Manchester and requested that he send it on here instead."

"But Boris can't drive an automobile," Titiana protested.

"I instructed Royce to send one of his English driver-mechanics with the car. He can teach Boris—or, if not, we'll keep the man on."

"Even the Tsar doesn't have one!" Titiana clapped her hands gleefully. "How fast will it go?"

"Last year a special model went one hundred and one miles an hour—but I think we'll stay well under that—I don't want to frighten Boris." Vasily was delighted with the success of his surprise. It was exactly the thing needed to take Titiana's mind off her arrival in a strange land where her disease would finally have to be faced. It had been worth all the effort and thousands of pounds expended to make sure that the automobile would be in Davos in time for their arrival.

It seemed perfectly natural to Titiana Valensky that her chalet in Davos should be a miniature of her palace in St. Petersburg, and that she should have the same quality of total service she had always taken for granted, service so complete that the same woman who risked her life on a horse without hesitation had never put on her own stockings. Women of her class never knew the price of anything, neither the price of their jewels, their shoes nor their furs. They would not recognize that piece of paper called a bill if they had ever chanced to see one. They chose everything they wanted without asking or thinking of cost. Expense did not exist for them, not even as an abstract concept, just as it never occurred to them to visit the kitchens of their own palaces.

Now that Titiana was confined to Davos, she set about regaining her health with as much blind determination as she had put into losing it.

Vasily, marooned as a mountaintop, kept in almost daily touch with events in Russia by means of mail and the telegraph, and Russian, French and English newspapers reached him twice weekly by a special courier from Zurich. In 1912, when five thousand workers in the Lena goldfields went on strike and incredibly held out for a month, he took note. This strike led to others, far more widespread until, in 1912, there were over two thousand strikes. The last time there had been such serious troubles in Russia had been in 1905 when troops had fired on workers in front of the Winter Palace, a day that would always be known as Bloody Sunday.

For long hours Vasily pondered in his library in Davos. It was evident to him, from the doctors' reports, that his family and his servants were not to leave Switzerland for many years. While his wife had not become dangerously worse, neither had she shown signs of improvement. Willpower was no match for fever, courage could not win a victory over a bacillus. Her nighttime temperature curve was slightly higher than it had been several months ago when they first arrived and the rales in the right lobe of her lung were as harsh as ever. The doctors never spoke of time; a question about the future was treated as if it hadn't been asked, as if it were the question of a fool.

Prince Vasily Valensky set his teeth and determined that if his family was to live in exile for years, they must certainly live without the bother of sending to St. Petersburg for money. He decided to sell his platinum mines in the Urals, and his sugar plantations, forests and sawmills in Kursk. He put the immense fortune thus realized into Swiss banks where it would be immediately available to him.

Tattersall, the Englishman from Manchester, who had failed utterly in instructing Boris in the mysteries of the Rolls-Royce, now taught Vasily to drive the Silver Ghost. The Prince discovered that while the great machine, the most famous model the firm of Rolls-Royce ever made, could negotiate any mountain road ever constructed, there were not enough roads around Davos for a good day's motoring. It was then that he sent to Russia for the great wooden troika. As soon as snow covered the ground, Vasily took the reins of three strong horses, and strapped little Alexander securely to the seat at his side. The father and son became a familiar and much admired sight in the shop-filled, festive streets of Davos, as they passed through the town on their way to the snow meadows.

There were other Russians of noble birth among the patients of Davos, as well as a good sprinkling of British and French aristocrats, and soon many of those who were ambulatory could be discovered at Princess Titiana's. It had never occurred to anyone in the family even to try to adapt themselves to this foreign country: cozy, quaint, comfortable, safe, dull, dull Switzerland. To enter the chalet was to walk into St. Petersburg where all things produced a distillation, profoundly nostalgic, of the profusion, the elaborate, careless abundance and warmth of their vanished home. Certain refugees who entered the chalet for the first time gazed about them, breathed in the scent of the dark, gold-tipped Russian cigarettes, listened to the sound of rapidly spoken French and burst into tears.

These elegantly dressed habitués, cheeks a shade too red, eyes a shade too bright, ate with unappeasable appetite. Here and there, throughout the reception rooms, stood long tables covered with food. The Valenskys kept open house, both at tea time and dinnertime, with dozens of Russian servants busy refilling glasses and plates and passing boxes of imported cigarettes and cigars. On those evenings when the Princess was not well enough to appear, none of her guests was so tactless as to remark on her absence. On the days when she felt strong enough, she was dressed by her maids in one or another of her two hundred tea gowns. Languidly Titiana decided whether to wear her rope of Burmese sapphires of the prized cornflower blue which matched her eyes or her triple string of matched black pearls, before she descended on Vasily's arm to reign over her guests.

The festive atmosphere of the Valensky chalet might have deceived a total stranger, but everyone in the huge house was trained to revolve around a sickroom. The inner weather of the family depended on whether the Princess had spent a quiet night or a restless one. The barometer of spirits, from the kitchen to Vasily's study, from the peasants' rooms to Alexander's nursery, rose or fell determined by Titiana's fever chart or the news that either she had been permitted out for a walk or was confined to her balcony. Every day two doctors attended her and, at all times, two trained nurses made up part of the permanent household.

From his earliest memories, the little boy, Alexander, never knew what it was like to have a healthy mother. His babyish play with her was always cut short by someone who was afraid that he was tiring her. When Titiana read out loud to him, a nurse would always close the book far too soon. When Alexander grew old enough to play simple games of cards with his mother, her chief doctor took him aside and gravely warned him of the dangerous excitement engendered by any games of chance. His love for her was imprinted, from earliest memory, by the terrible tension which lies between the sick and the well. From babyhood on he was crippled, permanently, with a resentment, a wordless hatred, and a deep and irrationally superstitious fear of any sign of illness. Even normal weakness was loathsome to him, although his frustrated child's love for his mother made him conceal his sense of horror.

From 1912 to 1914 this life, half enforced holiday, half devoted to the monotonous routine of the cure, endured. On that day of June 28, 1914, when the Austrian Archduke Francis Ferdinand was assassinated in Sarajevo, the Valensky family, attended by ten servants, was having a rare picnic in a green pasture from which they could clearly hear the sound of cowbells. Titiana was making the most of one of her brief and deceptive periods of well-being. Their world had just died although no one yet knew it.

Two months after that happy Alpine picnic, the defeat of Tannenberg took place, during which the finest and best of Russia's fighting men were lost. Within a year over a million Russian soldiers were dead, while in Davos, far from the sound of guns, Alexander received his first pony for his fourth birthday. In 1916, the year of Verdun, the year in which nineteen thousand British soldiers were killed in a single day in the Battle of the Somme, Alexander's chief interest was in the hours he spent in the garage, being surreptitiously introduced to the interior workings of a Rolls-Royce engine.

On March 12, 1917, after another long winter during which his father had rarely smiled, Alexander, six years old, and already an audacious skier, had gone to the slopes of spring snow with his school friends. On that day in St. Petersburg, now called Petrograd, and soon to be called Leningrad, a starving mob, waving the red flags of the revolution, was seen near the Alexandra Bridge. Opposing them, on the other side of the bridge, stood a regiment of guards, the nemesis of rioters. However, the mob continued to press forward and the guards held their fire. Then, in a moment which was to change the history of the world, the two groups merged. Like two drops of water, the masses and the army became one body. As Alexander climbed back up the shadowy slopes for the last run of the day, as Titiana poured hot water from the samovar and offered a cup of tea to a French count, as Vasily, haggard and sad from his years of involuntary internment in Switzerland, bent over newspapers that were three days old, the Russian Revolution began.

World War I had been over for almost three years when the decision was made to send Alexander away to school. He was only nine years old, and Titiana might possibly have allowed him to continue in the Davos school where he was the undisputed leader of the gang of village boys, self-willed, taller, rougher, stronger and more ready to take a reckless dare than any of them, but Vasily saw clearly that their son was running wild. He had been born a prince but he was in danger of becoming a peasant. Even in a world in which princes were considered obsolete—particularly Russian princes—if they had managed to survive at all, there was the Valensky tradition to honor, and the Valensky fortune to inherit. He must be educated like the noble gentleman he would become.

"We'll send him to Le Rosey," he told his wife. "I've already made inquiries. He can start in the fall, just before his next birthday. Now don't look sad, my dearest—it's only at Rolle, not far from here, and in the winter the whole school moves up to Gstaad. It's so near that Alexander will have no trouble coming home for holidays."

Eventually, Titiana accepted the idea as, with the necessary self-absorption of the chronic invalid, she had accepted the fact that her family was doomed to eternal exile, that the world of her girlhood no longer existed and that her disease never slept for long. Hope, in her soul, had been replaced with endurance.

Each time Alexander came home for vacations, his parents saw how he was being changed by his new life in the world's most exclusive and expensive boarding school. They noticed little by little how his manners, in the fashion of his international crowd of schoolmates—young potentates, heirs to dynasties—began to show that he was newly comfortable wherever he found himself. He was at ease in *their* way, a way which was based on a sense of hauteur that eventually turned into the special, superior kind of lofty amusement which clings to the elite of the Le Rosey students, a secret, inward smile. He even acquired a new name—Stash—to which both his parents objected because it was a Polish, not a Russian, diminutive, but which they had to admit suited him in a way that Alexander never had.

4

$\mathcal{S}$tash had just turned fourteen when he came home, as usual, for the Christmas
vacation of 1925. He had reached that age at which the
outlines of the man he would become were unmistakably
present to an attentive eye. His nose had been broken for
the first time in a brawl with the heir to a French
marquisate, his curls had been cut short and although he
was still far from reaching his full muscular development,
he was close to six feet tall. His lips were red with the
turbulent vitality of youth and permanently chapped from
outdoor sports. His eyes had exchanged their innocence
for a gaze in which a hint of the relentlessness of his later
years had already appeared.

As he always did, after a day of sport, Stash left his ski
boots outside the chalet for one of the servants to clean.
He put on a pair of after-ski boots and slipped into the
salon in search of something to eat. He was an expert at
moving among his mother's coterie with a kind of ward-
ing-off politeness which prevented them from detaining
him with unwelcome questions. Privately he thought them
all unworthy of his mother, this titled band of tuberculosis
patients whose illness alone brought them together. His
terror of disease expressed itself as contempt for the
invalids themselves. With an arrogance which made an
exception only of his mother, he even despised the courage
and resignation with which they faced their lives and he
told himself that he would rather die cleanly than live with
rotted lungs.

Deftly he helped himself to a big cup of hot chocolate
and a plate of pastries, and started to escape to his own

room. However, a languid hand raised from a far corner indicated to him that this was one of the days on which his mother had joined her guests, and instantly he turned to cross the room and greet her.

Princess Titiana was sitting deep in conversation with her close friend, the Marquise Claire de Champery. The red-headed Frenchwoman kept her lush body tightly girdled, her bright hair was carefully restrained, but nothing could conceal the feline expression of her sulky, green eyes, her small, pouting avaricious mouth or her malicious half-smile. She used very little make-up and dressed almost entirely in black with an uncompromisingly severe chic. On meeting her, men felt an erotic shock.

Although the Marquise had lived in Davos for seven years, she had no trace of sickness. She had originally traveled to the Alps with her husband, Pierre de Champery, expecting that a few months of mountain air would cure him of the bothersome cough he had acquired during his distinguished military service. This accomplished and polished Parisienne had never contemplated spending seven years waiting to return to civilization, but she was a prisoner in Davos, linked to a man she had never loved, even before her marriage, by one of the strongest of bonds, that of prospective inheritance. In order to maintain her position in Princess Titiana's salon, she worked diligently and knowledgeably before her mirror to conceal that flamboyant spoor of her sexuality, to maintain her guise as a lady of the highest class of society.

Claire de Champery's husband clung to her with all the determination permitted to a man of wealth who had married a penniless woman twenty years younger than himself. He lived in a sanatorium because he was far too ill to live anywhere else, but he had rented a charming little chalet for his wife. The doctors told her it would not be long . . . yet they had told her that for years.

Stash approached the two women, kissed his mother's hair and bent to brush the air above the Marquise's hand.

"So, my little Stash is home from school," mocked the sleek red-headed woman, sitting with disciplined decorum in an armchair. "Do tell me, my dear child, did you manage finally to do well in your examinations? And are you still a member of that fascinating inner circle you spoke of last summer—the little jumped-up American millionaires and the little British lords with bad teeth and the naughty baby cattle barons from the Argentine, and all the other grandees of your school?"

Stash tightened his lips in rage. One day last summer, when he was only thirteen, he had made the mistake of describing his best friends to her. She seemed to be taking a genuine interest in his school life. Most of his mother's intimates, occupied with the myriad intrigues of their hermetically sealed world based on illness and gossip, had learned not to pay attention to the difficult, unfriendly boy, but the Marquise had drawn him out until he allowed her a rare glimpse into his school life.

"And you, Madame la Marquise," he shot at her, ignoring her questions, "are you still the notorious *femme fatale* of this vast and cosmopolitan center? Or have you been replaced by someone whom I have not yet met?"

"Alexander," flashed his mother. "That is quite enough! Claire, you must forgive him—he's just fourteen you know, that impossible age when you think it's amusing to be impudent. Alexander, apologize at once!"

"No, Titiana, darling, don't be silly ... I was teasing him and the little one got angry." Claire de Champery was in the best of humors. She felt the congestion of blood rushing between her primly pressed together thighs, proof positive that she had been right to provoke the boy. From the moment she had seen him coming across the room, she had noticed that the childish beauty she had savored in secret for years had become that of a youth. She saw the faint beginnings of a mustache on his upper lip, she measured with her eyes the new physical development which had given a fourteen-year-old the muscle structure of a youth. No longer a boy, yet not a man—a most delectable, a most tantalizing, a most fleeting age. A moment in a man's life, she reminded herself, that did not last long. A youth—a pure and perfect youth—that most tasty morsel of all. He knew nothing yet, she was sure of that. Off at a boys' school all year long, what could he possibly have learned besides the little dirty games they might play with each other? But his fiery reaction to her mockery told her that he was ready to be taught.

"Claire," Titiana insisted, "he simply must apologize. I can't permit him to behave in such a manner."

"Let him do a penance instead, Titiana darling. An apology is too easily given. Ah, I have it—he shall take me for a troika ride—that is, if he is old enough to control the horses?"

"I have been driving the troika for over four years," Stash said with scorn.

"*Tant mieux*. Then I have nothing to fear. Be at my chalet at three tomorrow afternoon and I'll be ready to leave. Now, baby, go and eat your pastries . . . you look as if you're longing for them."

As the Marquise dismissed the sullen youth, she turned back to Titiana and resumed the conversation with the facile charm which had drawn the Princess to her in the first place.

The day after Stash's scene with the Marquise de Champery, he arrived on time to take the Frenchwoman for a troika ride, since his mother had continued to insist on it.

The maid who let him into the chalet told him that her mistress was not quite ready to leave. She took his coat and led the way to a little sitting room just off the Marquise's bedroom. A fire had been lit and the room was very warm. The maid pointed out a tray of bottles of different liquors and an assortment of boxes of various kinds of cigarettes, and left him. Stash tightened his lips in annoyance. He was not old enough to drink or smoke and he knew that the Marquise was aware of it. This was just more of her baiting, another reminder that he was still a child. He was still standing resentfully in the center of the luxurious nest of a room when the Marquise entered. She was dressed in a loose flowing tea gown of black chiffon trimmed with lace.

"Oh, so you're not coming driving then," Stash exclaimed in relief, at the sight of her unsuitable clothes.

"No, I have merely changed your penance, my boy."

"Penance! You mean charade! This whole thing is absurd. I'm not a child to be treated like this. I'm leaving . . . enough of this!"

"I think not," the Marquise said softly. "You spoke to me most rudely and your darling *maman* is still very angry with you." The woman knew well that the only influence to which Stash made himself subject was that of his mother.

"Come sit down on this couch with me and I shall tell you what it is."

The boy suppressed a sigh of anger and silently did as he was told.

"I have been thinking," she mused. "We've known each

other a long time . . . is that not so? You were only seven when I first saw you . . . a little boy. And now you are almost a man. Do you have any idea how old I am?"

Stash was startled and deeply gratified at being told he was almost a man. His anger forgotten, he answered shyly. "You're not as old as my mother . . . certainly, but I can't guess women's ages."

"I am twenty-nine," she said, lying by only three years. "Does that seem very old to you? Of course it must. No . . . don't protest, don't be polite, it doesn't become you. When I was your age, twenty-nine was unimaginably old. So I have decided, as your penance, to teach you a lesson . . . a lesson in relativity."

The Marquise's small and swollen mouth was fresh as a fruit and she licked her lips thoughtfully. She moved closer to where Stash sat stiffly on the rose satin upholstery she knew was in bad taste but nevertheless permitted herself in private apartments. One of her plump white arms reached out, the black lace falling away from it, and she placed her hand on his head. "I miss your curls," she said softly, rumpling his thick hair. He sat straight and motionless, his nostrils drinking in the unfamiliar scent of a woman in a low-cut gown. By the light of the fire, out of the corner of his eye, he could see the blue shadow where her breasts began. Her hand left his hair and began to caress his neck with the most neutral of touches, as if she were absent-mindedly stroking a pet. Stash felt, with horrified embarrassment, that his penis had become rigid inside his trousers. He did not notice Claire's glance at his crotch, her eyebrows lifting only slightly as her practiced eye told her what had happened. Idly, she played with his earlobe, not moving any closer to him.

"So, what is relativity? Can you tell me? No . . . I thought not. The lesson in relativity begins with the realization that my hand and your neck have no age at all. They are only flesh meeting flesh. But to appreciate the true meaning of relativity, we must go further . . . much further." She allowed her wandering fingers to touch the soft hollow at the base of his throat, exposed in his open-necked shirt, and then she slipped her entire hand into his shirt and found one of his nipples and started to circle it with one finger. Stash groaned aloud and she drank in the sound with gourmandise—that was his first groan as a man, she thought, feeling his nipple harden. Now he would never forget her. "Ah, little man, you are beginning to understand relativity," she whispered to the boy who still looked ahead, his mind spinning. What was she doing ... his mother's friend ... impossible ... another mockery. In confusion he thought—but he couldn't be certain—that her hand, which she had withdrawn from his shirt, had, for an instant, fallen lower, to his crotch, and brushed like a feather over the stiff lump of his penis. But then this same hand, quickly raised, now gently unbuttoned his shirt, revealing his strong youth's chest down the center of which fine blond hair made a straight, faint shadow. She moved closer to him, threw back his shirt, and ran the fingers of both her hands down his half-naked, already well-muscled arms and murmured to herself, "How very grown-up you are, after all, my Stash." The boy was stunned into immobility even when she caressed him under his arms, fingering the scant, silky tufts of hair that had so recently sprouted there. The painful tumescence of his penis seemed shameful to him, a confession of weakness before this dominant woman. He knew her, the sly one, she wanted to make him try to touch her and then she would remind him of what a child he was. He gripped the pillows he was sitting on in order not to move, not to give her that satisfaction.

Then he felt her unbuckle his belt and unbutton his fly. For a moment she seemed to hesitate, her head lowered in the firelight, riveted at the sight of the outline that reared under his restraining undershorts. The size of it seemed to make her decide. She slid to the thick carpet and looked up at him as he sat on the edge of the couch, his teeth biting into his lower lip in a grimace which hardened his face into a look it would not naturally wear for ten more years.

"Now ... now we come to the penance, Stash. You must stand up." She remained still, waiting patiently, steadily watching him, not repeating her command. Slowly he stood up, his trousers falling to his feet. Controlling her breathing with difficulty the woman looked at the slender youth who stood before her, not daring to meet her eyes. Through the opening of his undershorts the thick, jutting shaft of his penis was clearly visible.

"Pull down your shorts," she whispered. He obeyed. His body was marvelously made, pale except where the winter sun had touched his big hands and strong neck. All his joints and tendons were tender-skinned, yet firm and defined. A little blond hair grew on the legs and a deeper shadow of coarser hair curled at the base of his testicles.

"Step out of your pants and lie down on the sofa," she ordered. "Don't touch me, Stash, or I will stop what I'm going to do to you. I am the teacher here and you are doing your penance, so be obedient. If you move, even one little inch, I'll stop the lesson. I swear it." The threat in her voice was real. She pulled at her gown so that it dropped from her shoulders. Her breasts sprang out from the confining lace. She cupped each of them in a hand, leaning over him so that he could see how sumptuously heavy they were, tipped with the light brown nipples of a true redhead. He lay still on the rose satin, not daring to arch his back and thrust his agonizingly hard penis upward. She brushed her nipples tantalizingly over his chapped lips. "Don't move!" she warned again, adoring the sensation of the roughness of his young open mouth on her flesh. When he moaned in fearful desire and tried to touch them with his tongue, she moved away at once. "Ah! No! I've only begun . . ." Very delicately, with the lightest possible touch, she moved her full, succulent mouth down this body which had just emerged from boyhood, stopping to anoint each of his nipples with her pointed, flicking tongue. Finally she hovered over his penis for a long moment while he held his breath. Her sleek head hung, almost in meditation, as she observed how it strained upward, jerking toward her mouth. But, without even touching it, she passed on and went lower, tonguing the insides of his strong thighs. As she knelt on the sofa she had gradually slipped out of her gown so that her full body, with its rich bounty of lush perfumed flesh, was entirely exposed, but from his position on the sofa, he could not see her nakedness clearly without raising his head. She had not yet touched him with anything but her nipples and her mouth, nor had he touched her at all. He ground his teeth and clenched his fists in frantic frustration and heard her low, satisfied laugh, the laugh of the true gourmet.

"Oh, yes, indeed, yes, you are making progress. You are beginning to appreciate relativity. You are almost prepared for the end of the lesson."

The Marquise's tongue traveled leisurely from Stash's thighs back to his testicles. She blew on his pubic hair very lightly, and again, he couldn't prevent a groan from escaping his dry lips. Like a line of fire, the tip of her experienced tongue ran up the base of his straining penis and then rested for one whirling moment on its tip.

"No," she said, pensively. "No, you cannot control yourself well enough." With a little movement she positioned herself until she was straddling Stash's body, one knee on either side of his tensed thighs. Slowly, with the leisurely care of a woman of thirty-two, she parted her thick, red pubic hair and opened the lips of her vagina with the fingers of one hand and, with the other, she gently pulled Stash's penis back from his stomach until it was pointed straight up into the air. He was so hard that she had to hold it back firmly while, taking an infinite amount of time, she gradually lowered herself onto the swollen tip. She gathered her ripe body into a soft pillar of flesh and slid down on him. When he was completely enclosed within her, she leaned forward and whispered into his contorted lips, "Now, now . . ."

Stash, released from his bondage, grasped the kneeling woman around her waist with both his arms and, without removing his penis from her tight sheath, lifted her up and turned her so that she was under him. With one gigantic thrust he poured himself out into her while he bit her lips mercilessly and crushed her breasts in both hands. As soon as he could breathe again, he said, "Don't you ever dare to ride me again! I'll do the riding from now on!"

"Oh, ho," she muttered in a harsh whisper, "so now it's you who gives the orders? But, my friend, only one of us is satisfied . . . so relatively speaking, the lesson has not been learned."

"No?" She realized that his penis had never left her vagina. It was growing again, growing bigger than before. He ground it into her waiting body with unsteady strokes, until she reached a violent orgasm. And still he rode her, swollen with blood, pausing only once to wipe his sperm from her wet pubic hair with her black lace gown. This second time he had already learned much he needed to know and he took his time in pleasing himself, ignoring her protests that he was hurting her, that he must stop a minute, that he was too big. His second orgasm was much more intense than the first, coming, it seemed, not just from his penis and his testicles, but from his whole spinal column. The fourteen-year-old boy lay, momentarily exhausted, beside the voluptuous, satiated form of the woman. Neither spoke as the fire crackled in the fireplace. It was dark outside.

"Claire," Stash said. "I'm going to take a bath in your tub. Ring the maid for hot chocolate and bring it to me there. And then . . ."

"Then. . . ?" she interrupted, astonished at the voice of command which came from the youth to whom she had just given his first lesson in love.

"And then we'll have another lesson in relativity. In the bedroom. This couch of yours is too slippery for me." His voice was rough with new authority.

"But . . . you're crazy!"

He took her hand and put it on his penis. The hot sticky organ was already beginning to rise and fill. It moved under her touch like an animal. "Don't you want me to bathe?" he asked. "Shall we just go to the bedroom now?"

"No, Stash—no—go take your bath. I'll ring for the chocolate." She hastily covered herself with the bedraggled gown.

"Don't forget the pastries."

Every day of that Christmas vacation, Stash cut short his skiing and spent all afternoon in the rose-red sitting room or the lavender bedroom of the Marquise de Champery, leaving only when it was time to go home for dinner. She wrote a note to Titiana to say that a head cold prevented her from joining the usual gathering at the chalet and gladly gave up her dinner engagements to preserve the fiction.

Stash became familiar with the long slow strokes, the quick jabs, the excruciatingly disciplined pauses which only made them both more eager, the quiver, the holding back, the pulses beating together—all the ebb and flow of making love. The Frenchwoman taught him how to please her, and all the other women he would possess, with a sensuality that explored every detail. She taught him to be shameless, as she was, so that all the prohibitions of conventional sexuality never had a chance to make an impression on him. She taught him the many delicate uses of his mouth, his tongue, his teeth and his fingers moving urgently between her legs. She taught him the importance of patience and stealthy gentleness. She taught him nothing of tenderness or sentiment . . . between them there was none of that ... she was not false, whatever else she was. When they parted, as he left to go back to school, there were no promises exchanged or backward looks. He was a youth, she a woman who did not permit herself the luxury of believing for an instant that he would come back to her for anything except her body ... and then only if he did not find another he preferred. But she knew that in the entire lifetime which stretched ahead of Stash Valensky, she would occupy a place that no other woman would ever fill. When he was an old man and had forgotten a hundred other women, he would still remember the rose satin and the firelight and the lesson in relativity.

After the boy's departure, the head cold of Madame la Marquise vanished. However, she decided not to return every day to the claustrophobic tea-time group at the Princess Titiana's. Instead, she took up skiing. In the next decade, as her husband persistently, unforgivably lingered on the verge of death, Claire de Champery deserved credit for having been the instructor of an entire legion of naive village youths, those Alpine ski instructors who are, today, legendary animals of pleasure. Even if they have never heard of her, they owe much to her teaching, lessons which have been handed down from one generation of ski-school heroes to another.

In 1929 Stash Valensky graduated from Le Rosey. He spent that summer on a vast ranch in Argentina, owned by the father of one of his classmates. The finest polo ponies of the world were bred in South America and many of the best players lived there. They came up from Argentina to compete with the American or British teams, often bringing a string of forty ponies which they sold after the season for great prices. The golden age of polo lasted from 1929 to 1939, those years during which Tommy Hitchcock, Winston Guest, Cecil Smith, Pat and Aiden Rourk, the brothers from Ireland, Jai, the Maharajah of Jaipur, Eric Pedley from Santa Barbara and other equally great players were all in competition, all marvelously mounted, all devoting their lives to the game.

At Rolle, the spring and fall campus of Le Rosey, and during his summer vacations in Davos, Stash had become a consummate horseman. Now, in the Argentine, he discovered why. Polo might have been invented for him. Had he another life to live, he would have chosen to be Akbar, the Mogul ruler of India in the 1500s who loved polo so much that he played it in the dark, with balls of smoldering wood, galloping after the trail of sparks they left behind them. After three months of constant practice, in the "pit" and on the field, his hosts felt it safe to pay Stash the honor of asking him to play in a practice match. Filled with jubilation he wrote home and explained that it was absolutely necessary for him to extend his visit for another three months, since the South American polo season was just beginning.

Princess Titiana was desolate that her son was staying away for so long, but Prince Vasily took the request with equanimity. What else was there for a boy to do, after all?

"My dearest, had there not been the Russian Revolution or the Great War, your Alexander would have made a splendid cavalry officer. At least polo is becoming to a prince." He deposited a large sum of money in Stash's Buenos Aires bank account and wrote to him that he must buy his own ponies and no longer depend on borrowed mounts.

The essential element in a great polo player, once he has established the perfection of his horsemanship and his coordination, is raw courage. Stash Valensky, who had now reached his full height of six feet, two inches, was perfectly trained for the sport, but more importantly, his warrior spirit *needed* it.

Beginning in that summer of 1929 when he was eighteen, Stash roamed the world, following the polo seasons: England in the summer, Deauville in August, autumn in South America, winter in India, spring in the United States. With him went his household: his valet, an Englishman called Mump, his grooms, his trainer and, of course, most important of all, his ponies.

Mump's duties extended beyond the care of the Prince's wardrobe. He spent as much time at the florist's and delivering notes by hand as he did on his master's boots. Stash, who had been so precociously indoctrinated into carnal love, spent no time laying siege to marriageable virgins or even young ladies of good reputation, virgin or not. He had early learned a taste for another kind of woman, and such women were inevitably the wives of other men. A complication, but not one which couldn't be managed, particularly with the participation of Mump— who made sure that letters were discreetly delivered and received; that flowers only arrived before or after a party, so as not to arouse suspicion; that no lady who found herself alone for a minute in Stash's apartments would ever stumble upon evidence of another.

Stash discovered that polo had a way of confining him to a single love affair at a time, since the lady in question invariably considered it her precious prerogative to drive out to the field and watch the teams practice. Decency demanded that two women were not observed, each parked in a great open car, cheering him on at the same time. However, the teams never lingered long in any one country, and the glowing general's wife in Brazil never knew about the young maharanee in Delhi; the exquisite English countess had never heard rumors of the lovely San Franciscan who came out every day to the Old Monterey Polo Club.

The only interruption in the gilded years of pleasure Stash led after his graduation from Le Rosey came when Princess Titiana, worn and wasted, yet struggling to the end, died in 1934. Stash had always visited his parents in Davos twice a year and neither of them ever brought themselves to comment on the dash and heedlessness with which he lived. It made them too happy to see him full of health, brio and the joy of the chase. Now Stash paused long enough to realize that his father was sixty-five, a devastated man whose reason for living had vanished. For the next few months Stash remained in Davos with Prince Vasily, curbing his impatience to resume his life. Soon he saw that his father was slipping away, giving up, coming to an end of the exile that he had imposed on himself, an exile that had preserved his fortune yet left him only half a man, able only to watch, but never to participate in the great events of history, self-marooned, on the heights of Davos-Dorf.

After the death of Prince Vasily Valensky, the new heir found that besides the diminished but still great amount of Russian gold that had been deposited in Swiss banks twenty-two years before, he had inherited a huge houseful of terrified servants, all of whom had come from Russia with his parents and were now well into middle age. None of them knew anything but service to the Valenskys. Their greatest fear was of what was to become of them. Stash was their feudal lord as far as it was possible in the modern world. They neither accepted nor aspired to any other point of view. Their children had been brought up as

Swiss citizens, but nothing could shake the need these old Russians had to cling together in an atmosphere that reminded them of a country as remote as drowned Atlantis.

They were his responsibility now, Stash realized, with a grimace of astonishment. He had never considered what he would do with them if his parents weren't alive, never once thought realistically about the future. Now he called their leaders, Zachary, the former chasseur, and Boris, the former sledge driver, to him.

"I dislike Davos," he told them. "It has too many sad memories. Yet some of you have children in Swiss schools. What would you think if I were to move to a lower part of Switzerland—and take you all with me? Would you want to come or would you prefer to stay on here? In either case you all will continue to be paid during my lifetime."

"Prince Alexander," answered Zachary, "we have no home that is not your home. We are not too old to move, but we are far too old to change."

Soon Stash found the villa outside of Lausanne and, within a short time he had reproduced there the interior of the palace he had never seen in St. Petersburg, just as his father had brought it intact to Davos. But the Lausanne establishment was free of any trace of the sickroom, empty of the chatter of invalids, swept bare of any nostalgia except that which might cling to the increasingly valuable paintings and furniture. The treasure of icons remained sleeping in their velvet boxes, with the exception of the one his mother had always loved best, which Stash kept in his bedroom, and the humble ones the servants hung in their own rooms. Stash spent only a month or two of every year in Lausanne, just enough to reassure the servants, but they maintained the great house as if he were expected home every night.

In 1934 polo and women were almost eclipsed by a new passion. The lure of flying caught him after the English summer polo season had ended. A badly broken leg, souvenir of a match in September, had kept Stash from going on to South America that year and, on the 20th of October, 1934, he was among those who gathered at dawn at Mildenhall, Suffolk, to watch the start of the MacRobertson Race, from England to Australia, the single greatest sporting event in the short history of aviation. He was immediately caught up in the thrilling, exultant tension of the crowd of sixteen thousand, as it watched twenty of the finest, most experimental aircraft of the period take off toward the East and the first checkpoint at Baghdad. That same day, still on crutches, Stash joined the London Aero Club, an offshoot of the Royal Aero Club. By the following week, he had convinced his doctor that he no longer needed crutches, and he immediately drove to the Aero Club for instructions. He soloed after six hours in a little training biplane, the de Havilland Moth, and after another three hours of solo flying, followed by an examination, he earned his pilot's license.

Stash bought a monoplane, the Miles Hawk, and began the pursuit of speed which was to obsess him for the next six years. He entered his first race in France the next year, the Coupe Deutsch de la Meurthe, flying a Caudron racer, small-winged, slim and built of wood, with a supercharged Renault engine, a plane which could, at its peak, reach a record-breaking 314 miles per hour. In 1937 he went to the United States to compete in the Bendix Trophy race and returned to try again in 1938, to become one of the ten men to lose to Jacqueline Cochrane, a woman who set the coast-to-coast endurance record in ten hours, twenty-seven minutes, fifty-five seconds. He flew Severskys; he flew the madly dangerous, tiny Mignet Pou-du-Ciel or Sky Louse. He flew anything with wings, and he always flew alone, a predilection which prevented him from entering many of the distance competitions which required a flying partner. But being alone in the air was more than half of the joy of flying to Stash. It provided such a total contrast to the team play of polo. The sky meant solitude, a solitude which had become almost impossible to find on the ground. The next four years, spent in headlong pursuit, chasing almost mindlessly after speed records in the sky and women and polo balls on the ground, were scarcely interrupted when Stash read, one day at the end of September 1938, of Chamberlain's return from Munich with the promise of "peace in our time."

However, the following March, in 1939, as soon as he read of the German seizure of Czechoslovakia, Stash saw clearly that war was inevitable, and, immediately, he left Bombay for England. On his arrival he went directly to the headquarters of the Royal Air Force Volunteer Reserve and made his application for a commission. By June, Flight Officer A. V. Valensky was involved in full-time training of young pilots at Duxford in Cambridgeshire, most of them young university squadron members.

When Britain and France declared war on Germany on the 3rd of September, 1939, almost a month short of Stash's twenty-eighth birthday, he had been trained as a fighter pilot and was a member of the 249 Squadron, flying a Hurricane, powered, he saw to his delight, with a Rolls-Royce Merlin engine. But when his squadron was declared operational in July and qualified for night fighting, Stash, to his inutterably violent and bitter rage, was promoted to Flight Lieutenant and ordered to Aston Down where he was doomed to remain for one entire year, teaching young pilots the techniques of fighter flying.

Nothing he had ever experienced in his life of action had prepared him for those twelve maddening months in which men he had trained were sent off in batches, to "clobber bandits" as they cheerfully put it, leaving him behind to teach, not fight. Whenever he could, Stash went down to London to besiege RAF officials in his grim efforts to get posted to a fighter squadron.

"Be reasonable, Valensky," he was told with cold regularity. "You're a damn sight more useful to us right where you are than if you were busy getting shot up somewhere —*someone* has to teach the kiddies, after all."

Filled with pent-up frustration and feeling utterly worthless, Stash drank heavily for the first time in his life. When he met Victoria Woodhill, a WAAF, he put all his pent-up frustration into conquering the rather curt and aloof young woman whose chief attraction was that she was not interested in him. Anything he could batter, beat against and overcome was a target for Stash during those months that saw the Germans push deeper into the body of Europe. They were married in June of 1940 and almost immediately afterward lost sight of each other as Victoria was posted to Scotland.

Officially the Battle of Britain lasted almost four months, from the 10th of July, 1940, through the 31st of October. It was actually a series of battles, fought by six hundred RAF planes against the mighty *Luftwaffe* flying to dominate Britain with its three thousand bombers and twelve hundred fighter planes. Had the RAF lost, England would almost certainly have been invaded.

For Stash, the Battle of Britain lasted only three months, beginning in August 1940, when the powers that decided such things finally reached the last-ditch conclusion that they could no longer afford the luxury of Training Units, but sent their newly hatched airmen out to operational squadrons to be trained between and during actual combat.

At last Stash was posted to Westhampnett, near Portsmouth, where he arrived on a day which would be known as "Black Thursday," the day of August 15, 1940, the day on which Göring unleashed his "eagles" from all the flanks under his command in an all-out air assault. A vast armada of Dornier 17s and Junker 88s, escorted by fighter planes, had crossed the coast of England when Stash's new squadron was scrambled. In the blue English sky his first air battle was a maelstrom of diving, swerving, spinning, firing planes, thrusting and striking even as they died.

By the time the battle was over, Intelligence had confirmed that Valensky had bagged two German bombers and three German fighters. He had never even heard the shouting which filled his earphones as the other pilots warned each other of an attacker or screamed in jubilation when they'd made a hit—the cold, concentrated, lethal rage of his own flying made them inaudible to him. Nor did he realize that each time he shot down an enemy he uttered a harsh war cry which rang in the ears of the other members of his flight. After they'd driven off the Germans, with their tails between their legs, the air was full of comment.

"Christ, what in bloody hell was *that?*"

"The new chap—can't be anyone else—no one here but us chickens."

"Well, it sounded like a bloody condor to me!"

It was as Condor Valensky that Stash fought the Battle of Britain; and later, transferred to the Western Desert Air Force, he flew by day and by night in operation "Crusader" to relieve the port of Tobruk in November of 1941. It was as Condor Valensky that he flew a Hurricane "tank-buster" against Rommel at El Alamein; as Condor Valensky that he won the DFC and the DFO and became Squadron Commander in 1942. He was not called Stash again until the war had ended. And been won.

5

$\mathcal{A}$s autumn approached, Francesca and Stash, still deep in the first weeks of their honeymoon, began to plan for the future. They discussed the idea of traveling to India toward the end of November, in order to be in Calcutta for the December and January polo season which would be followed by the matches in Delhi in February and March. But, one day in the middle of October, Francesca became certain that she was pregnant.

"It must have happened that first night in the stables," she told Stash. "I suspected it three weeks after we were married but I wanted to be absolutely sure before I told you." She was resplendent.

"Then? In the stables? You're sure?" he demanded, transported by the sudden joy.

"Yes, then. I know it. I don't know how I know, but I do."

"And do you also know that it will be a boy? Because that *I* know."

Francesca merely murmured, "Perhaps." She knew why Stash wanted a boy so badly. He had a son by his brief first marriage, a boy who was now almost six years old. The boy had been born after Stash and Victoria Woodhill had separated. That hasty marriage, product of Stash's frustrated warrior spirit, had not lasted long into peacetime. They had waited only until after the child's birth to get divorced. The boy's mother had no intention of saddling her son with more foreign a name than the one he had been born with, so he was called George Edward Woodhill Valensky. However, as a baby, she had dubbed him Ram, because of his habit of butting his head against the side of his crib, and Ram he had remained. He lived with his mother and stepfather in Scotland and only visited Stash on infrequent occasions. Stash's hope, so strong that it was expressed as a certainty, that Francesca's baby would be a boy, was a way of ensuring himself another son, one who would not be taken from him.

Francesca had seen photos of Ram, a straight dart of a boy, with brows knitted together as he stared defiantly into the camera with a stern and unchildlike expression on his handsome face. She recognized little of Stash in this son who had an air of aristocratic coldness, a high-strung, almost bitter expression that already indicated that he would never allow himself to relax into the rough and confident stance of his father.

"He's a regular horseman, even now, even at this age," Stash said. "Ram's a perfect physical specimen, brought up like a little soldier—that damned British upper-class tradition." He looked at the photograph again, shaking his head. "However, he's intelligent and as tough as they make them. There's something . . . closed off . . . in him . . . like all his mother's family. Or perhaps it was the divorce. In any case, it couldn't be helped." He shrugged, put away the photos with the gesture of a man who doesn't intend to look at them again for a long time, and held Francesca close to him. His eyes searched her face and, just for a moment, his predator's gaze softened and she felt that it was she who was his rock in a stormy sea.

The villa outside Lausanne was so comfortable and spacious that the Valenskys decided to remain there until their child was born. Lausanne itself, with its excellent doctors, was only a short ride away, and, since there was no longer any question of going to India, Stash sent his string of ponies to be put out to grass in England. After the war, he had taken the larger part of his fortune out of Switzerland and invested it in the Rolls-Royce Company. Born in Russia, brought up in the Alps, a nomad of the polo seasons, he found that his nationality was emotional, dedicated not to a country but to an engine, the Rolls-Royce engine that had, to his way of thinking, surely saved England and determined the course of the war.

In the summer of the following year, when the baby would be a few months old, Stash assured Francesca that they would move to London, buy a house, get properly settled in and make that their home base for the future, but meanwhile they lived those first months of their marriage in a state of such incredulous adoration of each other, such passionate absorption in each other's body, that neither of them wanted to travel any farther than to Evian, just across Lac Leman, where they went from time to time to gamble at the casino. The trip by lake steamer in the early evening was a dream of pleasure as they stood together at the rail and watched the small boats, their yellow, red and blue sails like huge butterflies, heading for the harbor in the sunset. When they took the midnight steamer home to the Ouchy landing stage, they were never sure if they had won or lost at *chemin de fer,* nor did they care.

To mark the passage of the weeks, Stash gave Francesca more of the Fabergé rock-crystal vases from his mother's collection. Each one held a few sprays of flowers or branches of fruit worked in precious stones, diamonds and enamel: flowering quince, cranberry and raspberries, lily of the valley, daffodils, wild roses and violets, all fashioned with the most imaginative and delicate workmanship, so that the rich materials never overwhelmed the reality of the flower and fruit forms. Soon Francesca had a flowering Fabergé garden growing by her bedside, and, when he learned of the coming child, Stash gave her a Fabergé egg made of lapis lazuli mounted in gold. The egg contained a yoke of deep yellow enamel. When this yoke was opened it activated a mechanism that caused a miniature crown to rise up out of the heart of the egg, a perfect replica of the dome-shaped crown of Catherine the Great, paved with diamonds and topped by a cabochon ruby. Inside the crown still another egg was suspended, formed from a large cabochon ruby, hanging on a tiny gold chain.

"My mother never knew if this was an Imperial Easter egg or not," Stash told her as she wondered at it. "My father bought it from a refugee after the Revolution who swore that it was one of those presented to the Dowager Tsarina Marie but he couldn't account for how he happened to have it and my father knew too much to insist . . . however, it bears the Fabergé mark."

"I've never seen anything so perfect," Francesca said, holding it on the palm of one hand.

"I have," Stash answered, running his hands down the

length of her neck until they found her breasts which were growing fuller and riper with each passing day. The egg fell to the carpet as he fastened his lips on her darkening nipples and suckled as demandingly as any child.

In Lausanne, as winter closed in on the great villa, Stash exercised the large bays in his stable during the afternoon, and Francesca napped under a light, mauve silk eiderdown, waking only when she could tell, from the subtle smell of snow that invaded their room, that he had returned.

After tea, if the early evening was not too windy, Stash took Francesca for a horse-drawn sleigh ride, and often, seeing the moon rise as they returned to the huge villa, as welcoming, cheerful and brightly lit as an ocean liner, listening to the snuffling of the horses and tender music of the sleigh bells, warm under the fur-lined lap robe, with the hood of her full-length sable coat drawn up over her chin, Francesca felt tears on her cheeks. Not tears of happiness, but rather tears of that sudden sadness that comes at those rare moments of perfect joy that are fully realized at the exact instant at which they are being experienced. Such knowledge always carries in it a premonition of loss, a premonition which needs no reason or explanation.

Just as Francesca grew expert in the ways of the great silver samovar that occupied its traditional place of honor on a round, lace-covered table in the salon, she became accustomed to the ways of Stash's crowd of servants who treated Francesca with a mixture of irrepressibly loving concern and overbearing curiosity. She found herself virtually engulfed in—not "staff" she thought, nothing that starchy, not "help," nothing that casual, certainly not "domestics," nothing that removed, but rather a tribe of what she could only think of as semi-in-laws.

She had married into a way of life, a life which included Masha, who, as a matter of course, invaded Francesca's lingerie drawers in order to fold each object with exquisite care, Masha who hung up her bathrobes and then tied the sashes and buttoned the buttons, so that it was no longer possible to put on a robe quickly, Masha who had her own way with scarfs, arranging them according to color rather than according to utility or size, so that old favorites had a way of disappearing into the spectrum, Masha who appeared in Francesca's bathroom as she got out of her tub, with an enormous warm towel unfolded and ready to wrap around her.

Within a few weeks Francesca felt entirely comfortable with Masha's ministrations and allowed her to brush her hair and even help her into her underwear, quite, Masha told her, as she had been allowed to do for Stash's mother, Princess Titiana, when the Princess's own maids were unavailable for one reason or another.

"Is that so, Masha," said Francesca with lazy interest, but as she relaxed and gave herself over to the gentle brushing, she *saw* herself vividly, lying there on the heap of lace-covered pillows in a velvet dressing gown with her hair being tended devotedly. She had only to ask for a luxury in order to have it brought to her immediately—or, in the case of the men who came from Cartier to show Prince Valensky jewels for his wife, she had only to indicate which of the jewels pleased her, to own it. Yes, now when she walked, she walked like a princess, Francesca thought, and didn't even ask herself what she meant.

The inquiries Stash had made among his friends in Lausanne had indicated that Dr. Henri Allard was the most highly considered specialist in the city. He ran a private clinic which was, in effect, a small, extremely well-run, modern hospital, much favored by wealthy women from all parts of the world.

Dr. Allard himself was a compact, beaming, competent and energetic man who grew tulips almost as well as he grew babies. He told Francesca that she could expect her child sometime at the end of May. Her monthly visits to Allard were a small and mildly annoying interruption of the great dialogue on which she and Stash were embarked until February. That day Dr. Allard bent over Francesca's belly with his stethoscope for an unusually long time. Afterward, in his consulting room, he was more cheerful than this perpetually jovial man had yet been.

"I believe we have a surprise for the Prince," he announced, almost bouncing in his chair. "Last month I was not completely certain so I said nothing, but now I am. There are two distinct heartbeats, with a difference of ten beats a minute. You are carrying twins, my dear Princess!"

"A surprise for the *Prince?*" Francesca's voice rose in astonishment.

"Is there no history of twins in your family then?" he asked.

"History? I don't . . . no, no history. Doctor, is there anything special . . . is it harder to have twins . . . I can't believe . . . twins . . . you're *sure?* Don't you have to make an X ray to be sure?"

"I would prefer not to do so yet. Perhaps next month. But both heartbeats are there, each quite separate, so there can be no doubt." He beamed at her as if she had just won a gold medal. Francesca was unable to sort out her feelings. It was almost impossible to imagine the reality of one baby, let alone two. Lately she had been dreaming of a baby, always a boy, who lay in her arms looking a great deal like Charlie McCarthy, and spoke to her as if he were an adult—happy, funny dreams. But two!

"So, my dear Madame," the doctor continued, "you will now come to see me every two weeks for the next month and then, just to be on the safe side, once a week until the babies begin to manifest a desire to enter the world. Yes?"

"Of course." Francesca hardly knew what she was saying. Suddenly the bewitched dream of her world had been destroyed as easily as an iridescent soap bubble. She wanted only to leave and drive back to the villa and try to absorb this invasion, this new reality.

The entire chalet beat rapturously to the rhythm of the news. Twins! Stash, in his incredulous delight, hadn't been able to resist telling his valet, Mump, almost immediately. Mump had told the housekeeper, the housekeeper had told the chef, the chef had told Masha, who, bursting with excitement, ran to find Francesca in the library and reproached her mistress for not having announced the news herself.

"I should have been the first to know, Princess. After all . . . and now everyone knows about it, right down to the old laundry women and the men in the stable."

"Oh, for heaven's sake, Masha, *I* didn't even know it myself until yesterday. Why, oh why, do you all gossip so much?"

"Gossip? Why, Princess, we never gossip. We only say what we have happened to overhear or observed or have been told. . . . That's not gossip!"

"Of course not. Now Masha, we're going to need twice as much of everything now. Two layettes, dear God, even one seems too much! Bring me some paper please, and I'll start making lists."

"I think the Princess should lie down," Masha insisted.

"Masha, the Princess has work to do!"

February and March passed gaily, except for Francesca's ever increasing discomfort. At night she could lie only on her side, Stash behind her. Often, for hours, he stayed pressing closely the fragrant length of her body, his arms around her so that he could feel the movements of her swollen belly.

"They push you like two little horses," Stash murmured proudly. "When I was a baby Masha used to tell my mother that she had never heard of a child who suckled with such strength. She said no man had dared to treat her with such impudence, not even the one who gave her a bastard. My God, imagine two like me!" He gave a lofty chuckle.

Francesca smiled to herself at his absolute conviction that he was simply going to be reproduced in miniature, not just once but twice.

He took it for granted that the babies would be no less than extensions of himself. Already he had made plans to teach them to ride and ski, as if they would be born at the age of four, each a precocious Hercules.

One day, during the third week of April, Francesca's back ached particularly badly. That night she woke up as if she had been tapped on the shoulder in the dark. "Who. . . ?" she said, not really awake, and then she knew. "Well ... well ... what do you know?" she asked herself in a whisper and lay quietly, waiting. Half an hour later, after two more contractions had gripped her, she woke Stash gently.

"It's probably nothing, darling, but Doctor Allard said to phone him if anything happened at all. This must be false labor, nothing to get excited about, but would you call him for me, please?" She felt shy about waking the doctor in the middle of the night.

Woken from depths of sleep, Stash jumped out of bed with the instant reactions that had become second nature in the RAF.

"Wait, it's not a scramble—take it easy," Francesca said, basking in a feeling of heightened well-being.

Stash returned from the phone in a minute.

"The doctor said to come to the clinic immediately. Here's your coat and your handbag . . . oh, your boots."

"I'll brush my teeth and pack a nightgown and . . ."

"No," Stash ordered, bundling her into her coat and bending down to put her bare feet into her fur-lined boots.

"At least wake somebody and tell them we've gone," Francesca gasped.

"Why? They'll figure it out in the morning."

"I feel as if we're eloping." Francesca's laugh spilled out as she watched Stash plunge into his clothes. She continued laughing quietly as he led her through the quiet villa to the garage, clumsy as he tried to support her weight when she was perfectly capable of walking by herself.

By the time they reached the clinic Dr. Allard and his chief assistant, Dr. Rombais, were waiting for them right inside the door. Francesca was surprised to see her dapper obstetrician dressed in loose white pants and a matching smocklike top. She had never seen Dr. Allard without a vest immaculately piped in white under his excellently tailored jacket.

"So, Princess, we may have less time to wait than we thought," he greeted her, with his usual cheer.

"But it's too soon, Doctor. It must be false labor. You said not till May," she cried.

"Perhaps that is all it is," he agreed, "but we must make sure, must we not?"

From then on everything else was forgotten as Francesca was settled into a bed with side rails on it. As soon as she was comfortable Allard entered and closed the door behind him.

Allard knew his statistics. Any woman faced with the delivery of twins faces a twofold or threefold increase in the possibility that the birth will be fatal to her. However, this remote chance was not his chief concern, although his operating-room staff was prepared for all possibilities. Francesca was not exhibiting high blood pressure or any signs of a toxic condition. However, by his calculations, labor was five, perhaps even six weeks premature, and under such circumstances, particularly with twins, he had every reason to be cautious.

"Well, *Maman*," he said after he had examined her. "The great day is here." Allard always called women in labor *"Maman,"* feeling that it focused their minds on the future rather than the present.

"So it's not false labor?"

"Indeed, no. You are well on your way, but we must expect a certain number of hours to pass. After all, this is your first delivery, even if you are a bit early."

After the next half-hour of contractions, Francesca's calm acceptance of her physical discomfort began to disintegrate. Fun was fun, she told herself, but this was really hurting. There was no way in which she could visualize herself playing the role of a woman in labor. She was *in* it for real and she wanted to be out of it, and fast.

"Doctor Allard, could I please have something for the pain? I'm afraid I need it now."

"Alas, no, *Maman,* in your case we must avoid giving you any drugs."

"What!"

Beaming as if he were giving her good news he continued. "Anything I gave you now would affect the unborn babies adversely. It would be passed along to the babies through your bloodstream. Because you are more than a month early, they still have not reached their proper weight. To be frank, I can give you nothing at all . . ."

"No drugs!" Francesca was pale with terror. Like generations of American women, her idea of childbirth without drugs was firmly based on the long and fatal agony of Melanie Wilkes in *Gone With the Wind.*

"It is for the best, *Maman,* much for the best."

"But, my God, for how long?" she asked.

"Until you are ready to deliver the little ones. Then I can give you a saddle block and from then on you will feel no pain at all."

"A saddle block? My God, what's that?" she gasped in horrified apprehension.

"Merely a painkilling injection," he explained, thinking it best not to add that it was administered into the fourth lumbar interspace of the spinal column. The Princess was agitated as it was, without exact explanations.

"But Doctor, can't you use a saddle block now?" Francesca implored him.

"Alas no. It might stop the labor and your babies want to be born, *Maman.*" He was kind, but she knew then that absolutely nothing she could say would move him.

"Doctor, why didn't you tell me about this before? It just seems incredible that with modern medicine . . ."

Francesca stopped, unable to adequately express her outraged, fearful disbelief.

"But you are having premature twins, *Maman*. Modern medicine calls for precisely these measures." The doctor took her hand and stroked it paternally. "I will leave my head obstetrical nurse with you now, but I will be in the next room. If you need me or want me for anything, just tell her and I will come at once."

"The next room? Why can't you stay here?" Francesca begged, terrified at the idea of his leaving her for any length of time.

"For my catnap, *Maman*. Tonight I have already delivered two babies. You must try to relax completely between contractions—I strongly advise that you take a catnap, too."

The next eight hours passed in a kaleidoscope of emotions: physical anguish of a kind never experienced or dreamed of, which left no time for thought; anger that this was so much worse than she had expected; raging euphoria tinged with the knowledge that it would only last until the next contraction; fear, like that of a swimmer realizing that the tide is too strong and all hope of fighting it is gone and, above all the other emotions, *triumph* which painted those hours in their single unforgettable light; triumph at being fully alive, totally involved with every atom of her mental, moral and physical resources engaged in the most important work of her life.

Francesca endured without medication, helped only by the constant encouragement of the two doctors and the many nurses who came and went, busy with examinations which she soon disregarded entirely. When she saw the two orderlies appear with the cart on which they were to roll her into the delivery room, she was too dazed to realize what they had come for.

On the delivery table, Dr. Allard waited until Francesca was between contractions. Then he helped her to a sitting position for the saddle block. Afterward, she was placed flat on her back with a pillow under her head. The complete relief of pain, as astonishing as a clap of thunder, was so extraordinary that Francesca was startled and alarmed.

"I'm not paralyzed, am I, Doctor—it's not that, is it?"

"Of course not, *Maman*—you are doing wonderfully.

Everything is going just as it should. Relax, relax ... we are all here for you." He bent over her for the hundredth time with his stethoscope, listening for the fetal heartbeats.

"Oh, this is heaven..." Francesca sighed.

Although the delivery room contained Allard and Dr. Rombais, as well as three nurses and an anesthesiologist, silence was the rule for the next forty minutes except for Allard's instructions to Francesca. Allard's team were trained to work together without speaking, by eye and hand signals, since it was his belief that women giving birth were more than normally alert to any spoken words and almost certain to misinterpret them. "Remember," he would say to his staff, "a *Maman* may look unconscious under anesthetic but the sense of hearing is the last to go—say nothing."

After forty minutes Francesca was once again conscious of pain, but of a greatly diminished degree.

"Doctor, Doctor," she murmured, "I think the injection is wearing off."

"No, indeed—we are merely coming to the end," he reassured her in the most jocund of tones. "Now, when I say push, bear down as hard as you can. You won't feel the contractions but I can see them, so you must obey my instructions."

In another ten minutes Francesca heard him grunt in satisfaction. Almost immediately she heard the cry of a baby.

"Is it a boy?" she whispered.

"You have a ravishing daughter, *Maman*," answered Allard, hastily handing the baby to Dr. Rombais who carefully clamped its umbilical cord. Allard plunged back to his position between Francesca's thighs. The nurse who was monitoring the fetal heartbeats had just indicated urgently to him that the heartbeat of the unborn child was becoming slower. He saw, to his consternation, that the amniotic fluid which still appeared was yellow green in color instead of clear. The heartbeat of the second twin was growing slower every second. Allard palpated Francesca's uterus and discovered that it had gone completely rigid. All contractions had stopped. He signaled vehemently at Dr. Rombais to put immediate pressure on Francesca's fundus, the uppermost part of the uterus, while Dr. Allard squeezed with all his might on her now boardlike uterus. Using all the force at his command, he manipulated the second twin down the open birth canal into a position from which he could deliver it with forceps.

Within a matter of minutes, no less than four and no more than five, the second twin was delivered. She did not start to breathe spontaneously as the first one had, but had to be roughed up in a towel with considerable friction before a weak cry came from her mouth. As Dr. Allard cut her umbilical cord, he carefully noted that although the child appeared perfectly formed, she could not weigh much more than four pounds, a guess confirmed by the delivery-room scale. Worse, as he had feared, because of the sign of the yellow green amniotic meconium in the amniotic fluid, Francesca had suffered a massive internal hemorrhage due to an abrupt separation of the placenta from the walls of the uterus minutes before the delivery of the second twin.

"Doctor?" Francesca's voice implored. "What's happening—is it a boy or a girl?"

"Another daughter," he answered briefly. The terseness of his answer, the neutral quality of his normally merry voice, indicated to the others in the delivery room that their chief was deeply concerned about the second child. Something was gravely wrong.

Even as he spoke, the anesthesiologist who was watching Francesca's vital signs saw that her blood pressure had suddenly dropped and her heartbeat had risen markedly. Her pang of bitterest disappointment at Dr. Allard's announcement was forgotten as she became aware of feeling suddenly nauseated and dizzy. Sweat began to pour from her body. Still she persisted. "Show them to me . . . please show them."

"In just one minute, _Maman_. You must try to relax now." Allard motioned for two nurses to start simultaneous transfusions in each of Francesca's arms. She was beginning to go into shock, but within a short while the transfusions and the administration of fibrinogen brought her pulse rate and her blood pressure back to safe levels. As soon as he saw that his patient was stabilized, Allard told Dr. Rombais to bring the babies to the delivery table. Both infants' eyes were tightly closed, both of them had their fists firmly curled. On one twin the Saxon-white hair, which had just been gently dried, had already started to curl. On the other, the pale hair was still a bit damp.

Both of the babies were wrapped in soft white flannel

cloths and as Francesca, weak but alert, studied them, she felt a burst of astonishment such as she had never known before. The transition from the creatures with whom she felt a total connection and communication as she carried them inside her, to the sight of these two separate human beings who each possessed the individual authority to close their eyes and curl their fists and thus reject the brightly lit world in which they found themselves, was such a stunning and incomprehensible change that she couldn't grasp it intellectually, but only feel it emotionally.

"Are they identical, Doctor?"

"Yes, but your second daughter weighs less than the first. This one," he said, pointing to the smaller baby, "must go directly into an incubator until she gains some weight. But rest assured, we have counted and they both have all their fingers and toes."

"Thank God," Francesca whispered.

"Now, *Maman*, you must rest."

"Tell my husband."

"He must wait for just a while." The doctor had no intention of leaving Francesca until he was completely satisfied that the new blood running into her arms had done all its work. He didn't leave her until she was ready to be transferred to the recovery room. Then he left the empty delivery room untying the strings of his white cap wearily.

When the tired doctor entered the room in which Stash had been waiting, he saw that he had fallen asleep sitting up, his forehead pressed to the window out of which he had been peering, sightlessly, during all the long night. Dr. Allard stood behind the sleeping man for a long minute. Then he sighed and lightly pressed Stash's shoulder. The Prince woke instantly.

"Tell me!"

"You have twin daughters. Madame is well but very tired."

Stash stared wildly at the doctor as if there might be other information. The assault on his rigid expectations was so ruinous that he could say nothing. The doctor, after a short pause, continued blandly to answer the unasked questions with which other men would have bombarded him.

"One of your daughters is in excellent condition, Sir. As for the other . . ."

Stash finally found his voice. *"What* about the other. . . . Tell me!"

"There was a problem, a clinical condition, before the second child was born. The placenta separated from the womb just before birth and Madame suffered an internal, concealed hemorrhage."

Stash slumped against the wall. "So the child is dead. You can tell me, Doctor."

"No, the child is alive, but I must warn you that she is in grave difficulty. She is very small, only four pounds, two ounces, and because of the *placentae abruptio*—the separation—and the presence of meconium in the amniotic fluid, we know that there was a period during which no oxygen reached her brain. We acted as quickly as possible, Prince, but it was four minutes, perhaps four and a half, before we were able to deliver the baby safely."

"What are you trying to tell me? Just say it, Doctor!"

"There is the probability—no, the certainty—of brain damage."

"Brain damage? What the hell does that mean—what are you saying?" Stash took the doctor by the shoulders as if to shake him and then lowered his hands. "Forgive me."

"It is much too soon to tell. The extent of the damage cannot be foreseen until I have had an opportunity to examine the baby closely."

"How soon will you know—when will you examine the—the other?"

"As soon as I think she is strong enough. Meanwhile, as a precaution, she should be baptized. What name shall she be given, Prince?"

"I don't give a damn!"

"Prince Valensky! Calm yourself. There is absolutely no need to give up hope. And you have one healthy, perfect little daughter. Don't you want to see her? She's in the nursery. She weighed five pounds, ten ounces, so there was no need for an incubator. Would you like to visit her now?"

"No!" Stash spoke without thinking. All he knew was that it would be impossible to look at any baby. The doctor observed him shrewdly. This was far from the first time he had received such a response.

"My advice," he said kindly, "is that you go home and sleep and then return to visit the Princess. You have been up all night under great stress. And when you come back, no doubt the little princesses will also be awake."

"No doubt." Stash turned to go, turned back and said in

a tone which contained a hidden question, "I'm sure you did the best you could."

"Indeed, yes, Prince. But there are some things about which we can do nothing."

Still Stash glared at him. The little doctor drew himself up, offended in his art. "Accidents happen in nature, against which the utmost skill of man can do nothing except salvage as best it can."

"Salvage?" Stash said the word as if he had never heard it before. What had he to do with salvage? There had never been any allowance in his life for loss, so what room could there be for salvage? "Goodbye, Doctor."

He drove home at a dangerous speed, ignoring the servants gathered at the front door. He didn't stop at the villa but sped on farther to the stables. There he hurled himself out of his car, ran inside the stable and jumped on the back of the first horse he saw. As the groom saw his master about to ride off bareback, he ran up to Stash and shouted, "Prince? How are the twins—and the Princess?"

"The Princess is well. One child. A girl. Now get the hell out of my way!" Stash drove his heels into his bay's side and buried his hands in the beast's mane, with a command that was more a howl than a word. The animal, suddenly as savage as its master, reared with a great whinny and galloped off into the hillside with Stash kicking him on as if the devil were riding behind him.

6

In Dr. Henri Allard's clinic in Lausanne the month of April 1952 passed. The month of May passed too, and Francesca Valensky and her twin daughters had not left the clinic since the premature birth. It was on a June day, rather late in the month, that a nurse brought Marguerite, the firstborn of the twins, into her mother's room for the earliest of her two daily visits. The nurse, Soeur Anni, barely glanced at the passive woman with an extinguished face who sat, motionless as always, in an armchair. Soeur Anni had long ago become bored with the monotony of these useless, routine visits. All the other nurses in the clinic who had, at first, bulged with cautious gossip about this glamorous patient had become equally accustomed to the facts of the case. Princess Valensky never spoke and had not shown a minute's interest in her babies; she would not take the slightest care of herself although she wasn't physically sick, and she only left her bed if two nurses held her by the elbows and guided her, unprotestingly, around the little enclosed garden outside her bright, sunny room.

Postpartum depression in all its sad guises was nothing new to them. Poor thing, they agreed, but then even the doctors didn't know what to do. Sometimes they got better by themselves, sometimes they just never recovered—each nurse had some particularly lurid tale to tell about such cases—but they were careful not to indulge in them within earshot of the special round-the-clock psychiatric nurses who were in permanent attendance on this patient who must never be left alone, even while she slept.

Soeur Anni nodded to the special nurse who was knitting in a corner. "You might as well take your break now. I'll be here with the baby—no need for two of us to be hanging about, is there?"

"Not really. She's been quiet—as usual."

It was a particularly warm and sunny day. Holding Marguerite expertly in the crook of her arm, Soeur Anni opened the windows wide and drew aside the curtains to let in the fresh, flower-touched air. Then she sat down in the chair next to Francesca and after ten minutes, which passed in the customary silence, she began to doze off.

A ladybug flew inside the room and settled on the baby's forehead, right between her eyes, like a Hindu caste mark. The nurse, her eyes half-closed, paid no attention. Francesca glanced at the drowsy nurse and child without a flicker of interest. But, in one tiny part of her mind she waited, without knowing it, for the nurse to notice the insect. After a few minutes the nurse's faint snore still showed no sign of stopping. The ladybug promenaded around on the baby's face and finally lit on one delicate eyelid, close to the fine line of lashes. Too close, perilously close. Francesca reached out a tentative finger to brush away the bug. As she did so she touched her child for the first time, touched the baby skin and found it shockingly soft, shockingly *alive*. The child's eyes opened wide, looking straight at her, and she saw that they were black, as black as her own. She ran one finger over the almost imperceptible blonde eyebrows and then timidly curled a lock of the child's flaxen hair between her fingers.

"Could I . . . could I hold her?" she whispered to the half-slumbering nurse. The nurse slept on, unhearing.

"Nurse?" Francesca said in a low tone. Only a snore answered her. *"Nurse?"* This time her voice was stronger. At its sound something heavy shifted inside of her, some mass blew apart as she rediscovered her own voice. "My God, my God," she said out loud, stroking the baby's hair with fingers to which life and joy had returned.

"NURSE, GIVE ME MY BABY!"

The nurse woke up abruptly, disoriented and flustered. She held onto the infant firmly.

"What? What?" she stumbled. "Wait—stop—I'll call the doctor . . ." She scrambled to her feet, backing away.

"Come here," Francesca ordered preemptorily. "I want to hold her. Now. Give me my baby immediately. There was a bug on her eye!" she added, accusingly. Francesca rose from her chair and drew herself up with all the vivid authority with which she had once faced the cameras. As suddenly as if she had materialized out of a bottle, Francesca Vernon, the great star, stood in front of the nurse, holding out her arms with an imperious gesture.

The nurse was thoroughly startled but not daunted. "Forgive me, Madame, but I can't permit it. I have firm instructions to hold the baby at all times."

Now the woman changed again. Without lowering her arms she became, unmistakably, Princess Francesca Valensky, a princess who was never disobeyed, never questioned—a princess to whom all was allowed.

"Call Doctor Allard at once!" Francesca's voice was rusty but its power filled the room. "We'll see about this nonsense!"

Allard took only a few minutes to reach Francesca's room. He entered running, stopping abruptly as he faced the suddenly beautiful woman, as dark and passionate as a puma, who gazed hungrily at the baby. Charged with adrenaline, she stalked around the bewildered but still defiant nurse.

Mildly, but hiding as much excitement as he ever permitted himself, the doctor spoke. "Well, *Maman,* so we are beginning to feel better? We are making friends?"

"Doctor Allard, what the hell is going on? This crazy woman won't give me my baby."

"Soeur Anni, you may give Marguerite to her mother. Perhaps you might leave us for a moment." Without a word the nurse passed the baby to her mother. Marguerite was wearing a light shift from which her delicate arms and legs, just beginning to show signs of plumpness, wriggled freely in pleasure at the sunshine and the light breeze. She was an inexhaustible treasure of pink and gold, so tiny and yet so definite that even jaded doctors and nurses hung over her crib.

Allard watched carefully while Francesca gazed into the baby's eyes. "Who *are* you?" she asked. Hearing the human voice, Marguerite stopped wriggling for a second and looked at her mother's face. Then, to Francesca's stunned disbelief, she smiled.

"She smiled at me, Doctor!"

"Of course she did."

Francesca ignored the remark. "Doctor, what's this nonsense about not leaving me alone with the baby? I simply don't understand."

"You have not been well, Princess. Until today you didn't want to hold her."

"But that's impossible! Ridiculous ... simply ridiculous. I've never heard anything so absurd in my whole life!" Francesca looked at the doctor as if she had never properly seen him before. "Where's my other baby?" she asked. "I don't understand what's been going on around here and I don't like it one bit. Where's my husband? Doctor, call Prince Valensky and tell him to come here at once," she commanded. "And tell me where my other baby is ... I want to hold her, too."

"Your smaller daughter is still in the incubator," the doctor said quickly. There could be no question, no question at all of his patient visiting the other child. The infant had had a convulsion only that morning, the second since her birth. The sight of the sick, piteous mite could well upset the mother to such an extent that she would relapse into the depression in which she had been plunged for so long. Nothing could make him risk that.

"Where's the incubator, Doctor?" asked Francesca, starting to walk toward the door with Marguerite in her arms.

"No! *Maman*, I forbid you! You are not yet well, not as strong as you think. Do you have any idea how long you have been here, my dear lady?"

Francesca stopped, puzzled. "A while? I'm not exactly sure—perhaps—two weeks?"

"Almost nine weeks ... yes, nine weeks.... It's been what you Americans call a long haul," the doctor said gently, seeing that his patient had given up her idea of going to the incubator.

Francesca sat down, still gathering her child close. She had the impression that she had been some sad place far away, locked in a world as dismal and colorless as rain in winter; some place lost, in which dim events passed before her eyes like a remote shadow play glimpsed through a distant window. But nine weeks! Suddenly in every bone and muscle, she felt her force drain away. Mutely, she held the baby out to the doctor.

Allard took advantage of the moment. "We must regain our strength, *Maman*, before we start to go visiting." Francesca nodded tiredly in agreement. "In a week, perhaps even less if you do not overtire yourself. You have a long way to go, my dear, before you get back to normal.

Now, we have talked enough for the moment. You must try to sleep, heh?" He brought the baby close to her. Francesca brushed her lips over the choicest part of any baby, the fragrant, silky little folds that will one day become a neck. "She will come back to you this afternoon —you can give her the next bottle," the doctor promised, opening the door so the waiting nurse could come in. He carried Marguerite back to the nursery, saying over and over to himself, "Thank God! Thank God!"

As soon as the doctor telephoned, Stash raced to the clinic at ninety-five miles an hour. During the past weeks he had spent hours every day with Francesca, trying vainly to penetrate her withdrawn silence, her fathomless misery, so thick that it seemed to come from without, like a cloud which had enveloped her and made her invisible. His vigil had been made bearable by the visits Marguerite made to her mother, visits ordered by Dr. Allard whether Francesca responded or not.

Stash had fallen passionately in love with his daughter. He played with her for as long as they would let him. He insisted on unwrapping her completely so that he could see her naked. He displayed her enchanting little body to Francesca, hoping that the sight of this newborn perfection must move her as much as it did him, but to no avail. He had had long conferences with Allard, demanding constant reassurances that every precaution had been taken to prevent Francesca from doing herself harm.

When he wasn't with Francesca, Stash shut himself up in the villa, seeing no one from the outside world. Just as he and Francesca had managed to escape, undetected by reporters, on their honeymoon, so he was able to prevent news of the birth of his children from appearing in the press. Dr. Allard's clinic offered complete privacy and the only people who had known that Francesca was pregnant were Matty and Margo Firestone. Stash had written them during the first week after the premature births, telling them only of Marguerite and of Francesca's postpartum depression. He had asked, and obtained, their silence on behalf of the sick woman.

But now ... now! he thought to himself, as he waited impatiently in Dr. Allard's consultation room, at last life could begin again. He had known, from the beginning, that he must *win* this cruel game. He had promised himself a thousand times that it was only a matter of time before he could take Francesca and Marguerite home with him. Stash had never permitted himself the slightest doubt.

At length Allard appeared, fairly waltzing in satisfaction.

"Can they come home with me now?" Stash demanded, without even greeting the doctor.

"Soon, soon, when the Princess is stronger. But first, my friend, we must talk about the other baby, about Danielle." Even the doctor had not been able, during the time of Francesca's depression, to force Stash to discuss his second child. Good Catholic that he was, Dr. Allard had seen to it that she was baptized the day after her birth, since he was not sure she would survive another twenty-four hours. He himself had chosen the name, that of his own mother, hoping that it might bring some good luck to the unfortunate infant.

"Danielle." Stash said the name as if it were a foreign word which had absolutely no meaning for him. "I do not expect her to live." His voice carried a tone of finality, of utter dismissal.

"But if she lives, and she *may*, you will have to deal with the neurological complications . . ."

"Doctor, not now!"

The doctor continued imperturbably, with emphatic gestures and formal intonation. "I have examined both of your children, Prince. There is a precise set of tests used to determine the extent of nerve development in newborn babies. Doctor Rombais and I have examined them together in order to compare their reactions and . . ."

Stash interrupted him with the savagery with which he confronted any obstacle in his path. His neck and head became the hunting beak of an angry, vicious bird as he spoke.

"Just give me the results!"

"Prince," the doctor replied, without changing his measured lecturing tone, "you must become aware of what we have to deal with, no matter how little you wish to know about it. I assure you that there is no way in which I can give you the results, as you put it, in two words. Now! If you will permit me to continue—Marguerite responds in all ways like a normal, strong infant. She sucks vigorously, her rooting inflex is strong and the Moro reflex was normal. To obtain it I put her on her back and slammed my hand down loudly near her. She extended her arms and legs abruptly and fanned her fingers and toes. When I held her up with her feet touching the examination table, she made stepping movements, and when I pulled her to a sitting position for the Traction Response, her shoulder and neck muscles contracted. All in all, it was a lively session."

Stash followed every word the doctor said with painfully reined-in attention. He needed no doctor to tell him Marguerite was perfect. There was a slight pause while Allard collected his words for what he had to say next. He sighed heavily, but resolutely.

"Danielle showed very little reaction to all of these tests. I repeated the examination twice at a three-week interval and the results obtained were no different. There is a paucity of movements, she rarely cries, she has not yet held up her head and she has put on only a little weight ... what we call a failure to thrive."

"Failure to thrive! You mean she's a vegetable!" Stash could contain himself no longer.

"Certainly not, Prince! She is only nine weeks old and there is still positive hope that her body will, with the best of care, develop along normal lines. If she should continue to gain weight at the rate she is gaining, slow though it is, there is nothing to stop her from eventually becoming a physically active child. She is not deformed in any way, merely weak, very weak."

"And mentally?"

"Mentally? Mentally, she will never be normal. We have known that from the beginning."

"But what are you telling me *exactly*, Doctor? How far from normal will she be?"

"She will be retarded, that much is certain. The exact degree of retardation is something which I can not possibly estimate at this time. We cannot even give your daughter an I.Q. test until she is three years old and even then the judgment may not be final—in this problem, Prince, there are so many, many variations, from mild to moderate to severe ..." Dr. Allard paused abruptly and lapsed into silence.

"Could it be ... mild?" Stash finally forced himself to ask, in a low, disbelieving voice, each reluctant word acid on his lips.

"Prince, there is so much room for possibility in these cases. Sometimes only a few percentage points of I.Q. can make the difference between a child who is only barely trainable and a child who can develop certain skills—no one can predict where the strengths might be . . ."

"Spare me these vague generalities!" Stash bit out. *What is her future, damn it!*"

There was a short silence. Dr. Allard finally answered with the most precise information available to him.

"The most we can hope for is that little Danielle will be somewhere on the borderline from low-mild to high-moderate retardation, that she will manage some personal care, that she can form some social relationships, that she can express some simple phrases on a prereading level—perhaps that of a four-year-old . . ."

"A four-year-old—Doctor, you're talking about a *kindergarten mentality!* And you call that 'moderate'—no matter *how* old she gets to be?"

"Prince," answered the doctor, facing the question squarely, "that is probably the best, the very best you can hope for. Because of the little one's lack of oxygen before and during birth, the poor response to the tests—the convulsions—no, Prince, we cannot possibly hope for more than that."

There was total silence in the room for minutes. Finally Stash spoke again. "What if you're wrong, what if she's severely retarded? What then?"

"Don't borrow trouble. There will be, in any case, the question of constant care, even with moderate retardation. With severe retardation the problem becomes enormous. Great watchfulness is necessary in all cases, throughout the child's life. Once the child can walk, there will always be danger. As puberty approaches, the problem becomes aggravated. Often an institution is the only answer."

"If . . . if she lives, Doctor, how long can she remain here in your clinic?" Stash asked.

"Until she gains enough weight to go into the nursery with the others. Not until she weighs five pounds, eight ounces, Prince, which is a question of only a few months, in my opinion, if there are no complications. While she is still in the incubator, of course, we are in complete charge. But once she grows large enough for the nursery, we can't continue to keep her. At that point you should make preparations to take her home."

At the word "home" Stash's face hardened. "Doctor Allard, I don't intend to speak of this to my wife until she's stronger."

"I agree. In fact, I advise great caution at the moment. There has been massive denial, on the part of the Princess, of either child. However, now she has made normal contact with Marguerite and the prognosis is extremely good. However, her depression was severe, most severe, and in such a case she must not have any further shocks. If the Princess continues to do well, you can take her and Marguerite home in a few days. I shall see to it that she doesn't see Danielle until the baby is, as you put it, 'out of the woods.' Nature will decide the timetable."

It was on a brilliant day, almost the last in June, when Dr. Allard declared Francesca well enough to go home. From the instant that Stash had hired a baby nurse from a Lausanne agency, it seemed as if every international newspaper correspondent in Switzerland had been alerted to the news. A crowd of reporters and photographers waited with increasing impatience outside the impenetrable gates of the private clinic. They had been keeping vigil since early morning, and now, seven hours later, when Stash and Francesca Valensky appeared at last, carrying their baby, there was an uproar in a dozen languages, demanding that the child be held up for the cameras.

In spite of the protective scowl of her husband, the pale woman, whose prodigal beauty had vanished from print many months ago, carefully tilted the white lace cocoon so that the infant's sleeping face could be seen. A quilted, white silk cap covered the tiny head but wisps of hair escaped and flared silver in the breeze like delicate petals. Although the child had been christened Marguerite Alexandrovna, she seemed in her mother's arms so much like a flower in human form that the imagination of the press was fired. In every one of the pictures that appeared of that moment she was crowned Princess Daisy.

The convoy of photographers and reporters followed Francesca and Stash all the way back to their villa. They besieged the great house, standing outside the locked gates in a large group and shouting, over and over, "We want Daisy." When, at last, they left, persuaded only after a long wait that there was no chance of getting any stories or even any more pictures than those they had snapped on the steps of the clinic, everyone had forgotten that the baby had ever been named Marguerite, even her parents.

She was Daisy to Stash and Francesca, and Princess

Daisy to most of the servants who still clung to the old ways.

She was a circus of a baby when she was awake, distributing smiles to all her hovering adorers, lifting her head halfway off the mattress of her crib if she spied a butterfly or a flower or a friendly finger, making music with the collection of rattles which hung on the side of her crib, kicking her legs for joy when she was touched. She slept almost eighteen hours a day, by Francesca's reckoning, and ate for two hours, but the remaining four hours in every day she held a royal court.

For several days all of Francesca's attention was focused on Daisy. Each morning she asked to be driven into Lausanne to see her other daughter, but Stash managed easily to convince her that she wasn't strong enough yet to make the trip. Indeed, her vitality was exceptionally slow in returning. She was so weary by late morning that she spent most of each day on the chaise longue in her room. But finally, after a week, exhausted though she still was, Francesca fretfully demanded to be taken to visit Danielle at once. The moment Stash was dreading had arrived. He had prepared his words over and over.

"Darling, the doctor and I have agreed that it is a very bad idea for you to visit Danielle yet."

"Why not?" she asked in quick alarm.

"The baby is ... very small, extremely weak ... in fact, my darling, she's ill, very ill."

"But that's all the more reason. ... I might be able to *do* something, maybe I can help ... why ... *why* didn't you tell me before that she was *sick?*" Her face was contorted, her eyes jagged with shock.

"Christ! Look at you!" he cried in fear and anger. "I knew I shouldn't have told you! You're much too upset. You haven't been well enough to be told, and damn it, you aren't well enough now."

"Stash. *What's wrong with her?* Tell me! You're only making it worse!"

Stash took Francesca in his arms. "She's too small, darling. You wouldn't be even allowed to touch her. Now, listen to me, my dearest, since you know she's not well, I'm going to tell you the whole thing. That's the only way you'll understand why you shouldn't see her yet. The chances that the baby will survive are almost nonexistent. Allard feels, and I totally agree, that for you to become attached to the baby now might plunge you right back into your depression . . . when . . . if . . . anything happens to her."

"But, Stash, my own child . . . my BABY."

"No, Francesca! No! Don't you realize how sick you were? It's absolutely out of the question to risk anything like that again. You just can't be the judge—you're not well enough yet, no matter what you believe. Think of Daisy if you won't think of yourself, think of Daisy and think of me."

He had found the magic argument. He felt Francesca stop struggling in his arms, saw her relax her fight, watched with relief as she gave in to her grief. Let her cry, cry and cry, for it was just no good, no bloody good and no way to make it better.

Week after week passed. Stash went faithfully to the clinic and reported to Dr. Allard that Francesca was making a very slow recovery and that, in his opinion, she was still too close to her long depression to allow her to chance a visit to a baby who was visibly not well. "She's too fragile, Doctor," he said. "It would be the worst thing for her."

When he returned from these excursions he told Francesca that the baby was still in the same condition as before, holding on to life only by each breath she took and that the doctor refused to hold out any false hope. Her misery was such that after a few weeks she merely looked at his somber face and forebore to ask about Danielle. She knew that if the news was better he'd tell her immediately.

At the clinic Stash never once went into the incubator room to look at Danielle. After what the doctor had told him about her future he had discarded her. She did not exist for him. She could not exist. *She must not exist.* He had never seen her and he had no intention of ever seeing her. Nature was cruel, accidents happen, but a strong man could override the blows of fate. The mere idea of a child of his—a child of *his*—in *his* home, growing up, yet *never* growing up, growing into something he refused to contemplate—*no!* When that thought touched his mind he rejected it with all the power of his warrior's nature. After his childhood, so distorted by the overwhelming concentration on his mother's slow dying, compassion, that most human emotion, had died totally within him. The fate that awaited the child he never saw was so dreadful that he determined to eliminate it from his life. It was the one thing in the world of which he was in fear.

With ease Stash concealed these emotions from Dr. Allard and, little by little, he asked the subtle questions which brought him the answers he needed to keep him to his resolve. Yes, it was most possible that the Princess would become enormously devoted to Danielle; yes, the mothers of retarded children often spent much less time with their normal children in favor of the sick one; yes, it was not at all impossible that the Princess would refuse to have the child institutionalized no matter how necessary it was. Indeed, there were many such cases. The maternal instinct was often strengthened beyond the imagination of man by the care of a sick or retarded child and there was no force as strong as that instinct. Nature was indeed marvelous. Mothers were self-sacrificing, the Prince was right. Yes, even beyond the point where it was reasonable or even wise. But that was the way of life—what could man do in the face of it?

Grimly, Stash received news of Danielle. She had begun to put on weight. She had had no further convulsions. In Dr. Allard's opinion it was perfectly safe for the Princess to come and visit the little one. In fact, he had expected that the Princess would have come sooner, in spite of her weakness, knowing her determination as he did.

"My wife does not *intend* to see her, Doctor." For many days Stash had rehearsed various replies for the inevitable moment which had now arrived.

"Indeed?" The little doctor expressed his astonishment only by that one word. He had, in the course of practicing his profession for many years, almost learned not to show surprise.

Stash turned his back on the doctor and went to stand by a window, looking out as he spoke. "We've been talking it over, and over, from every angle. We've agreed that it would be a serious mistake to try to bring up—Danielle —in our own home, and that the time to make this decision is now, not later. A clean cut, Doctor." Stash sat down solidly, relieved to have met the charge head on.

"But what do you intend to do?" the doctor asked. "Danielle weighs over five pounds now. Soon she'll be able to leave the clinic."

"I've made thorough inquiries, of course. As soon as she's old enough, she'll be sent to live in the finest of institutions for children in her condition. I understand that excellent ones exist when money is no problem. Until then I believe she should be boarded with a foster mother. In fact, I've heard of several right here in Lausanne. Could you just look at this list of names and tell me if there is anyone here you particularly recommend?"

"And this is what you are *resolved* to do about Danielle?" the doctor asked intently. "And the Princess agrees?"

"Absolutely," Stash said, handing the doctor the sheet of paper. "We always agree with each other in family matters."

Madame Louise Goudron, the foster mother most highly recommended by Dr. Allard, had been available to take over the care of Danielle. As long as the banker's check for the child's care that arrived each week continued to come, she required no further information than Dr. Allard's request. Danielle was far from the first imperfect baby she had sheltered in her home, which was both comfortable and cheerful, but would have been neither if this childless widow had not discovered that some people, whose names were no concern of hers, preferred not to be burdened by their own children.

Only a few weeks after Madame Goudron had fetched Danielle home from the clinic, Francesca reached a decision. She was feeling so much stronger physically, so much more able to cope with her emotions, that she knew she had to see her second daughter, no matter what Dr. Allard or Stash thought. Neither of them had any idea of what she could endure. They were both sheltering her too much and she'd had enough of it. She must see Danielle whether or not the baby's life was in danger, whether she could touch her or not. It would be far worse if her child died and she'd never even seen her alive again since her birth—why couldn't they understand?

"But it's impossible, my poor love," Stash said.

"Impossible? I tell you I'm *ready*—you don't have to worry—I can take anything—except this awful limbo, Stash. Don't you realize it's been over five months and she's still alive?"

Stash didn't falter. The expression on his face was the expression he had worn in a battle in the sky when he pressed the button of the machine gun that would shoot the enemy out of the sky. He took Francesca's hands in his and pulled her toward him.

"Darling, darling—the baby is dead."

She screamed just once, waiting in the fearful anguish of someone who has cut herself deeply, to the bone, but who has not yet seen the blood begin to flow. Her eyes flashed and then dimmed as if the last candle had been extinguished in a dark room. Stash held her so tightly that she couldn't see his face.

"She died soon after we brought Daisy home," he continued. "I waited to tell you until you were able to hear it. . . . She was far worse off than you ever knew. . . . She would never have been well, darling, never, never in all the world." He spoke rapidly, tenderly caressing her hair. "She was seriously ill from the minute she was born. We didn't want you to know but there was no future for her, she would never have been normal—brain damage during birth—nobody's fault—but you might not have recovered if I'd told you while you were still so emotionally disturbed."

"I *knew*," Francesca whispered.

"Impossible."

"No . . . there was always a feeling . . . I knew something was wrong, something was being kept from me . . . but I was too cowardly to find out . . . I didn't want to find out . . . I was afraid . . . a coward . . ."

"Oh, my love, don't blame yourself, your instincts were right, you were saving yourself . . . and saving the rest of us. What would Daisy do without her mother? What would I do without you?"

"But I *knew!* I must have known all along." She was sobbing frantically, pulling herself away from him, kneeling on the rug, doubled up in the cramp of her grief. It might be hours, he thought, before she could be persuaded to allow him to comfort her, to press her to him again, but already Stash could anticipate the gradual acceptance of the child's death—to him a reality—which would eventually enter her body and make her cling to him as she had from the moment they had met. He waited patiently, this man who so rarely waited for anything.

Within several weeks Stash, who had been observing Francesca closely, judged that the worst of her grief and shock were over. He allowed *Life* to send Philippe Halsman to come and take pictures for their cover. Francesca now spent almost all of her time with Daisy, who had progressed from shaking her rattles to an insatiable inter-

est in her mother's glittering, tinkling charm bracelet. The
baby had developed a genuine belly laugh and nothing
pleased her as much as being allowed to grab at the
dangled bracelet. It was a game, a real game, and she
squealed with rapture every time she caught it and tugged
almost hard enough to pull it off. Stash and Francesca
watched, holding their breath, while the fat, fair bundle
actually rolled over from her back to her stomach. Wonder of wonders, she seemed to talk to her tiny stuffed
animals, although it was no language known to man. Her
enormous eyes were alert and happy from the instant she
woke, and when she slept on her stomach, her minute
heels drawn up under her diapered bottom, Francesca
decided that she looked like a heavenly jumping frog.
They put her on a heap of Francesca's furs, naked except
for her diaper, and she lifted her head up with her chest
high and crowed in surprise.

"She might as well know what sable feels like," said
Stash.

"You'll spoil her rotten."

"Of course I will."

"But why not start her on the mink? Show a little
restraint?"

"Nonsense. She's a Valensky, and don't you ever forget
it. And speaking of that," Stash said, suddenly serious, "I
really think we've had enough of country life, don't you?
I'm bloody sick and tired of Switzerland. What would you
say to moving to London? I know damn near everybody
there who's much good. We could get back into the swing
of things, go to the theater, entertain, see friends . . ."

"Oh, yes! Yes! I've been wanting to get away. And now
. . ." Francesca stopped, thinking that she never wanted to
see Switzerland again.

"Now it's time for London, now it's time for that house
I promised you. And then we'll go adventuring—all three
of us!"

"They warned me about you, the playboy prince! Don't
think I don't know the way you used to roam the world.
Oh, the stories I've heard . . ."

"All true."

"But over now? You're not restless in domesticity?" She
teased him, more beautiful than she had been in many
months.

"All over. I have everything I want." He was staggered
again at the pleasure she was able to give him, the way

every angle and every curve of her face was illuminated for him as no other face had ever been. Again, the lawlessness in him met the lawlessness in her and they joined in outrageous delight. The sooner they left Lausanne and the clinic of Dr. Allard, the better, he thought, as he plucked Daisy off the sable coat and tickled her stomach.

"Let's go to London and buy a house. Can you be packed by tomorrow?" he asked.

"No, you go alone, darling. I don't want to leave Daisy by herself, not even with Masha and the servants—I just wouldn't have a second's peace of mind."

"Right. But if you don't like the house I choose, you'll be stuck with it."

"Spoken like a true prince," she laughed. "The last man in the world without servant problems. I'm sure you'll pick the best house in London—they expect it of you."

"What the devil are you complaining about? I know some women who would have killed to be in your position," he grumbled.

"Don't get so indignant—at least the silver is always polished." She threw a cushion at his head. "Give me my baby. You've had her long enough. Poor baby—six months old and jaded already."

The day Stash left for London, Francesca sent Masha into Lausanne with a precisely detailed list of shopping to do for her. She should really have gone herself, she thought, for without doubt Masha would manage to buy the wrong shade of nylons, but she had plotted to arrange this afternoon completely alone with Daisy. Although the trained baby nurse had been discharged weeks before, Masha, with her position of former wet nurse to Stash, with her decades of devoted service to all the Valenskys, had never learned to properly knock at a door. She kept coming in and hovering over them when Francesca was tending Daisy, making well-meant but vaguely critical comments all the while. It would have been impossible to ask her to leave without hurting her proprietary, grandmotherly feelings, and Francesca, so recently returned to the world of everyday joys, was reluctant to cause anyone pain.

She looked up in annoyance when Masha returned, an hour before she was expected. The Russian woman clumped into Daisy's room, her broad, kind face flushed with anger, her mouth working silently, every inch of her sturdy, reliable body conveying an imminent explosion.

"Masha—what's wrong with you?" Francesca whispered. "Daisy's just gone to sleep—hush, now."

Masha was so disturbed that she could only keep her voice low with difficulty.

"She—that nurse—Soeur Anni—I saw her in the store —that, that *creature* had the nerve to say to me—I've known her for years, mind you, and she, oh, it's not to be endured . . . to *me* . . . ach, I can't even say it myself, it's disgusting, the gossip, the things people will say . . ." Masha stopped abruptly and sat down squarely in the yellow rocking chair, unable to continue for sheer anger.

"Masha, what exactly did Soeur Anni say?" Francesca asked quietly. She knew that in the nine weeks of her depression she must have been worse than bizarre, strange in ways of which Masha couldn't be aware. It was unprofessional of the nurse, to say the least, to discuss a former patient, but her years in Hollywood had hardened her to the blows of gossip mongers.

"She told me . . . she said . . . she . . . *ach*—the things these crazy people believe! She said that our poor little baby who died—that the baby wasn't dead at all!"

Francesca went gray. Gossip was one thing, but this was of such vileness, such palpable evil, to speak of her tragedy as if it hadn't happened, to use her grief as material for a rumor. One look at Masha's face told her there was more.

"I want every single word Soeur Anni said. She's a dangerous woman—the whole story, Masha, out with it!"

"She said that little Danielle, that our baby, was in the clinic for months—months—after you left, until she got big enough and then they sent her away to be boarded at that Madame Louise Goudron's, a woman who takes in children . . ."

" 'They?' Did she say who 'they' were?"

"No, she didn't know, but the worst of it, Madame, the worst was what she said to me when I told her it was the foulest lie I'd ever heard. She said I could say what I liked but she knew some people who are so rich and high and mighty that if they don't like the baby they have, if something's wrong with it, they just get rid of it! I damned her to burn in hell, Princess, right to her face!"

"Masha! Now just calm down . . . you'll wake Daisy. . . . It's not possible that Soeur Anni—of course, I was rude to her, but still, to be so vicious, to dream up a story like that. . . . She's mad, utterly mad. I've got to do something about her. She must *never* be allowed around sick people again. She's crazy, Masha, don't you see, really and truly insane."

"Oh, Princess, Princess . . . the wickedness of it. What if she's told other people, what if they believe her?"

"Nonsense. No one in his right mind would listen to her. The Prince would strangle the woman if he even heard—is that everything she told you?"

"Yes, every word. I left the store and came right back to tell you."

"I'm going to call Doctor Allard right away. . . . No . . . wait. I'll sound as mad as Soeur Anni. You'll have to be my witness. We'll go into town and see him tomorrow morning, first thing. That way she can't deny what she told you. That bitch. That utter bitch!"

Stash's valet knocked at the door.

"What is it?" Francesca said, angrily.

"Princess, you're wanted on the telephone. It's the Prince, from London."

"I'll be right down, Mump."

The telephone was in the library of the villa. Francesca rushed down the stairs and picked up the receiver.

"Darling, I'm so glad to hear your voice! Why? Oh, I was just feeling terribly lonely for you, that's all. It's been a whole day." As she spoke she thought that there was no reason to tell Stash about Soeur Anni. He would go into one of the cold, devil-sent rages she had seen overcome him when someone or something challenged his power over his life, and heaven knows what he would do to that crazy woman. She was perfectly capable of handling this nasty incident herself. "Daisy?" she continued. "She just went to sleep. We had a wonderful afternoon, all alone together. No, darling, nothing new . . . two more days . . . maybe three? So, it's not that easy to find the perfect princely residence. Just don't rush it. . . . I'm being well taken care of. Goodnight, my dearest heart. I love you."

The next morning Francesca and Masha were driven by the chauffeur into Lausanne. Francesca told Masha to stay in Dr. Allard's waiting room while she went into his consultation room. As the receptionist ushered her in, the little doctor bounced up from behind his desk at the sight of her.

"Ah, ha, *Maman*, you've had a change of heart! I was sure of it! I knew it! I knew it! I was certain you'd never really give up your baby, not a woman like you! Of course, at the time—but, my dear, what's wrong?" Dr. Allard caught Francesca just as she stumbled to a chair. He busied himself reviving her from her faint, murmuring, "Naturally, the emotion, the emotion . . ."

As she came back to herself, the horror was all around her, a sick whirl, yet without a name, without specifics, generalized, surrounding, stifling. She knew nothing except that something very bad had been done, something criminal. Every ounce of acting ability Francesca possessed was mustered as she slowly realized where she was and the full implications of what Dr. Allard had said. Instincts of cunning she hadn't known she possessed took over.

"I'm sorry, Doctor . . . it must be the reaction to coming back to the clinic. I'm perfectly all right now. No thank you, no water, I'm fine. Well! How are you?" She was gaining time settling down into a natural rhythm, her words coming from her numb lips as if she really were in full command of herself.

"I? I am a happy man today, Princess. When the Prince told me that you had decided never to see Danielle, that you refused to bring her up, I must confess that I was deeply disappointed. But I do not consider it my business to comment on such decisions, you understand, that is always a matter the parents must decide. But somehow, something told me, yes, even at the time, that when you were quite well again you would reconsider."

"Doctor, I went through a very difficult time. I'm not sure that I really understand now, even though I've recovered, exactly what happened. Could you straighten it out for me, tell me just what occurred? I didn't pay enough attention to the whole thing and I'm ashamed of myself. . . . I don't want my husband to know how little I listened to him." She smiled at him, composed, charmingly helpless.

When the doctor had finished the long recital, filling in every detail with Swiss precision, remembering with no trouble all of his interviews with Stash and all the details of Danielle's condition, Francesca sat numbly. Every word was a heavy spiked object that fell straight on her heart, blow after blow. The foreknowledge of approaching doom was as palpable as an open casket. She wanted to scream, to scream and never stop screaming, so that she would never have to think about what the little doctor had told her. Instead, calmly, out of a cave on the dark side of the moon, she heard her voice asking, "You still haven't told me exactly what sort of special care Danielle will need."

"Only what you've given Daisy—I see that is what the newspapers call her now, our little Marguerite. At the moment, before Daisy starts to walk, the differences between them will be less than they will be in the future. Danielle will, of course, be slow and late to develop in every way, and a good deal less active than her sister, but, as I have assured you, she will look normal. Soon, very soon, it will be time for speech . . . the first major problem. Then, in a few years, Danielle can be tested. With luck there are many, many things the little one can be taught to do for herself, but all that's in the future. For now it's only love and attention that she requires."

"Doctor Allard, I foolishly gave away her crib and all her clothes . . . everything that might have reminded me. . . . I'll need just one more day to get ready for her."

"But of course . . . one day, two days, what do they matter now?" The doctor looked at her keenly, thinking that perhaps what she really needed was time to get used to the idea, now that her difficult decision had finally been made.

When Francesca came out of the doctor's consulting room, Masha was waiting with fiery impatience to be summoned as a witness against Soeur Anni. Francesca intercepted her before she could say anything.

"Masha, it's all settled, our business. Come on, right away, we've got a lot of things to do." She grasped the older woman's arm and tugged her out of the door, hurrying down the clinic corridor into the street.

"Princess, did you get that woman thrown out? Why didn't you let me tell him? You were in there so long I was worried."

"Masha," Francesca began and then stopped. In the space of an hour everything on which she had based her beliefs had vanished. Nothing was as it seemed. Deception, lies, cruelty, impossible hurts, a vast, confused landscape surrounded her.

"Masha, she didn't lie to you. Danielle—she's alive!" The strong peasant woman tottered. Francesca held her up with all her strength. "Masha, come, we'll sit in the park. I'll explain it all."

At the end of Francesca's recital, broken as it was by incredulous cries of denial from Masha, the two women sat silently on the park bench, eyed with mild curiosity by the chauffeur who was still parked in front of the clinic.

Slowly Masha turned to Francesca. "You must understand, Princess, even as a little boy he was in terror of weakness, sickness, only that, no other failings. I've watched him over the years—oh, I know he pays no attention to me, but I've watched and watched. He has to have everything his way. He always wins, always. There is no hope, Princess. He'll never admit the poor baby to his heart."

"He won't have to," Francesca said in a voice that was almost a howl of potent, rending rage. "He's lost every chance."

Masha's subservient reaction to Stash's point of view had mobilized her as nothing else could have. The old woman was actually trying to explain what he had done, as if his actions could be accepted, *had* to be accepted.

"I'm going away, Masha. I'm taking my children with me. Nobody can stop me, I warn you. He *lied* to me. He let me think she was dead! He *stole* my baby. If I don't protect her, who knows what evil thing he might do next? Think what he did, Masha. Think what he *is*. I never want to see him again. I'll be gone before he gets back from London. All I ask from you is to say nothing until I've left."

Masha's eyes filled. "What do you take me for? Once I had a baby ... but he died. Still, I have always had a mother's heart, Princess. Anyway, you can't manage without me. Just how do you think you are going to take care of two babies all by yourself? I'm going with you."

"Oh, Masha, Masha!" Francesca cried. "I hoped you'd say that—but I would never have asked you to leave him."

"He doesn't need me. You do," Masha said with stately finality.

Francesca spent one day at the U.S. Embassy in Geneva making emergency passport arrangements, assisted by a bored and incurious clerk, bought airline tickets in a Geneva travel agency, returned to Lausanne to cash a large check at their bank and hurried back to the villa to pack. For herself she took almost nothing but her traveling clothes, but she filled two big suitcases with all of Daisy's clothes and necessary temporary supplies. She took out all her jewels and looked at them speculatively. No, she was no longer the wife of the man who had given them to her. Her garden of Fabergé crystal vases, filled with jeweled flowers? Yes, somehow they belonged to another life—a life before the lies—and they rightfully could go with her. The lapis lazuli egg with the diamond crown of Catherine the Great inside, bearing a ruby at its heart? Yes! That was undeniably hers, hers for bearing the twins. She shut the vases and the egg into their boxes and put the small packets in the bottom of her vanity case. Each of her actions, all day long, had been executed with precision, perfection and perfect ease. She had been taken over by a molten core of anger which powered her like an enormous engine. Her strength knew no limits, her brain worked at ten times its normal efficiency, she was a living fire, burning, burning toward the moment when she would take her children to safety. Should she cable Matty Firestone to meet her in Los Angeles? No. Absolutely no one must know she was leaving until she'd gone.

She answered Stash's next phone call that evening with such a perfect imitation of the tone of the night before that, from the observing part of herself, she was astonished. But all that night she prowled back and forth in her bedroom, hurling words of loathing and bitter blame at him. A man should die for what he had tried to do—had done. How frighteningly little she had really known him, how trusting she had been, how easily she had been duped, used as if she were a figure on a chessboard. How she hated him!

The next morning she telephoned Dr. Allard. She would be sending a nurse to Madame Goudron's to pick up the baby in two hours, she told him. Would he have the kindness to telephone the lady and ask her to have Danielle ready, and warmly dressed? It was such a chilly day. Yes, yes, she was happy, very happy and very excited. The doctor was perfectly right. It was a wonderful day. Yes, she would give the Prince his best wishes for them all ... how very kind.

Precisely two hours later Francesca sat hidden in the back of a taxi, holding Daisy, while Masha went into the neat little house. No one would have recognized the woman in a bulky travel coat, wearing dark glasses and a deep-brimmed hat, a woman without make-up, her hair pulled back into a tight bun, as that lyric, famous beauty, her long hair flying, who responded in such carefree, innocent delight to the cheers of her fans on her arrival at Cherbourg, just a little less than a year and a half ago.

Five minutes passed before Masha emerged, waving at the woman at the door who lifted a wistful hand. As the taxi started toward the airport, Masha and Francesca exchanged babies. Francesca lifted the hood of the carrying blanket which almost covered the child's face. How small she was. How incredibly sweet. Silver blonde hair, curly and fine. A grave face, a bit sad, but so marvelously familiar. And the eyes—the same velvety black, the black of a purple pansy, Daisy's eyes. But dull. Just a little dull. Perhaps only dull if you compared her to Daisy ... and that was something you must never, never do, never again.

In one glance she committed herself irrevocably to protect and cherish her child, knowing that whatever happiness this attachment would bring, it would always be linked to shadows and a vast sadness that she rejected even as it was stitched tightly into her soul.

7

$\mathcal{N}$one of the servants dared to say a single word to their master. Stash Valensky's face, as he went about the business of selling the huge Lausanne villa and moving them all to London, was set in lines of pain which made him almost unrecognizable. Even among themselves they only whispered a few words of speculation. The unexplained disappearance of the Princess, with Daisy and Masha, was so threatening to their sense of security that they tried to ignore it. They closed their minds to the mystery. A family quarrel, they prayed, that would be resolved as suddenly, as mysteriously, as it had sprung up.

Stash could do nothing. Any legal action to recover Daisy would instantly become public knowledge, and then the whole story would have to be revealed. He had entirely justified his actions to himself, but, armored with scorn, he accepted the fact that the great majority of people, people who allowed unfortunate accidents to control their little lives, would never understand what he'd had to do about Danielle.

They would never understand how right he had been. How right he *was*. He reasoned that the situation couldn't last long. Francesca had acted emotionally, out of the shock of the moment, but she'd come to her senses soon and realize that he had merely *shaped* events for her sake and for Daisy's sake, that he had taken the only rational, the only right course to ensure a happy life for the three of them.

Yet Stash had no idea where Francesca was. By the time he had returned from London and discovered that she was gone, he could only trace her as far as Los Angeles. He called Matty Firestone. Whatever further information existed, her former agent was the obvious first source.

Matty expressed his almost incredulous contempt for Stash by informing him that *both* of his daughters were very well; in fact, Danielle was beginning to hold her head up nicely for a second or two. Daisy? Oh, yeah, Daisy. She was sitting up and saying mama, but that little Danielle, now she was amazing. He could almost swear she'd smiled at him the third time she saw him.

Stash spoke as coldly as possible. There was nothing to be gained by rising to the bait. Would Francesca see him? Could he write to her? There had been a misunderstanding which could be worked out.

"Well," said Matty, enjoying himself viciously, "there's no way on earth that I'm going to let you know where they are. They're safe and they're well and they're not starving and that's all you get out of me. And it's more than you deserve."

Months passed. Stash went to California, but Matty was obdurate. He was acting under orders from his client. Mr. Valensky would get nothing from him. Of course, he could sue for divorce if that's what he wanted. The newspapers would bless him. There hadn't been any juicy scandals lately.

Stash spent New Year's Day of 1953 alone in his great house in London. His wife and child had been gone for just over four months. He was a prisoner in his own home. He knew that if he appeared in public without Francesca the rumors would start. Already he had received telephone calls from the British press requesting interviews with Francesca. Everyone, they assured him, wanted to know how the movie-star-turned-princess was enjoying London. They all clamored to photograph her with Daisy again. The *Life* cover picture was many months out of date. He ran out of credible excuses. He knew that soon his postponements would be futile and that any day now the press would be watching outside the house to see if they could spot a nanny with a pram.

Stash fled to India, where the polo season was in full swing, but this year he didn't play. There were palaces into which no reporters had ever dreamed of being allowed to penetrate, a dozen maharajas who were delighted to have their old friend as a houseguest. Calcutta was safe during all of January; February and March could be spent in

Delhi, Bombay and Jaipur. But in the spring where would he go?

By April he had had enough. Stash announced that he and Francesca had separated and that she had returned to the United States. He had no plans for a divorce. And he had nothing else to add. In a week, for lack of details, the story faded, disappeared and was soon forgotten.

That summer of 1953 Stash played polo again. The thin line between riding fairly and riding to intimidate grew even more questionable than it had been before, but he still kept on the right side of it. He flung himself into the purchase of new ponies and the establishment of a stable in Kent, within an easy drive of London. He sold the British fighter jets, both the Gloster Meteor and the de Havilland Vampire, which he had bought after the war. He acquired an Argentinian plane, the Pulqui, another fighter jet of a later vintage, which was powered by a Rolls-Royce Derwent engine. He tracked down and bought the most recent model available of the Lockheed XP-80, known as the Shooting Star, a jet which for many years could outmaneuver and outperform almost every other aircraft in the world. He invented excuses to fly these warplanes: keeping his pilot's license current, recreation and relaxation. What he never admitted to himself in the years after Francesca left him was that he would welcome another war. Only an aerial duel with an enemy, with death the inevitable outcome for one of them, would have given him the terrible release he sought. Girls, fresh desirable girls, at the peak of their youth, were everywhere he looked. There was so little struggle and even less pleasure in their capture that he sometimes wondered why he bothered.

Anabel de Fourment was a member of a unique, little-known breed of woman, the great modern courtesan. Few women other than her own kind ever managed to comprehend her ruinous charm. She was not a great beauty, she lacked chic and she was close to forty. Yet, stretching from her nineteenth year there existed a history of notable men who had spent fortunes for her favors. One brief, youthful marriage had convinced her that the role of lover was far more agreeable than the role of wife. Ravishing young woman anxiously asked each other what her secret was, but only a man who had lived with her could have told them.

Anabel wrapped a climate of utter comfort around the man who possessed her. With her possession—and it could belong only to the very rich—came entry into a hitherto unknown country of harmony, ease and a level of good humor which seemed Edwardian in its mellow patina. She made it her business to find and keep the best cook in London. Her home was arranged with such art that no man ever managed to analyze why it was so supremely relaxing: all they felt was that the problems of their world stopped at her door. Anabel didn't know what a neurosis was. She had no complexes, no phobias, no obsessions. She was never depressed or out of sorts or annoyed or short-tempered. She had iron health and no one had ever heard her complain of so much as a broken fingernail. In fact, she had never been known to speak in anger, yet she managed her domestic affairs with absolute dispatch. Below Stairs she was a benevolent dictator who maintained absolute rule.

She was never, never boring. She was rarely witty, but she was often just plain funny, with a fresh felicity of phrase. She couldn't remember the punch lines of even a single joke, so she laughed as much the tenth time as the first time she had heard the same man tell one—a laugh that might alone have ensured her fortune, a laugh so generous, so full-bodied, so *admiring* that to hear it was to sit at a fireside and expand in its welcoming warmth. She was not shrewd but she understood instinctively why people acted as they did. Anabel was not outstandingly clever nor particularly intellectual, but she had a way of looking at people as she spoke to them which invested the straightforward, uncontrived things she said with significance and grace. She always asked precisely the questions a man was most anxious to answer. Perhaps it was her intensely personal voice, perhaps the rhythm of the words themselves, that explained the sense of utter agreeableness men found in the way she expressed herself. They looked forward to a peaceful chat with Anabel as they never looked forward to a *tête à tête* with women known to be far more brilliant and sparkling.

Anabel de Fourment had a *bounty* which made her only average prettiness seem like beauty. Her skin was flawless, and so were her teeth. Her hair was straight and Titian red and always incredibly clean. She had a wide, happy mouth, a rather long nose and nice gray green eyes, remarkable only for their kindness. Her body was so soft and supple, so subtly perfumed, so well-tended, that it was unimportant that she was always just a little too plump. Her breasts were sumptuous and her bottom was full and dimpled and no man ever noticed that she was short-waisted and just a bit dumpy.

Anabel had been born to an improvident French portrait painter, Albert de Fourment, the black sheep of a good, old provincial family of minor nobility. Her mother, a fey, rebellious daughter of a stuffy English lord, was an art student at the Slade who had hung around the fringes of Bloomsbury, trying wildly to be let into that feverish, incestuously tangled circle, but found herself only marginally accepted as an artist's model, valued for her beauty but judged of little talent. She married the first real artist who asked her, only to discover that his was merely a small talent, too, scarcely greater than her own.

Their only masterpiece was their daughter Anabel, whom they brought up on a diet of crusts and caviar. Anabel's earliest memories combined, in a confusing mixture of place, delicious, improvised meals in a shabby Paris studio where there was always enough wine for the multitude of guests, even if the food ran out, and Christmas visits to a grand English country house. There the little girl was allowed up for Boxing Day dinner, and looked with wonder at the grownups wearing evening gowns and funny paper hats, pulling snapping crackers and blowing horns at each other as if they were as young as she. As she grew older she decided, very quickly, that she liked the ease of her parents' bohemian life but didn't like being poor: that she liked the wealth of her grandparents, but didn't like doing what was expected of her.

Her only marriage, at sixteen, was a mistake. No amount of money could compensate for being as bored as she had been, Anabel decided. After her divorce at nineteen, she had been discovered by the first of the men who would be able to afford the enormous private extravagance of keeping Anabel. He was a member of the House of Lords, a friend of her grandfather's, a distinguished man in his sixties to whom she remained faithful for the last ten years of his life, years that were the best he'd ever known. It was he who introduced her to the succulent details of her true career, he who patiently educated her in the complex expertise of wine and food and cigars, he who hired a clever Frenchwoman to "maid" her, he who took her to Phillips of Bond Street and trained her to recognize and use only the best Georgian silver, he who explained why the banked fires of old, rose-cut diamonds were so much more becoming to her than anything from Cartier no matter how sumptuous. It was during those years with him that she learned that old money, aristocratic money, was the kind of money she understood. She hated all that was flashy and modern and obvious. The ambience she created always had, lingering in its perfumed leisure, the honeyed graciousness of some other better time than the present.

Anabel was not a daytime woman. She slept very late, lunched alone and spent much of every afternoon regulating the perfect functioning of her household and arranging large bunches of flowers in great, seemingly careless bouquets which gave all her rooms the feeling of being inside a Renoir. To her cook's jealous dismay, she particularly enjoyed marketing, personally picking out the ripest fruit, the best meat, the most aromatic cheeses. The merchants who enjoyed her custom saved their finest produce for her because Anabel de Fourment not only paid for quality but she made the transaction a pleasure in itself. She entertained frequently; small dinner parties of an interesting composition. The men were always invited by her protector, the women by Anabel. These women were wellborn —or at least always seemed to be—but either they were not English or they were not members of London society. They were a worldly, raffish, reckless, amusing lot and they set Anabel off as a collection of costume jewelry would set off one perfect gem. Her dinner parties became a delightful club to which only a few important men belonged, a club whose very existence was a secret. When Anabel needed a woman friend for woman talk, which wasn't often, she could always count on the members of her loyal, if unconventional coterie.

Somehow Anabel never looked chic or even elegant in her expensive day clothes. She knew it and didn't care in the slightest. She was at her best at twilight, in her own house. There she was superb. She spent a fortune on what her lingerie maker called "at-home garments," long robes of velvet, silk, chiffon and lace, of no particular period or style, brilliantly designed to expose the wonderful skin of her bosom with a flattery so subtle that it was never recognized. Her underclothes and nightgowns were custom-made for her with equal skills from a treasury of fabrics. Her bed linens were those of a queen and on them occurred an astounding number of what Anabel called, but only to herself, "nice, comfy fucks." She didn't much care about sex. She was a courtesan, not a full-blown *grande amoureuse,* a type who could be so showy and drearily full of troublesome passion, always getting involved and making messes. The worst thing that could happen to her, she knew, would be to fall profoundly in love. That was not at all her line of country. Young, ardent men were as schoolchildren to her, schoolchildren on whom she had no time to waste. Oh, she loved the sensuality of being made love to, but sexuality was another story—hardly worth the trouble it took. She purred and sighed and moaned softly and thought that really it *was* rather nice.

After the death of her first protector, Anabel found herself, at twenty-nine, in possession of a private income which, though generous, was not quite enough for her needs. The way she lived, unostentatious as it seemed to her, cost an astonishing amount of money. She also owned the leasehold, good for another eighty years, of a good-sized house in Eaton Square which presented to its neighbors a columned façade precisely like those of all the others in that grandest part of Belgravia, but, on the inside, was decorated with a concentration of comfort that few of them could boast. Although Anabel's quintessentially feminine presence was central to it, the house was, for all its greens and grays and taupe tones, for all its flowers and silver, profoundly a man's house.

She made plans for her future. She had no desire to ever marry again because marriage had been so excessively boring. She would have rather enjoyed a child or two, she thought, but babies were even more boring, if such a thing were possible, than marriage. She knew the limitations of her looks, just as well as any of the women who lunched together and picked her to pieces in irritation at not being able to understand why all their husbands and lovers found her so attractive. But she knew that simple truth that they could never comprehend: she could give the most complicated men simple happiness. A great courtesan in a day when courtesans were no longer in style? Bosh, thought Anabel. I'm a classic type—good forever. She had not the slightest doubt that the day when her kind of women went out of fashion would be the last day of civilization as she knew it. And after that, who cared?

Placidly, enjoying the privilege of selection, she waited for her next protector to identify himself, rejecting any homage which didn't please her fastidious tastes. In the following ten years she belonged to three men, one following the other, each in his own right as worthy as the lucky old lord who had formed her. Her private income did not grow, for none of them died, and the only gifts she ever accepted were of jewels or pictures, but she continued, in a time of inflation and rising taxation, to live as well as ever in utter disregard of money. In the late fall of 1955, she was thirty-nine and, for the moment, without anyone who could say she belonged to him.

"Anabel?"

"Sally, sweet Sally—how are you?" Anabel recognized the anxious American voice immediately. Sally Sands, scatty, droll Sally, was the London editor of an American fashion magazine and she was usually anxious, frequently over the nasty necessity of breaking a solemn engagement to be married. She had been engaged six times in the past two years.

"Anabel, would you do me an enormous favor?"

"If I can, but first tell me what it is. . . . Oh, well, all right, why not, after all?"

"Thank God. Then you'll be my maid of honor."

"Now, Sally, you've gone too far—that's utterly ridiculous." Anabel laughed her valuable laugh.

"Be serious . . . I need you, Anabel. *Please*. He's terribly British and I adore him and his family'll be there, but mine won't be, so you'll lend me class, darling—there's nobody else I know who would do at all."

"It's most unsuitable—maid of honor, indeed, when the bride's a mere twenty-six! But every year I do go to *some* sort of wedding just to reaffirm my belief that holy wedlock isn't for me—and your wedding will do as well—in fact, probably better—than any."

"Oh, but Anabel, this is the real thing." Sally reproached her.

"Of course, poppet, for you, but I just don't believe in the drill myself. It's not going to be big do, is it? I don't have to carry your train or something?"

"Just a Registry Office for now. We'll have a church wedding back home. He's a viscount and I couldn't cheat mother of that. Afterward, I'm planning a little, simple reception at the Savoy."

"Oh, no, Sally, I don't think a hotel is ever really much good. The walls reek of too many other parties. I'll give the reception here—it'll be my wedding present to you."

"Oh, I was hoping you'd say that! Anabel, thank you!"

"I know you were." Anabel laughed again. She liked to be generous in anticipation of being asked a favor.

"Just don't change your mind again, Sally. I've never given a wedding reception before and I don't want to have to cancel it at the last minute and drink all the champagne myself."

"I promise, Anabel, *honestly*. Oh, you're an angel!"

"Sally, one thing . . ."

"Yes?"

"Relax."

"Relax? My God, you're amazing. How can I relax at a time like this?" Sally's voice scaled new peaks of anxiety.

"Sit down in a chair and say 'viscountess' over and over for a half-hour . . . that should be very relaxing indeed."

The Registry Office had been as unromantic a place as you could find for a wedding, Anabel thought, surveying with satisfaction the success of the reception she had arranged. The groom's entire entourage had brightened visibly as they had entered her flower-filled house and now, hours later, stuffed with caviar and pâté and an elaborate cold buffet, they were making a real party out of it. The bride and groom as well as the tall, grand parade of the groom's relatives had long since left, but the remaining guests had passed into the stage of singing old songs.

Apparently, the men had all served in the war together, Anabel decided, since her drawing room now was filled with musical sounds from an airforce film of the late 1940s. Fortunately, she didn't have the kind of breakable objects around with which many women filled their homes.

She had been too busy being a maid of honor, a duty which had finally boiled down, as she had fully expected, into forcing a recalcitrant, hysterical Sally to show up for the wedding, to pay much attention to the other members of the wedding party. She kept a stern eye on Sally until the final vows were said and then raced home to change and be ready to greet the reception guests. The small, simple reception Sally had spoken of had ballooned, once she knew that Anabel was giving it, to a party of over a hundred guests, and now Anabel patiently waited until the last song had been sung and the last bottle drained, to usher her guests out.

Finally, after midnight, she went upstairs to her bedroom. As usual, her maid had taken off the heavy, yellow damask bedspread and turned back the lace-trimmed sheets, made of linen so smooth that it felt like silk. As usual, her chiffon nightgown was spread on the bed and her embroidered slippers were on the carpet. But, not as usual, there was a man asleep in her bed, face down on the mattress, his naked shoulders burrowed snugly under her white wool blankets.

The next time Sally gets married she can jolly well have her reception at the Savoy, Anabel thought. Helplessly she looked at the morning coat, one sleeve inside out, the striped trousers, the shirt, the four-in-hand, the shiny black shoes, even socks, and God save us, undershorts, all strewn on her carpet. She started to ring for the maid and decided against it. No point in waking the butler either. He and the cook had had a busy day, even with the caterers doing most of the work. She went to the bed and inspected the usurper. From the color of his hair she realized it was the best man. Their only exchange had been one vivid flash, an ironic look they had exchanged during the ceremony which conveyed that they both shared an equally dim view of the entire performance.

Well, she thought, he *had* seemed a gentleman, and she was damned if she was going to make up a bed in one of the guest rooms at this hour. She undressed in the bathroom, put on her nightgown and slipped into the other side of the big bed. At least he doesn't snore, she thought, and went to sleep.

Sometime during the night Stash woke and realized he was in bed with a sleeping woman whose identity was unclear . . . in fact, unknown. Since this was no novelty he went back to sleep.

Both Stash and Anabel woke late, within a few seconds of each other. She leaned on her elbow, her dark red hair spread loose on her shoulders, and said, "Shall I ring for breakfast, Prince Valensky, or don't you feel up to anything but an Alka-Seltzer?"

"Breakfast, please, Miss de Fourment."

"Eggs? Coddled in cream? Freshly-baked croissants? Irish ham? And honey? In the comb?"

"Please."

"Tea or coffee?"

"Tea, please."

"You're very polite this morning. I'll say that for you."

Anabel spoke on the bedside phone which was connected to the kitchen and ordered.

"You wouldn't happen to have a bathrobe handy . . . a man's robe?"

"Certainly not. I live alone."

Stash got out of bed, stalked naked to the bathroom, and closed the door behind him. Anabel rocked with laughter in the bed. The test would be what he wore when he came back. She had huge towels piled in heaps by the tub. The bathroom door opened and he returned to bed, as naked as before. He'd passed one test, at least, and very, very handsomely indeed, she thought.

"Good morning, Marie," she said to the maid who entered with one tray. Landon, the butler, stood behind her carrying the other.

"Good morning, Madame."

"Marie, give that tray to the Prince. Landon, that's for me. Yes, here, thank you. Is the sun out?"

"Lovely day, Madame. Shall I open the curtains?"

"No, thank you, Landon. I'll ring if I need you." She poured herself a cup of tea. Stash ate with concentration.

"Wonderful eggs," he said.

"My dairy man keeps chickens and lets me have them the day they're laid."

"Really."

"Really."

"Stop laughing at me," he said fiercely.

"You're so terribly funny. Why shouldn't I laugh?"

"I'm not used to it. I don't like it."

"Oh, God. You do take yourself seriously." She laughed harder than ever.

"Look, the morning after you've slept with a man, you don't treat him as if he's the new comic from the Palladium. It's simply bad manners, if nothing else."

Now it looked as if her laughter was going to pitch over the tray, if not cause her to fall out of bed. Stash put their trays on the floor, grabbed her and shook her. Anabel subsided enough to gasp out three words.

"But we *didn't* . . ."

"Well, that was a mistake. Set that right in no time."

"Damned if you will. You're not my type."

"Try and stop me."

She couldn't. In fact, she reflected, hours later, she probably, in all fairness, hadn't tried as hard as she might have. Although he had made her miss breakfast—and lunch as well.

Anabel de Fourment, Stash realized, was exactly, precisely, positively what he needed. And what he needed, he got.

It wasn't that easy. It took him another month of proper courtship before she would allow him more than a goodnight kiss. And still another month before she allowed him back in her bed. Anabel could be taken by surprise only once ... after that the game was played on her terms. There were practicalities which had to be settled first ... certain financial understandings which had to be reached, provisions made. Once all of her exceptionally stringent conditions had been met, and properly, she permitted herself to wonder if perhaps she would have taken him on for nothing. Just for fun. No, probably not—she couldn't afford that sort of luxury. But there had been a moment of temptation, about which she'd never tell him. Stash didn't want to be responsible for a woman's emotions, and, from the very little he'd told her, she could understand why.

With Stash came an occasional bonus; infrequent visits from his son, Ram, who was now eleven, and in school at Eton. There was something irreducibly stubborn and unreachable in his dark, slim face, that troubled Anabel's kind heart.

Ram's mother, Stash's wartime bride, had remarried and lived in a half-tumbled-down castle in Scotland. Occasionally the boy spent a rare school holiday with his father, whenever Stash was in London. The relationship between the boy and the man was as strained as such arrangements were bound to make them. Stash hadn't seen Ram grow up, he hardly knew how to communicate with him. The boy already bore him animus because of the small, malicious remarks his mother had made for as long as he could remember; he felt neglected when, as often happened, his father was away playing polo during those times when he could have visited him; he felt cast off from his rightful heritage when he compared the way in which Stash lived with the shabby, faded, ramshackle Scottish life which he had to share with three half-sisters and a stepfather he didn't like.

And yet he had such towering pride in being a Prince

Valensky! He had cultivated this pride as one cultivates an ultimate, only possession. During his three years at Eton, he had had the bad luck to fall in with a crowd where the choice was clearly to bully or be bullied. Of course he had become a bully, strong as he was, with his father's soldier's temper. He had lessened the disadvantage of a foreign name by stressing the fact that he was a prince, rubbing their noses in it, making up tales about his ancestors when the real ones would have been more than impressive enough, had he but known them.

At eleven he was well grown, but with a tightness, a withheld quality in his approach to people which didn't go with his age. A diffuse, generalized, but biting envy of happy people—all happy people—made him shy and guarded, quick to amass grudges and hoard bitterness. He knew, without articulating the exact words, that he had been cheated—cheated since he was born, and he chewed over that fact endlessly. It was a constant, dark rhythm which went with him everywhere.

And yet his face betrayed nothing. He was an exceptionally beautiful boy with none of the Valensky blondness except for his gray eyes which looked so much like Stash's eyes that Anabel was drawn to Ram immediately. He was dark, like everyone in his mother's family, with skin so olive and a nose already so aquiline and haughty that he could almost have passed for one of those young Hindu maharajas whose labyrinthian genealogies stretched back thousands of years and were known only to the Brahman priests in the sacred town of Nasik. He was a boy of mystery, Anabel decided, an unhappy boy, and it went against everything in her nature to have an unhappy male of any age in her vicinity. She bent all her arts and wisdom to making a friend of Ram. Soon he loved her, as much as he was able to love, and he found, when she invited him to special private lunches alone with her in her house, a spontaneity and well-being he hadn't known before. Only with Anabel could he stop envying happy people because with her, he became—for a short while—one of them.

8

$\mathcal{W}$hen Francesca had fled Lausanne with the twins and Masha, her only clear intention had been to get away from Stash. But, as she flew westward, to New York, she realized that the only people in the world who could help her now were the Firestones. As soon as they had passed through customs at Idlewild she telephoned Matty in Hollywood and asked her former agent to meet her at the airport in Los Angeles.

"Please, Matty, don't ask me any questions. I'll tell you everything when I get there," she begged.

"But hon ... never mind ... we'll be there, don't worry." I knew she'd be back, he thought, as he hung up the phone. I knew that shit would make her miserable. But none of his premonitions prepared either Matty or Margo for the sight of two babies. Their astonishment went beyond questions, particularly since Francesca and Masha were both so exhausted by the hours of travel that they were too tired to make sense. The Firestones drove the huddle of women and infants back to their home as fast as they could and fed them and put them all to bed at once.

"Now sleep! We'll talk about it in the morning," Margo ordered.

As soon as she woke up, Francesca told the Firestones the whole story, pouring out the words with fresh incredulity. During the achingly long trip, in order to shepherd her band to safety, she had had to concentrate on practical details and prevent herself from dwelling on the facts she had discovered so recently, but now, as she put the words together for Matty and Margo, she became hysterical.

Only Margo's assurance that there existed a safe place for her and her children kept her from breaking down.

"We'll go there tomorrow," Matty said.

"No, *now!* I can't stay here—he'll find me here!"

"But it's a six-hour drive, hon."

"Can we make it if we leave in fifteen minutes? We haven't even unpacked."

Matty glanced at Margo, and then turned back to Francesca. "Sure—so we'll arrive after dark—no big deal, we'll turn on the lights."

In Matty's big Cadillac they drove up Route 101 to Carmel. There Matty turned back down the coast, taking Route 1, the narrow, twisting, dangerous coast road, and drove thirty miles to a vacation cabin he and Margo owned in the Ventana Wilderness of Big Sur.

The cabin, almost invisible from the steeply rising dirt road which climbed up to it, was built of weathered, local redwood. It had running water, electricity and heat since the Firestones had discovered that even in the summer Big Sur can be bitterly cold at night. Margo had furnished it with sturdy American antiques from Carmel and had used old quilts for bed covers and upholstery. From the small clearing of wild grasses in front of the cabin, which was tucked among redwoods, aspens and sycamores, there was a view straight out over the Pacific Ocean, a thousand feet below. At that height the wild waves and breakers flattened out and the ocean looked calm and harmless.

When Francesca gazed down at the sea on the following morning, she saw a coastline that is not equaled for elemental beauty anywhere on earth. She sensed that gods and goddesses had walked there and she felt an intimation of safety beginning to grow in her. She had never been to Greece but something about the absolute serenity of the steep wooded knolls that rose directly from the water made Francesca feel that this was a place protected by forces of which she knew nothing. The cabin was part of nature. After the Firestones went back to Los Angeles, blacktail deer began to appear at the edge of the clearing and the coast jays soon learned to join them when Francesca and Masha fed the babies outdoors, stealing food from their plates.

There, in the Ventana Wilderness, Francesca held her little household together. Sometimes in the all but overwhelming remoteness of the Big Sur country, Francesca thought that she had bitten right out into the very edge of her soul and that the next day would find her with no more courage, no more patience, no more strength to give to her children, but she never broke. *Intact.* That was the word that was always on her mind. Year after year she kept them intact; Daisy, who crackled so with energy that when Francesca managed to capture one of her busy hands she expected to receive an electric shock, and Dani, who, at three and a half, could walk upstairs only if she held on to the railing, and then only by putting one foot on each tread and then the other so that it took her an eternity to creep to her bedroom; Daisy who sang long, rhyming songs to anyone who would listen and could name every animal in the picture books and every flower in the woods and could put away every object in the kitchen in its proper place and take her own bath and brush her own teeth; and Dani who built towers only two blocks high, who knew how to turn three or four pages of a book at once, but never managed one page at a time, and who understood only the simplest of verbal instructions.

Yet it was with Dani that Francesca found her most peaceful and harmonious moments. Dani's eyes, like a baby's eyes, seemed to remember something of a previous life which couldn't be communicated, but which reassured and comforted her. Dani's vulnerability was her strength, since no one saw her without feeling the impulse to protect her. Dani was never unhappy because she was never frustrated. If she couldn't do something, she didn't bang furiously on the table the way Daisy did when she first discovered that she didn't know how to read. Dani didn't ask endless questions, didn't plague Francesca with demands to climb a tree, catch an earthworm, make cookies, train a hummingbird, take a walk in the woods and collect pebbles on the beach—all in the same breath, as Daisy did.

Every week Margo or Matty Firestone would telephone to find out how they were faring, and Francesca was able, with honesty, to tell them that all was well with her. She was so caught up in the intensity of her maternal feelings that she had no time to regret the years during which she had been a movie star or the months during which she had been a princess. Love for Daisy and Danielle—and fear for them—isolated her more than any other emotion she had ever known. She, who had had within her something as powerful as a huge magnet that had irresistibly attracted many, many men into her field of force, now allowed that magnet to become just another piece of inert material. Occasionally she would consider briefly her solitary life, hidden from the world, and remember the days when she had loved Stash. She would murmur a few lines from Hamlet—

> *There lies within the very flame of love*
> *A kind of wick or snuff that will abate it,*

—and return to the present, remembering only that Ophelia had always been a part she had disliked.

"I don't understand her," Matty said to Margo. "How can a woman like that not go totally bananas stuck up there all alone with only Masha and the kids to keep her company? What kind of life is it for her, I ask you? It doesn't make sense."

"She's playing the greatest role of her life," Margo answered.

"Bullshit. That's what you said when she was doing the princess number."

"Matty, you really still don't get it, do you? That whole princess thing was a lightweight farce compared to being the tigress mother. Now she has those two precious babies to protect and bring up and she doesn't *need* anything else—not men or acting or even friends. It'll change as they get older, I guess, but right now she's absorbed in them to the exclusion of everything. Nothing, *nothing* has any other meaning for her."

"That was some great idea you had, to take her to Europe," Matty sighed in incurable despair. "If it hadn't been for that trip she'd still be the greatest star in the business . . ."

"Don't look back, Matty. It doesn't help."

Daisy had started to talk a steady stream of jargon at about fifteen months, spaced with clear-cut, well-pronounced names and a few demands. By the age of two she was spontaneously combining words into short sentences, using pronouns and verbalizing her immediate experience. "Daisy not afraid of thunder," she would announce, grabbing Masha's hand and squeezing it hard. Anxiously, Francesca waited for signs of speech development in Dani, who could say "Mama," "Asha" for Masha and "Day" for Daisy, but instead she heard only occasional sounds which were utterly without meaning, gibberish composed of distorted and unarticulated syllables. She waited and patiently tried to teach Dani, but the little girl added only a few basic words—like "yes" and "no" and "bird" and "hot"—to her vocabulary. However, to Francesca's horror, Daisy started to use Dani's gibberish. She listened, fear cold in her bones, as the twins communicated with each other in the way of idiots. She was afraid to say anything about it to Daisy, hoping that if she didn't mention the strange phenomenon it would go away. Instead, it got worse. Finally, when they had passed their third birthday, Francesca asked, as casually as possible, "Daisy, what are you and Dani talking about?"

"She wanted to play with my dolly but when I gave it to her she didn't want it anymore."

"Why do you talk to Dani that way, Daisy?"

"What way?"

"The way you just did—all those funny noises. Not the way you talk to me."

"But that's just the way she talks, Mama."

"Can you understand everything she says?"

"Of course."

"What else do you talk about?"

"I don't know." Daisy looked puzzled. "We just talk."

That night, as she was putting the twins to bed, Francesca heard the strange sounds start up again.

"What did she say just now, Daisy?"

"Dani said, more kiss. That means she wants you to give her another goodnight kiss."

"Couldn't you teach her to say kiss, Daisy, the way you say it?"

"I don't know. I don't think so."

"Will you try?"

"Yes, Mama. More kiss for me, too?"

That night Francesca spoke to Masha about the twins' strange form of communication.

"Yes, I've noticed it many, many times, Madame," Masha answered slowly. "It reminds me of something from Russia—something I heard when I was growing up—it must have been about fifty years ago. There were twins—boys they were—who lived in the village nearest to ours and I still remember my mother and my aunt whispering to each other about them. The twins talked to each other all the time in a language nobody could understand. People thought perhaps they were . . . they didn't know—"

"Were they normal, Masha?"

"Oh, yes, Madame. They stopped doing it when they got older and by the time they were six or so everyone thought they had just forgotten it. They talked just like everyone else. But then I left, to go to St. Petersburg, and that's all I can tell you—about them or about anyone else in that village," she finished sadly.

Francesca knew few other people to consult about this problem, or any other problem in her life. She was living in the most isolated way possible, except for the phone calls from Matty and Margo. Francesca understood that if reporters were to come across the fact that Francesca Vernon Valensky lived in Big Sur with two identical twin children, she would be hounded to the ends of the earth, until the whole evil story was discovered. She was not protecting Stash, but protecting Daisy from ever knowing what her father had done.

Whenever she had to drive into Carmel for supplies that couldn't be found in the tiny general store that supplied the few, scattered permanent residents of the area, she left both children at home with Masha and wore such concealing clothes and head scarfs and sunglasses that she was never recognized. She dared not make friends. No friends, old or new, could be trusted except Matty and Margo. She lived frugally, accepting the cabin without shame, for her children's sake. One by one, through Margo, she sold the jeweled flowers in the crystal vases. Each object was worth only some fifteen hundred dollars to a Beverly Hills dealer, but fifteen hundred dollars could keep the four of them for six months. She guarded the lapis egg for last, when the flowers would be gone. Margo had described it to a salesman at *A la Vieille Russie* in New York, who said that if it were genuine Fabergé it might be worth up to twenty or thirty thousand dollars to them. That it was genuine Francesca didn't doubt—it was her only security. She cursed herself to sleep night after night thinking of the jewels she had so proudly and foolishly left behind, thinking of the money she had made in Hollywood and casually spent, every penny of it, on clothes and cars and books and extravagant presents to her parents and friends.

From time to time Matty would send her a script some hopeful producer had given him to "pass on if you can." For the first three years Francesca refused all these offers without thinking about it because she couldn't dream of leaving Masha alone to cope with the two children for months at a time.

Two years after Francesca's flight, Stash had a letter from Matty Firestone. He was informed that Francesca believed that Daisy, now three years old, needed to know her father. She would permit him to visit the child four times a year, for three consecutive days, four hours at a time, provided that he do so without making any attempt to see Francesca or discover where she lived. He was told to go to the Highlands Inn in Carmel and wait.

Stash left London that same morning. A few hours after he arrived, the desk clerk told him that he had visitors. In the rustic lobby Masha was waiting for him with Daisy holding her hand tightly.

There was no sign of Francesca or Danielle. Stash asked Masha no questions, none at all, and she volunteered nothing but a quiet greeting to the man she had once suckled at her breast.

At the end of the first hours with his strong, brave and beautiful daughter, Stash drew pictures for her, stick figures of a man and a little girl adorned with big red hearts. He explained to her that whenever she received one of these in the mail it would mean that he had been thinking about her every day. He mailed one every two or three days until his next visit. The minute he was alone with her he asked her if she had received them.

"Yes, Daddy."

"Do you like to get them?"

"Yes."

"Do you remember what they mean?"

"That you think about me."

"Do you keep them?"

"Oh, yes, Daddy, I keep them."

"Where do you keep them, Daisy darling?"

"I give them to Dani."

"Oh."

"She likes to play with them."

"Daisy, let's go and look at the kitten."

Each time that he returned to London from California, Stash willed himself not to start counting the weeks until he could see Daisy again. He failed utterly. He was unable to resist the temptation of consulting a judge he knew personally, telling him nothing of the existence of Danielle, but merely explaining that after his separation, his wife had restricted his access to his child. The only remedies open to him, he soon was made to understand, would have to involve publicity. Stash was advised to wait. Often, in cases such as his, as a child grows older, access is made easier, particularly as the child herself can be influenced more strongly as she gains in maturity. So he waited, with the same wolfish, undefeated yet helplessly impotent fury that he had known during his first year in the RAF; yet he never contemplated anything but victory. If not now, then soon.

By the time Daisy was five, the child was providing real help around the cabin, making both her bed and Dani's, cleaning the room they shared, drying dishes, watering and expertly weeding the vegetable garden. Francesca, who had just received a letter from Matty enclosing yet another script, a good one, explained to Daisy that she might have to go away for a short time to do some work which would earn some money for all of them, but that she would be back very, very soon. "How long?" Daisy asked fearfully.

"Only six weeks," Francesca answered and Daisy burst into tears.

"Daisy," Francesca reproached her, "you're old enough to understand now. Six weeks isn't very long and I'll come home as soon as they're over. Just six Sundays and six Mondays ... it's not so much."

"And six Tuesdays and six Wednesdays," Daisy said sadly. "Would you make a lot of money, Mama?"

"Yes, darling."

"And then you'd come right home?"

"Yes, darling, the minute the work is finished."

"All right, Mama, I understand," Daisy said reluctantly.

Later, Daisy and Dani exchanged a long stream of sibilant babble, with Daisy saying almost everything and Dani asking what obviously were questions. At the end of the conversation Dani, who could walk perfectly well by now, went down on all fours, like a baby, crawled into a corner of the room, pulled up a rag rug, and lay under it, her silent, wretched little face turned toward the wall.

"Daisy? What did you say?" Francesca demanded, alarmed.

"I told her what you explained to me, Mama. She didn't

understand. I couldn't make her understand. I tried and tried, really I tried. She doesn't know what coming back *means*—she doesn't understand about earning money."

"Try again!"

"I tried ... now she won't listen to me. Oh, Mama, I tried so hard."

"All right ... it's all right, Daisy darling. I don't really have to go away. It was just an idea. Would you tell Dani that I'm not leaving, that I'm not going anywhere?"

Daisy put her arms around her mother's neck and pressed her warm, soft face into Francesca's cheek. "Don't be sad, Mama. Please don't be sad. I'll help you work. I'll help you make some money. I promise I will."

Francesca looked at the courageous little figure with the eyes like flowers, her white-blonde hair in one long braid which reached halfway to her waist, her tan knees scratched from adventurous rambles in the deep forest, her hands beginning to lose their baby fat, to become capable, caring and strong.

"I know you will." She smiled without a trace of sadness. "We'll figure out something ... something fun."

"Can't we ask Daddy?"

"No! Daisy, that's the one thing we can never, never do."

"Why not?"

"I'll explain—when you're older."

"Oh," said Daisy, with an air of resignation. "That's one more thing I have to remember, for you to explain when I'm older."

"Do I say that a lot?"

"Yes, Mama. But it's all right. Don't be sad again."

Suddenly Daisy changed the subject. "Mama, am I really and truly a princess? Daddy said I was."

"Yes, you are."

"Is Danielle a princess?"

"Of course she is—how could you be a princess if Dani weren't a princess too?"

"But you, Mama, are you a queen?"

"No, Daisy, I'm not a queen."

"But in stories the mother of a princess is always queen," she said stubbornly.

"Once—I was a princess, too, Daisy," Francesca murmured.

"'Once'.... Aren't you a princess anymore?"

"Daisy, Daisy, it's too complicated for you to understand right now. And anyway, it's just a word, it doesn't mean anything really, nothing important, nothing for you to bother about. We don't live in a world of princesses here—just the two of us and Masha and Dani and the deer and the birds— Isn't that good enough for you, my Daisy?"

Something about Francesca's face told Daisy to agree with her mother. But it wasn't good enough for her, she didn't understand it at all and no one seemed to ever give her an answer to her most important questions, particularly the ones she had never dared to bring up: why did her father only come to see her at long intervals? Why did he never see Dani? And most important of all, what had she, Daisy, *done wrong* to make him go away each time after only a few days? It was never discussed, never even hinted at, and somehow she understood that she must never ask, never.

"Masha, look, I've shelled all the peas."

"How many did you eat, little one?"

"Only six. Eight. Maybe ten."

"I know, they are better raw. I always thought so, too."

"Oh, Masha, you know everything!"

"Ah, will you tell me that in ten years?"

"Masha, Masha . . . why is Dani different from me?"

"What . . . what do you mean?"

"She's my twin sister. That means we were born at the same time. Mama told me that. That's what twins are, two babies in the same mother. But Dani doesn't talk like me and she can't really run like me—not as fast—and she can't climb trees and she's afraid of thunder and rain and birds and she doesn't draw pictures like me or cut her own meat, and she can't count like me, or tie her own shoes. Why, Masha?"

"Oh, Daisy, I don't know."

"Yes, you do, Masha, you know. Mama won't tell me but you will. You always tell me everything."

"Daisy, you were born first, that's all I know."

"Born first?" Daisy was astonished. "Twins are born together, that's what makes them twins. You're silly, Masha."

"No, Daisy, one twin is born after the other. You are

both in the same mother, the way your Mama told you, but one has to come out of the mother first and then the other. You were born first."

"So it is my fault." She spoke slowly, as if something she had long suspected had, at last, been confirmed by adult authority.

"Don't be silly, little one, it's God's will, not anybody's fault. You should know better than to talk like that! Daisy?"

"Yes, Masha?"

"You understand, don't you?"

"I understand, Masha." Yes, she understood. She *had* been born first so it *was* her fault. Masha always talked about God's will, but Daisy knew that when Masha said that it meant that Masha didn't understand either.

As 1957 wore on, the winter storms brought driftwood to the hidden beaches of Big Sur, wild, windswept beaches where sandpipers jittered and great waves carved strange bridges out of giant rocks; where sea lions often roared; beaches from which migrating whales could be sometimes seen in their benign, silent flotillas.

Francesca had found a craftsman in Carmel who made lamps out of driftwood and she made a little money collecting it from the beaches, polishing the best pieces and bringing them in to him from time to time. She usually went alone to the beach, but one early spring day in 1958, she took Daisy and Dani with her. She left Dani in Daisy's charge and wandered along the beach, one piece of driftwood luring her to another, until she suddenly realized that the children were out of sight.

"Dear God!" She ran back the way she'd come and stopped suddenly. Daisy was sitting on the warm sand out of range of even the farthest lapping wave. She held Dani in her little lap, awkwardly since they were almost the same size. Their sixth birthday was only a week away. Daisy was rocking Dani back and forth and from the shape of her mouth, Francesca could see that she was singing to her sister. From time to time Daisy patted her hand over Dani's hair and kissed her cheek, with a maternal gesture. Dani's beautiful face wore its usual sweet, contented expression. A great inner peace descended on Francesca, a feeling of joy so simple and so deep that she almost fell on her knees. She had been right.

She had done the only possible thing. She had been blessed.

One week later Stash received a long-distance call from Matty Firestone in California. The agent was sobbing unashamedly.

"You get here as quickly as you can. Francesca's gone ... she's dead. She was driving back from Carmel, on the ocean side, Route One, I always warned her—some madman in a pickup truck swung wide, she went off the road ... into the sea."

"Daisy!" Stash screamed.

"Francesca was alone. I went up and brought Masha and the kids back. They're here at our house. Come and get them, Valensky.... You're all they've got left, God help them."

9

$\mathcal{O}$n a spring Sunday in London in 1963, Stash Valensky and Daisy, who was now eleven, entered the Connaught Hotel for their regular Sunday lunch alone together.

Lunch at the Connaught is one of the premiere experiences of Western civilization, the Uffizi Gallery of dining, and Stash, still absorbed in taming his invincible child, thought that the Connaught, with its richly subdued air of comfy pomp, its air of being not a hotel but a lordly private house, in which one always feels the subliminal ticking of a soberly friendly Victorian grandfather clock, provided the best atmosphere for his purpose. The doorman greeted them as old friends; they walked through the small, deeply carpeted, russet-toned lobby dominated by a sweeping, prodigiously polished flight of mahogany stairs, and turned right to pass through the corridor which led to the restaurant, recognized as one of three finest in England. As usual, Stash had to keep a firm hand on Daisy's elbow, for the passageway was lined with a series of tables bearing silver platters laden with a dozen different kinds of cold hors d'oeuvres, melons, salads, lobsters, stuffed crab and a selection of game pies. The tables laden with food were crowded in that wide corridor, which also held a little mirrored bar and tall vases of spring flowers, in a way that suggested an overflowing abundance that caused Daisy to linger inquiringly over each dish, trying to decide, even before she read the menu, what looked most interesting today.

The restaurant had walls of highly waxed, dark honey-colored wood, on which glowed crystal sconces with apricot shades. The chairs and banquettes were covered with burgundy-striped velvet and large screens broke the restaurant up into sections, at the same time imparting an Alice in Wonderland feeling to the substantial room since the bases of the screens were carved wood to the height of a seated diner, but above they were made of engraved glass, so that standing up, one could see through them. Stash and Daisy's favorite table was in the center of the restaurant rather than at one of the banquettes because it provided a vantage point from which they could see all their fellow gourmets and speculate on them.

Many people looked up from their plates as they entered. Stash had changed almost not at all. At fifty-two, his hair was as blond, as thick and as close cropped as ever; his features as strongly marked with an air of valor and resolution. Alone, he would have attracted attention, but with Daisy he aroused the most lively inspection, even in this sanctuary of solid, upper-class lack of curiosity, for she was a child out of fairyland. Daisy was five feet tall now and possessed the slim roundness of prepuberty which is so tender, so free of the slightest fault, so pristine and yet so full of rushing life, that it causes the most hardened adults to give a sigh for a vanquished vulnerability and strength they must have once possessed. She wore an ivory dress of the thinnest wool challis printed with clusters of pale pink flowers and pale green leaves. It was pleated down the front, with a sash that tied in the back, and the collar was like a little garland around her neck, where the flowers of the dress had been cut out and thickly appliquéd.

Her gilt-blonde hair almost reached her waist and it was brushed back and held by a simple band, but nothing could restrain the individual curls that sprang from her forehead and escaped above her ears. The light coming from the great Victorian windows of Carlos Place seemed to attack Daisy's hair, snatching and catching it with a rollicking freedom, all the planes and shafts of the watery spring sun finding an object worthy of their focus. It was the hair of an old-fashioned heroine, tresses that looked as if they had been lovingly brushed by a mother and admired and envied by aunts and sisters; hair precious enough to be kept in lockets and treasured for decades.

Stash guided her to their table with an air of possession that he couldn't conceal. He cherished Daisy in a way that deeply frightened him. He had long ago learned that it was unbearably dangerous to invest so much emotional capital in another human being, but he was helpless in the face of the mere existence of this daughter of his, this treasure he had almost lost, this obstinate, bold-hearted, loving female creature he had worshiped from the first, never-to-be-forgotten sight of her, as he had never worshiped another female in all his life.

Now, in Daisy, he saw himself as a young boy, the forever lost, forever innocent, forever hopeful self which can only be recaptured in a dream, the forgotten self that vanishes as one wakes, leaving only a feeling of impossible brightness and unreasoning happiness, a feeling that rarely lingers for more than a few seconds.

As the tail-coated waiter handed Daisy the white menu bordered in brown and gold, with the date printed at the bottom, she gave a sign of anticipation, although she knew it nearly by heart now, after almost three years of such lunches. She had long since passed the stage of chicken pie, of lamb chops, even of roast sirloin of Scottish beef, the three favorites on which she had first settled. Stash had, in the beginning, tried to lead her carefully through the menu, but he quickly found out that there was no way he could convince or cajole her into ordering something new. She had no interest in "training her taste buds," she said to him, repeating his pedantic phrase with a teasing look. He often wondered where his nimble girl, who never faltered in her attempts to make her own decisions, had learned to be so adamant in those backwoods in which she had spent those early years of her life. But even when she was first confronted by the grandeur of the service of the Connaught, Daisy's smile informed the maître d'hôtel that she represented no one on earth but herself and that since she had wanted chicken pie every Sunday for a year, that was what she would order.

"Well, Princess Daisy," the maître d'hôtel greeted her with relish, "what is your choice today?"

"What," she asked, "is the 'croustade d'oeufs de caille Maintenon' besides eggs?"

"Tiny quail eggs, served with creamed mushrooms and hollandaise on little pastry barquettes."

"Daisy, you had eggs for breakfast. Why don't you start with some smoked Scotch salmon?" Stash asked.

"That's listed under the 'extras,' Father," Daisy rebuked him gravely.

Stash sighed inwardly. No matter how often he explained to her that she was permitted to order from the extras, she never would. Her habits of thrift, learned so young, couldn't be forgotten even in this restaurant in which the final bill would represent such an astonishing total that one or two extra dishes wouldn't be noticed. She went to the Connaught because he took her there, but nothing he could say had ever convinced her to order an extra, not even the *Salade Caprice des Années Folles*, surely the most delightfully named dish in the world.

"If I might suggest," said the maître d'hôtel, "the trolley of hors d'oeuvres so that you have your choice, and then, perhaps, the lobster grilled with herbs—we have just received a superb shipment from France—"

"Are they still alive?" asked Daisy.

"But of course! They *must* be alive before we cook them."

"I'll have a Lancashire hot pot then," announced Daisy, not knowing what on earth it was but determined not to directly cause the immediate death of a single lobster.

Ah, thought the headwaiter, Prince Valensky must take care. If the little girl should become, disaster of disasters, a vegetarian, we might not see her every Sunday.

Lunch finally ordered, Daisy and Stash settled into the easy conversations he enjoyed now more than any other single thing in his life. He was teaching her his world, little by little, and she, in turn, brought him all the excitements of her life at school and acquainted him with the small adventures of her friends. But today she had something special on her mind.

"Father, in your opinion, do I have to do maths?" asked Daisy.

"Naturally—they teach it in school, don't they?"

"Yes, but I hate it and I can't study my maths and do a proper job on my new pony. How can I ride Merlin every afternoon after school and then muck out her stall and turn over her bedding, groom her with the curry comb and vacuum her all over and use the body brush and the rub rag and the hoof pick and . . ."

"All that takes exactly one half-hour and you know it," Stash said, laughing at the dramatically detailed list she'd presented him in the hope that he'd be impressed. "You still have time for maths."

Daisy, a seasoned strategist, abandoned Merlin instantly. "Anabel says she doesn't see why I have to do maths—she never did and she says she never missed it. Anabel says she's never balanced a checkbook in her life and the only reason for maths is to balance checkbooks or find out if the fishmonger is cheating you and if you tell him he is, you won't get the best fish so you might as well resign yourself."

"So Anabel has become your authority on education?"

"Anabel is my authority on many things," said Daisy with dignity. "However, if you gave me three good reasons why I have to do maths, I'd try, even though I think there's something missing in the place in my brain where most people have maths."

"I'll give you only one good reason because I don't need another—Lady Alden *requires* that all girls at her school do maths."

"I think it's most unreasonable of Lady Alden ... most unreasonable," Daisy grumbled.

"Did Anabel teach you to say things are unreasonable?"

"No, you did. You said it was most unreasonable of me to want to jump Merlin over the railings in Wilton Crescent." Daisy's face crinkled in mischief. She changed her moods so rapidly that Stash sometimes wondered if he was talking to a child, a grown woman, a scruffy farmboy or a sage member of Parliament.

"I'm afraid you're a pagan, Daisy."

"I wouldn't mind. Don't they dance around trees and do strange things when the moon is full?"

"I believe those were Druids. Pagans are like the ancient Greeks or Romans, people who worshiped many gods, not just one."

"Oh, good, I think I'd like to be one. Like you are, Father."

Heading her off this unpromising subject Stash asked quickly, "How's Merlin getting used to the stable?" Merlin, the latest in a series of ponies, each taller than the last, was named after Stash's old favorite, now retired from the fray. Daisy's horse was stabled in Grosvenor Crescent Mews, a few minutes away from Wilton Row, where the Valensky house was located. The stable had been run by Mrs. Leila Blum for twenty years. It was dark, with cobbled floors, and Merlin occupied one of the four loose-boxes rather than a less spacious stall where she would have to be tied up.

"She's as happy as the day is long," Daisy said importantly. "There're a few black cats hanging about and she gets along very well with them, but Merlin really and *truly* wants a dog. She *craves* a dog, passionately."

"She does, does she? Did she say what kind of dog?"

"Just a dog."

"She 'craves' it passionately?"

"Absolutely."

"Something tells me that Merlin's been talking to Anabel."

"No, Father, she communicates with me. You know horses can, if they like."

"Hmmm. Daisy, isn't it time for a sweet?"

Daisy inspected her father's face closely. For three years she had been trying to get him to buy her a dog. He wasn't a man who loved dogs, he wasn't a man who even liked dogs, and he had resisted her successfully. Today, by the light in his eyes, she realized it was hopeless to pursue the subject.

"I'd love a sweet," Daisy said. The matter was not yet settled, but it was only a question of time. She had no intention of giving up.

Stash signaled the waiter who wheeled over one of the dessert trolleys, shining objects of solid mahogany on four silent ball bearings, with several levels of trays, each covered in an array of desserts: chocolate, lemon and raspberry mousse, bread-and-butter pudding, rice pudding, apple tarts, assorted pastries, poached fruit in port, fresh fruit salad served with thick cream from Normandy, large, rich cakes and *mille feuilles aux fraises*. The doting waiter, worthy inheritor of the Connaught tradition, never waited for Daisy to make the agonizing choice but simply filled a plate with small samples of every dessert on the trolley, except for the rice pudding. After dessert, while Stash had his coffee, the waiter, as he did at each table, brought a silver compote on which lay a variety of miniature sweets: fresh strawberries dipped in chocolate, tiny eclairs and cherries iced in frosting. Each one of them lay in a fluted paper cup. While Stash stared fixedly at the floor, Daisy deftly swept every single one of these delicacies into her small handbag, which she had lined with her best handkerchiefs in anticipation of this loot. The first time she had done it Stash had been horrified.

"Daisy! A lady can eat as many of those as she likes *at* the table, but she doesn't take them away with her!"

"They're not for me."

"Oh." Stash knew immediately for whom they were

intended. She was taking them to the other. He never mentioned them again but endured in silence the humiliation of the weekly incident. Daisy would not have allowed him to order a box of the candied treats for her, he knew, because then they would be "extra" and he couldn't bring himself to deprive her of the pleasure she took in her gift to her sister.

When Stash had received the telephoned news of Francesca's death from Matty Firestone, he had started to consider his options even as he booked the flight to Los Angeles. Almost immediately he realized that someone had to be told the story which had been, until now, kept absolutely secret from all the world. He needed help in managing the future and Anabel was the only person he trusted. During the few days that Stash was away in California, Anabel managed to find Queen Anne's School, the best home for retarded children in England, and make arrangements for Danielle to live there.

She drove Stash's big car to the airport to meet the little band since he had been adamant about the need to keep the arrival of the children hidden, even from his chauffeur. As they came through customs she saw Stash, walking ahead, with Daisy's hand in his. The little girl was as confused by the rapidly changing events of the last week as she was grief-stricken. She still didn't quite understand how it was possible that her mother had driven off one afternoon and had not come home. How could she be dead? Neither Matty nor Margo nor Stash himself had yet been able to bring themselves to explain the details of the accident to her, and Daisy was engulfed in the reality of her childish fears of abandonment. Behind Stash walked Masha, carrying Danielle who had retreated into a world of silence and immobility. Quickly, without asking questions, Anabel drove them to the school which was located in the country outside of London.

When they arrived at the large building which had once been the main house of a great private estate, and was still surrounded by wide lawns, fine old trees and flower gardens, Stash told Masha, Daisy and Anabel to wait in the car for him. He picked Danielle up, the first and last time he ever touched her, and stepped out of the car, putting Danielle's feet firmly on the driveway. Daisy jumped out and followed him, hanging on to his leg as he started up the steps, Danielle silently trailing behind.

"Daddy, where are we going? Is this where you live? Why isn't Masha coming, too?"

Stash kept climbing the wide steps. "Daisy darling, your sister's going to live here for a while. It's a wonderful place, a school for her. You're coming to live with me in my house in London."

"NO!"

He stopped, bent down and spoke earnestly to the disbelieving and defiant child. "Now, listen to me, Daisy, this is very important. All the things you know how to do that she can't—like telling time and reading the cards I send you and jumping rope? Well, if she lives at this school for a while she'll learn how to do all those things from the best teachers in the world and then you'll be able to play together the way you've always wanted to . . ."

"I *love* to play with her exactly the way she is—oh, *don't make her, Daddy, don't*—she'll miss me so much. I'll miss her—please, please, Daddy!" As she began to understand the implacable extent of his intentions, Daisy's defiance turned to terrible fear.

"Daisy, I understand that it's hard, but you're thinking only of yourself. Danielle will get to like it here very quickly and there are many other children for her to play with. But if she doesn't live in a special place like this, she won't learn. Now, you don't want that to happen to her, do you . . . you don't want to keep her from learning all the grown-up things that you can do? It wouldn't be *fair*, you know that. Now, *would that be fair, Daisy?*"

"No," she sobbed, tears running down her face, down her neck and disappearing down the front of her dress.

"Come along and you can see her lovely room and meet some of the teachers."

"I can't stop crying . . . I'll make her cry, too."

"You *have to stop*. I want you to tell her all the things I said. You've always said that she understands you, best."

"She won't understand now, Daddy."

"Go ahead and try."

Finally Daisy controlled herself enough to communicate with her sister in their private language. After only a short while Danielle was weeping huge tears and howling like a small animal.

"She said: 'Day, no go!' "

"But didn't you tell her about all the things she'd learn?" Stash said impatiently.

"She didn't know what I meant."

"Well, that just shows I'm right. If she learns the things they can teach her here, she *will* understand. Now come on, Daisy, get her to stop that terrible noise she's making and we'll both take her to her nice room and she'll be fine, just fine, before you know it."

The dedicated professionals who ran the institution were accustomed to, as they put it, "unfortunate scenes" when a child was finally left in their excellent care, but nothing had prepared them for the parting of Daisy and Danielle. All of them who were unlucky enough to be present found themselves in despair and some of them were reduced to unprofessional tears by the time Stash finally pried Daisy away, as gently as he could, although he eventually had to use brute force.

After Daisy, shrieking and struggling and kicking, had been bodily carried down the corridor from Dani's room and bundled into the car, Stash determined that such emotional traumas could only be bad for her. The following Sunday, when he had promised Daisy that she could visit her sister, he refused to take her, carefully explaining that it was for her own good and for Danielle's good, too. The little girl listened intently to every word he said and, deigning no reply, merely turned away and went to her own room.

After one day Masha knocked on his door.

"Prince, little Daisy won't eat."

"She must be sick. I'll call the doctor."

"There's nothing wrong with her body."

"Then what is wrong? Come on, Masha, stop giving me that disapproving look of yours . . . it hasn't had any bloody effect on me since I was seven."

"She won't eat until she can visit Dani."

"Ridiculous. I'm not going to be dictated to by a six-year-old child. I've decided what's best for her. Now, go and tell her it didn't work. She'll eat when she gets hungry."

Masha left the room silently. She didn't return. Another day passed, and Stash sought her out.

"Well?"

"She still won't eat. I warned you. You just don't know Daisy." Masha looked at him grimly until he looked away, still resolute.

It took still another day of the hunger strike before Daisy brought her father to terms. Not one bit of food entered her mouth until she had his sworn promise that she could visit Danielle every Sunday afternoon. Stash had learned, once and for all, not to thwart her in anything to do with Danielle.

For several months after Francesca's death, Stash had received letters from Matty Firestone, asking about the children and how they were settling down in London. This was a complication that Stash decided to put behind him. He could not contemplate the possibility of a continued correspondence with the agent and his wife, whom he regarded as his sworn enemies. Eventually he composed a letter in which he demanded to be spared any further inquiries into his private affairs, a letter that was so curt, so profoundly unpleasant, so thoroughly nasty and peremptory, that both Matty and Margo decided that there was no further reason to write Valensky. Daisy and Danielle were his children, he had every legal right to them and, as Margo asked Matty sadly, realistically, what could they do about it? It was best to forget now; forget Francesca, forget the twins, put the whole tragic chapter in their lives behind them. It was over, gone, lost and they had done the best they could. Now it should be left alone.

"You mean *try* to forget," Matty said bitterly.

"Exactly. The only alternative is to sue for custody and you know we'd never get it."

"But those little girls—they were *family*, Margo."

"For me too, darling, but not legally. And that's what counts."

The Firestones stopped writing, and Daisy, in London, continued to visit Dani every Sunday. Stash never took her to Queen Anne's School himself. Rather than risk having to see the other, he sent Daisy, accompanied by Masha, on the hour-long trip, by train and cab.

During the summer months of the following years, when Daisy was on vacation from school, Stash took her with him to the house in Normandy, *La Marée*, that he had bought as a gift for Anabel soon after she had come into his life. However, every two weeks Daisy insisted that she must go back to England for the weekend so that she could visit Dani. His lips pressed together in an unwilling line, Stash saw his daughter and Masha off at the Deauville airport on a Saturday morning and returned on Sunday evening to greet them, never asking any questions about the time they had been away.

Stash received monthly reports on Danielle from Queen Anne's School, reports which he often left lying about for weeks before he brought himself to open them. They would all be the same, he told himself, and indeed they were. She was well, she was happy and well-behaved. She had learned to do a few simple things, she enjoyed music and played with some of the other children and she was particularly attached to several of the teachers. She knew a few new words and communicated with the teachers she liked, but it was only with her sister that she seemed to have any sort of conversation.

Curiously, Daisy never spoke to Stash about her twin, after she had forced him to capitulate in the matter of the visits. There was no one in her life except Masha with whom she had the slightest impulse to discuss Dani. She never spoke of her to Anabel although she knew that Anabel was aware of Dani's existence. Nor did she ever try to tell any of her school friends that she had a twin sister. She did not dare. It was a prohibition so strong that it had nothing to do with an ordinary secret. It was taboo in the most primordial sense. *Her father did not want it.* In some mysterious way Daisy was convinced that her *survival*— and Dani's too—depended on her silence. It defied her comprehension but she *knew*. She could not risk losing her father's love, that love that had been given and then withdrawn so inexplicably for the first years of her life. He was wrong about Dani, but Daisy was aware of the limits of her powers. She could tease Stash about some things, she could act the playful tyrant, but only within certain well-defined borders. Motherless, she had to cling to her father and accept the way he felt about her sister without discussion, or be totally orphaned.

The compromise they had reached in that first week, that enabled Daisy to visit Danielle, slowly became more and more acceptable to her as her sister's pliable nature adjusted happily to the teachers and the other children at Queen Anne's School. Daisy couldn't help but realize that she couldn't go to Dani's school and Dani certainly couldn't go to Lady Alden's.

The five years of seclusion in Big Sur grew ever more remote and far away as her new life in London unfolded itself, a life she found constantly less possible to even attempt to explain to Dani. Their conversations were limited to Dani's small circle of comprehension and, every year, Daisy felt more like an adult talking to a child, than one child talking to another. Daisy often drew pictures for Dani, until the walls of her room were almost papered with them.

"Do pony" was one of Dani's constant requests, because of the old horses that grazed in a meadow near Queen Anne's School. At a time when Daisy's peers at Lady Alden's were struggling to draw presentable apples and bananas, Daisy was already able to do a lively sketch of one of the most difficult of all objects to draw well, a horse.

When Daisy had first appeared in London, Ram had been a precociously alert thirteen. He had always rejected the existence of this half-sister, a product of a marriage made after his own birth. He did not accept the fact that this usurper had any rights. She was nonvalid. Worse, far worse, she was a *rival*.

Ram was preoccupied, even more than most of his friends, all upper-class, public-school boys, by the importance of being an "heir."

At Eton, enormously important distinctions concerning inheritance had been made since the school was founded by Henry VI in 1442. In 1750 the lists of pupils at Eton still appearing in order of rank, with dukes' sons coming first. Titled boys wore special clothes, had special seats and special privileges of all kinds. In the supposedly democratic 1950s and 1960s, certain of these out-of-date marks of a rigid caste system had been abolished, but the orderly passage of property and titles from one generation to another was deeply ingrained in the collective unconsciousness of Eton and the other great schools of Britain. They were as much in the air as the importance of cricket or the bad form of "showing off."

Ram couldn't remember a time when he hadn't looked forward to inheriting Stash's property, *all of it*. He didn't consciously wish his father dead, he didn't even consciously realize that only his father's death could make that property his, he simply lusted after it without any of the complications of guilt. He believed, in his heart of hearts, that the acid feelings of injustice from which he suffered —and which he never recognized were envy of happiness —would disappear when he was the possessor, the undisputed owner, *the* Prince Valensky.

The fact of Daisy meant that he would never have it *all*. No matter how many times he reassured himself that even if she got something, there was more than enough for both of them, still she had destroyed the splendid fullness of his prospects. However, he was too crafty and too wise to ever allow any of these feelings to surface and reveal themselves to grown-up eyes.

As for Daisy, from the first moment she saw Ram, he filled a great place in her imagination. He was like the young heroes in the tales that her mother used to read to her, someone who could leap across dangerous rivers and tame the wildest horses, climb up sheer mountains of glass, ride on the wind and battle with giants. To the little girl who had lived for as long as she could remember in the solitude of far-off Big Sur, this straight, tall, darkly handsome boy with his slim, stern face, his dark eyebrows and haughty Etonian air, was the most fascinating person in her new life, particularly since he had an offhand manner with her which lacked the indulgence she received from everyone else.

She could never have imagined the worm of obsessive envy that ate at Ram. At Christmas, while they were each opening their presents, he watched, behind lowered eyes, and saw that although both he and Daisy received equally expensive presents, Stash's eyes were only on Daisy as she opened the gifts, waiting to drink in *her* pleasure. Immediately Ram's own presents lost all meaning for him. When he received Daisy's letters at Eton, and she innocently wrote describing a Sunday Connaught lunch, Ram thought bitterly that the only times Stash had taken him to the Connaught had been on his birthday or to celebrate a school holiday. Twice, at Christmas, his mother insisted that he come home to that cold, drafty castle near Edinburgh instead of staying with his father, and those were the two times that Stash chose to take Daisy away to Barbados for a month of sun ... a deliberate choice, without doubt, Ram told himself, feeling the pain of being left out burn deep, although he never said anything to anyone.

As Daisy grew older, every time he went to London he hoped to find that she had finally broken out in adolescent pimples or started to get fat. He received the admiring looks she gave him without any flattery and when she asked him questions about his life at school, he answered as briefly as possible. He watched, missing nothing, as she stole all the attention that should have been his, took the place by his father's side that was Ram's by right. And all the while, Daisy, who never had any idea of how he felt, was impelled by his manner to continue to try to form a connection with him, inspired by a deeply feminine impulse that was so strong it positively tugged at its moorings in search of his love. She drew his face so often that Dani began to say, "Do Ram" although she hadn't the glimmer of an idea who Ram might be.

Stash had bought a house that was not typical of London houses, the finest of which tend to have those identical classic exteriors which are the cause of the remarkable architectural unity of London's squares and crescents. He had discovered a house in Wilton Row, a small cul-de-sac off Wilton Crescent, a street within a short distance of Hyde Park on the left and the gardens of Buckingham Palace on the right, that, nevertheless, had a quality of remoteness, an almost secret existence.

In that sedate, supremely aristocratic part of London, with its concentration of imposing foreign embassies, Stash had managed to find an exceptionally large house, low and rather wide, painted a pale yellow with gray shutters. It had a distinctly foreign look about it, this house that might have fit easily into many parts of the European countryside. The three sides of Wilton Row surrounded a cobbled space with a pale blue lamppost at its center, where no cars were allowed to park unless they belonged to the other homeowners, all of whom had painted their houses in pastel, altogether un-British colors.

There were bow windows on the ground floor of Stash Valensky's home and the rooms inside had fine proportions. He had filled them with the contents of the Lausanne villa; those rare and valuable French rugs, furniture, paintings and jeweled bibelots which had once made the journey from St. Petersburg to Davos with his parents. It never occurred to Stash to decorate his home in any way but the one he had been used to as a child.

The noise of London was extinguished in Wilton Row, and an air of rustic peace prevailed. At the corner, where Wilton Row joined a tiny alley called Old Barrack Yard, stood a pub, the Grenadier, bravely painted in red and gold, with benches in front, sheltered by a twisted, venerable wisteria vine. A sign announced that only customers who had entered Wilton Row by taxi or on foot were allowed to be served. All in all, there was scarcely a more private dwelling place in all that great, gray city than the Valensky home.

For many years Stash and Daisy spent a large part of Saturday in Kent, where he owned stables in which he kept many of his horses. It was after one of their companionable rides through the country, on a day when Daisy was almost twelve, that father and daughter spied two gypsy caravans. They were parked close to Stash's property and, mistrustfully, he eyed the wagons with their painted canvas tops stretched over hooped ribs. They hadn't been there last week. Stash went over to investigate.

"Daisy," he ordered, "you go back to the stable. I'll just be a minute."

"Oh, Father, you wouldn't deprive me of seeing gypsies?!" she cried in dismay.

"They're just tinkers, Daisy, but I don't want them around my ponies. They can always use an extra horse or two or five."

"Please, Father," she said longingly.

"All right," he sighed, not in the mood for discipline. "Just don't let anyone tell your fortune—I detest that."

The gypsies were friendly, overfriendly, thought Stash, and easy about answering his questions in their accented English.

They would move on if he liked but they were only planning to stay another day or two anyway. Just the time to do a bit of tinkering in the local village.

Not really reassured, but not able to order them off a field he didn't own, Stash turned to leave, but Daisy was no longer at his side. She was on her knees in front of a box crooning a love song and both hands were full of a puppy which looked to Stash like a beanbag. The puppy's bottom and hind legs drooped down from one of Daisy's hands, his head and front legs flopped from the other. In the center of Daisy's palms he rested his bulging belly. The puppy's color was at one and the same time gray, brown and blue, with white paws and white ears. He looked as if he could be any kind of dog at all except some recognizable breed.

Damn and bloody blast, thought Stash, puppies! I should have guessed.

Stash was not a sporting man, not for him the joys of the turf or the pleasures of the hunt, both of which seemed so inferior compared to polo. He hadn't the faintest interest in animals other than horses and he had no knowledge of the part that hunting game on foot plays in the lives of many country people.

"He's a good lurcher," said the gypsy. "And for sale."

Had Stash any knowledge of dogs or the hunt this statement would have caused him to take Daisy by the arm and leave on the instant. No gypsy can sell you a "good" lurcher puppy. It is a definition without meaning since no lurcher can be called "good" until it is old enough to hunt, for that is a lurcher's role in life. It is a poacher's dog, a gypsy's dog, a tramp's dog, silent, swift, deadly. A good lurcher can catch a low-flying seagull in one jump; a good lurcher can support a family in its deadly nightly raids on the countryside, can leap high barbed-wire fences, gallop miles over frozen ground and kill a deer by itself.

"Looks like a mutt to me," said Stash.

"No, a lurcher. Dam's half Irish wolfhound crossed with greyhound, and his dad's a cross of deerhound and greyhound with whippet and sheepdog both in there one generation back. Can't ask finer than that."

"That's just a mongrel."

"No, sir, lurcher. You won't find them in dog shows, but you can't ask for a better dog."

"If he's such a prize, why are you selling him?"

"Got eight in the litter. Can't take them all traveling, now, can we? Still, a bargain for the man who buys him." The gypsy knew that the puppy Daisy was holding with such adoration had one hind leg shorter than the other. Such a lurcher probably couldn't outrun a hare and wouldn't be worth feeding. The gypsy had planned on abandoning him when he moved on, but the puppy's ancestry was exactly as he had reported it and had it not been for that short leg, he wouldn't have sold him for a hundred pounds.

"Come on, Daisy, let's get back."

Daisy didn't have to say anything. The appeal in her eyes was enough to make Stash suspect that he had postponed the dog question too long.

"All right," he said hastily, "I promise I'll get you a dog. Next weekend, Daisy. We'll go visit some good kennels and you can pick any dog you want. That's a mutt, some kind of hound and God knows what else. You don't want him. You want a purebred puppy."

"I want Theseus."

"Theseus?"

"Father, you *know*, the boy who went to fight the minotaur in the labyrinth—we're doing the Greek myths this term with Lady Ellen."

"And *that* is Theseus?"

"I knew the minute I saw him."

"Funny name for a lurcher," said the gypsy.

"Never mind about that," snapped Stash. "How much are you asking for him?"

"Twenty pounds."

"I'll give you five."

"I'll give you the other fifteen. I've got it from my Christmas money, Father." Daisy rushed into the bargaining, shocking both men who had been ready to settle for ten pounds right from the beginning.

And so Theseus the lurcher, for whom Stash eventually had to give twelve pounds, came to live in London, where Daisy now added the duties of feeding him and training him and exercising him to her other activities, managing somehow to get over the first few difficult weeks when Theseus often collapsed on the floor from the weight of his full stomach and wasn't able to get up without assistance. However, with enough minced beef and raw eggs and milk and honey he soon grew stronger and finally came into his lurcher heritage on the day he slipped like a shadow into the big kitchen larder and without a sound which might have betrayed him, snatched clean a platter of stuffed, boneless chicken breasts, leaving a raging cook with suspicions but no proof.

He soon accommodated himself to his shorter rear leg which only showed up in a rolling gait, like that of a hard-drinking man who's had three martinis but is still good for a few more. He slept in a basket next to Daisy's bed, often on his back with all four legs up in the air, and quickly was on the most intimate and friendly terms with Daisy's pony, sniffing Merlin's nose like an ardent lover and curling up at her hooves.

However, he divided the Valensky's servants into two camps: those who wooed and spoiled him, victims of his con-man tactics of wild affection combined with a certain morose look of incredible pathos he knew how to give them that melted their hearts, and those who detested him on the solid grounds that nothing was sacred to Theseus, not their roasts of beef nor their blinis, nor their rashers of bacon, nor their piroshki nor their fondue, and certainly not their mugs of stout.

Stash's Russian servants were now all in their seventies, many of them had died and others retired, but those who remained, those who had left Russia as very young people in 1912, now enjoyed a diet that combined English, Swiss and Russian culinary delights. Age had only improved their hearty appetites.

Theseus seemed to eat his weight every day, and in a short time the floppy puppy became a lean dog, the size of a large, strong greyhound, two and a half feet tall at the shoulder. Short of locking and barring the doors to the kitchen and larder, it was impossible to keep out the crouching, sidling, slinking, all-but-invisible animal who pounced silently, consumed his prey in a gulp, and disappeared before the theft could be discovered. He was merely performing his function in life, but few of them were sympathetic to this inborn criminality, a lawlessness which had been carefully bred into him throughout centuries.

Yet lurchers, for all their stealthy ways, are noble dogs. Many hundreds of years ago the ownership of these rough-coated, mixed-blood greyhounds was confined to princes. They wore collars of gold, they were indispensable at court, where hunting was the principal pastime, and many an antique tapestry is adorned by their royal presence.

Daisy's school, Lady Alden's, was the most fashionable in all of London. It operated on two principles which, extraordinarily enough, turned out well-educated young women. The teachers all were required to come from aristocratic backgrounds; Lady Alden had a decided preference for the daughters of impoverished earls—Lady Janes and Lady Marys abounded. The girls, from six to sixteen, did not need to fill such requirements. All they needed was parental money, preferably on a monarchical scale. That many of the parents were also wellborn was merely a happy coincidence.

During all the nine years that she was a pupil at Lady Alden's, Daisy wore the expensive uniforms bought in different sizes every year at Harrods, but always exactly the same design: navy blue sailor dresses with white collars and piping, covered by pale blue pinafores that buttoned down the back.

She arrived every day before nine o'clock at the entrance to the school's three adjoining buildings on a quiet street not far from Kensington Gardens and the Albert Memorial. After prayers Daisy and all the other students, some hundred girls in all, filed out past Lady Alden, dropping her a curtsy and saying good morning in a voice which had to be clear, audible and well-articulated. Lady Alden, a former beauty, was a firm disciplinarian, and when her attention turned toward any individual girl a heart palpitated instantly. She wielded a formidable ruler which she never hesitated to use on the knuckles of her pupils, and even the titled teachers quailed before her.

When Daisy left for school one fall day, shortly after Theseus had come to live in her room, the cook and the ancient butler carried out a plot to get rid of Theseus. The cook lured the dog to the front door by holding a chicken high in the air. She flung the chicken outside, onto the cobbles, and when Theseus flashed through the open door she closed it behind him and locked it. The two conspirators waited for sounds of the dog's paws on the front door, determined to ignore him until he wandered away. Theseus merely engulfed the chicken, briskly shook his coat of longish hair that was rough to the touch, perked up his white ears, and followed Daisy to Lady Alden's by smell. When she emerged that afternoon she found him there, patiently curled up outside the entrance to the guard box from which Sam, the porter, protected the school and its precious young ladies from contact with the world.

"So that's your dog, Miss," said Sam, who called all the students Miss because he couldn't be bothered to remember the great variety of titles they bore. "Well, he can't stay here every day, if that's what you're thinking. Against the rules. Lady Alden'd have a proper fit if she knew." Theseus, in a delirium of delight, was hurling himself at Daisy, putting his front paws on her shoulders and passionately nuzzling her face, all in proper lurcher silence.

"No, Sam, of course not," said Daisy thoughtfully.

Had a dog ever gone to Lady Alden's school before? No one knew. Such a violation was beyond the realm of imagination, rather like the possibility of the art students having a naked man to pose for them, or for that matter, a naked woman. But go to school Theseus did for three years; smuggled in through a tiny door at the back of the shed that was reserved for the gardener. Tactfully, he slept all day on a bed of cushions Daisy brought, one at a time, from her own room, so totally hidden in one dark corner that he went unnoticed except for the cooperative gardener who loathed Lady Alden as much as he loved dogs and never asked any questions, but made sure he carried his own lunch in a buttoned pocket, having had much experience with lurchers before he came to the City.

Daisy was fifteen. It was April of 1967 and London was at its peak, the center of all that was new and vital. Daisy was equally in love with all the Beatles, Vidal Sassoon, Rudolf Nureyev, Twiggy, Mary Quant, Jean Shrimpton and Harold Pinter. She was not in love with Andy Warhol or Baby Jane Holzer or even Mick Jagger.

Yet in a year in which any shopgirl could choose between dressing like an American Indian in leather and beads and headbands, or like a romantic trollop in *Viva Maria*-inspired lacy, tucked bloomers and frilly blouses, in a year in which the mini-skirt became a micro-skirt and eventually turned into shorts, she was still confined to a navy sailor dress and a pinafore.

"I'd have to wear my school uniform all the time, if it were up to Father and Masha," she exploded to Anabel after lunch in Eaton Square one Saturday, tucking her long slender legs up under her on one of Anabel's gray green couches.

"Hmmm. You don't look so terribly underprivileged to me," Anabel answered, surveying her from top to bottom. Daisy was wearing black velvet knee breeches and a matching jacket trimmed with gold buttons and black braid, over a ruffled blouse of white silk. She had on white ribbed tights and flat black slippers with a rosette on the front. Today she had dressed her incomparable hair in curly bangs and tied it back on each side of her face with bunches of shiny black ribbons. She had darkened her blonde eyebrows a little and wore a hint of mascara, but no other make-up.

From the time Anabel had first seen Daisy, a six-year-old whose mother had just died, a six-year-old who was about to be separated from her twin sister, and who had come to live in a strange country with a father she knew only from fleeting visits, Anabel had been fascinated by the little girl's indomitable sense of what was right. She could scarcely believe that a child was capable of the absolute loyalty that had enabled her to force even Stash, that man of hard metal who, in Anabel's opinion, had never quite gotten the hang of life, to give in to her insistence that she visit her sister every week. She had watched Daisy grow up with intense interest, missing nothing. Often Anabel wondered how Daisy managed to slip, seemingly without too much difficulty, into a life that must have been utterly foreign to her. Anabel was too wise to think that she understood everything about Daisy—she was not a child who confided, who poured out her troubles. She was not a child without secrets. She *must* have paid a price.

Would Daisy, Anabel wondered, burn out this early promise and become just another pretty teenager? Now at fifteen, Daisy had not only retained the purity and fire she had always possessed but approaching adulthood could be clearly read on her face. There, thought Anabel, is a girl who is going to cause all kinds of perfectly wonderful trouble. Even another woman was forced to imagine the pulse of curiosity which must beat in the hearts of the men who saw her ... that full, enigmatic mouth, so ripe with promise and yet so innocent, and those eyes that, no matter how frank they were, contained unfathomable, never to be analyzed depths in their velvety blackness ... and, oh, a body, a faultless body, strong and slim, and lucky child, she came naturally by the romantic and wild look which was the fashion of the day. Yet here Daisy was, suddenly painfully full of the pent-up turmoil and ferocious misery of adolescence, now focused on clothes, which had never meant anything to her before.

Indignantly, Daisy continued, "You just don't know how I had to fight like a mad thing to get Father to let me go shop at Annacat—can you imagine it, Anabel, Father wanted me to go to Harrods' young ladies' department and buy plaid skirts and twin sets. *Twin sets!*"

"That's what English girls are still wearing, some of them anyway," Anabel observed mildly.

"Only in the country, only if they're parsons' daughters, and *then* only with jeans," Daisy said rebelliously. "He doesn't realize I've grown up. I'm not allowed to go out with boys yet, not that I know any! It's just impossible!"

She was at the rebellious age, no doubt about it, Anabel thought. Trouble in sight for Stash with his old-fashioned ideas. At fifty-six he had become as conservative where Daisy was concerned as he was unconventional for himself. Not an uncommon fix for the fathers of beautiful daughters to find themselves in, she ruminated with a touch of inward glee. Why, when she was only a year older than Daisy was now she'd run away and married that awful bore, what's his name. He'd died last year . . . yet if she'd stayed married to him, she'd be the Dowager Marchioness now. At the thought Anabel couldn't help but smile, although she was trying to be as serious as possible since she truly loved the girl and knew how adolescents hate it if they aren't treated with appropriate solemnity. Anabel had arranged their intimate lunch on purpose for just such conversation, because she sensed the essential, the irremediable loneliness of the age Daisy was going through.

Both the girl and the woman were surprised at the sound of the doorbell on the floor below. Anabel expected no visitors until Stash that evening. In a minute Ram entered the drawing room and Daisy rose to her feet in delight. Now that he had his own flat and was working in the City she rarely saw this twenty-two-year-old half-brother.

"What's that God-awful fancy dress you've got on?" he asked. He looked annoyed. He'd dropped by unannounced, hoping to find Anabel alone, so that they could have a chat, and here she was closeted with Daisy. He didn't even notice that Daisy's expectant look of joy, her open smile at the sight of him, a smile that had such completeness to it, faded and shrank with hurt at his careless words.

"You don't know one damn thing about fashion, Ram," Anabel snapped in an irritated voice he'd rarely heard her use. "Daisy looks divine, as any fool would know."

"Only if you say so, Anabel darling," he said absently, ignoring Daisy. "I've got to get home," Daisy said hastily. She couldn't wait to take off the velvet knee breeches and ruffled shirt she'd been so proud of. Now this ravishing pageboy, this festival of a girl felt ashamed of the way she looked. Ram's approval, which she had sought so fruitlessly for the last nine years, meant almost everything to her, no matter how often she told herself that for reasons she couldn't understand he didn't like her and would never like her. He had the power to hurt her as no one else could. Ram, unattainable, detached, withdrawn, undemonstrative Ram, who showed so little emotion on his dark, haughty face, made her helpless with love and passionate with the desire to please.

At Lady Alden's, where Daisy was in her next to last year, she was the acknowledged leader of her class, the champion jacks player of the school, one of the only girls who had never been reduced to tears by the application of Lady Alden's ruler, and the center of a group of special friends who were as physically daring and as horse-mad as she. They formed a potentially revolutionary society within the docile body of the school, which, had Lady Alden known of it, would have caused the dreaded ruler to fly as it had never flown before.

Now Daisy, still smarting with the reception her first venture into grown-up clothes had drawn from Ram, contemplated taking out her feelings with a devilment which would exceed anything in the annals of the school. Her emotions were almost adult but she still only knew childish ways to relieve them.

Even her best friends were aghast at her proposition.

"A gymkhana! Daisy, you're bonkers. You know as well as I do a proper gymkhana's got to be a field day, with horsemanship, exhibitions and all sorts of pageantry. Lady A would never hear of it."

"Lady A doesn't own Belgrave Square."

"Oh, Daisy! Oh, how perfectly awful! Oh—could we really do it?"

"Why not? If you're all with me, that is. It's merely a question of organization."

The Metropolitan Police were never able to explain the Great Belgrave Square Gymkhana to their superiors. How were they to know of the cunning resources of two dozen fiery young equestrians, who stole into that august park in the early morning hours and set up jumps and flags and brilliantly colored pennants and all matter of gates and fences? By the light of dawn in their beige breeches and polished boots and stocks and tweed jackets, looking like all the other proper young ladies who ride in London, these she-devils quietly collected their horses from various stables all over Mayfair and assembled at the entrance to that beautifully groomed square of turf and trees onto which face the embassies of Portugal, Mexico, Turkey, Norway, Germany, Austria and, appropriately enough, the Royal College of Veterinary Surgeons and the Imperial Defense College.

One of the fearless number lived on the Square and had a key to the high iron entrance, and before the police had collected their wits not only had the Gymkhana started, but the entrances to all the main streets which led to the Square—Upper Belgrave Street, Belgrave Place, Wilton Terrace, Wilton Crescent and Grosvenor Crescent—were blocked with cars, abandoned by their passengers who had flocked out to see what was going on. And what were a handful of policemen to do with a horde of whooping, hurrahing wild teenagers, veterans of dozens of horse shows, as tough as cavalry and twice as tenacious, all mounted on swift horses, galloping madly about in the vernal sunshine as if a troop of Amazons had suddenly materialized from another time in history? Led by Daisy, her bright braids flying behind her, they jumped fence after fence in a bacchanalian circle, holding their pennants high in the air and brandishing them at the London sky with no lack of pageantry. Yet there was discipline in their ranks and Daisy's whistle could make them all slow to a canter or form into a double line at a trot. The police could no more have arrested them than if they'd been a Guards' Regiment, coming to Troop the Colors. Nor could they be caught. The Gymkhana ended only when the sound of police sirens started to get close to Belgrave Square. At that moment, Daisy raised her arm and shouted —and all her inspired band scattered, jumping their horses over the railings and fleeing into the friendly, cheering carnival crowds who had surrounded the square.

It was perfectly true, as Daisy had said, that Lady Alden didn't own Belgrave Square. The Earl of Grosvenor did, just as he owned almost every square inch of Mayfair and Belgravia. The Grosvenor family is the wealthiest private landlord in England, with these three hundred acres in the heart of London representing only one of their holdings all over the world. The Earl of Grosvenor most certainly owned Wilton Row . . . Stash only leased his house from the Grosvenor Trust.

In the offices of the trustees of the Grosvenor Trust there was little amusement concerning Daisy's Gymkhana. The gardeners of Belgrave Square had reported that the turf was damaged to the tune of hundreds of pounds. However, that wasn't their chief objection . . . it was the principle of the thing. A typical sign on a typical park in Grosvenor territory reads like the one which adorns the entrance to Wilton Crescent's semi-oval green space. Some of the injuctions written thereon forbid any game involving noise, prohibit any children under the age of nine who are unaccompanied by adults and outlaw all dogs. Although tricycles and scooters may be used by accompanied children, they must be ridden only on the paths, no flower beds may be trodden upon or dug, and, in particular, organized groups of children cannot be admitted to the park at all.

The tradition of these sedate and quiet parks had been violated—shaken to its depths—by Daisy, who had been recognized and identified by one of the Grosvenor traffic wardens who had helplessly observed the Great Gymkhana. She was, he reported in an outraged voice, a young lady who owned ... a lurcher! That news alone was enough to cause a hush and raise the eyebrows of the trustees, landowners all and therefore victims, down to their last remembered ancestor, of poachers and their dogs. A lurcher indeed! Just what kind of young lady could possibly own a lurcher?

It was not, as one of the trustees soon explained to Stash, that they wished to punish his daughter, but if she was capable of such insurrection, what might she do next? Stash thought about his lease, which had only three years to run before it would revert to the Grosvenor estate, and agreed with the trustee that certainly he would have to do something serious about the discipline of his daughter. In addition, Stash was genuinely shocked at Daisy's behavior. It was more daring than anything he remembered ever having done himself, at her age, even making allowances for the fact that she was a female.

After the trustee had left, with a check for the damages and Stash's assurances that the matter of Daisy would be attended to, he sat alone for a long time, thinking about his foolhardy daughter. How was she to grow up properly with, as adult examples, only himself and Anabel? Neither of them was immoral, it was true, but they were certainly amoral, both of them heedless of the laws of ordinary society. Eton had turned Ram into a sober, unemotional, hard-working young man, but Lady Alden's had missed having a salutory taming effect on Daisy. What would happen to Daisy when she no longer lived under his roof? This matter of the Gymkhana went far beyond an irresponsible childish prank, Stash thought, feeling every one of his fifty-six years. He blamed himself. There was no doubt in his mind that he had spoiled Daisy. But what to do about the future? He would not always be there to get her out of trouble.

During the rest of April and May Stash considered the problem of Daisy as he attended to his affairs. Eventually, he sent for his solicitor and made certain thoughtful changes in his will, and then forgot about the matter, satisfied that he had acted prudently. A great deal of his fortune was now invested in Rolls-Royce and Stash watched with deep interest as the company attempted to break into the American-dominated manufacturing of airplane engines. In 1963 his faith in Rolls had been bolstered as their Spey turbofan engine was being widely bought and now in 1967 they were going after a contract with Lockheed to produce the engine for its TriStar Airbus, the RB. 211. His investments had always been made on an emotional basis rather than on that of cold financial judgment, and Stash poured even more capital into the company he loved.

However, the training of his stable of polo ponies occupied most of Stash's time. He flew less and less now, having lost the need for the release from fury he had found in the air after Francesca had left him, fourteen years ago. All that seemed very far away and unimportant. Still he kept his jet license current and occasionally he flew aerobatic exhibitions in the many air shows which were so popular all over the country, returning for a few nostalgic hours to the cockpit of a lovingly preserved relic of a Spitfire or a Hurricane, with their Rolls-Royce Merlin engines, still as trustworthy as ever.

On a fine Sunday in May, there was no fault in the engine of the Spitfire he was flying at the Essex Air Show. The undercarriage of the twenty-seven-year-old plane stuck and the landing gear could not be released. Stash headed for the woods beyond the runway, hoping that the trees might cushion the crash. Many a fighter pilot had crash-landed in these planes and lived to tell the tale. He did not.

10

In the weeks right after Stash's death, Anabel, who grieved for Stash in her own way as she had never grieved for anyone before, Anabel, who had a premonition that Stash would be the last man in her life, pulled what was left of the family together.

She insisted that Daisy and Ram spend the summer at the house near Honfleur that Stash had bought for her seven years before. Seeing Ram so unlike himself, functioning without his usual effectiveness, she persuaded him to take a leave of absence from his job in the City for all of June, July and August. However, with her great virtue of good sense, Anabel realized that three mourning people should never be alone together and she arranged for a constant stream of houseguests to come and stay in the large house; friends from both her London life and her French summer world, people who would distract and beguile the sad household.

Daisy, Anabel realized, was feeling the loss much more than Ram. It was she who was absolutely orphaned now —even Masha had died two years ago. When Daisy went to visit Dani for comfort, her twin, with uncanny intuition, seemed to smell her grief even though Daisy smiled as she hugged and petted her. Dani became so upset that she was reduced to silent tears. "Day, no *do*," she said, drawing away, and finally Daisy sent her running gladly back through the gardens to her own friends.

Ram was *the* Prince Valensky at last. Not only had he inherited the London house and its valuable antique contents, with the exception of the Fabergé animals which had been left to Anabel, along with a certain amount of

Rolls-Royce stock, but he had inherited all the polo ponies and the stables in Trouville and Kent and one half of Stash's fortune, both in Rolls-Royce stock and all that remained of the Swiss gold. Stash had left Daisy the other half of his fortune, all of it invested in Rolls stock. Several weeks after the Belgrave Square Gymkhana had convinced him that Daisy shouldn't be in charge of her affairs until she turned thirty, he had made Ram, that dependable, clever boy, co-trustee of her inheritance, along with the Bank of England.

Ram was rich and he was in charge. Yet he had a nagging sense of incompletion, as if his father, in dying so suddenly, had remained intact, as if Stash were still *the* Prince Valensky. There was a sense of unfinished business about the whole thing—something not done, something not finished, something not *won*.

That summer, at Anabel's house, *La Marée*, there were never fewer than eight people at any meal, and often more than a dozen. Anabel's invitations were eagerly accepted by everyone she knew. As she had grown older—she was now almost forty-eight—she collected around herself an atmosphere more filled with intimacy than ever before, as more and more people found her the perfect confidante. She wore their secrets like priceless pearls tucked inside the neckline of a thin dress so that only a faint glimmer of them showed that they were there, but they added constant new depth to her ageless charm and the comfort of her presence. One of her friends, a recently lapsed Catholic, had told her that he felt as cleansed of sin after he'd talked to her as if he'd been to confession, only—and this was the best of all—he had not had to promise never to sin again.

La Marée was a house which could be described by no other word in the language except *enchanted*. There must be in the world many great houses on the top of thickly wooded hills overlooking the sea, but no one who had ever spent any time at *La Marée* had failed to be marked for life by its strange, poetic, nostalgic, tenderly mysterious atmosphere.

It stood behind high walls and acres of overgrown gardens, on the Côte de Grace, the thickly shaded, narrow road that mounts up steeply from Honfleur in the direction of Deauville. From the windows of the house, on all but the front façade, there was a high view over the entire estuary of the Seine, with Le Havre clearly visible in the opalescent distance. Behind the house was a wide gravel terrace from which tangled, fragrant woods led steeply down to the boundaries of two small farms. These woods were crisscrossed by a maze of hidden paths. Beyond the farms was the sea and on the sea was a constantly changing, gay armada of fishing and pleasure boats going in and out of the port of Honfleur. Farther out, great ocean liners and cargo ships passed back and forth. The terrace faced due west, and in the evening, when the sun was finally eaten by the horizon and the lights of Le Havre became visible, there was an almost unbearable poignancy about the moment which caused people to speak in lowered voices, or not at all.

La Marée itself proved that magic still existed. It had grown out of an ancient farmhouse, little by little over the centuries, and by the time Anabel became its owner it possessed thirteen different levels of roof, each covered with thatch, from which, in the spring, seeds left in the straw would sprout and send up wild flowers. Some parts of the house were three stories high; the kitchen wing, which was the oldest part of the house, was a single story; but all the various parts of the structure were unified by being built from exposed wooden beams and plaster, most of which wore a rippling mantle of the big-leaved ivy called *la vigne vierge,* which turned bright red in the autumn. The enormous house looked more like a growing thing than a building, and the feeling inside of it was that of being part of a living, breathing space which belonged as much to the outdoors as the indoors. All day long the tall windows were thrown open to the sun and Anabel went out early to gather the basketsfull of columbine, coreopsis, roses, asters, lupines, delphinium, dahlias, heather, baby's breath and the *pied d'alouettes,* an old-fashioned flower that appeared in Breugel's paintings, from which she filled vases even more imaginatively and abundantly than she did in London where she was dependent on her florist's stock to choose her blossoms.

Although Anabel expected her guests to live at *La Marée* in an informal, holiday way, the house itself was well-staffed and decorated with a certain formality. Each bedroom had walls of finely pleated damask, color on color, woven in flower motifs and hanging from floor to ceiling. The same fabric that covered the walls was draped on the four-poster beds and at the tall windows. Daisy's room was all sea-green, Anabel's rose and cream and Ram had the blue bedroom. The main salon of the house was enormously high and, in one corner, a circular staircase led up fourteen feet to the balcony that surrounded the room on three sides. The back of the balcony was lined with bookshelves and there were many recesses, invisible from below, in which one could spend all day on comfortable loveseats, reading from the slightly musty volumes which had been there when Stash acquired the house as a surprise for Anabel. It had suited him well because of its nearness to Trouville, where he had still owned the stables to which he had once taken Francesca. He had also been attracted by the legend of the house in which, as everyone in Honfleur knew, its former owner, Madame Colette de Joinville, had hidden eleven British soldiers after Dunkirk. Unable to reach the evacuation beach, they had been guided to her by the Resistance, of which she was a member. At great personal risk, she kept them safe in her attic for nine months until they were all able, one by one, to make their way to Spain, through the Underground, and return to England to fight again.

Soon the routine life of *La Marée* established itself: late breakfast at the long wooden table in the big kitchen, to which they all drifted when they pleased, dressed in bathrobes or peignoirs, after which, Daisy and Anabel, with sturdy market baskets on their arms, went shopping for fresh produce in the port of Honfleur. Lunch was preceded by sherry on the terrace, lasted for two hours and was followed by coffee, again on the terrace. After coffee each followed his own pursuit: antique hunting, sightseeing, napping or rambling in the countryside. Finally cocktails, dinner, a few games of poker or liar's dice, and an early bedtime ended the lazy day.

Daisy found that she was least unhappy when she was alone with her sketch pad, drawing the unforgivably picturesque houses of Le Vieux Bassin in Honfleur, a favorite painter's subject for the last hundred and fifty years, or in trying to capture on paper the three umbrella pines that guarded the ocean side of *La Marée*.

When Daisy took her bath she saw that day after day in the open air had tanned her to the color of a freshly baked croissant. She was not used to looking at herself naked she realized, as she studied with fascination the interesting contrast between her white breasts and her tan shoulders, marked with white only where the straps of her jerseys covered them. Then she was white again right down to the place where her tennis shorts ended and from then on, her legs were even tanner than the rest of her. She turned around and around in front of the mirror, half amused by the comic effect of being colored like a piebald horse, and half admiring the new high fullness of her well-separated breasts and the sleek, long curve of her flanks. Daisy was sexually backward for her age of fifteen and a few months. She had led a severely protected life dominated by a father who had not allowed her contact with boys of her own age. Her friends at school had been those whose sexuality was still invested in horses and dogs. She had often been restlessly aware of physical desires but they had been either suppressed or released in sports. She rubbed her hand questioningly over her white-blonde pubic hair and hastily removed it when she saw what she was doing in the mirror. It was softer than the hair on her head, Daisy thought, oddly embarrassed, and she quickly dressed herself in her summer uniform: worn, tight tennis shorts from the year before that she hadn't bothered to replace and one of the sleeveless striped fishermen's jerseys she had bought in Honfleur. She wore her hair loose, and often, after one of her rambles in the woods, a twig or a bud would be caught in the tangled excess of her curls.

Ram was violently critical of the way she looked. "Christ, Anabel, can't you speak to her about the way she goes about? She's like some sort of savage. It's not only disgraceful, it's damned near indecent. I can't stand to look at her! You're not doing the job you should be with that girl—I'm surprised at you letting her get away with being such a pig!"

"Ram, come on, relax. Honfleur's a resort—everyone dresses like Daisy," Anabel chided him gently. "You're the one who should let down a bit and get into the spirit of things—do I see the playing fields of Eton around your neck, my dear?" Ram refused to even smile but stalked off, stiff with outrage. Hurt, Anabel shook her head sadly as he disappeared. Every time Daisy tried to talk to him, she thought, Ram found something about her to comment on in an unpleasant way, until the girl had almost stopped trying to include him in her conversations. Still, there was nothing Anabel could do except try to reach Ram through gentleness . . . she thought that this was probably his own strange way of reacting to Stash's death, this anger, this . . . almost . . . cruelty.

A few days later, at breakfast, as Ram unwisely tried to

take a glance at the newspaper before he'd started his bacon and eggs, Theseus gobbled down everything on his plate. Ram lashed out at the dog with his fist but Theseus was long gone. "Damn it to hell, Daisy, that goddamned verminous mongrel of yours has got to go!" Ram's face was knit in thundering fury. "I'll kill that creature when I catch him!"

"If you touch him, I'll kill you!" Daisy shouted.

"Children, children," Anabel murmured ineffectively.

"I'm warning you, Daisy—I won't stand for that filthy animal," Ram continued. "He's not a joke anymore."

Daisy held out her own plate at him. "Look, take my breakfast, it's just the same as the one Theseus had—Ram, you put temptation in his way—you ought to know him by now. And he's *not* dirty! Here. Don't be mad."

Ram thrust away the proffered plate. "I'm not hungry anymore. And I'm sick of your excuses for that filthy beast. Just keep him away from me." Abruptly he got up from the table and went to his room.

"Oh, dear, oh, dear," sighed Anabel. If only people would be kinder to each other. Of all human sins, the only one Anabel really found unforgivable was unkindness.

Toward the end of the first week in July, Anabel awaited with particular anticipation the arrival of her friends Guy and Isabelle de Luciny, who were bringing their children; Valerie, who was a little over a year younger than Daisy, and Jean-Marc, who was almost eighteen. She hoped that their company might entice Daisy away from her solitary expeditions. She remembered Jean-Marc as a sturdy lad of fifteen, rather short and plump, but pleasant and well-spoken.

She scarcely recognized the tall, attractive Frenchman with fine brown eyes who got out of the car and came toward her as she stood, welcomingly, in the circular entrance hall of the house. His manners were as polished and suave as only those of an almost adult, well-bred French youth can be, and it amused Anabel wickedly to see this self-possessed and rather lordly young sprig fall for Daisy as acrobatically, as dramatically as if he'd been hit over the head in a silent movie. He followed her around more closely than Theseus; he literally couldn't move his eyes away from her, which made him difficult at meals since he ate without looking at his food and he never heard a word anyone else said, not even a request to pass the salt. At first Daisy seemed more interested in his sister Valerie than in Jean-Marc, who insisted on accompanying them into Honfleur each morning for their shopping, carrying Daisy's basket, but eventually she began to respond to the smitten youth, with a kind of mischievous pleasure, the first she'd shown in many weeks.

"Honestly, Jean-Marc, I think I'm going to have to take legal measures. There's something curiously adoptable about you," she told him after lunch one day as the whole houseful of guests lay lazily on the terrace, except for the young man who was busily dragging his striped canvas deck chair closer to Daisy's. Her clear voice was heard by all the others, and Isabelle de Luciny and Anabel exchanged hopeful glances.

Under the influence of Jean-Marc's admiration, a new Daisy appeared at dinner, a Daisy who had taken the time to change into a mini-skirt and a thin summer sweater and offered to pour the coffee after dinner, a grown-up duty which she had occasionally attempted with a lack of interest, but which she now accomplished with finished grace. When this new Daisy was complimented by Guy de Luciny she received his words with the poise of a much older woman, sliding her black eyes toward Jean-Marc with a look that seemed both insolent and alluring, as if to ask why he had left it to his father to say the things he was thinking.

Now Daisy permitted Jean-Marc to go with her on her trips into Honfleur to sketch, and several times the two of them were late for lunch, returning flushed with the sun and still trembling with laughter over jokes they assured the others they wouldn't understand.

On the night of Bastille Day, the *Quatorze Juillet*, there is dancing in the streets in every city in France. In Honfleur the square in front of the town hall is turned into an outdoor ballroom and everyone, townspeople, tourists and the owners of the houses in the surrounding countryside, all come and dance with anyone who asks them, stranger or not. Daisy wore her best dress, from a London boutique called Mexicana, a long, demure, fragile white dress. The closely fitted bodice and full milkmaid sleeves were both made of bands of lace alternating with bands of finely tucked cotton. The lace and cotton formed a high, frilled collar. A hot pink satin sash with a big bow at the side was tightly clasped about her waist and below it fell a tucked cotton skirt with a wide lace hem which swept the floor. She had taken just the top layer of her hair, divided it into six sections and braided each section with white silk ribbons which ended in bows at the end of each braid.

The innocence of the covered-up white dress and the beribboned braids contrasted strongly with Daisy's straight, thick brows and excited pansy-centered eyes. Her full mouth was endowed with a new maturity as she felt for the first time in her life the intoxicating bone-deep assurance that tonight she was the unquestioned center of the group, the key to the romance of the evening. She had become an enchantress; in one stroke, she had absorbed and embodied the spirit of *La Marée*. None of the guests could stop looking at her. It was, thought Anabel gleefully, as if they had all turned into a band of besotted Jean-Marcs—all but Ram, whose disapproval of his half-sister seemed to have been accentuated by her success. He stood aside, an unpleasant expression crossing his aquiline features, his gray eyes colder than those of his father had ever been.

Anabel was glad that Daisy had always had courage. It takes courage to be a beautiful woman, she thought. Beauty, in Anabel's estimation, is the female equivalent of going to war, bound, as beauty is, to put a woman in hundreds of unwanted situations that otherwise she could have avoided. And Daisy was almost a beautiful woman —she had only a year or two of girlhood left, Anabel thought, with pity . . . and a little envy.

The entire house party, some fourteen people, drove down to town to dance and watch the fireworks. Daisy, as conspicuous as a bride, and as lively as the traditional *guinguette* music which demands no other knowledge of dancing than whirling, passed rapidly from the arms of a fisherman to a local painter to the Mayor of Honfleur to Jean-Marc; from the arms of the butcher to the arms of the sailors from the French Navy vessels moored in the port and then back to Jean-Marc again. She held herself as proudly as a young tree in its first season of spring bloom, her silvery hair flew and flew and even the braids couldn't prevent it from getting tangled as she danced. Her lips were parted in a smile of pure, unthinking, undirected pleasure. Her cheeks were flushed a deeper pink and the punctuation of her black eyes made the vivid, flying figure in its white dress elementally alluring. As the music went on and on far into the night, Daisy danced with every man in Honfleur except Ram, who had danced not at all, preferring to stand aloof on the edge of the crowded circle of jostling figures, arms crossed, eyes baleful, watching the merrymaking with an oddly malevolent expression on his face. Finally, Anabel and Isabelle de Luciny persuaded everyone that it was time to drive home, if only out of pity for the band, which was starting to look as if they would be glad to stumble back straight into the Bastille if only they didn't have to play another tune.

The next morning everyone was late for breakfast. Jean-Marc missed the meal completely. It wasn't until after he'd also been absent for lunch that his mother finally went to his room to wake him. She found his bed empty and a note addressed to her on the pillow.

Dear Maman,
   I had a discussion with Ram last night which makes it impossible for me to remain here one minute more. I'll be back in Paris by this afternoon. I have a key to the apartment so don't worry. Please make my apologies to Anabel and thank her for the time I've spent here. I'd rather not explain any further, but I couldn't stay. Don't be upset.

                                                                Love,
                                                                Jean-Marc

Astonished, Isabelle took the note to Anabel.
"*Ma chérie,* does this make the slightest bit of sense to you?"
"Ram? I don't understand it at all. What on earth could Ram have had to do with it? If he'd had a fight with Daisy I wouldn't be a bit surprised if poor Jean-Marc disappeared—but Ram?"
"I'm going to ask him," said Isabelle, with serious maternal irritation. She and Anabel began to search the house.

Before lunch that day, Daisy had taken her sketch pad and gone to one of her favorite, secret places in the woods, a sweet-smelling eucalyptus grove thickly carpeted with aromatic leaves, from which there was a clear view of a small farmhouse. She often spent long hours drawing there, listening to the faint sounds of the barnyard far below, completely hidden from the world. Her triumph of the night before had left her languid, too lazy to get down to work, and she had stretched out on the leaves and slept for hours. She woke to hear footsteps crashing through the wooded trails. Curious, she peered out from her hiding place and saw Ram walking at a fast pace.

"Ram, I'm here," she called, sleepily.

Ram entered the grove and stood directly in front of her, without a greeting. Daisy looked up at him and laughed. "If you've come to see my view, you happen to be blocking it."

He threw himself down at her side, on the leaves, and roughly, silently, knocked the sketch book out of her hands. Then he took all her precious pencils and broke them in two and threw the pieces away furiously. Daisy watched him, speechless, incredulous.

"I've gotten rid of Jean-Marc so you needn't bother to go dangling yourself in front of him like a slut anymore!" he burst out in a strangled voice. "That exhibition last night was the last straw—I've never seen anything so disgusting, so degrading in my life—the way you slobbered over every sailor, every fisherman, every damned farmer —they must be calling you the cock tease of Honfleur!"

"What?" Daisy didn't know what he was talking about.

"Don't pretend that you don't understand exactly what I mean—all dressed up, pressing yourself against the local idiots—everything for everybody! And as for your love, your precious Jean-Marc, I told him that maybe it's done in France to come to visit and seduce the daughter of the house, but only a filthy, rotten swine would be such a shit."

"Seduce? But you're insane. Oh, Ram, I only let him kiss me on the cheek—he's fun, that's all, I swear it. How could he be my love? You've got it all wrong," Daisy said, gazing indignantly at Ram, her voice ringing with truth and surprise. He kept his eyes fixed on the ground, stubbornly holding on to his jealous anger, his face set in disbelief. "Ram, look at me," Daisy commanded. "Do I look as if I'm lying to you?" She put out her hand and tried to turn his head toward her, but, at her touch, he flinched away, making an animal sound of protest. "No, no, Ram, that's just not fair!" Daisy cried out. And innocently, out of her lack of sophistication, moved by an impulse to heal the hurt she saw on his beloved, sullen face, with fatal simplicity, she kissed him full on his stern mouth.

The gesture obliterated sanity for Ram. Groaning, he

took her into his arms and buried his face in her hair. He kissed her hair over and over again, shaking in every limb with repressed emotion, half-rage, half-desire. He tried, for one brief moment, not to kiss her lips but a red wind of passion drew him to them.

He gave up the struggle and devoured her lips with his own, kissing her as if he were dying of thirst and her mouth were a moist fruit. Daisy, amazed, innocently and awkwardly returned his kisses giving herself up to the joy of realizing that Ram, whom she had never stopped loving since she first saw him, Ram who had always been the secret hero of her dreams, Ram from whom she had hopelessly begged a smile or even a mere word, was holding her tight, being kind to her, good to her, kissing her.

She abandoned herself to the comfort of this fulfillment of years of yearning, all thoughts blotted out. Daisy, who had never been kissed on the lips before, made the discovery of the mouth of another, of the roughness of his shaven cheeks, of the hardness of teeth, the wetness of his tongue. She kissed him back as if each kiss could bring back the life she had carelessly romped and reveled in, bring back happiness, kiss it into returning.

Daisy gave herself so completely to the happiness of being—after so many years—held and kissed by Ram, that she didn't realize that he had opened the buttons of her thin shirt until she felt his mouth move down to the nipples of her breasts. The feeling was the most exquisite she'd ever known—his beloved mouth tugging on the tender, sensitive buds—a feeling too new, so rapturously new and good that tears stung her eyes. In a flash Daisy felt all the intimations of physical passion she had never localized before, this girl to whom a gallop on a bright morning had been the height of pleasure of the body. Her pale, pale pink nipples grew firm and pinker as he kissed them, holding her breasts in each of his hands, and her head fell back on her willing neck as she surrendered to his lips and his fingers, feeling his hair against her shoulder, unhearing, unthinking, a creature of feeling only. She was dazed, almost paralyzed by the electric flashes of desire which were whipping through her body, when suddenly she returned to reality. Ram was fumbling at the waistband of her shorts, trying to take them off. She pushed him away as hard as she could, but he used all his strength against her sudden panic, her belated realization.

She struggled with him, her mind a jungle of confusion. What had happened? How had it happened? What was going to happen? Soon, in spite of all her efforts, she was naked, her brown and white body revealed in all its terrified beauty.

"No! No!" she panted, "please, no!" But Ram was deaf to her pleas, deaf to her sobs. His face was as inhuman as a spear as he bent over her body. Nothing, no one could stop him now. In an ecstasy of lust he pried open her thighs and quickly, pouncing, found the opening he had to find, and drove himself into her, pounding brutally through the tender flesh because she was a virgin and he had to have her or die of anger and need.

Daisy's mind stopped working. Spangles of red and white and black exploded in her brain like the fireworks of the night before. Even as she groaned, even as she grunted in violent protest, she clung to his plunging body because, more than anything, she was desperate for reassurance that this cruel stranger was Ram, her Ram—only that knowledge would prevent her from being annihilated.

Afterward it was the man who sobbed and the girl who held and comforted him, kissing his dark hair and whispering, "It's all right, it's all right," clinging to him like the survivor of a vast tempest, eucalyptus leaves sticking to her back, the mingled smell of sweat and sperm rising to her nostrils for the first time in her life, her thighs stained with blood which she blotted away with pages of the broken sketch pad. When Daisy looked at Ram, his head hidden in her arms, prodigal flares of dark light came from her eyes. Although, instinctively, she tried to reassure him, she was herself drowning in a murky pool of feelings, totally foreign in a life in which she had always seen her way clearly and cleanly. Daisy was filled with her awakened knowledge of physical desire but it was mixed with a kind of shame she had never known before. Her whole mind and body ached with acute conflict and resentment. She wanted to bite, to kick, to shriek to high heaven, to faint, to run away. She wanted to go back to where she had been only an hour ago, but she knew already that there was no return. Deep within her something sounded, as if the string of a great cello had been plucked, a note of remote, mysterious but unmistakable warning.

When they finally returned to the house, the sunset was so brilliant that it partially blinded the eyes of anyone looking toward the woods which lay between the house and the horizon. The rest of the de Luciny family, having been unable to find Ram or come to any satisfactory explanation of the mystery of Jean-Marc's departure, had hastily packed and left for Paris. Anabel was in the salon, as Ram and Daisy materialized out of the woods, several feet separating them from each other. Daisy turned quickly and disappeared, entering the house, almost running, but Anabel was able to collar Ram before he started up the stairs.

"Ram! We've been looking everywhere for you. For God's sake, what happened with Jean-Marc?" she demanded.

"It's not something I want to talk about."

"What nerve—you drove him away somehow—you'd better have a good reason."

"Anabel, I'm telling you that it's best left alone."

She stood up, moved to unusual anger. "Now, just what the hell happened?"

"Since you insist—Jean-Marc made some disgustingly improper remarks about Daisy and I told him he wasn't a gentleman."

"Oh, for heaven's sake, Ram, you sound like something out of the eighteenth century. Improper remarks? What on earth are you talking about? Just what did he say?"

"Look, I refuse to have Daisy insulted, that's all. Jean-Marc apparently thinks English girls are pretty hot stuff, Daisy in particular."

"He never said that!" Anabel cried.

"You weren't there. You would have been as revolted with him as I was," Ram insisted coldly.

"Oh, what a total mess! He probably didn't mean what you thought at all. And since when have you been Daisy's champion? And now they've all gone off three days before they were supposed to leave and there's been *such* an unnecessary scene. I do wish, Ram, that you'd try to develop a sense of humor," Anabel said with unaccustomed asperity.

"The fact that he ran off with his tail between his legs speaks for itself," Ram answered, obdurate.

Anabel looked at her watch and was startled. "Ram, don't you realize that we still have a houseful of guests and that it's time for drinks? At least make yourself useful and run down into town for me and get some ice—the fridge is acting up, as if we hadn't had enough confusion today...

quite seriously, Ram, I'm fed up!" As he left on his errand, Anabel thought that difficult as he had been since she'd known him, she had never been quite as angry at Ram as she was now. Nor had he ever seemed more indifferent to how she felt, now that she thought about it.

Nevertheless, as she surveyed her dinner table an hour and a half later, Anabel had to admit to herself that whatever it was that had been changed in the atmosphere of *La Marée* by the departure of Jean-Marc and his family, only good had come of it, unpleasant as the preceding day had been. It was the most agreeable evening she could remember of the entire summer. Everyone seemed touched with kindness and good will and jovial spirits and they were not caused just by the four bottles of champagne Ram had brought back from his errand to buy ice. Perhaps, she mused, it was because Ram himself had finally relaxed and lost that cruel, unforgiving look she was so sadly accustomed to seeing on his face. He played the host with charm and a grace which Anabel, herself the consummate hostess, could thoroughly appreciate. Although only his gray eyes physically reminded her of Stash, there was something of Stash in the way he dominated the table, yet refrained from taking over, allowing each guest to shine. He had a special air of being at home that Stash had always adopted unthinkingly wherever he went; he was gracious and gallant to all the ladies and with the men he seemed more mature than his twenty-two years, almost their equal, yet he retained a flashing, youthful gaiety that she was touched to see in him, in spite of her fading anger. It was so unlike Ram to express easy happiness that she couldn't begrudge it. As for Daisy, although her cheeks were red and her eyes almost feverish, she was subdued. Anabel made a mental note to have a serious talk with the child about getting too much sun: did she want that skin of hers to be tanned like a piece of leather by the time she was thirty? Tonight Daisy didn't offer to pour the coffee but gladly left it to Anabel, and the capriciousness which she'd been practicing on poor Jean-Marc was absent. She seemed disoriented and far-away, as if she had been sapped of her usual energy, and no wonder, Anabel decided. That riotous, nonstop night of dancing yesterday would be bound to cause a reaction in such a young girl. She wasn't surprised when Daisy decided to go to bed almost as soon as the late dinner was over.

Once she had shut herself into her sea-green refuge, Daisy collapsed on her bed. She was in such confusion of mind and body and spirit that it had taken all her resources to get through dinner. Too much had happened for her to think about it coherently. In her mind she was still lying in that eucalyptus grove, still hearing Ram's voice saying her name. Uncontrollable vibrations swept over her newly awakened body. She quivered from her toes to her scalp. She unbraided her hair and brushed it hard, she took off her dress and flung open the windows, hoping that the sight of Le Havre gleaming in the far distance might calm her, but the slightly misty air was too soft and the stars over the sea hung too low and the crickets were chirping in a way which she had never noticed before, a way that she could barely endure. She had never understood why adults asked each other how they had slept. That night Daisy was initiated into the great company of those who have passed sleepless nights. "White nights" the French call them, a night filled with thoughts she couldn't escape. The thing that had happened —Ram hadn't *meant* to do it! He was sorry—had he not wept, had he not said he was sorry, over and over? Of course it would never happen again. Of course they must never let anyone know. These tormented thoughts mixed and whirled with thoughts of Ram's lips, Ram's words of love, above all his words of love. He had told her he loved her. *He had said he had always loved her.* First one thought attacked her, then another, then they twined painfully round and round in her brain until, blessedly, at last the sun rose and touched the tops of the umbrella pines in front of her window, and she knew she could get up and find Theseus, who now slept outside, and take him for a good long run before breakfast.

Ram had never been so happy in his life. He felt as if only today had he become himself. He had come into his full heritage. He finally was *the* Prince Valensky with all the prerogatives that title implied. Of course, Daisy was *meant* to belong to him, just as everything his father had had was meant to belong to him. He looked back at the past weeks and realized what a fool he'd been, how he'd been angry and cold and unkind to her when it was only the simple injustice of not possessing Daisy that was the cause of his feelings of incompleteness, of unsecured happiness.

As for Daisy being his half-sister, it simply didn't matter. There could be no barrier, when two people are not brought up together, Ram told himself. Why, he hadn't even given a thought to Daisy's existence until he was fourteen. Not for them the shared family warmth, the well-worn jokes, the cloying familiarity of ordinary people. They had seen each other only on scattered holidays, almost totally separated by age and interests. In fact, he smiled to himself, they had been the closest thing to born enemies that two children of the same father could be. No. Ordinary rules for ordinary people did not apply to him and he most certainly wasn't going to concern himself with them, just as his father never had. Of course, he would make sure that other people—particularly Anabel who was basically conventional, in his opinion, in spite of the fact that she'd been his father's mistress—didn't meddle in business that didn't concern them—his business. He was so grandly happy, so sublimely conscious of everything he was and would become, of everything that, at last, he owned, that he, too, spent a sleepless night.

"Let's go to the stables and decide what to do about the polo ponies," Ram said to Daisy the next morning. They were the only ones in the kitchen. Even the cook was still asleep and they had made breakfast for themselves, each unexpectedly shy and glad of the business of frying eggs and looking for the wild strawberry jam the cook always hid.

"I thought you didn't want to make any decisions about them— That's what you said to Anabel."

"That was the other day—but I can't have that whole lot, not just the horses but the men, too, eating their heads off in Trouville and not do something about it. Either I'll keep them or I'll sell them—but first we'll go take a look."

"I'll be ready in fifteen minutes. Will you leave a note for Anabel?" Daisy ran upstairs to get into her riding clothes, her heart beating lawlessly.

They were gone all day, like truants, riding for hours in the green fields, changing from one pony to another, and finally, worn out, they flung themselves under a tree to eat a picnic lunch of long, mild, buttered radishes and a crusty loaf filled with ham and cheese that had been provided by the wife of the stable manager.

Eventually Ram decided that since he didn't play polo

he'd put all the ponies up for auction at the first opportunity. There was no point in keeping even the best of them for ordinary riding; they were too finely bred, too nervous for his taste; he liked a larger horse, a good jumper, and Daisy had just acquired a fine pale bay with a black mane and tail who was stabled back in London, so she didn't need another mount.

During the long day and the drive back neither Ram nor Daisy referred to what had happened in the woods. Then, just as they turned into the driveway of *La Marée*, Ram took one hand off the steering wheel and laid it, heavy with authority, on top of her thigh.

"I'm going to kiss you there, right there, tonight," he said brusquely. She didn't dare look at him. Her whole body was blushing. Emotions spilled over which had been trembling near the surface all day, held in check only by the constant exercise into which they had thrown themselves.

"No, Ram!" she said in a low tone of prohibition which blotted out everything else, even the sight of some of the guests playing badminton in the garden.

"Be quiet," he ordered her, and she was quiet, finding, from somewhere, a smile with which to greet the others, an expert smile she didn't know she owned, a social smile and a social voice.

That night, after all the lights of the house were off, Ram tapped on the door of Daisy's bedroom and came in without waiting for her answer. He locked it behind him. Daisy was on the window seat, her knees drawn up under her, her arms circling her legs, her chin on her knees, as if she'd been sitting there thinking for a long time. He walked over to her and swept back the pale curtain of hair which fell over the near side of her face. She didn't move as she tilted her face so that he could see her eyes.

"We must *not*, Ram," she said.

"Daisy, you're still a baby. There aren't any stuffy musts or must nots for us—except that we must love each other."

"But not like . . . *not* what you did yesterday . . . Ram, just . . . sweetness, just being together," she said, hope and supplication mingled in her voice.

"Darling Daisy," he said, "just being together." He put both his arms around the entire slim circle of her body and carried her over to her bed. She lay there, hugging herself, stiff, silently resisting, abashed. When he kissed her the first time she pressed her lips tightly together and tried to turn her head away, but he wouldn't allow it. Very gently, very tenderly, but with absolute conviction, he parted her lips with the tip of his tongue. Now that he owned her he could take her slowly, surely. Her breath caught in her throat as she felt his tongue press on her clenched teeth and then felt it retreat to circle her lips, until she felt that her mouth was a ring of fire. Gradually, in spite of herself, she uncoiled her limbs as his lips traveled up her neck to her ear lobe. "Daisy, my Daisy," he whispered into her ear in a voice so soft that she could barely hear him. With a plaintive sigh she threw her arms around his neck and held him with all her strength. Oh, how content she was with this, nothing more, just this closeness, this dear affection. She felt sheltered, protected, safe from everything and everyone, a security she had thought she had lost forever when she was told of her father's death.

"Hug me tight," she asked. "Just hug me tight, only hold me, Ram, promise me, promise me . . ."

"Yes, Daisy, yes," Ram answered, while his fingers stealthily untied the ribbons of her long peignoir. "Yes, I'll hug you, my darling, I'll hug you." And he felt the outline of her small, firm breasts with careful, traitorous hands, brushing lightly over the tips of her nipples again and again until they rose to his touch and became so singingly sensitive that he knew he could bend his head and suck them and she wouldn't beg to be hugged anymore. He filled his mouth with the delicate rosettes, remembering their pale pinkness, still gently, still tenderly, until she lay back on the pillow giving herself in fresh astonishment to the darts which shot throughout her body from each nipple to her vulva, as if some crucial nerves had been activated, connections she'd never known existed.

Ram had been erect from the second he'd touched Daisy on the window seat but instinctively he had known to keep his rigid penis from touching any part of her, until she was led, step by step, into desire. Now he took one of her hands in his. "Daisy, feel how much I love you." He guided her hand to his penis and closed her hand around the quivering organ. She jerked her hand away immediately, shocked, struck with fearful alarm. He didn't try to make her touch him again but covered her lips with deep, slow, hot kisses, until he felt her mouth open of its own accord, until he felt her tongue tentatively reach out to touch his.

For half an hour he kissed her mouth and sucked her nipples until he could feel her beginning, just beginning, to stir her hips, unconsciously rotating them in a rhythm as old as time. Then he whispered again, "Daisy, touch me, touch me ... you'll feel how much I love you ... please touch me," and he took her hand again. This time she was too deeply bemused by her own aroused passion to resist. He took her hot fingers and tried to show them how to clasp his painfully engorged penis, but he had reckoned without his own towering desire. At the touch of Daisy's hand he realized that he was about to come to orgasm. Ram clutched his penis in one hand and shoved it roughly into the girl, just as the spasms overtook him. He bit his tongue to keep from crying out in the silent house. Bewildered, and hurting, she felt him quake in great, silent tremors.

After a brief time in which he lay panting, he kissed her once more. "Now, I'll hold you, my little Daisy," he muttered, and he lay, half asleep, clasping her in his arms for long, quiet, motionless minutes. Daisy didn't dare to move or speak. She was an accomplice. She had *let* him do it to her. If she protested he would fall into one of his sudden rages, or even worse, turn away from her and leave her all alone. But she could not be alone again. She had believed that all she wanted in Ram's arms was protection, security and the feeling that someone loved her but now, painfully excited, and shipwrecked anew, she wanted ... she didn't know what she wanted. Furtively she pressed her lips to his bare shoulder, and as she did so they heard someone open, and a minute later, shut a door along the corridor.

"I'd better leave," Ram whispered.

"Yes."

He left her with a hurried kiss, left her high and dry, burning, burning, sickened with desire, sickened with shame, burning, burning.

The next day, after lunch, Anabel told Daisy that so many of the guests she had invited for the next week had announced that they were coming that Daisy would have to share her room, since it had two beds in it.

"I never dreamed they'd all say yes, but it's too late

now. You'll like your roommate, I hope—she's an American girl, Kiki Kavanaugh, the daughter of an old friend of mine. Her mother is American too—she was Eleanor Williams when I first met her. She married a man who's in the motor business in Detroit."

"I'm half an American girl, too, Anabel—although I don't feel it."

"Do you remember much of it, Daisy?" asked Anabel, struck by some note of pathos in the girl's voice she didn't remember ever having heard before.

"So little. Mostly this feeling of having *been* with Mother and Dani and Masha—and sort of a dream memory of the way things looked, the big waves on the beaches, the forests, the light—I've never seen such light in England. I wish I could remember more. It seems as if my life was just split in half." There was a wistfulness in her voice like the residue of sugar in an empty cup, the memory of uncomplicated sweetness. Anabel wished sharply that she hadn't asked if Daisy remembered her American years—the girl looked even more weary than she had at dinner the night before, although at her age it was difficult to detect signs of fatigue.

Ah well, the death of Stash was a period they all had to live through, no way of skipping it and just carrying on as if nothing had happened. Anabel herself had had to strain every emotional resource she possessed to keep the house full and lively. Her own impulse was to crawl into a quiet room and just let desolation wash over her, but she couldn't permit herself to do that, mainly for the sake of Daisy. There were no more words between them as they sat on the striped canvas deck chairs on the terrace, their backs turned to the sea which, at this hour, was too bright to look at. Anabel had the gift of reposeful silence and she never asked what anyone else was thinking, a simple combination which had been only one of the many things men loved, that few other women had ever understood.

11

*I*n the course of the following week, Ram came to Daisy's room every night. Now that he possessed her the feelings he had repressed for longer than he realized had been freed. They burst, full blown, into obsessive madness. He could think of nothing else but Daisy. At last he had her to himself, at last his father didn't come first with her, at last he could do as he wished with her.

At night he waited only until the corridor was clear before he slipped through her door. He no longer cared if other lights were on in the house once he had locked the door. As soon as he saw the secret, tender whiteness of her breasts and her belly, as soon as he smelled the smoky, sweet wine of her hair, as soon as he felt her amber arms around him, he became so inflamed with the need to take her that all consideration, all caution, all vestiges of reason left him. And she was dominated by him, totally suffused with a strange mixture of wanting, still wanting, his kisses and yet dreading what she now knew he would eventually do to her. Each night, in torment, she waited for him, thinking that this time she would have the will to prevent him, and each night she failed.

There was never any physical release for Daisy, and she was so naive, so untutored that she had no clear idea of what there might have been. Even if she had known, she would have been too ashamed to ask for it, because to ask for it would have been to participate even more than he forced her to in the thing he did to her. She concentrated only on the minutes of kissing and holding and being held and blocked the rest out of her mind as best she could.

And afterward, there was her punishment; the dizzy fog of misery and sticky, blood-heavy frustration that enveloped her throughout the long, hot days.

Unlike Ram, Daisy felt intolerable guilt, although she was too innocent to identify the emotion clearly, experiencing it as crushing fatigue and a black sadness. But she was torn by her continuing need for Ram, a need as strong as her guilt. She had loved him since she was six and she didn't know how to break away from his hold on her. Guilt and her fear of having no one to hold on to, no one to belong to her, fought inside of her daily and she grew more unhappy and confused and unable to think things through ... to think at all.

"Daisy, let's go into Deauville for the day, just the two of us, and do some shopping. The boutiques are full of fall clothes—we could see what's going on at Dior and St. Laurent and Courrèges—you've grown so much that you need new things," Anabel said, looking anxiously at the signs of something very wrong on Daisy's face.

"I'm not in the mood to buy anything, Anabel—I'm so worn out I don't think I could stand to try on clothes."

"Then I have a great notion. I've always wanted to try that spa near the boardwalk—it's supposed to make you feel marvelous—rejuvenation therapy. First they pound you with sea water from a giant hose and whip up your circulation, then you soak in a hot tub full of bubbling sea water, then a long massage and finally they wrap you up in towels like a baby and make you rest in a deck chair for half an hour. It's all over by tea time, and, afterward, we'd go directly out to tea and chocolate eclairs. Why don't we try it?"

"It sounds like water torture to me," Daisy said indifferently.

Anabel, not defeated, proposed a drive to Pont-l'Evêque to buy the cheese that has been prized since the thirteenth century, or even just lunch at the Ferme St. Siméon, at the bottom of their hill, where the Impressionists used to meet, a favorite treat for Daisy in former years. But Daisy refused all of Anabel's suggestions, on one pretext or another. She didn't want to be alone with her secret and Anabel. She was afraid that Anabel, always so sensitive to mood, might divine the truth. She was even more afraid that she might *tell* Anabel. And then—what would Ram do to her?

One afternoon, disconsolate and restless, Daisy secluded herself in one of the deep recesses of the balcony of the salon, intending to attempt to read Balzac in French, something the honorable Miss West, French mistress at Lady Alden's, had suggested for all the girls' summer vacations. Before she was more than three pages into the dusty volume, barely understanding a word of what she read, Ram discovered her hiding place.

"I looked for you in the woods," he said, with reproach in his voice. "Why are you stuck away up here—it's gorgeous out."

"I wanted to be alone."

"Well, I want to talk to you. I've decided what to do with the house in London. It's far too big for us—Father never needed all that space—and the real-estate market's never been better. I'm going to sell it and buy a house that makes sense; one that doesn't need more than three or four servants to run. I think we should live in Mayfair, Upper Brook Street or South Audley Street—somewhere in that general area."

"You mean—live together?" She gaped at him.

"Obviously. You have to live somewhere. Do you think you're old enough to live alone?"

"But, I thought, I assumed—I'd be living with Anabel, Ram, not with you," Daisy said with all the grown-up dignity at her command.

"Impossible. I won't permit it. Anabel will have found another man to keep her within a few months and you can't be exposed to that sort of thing."

"Ram! That's a beastly, stinking thing to say—Anabel's like my mother!"

"That only proves I'm right—you're too much of a baby to understand that Anabel lives off rich men—always has and always will."

"It's not true! How can you be so awful?"

"Then why did Father never marry her?"

Daisy faltered, unable to answer his question. Frantically she turned to another objection. "What about the servants? What are you going to do with them?"

"Pension them off, of course," Ram said in an indifferent voice. "They're far too old—every last, decrepit one of them—and there's no good in thinking that we're doomed to keep them doddering about until they drop dead one by one in the pantry—they were all just another of Father's crazy extravagances, like putting all his money into Rolls-

Royce for sentimental reasons. I'm getting out of Rolls, Daisy, and I'm taking your money out, too. It's high time we put that money to work—and time to get as much of it out of England as possible!"

"Ram, no! You can't sell my stock . . . Father left it to me and I'm not going to sell."

"Daisy," Ram said reasonably, "the market's no place for emotional attachments. I'm the legal trustee of your money and if I want to sell your stock I can."

"Would you do that to me? Against my will?" she blazed at him. The stock in Rolls-Royce suddenly seemed all she had left to cling to, a real and tangible relic of her father's concern, of his caring protection, of the fact that she still possessed a link to the past that Ram was so abruptly dismantling.

"Oh, to hell with that," he barked. "Keep the stock if it means so much to you."

"And my horse? Where will I keep her?" Daisy asked, struggling to find another fixed element of her life that Ram couldn't wipe away with a word.

"We'll find another stable, nearby our new house—don't worry. You can have two dozen white horses if you want, Daisy, and a kennel full of lurchers," Ram said, relieved that Daisy seemed to be running out of reasons why they could not live together.

"But your flat," she said feebly, "you were so pleased with it."

"It's far too small for the two of us. I can get rid of it in a flash, and at a profit. Father's pictures will fetch a fortune at Sotheby's, even though I'm going to keep at least two Rembrandts and the furniture—my God, do you have any idea what signed French pieces like that are going for these days? To say nothing of the icons—that will be a major sale just in itself."

"So you're going to sell *everything*—everything I love, everything I grew up with," she gasped, with stricken eyes. She wanted to writhe and tear at Ram, but she knew he could do whatever he wanted with his own property. He took her in his arms and crushed her body to him.

"We'll be together, just the two of us, and no old servants around to poke and pry and treat you like a child—you want that, don't you?" She didn't answer, gasping in outrage, and taking her silence for agreement, he thrust his hand under her shirt and cupped one of her breasts firmly, his thumb making circles around her nipple.

Furious as she was, her nipple hardened and he pulled her shirt higher and fastened his mouth on it, sucking with a desperate, hasty need. His other hand was reaching under her shorts, searching for the downy hair, fingertips blindly reaching for her special warmth. Daisy froze as she heard a light footstep mounting the staircase to the balcony, but deaf to everything, Ram pulled on her nipple harder than ever, as if he wanted to inhale her all in one mouthful. Daisy, with a terrified force she didn't know she possessed, pulled away and flung herself as far from him as she could on the loveseat, pointing frantically in the direction of the footsteps while she pulled down her shirt. Dazed, Ram finally understood, and when Anabel appeared with a vase of flowers, she found the two of them sitting several feet apart, Daisy apparently engrossed in Balzac.

"Children! Oh, you frightened me! I thought I was alone up here. Just look—aren't these Queen Elizabeth roses marvelous? Daisy, they're for your room. The Kavanaughs are coming tomorrow early and I'm filling the house with flowers for them."

"Christ! Not more people. This is becoming a boarding-house," Ram said in disgust.

"You'll like them," Anabel said lightly, not, at the moment, really caring if he did or he didn't. She supposed they'd been fighting again from the way they looked. Well, they'd have to work it out between them, whatever it was.

That night, as soon after dinner as possible, Daisy went upstairs to her room and locked herself in. Later Ram knocked several times, each time a little louder, and whispered her name. Defiantly she glared at the door and neither opened it nor answered him. Only when she heard him stride off did she allow herself to whimper in fear.

Daisy fled *La Marée* at dawn the next morning, putting a big chunk of bread and an orange in her pocket. She roamed the country lanes of Honfleur with Theseus, keeping him firmly attached to a leash so that he didn't take off for any of the kitchens or farmyards of the neighbor-hood.

She felt that she could somehow, in solitary companion-ship with her dog, retreat into a time when life was simple, when rules were made for her, when she knew the guide-lines and lived within them happily. But as hours passed and the sun rose high overhead she realized that Anabel would be expecting her back for lunch. This was the day of the arrival of the new guests, Eleanor Kavanaugh and her daughter, with some sort of silly name, the one Anabel thought she'd like. The idea of meeting new people was an almost unbearable complication right now, yet the girl would be sharing her bedroom, and that was a profound relief to Daisy, a respite she couldn't have arranged herself.

The Kavanaughs' arrival at *La Marée* was announced from the driveway by an enormous, dark burgundy Daimler, parked in front of the door, with a dozen suitcases still being carried inside by their uniformed chauffeur. "Oh, bloody hell!" said Daisy to herself, as she contemplated the scene. It was the most violent expression of disgust she knew. Anabel hadn't said they were on an official tour of the native islands. Did they think they were royalty? She looked down at her dusty tennis shoes, her outgrown shorts, and her worn jersey. Her hair, she imagined, must look like a vulture's nest. With luck, she judged, they might all be outside drinking sherry and she'd have time to make herself presentable before she met them.

Seeing no one, Daisy slipped up the staircase and quietly approached her room. She heard no noise inside, no sounds of unpacking, so she entered briskly, and then stopped, almost falling over her feet, at the sight of a girl curled up on her window seat, looking out at the sea. Too late. The girl turned and looked at Daisy with an expression of amazement.

"You can't be Daisy!"

"Why not?"

"Daisy's a little girl—fifteen or something."

"How old are you?"

"I'm almost seventeen."

"Huh—you don't look it."

Kiki Kavanaugh drew herself up impressively. Five feet, two and three quarters of an inch of audacious female. She had frolicsome eyebrows, the face of a kitten who knows she's the pick of the litter and a short, fluttering mop of once brown hair which she had just had streaked in Kelly green, à la Zandra Rhodes. Her big eyes were umber, a dark, dusky brown with yellow lights in them—the eyes of a waif—spawn of a devil—and her beautifully shaped head was adorned with a pair of small, perfect, almost pointed ears. She was wearing what might have been either a Ukrainian wedding dress or something invented by a newly rich Afghanistani princess, made of red pleated linen, largely embroidered, appliqued in gold lace, fringed, wrapped, and tied here and there with multicolored beads. She lacked only anklets of bells.

"You're absolutely sublime, whoever you are," this apparition told Daisy. "I tried to convince Mother it was time to get back to classics but she never listens—after all, what could *I* know compared to the Queen of Grosse Pointe? Wait till she sees you—will she be sorry she let me keep this hair."

"Can't you have it, ah . . . put back?" Daisy suggested.

"Try that and it falls out—I'll just have to wait till it grows. Oh, balls! I can't go out there and meet all those people like this. Will you lend me something to wear—shorts and a shirt? And some of your hair?" Kiki circled Daisy in rapt admiration. Even Daisy's old shoes seemed to her to be the ultimate in throw-away chic.

"But they'd be way too big . . . of course, I would, but you'd swim in them," answered Daisy, enthralled by this gypsy who had camped in her bedroom.

"Oh, never mind, I'm always like this when I see someone divinely tall and naturally silver-blonde and absolutely, incredibly beautiful—it gives me a swift rush of shit to the heart but I'll be okay in a few minutes. I mean, I actually have a fairly healthy ego but bugger it all, wood nymphs set me back to square one. Do you like 'bugger'? I just learned it in England and I think it's an awfully useful word." She looked at Daisy, her raffish smile inquiring.

"Lady Alden disapproved of 'bugger'—very strongly—so it must be a good word. We got the ruler if we ever used it."

"The ruler! Capital punishment? No, corporal punishment—or whatever. They'd do that to you? How dare they? But then . . . you *must* be Daisy."

"Well, what would I be doing in this room if I weren't?"

"I thought . . . well . . . never mind. No, scratch that. I made a resolution never to say 'never mind' again. It drives people crazy and they always get it out of you anyway. I thought Daisy was a perfectly dumb name, so sickeningly pristine, an anachronism. But now it's just right for you, since you're she . . . or her?"

"She."

"Lord have mercy, I just guess at grammar. You realize, I had this mental picture of a little girl called Daisy, a princess no less, and what do I find but a fucking goddess

—I tell you, it's enough to make me try to be mean—but who could be mean to you? Listen, do you know what I hate the most in the world?" Daisy never took her eyes off Kiki. She had just realized that Kiki had on green nail polish, green mascara, and green eyeshadow. "It's those frantically well-dressed people in *Vogue* who say they live in only three wonderful old skirts they had made to order fifteen years ago—by Main, of course, who else?—and just two plain black cashmere sweaters and then they add one perfect jewel of an accessory every year, like a pair of priceless, antique Chinese slippers—you know it's a filthy lie but how can you prove it? Shit, I'll never get it right." She slumped despondently in the middle of her elaborate costume.

"Don't change, don't move, don't despair," said Daisy, suddenly restored to her role as the leader of Lady Alden's. "I'm coming right back."

She returned in five minutes, her hair all pulled up on the top of her head, skewered by pins into which she'd tucked some of the purple bougainvilla which grew on the walls of the house. She wore a mini-dress of flashing silver paper which she'd bought for three pounds at Biba. It could only be worn once and she hadn't dared to take it out of her wardrobe until today.

"Do you have any Paco Rabanne jewelry?" she asked Kiki.

"Doesn't everyone? Just a minute." Kiki rummaged in one of her seven suitcases and pulled out a space age, cast-metal neck sculpture which looked like a large, elaborately framed mirror, a chastity belt for the upper body. She clasped it around Daisy's neck. "Earrings?"

"No—I think that might be too much. I'll just wear bare feet—same effect but less fuss."

"You can't be fifteen," said Kiki flatly, admiringly.

"I'm wise beyond my years. Come on—let's give the old people a shock they won't forget."

During the week of the Kavanaughs' visit, Ram, for the first time in his life, found his generalized bitterness against the world turning to actual fantasies of murder— Kiki's murder.

Her mother could have told him that it couldn't have been done without a silver bullet. Kiki, a brisk, practiced and roguish prankster, stood for having fun in a way which, in spite of her intelligence, had caused four of the best girls' boarding schools in the United States to fail to "invite" her to reregister for the following year. She had survived the inestimable damage of immunity enjoyed from earliest childhood, the damage which might have been caused by knowing, almost from the playpen, that she was a member of the only local aristocracy worth belonging to in Grosse Pointe, that of the motor industry; as well as the damage which could have occurred as a result of being the longed-for daughter in a family of three older brothers—she had survived because of a stern, inborn, incorruptible honesty. Kiki told the truth, to herself and to others, a trait so rare as to make her seem eccentric. Her honesty went hand in hand with her impulsiveness, and she and Daisy, separated in age by little more than a year and a half, fell into instant complicity. They were a match in their love of a dare, their fancy for the improbable project. If Kiki was far more worldly and sophisticated, Daisy was the braver and more stalwart of the two; where Kiki was spoiled—or as she liked to put it, "divinely rotten"— Daisy was merely stubborn. The greatest difference in the two girls was in their emotional attachments. Kiki admitted to many, none of which troubled her—she took her father, her brothers and especially her mother for granted and found them, all of them, *amusing*—an attitude which puzzled and entranced Daisy.

However, during the week Kiki and her mother spent at *La Marée*, the two girls spent little time in serious discussions. Like fillies let loose in a pasture, they were busy exploiting their new camaraderie. Daisy, after a long night of uninterrupted sleep, suddenly felt full of her old laughing vitality, as if she'd had her youth returned to her, an unquestioning, untormented youth which led the two of them on expeditions into Honfleur to banter with the fishermen, to fill themselves with the Coca-Colas Anabel wouldn't have in the house, to buy coarse garlic sausages that they ate on the street, taking huge bites and talking with their mouths full. They hired a taxi and went to Deauville at teatime and paraded slowly through the lobbies of the great hotels, like strolling players in their rich-hippie rig-outs, enjoying the outraged looks of the middle-aged women in their safe, laughably expensive Chanel suits. They kept a score of how many women they could stare down in any given lobby on any given day. They exchanged clothes avidly, finding that Daisy's shorts and shirts would fit Kiki if she hitched them up with a belt and folded over the waist bands. Dressed alike, they ran up and down the beach at Trouville treating placid family groups to rude shouts. From a rented cabana they swam in the cold, northern waters, often arriving back late for meals at *La Marée*, with barely an excuse except to Anabel who didn't need one, since she was so delighted with the success of her hopes for a friend for Daisy.

Kiki had only one complaint. "That brother of yours must simply loathe me," she said to Daisy. "I've been flirting with him like crazy. I've invited him to come with us and I've been getting absolutely nowhere with him— and that, I promise you, is something that doesn't happen to me a whole lot. If at all! Does he have something against Americans? Or is it my green hair? Is he queer? I just don't get it."

"Oh, Ram's hopeless—forget him, it's that Etonian superiority of his. He doesn't mean to be rude . . . it's just his way," Daisy answered evasively. Couldn't Kiki see how jealous he was, she wondered? Of course not—how could Kiki imagine that she, Daisy, was clutching at her companionship in an effort never to be alone with Ram. She watched him at the dinner table staring at her, his eyelids hooded like those of a sculpture of a knight, killed long ago on a Crusade. Just the thin slivers of pupils peered out from his closed face, but she could feel Ram pulling at her across the table.

Several times he'd trapped her alone on the staircase, and had been about to fall on her with kisses but the sound of Kiki, faithfully following her, had forced him to let go. Ram was both malignant and reckless in his powerlessness but Daisy managed to never be far from Kiki, admitting to herself that this shield couldn't last for long, but using it to the full while it did. She needed this time apart from Ram, she needed it so much that she was willing to risk the punishment she knew she'd have to face when it was over. Every night, for long after Kiki had fallen asleep, Daisy lay awake thinking, trying to put her emotions in some sort of order, but not succeeding. She sorted over and over the facts of her long love for Ram, her need for Ram, and her conviction, which grew every day, that what Ram did to her was utterly bad, utterly wrong, no matter what he thought. She once toyed with the idea of consulting Kiki, but the mere realization of the words she'd have to use convinced her that it was impossible. The burden was one she had to bear alone, in shame. Dreadful, inescapable shame, shame unending.

Finally the day came when the Kavanaughs had to leave for the Côte d'Azur, where they were to meet Kiki's father, who was flying there from Detroit, via Paris. They planned to break the trip at Limoges and drive the distance in two long days on the roads. In a few weeks Kiki was going to enter the freshman class at the University of California at Santa Cruz. Although she hadn't officially graduated from any of her various schools, her college boards had been good enough for Santa Cruz and she had been welcomed by that most liberal and free-spirited of universities. Her parents had carefully coordinated this summer's trip so that they could spend time with their daughter before, as Eleanor Kavanaugh almost tearfully put it, "we lose her to higher education." There was no question of her disappointing her father and staying on at *La Marée* as Daisy and Anabel had asked her to do.

"Daisy, I promise you that, at Christmas, you can go visit Kiki in the United States," Anabel told the miserable girls.

"Christmas is a million years away. Why can't Daisy come to Santa Cruz, too?" Kiki asked rebelliously.

"She has another year at Lady Alden's before she even takes her university examinations," Anabel said, patiently.

"Oh, balls, balls and bugger! Excuse me, Anabel. I feel like a star-crossed lover or something," said Kiki.

"You don't quite sound like one," Anabel laughed kindly. She had taken a great liking to this unlikely creature, such a strange daughter for her old friend Eleanor, who had been, before her great automotive marriage, a conservative and well-bred American miss.

That night, when Ram rapped on her door, Daisy opened it immediately. The departure of Kiki had made her realize that, in the course of their tomboy week, she had made a decision about her future she wasn't conscious of having reached. But now she felt a need, as sharp as thirst after a long day on an empty boat, to return to her lost girlhood, to become again as chaste as she had been on the *Quatorze Juillet*. She was calm, determined and possessed by the certainty that everything must be sacrificed to that end. Her confusions had fallen away. She could do without Ram. His protection was infinitely worse than being alone in the world. All the corners of her mind seemed clear and in focus for the first time since her father had died.

Ram came in and locked the door behind him. Hurriedly, he tried to take Daisy in his arms but she retreated to the window seat. She hadn't changed from the yellow cotton dress she wore at dinner and the lights in her room were all on.

"Sit down, Ram. I have something to say."

"It can wait."

"No. Not another second. Ram, what we've been doing is over—finished. I'm your sister. You're my brother. I won't do it ever again because it's wrong and I don't like it."

"It's that bitch, Kiki—you told her, didn't you?" he said in a voice of white revenge.

"Not a word. No one knows and no one will ever know, I promise you. But it's over."

"Daisy, you sound like some little bourgeoise—'it's over'—how can it ever be over? We love each other. You *belong* to me, little idiot, and you know it."

"I belong to no one but myself. You can do whatever you like, you can sell everything Father ever loved, you can live any way you choose to live, but I intend to stay with Anabel in Eaton Square—I'm sure she'll have me—and that's the end of it. I don't need you anymore!"

Ram came closer and put one large hand around the top of her arm, just below the shoulder, hurting her with his fingers. She sat as silent as a marble girl. There was enough light for him to look right into the velvet centers of her eyes and what he saw there, utter, indomitable conviction, clear and hard, maddened him.

"Ram, take your hand off my arm," she ordered him.

Her words, still delivered with the calm and composure she was hanging on to desperately, only acted as goads. He fastened both his strong, bony hands on her arms and jerked her sharply to her feet, as if she were a mere beast who had to be taught a lesson in discipline. Still she stood fearlessly in his grip, looking him straight in the eye. With relentless force he pulled Daisy close to him and kissed her lips. Her mouth didn't move under his. She scarcely breathed. He appropriated her mouth, consuming it with calculated skill, and held back his anger. He gave her the long, delicious, unthreatening kisses she had craved only a week ago. But she remained passive and detached, her lips closed and cool under his skillful mouth. He stroked her hair with a hard, possessive, demanding hand and whispered in her ear, "Daisy, Daisy, if you don't want more than this I won't do anything else ... just kissing and being close—I promise ... I swear." Yet, as he clutched her to him and battered her cheeks with scorching kisses, she felt his penis rise and press dangerously against her belly. With a violent summoning of her energy Daisy flung herself away from him.

"No good, Ram. I don't trust you. *I don't want you!* Nothing of you—no kisses, no hugs, no more lying words. Just get out of my room." Her voice was low, because of the others in the house, but tense with a wounding distaste.

She had backed away until she reached the far wall of her room and now he came at her, his features blunted and swollen with lust, his eyes dulled by the intensity of his need to possess her. Ram was out of control. He pressed Daisy against the wall with all of his weight, lifted her skirt with a brutal hand and ground the hard butt of his penis against her underpants. With his other hand he snatched at her breasts in a frenzy, viciously bruising the young nipples.

"You wouldn't *dare* if Father were alive, you filthy coward!" Daisy gasped.

Ram hit her on the face with his open hand. She felt her teeth cut into the inside of her cheek. She felt the blood begin to flow onto her tongue. He hit her again and then again, and while she was trying, in a panic, to get the breath to scream, he put a hand over her mouth and dragged her to the bed. With every bit of force she possessed, Daisy wasn't able to pull his hand away from her mouth during the brief, hideous minutes which followed. As she swallowed her own blood to keep from choking, Daisy felt him rip off her underpants. He had to hit her twice again before he could wrench her legs apart with his knees and then there was the searing, rasping eternity of a nightmare as he stabbed his penis into her, again and again, with the inhumanity of a madman, dry and closed as she was. Then he was finished, and gone. Daisy lay inert, blood seeping from her mouth, so extinguished, so obliterated, that it was many minutes before the tears she longed for finally came. After the tears, painfully, resolutely, Daisy got off the bed and went to wake up Anabel.

Anabel gave Daisy warm water and soft towels and stopped the bleeding and listened, holding her close, as Daisy told her the entire story, again and again, until she had finally calmed down enough to fall asleep on Anabel's bed. Only then did Anabel give way to the sobs which were more piteous, more tormented and far more furious than those Daisy had shed. She had failed Stash, she had failed Daisy. Ram's crime had to remain secret, depriving her of the revenge she would have taken. She would never speak to him again—he was dead to her forever—but there was no way to bring him to justice. What was done was done—she cursed herself, her blindness, her assumptions, her trust.

As soon as daylight appeared, Anabel telephoned to the hotel in Limoges where the Kavanaughs were spending the night on their trip south.

"Eleanor, it's Anabel. Don't ask me any questions but do you think that Daisy could possibly get into Santa Cruz?"

"This year? Isn't she too young?" Eleanor Kavanaugh answered with her habitual direct approach to the fundamentals.

"Age isn't the question now—it's whether she could pass the exams. It's *very* important, Eleanor, or I wouldn't let her go so soon."

"I'm sure she could pass the college boards, Anabel. Her education is already beyond an American girl's of seventeen, thanks to our atrocious high-school system. Look, I'll find out if there's still room and where she can take the exam—all right?"

"Could you do it tomorrow—today, I mean. Don't wait till you get home," Anabel pleaded.

"Count on me." Eleanor had never been a person who asked unnecessary questions. "Whenever that admissions office is open in California I'll telephone them—and then I'll call you, and you can send them Daisy's records."

"Bless you, Eleanor."

"Anabel, we're old friends, remember? I haven't forgotten . . . and don't worry. Daisy'll get into Santa Cruz, I guarantee it. After all, I made them take Kiki, didn't I? Just realize, it's not exactly Harvard."

But it is six thousand miles away from Ram, thought Anabel, as she hung up the phone.

12

Handwoven!" Kiki proclaimed excitedly.

"What?" Daisy looked up from the catalogue of courses offered at the University of California at Santa Cruz. Kiki had been ruminating for a good half-hour as she cast a disgusted eye on her still-unpacked suitcases sitting in one corner of their dormitory room.

"But that's it! That's the key! Handmade, homespun, second-hand, third-hand, stolen or bartered for—but above and before all else, *handwoven*. I mean, we don't want to stand out like a couple of nerds, do we?"

"I thought I'd gotten away from uniforms once I was freed from Lady Alden's—don't tell me I've got to get back into another one here? And anyway, why is how we dress so important?" Daisy inquired. "I thought this place was casual."

"Daisy, you just don't understand yet," Kiki sighed patiently. "Once you know how to dress for a place or an event—once that's figured out, the rest takes care of itself. You spent too much time at the same school so you never had to worry, but if you'd been to as many schools as I had, you'd realize that you can only survive and be yourself if you *blend* into the surroundings. Now neither of us is exactly inconspicuous and we both want to spend the next four years sort of incognito—no princess for you, no Miss Grosse Pointe Automotive Heiress shit for me—so we've got to get into handwoven right away, even if it itches."

"Done. Now how about deciding what courses you're

going to take? That won't take care of itself," Daisy said, waving the catalogue at her meaningfully.

"There's a course in surfing that sounds intensely interesting. Also kayak handling, bike maintenance and jazz dancing. But the only one I'm absolutely definite about is trampoline."

"Kiki—you're impossible. There's no credit given for any of those."

"Bugger."

"I'm taking pottery, drawing, print making and painting —all necessary for an art major," said Daisy smugly. "And, since we have to satisfy something called the Social Sciences requirement, let's both take Dreaming S. Oh, hell, it says here that we have to take Western Civilization too—a must for Freshmen."

"I'll sign up for anything to stay here. I think we've landed in Camelot," Kiki said, looking out of the window blissfully.

"Look, take trail riding with me. We've got to get some phys. ed.—oh, blast, no credit for that."

"Give me that catalogue," Kiki demanded. "Ah ha! Workshop in Theater Production satisfies the Humanities requirement—how about that? We get to be in a play—I think I'll major in Drama."

"Good. Our education's settled," Daisy said in satisfaction. "Now let's go shopping. Or should we just buy our own loom?"

Daisy had given an entirely adequate performance on the College Board Examinations—Lady Alden's ruler had not been plied without a purpose—and Santa Cruz had been glad to welcome the fifteen-and-a-half-year-old student from London.

Kiki and Daisy were roommates at Cowell, the first of the largely self-contained residential colleges to open in Santa Cruz which was, itself, the most beautiful baby of a great university system. It had been founded in 1965, just two years before Daisy and Kiki entered this experimental school built on two thousand dreamingly lovely acres overlooking Monterey Bay, seventy-five miles south of San Francisco.

A visitor, driving toward the university from the Victorian seaside city of Santa Cruz, grows dizzy with the rich, lazy, untouched sweep of open fields and deep forests of a former working ranch, still guarded by old fences, dotted with limestone kilns and graced by a few ancient farm buildings. The university is made up of separate residential colleges, modeled after Oxford or Cambridge in their conception of community but designed by some of the greatest modern architects in the United States. The colleges are so cleverly hidden in the trees that they can almost be overlooked entirely, although the students, who could be dress extras in a lumberjack movie, contrive to stay visible as they lope from class to class, bearded genial boys and gilded, if messy, girls.

Daisy and Kiki romped through Santa Cruz, taking courses that always sounded easier than they turned out to be, and working much harder than they had planned to, but, in the course of it, becoming increasingly drawn into the worlds of art and the theater which opened up to them.

Daisy discovered that her talent for drawing, which she had reserved for the sketches she made for Dani and her moments of solitude, was a substantial talent, a far greater gift than she had realized, a serious potential. She immersed herself in drawing and painting, watercolor, pastel and oil, never tempted by the abstract-expressionist mode, but rather sticking to what she did best: realistic and sensitive portraits, studies of nature, and, of course, drawings of horses. Kiki found an outlet for her randy, inquisitive and honest self in the theater where nothing she could do or say aroused any surprise from her peers. They were all "into self-expression" which suited Kiki very well. This was finally the "fun" she had always searched for everywhere, and at Santa Cruz she could get academic credit for it.

Kiki was a spendthrift with her small delicate body. She had many love affairs, caring nothing for her Grosse Pointe indoctrination into the nature of virtue, her good name or public opinion. She cared for no opinion of her actions but her own, and her strict code was satisfied by personal generosity and absolute sincerity. She had a talent for falling for the wrong men, but she reveled in her errors, getting out before she hurt anyone but herself. She observed, in sinful amusement, the efforts of others to try to make her feel guilty. Fun came first—why couldn't people just admit it—take their fun, take their lumps and go on to the next adventure? Why did you have to *learn* from your mistakes? You'd only find a different one to make the next time anyway.

Daisy and Kiki roomed together during all their years at Santa Cruz, often talking far into the night and sharing their experiences, yet Kiki, whose many antennae seemed to sprout like a network from her whimsical head, knew that there were large areas in her friend that she didn't understand. Daisy was, even in their senior year, still something of an enigma and Kiki had little patience for enigmas.

"Daisy," she suggested one day in 1971, the winter of their senior year, "think about the clitoris."

"Before lunch?"

"Why, I ask you *why*, is it where it is? All tucked away, practically invisible, impossible to find without directions that I, for one, am fed up with having to provide."

"I thought you just told them what you wanted them to do and they did it," Daisy said, incuriously. Her friend's complaint was not an unfamiliar one.

"Why should I have to give them a goddamned road-map? A man doesn't have to show a woman where his cock is! It's not fair!"

"Just where do you think it should be moved to?" Daisy inquired reasonably. "The tip of your nose?"

"I'm not giving up sex," Kiki answered her quickly, "but there's a real need for reform."

"Hmmm." Daisy waited patiently for the real purpose of this conversation. Whenever Kiki talked about the clitoris she was leading up to something.

"While we're on the subject, Daisy, there's one thing I really don't understand about you," Kiki continued.

"Only one?"

"Yup—how come you're still a virgin? Everyone's talking about you—did you realize that? They call you Peck-on-the-Cheek-Valensky."

"I know. It's un-American . . . I'm an embarrassment to you, aren't I?" Daisy laughed.

"It's getting that way. Do you realize that you're going to be nineteen on your next birthday? In a few months? And still a virgin? Forget un-American—it's unhealthy and unwholesome. Really, Daisy—I'm serious."

"I'm waiting for Mr. Right," Daisy said annoyingly.

"Bullshit. You go square dancing with Mark Horowitz

who's having a mad thing with Janet except she hates square dancing; you go riding with Gene, the Gay Caballero; you go to the movies with absolutely anybody so long as it's a mob; you let Tim Ross buy you pizza and he's so in love with you that he's happy just for the honor of paying for your pepperoni; you go into San Francisco for Chinese food with three *girls,* for God's sake, and yet every *one* of the most attractive guys at school has been after you! And I'm not even counting the men you've met when you come home with me for vacations—the most eligible bachelors in Grosse Pointe have all been spurned by you, kid, including my poor brothers, those sweet assholes, and what about the men you meet when you go to Anabel's for the summers? I've seen the letters they write which you don't even bother to answer. What's with you?" Kiki finished, her arms akimbo under her tattered poncho, her pointed ears pink with indignation.

Daisy looked at her, suddenly serious. Kiki had been sounding this note for well over two years now and evidently it really bothered her enough to make an issue over it. And when Kiki made an issue she was capable of bringing Napoleon back from Elba.

"Okay, you're right. I don't want to get involved with a man, not at all. I don't want anyone to have any power over me. I don't want anyone to think he is entitled to any part of me. I don't want any man to get that close. I can't stand it when they think they have a right to kiss me just because we've spent an evening together—who the hell asked them to—who gave them any permission, how *dare* they act as if I owed them anything?"

"Hey, take it easy—calm down—we're not talking about the same thing. You're supposed to *like* getting close to a guy—or didn't they ever tell you when you were growing up? Haven't I gotten through to you, ever?"

"But I *do not* like it—I don't want to try it—and that's the way it is. You should be able to accept that about me by now," Daisy said with finality.

"You're right, I should. But I don't."

"Well, keep trying," Daisy advised her.

Since Daisy had arrived at Santa Cruz she had been plagued by the romantic passions she inspired in various young men and, as far as she was concerned, their romantic passions gave her less sympathy for them than if they'd lost a shirt in the laundry. No one, *no one* was to be allowed to have the faintest hope of possession—she stamped out their feelings without the slightest remorse. She wasn't responsible for them and if they wanted to be miserable because of her, let them. The minute anyone she went out with started to try to turn the neutral peck on the cheek into a larger embrace was the minute her relationship with him ended. There were always others to take his place.

At almost nineteen, Daisy had consolidated her early beauty. Her spun silver-gilt hair, which she rarely cut except to have a quarter of an inch trimmed off the ends from time to time, reached almost to her waist. No matter how she tried to control it, to braid it or bunch it or tie it in neat clusters, it was impossible to do anything to keep her nape, her temples and her ears from being tickled by wisps, cowlicks and curls of shorter hair which escaped her firm hand and created a halo around her face. Her skin still held the warmth, that of a ripe peach, that she had inherited from Francesca and those generations of beautiful women of San Gimignano, and men found themselves impaled on her eyes. Eyes as large, with pupils of such a blackness as Daisy's, were almost impossible to penetrate ... yet the men of Santa Cruz never gave up trying. The touch of strangeness, which lent her beauty the necessary counterpoint, was her eyebrows, which were so straight and determined above the mystery of her eyes. As she grew older, her full, Slavic mouth, the one feature, aside from the color of her hair, that she had inherited most noticeably from Stash, became more firmly marked. At Santa Cruz she had grown taller until she reached her full height of five feet, seven inches, but her body had not succumbed to institutional food. She was as slim and limber as ever: she rode every day in every kind of weather, and she had the firm, graceful arms, thighs, calves and shoulders of a horsewoman. Her breasts were fuller than they had been four years before but were still high and pointed.

Both Daisy and Kiki wore the uniform they had settled on in their freshman year—jeans and handwoven tops, the jeans as battered as possible, the tops as ethnic. The two of them, known as Valensky and the Kav, were a legend on a campus where almost everyone was eccentric, because of the contrast in their personalities and their looks, to say nothing of Theseus who slept in their room and accompanied Daisy to all her classes. The only place from which he was barred was the eating commons, by demand of the other students.

In spite of the intimate friendship between them, Daisy had never told Kiki about Dani, to whom she mailed, twice each week, a detailed drawing, sometimes showing a scene from her own life, sometimes a scene from Dani's life, drawings which included those teachers and friends of Dani's she had come to know so well. Sometimes Daisy asked herself if there might have been a time when she should have told Kiki about the existence of her twin sister, but, year after year, that moment had never presented itself. She still felt the power of the absolute prohibition which had been imposed by her father, that prohibition which she had been under since she was six, a prohibition she understood to be total, without knowing or questioning why it should exist. The longer it lasted, the more binding it became, and it was all the stronger for never having been discussed or explained—a terrifying taboo, that *must* be served because of consequences that were unthinkable, irrational, but entirely real.

The only person left alive in the world who knew about Dani was Anabel, but Daisy never discussed Dani even with her. After Stash's sudden death, Anabel had assured Daisy that Danielle had been provided for. Nevertheless, Daisy knew, in the deepest part of herself, that Dani was a secret she was under a compulsion to bear by herself. *She had been born first*—nothing had changed that fact, and her deepest loyalties and sense of responsibility still went to Dani. Often, when she was in the midst of some special enjoyment, she would imagine Dani, her double, her other self, more her child than her sister, playing in the garden or singing the simple songs she had been taught, and hot tears would fill her eyes at the realization of all her twin was missing, all the new knowledge and experience she would never have. Her only comfort was the realization that Dani was as happy as she could possibly be, that Queen Anne's School was truly home to her and that the staff and other patients had become her family.

Daisy had not, of course, been able to visit Dani from Santa Cruz, but during the long breaks at Christmas and Easter she always flew to England to see her, and every summer was spent with Anabel at *La Marée* so that she could be within a few hours of Dani by plane. The staff at Queen Anne's School took photographs of the two sisters together whenever Daisy visited, and these photos, which covered a period of thirteen years, were pinned up on a special cork board in Dani's room. Often she pointed it out to her friends and teachers with great pride. "See Day? See Dani? Pretty?" she would ask, time after time, knowing that their answer would always be, "Yes, yes, pretty Dani, pretty Day!"

During her years at college, Daisy had received letters from Ram, since all her school bills, all her travel bills and clothing bills were sent to him for payment, and her allowance checks had to come from him, too. Daisy could not tear up the letters and throw them away unread. Unfortunately money matters still gave Ram a hold on her and she could barely wait to graduate to get a job and become completely self-supporting.

During 1967 and 1968, Ram's letters had been totally impersonal, noting only that he had paid the various bills she had sent him out of her income from her stock. Then he had started dropping disquietingly intimate sentences into his communications. The first time this happened he had written, after disposing of business, "I hope that my actions of the past won't be held against me for the rest of my life. I've never stopped condemning myself for what could only have been a case of temporary insanity." The second quarterly letter was even more upsetting. "Daisy, I've never forgiven myself for what I did to you. I can't stop thinking of how much I loved you and how much I still love you. If you would only write to say you forgive me—and that you are now able to understand that you *literally* drove me crazy, you would relieve me of a great burden." This letter had struck a chord of terror into Daisy. It was as if Ram had reached out and tried to touch her. She looked around the room she shared with Kiki, trembling at the thought that her only safe refuge was here, and yet even here he was able to enter, if only in a letter.

When she opened the first letter Ram sent her in 1969, she hoped that her lack of any answer to his last two letters would have caused him to return to simple business matters. But instead, he wrote, "I understand why you don't feel ready to answer me yet, Daisy, but that doesn't change the way I feel about you or the fact that I feel I *must* have, some day, a chance to gain your forgiveness *in person*. No matter what you think, I am still your brother and I always will be and nothing can change that—just as nothing can change my memories. Can you really forget the eucalyptus grove? Have you really no feelings toward someone who loves you so much?"

The next time a letter came from Ram, and every time thereafter, Daisy dropped them, unopened, into the big trash basket in the coffee shop, unwilling to put them into the wastebasket near her desk. The arrival of one of them in her mail cubbyhole was like the sight of a curled-up snake. Her fear and loathing of Ram had grown stronger every year and his pleading words were vomitous, somehow menacing even in their humility.

Long hours of introspection had permitted Daisy to understand that her premature sexual experience had been possible only because of an incompleted mourning process for her father that had catapulted her into a state in which she felt that she had lost a part of her own *self*, and so had fled to Ram to become whole again. She could never stop blaming him, never stop reassuring herself that *it had not been her fault*, but his. And yet, somehow, the guilt lingered, the guilt she knew she had no reason to feel, and she was angrily unwilling to venture into sexuality again. Daisy walled off and defended herself against sexual feelings—they caused pain, confusion, shame. She knew that she wasn't being rational, but her emotions could not be reached by logic.

Instead, she threw herself into a schedule of activities so full that her energy was consumed. Besides her regular classes and her daily trail ride, she became a member of the crew responsible for the stage sets of the many performances put on in the various Santa Cruz University theaters. She was so eager and ready a volunteer that more and more of the work fell on her shoulders until, by the fall of senior year, she was in full charge of all scenic design, and leader of a crew of scenery painters and builders called "Valensky's Vassals" because of their devotion to their demanding chief. During her time at college Daisy created many stage sets which combined ingenuity with illusion in a highly professional manner. She also became familiar with all the varied crafts of stage décor: lighting, set dressing and costume design, as well as her own specialty of scenic design. She loved the stage of a theater as much as Kiki did; Kiki, who had become such an iridescent personality, as she acted in play after play, that to most people but Daisy, she seemed a splashy, spangled creature, so colorful that the details of her real self were overlooked in the glitter. But while Kiki appeared in front of an audience, Daisy's feelings for the stage were based on the handling and working of actual materials and seeing what could be made of them. She took rich pleasure in seeing a freshly painted backdrop laid out on the grass of the sculpture garden of College 5, and later transforming it, with furniture and props, into a startling reality, as much as she loved creating a set for a dance group, using nothing but a curtain of long ropes of Christmas tree ornaments and spotlights. Daisy didn't know what kind of job she would eventually get in the theater, but that was her ambition, and, until graduation, she planned to cram as much of stagecraft into her life as possible.

Early in the fall of her senior year at college, Daisy was engrossed in sketching costumes for a futuristic version of *The Tempest* when an excited Kiki, shouting, "Hey, Daisy, where are you?" burst into their room at a run. "Oh, great—you're here. Listen to this, I just got a letter from Zip Simon, head of advertising at old Dad's company and he's coming out next week and we're invited!"

"What does an executive of United Motors want with our humble, but admittedly lovely selves? And by the way, you've interrupted me. How do you think Prospero would dress on a spaceship?"

"In a spacesuit—just leave that alone for a sec—I told you ages ago that Zip promised me that the next time they shot a TV commercial anywhere near here, he'd let us watch—and they're going to do one in Monterey next week. It's to introduce the new model of the Skyhawk. You know, the car that's been such a secret."

"A television commercial! Oh, really, how *gross!* Stop kidding, Kiki," Daisy said disdainfully.

Students at Santa Cruz made it a fetish not to watch television except for an eccentric few who followed "As the World Turns" and insisted on being proud of their addiction. As far as commercials—all commercials—went, their contempt knew no bounds. Kiki, as an heiress to a vulgar Detroit fortune, was often hard-put to swallow her thoughts when she heard the lofty, utterly impractical ideas of her fellow students on American industry in general, and television advertising in particular.

"Daisy Valensky!" she said indignantly. "Don't you know that Marshall McLuhan said that historians and archaeologists will one day discover that the ads of our time are the richest and most faithful daily reflections any society ever made of its entire range of activities?"

"You're making that up!"

"I am not! I memorized it because I'm just so sick and tired of the way everyone goes on around here—talk about ivory towers—wait till they try to get jobs, they'll find out. Oh, come off it, Daisy, maybe you'd learn something from seeing them do the commercial."

"I suppose one can always learn something—like how not to do things."

"Oh, you're so fucking condescending! You've been at Santa Cruz so long your brain's decayed."

"Spoken like a true daughter of noble Detroit."

"Elitist swine!"

"Capitalist pig!"

"I got to say swine first, so I won," Kiki said, delighted at her victory in their long-playing game of insults.

A week later, on historic Cannery Row in Monterey, less than an hour's drive from Santa Cruz, the two girls approached a roped-off section of the street where a small crowd of spectators had already collected. A gigantic truck, with the word "Cinemobile" printed on its side, was parked close by. There was also a large Winnebago, and a truck carrying the new Skyhawk that was draped in heavy canvas. A vintage Skyhawk, in perfect condition, stood on the street.

Kiki and Daisy edged cautiously through the crowd up to the ropes and inspected the scene of the commercial shoot.

"Nothing's going on," Daisy observed.

"Weird," Kiki whispered, looking at the crowd of people inside the ropes who were frozen in widely separated groups. Two of the groups were made up of conservatively dressed men in dark suits and ties muttering together in low tones. She pointed to them with knowledgeability. "Our gang's from the agency, the other's from the client— my old dad's guys."

"Those must be the crew," Daisy said, indicating a tangle of men and women in jeans so shabby that they wouldn't have looked out of place on campus, all of whom were drinking coffee from plastic cups and munching leisurely on doughnuts as if they were on vacation. Both girls looked with more interest at two people, isolated from everyone else who, at least, showed signs of animation. One was a tall red-haired man and the other a young, plump, severely tailored woman.

"This doesn't look right to me," Kiki said snappishly. "I've seen them shoot commercials before and they're not supposed to be just *standing* there."

"Look, you're not in charge here," Daisy reminded her.

"Yeah, but Zip Simon is. Hey, Zip! Over here!" Kiki called boldly, with all the assurance of the client's daughter, which is second only to the assurance of the client's wife.

A short, bald man broke away from one of the groups in business suits and came over to escort them through the ropes which were being guarded by policemen.

"Kiki, how are you, kid?" He hugged her. "Who's your friend?"

"Daisy Valensky."

Zip Simon sighed gloomily. "Well, gals, it looks like you're not going to see a commercial made after all. We've got big, big trouble. And I still can't believe it. North is the best damn commercial director in the business and he can't shoot. It's a disaster."

"What's the disaster? Is someone sick?" Kiki asked.

"Unfortunately not—that we could ignore. We've had this fucking commercial—sorry, Kiki—planned for months and now we've blown the location."

"What's wrong with it?" Kiki asked.

"It's been fucking *renovated*—that's what. North used a location scouting service and the bastards showed us perfect photos—Cannery Row in its prime. When we got here we found it'd been turned into a Design Research store, and there isn't a building left in this whole lousy town that looks old anymore. Oh, shit! Sorry, Kiki. Excuse my language, Kiki's friend."

"Why does it have to look old?" Daisy ventured.

"Because of the story board," he said, as if that would tell them everything they wanted to know.

"What's a story board?" Daisy asked. He looked at her incredulously. Such ignorance was not possible. On the other hand, she was another person he could complain to.

"The story board, Kiki's friend, is a big piece of paper

with cartoon figures drawn on it and balloons coming out of people's mouths with words written on them. Got it? It's like the Bible to us simple folk in advertising. And in this story board you see an old Skyhawk convertible parked in front of a restaurant on Cannery Row forty years ago, see, and then a couple in period costume come out and drive off, and then you have another funny picture and you dissolve into the new model Skyhawk, in front of the same old place, and a couple in modern clothes walk out and drive off and voice-over you hear—now get this: 'The United Motors Skyhawk—*still* the best car you can drive!' "

"I love it," Kiki squealed.

"It's a gem—simple but eloquent... and we're going to shoot the same scene all over the country in historic, picturesque locations—or, at least, we were.... Now, who knows?"

"But, why can't you un-renovate the building—build a set?" Daisy wondered.

"Because we don't have time. Tomorrow the new car has to be on a plane headed back to the factory in Detroit for the unveiling at a stockholders' party—a gigantic affair—don't even ask how many people are invited. And if we don't get this shot done today, we'll blow our first air date. Does it hurt to commit hara-kiri?"

"Oh, Zip, don't be so hard on yourself—you didn't screw up the location," Kiki said fondly.

"I was going to do the hara-kiri on North, not me."

"Which one is North?" Daisy asked curiously. Zip Simon pointed to the red-headed man. "That's the son-of-a-bitch, and the gal with him is his producer, Bootsie Jacobs."

Forty feet away from Simon, North was speaking so quietly that no one could overhear.

"Bootsie, this is as careless as expecting an ear, nose and throat man to look up your ass with a flashlight and tell you why you've got a sore throat."

"That location scouting service will be out of business next week," she said, struggling for her usual taut composure. "Palming off pictures that were two years old—*two years!* Okay, okay, North, it was my fault for not double-checking. There's no one you can trust—I know it, it never fails—especially when you have the client and his whole mob and the agency and their shitheads all watching this little road show. Wonderful! They outnumber us two to one, even counting all the models and hairdressers and make-up people—I told that lot not to set foot out of the Winnebago. It looks bad enough already." Panic was seeping through her crisp tone. "If they'd only let us keep that new Skyhawk for a couple of days, we could go to EUE's big Burbank studio and shoot down there—but that's absolutely not possible."

"You'd better think of something to pull this one out, Bootsie," North said angrily. "That's your job, not mine."

Frederick Gordon North was the best director of television commercials in the United States. He knew he was. Everyone in the business knew he was. What's more, he charged a thousand dollars a day more than any of the other top directors in the business and got it, as many days a year as he wanted to work. While the likes of Avedon, Steve Horn and Bob Giraldi all charged four to five thousand dollars a day as their personal directorial fee, North got six thousand. Even Howard Zeiff had never charged as much in the days before he became a film director, during which he was the undisputed king of commercial directors.

Why were they willing to pay so much? Why would advertising-agency creative directors pay North a thousand dollars a day more than directors *almost* equally good? Everyone had a different answer. Some talked about his "eye"—the way he *saw* things as they would appear on film with just a little more originality, a little more visual interest than anyone else saw them. Others talked about the way he worked with actors, bringing out more than they knew they had to give. There were those who insisted it was his matchlessly innovative use of lighting, and still others spoke of the way he managed to telegraph more of a message in thirty seconds than other directors could in a full-length motion picture.

The truth lay in the blood he spilled. North would do anything to make a good commercial, and he put his blood and that of everyone else he worked with on the line. He didn't secretly want to make "real" movies, like the majority of commercial directors, nor did he hanker to do the most marvelously artistic still photography. To Frederick Gordon North *THE perfect art form* was the television commercial, whether it was thirty seconds, sixty seconds, or even only ten seconds long, and that quality of utter commitment made clients slaver for him. Of course, it was essential that his work was technically superior, but that wasn't the real lure—the hook was, had always been, the smell and sight of blood.

Daisy turned away from her inspection of North and his producer to speak to Zip Simon.

"Excuse me, but do you have other problems besides the set?"

"No, just that minor detail," Simon said bitterly. "But we can't get a set built by tomorrow, and the car leaves in the morning, even if we could work all night."

"I can get it done," Daisy said.

"Sure you could. Two minutes ago you didn't even know what a story board was, Kiki's friend."

"My name's Daisy Valensky and I'm the head of Scenic Design at the University of California at Santa Cruz," Daisy said with dignity. "I have a crew of forty top workers who will be here in an hour if I make just one phone call. They'll work all night."

"Is she for real?" Simon asked Kiki.

"Of course! They're professionals, for God's sake, Zip," Kiki said, quivering with the unmistakable imperiousness of her old dad's daughter, an unfamiliar guise to Daisy, but one which Kiki knew precisely when and how to assume.

"So, what the hell, Daisy, let's talk to North. It's worth trying—at this point anything's worth trying." Zip Simon was so disgusted that he didn't mind confronting even Frederick Gordon North with this absurd idea. The shoot couldn't get more fucked up than it was.

North and Bootsie Jacobs watched them approach with lively suspicion. Zip Simon, Vice-President in Charge of Advertising at United Motors, did not communicate with the director of his commercials casually. And, at a moment like this, accompanied by two hippie girls, he was particularly unwelcome.

"North, this is Kiki Kavanaugh, daughter of my boss and your client, and her friend, Daisy—ah—Valensky."

North frowned. If there was anything worse than having a client on the set it was having the client's daughter, and after that came the client's daughter's friend.

"Hi. Sorry we don't have time to chat today. Nice to see you." He turned away, leaving them with the impression of supreme indifference and wrathful blue eyes.

Daisy tapped him on the arm. "Mr. North, I can have

this place looking any way you want it by tomorrow or sooner."

He turned and gave her a look of freezing irony. "Who let you on the set?"

"Listen," said Simon, "this kid's head of stage sets or something at Kiki's college. She's got a thousand willing nuts who want to build you a set."

"Kids?" North asked Daisy.

"People. Good people. They like to work."

"I don't care who they are. Do you seriously believe that you can take this building and make it look exactly like the outside of Cannery Row fifty years ago, before eight tomorrow morning?" He gestured in disgust at the spanking-new brick, the gleaming paint, the huge, modern windows.

"We can certainly try," Daisy said resolutely. She looked boldly at North as she spoke. He had shockingly red hair, a fox of a man with a long, pointed nose, lots of freckles and blue eyes which told her that no matter how bad this moment was, it could not possibly end in failure. He was a man of sharp, clear edges. There was nothing indistinct or rounded or even comfortable about his clever features. He turned to Bootsie Jacobs and asked calmly, "What do you think?"

"We'd be breaking about sixteen union rules I can think of and about sixteen I don't know about yet. Using nonunion labor would be the least of it, and that's big trouble. Anyway, how can it work? They've got to be strictly amateur time. I think I'll kill myself," Bootsie said grimly.

"Why not let us get to work?" Daisy said eagerly.

"North," Zip Simon said angrily, "you've come up empty. Now here's a chance to get something on film before I put the new Skyhawk on that plane tomorrow. I don't care if you shoot the damn thing upside down, sideways or hanging from a tree—it's up to you to *do it!* That's why we hired you. I don't plan to go back to Detroit and have to tell my boss that the location just 'happened' to be renovated and we couldn't do a single thing about it. Miss Kavanaugh says that this young lady can help—so let her! Unless, of course, you have a better idea." His bald head had gone almost purple with aggravation.

Bootsie glanced briefly at North. "Go call your crew,"

she said to Daisy. If Zip Simon thought he'd be in trouble if they didn't get the film, what did he think would happen to *her* if she couldn't make this shoot happen? She'd begged and begged the agency to let her build a Cannery Row set at the automobile plant just to avoid trouble, but no, they had to be authentic—fuck authentic—and fly the prototype all over the country for historic streets to shoot on. What an utterly corny idea—but how many clients did sixty-second spots these days? And now here was the client's bossy daughter with her helpful suggestions—well, if this long shot didn't work, wouldn't it be partly the client's daughter's fault, instead of hers alone? And who knew, with the right lighting and the right filters and a stiff breeze . . . who knew?

Daisy was already headed toward the phone.

Santa Cruz didn't have a football team, but it had one hell of a Theater Arts department. And, as Daisy knew well, they had stored backdrops and props and varied other bits and pieces from past performances of *Camino Real* and *Streetcar Named Desire* and *Petrified Forest*. She told her people to bring everything, whether they thought they'd need it or not, and bring it fast. She ordered them out in full strength, not just the scenery painters, carpenters and prop people, but the stage hands, the lighting crew and even the costume and make-up teams. They could all help, including Kiki.

They swarmed to the location loaded with all the stuff that had been stashed away in the storeroom, including paints and tools, as thrilled to get their hands on an honest-to-God, real live television commercial as if they'd never looked down their idealistic noses on the entire medium.

An hour and a half after Daisy's phone call, they reported to their chief ready for a night of work. The art director from the advertising agency handed over the photos of the demolished location to Daisy who snapped her orders and deployed her forces throughout the long hours before dawn. Zip Simon, the art director and Bootsie stayed up all night watching, while the cast and crew drifted away to sleep. North coolly went to his hotel to have dinner and get a night's rest. The catering service was on duty all night long, and by sunrise the set was ready. A Monterey which had long vanished had reappeared, if not absolutely authentic in every detail, still echoing the period and the mood of the old photos. It was jerry-built and a strong breeze might have destroyed it—but, somehow, it existed. It was usable.

Exhausted, but too delighted with her success, and, by now, too interested in what was going on to leave, Daisy stayed throughout the shoot, understanding very little of what was happening. It was as different from a stage production as a stage production is from a basketball game. She watched the coffee-drinking rabble of yesterday become a crew such as she had never seen before, intimately connected to one another as members of a primitive clan, working together with the precision only enormous discipline can bring, more quietly expert than she had ever imagined technicians could be. They were all satellites of North, who controlled the set by the force of a hypnotic power, pleasure and displeasure shooting out from him as he rehearsed the actors to the constant accompaniment of asides to a girl who sat on a box seemingly chained to an enormous stopwatch which she wore around her neck.

"We have four seconds here," he said to her. "How many have I used?"

"Three and a half."

"Yell when I've got four."

As Daisy watched him, she realized that this man in his early thirties, tall, lean and tense, was a battered lion tamer of diehard toughness. He wouldn't be daunted by a cage of mixed rattlesnakes, porcupines and polar bears, to say nothing of lions. No matter what problems circled, prowling and growling, around him, North never put down his whip and chair, invisible though they might be, and once he began directing, every person on the set was convinced that his eye was on them at all times, even when he was looking through the camera.

The client group and the agency group stood at a respectful distance, glancing constantly at their watches, but drinking in the electric tension of the curses, the frenzy, the lightning flashes of temperament, the freely opened veins. They were in show biz, they thought, not realizing that as far as North was concerned, this had nothing to do with show biz and everything to do with advertising.

The crew combined alertness and stillness in equal combinations, as people do who are sure of their skills and aware of when they are needed and when not. The technical jargon Daisy heard was strange to her in spite of her knowledge of stagecraft, and many of North's directions to the actors sounded odd.

"Four seconds," Daisy muttered to Kiki, "what can you do in four seconds?"

"Sell cars," said Kiki smugly.

Over and over and over she heard North say, "Stand by . . . and . . . action!" The word "and" was drawn out almost unbearably. Many times it seemed to her that everything had gone perfectly, but he never seemed satisfied until, abruptly, he was. He coaxed, he warned, he encouraged, he grew taller, he grew shorter, he got violently angry, he became suddenly gentle and calm, he screamed for quiet in a terrifying voice and, seconds later, looking through the lens and talking to his cameraman, he was as loose as if he had been alone on the street. Once he caught her eye with a raking glance, unexpected and startling.

Pointing to the couple in modern dress about to get into the new Skyhawk, he said to them, "Now the intention here is that you're going to take her home and give her a zatch—I haven't been out myself since 1965, but am I wrong about the intention here?" Odd direction or not, the actors immediately grew into a couple in love when before they had only been a couple.

Everyone worked without a break, not even for lunch, because of the pressure to send the new Skyhawk back to Detroit. The auto carrier that would take the car to the cargo plane was delayed until the last possible second before the automobile, again hidden in its canvas covering, was carried away. Only then did North call a break.

Daisy expected that after lunch the set would become more relaxed, since they had the use of the vintage Skyhawk for as long as they needed it, but the tense time pressure was as strict as before. Time, on a commercial shoot, is always the enemy—there is never enough of it, and both North and Bootsie had to be back in New York for a production meeting with another client on the following afternoon.

Finally North said quietly, "Right, it's a wrap," and the technicians began to dismantle their equipment, the models vanished into the Winnebago with their attendants, and the large lights, cameras, sound equipment and other tools of the trade were quickly stowed away in the Cinemobile.

It was like the dismantling of a circus and Daisy felt sad as time turned back into an everyday beat, time which had been counted in seconds and half-seconds, all day long.

"Hey, they're leaving without saying goodbye," Kiki said with astonishment.

"No, they're coming over here," Daisy said. "How could they not say thank you?"

North and Bootsie, almost running, approached the two girls.

"Be sure to strike the set and make certain everything is back exactly as it was," North ordered.

"Uh—sure," said Daisy.

"Sorry, but we have a plane to catch," Bootsie said rapidly. "You were really great—Daisy, you'd make a terrific production assistant if you ever want a job."

"Thanks—but no thanks," Daisy answered.

"Come on, Boot, we haven't got time to talk," North snapped impatiently. "So long, ladies." He took Bootsie by the arm and turned her toward the waiting car. As they drove off Bootsie Jacobs said, "You could have been a little nicer to them—they really helped, for Christ's sake!"

"They wouldn't have been necessary if you'd done your job," North answered absently.

No one, but no one impresses him unless they get in the way of his blasted parade, Bootsie thought wrathfully, and then . . . watch out!

Four months later, in February of 1971, with graduation only four months away, Daisy received a letter from Anabel.

Daisy dearest,
    Isn't it frightful! I'm in such a state of shock at the news. Honestly, I know just how the Minister of Aviation felt when he spoke in the House last week— "never in my wildest dreams or nightmares did I dream it was as bad as all this." I can imagine how you feel, too—Rolls-Royce in receivership! It simply does not seem possible—only three months ago the government said that they were going to simply pour money into the company—but when they saw the books!! I've been wiped out, of course, financial idiot that I am—but I assume that Ram got your money out ages ago. I hate to say it but when he told me to sell I thought he was too young to change Stash's invest-

ments, but it's no good even thinking that way. Do you know what he put your money into? I detest asking a question like that but, darling Daisy, there's a reason. Although your father and I never married, I considered myself responsible for Danielle's upkeep and, from the income of the stock he left me, I've been paying her bills since he died. When the stock became worthless I went to see Ram. Daisy, I know what you're thinking but it was the only possible thing for me to do. I had to tell him . . . after all, she's his half-sister too. It was almost impossible to convince him that she existed. And then he refused to do anything! He said that if Stash had never seen fit to bother him with Dani he must not have wanted him to know about her . . . he even said that as far as he was concerned she simply wasn't real. She was no responsibility of his. And he's rolling in money . . . simply rolling! He categorically rejected contributing a shilling to her school bills. Forgive me for telling him, Daisy, but I was sure he'd help, fool that I was. I should have known how he'd react, but I had to try.

Anyway, I'm going to have to retrench severely. I'm selling Eaton Square and moving permanently to La Marée. With the few investments I still have and the sale of my paintings and the Fabergé animals there should be enough of a nest egg so that I can invest it in something safe and live off it for the rest of my life. Even a modest income would be enough, particularly if some of the friends who used to visit me will want to come and stay as paying guests. Well, darling, next summer I'll find out.

The problem isn't what's to become of me—of course I'll manage one way or another—but what will happen to Danielle?

The school has sent in their quarterly bill for what amounts to almost five thousand dollars in American money and I find that I simply can't put my hands on that sum. I just can't believe it! It's no more than I used to spend on underclothes without thinking twice. How our vanities catch up with us. But, oh, it was glorious while it lasted. Never forget that.

Now, to business. Can you take over some—in fact most—of the Queen Anne's bill? I do hope that Ram invested wisely for you? But enough of this. I've never *thought for so long or written so much about money in my life. It makes me fairly lightheaded—how can people stand to be bankers? And to think that I still must spend a whole afternoon with an estate agent about Eaton Square! I find I don't mind selling this house as much as I thought I would—the idea of living all year in La Marée is so appealing. You'll be coming at Easter, of course, my pet, won't you? Perhaps all the apple trees will be in bloom as they were last year . . . but that was an early spring.*

My dearest love always. Je t'embrasse très fort!

Anabel

Daisy read the letter over three times before it made complete sense to her. She hadn't bothered to look at a daily newspaper in weeks, and this was the first she had heard of the bankruptcy of the Rolls-Royce Company. Ram had never, in the letters she had read before she started throwing them away, again suggested that she sell her stock, but she had always assumed that she possessed more or less what the stock had been worth right after her father's death, when it had amounted to roughly ten million dollars.

Daisy realized with wonderment that she had not the faintest idea of where her money was. Even though she had cut off communication with Ram, she had remained in his power financially. What had he said in the letters she had found too distasteful to open?

Daisy went to her desk and wrote Ram a brief note asking for a complete statement of her financial position, and then wrote a much longer letter to Anabel saying how unhappy she was about the changes Anabel was going to have to make in her life, but assuring her that she must not worry about Danielle's future expenses. From now on, Daisy wrote, she would be responsible for her sister. It was out of the question that Anabel should beggar herself for Dani—her generosity had been already enormous. She'd had no idea where the money for Dani's bills was coming from or she would have taken them over long ago. And of course she understood why Anabel had told Ram. As for La Marée at Easter, she wouldn't dream of missing it.

She posted the two letters and rushed off to the playhouse where she was already a little late for a dress rehearsal of *Hamlet* performed entirely in mime and jazz dancing. All the parts were being played by females, and Elsinore had been relocated to the island of Lesbos.

Daisy felt a persistent uneasiness as she waited for Ram's reply, but she dismissed it and immersed herself in work. Five days later she received a cablegram.

HAVE WRITTEN THREE TIMES IN LAST YEAR FOR PERMISSION TO SELL YOUR STOCK. HAD NO REPLY SO ASSUMED YOU INSISTED ON HOLDING. UNFORTUNATELY, COMPANY IS NOW NATIONALIZED. STOCK WORTHLESS UNLESS GOVERNMENT REIMBURSES BUT DOUBTFUL SINCE YOU HELD COMMON STOCK NOT PREFERRED. HAVE ADVANCED FROM PERSONAL FUNDS MONIES FOR ALL YOUR EXPENSES FOR PAST FOURTEEN MONTHS SINCE ROLLS INCOME NOT SUFFICIENT. INTEND TO CONTINUE TO SUPPORT YOU. CONSIDER IT APPROPRIATE IN VIEW OF OUR RELATIONSHIP. R.A.M.

Daisy dropped the cable on the floor and ran to the communal bathroom. She felt as if someone had come upon her in her sleep and hit her head with tremendous blows. She reached a toilet stall just in time before she started to vomit. She hugged the chill bowl as if it were the last refuge on earth. After the final dry heaves had stopped she remained kneeling in the bathroom, mercifully empty of students, clutching the friendly porcelain. She felt that there was still an unexpelled mass in the back of her throat, a solid ball of disgust and panic, like some monstrous embryo clinging to her breathing passage as it might cling to a womb. Her aching stomach muscles tried to clench again but failed to dislodge the mass. There was nothing left, not even bile, to throw up. Her sense of life being safe and good had evaporated in the lethal gas of Ram's message. She felt as if she had fallen far down into one of those dark places, unbearably sad, filled with danger and threat and fear of the unknown, the places she had lived in for so long after her mother had disappeared, after Dani had been taken from her, when her father had died—all the great and sudden losses of her life seemed concentrated again in the news she had just received. All the victories she had won, all her stubborn refusals to be controlled, felt hollow and tawdry now that she knew Ram had been giving her everything she thought she had paid for with her own money. She was in his debt now, God help her, and her stock was worthless. Why hadn't he simply sold without her permission? As her trustee he could have done so and he must have known what was happening to Rolls-Royce. Was it possible that he had *let this happen* just to put her where she was now? She would never know, Daisy realized, and it really didn't matter. She *had to manage* somehow. With this thought her fighting spirit began to return. She stood up, her flesh and bones so sore that they seemed to be in conflict, and went to one of a row of washbasins to brush her teeth and splash her face with cold water. She met her eyes in the mirror and willed them to be undefeated, and they were. She left the bathroom and went to her room to think.

There were four more months until graduation and the chance to get a job. That meant, Daisy told herself, that she just wouldn't graduate—she didn't have the luxury of time. She had one asset and one only, the lapis egg which still sat in its box in the bottom of her chest of drawers, the egg Masha had given to her as she lay dying six years before, the egg Masha said that her father had given her mother when he found out she was pregnant. The time to sell the egg had come—it would buy at least a year, perhaps a little more, for Danielle.

A job. She knew enough about the theater to know that she stood almost no chance of finding employment except in an experimental playhouse which would pay almost nothing. The only time in the last four years that anyone had mentioned any other form of employment was last fall, when that woman commercial producer, Bootsie somebody, had told her she'd make a good production assistant. Whatever that was, precisely, it had to pay more than the theater. Get the name of the commercial company from Kiki or that nice fat man, Zip Simon, who worked for Mr. Kavanaugh, call what's-her-name, and ask for a job. What do I have to lose? thought Daisy. The worst they can say is no. And maybe they'll say yes. Even if they never did say thanks.

13

$\mathcal{T}$he catfood people called again," Arnie Greene, business manager of Frederick Gordon North's commercial studio, said hopefully.

"And?" North asked.

"This time it's for six spots, thirty seconds each, big, *big* budget. Easy to do—no way we couldn't make lots of very pretty money."

"How many times have I told you, Arnie? *No catfood!* There's no budget big enough to make me shoot that stuff. I can't stand the way it looks."

"And what should I tell Weight Watchers? They want us to bid on their new business."

"You can tell them to stuff it. I saw the story board they're going with—spaghetti, cheeseburgers and strawberry shortcake in drippingly edible closeups with a voice track saying that if you join Weight Watchers you can enjoy your favorite treats and *still* break the habit of eating fattening foods—and those sadistic bastards are going to run the spots at night, *after* dinner, just when fridge orgy time starts. I'm not against it on humanitarian grounds—I think the concept's basically bad and while I can choose, I choose not to do Weight Watchers."

Arnie Greene sighed mournfully. He was in charge of all financial transactions at the studio, and he turned down more work than North could possibly turn out without expanding his operation from its present size, but he still hated to send a potential client packing.

"Where's Daisy?" he asked, looking around the conference room.

"She's out nailing down the Empire State Building for the Revlon hairspray spot—then she's through for the week—it's Friday, remember?" North answered. "Why do you want her?"

"She's got the bills from the catering service. She took them home last night to check them, said we were being overcharged. Won't let me pay them until she found out where. Honestly, North, I think she's paranoid—she always says they're ripping us off on Jewish fish. I told her we *have* to give the clients smoked salmon for lunch—they come all the way in from Chicago, they *expect* smoked salmon. Four years now and she's still checking the bills."

"It keeps her off the streets," North said curtly. It irritated him, for no rational reason, to think that Daisy still had the determination and willingness to spend her free time worrying about bills after the exhausting days she put in on the job . . . it irritated him almost as much as the weekends she frequently managed to spend in the countryside enclaves of the horsy set. Leave it to Bootsie Jacobs to hire a production assistant who turned out to be some kind of White Russian princess with revoltingly classy friends. If she weren't so fucking good at her work, he'd never have given her Bootsie's job when it became available. But then, who would have thought Bootsie had it in her to get knocked up? And want to keep the brat? Of course she had been married ten years, so he guessed she was entitled.

"North," Arnie said, handing over two checks, "sign these please and just don't bother to look at them." North signed the two alimony checks grimly. Arnie went through the don't-bother-to-look-routine every month.

"Can you tell me why I married the two most beautiful models in New York and why they both turned out to be raving neurotics in less than a year and why I have to support them?"

"Why ask me, do I look like a shrink?"

"You look so much like the shrink I went to with the same questions that you could be his brother—probably are for all I know."

"Well—what'd he say?"

"I didn't wait around to find out."

"Why not?"

"He asked too many personal questions."

"Yeah, that would do it."

Frederick Gordon North was known simply as North because he wouldn't permit the use of his first two names, foisted on him by family-proud parents from old and comfortable Connecticut families, and Fred, Freddy, Rick, Ricky, and Gordy had all been ruled out as well. A timid movement at Yale to dub him Flash—which would have suited him best—had only lasted one day. His parents still called him Frederick, but he was North even to his brothers and sisters, who, in any case, only had occasion to use the name at Christmas and Thanksgiving since they were an unclannish family, of which he was the most unclannish member.

He had been a loner almost from birth, and throughout Andover and Yale he had been persuaded to perform only a minimum of the obligatory extracurricular activities. The first thing he ever set his solitary heart on belonging to was the Yale Graduate School of Drama. His goal was clear to him—he wanted to direct: Shakespeare, O'Neill, Ibsen, maybe even a little Tennessee Williams. But he had set his course without understanding his own inner pace. The mounting of a theatrical production takes many months, and North's viciously concentrated attention span demanded quicker results.

Soon after graduation he met a third-rate veteran commercial cameraman who was willing to try him out as director on a commercial with a budget so low that any profit that could be wrung out of it would have to come from using a nonunion crew and director, all at bargain-basement rates.

That first commercial, a thirty-second local spot for a chain of discount clothing stores, caught North as firmly as if it had been a chance to work with Lord Olivier at the Old Vic. He had found his métier, a medium that throbbed with a beat that matched his pulse, his heart and his inner eye. Now that he knew what he really wanted to do, remorselessly North jettisoned his baggage of the world's greatest playwrights and headed straight for Madison Avenue where he spent four years learning all the technical ropes at the knee of Steve Elliot, the dean of commercial directors, a violin-playing, bulldozer-driving, Renaissance man who, with his brother Mike, had been among the first commercial directors to get their cherished cameraman's cards back in the early 1950s. The Elliot brothers had founded Elliot, Unger and Elliot, a firm which later became EUE/Screen Gems, then and now the giant of the commercial-making industry.

At twenty-five, North went out on his own, living for the first six months on money he'd saved, hustling every contact he'd made at EUE, until a few small accounts came his way. By the time he reached the top he was only thirty. When Daisy went to work for him, she was barely nineteen and he was thirty-two, a scratchy, cantankerous, impatient perfectionist of extraordinary talent and equally astonishing charm, which he saved for the rare times he had unavoidable social contact with his most important clients, and the frequent times he had deliberate carnal contact with a long and lovely parade of women, two of whom he had had the bad judgment to marry. He was no more of a joiner in a marriage than he had been when his father had tried to get him to become a Boy Scout, but, fortunately, he had avoided having children, as Arnie Greene frequently reminded him when it came time to sign the alimony checks. "At least there's no child support, you should knock on wood."

Daisy, once she was assured that there would be no further problems with Mr. Jones, supervisor of the Deck of the Empire State Building, headed downtown to the SoHo apartment she shared with Kiki.

Something about the arrival of spring had put her in a reminiscent mood that even the subway ride couldn't modulate. She found it hard to believe that four years had passed since she had left Santa Cruz.

Bootsie Jacobs had answered her letter immediately. They not only needed another production assistant, they were desperate for one. When Daisy found out what the job entailed she realized that their desperation was permanent and well-deserved, since few people lasted more than two months in the incredibly demanding and underpaid job. However, she had had no choice. She was paid one hundred seventy-five dollars a week for the nonunion job at which she worked at least twelve hours a day, but it was enough to live on and still save money for Danielle's bills, provided that she lived on next to nothing, a style of life she had perfected until it had almost become an art form. Of course, without the thirty thousand dollars that she had received for the lapis lazuli Fabergé egg she could never have met the bills until she developed another source of income aside from her job. Thank God, thought Daisy, for kids on ponies.

She remembered how it had started. Jock Middleton, who had played polo with her father, had received a letter from Anabel asking him to keep an eye on Daisy in New York. He'd invited her out for a weekend with his family in Far Hills, a horse-crazed part of New Jersey which rightfully belongs in the Bluegrass country. Daisy had packed her riding clothes, just in case they had a mount for her, and spent a happy Saturday riding with a flock of Middleton grandchildren. At an elaborate dinner party that night, Mrs. Middleton had introduced her to everyone as Princess Daisy Valensky. On Sunday, when Daisy had made a sketch of the oldest Middleton grandson on his pony, as a thank-you present, she signed it as she had always signed her work, with a simple "Daisy."

A few weeks later she'd had a letter from Mrs. Middleton. The sketch had been so much admired that she wondered if Princess Daisy would consider doing one of a neighbor's ten-year-old-daughter, Penny Davis? Mrs. Davis was willing to pay five hundred dollars for a sketch, or six hundred and fifty for a watercolor. Mrs. Middleton made it plain that she was embarrassed to mention money to Prince Stash Valensky's daughter, but Mrs. Davis had insisted. Mrs. Middleton blushed to make such a commercial proposition, but her neighbor had just not given her a second's peace. Daisy had only to say no and she wouldn't be bothered again.

Daisy rushed to the phone to accept, wishing she could suggest doing it in oil and charging another hundred dollars. No, better not—she didn't have the money to buy oils and canvas.

Any well-trained, competent artist should be able to draw a horse, but there are special abilities involved in understanding the movements, the stance, the anatomical differences and the variations of color necessary to make one horse look entirely different from another. Daisy had been drawing and riding horses most of her life. As for the children, she'd drawn them too, by the thousands, during all those years of making drawings for Dani, and she'd taken advanced courses in portraiture at Santa Cruz. Her sketch of the Middleton grandson had revealed an innate and pronounced knack which was to give her equestrian portraits a lively quality of sympathy and immediacy.

When she arrived at the Davises, a larger and more luxurious Monticello, Daisy was introduced to Penny Davis, who was already dressed in her best riding clothes. Daisy took one look at the child's rigidly set face and apprehensive eyes.

"I thought we'd all have lunch together before you get started, Princess Valensky," Mrs. Davis said. "And you must be ready for a Bloody Mary after the trip out."

"That's awfully thoughtful, but what I'd really like to do first is ride with Penny," Daisy answered. She wasn't about to work with a model who not only was miserably shy but didn't want to have her portrait painted under any circumstances.

"But what about lunch?"

"We'll manage. Penny, why don't you put on some jeans and show me the stable?"

When the girl returned, looking a tiny bit less uncomfortable, Daisy whispered to her, "Is there a McDonald's near here?" Penny looked around quickly to see if her mother could hear. Out of the corner of her mouth, she confided, "It's only five miles if you ride across country. But I'm not allowed to go there."

"But I am. And you're my guest. Let's just git!" The little girl's eyes lit up as she glanced with surprise at Daisy.

"Are you really a princess?"

"Sure. But to you I'm Daisy."

"Do Princesses like McDonald's?"

"*Kings* like McDonald's. Come on, Penny, I'm having a Big Mac fit."

Penny led the way over fields and fences. Within ten minutes and double Big Macs, Daisy discovered that Penny thought portraits were dumb. Worse than that, who would want to have a picture of herself with braces on hanging around for the rest of her life?

"Penny, I promise, cross my heart, I won't paint your braces. In fact, if you want, I'll paint you the way you're going to look when they come off—with a gorgeous smile. But think of it this way: an equestrian portrait is as much a portrait of the horse as it is of the person. You'll have to sell Pinto in a year or two, the way you're growing, and now you'll always have a picture of her to remember her by. Hey, could you eat another of these—I'm having one. Good—maybe I can get them to give us extra sauce."

"They're all having trout in aspic for lunch at home."

"Ugh, ugh, ugh! Wonder what's for dinner?"

"Roast duck—it's going to be very fancy—she's invited practically everyone we know."

"Oh, well," said Daisy philosophically. "Duck's better than trout."

That afternoon, as the young girl posed, relaxed and willing, Daisy made dozens of sketches to pin down the natural, spontaneous gestures and characteristic expressions of Penny Davis. She also took many pictures with the Polaroid she'd borrowed from the studio. They would be used as visual aids for the watercolor she planned to complete at home. She blessed the classes in anatomy she'd taken as she carefully sketched Penny's hands holding the reins, and further blessed the natural limitations which surrounded an equestrian portrait, since they ruled out too great a variety of pose or attitude. She sketched lightly, without any tightness or stiffness, not trying for perfection, but for a feeling of the child in relationship to her pony.

On Sunday, as Daisy traveled back from the Davises' estate, driven home by their chauffeur, she reflected on the fact that Mrs. Davis, like Mrs. Middleton, had ceremoniously and importantly introduced her as Princess Daisy Valensky at the big, formal dinner party last night. After her four years as Valensky at Santa Cruz, Daisy had almost forgotten that she had a title. Obviously it was a business asset—in Horse Country, anyway. Since painting kids on ponies was probably the most commercial way in which she could use her talents, Daisy ground her teeth and resolved to milk the princess routine for every penny it was worth. When she had finished the watercolor of Penny Davis, she signed it in clear, careful lettering, "Princess Daisy Valensky." It meant six hundred and fifty dollars for Danielle.

Slowly, through word of mouth, after the Middleton sketch and Davis commission, Daisy got requests to paint other kids on ponies. Her prices rose steadily. Now, not quite four years later, Daisy was able to ask and get two thousand, five hundred dollars for a watercolor. These commissions, which had started to come just before the Fabergé money ran out, represented the difference between being able to support Danielle and being forced to try to get Ram to pay, any way she could. Daisy had never told Anabel where her money came from, because she didn't want her to know that she had been left penniless after the bankruptcy of Rolls-Royce. Nor did Daisy tell anyone at the studio why she spent so many weekends flying to Upperville, Virginia; Unionville, Pennsylvania; and estates near Keeneland, Kentucky. She knew they considered her to be a full-fledged member of the social, horsy set, but as long as she did her job, she didn't see that it was any business of theirs what she did with her own time. Of course, Kiki, who saw her working night after night to finish the watercolors, knew about her work, and in certain circles a portrait of one's child on a pony by Princess Daisy Valensky was quickly becoming a status symbol.

When Daisy had had to leave Santa Cruz to get a job, she finally told Kiki about Danielle. There was no other possible way to explain her leaving college a mere four months before graduation except by telling the truth—or part of it.

She remembered the scene as she had told the strange, sad story, the variety of expressions that crossed Kiki's winsome, urchin's face; disbelief, astonishment, sympathy, indignation and wonder replacing each other in quick succession. Daisy had anticipated the two questions she knew her friend would eventually ask when the reality of what Daisy was telling her finally struck home.

"But why *won't* Ram support Danielle?"

"It's a way to get at me. We had a serious and permanent quarrel over a family matter, and nothing can change that or make us friends. Believe me, it's final. He doesn't consider Dani his sister anyway—he's never even met her. It's out of the question."

"Then why won't you let me help?" Kiki asked, warned by Daisy's tone not to pry into the nature of the family quarrel.

"I knew you'd get around to that. First of all, I have to do it alone because it's going to be a permanent thing—even you, generous as you are, can't take on someone else's relative for an indefinite period. But I'm not too proud to borrow a couple of hundred dollars just until I get my first paycheck."

She hadn't expected Kiki's last reaction. "I'm leaving school, too—we'll go together," she proclaimed, when Daisy had finally managed to convince her that she wouldn't let Kiki support Dani on a regular basis.

"Never. No way. That's out! I refuse to be the reason why you don't get a diploma from *somewhere*. Your mother'd never forgive me. But I'll rent someplace that's big enough for the two of us and the minute you graduate I'll be waiting for you with open arms and half the rent bill—retroactive. It's only four months. Do we have a deal?"

"Christ, you're bossy," Kiki complained. "Can I pay for the furniture? At least?"

"Half of it."

"I assume it'll be Salvation Army."

"Unless you can get your mother to ship us some of her extra stuff—anyone who redecorates once a year must have leftovers. The idea is that we'll accept donations of *things*, just like any other deserving organization, but we won't take money—because that gives people a right to say what we *do*. Got it?"

"Can we take money on Christmas and birthdays?" Kiki asked wistfully.

"Definitely. And we never go out with anyone who doesn't pay for dinner. Dutch treat is out. Together, we'll bring back the fifties."

As Daisy climbed up the steps to their third-floor apartment in a shabby building on the corner of Prince and Greene Streets she sniffed the pervasive smell of fresh baking in the air. Cinnamon rolls today, she decided. SoHo, only fifteen years before, had been declared the city's number-one commercial slum. Now it was the boiling, self-conscious main outpost of Bohemia, a boom town for artists where the current dress code called for paint-encrusted overalls, whether, as Kiki remarked disdainfully, you had ever held a paintbrush or not.

But then Kiki had finally discovered how to cope with her preoccupation about the right way to dress in any given locale. Thanks to the timely death of her grandmother, she was rich enough in her own right to become the owner, producer, and permanent leading lady of her very own off-off-off Broadway theater, The Hash House. She was, in fact, the recognized Ethel Barrymore–Sarah Bernhardt of SoHo, and she dressed to suit whatever play she was currently mounting. Her latest production, *The Lament of the Pale Purple Faggot,* was keeping the theater comfortably full, especially on weekends when the up-towners came down to see what was going on in playland. Casting herself as the protagonist's only female confidante, Kiki had been drifting around for the last few weeks in an arrangement of a lavender leotard, pink tights, purple suede boots and a mauve feather boa, all of which suited her admirably.

Daisy unlocked the door and looked around. The apartment was empty. That meant that Kiki was probably still at the theater and Theseus was with her. He consented to spend the day lying on a bean-bag pillow at Kiki's feet or following her around the theater. He was only totally happy when Daisy came home, but it was impossible to have a lurcher on a set. The caterer's table would have been denuded before the first sleepy grip asked for a cheese Danish in the morning.

Kiki and Daisy's place in SoHo wasn't one of those enormous lofts that many artists had carved out of former cast-iron, palazzo-styled, industrial buildings. It was an apartment on a human scale in a shabby building that boasted a small art gallery on the first floor. But it was large: big enough to contain a rambling living room, three bedrooms, a studio for Daisy, a fairly large kitchen and two bathrooms which unfortunately seemed to still have their original plumbing. The style could only be called free-floating. At various times their apartment contained bits and pieces from the sets of Kiki's plays; odds and ends from the junk dealers of the neighborhood, and much fine furniture from Grosse Pointe. The only constants were a fireplace, Daisy's working materials, decent-enough beds and the mural with which one of their friends had been inspired to decorate a living-room wall: a pastoral scene featuring Theseus engaging in various criminal acts in a series of farmyards. Neither Daisy nor Kiki had the instincts of a homemaker, and when they weren't invited out to eat—a rare situation—they bought something from a local delicatessen for dinner. When they bothered about breakfast, they snatched it at a little street stand right around the corner which sold a doughnut and coffee for fifty-five cents, and, mysteriously, featured fresh coconut.

Daisy flopped down with a sigh of relief on the latest couch, brown satin and agreeably overstuffed, that had recently arrived from Kiki's mother. Every time she sent them a new shipment they promptly sold their old furniture. Eleanor Kavanaugh found it strange that they'd been able to absorb such *quantities* of objects, but she said, sniffing in disapproval, she supposed Kiki needed them for *that* theater. . . . Thank heaven Grandmother Lewis hadn't lived to know what had happened to her money. Although, of course, if she *had* lived, there wouldn't have been—oh, never mind, just don't tell her all the ghastly details.

"She's actually thrilled," Kiki declared. "I know that she boasts about me at the country club—she calls me a patroness of the arts."

Daisy roused herself from her comfortable place on the couch long enough to take off her baseball jacket. She'd bought it right after going to work as a production assistant for North. She'd appeared on that first morning in her newest jeans, freshly pressed, her best beige cashmere turtleneck sweater and a checked hacking jacket that had been made for her in London years before.

"Oh no!" hissed Bootsie, when she saw Daisy arrive.

"What's wrong?" Daisy asked, alarmed.

"Christ—do you have to look so much like old money?"

"But it's my oldest jacket."

"That's the point, dummy. It reeks of that good green stuff. And besides doing your job, you have to spend as much time as possible getting friendly with the crew so that they'll tell you everything you need to know, something I positively do not have the time to do. You're going to be pestering them with questions from morning to night and you're going to be dependent on their good will. They're the sweetest guys in the world if they think you need help, but no way do you look like a working girl who needs a job. That jacket says that you ride, you've ridden for years, you have better riding clothes somewhere else, and you're probably still using them. And they're hip to that. So get rid of it!"

"But *you* look very put together and expensive," Daisy objected.

"I'm the producer, kiddo. I can wear whatever I want."

Now that Daisy had Bootsie's job, which paid four hundred dollars a week, she still wore the baseball jacket from time to time. It reminded her of those first frantic, panicked months when, just as Bootsie predicted, she floundered around from grip to gaffer, from the sound man to the assistant cameraman, from the hair stylist to the set designer, from the prop man to the script supervisor, asking what now she realized must have been incredibly stupid questions, and writing down all the answers in a little notebook. Her jacket had won her friends by its mere existence, developed dialogues, created innumerable opportunities to join in mutual nostalgia for the lost team. It had made her one of the boys at a time when she desperately needed to be one of them.

She looked at her watch. In one hour she would be picked up for dinner at La Grenouille, followed by the opening of the new Hal Prince musical. Her hostess, Mrs. Hamilton Short, lived on a large estate in Middleburg, and she had three children, none of whom Daisy had been asked to paint...yet. Cinderella time, she thought, and reluctantly got up and went to her room to start the transformation from working stiff to princess. Or rather, from working stiff to working stiff, if the truth were known.

Ram was thirty. He lived in a perfect house on Hill Street, only a step away from Berkeley Square, a house decorated by David Hicks in severe bachelor sumptuousness. He was a member of White's Club, far and away the most exclusive and difficult to enter of British gentlemen's clubs, and he was a member of Mark's Club, that private restaurant which is the haunt of the most languid and most privileged of the young elite of London. His suits, which cost nine hundred dollars each, were made at H. Huntsman and Sons, the best tailor in England, as were all his riding clothes. He was counted as one of the best shots in the British Isles and owned a pair of shotguns, made to his measurements, from James Purdey and Sons, a firm that had existed in the time of George III. It had taken three years before they were completed, at fifteen thousand dollars the pair, and they were, Ram thought, well worth waiting for. His shoes and boots came, of course, from Lobb's and cost from two hundred and fifty-five dollars a pair upward, depending on the style and the leather. He collected rare books in a major way and avant-garde sculpture in a minor way. He wore white silk pajamas piped in a sober burgundy, heavy silk dressing gowns and shirts made from the finest Sea Island cotton, all made to order at Turnbull and Asser. He considered Sulka vulgar. He never left the house without his umbrella from Swaine, Adeney, Brigg and Sons. It was made of black silk and the handle and shaft were carved out of a single piece of exceptional hickory. He drew the line at a hat—perhaps in ten years, but not now, except for fishing, riding and yachting, and his dark hair was cut in the privacy of one of the ancient wooden rooms at Trumper on Curzon Street. He dined out every night, except on Sunday.

Ram's name appeared with frequency in those sugary columns about society written by "Jennifer" for *Harper's* and *Queen* magazine. Jennifer invariably described him as "the notably handsome and totally charming Prince George Edward Woodhill Valensky." He also often was mentioned in Nigel Dempster's purposefully bitchy column in the *Daily Mail*, where he was sometimes called "the last, dare we hope, of the White Russians," although Ram had made it a point not to join the Monarchist League run by the Marquess of Bristol. He had no interest in a group he considered fundamentally frivolous, nor did he care to rub elbows with archdukes in exile, who, even if they might be cousins, would almost surely prove to be needy. His business sense had led him to multiply his fortune many times. Ram was a full partner in an investment trust, Lion Management, Ltd., which had had impressive success in supervising the placement of large amounts of money from the pension funds of trade unions and corporations in highly imaginative and productive international investments.

If he had wanted to spend a weekend at one of the country estates which still, in spite of taxes, exist in Great Britain, Ram had but to pick up a phone and call any one of dozens of the young lordlings he had known at Eton. An equal number of the most spirited and desirable young beauties of 1975 would have invited him to their beds with enthusiasm, for Ram was one of that small group of rich and wellborn young men whose name appeared on every list of the Most Eligible Bachelors in England.

However, his status in British society had nothing to do with his money or his title. It rested on the one indispensable thing he had never even bothered to covet during his youth—land. And the land came through his mother's family, the family he had barely considered as he grew up. His mother was the only child of an untitled family, the Woodhills of Woodhill Manor, in Devon; quiet squires who had lived in one spot since before the Norman Conquest, looking down their noses, with pastoral certainty, at all parvenus, whether they were recently created earls whose titles didn't go back further than the eighteenth century, or merely merchant princes whose businesses had made England great in the Victorian era. As far as the Woodhills were concerned, they were all "fearfully recent" people.

The important thing about Valensky, everyone agreed, was that, when his grandfather died, he had inherited Woodhill Manor and the nine hundred acres of farmland that went with it. It was the ownership of this small piece of England that put Ram on the same lists as H.R.H. Prince Michael of Kent; Nicholas Soames, grandson of Sir Winston Churchill; the Marquess of Blandford, who would one day become the twelfth Duke of Marlborough; and Harry Somerset, heir to the Duke of Beaufort. Without Woodhill Manor and its pleasant fields, Ram's fortune and title would have always been just a bit *foreign,* but with Woodhill backing them up with the reassuring solidity of county status, they could be appreciated fully.

Ram went to his office in the City every day and worked hard. He returned home on foot, considering the walk as necessary exercise, changed for dinner, went to the entertainment of that particular evening, drank little, came home at a reasonable hour and went to bed. He rarely picked up his phone to arrange a country weekend, nor did he often ask for admittance to any young woman's bed. When he did it, he never asked a second time, not wishing to encourage bothersome attachments or raise false hopes. If he had had a cat, he would have kicked it.

When he reached his thirtieth birthday, Ram decided he must consider the idea of marriage to someone suitable. Not immediately but eventually. Looking around White's one night, when he'd taken a partner there for dinner, he'd noticed how different the club's atmosphere was from the busy, cheerful lunchtime scene. Only a handful of tables were occupied, many of them by solitary, older men who were far more interested in their wine and food than struck him as entirely decent. Ram didn't care for that fate. He began to consider the available crop of possible wives in the intense, humorless, practical manner that fit his outward demeanor.

Ram knew perfectly well that eligible as he was, he was not really liked. He didn't know why and he considered it of little importance. Some men spent their time being liked, others had better things to do. He was, however, highly and widely *respected,* and that, he felt, was the important thing, the *major* thing.

When Daisy's picture appeared in *Vogue* or any of the other publications, English, French and American, which kept an occasional eye on her horsy weekend parties, Ram looked at them with bitter disapproval. He felt absolute disgust at her job with North, working in a field he considered low, common and contemptible. Her social life seemed, to him, to be devoid of discrimination. Whenever any of the people he knew questioned him about her, he took pains to inform them that she was only a half-sister, with no English blood, and that he knew nothing and cared less about her private life. If it were not for the dreams about Daisy, dreams of love; hopeless, endless, devouring, destroying, never diminishing love, that tormented him ceaselessly, week after week, year after year, he might almost have managed to believe what he told his acquaintances. How he wished she were dead!

14

$\mathcal{C}$onference rooms are, almost by definition, designed to impress, but few of them were as explicit, Daisy thought, as that of the Frederick Gordon North Studio. It always amused her to look around and appreciate its purposefully spare and unornamented severity, its deliberately unemphatic and austere whitewashed brick walls and bare wooden floors lacquered in shining black. No one of any sensitivity could fail to be susceptible to the astringent luxury of the chrome Knoll chairs covered in pewter suede and the ascetic sweep of the huge, bare, oval conference table of white marble. From his place at the table, North could operate a concealed console of pushbuttons that signaled to the projectionist in the booth outside, telling him when to darken the room, when to lower the screen from the ceiling and when to roll film, a device which rarely failed to make even the most sophisticated clients sit up and pay attention. The conference room was on the top floor of a three-story building which had once been an abandoned music school in the East 80s, between First and Second avenues. Seven years ago North had bought it and converted it into one of the few privately owned commercial studios in the city. The first and second floors formed one huge sound stage which could be arranged in a thousand ways. Only the top floor was used for offices. North also owned his own cameras, lights and equipment. Since the vast majority of commercial directors had to include the cost of rental of studio space and equipment when they bid on a job—and most advertising agencies asked for at least three bids on each assignment they award—North was able to underbid on almost every commercial he went after, and still make a larger profit than his competitors despite his high fee.

Now, in the fall of 1975, six months after the hairspray commercial had been shot, an important meeting was being held in the conference room. Before the average commercial job, North usually met only with Daisy and Arnie Greene, but today he had insisted that all of his key employees be present for the first planning session of the Coca-Cola Christmas commercial.

By now Daisy knew the people gathered around the table so well that they felt almost like extensions of herself. There was Hubie Troy, the free-lance scenic designer with whom North worked so often that he might just as well have been on staff; Daisy's two young male production assistants, both recent Princeton graduates who would learn, or try to learn the business, and then go on to something which paid better; Alix Updike, her assistant for wardrobe and casting, a tall, quietly dressed and reserved girl, who used to be the lingerie editor at *Glamour;* and Wingo Sparks, the twenty-nine-year-old, full-time cameraman, in his Ivy League, unpressed duck trousers and splotched tennis sweater which was unraveling in six places. Daisy was sure he'd plucked out the threads himself.

Wingo was a Harvard graduate, the son of one top cameraman and the nephew of another. Had it not been for these family connections he wouldn't have been able to enter the cameraman's union, as tightly controlled as any medieval guild. He'd served as an assistant cameraman to his uncle for the necessary five years before getting his own union card. North infinitely preferred working with young men because they were receptive to even the wildest of his innovative ideas, and although, as the owner of his own business, he was entitled to operate a camera himself, without a union card, he disliked being responsible for all technical considerations in the heat of filming, while he had to concentrate on the actors and an overview of the entire set.

Daisy's eyes rested with affection on Arnie Greene, the business manager, who still found it hard to believe that after working most of his life for EUE with its four hundred employees he was now part of a "boutique" operation like North's. However, many of the top directors in the business preferred to work in small, compact shops, and although Daisy knew that Arnie hated the term "boutique," a word that was totally inappropriate for what was a mini-movie studio, it was used by the entire industry.

Finally, Daisy considered the flamboyantly elegant figure of Nick-the-Greek, North's full time "rep" who worked on commission getting new business. Nick was, to Daisy's knowledge, the only rep in the city who had found his way into the advertising business via a spitball. In the mid-1960s, when the big advertising agencies were each fielding a baseball team, and competing ferociously against each other, a copy writer at Doyle, Dane Bernbach had heard of a Puerto Rican high-school kid from the Barrio who was the best pitcher north of 125th Street. He'd given him a token job at the agency after school just to secure him for the team. But Manuel took one shrewd look at the agency business and liked it a lot better than any possible future in Spanish Harlem. The tall, flashingly handsome teenager baptized himself Nick-the-Greek and here he was now, earning over one hundred thousand dollars a year, wearing seven-hundred-dollar suits and drifting over to "21" for lunch every day, catching top jobs as easily as a lizard catches flies on his tongue. He could handle clients as carefully as any mahout ever handled a royal elephant during a lion hunt in India.

Now, just as North was about to call them all to order, Nick took the floor.

"*Compañeros* all—I have here the results of a new Gallup poll," he said, taking out a clipping from the *New York Times* and brandishing it at them.

"Can it, Nick," Arnie begged, knowing that when Nick-the-Greek got started, time got wasted.

"Wait! You don't understand. This concerns all of us, Arnie. Those of you who suffer from Jewish Guilt or Italian Shame or Wasp Resignation—come to order, *por favor*, and pay close attention. This poll concerns honesty and ethics in various professions as perceived by a cross section of the American people."

"That has *nothing* to do with Coke, Nick," said North, impatiently. "So why don't you just go away and hustle? Haven't you got some hungry, rich, potentially profitable client to take to lunch? *Vámonos*—we've got work to do."

"Not until I give you good tidings" said Nick, who, like all reps, made it a point of honor to be far more grandiose than the working stiffs for whom they labored. The reps of

New York, a mafia of superslick, ultra-fashionable sales-men, consider themselves to be to the actual commercial makers as Russian wolfhounds are to a pack of mon-grels.

"Here it is—clergymen, you'll be thrilled to hear, rate highest in the poll. Doctors and engineers come next. Out of twenty professions, *twenty,* the *next to last* rating is given to something called 'advertising practitioners.' That means us, *compañeros,* boys and girls included. Forty-three percent of the whole, fucking American public gave us a very low, repeat, *very low* rating for, and I quote, 'honesty and ethical standards.' The only people they rate lower than us are *car salesmen!* We even rate lower than state officeholders! Don't any of you guys feel we should protest? March on Washington, take out ads to say how clean, upstanding, patriotic and plain, down-home good we are? I don't think we should sit here and let them dump on us. Have you people no pride? Nor moral indignation? Don't you give at least a little, tiny shit? This can't be allowed to go unchallenged." His faultless teeth gleamed in his swarthy face, as he stood there, mockingly listening to the burst of hooting, catcalls and derisive whistles that filled the room.

"Nick, for a man who suffers from Greek Fire, when he's never been to Athens, you'll have to muster the indignation for all the rest of us. Out! The headwaiters of the world are waiting eagerly for you," North said firmly.

As the rep left, Arnie Greene said aggrievedly, "If doctors rate so high, how come there are so many mal-practice suits?"

"Nobody pays attention to Gallup polls anyway." For a second North's wily grin appeared. "Forget it Arnie. Now that Mr. Wonderful has boogied off, let's talk advertising for a change. And I'm warning you, anyone who isn't taking notes will regret it. This is a ninety-second commer-cial, and the story board makes a Max Rhinehardt produc-tion look like batshit. Not only that, Luke Hammerstein is going for humor, and they're not even going to show the product—which makes the whole thing different from what anyone else is doing."

"Not show the product?" Arnie Greene asked, in such astonishment that he squeaked.

"Nope—not show it and not *mention* it for one whole incredible *minute and a half!* Then, at the very end, we'll hear Helen Hayes saying, 'No matter how your family spent the night before Christmas, Coca-Cola wishes you wonderful holidays all year round.' "

"Did you say humor?" Daisy asked.

"Yup—Luke calls this the 'Flip Side of Christmas,' and he is seriously nervous about his idea. Luke talked Coke out of going with a big montage of Christmas dinners all over America, very mixed ethnic, your standard Mid-American big-yawn time, but Luke managed to sell them this—haven't I always said he was the best creative director in the world?"

"Yeah—but the two of you don't usually work together. You fight all the time," Daisy murmured, still dubious.

"True." North gave her a disapproving look for her interruption. "Luke *is* my close friend, but he has the conviction, unfortunately shared by most agency people, that the *concept* is what sells the product and that the concept begins and ends with the agency. As far as they're concerned, all a director does is bring the concept to life. I say it's both the concept *and* the way I make it make it work—my taste level, if you'll excuse the expression. That's why we fight. I want my share of the credit, Luke wants his share, and unfortunately together they add up to a hell of a lot more than a hundred percent. However, this commercial is a clear-cut case. He needs my help. And he knows it! With the story board they've got here it's either going to be a mild giggle or a fucking classic." The sharp planes and angles of North's face, his nose which ended so abruptly, even his freckles, all seemed to quiver with eagerness. North could hear the roar of the crowd under the circus tent, he was getting ready for the moment when he'd go into the cage and show the monsters who was boss. Daisy had seen him like this before, many times, but rarely had she seen him so excited by a challenge.

"May one ask what the 'Flip Side of Christmas' is?" asked Wingo, in his usual cheeky drawl.

"It's the shit that really goes down—thirty seconds backstage at a grade-school Nativity play, thirty seconds of a family of eight trying to get into a car meant for five small people, loaded with bulky presents, skis, what-have-you, all on their way to Christmas dinner at grandmother's, and last, thirty seconds of the sheer, hideous trauma of decorating the goddamned tree and everything that can go wrong—beginning to get the picture? And soft, soft sell—

Coke doesn't want to be hustling during the CBS Christmas special, so that, Arnie, is why we don't show the product."

"Is any of this location?" asked Hubie, who was already sketching rapidly on the pad he always carried.

"No, thank God, we're doing it all in the studio. Hubie, you've got not one, not two, but three—count them—*three-walled* sets to build. Nobody's seen three-walled sets used in a year, so get lost, you know what you have to do—here's a Xerox of the story board. I want everything middle-class but nice, and authentic, so fucking authentic you can smell the Christmas tree, smell the kids backstage, even smell that car with too many people in it."

As Hubie left, North fixed what was left of his audience with a stern eye and continued. "Daisy, you and Alix pay attention. Casting is of major, major importance in this—you know what the Coke commercials usually look like—everybody totally all-American, too many teeth, so much blond hair you could repopulate half of Scandinavia with the models—I don't want that. This is going to be different—we're not selling Coke to make you popular or happy, we're selling all that funny-awful crap that happens at Christmas, and telling everybody that maybe they should just laugh at it. So don't cast all-American Prom Queen. Most people get depressed enough at Christmas just seeing too much gorgeousness. For the kids' Nativity-play scene, I don't want little Jamie from Ivory soap or little Rusty from Crest toothpaste, I want real kids, nearsighted, fat, pimply, snot-nosed—cast sideways, not straight ahead, cast *bent*, as bent as you can get. Don't give me those looks. You think I don't know how much harder it's going to make the job? Shit, ladies, if a kid can't sit still, concentrate and follow directions, it's home-movie time. That's a chance I'm willing to take because this has to look like a real Christmas play in a real place—not TV-commercial heaven."

"North," Daisy asked suspiciously, "is this *all* in the story board—you're sure the client wants bent kids? Coke *always* goes for more-beautiful-than-life people."

"Daisy, just do me one small favor? Stop trying to second-guess me," he snapped, thoroughly annoyed. "This story board calls for a dozen kids, good mix, three black, five white, all colors of hair, two Oriental and two Chicano. On the other thirty-second scenes you need nine people for the tree-trimming episode and eight for the family in the car, plus a dog, a really big, awful-looking one—a crummy, slobbery, hairy dog . . . not a cute one . . . also a baby, nine months old. Get me the quietest babies in the world—remember we can't keep them under lights for long, so we may need a dozen in reserve. Check it out. But bring me just one familiar face and I'll tear your heads off! This is going to be the Dickens *Christmas Carol* of Christmas commercials."

Arnie Greene rolled his eyes to heaven. He knew what could happen when North got really excited about a job. No matter how he insisted that he was in advertising, not show business, they might go over budget to get just exactly what he wanted and he wouldn't be satisfied with a millimeter less. He didn't know what the words "good enough" meant. Well, he owned the business and this year they'd net enough so he was entitled to play a little.

"Wingo," North turned to the young cameraman. "There're three Hollywood studios in town now shooting movies. You may have trouble getting the crew we want, so get off your ass and start phoning. Tell 'em it's four days work, starting ten days from today."

"Four days—since when can't we do ninety seconds in three?" Wingo objected.

"With kids and dogs and babies? We'll run over—it's inevitable. And if you say three days they might have other jobs on the fourth—how'd you like to lose your crew before you finish?"

"The thought," said Wingo, "is not attractive."

"So why are you still here?"

"Excellent question," he said cheerfully, rising from his seat. "It all sounds easier than it's going to be, North, but at least Luke didn't ask us for the 'Robert Altman look'—not, of course, that you couldn't give it to him."

Before Wingo reached the door, North caught him with a last goad. "Wingo, young man, I hear from my secretaries that that lady of yours named Maureen has been calling you every ten minutes. Why don't you just throw it into her and get her off our back?"

"Sorry, but no time for social chatter this morning, boss," said Wingo, closing the door quietly behind him.

"That boy will go far," North said in satisfaction. "I like his fucking nerve."

Sure you do, Daisy thought balefully, in a man. But let a woman try it and you wouldn't merely threaten to tear her head off, you'd cut her heart out and eat it for breakfast.

"Daisy," North said, "tomorrow, we go to the agency for a meeting with Luke and his people. Do you think you could try to look like a lady, or at least a female?" He shot an unmistakable glance of disapproval at Daisy's habitual working costume.

"I'll make every effort, but I can't guarantee it—not on what you pay me," Daisy retorted. It was a never failing source of irritation that although she was the "producer" of the commercials, and in charge of coordinating every detail of every shoot, her job was nonunion and she was paid less for working more hours than anyone else in the studio. North ignored her remark, as he always did, refusing to acknowledge the fact that Daisy's clothes made good sense.

Soon after she had learned her trade she discovered that since someone was always looking for her to solve a problem, her jeans and work shirt made her difficult to spot in the denim-clad multitude of the crew. She had worked out an outfit that had three virtues: it was cheap, practical and highly visible. In cold weather she wore U.S. Navy, World War II, ordinary seaman's pants with their complicated set of thirteen buttons and their sturdy fabric. In summer she wore white Navy bellbottoms. To go with these basic trousers she had a dozen boys' Rugby jerseys in the boldest stripes and brightest colors she could find. In the huge, grubby confused studio she always wore tennis shoes and thick white socks, and braided her hair into one fat pigtail that fell over one shoulder, but at least it stayed out of her face.

If it's ladylike you want, North, she thought, I'll give you ladylike till your fillings fall out. The meeting ended while Daisy was planning her look for tomorrow—the 1934 Mainbocher suit, she thought, high heels, a tight chignon and *gloves*, you rotten bastard.

No matter how she railed at North in her mind, Daisy never failed to be astonished as he unpacked one fresh idea after another from the inexhaustible stock he seemed to possess, closely folded in his mind. His highest praise after a complicated, difficult commercial had been completed was to say to her, "It'll probably work," yet, for these three words, like a horsewoman trying out for the Olympic jumping team, she was game to attempt any fence, no matter how high. She could understand, she told herself in an attempt at fairness, why so many models insisted on telling her how devastatingly, divinely attractive her boss was, but then they didn't know him as she did. How could they begin to imagine the hardness of the man, the lack of warm humanity? His brilliance gleamed, but with a cold light. Nevertheless Daisy was unable to keep herself from trying to please him in her dedication to her job. As she had mastered her skills over the past years she took a craftsman's pleasure in her work, in each full, clean, well-organized day of shooting, the details of which, without her, would never have come together. She gloried in the flashes of inspiration that enabled her to solve the inevitable emergencies that plagued any shoot. With all modesty, she knew she was very, very good at what she did. Damn him, if only, just once, he'd *admit* it!

It is not often that the creative people who make television commercials have a chance to break the rules. Normally they are limited, almost entirely, to working in a world in which moldy grout can ruin a woman's life, while at the same time, perfectly white teeth can guarantee her love and happiness; a world in which her husband's morning is destroyed by a weak cup of coffee yet his virility can be validated by the brand of beer he drinks; they inhabit a cosmos in which thick, bouncy hair is life's dearest treasure and moist underarms are a constantly lurking menace; a territory in which best friends exist only to make critical remarks, and the choice between one kind of tampon or another is the difference between a carefree, athletic existence or being haunted by relentless anxiety. It's a threatening world in which the only real hope is the right kind of life insurance or a new set of steel-belted radials; a world of unending physical effort in which perfectly nice women are given life sentences in which they must produce immaculate floors, pristine toilet bowls, and even impeccable laundry; a world in which the people who depend on iron supplements to give them vitality barely look old enough to vote, in which the best filled medicine cabinet is certain to lack that one particular preparation which will make pain and head colds not just bearable but almost enjoyable. When this world isn't scary, it is frustratingly filled with too-healthy people having impossibly delightful fun in far away places, all thanks to an after-shave lotion or the right eye make-up. In advertising land it's quite all right to use obscenity to sell cigarette lighters—they couldn't dare mean anything dirty by "Flick my Bic," could they? But bra ads can't show women wearing bras, navels don't exist, and a pregnant woman may never seem to have the desire for physical contact with a man, not even her husband. There is even a regulation preventing a woman from sucking her own forefinger on camera. Singing cats can sell cat food better than any other commercial in history and creative advertising men write their copy in a cold sweat of fear and angst, not knowing whether a new idea will make them a hero or get them fired. With ten-second commercials becoming more and more popular, with research showing that viewers don't remember commercials that contain more than one single message, and with prime *seconds* on television costing hundreds of thousands of dollars, the opportunity to make expensive mistakes continues to multiply and the pressure to play it safe grows.

Luke Hammerstein had persuaded his bosses to go with his intuition on the Coca-Cola Christmas commercial, and intuition could mean disaster. If anyone had ever told Luke Hammerstein, when he was a wild, brilliant graduate of the wild, brilliant School of Visual Arts on 23rd Street in New York City that one day he would routinely send his most original ideas off to be tested in front of a carefully chosen target audience at Audience Survey, Inc., *before* he elected to use them or not, he would have sneered in outrage. But that was in the early 1960s when boy wonders in Edwardian clothes were grabbed up by the big agencies and started as assistant art directors when they were just out of school, the free-spending, innovative, let's-build-an-igloo-in-the-Mojave-Desert-and-see-if-it-melts days of commercials. Many of the other boy wonders didn't survive into the tighter-money, harder-sell days of the 1970s, but just as Luke had seen the change in the spirit of commercials coming long before it happened, he had traded in the poetically dandified elaborations of his attire for severely tailored suits with matching vests, started to wear solid blue shirts with starched white collars and French cuffs, begun to sport a stickpin in his dark, plain tie, and grown the perfectly trimmed Van Dyke beard which lent the final touch of authority to his aesthetic features. The distinguished aura of a young Oxford don replaced the graces he had cultivated in his early days as he progressed, in an amazing ten years, from assistant art director to art director to art supervisor and finally to creative director, with fifty people working under him, and eighty million dollars of annual billing under his supervision. Luke Hammerstein, only son of a conservative German-Jewish investment-banking family, was a superstar on Madison Avenue, even if his mother—who thought all advertising unnecessary and common—would never believe it.

Luke knew, from the beginning, that if an art director is ever going to advance in the agency business he has to be more than an art director; he has to also be a source of original ideas, a copy writer, a salesman and an expert on media and research.

Luke was in the center of the creative revolution when the power in the agencies passed from the people who created the words to the people who created the pictures. He had risen to a position of enormous power. But no power on Madison Avenue can survive unless it sells the product. The chance to do a Coca-Cola commercial without having to sell the product left Luke light-headed with the sheer freedom of it, and as antsy as he'd ever been.

Luke was almost never present at the shoot of one of his ordinary commercials, but during the four long days it took to finish the Christmas commercial, he showed up at North's studio every day, accompanied by the account supervisor, the assistant account supervisor, the copy writer and the art director, all of whom had been involved in the working out of Luke's commercial before he ever truly believed he could get the client to go for it. His agency group arrived no earlier than 10:45 A.M. although the cast and crew's call was for 8:00. Wise to the ways of commercial makers, Luke knew that the first take couldn't possibly take place before 11:00. In the words of one advertising immortal discussing the first three hours of every working day, "We shoot a commercial the way we used to build pyramids . . . everything is improved except the equipment . . . it's two guys carrying things on their backs, like over the Burma Road . . . you pull and you push."

The clients, the men from Coke, were there in force, too. Sometimes as few as six, invariably, just before lunch, as many as twelve. Although Daisy had been involved in dozens of shoots where the agency and client contingents —the "hungry worriers" as North called them—outnumbered the commercial makers, this time the cast, crew and observers were so numerous that the big studio was strained as it had never been strained before.

Looking back, after it was all over, Daisy couldn't be sure what had been, for her, the high point of the whole enterprise. Was it her canny method of casting kids who looked "real" but were actually professional models? She and Alix had spent four days searching out those unfortunate child models who'd had to stop work because of broken limbs, the early onset of acne, acute obesity problems, missing teeth, braces, growing out of their cuteness —even a month could do it—and just plain discipline difficulties, kids who were considered troublemakers. She winnowed out a gang of authentic misfits, none of whom could have sold a single box of cereal, no matter how sugar coated. These rejects provided enough difficulty on the set to convince North that they were normal, but without their foundation of professional training, the Nativity scene could never have been shot, not just in the agonizing day and a half it eventually took, but not in a week or perhaps not in a month.

Or was the best part, she asked herself, the satisfaction she had in casting Theseus as the dog in the car scene? Since North had wanted a difficult dog, Daisy reasoned there was no reason why she shouldn't make the money which would otherwise have gone to a recognized dog model. It came to her share of two months rent and, as usual, Dani's expenses had left her with no money to spare. She enlisted Kiki as dog wrangler for a day, with strict instructions.

"Keep him on the leash at all times until North signals for him. That'll be when the family's finally all stuffed into the car—one of the kids is going to whine, 'We forgot my dog.' Then let him go."

North inspected Theseus superciliously. "Where did you find that beast, Daisy? I've never seen anything like him before."

"Not to worry, he comes highly recommended."

"But I wanted a more *annoying* dog, something really shaggy. Something sloppier," he complained.

"This dog is guaranteed to be annoying," Daisy assured him. Since she had carefully hidden tiny bits of raw sirloin in various pockets of the clothes worn by all the actors in the scene, clothes she had chosen for the fact that they had pockets that buttoned, she had total confidence in Theseus's performance. With his hunting blood at boil he'd be all over those unfortunate people, loose in a lurcher's potential paradise.

Theseus didn't let her down. Take after take, he bounded into the packed car and wormed his way around the eight "family" members, poking his nose into their most private places, wagging his tail in their outraged faces and amorously pawing all over them in an unceremonious delirium of confusion and quest. All around was the smell of meat—but where was it? At the end of each take, Kiki dashed in with the leash to lead him out, slipping him a piece of meat from a Baggie full of beef tidbits which Daisy had given her, so that Theseus wouldn't get too frustrated—never enough to satisfy him but just enough to keep his appetite at its height.

By the middle of the day North said in admiration, "That's the worst behaved mutt I've ever seen in my life. He's driving them up the wall—perfect, Alix, perfect!" Naturally, thought Daisy, he doesn't even give me credit for casting my own dog, the son-of-a-bitch! North was even more pleased when the model playing the mother of the family developed a violent allergy to Theseus and couldn't stop sneezing.

"Write it in," he told the hovering copy writer. And for the next twenty-nine takes, between constant sneezes, the woman had to say, "You *know* that dog makes me sneeze!" and the impossible teenage son had to reply, scornfully, "Oh, *Mom!* It's just psychosomatic!" There was no question that Theseus was the star of the thirty seconds which everyone called "Over the Hill to Granny's Pad."

By the last day of the shoot, when they reached the tree-decorating scene, a childish spirit of fun had overtaken even the hungry worriers. They started to suggest lines and situations which weren't on the story board.

"This is getting like the Yiddish Art Theater," North told them. "Fellows, we have enough problems right here —nothing is going to go right, I promise you, so could I bother you guys for some fucking quiet?" He was prophetic. Nothing did go right. It took forty-five takes before the gaffers could manage to get the tree lights to blow all the fuses inside the set without having them blow all the lights outside the set as well, plunging the studio into total darkness each time.

Long after the Coca-Cola commercial had won a Clio, the commercial world's Oscar; long after it had won the New York Art Director's Club coveted annual award; long after it had been exhibited at commercial film festivals all over the world and brought back awards from Venice and Cork and Tokyo and Paris, Kiki had no doubts at all about the high point of those four days. What were the awards compared to the moment she had met Luke Hammerstein?

Kiki had felt so sorry for poor Theseus, after he'd spent all day sniffing for hidden meat, that as soon as the scene was declared a wrap, she'd let him off the leash.

"Excuse me, dog handler," Luke said to her, "are you aware that your animal is on top of the caterer's table, creating consternation and famine?"

"Don't worry about that food," Kiki said. "If you're hungry, I'll take you out to dinner. If you're not hungry, we can go to my place and just talk." Luke Hammerstein was sinewy and of medium height. He had green eyes which were both audacious and dreamy, insolent and kind. His eyelids were melancholy and his manner detached.

"Jesus," said Luke. "Is that a pass?"

"You'd be wise to consider it as such. I don't just kid around," Kiki said, with open admiration in her umber eyes.

"But what about the dog?"

"Forget him—I was just babysitting him for a friend. Coming?" Kiki was still the diabolic tatterdemalion, the elfin gypsy she had been when she and Daisy met eight years ago, but now she was far more aggressive and self-assured. Her excesses were harmless, her frivolity and self-indulgence basically benign, but she avoided the serious moment as if even one might turn her into a pillar of salt. In all her unsheltered years she couldn't remember meeting a man like Luke. She reached up and stroked his pointed, silky beard. What possibilities, what fantasies, what lubricious potentials it presented!

"Well . . ." Luke hesitated. All day long he'd seen Kiki on the set until she'd become part of the scenery, and suddenly, she had transformed herself into a peremptory female who seemed to have a specific intention regarding him and no problem about showing it. In fact, in the black pants tucked into the black boots and the severe black shirt Kiki had decided were right for her background role today, she seemed to him to be an apprentice highwayman, or rather, highwaywoman.

Every poll he'd read recently indicated that when women made the first approach it had a desirably erotic effect on men.

"Do I have a choice?" he wondered.

"Not really," Kiki said in a voice of despotic allure.

"I guess I don't at that . . . anyway, what do I have to lose?"

"Nothing you want to keep," Kiki assured him with her low laugh which was as fresh and aphrodisiac as a puff of spring air. At a distance Daisy was trying to decide who was doing the most damage, Theseus or Kiki. From the look on Luke Hammerstein's face, she decided it was too late to save him . . . anyway, he was a grown man and should be able to look out for himself . . . but she still might salvage enough from the caterer's table to feed the crew who had worked long over their normal quitting hour and would be expecting their dinner, as well as their extra money. She collared Theseus with one practiced gesture, pulling him from his perch on top of the platters of roast beef, corned beef and ham.

"Christ, Daisy, don't you have the sense to keep your hands off that wretched animal?" North said, as he passed by.

"Theseus, my own precious," Daisy said, with a hand signal she'd taught him ten years ago, "go give your Uncle North a nice big kiss."

Daisy had been invited to Middleburg, to Hamilton and Topsy Short's, for the weekend following the Coca-Cola shoot. As she considered what to pack she realized how important it could be—*must be*—to her. Daisy needed money badly. The Horse People had been scattered all over the world the past summer and she hadn't had a commission for a kid on a pony in months. Mrs. Short had hinted, in that dangling way in which certain rich, prospective patrons torment artists, that if the small sketch she had asked Daisy to do of her eldest daughter was satisfactory, she would consider commissioning an oil painting of all three of her children as a birthday present for her husband. That, Daisy calculated, would be at least a six-thousand-dollar job, although it would take several months to complete in what little spare time she had.

But there was no doubt about the utter necessity for earning some money. The quarterly payment for Danielle's care was due in a month. The prices at Queen Anne's School had gone up gradually, over the years, more than keeping up with the sums Daisy made through her painting as well as whatever was left over from her salary. Danielle's continual care now cost Daisy almost twenty-three thousand dollars a year and she hadn't been able to afford to fly to England to see her twin in the past eight months. Although she still faithfully made drawings to send Dani, sometimes she had so much work that she had to substitute one of the postcards she bought at a store in SoHo called "Untitled Art Postcards," postcards she knew Dani would like: the original illustrations from *Alice in Wonderland*, Odilon Redon butterflies, the carousel figure of an ostrich from the Philadelphia Museum of Art, three Edward Lear cartoons of Foss the Cat from Lear's *Nonsense Songs and Stories*, the strange fairy painting by Anne Anderson which illustrated Charles Kingsley's *The Water Babies*.

And now, just when she needed advice, Kiki wasn't exactly being helpful. Ever since she'd met Luke Hammerstein yesterday she'd been acting as if she were a moonstruck female satyr.

"Kiki," she'd objected, "I saw you coming on to Luke Hammerstein yesterday—you just can't behave like that ... it isn't ladylike."

"My dear Daisy," Kiki answered loftily. "It worked and that's what counts. And, in any case, your language shows the deplorable effect of association with that person you call Nick-the-Greek, if I may say so."

"What does that mean, 'worked'?" said Daisy suspiciously. "Where did the two of you go last night?"

"Out to dinner." Kiki's face was a circle of merriment and secret humor.

"And?"

"Princess Valensky, the fact that at the advanced age of almost twenty-four you only have had two unimportant love affairs with shy, undemanding, easily handled, and essentially passive men hardly makes you a person to consult on romantic matters. I'll answer your question when there is more to report."

During her years in New York, Daisy had, by dint of persuading herself that it was necessary to overcome her feelings about sexual involvement, allowed a few of her most persistent suitors to make love to her. She found that she could respond to them physically but not emotionally, and the relationships had not been important or lasting.

"I've had *three* love affairs," Daisy said angrily. "And one was with your own cousin."

"But did I describe the gentlemen properly?" Kiki demanded.

"You didn't say that they were all very attractive."

"I stand corrected. They were, but not my type. Now Luke Hammerstein on the other hand . . ."

"Spare me. Kiki, come on. Help me out. I've only got an hour to pack. The car's coming to take me out to the airport at six—the Shorts' jet leaves promptly at seven. Now, what do you think I should wear on Saturday night? It's that usual nonsense of 'Don't bother to dress, dear, because we're only having sixty for dinner.' In Middleburg they think dressing for dinner is 'pretentious' so they compromise—you know, silk blouses, long tweedy skirts, granny's pearls, everything fabulously expensive and just the right amount of dowdiness. You know I don't have that sort of drag—I wouldn't even if I could afford it," she said in a worried tone.

When she had first started spending weekends with the Horse People, Daisy had been forced to carve out a unique style for herself. She couldn't possibly buy fashionable dinner clothes so she became an old-clothes aficionado, avoiding the antique-clothing boutiques with their exquisite garments which only a Bette Midler or a Streisand could afford; avoiding the almost-new shops which were crammed with last year's couture clothes, already dated; and avoiding as well the flea markets at which only a miracle could uncover a garment in good condition.

Her buys all came from London jumble sales in church halls that she found time to go to each time she visited Dani. There she specialized in unearthing English and French couture originals, preferably over forty years old, clothes that had been made in the great dressmaking decades of the twenties and thirties. She researched them after she brought them back in triumph, for nothing she owned had cost over thirty-five dollars.

Daisy led Kiki into the third bedroom of their apartment in which she kept her nonworking clothes hanging on a horizontal pipe which crossed one end of the room.

The two girls stood and contemplated the garments that hung there. "It wouldn't be so hard if you only had regular clothes, like other people," Kiki sighed.

"Ah . . . that . . . how right you are. But it's simply too expensive and too dull, although I admit it would make life easier," Daisy replied.

"The Vionnet?" Kiki suggested.

"Too dressy," Daisy said regretfully, fingering the pale violet satin dress, cut on the bias and dating from 1926. "What so you think about the striped Lucien Lelong?"

"To be honest, I've never really liked it on you. Your essential wood nymphishness is not enhanced by zebra stripes, no matter how well done. How about the black velvet Chanel suit? It may be forty years old, but it looks as if it had been born yesterday," Kiki answered.

"It's not the right time of year for black velvet, especially in bluegrass country."

"Wait, *wait*, I see those Dove tea pajamas—you said they were around 1925? Just look, Daisy, cyclamen brocade and green satin with a black satin jacket—it's a smash!"

"They're Locust Valley maybe or Saratoga, but definitely not Middleburg."

"So that lets out the white satin pajama suit from Revillon too?"

"Afraid so. Oh, rot!"

Kiki carefully pushed the hangers aside, sighing wistfully over Daisy's treasures—they were all too long for her, but she itched after them.

"Ah ha!" Daisy pounced. "How could I have forgotten? Schiaparelli to the rescue, as usual." Triumphantly she held up an ensemble from the late 1930s when the daring Schiaparelli was doing clothes which were four decades ahead of their time. There was a jacket in lettuce green tweed touched with sequins at the lapels, worn with a pair of corduroy pants in a darker shade of green. "Just right, don't you think?"

"It's heaven—really a fuck-you number, as in 'fuck you, Mrs. Short, I know it's tweed and I know it's sequins and I know you didn't think they can be worn together, but now you do.'"

"In a nutshell. I really need this commission, so it's important to look as if I didn't."

"Then you'd better take my fake emeralds again."

"Emeralds with green sequins?"

"*Especially* with green sequins!"

15

$\mathcal{O}$f all the potential differences in human tastes, habits, interest and predilections, among the strongest is that which divides people who care about horses from people who don't. People can love cats or dogs and not feel as if they exist on an entirely different plane from those who are indifferent to these animals, but Horse People not only do not care to understand people who don't give a damn about horses, but the mere idea that such people exist—and are the vast majority—makes them wonder about the future of the human race. Horse People may be heads of state or professionally unemployed in their ordinary lives, but horses are their passion, as Jerusalem was the passion of a soldier in some ancient Crusade. The cult of the horse as their idol is as central to their lives as cocaine is to some and applause is to others. Perhaps not all of them know that the earliest work of art known to archaeology is a two-and-a-half-inch sculpture of a horse, made from the ivory tusk of a woolly mammoth, a masterpiece of supple grace which is thirty-two thousand years old—but this fact would seem only fitting and right to any Horse Person. It is only normal that the Cro-Magnon people of the Ice Age appreciated the horse twenty-five thousand years before the dawn of our civilization—normal and to be expected, since they believe that the horse is nature's finest achievement, not excluding man.

"Stupid, *dumb*, moronic beast!" Patrick Shannon told his horse quietly. He didn't want to be overheard. He was taking a private riding lesson in an outdoor ring at a stable in Peapack, New Jersey, only an hour and fifteen minutes from Manhattan. During the last month his chauffeur had driven him out to the school every night, right after he finished his heavy schedule of work as president and chief operating officer of Supracorp, a two-billion-dollar corporation. This had meant giving up all social life and the after-work squash games at the University Club that were one of the only chances he ever had to release his tensions, a cherished respite that he had now abandoned, in favor of this enraging, ridiculous, humiliating pursuit of something at which he would never be really good. At thirty-eight, Patrick Shannon was a natural athlete who had a way with a ball, any ball . . . but growing up in an orphan asylum had given him lots of ability with balls and none, none whatsoever with horses. He hated the things! They drooled and they snorted and they huffed, they turned their heads and tried to nip at his legs with their ugly, big teeth, they reared like silly girls if they saw something they didn't like, they walked sideways when they were supposed to go forward, they stopped to eat the grass when you hadn't pulled on the reins and wouldn't start when you kicked them.

They smelled good—that was all he would say for them. Horseshit was the best smelling shit he'd ever come across, oh, he'd grant them that.

The trail of events that had put Patrick Shannon on the back of a horse was clear. He had set his heart on acquiring for Supracorp another real-estate company, one solely owned by Hamilton Short. Ham Short had suggested that Shannon come next month to spend a weekend in Middleburg, Virginia, while the wooing of his business was going on. Short, assuming that Shannon rode, had spoken of "a little hacking about." Shannon, after committing himself to the weekend, had realized too late that he hadn't said he didn't ride. He didn't know just how crazy Horse People were, but he certainly knew enough about them to guess that the only excuse they would find understandable for an able-bodied man who did not mount a horse was a broken leg. He assumed that many of them rode even with broken legs, and he was perfectly right. Horsemanship, from the moment he accepted Short's invitation, became a challenge, which was next best to the thing he loved most—a risk.

Pat Shannon was a born risk taker who understood that the ability to cope with an occasional failure was a vital part of successful risk taking. But his failures, few as they were, had been business failures, and they had never been due to lack of effort or preparation. Since it was clearly possible to learn to ride, ride he would.

Short had said that he had some "fairly pleasant trails" on his place. Shannon had had one of his secretaries check the place out and discovered that it was called Fairfax Plantation, covered eighteen hundred acres, boasted a private jet airstrip, housed twenty servants and was worth, conservatively, four million dollars.

Shannon didn't have to be very clever to realize that if he were to go hacking about on almost two thousand acres, he had to count on fairly long hours in the saddle. And Shannon was clever, indeed exceptionally so. And a clever Irishman can be counted among the cleverest kind of man the human race produces. Hadn't Shannon's favorite Irishman, George Bernard Shaw, said, "A lifetime of happiness! No man alive could bear it; it would be hell on Earth." Pat Shannon grimly reminded himself of these words as he gave his horse the signal to canter for the fiftieth time that evening.

"You're making progress," Chuck Byers said drily, in a tone of voice which took any approval out of the remark. He had never had such a pupil before. He hoped never to have such a one again. Shannon had told him he wanted to learn to ride. Fair enough—lots of people did. But no one else had ever demanded that he be able to trot at the end of the first lesson, canter at the end of the second, and gallop at the end of the third.

Byers had told him it was impossible. Byers had said he'd break a bone at the least and he had made Shannon sign a paper saying that the stable wasn't responsible for any injuries to the man and that Shannon was responsible for all injuries to the horse. But the bastard had galloped after three lessons although Byers could tell by the way he walked back to his car that every muscle in his body was killing him.

The man was a demon, Byers thought. After the third lesson Shannon had sent out a crew of electricians to rig up lights around the ring so that he could ride late into the night, and he had insisted on a three-hour lesson every single night, paying so much that Byers had had to accommodate him in spite of his family's objections. He hadn't spent any time with his wife and kids since Shannon had started this nonsense.

Something about the single-minded way in which Shannon tackled the business of learning to ride made Byers feel downright vindictive toward the man. To Byers riding was the last vestige of chivalry in the world, a realm of magic which linked the past to the present as nothing else did, a sport that was both his religion and his romance. He grew more and more disgruntled as he watched Shannon make incredible progress of a mechanical kind, but without falling in any way under the spell of horses—the son-of-a-bitch acted as if mastering horsemanship was simply another form of locomotion. And not for him the ritual, pleasant half-hour of discussion after the lesson was over. No, the man just said a brief goodnight and disappeared into that big black Cadillac in which his bored driver had been reading all the while, and sped off to the city. Byers was a proud, sensitive man, and he knew he was being treated as a mere convenience. If a robot could teach riding, he was convinced that Shannon would have preferred it. He never realized, nor did Shannon tell him, that Pat Shannon didn't think of learning to ride as a human occupation which made human contact with his instructor necessary. It was merely a challenge he had chosen to confront, an obstacle which he had to conquer, a necessary nuisance which he had to put behind him. He went at it with total concentration, as if he were breaking rocks on a chain gang with an overseer watching him. He resented having to spend these hours in the ring just as much as Byers resented teaching him.

They had only one moment of non-instructional discourse in the past month. Shannon was limping badly, Byers noticed, in his new boots from M. J. Knoud, Inc., the venerable firm which had also made his handsome riding clothes.

"Trouble with the boots, Mr. Shannon?" Byers remarked, not without malice.

"My ankle bones are bleeding," said Shannon in a matter-of-fact fashion. "I suppose it's always like that when you break in new boots."

"Not necessarily—people don't all go at it the way you do."

"What size foot do you have, Byers?"

"Twelve-C."

"That's my size. Will you sell me your boots?"

"What? No, Mr. Shannon, you don't want these boots."

"It happens that I do—they're exactly what I want.

Beautiful leather and well-broken in. We wear the same size and you certainly have other pairs."

"I do indeed."

"I'm willing to pay whatever you ask, but I want your boots, Byers. I'll give twice what you paid for them, hell, make it three times."

"You're absolutely sure about that, Mr. Shannon?" Byers didn't show he was offended.

"My God, they're not sacred objects, man, just boots. What's all the fuss about?" Patrick demanded, more harshly than he realized. He'd been in considerable pain for three hours, although he would never have admitted it.

"They're yours," said Byers curtly. "No charge." He had been many things in his life but never had he bargained over second-hand boots.

"Thanks, Byers," Patrick said. "I really appreciate it." As far as he was concerned, it was the least the man could do, although he would not have grudged him any profit he cared to take. Business was business. He had no conception of the cult of tack, the preoccupation with all the leather appurtenances which belong to the equestrian world.

As Byers handed over the worn pair of boots he thought to himself, screw you, Pat Shannon. Who the fuck do you think you are?

It was a thought many people had had about Shannon in the course of his life, and all of them had eventually realized that whoever Shannon thought he was, he turned out to be. This had not endeared him to a rather large group—and if he'd bothered to consider this he would not have been astonished. Particularly since he'd forgotten all their names in the course of his climb to the top. A dedicated nonconformist, a maverick by deepest instinct, his success had depended on his following no one's plans but those he chose for himself, without consultation.

There were only a few men Patrick Shannon considered his equals in the corporate world. No man, no matter how powerful, who had inherited his business, belonged in his peer group. They had to have made it on their own. God knows he had.

From the orphanage in which he'd grown up he had won a scholarship to St. Anthony's, a minor Catholic boys' prep school. The scholarship had been established by a former student, now an elderly and childless millionaire, for a parentless boy who showed equal excellence in academics and athletics.

At St. Anthony's, Patrick saw immediately that he had found his first world to conquer. Nothing about the upper-middle-class East Coast boys he found himself among was familiar; their points of reference and the things they took for granted were all unknown territory to him.

For the first two years, he watched, listened and learned, always more comfortable with the adults in the school constellation than with boys of his own age. His speech had always been correct, taught, as he had been all his life, by nuns, and fortunately, the school required a uniform so that all the boys dressed alike. He learned that his black hair had always been cut too short, that his aggressiveness on the football field and the baseball diamond was acceptable, and as much as he relished the exercise of his brain, it was preferable to save demonstrations of intelligence for exams and term papers rather than display it in the classroom.

By junior year he was ready to emerge from the unobtrusive place he had taken everywhere except in sports. Pat Shannon had carefully marked out the boys he wanted to become friends with, singling out from the herd of his classmates the half dozen who displayed excellence, not merely in their achievements but in their character. By the end of his four years at St. Anthony's, he had made six friends he would never lose. Loyalty was his religion. If any of his friends had asked Pat to meet him in Singapore by noon on the day after tomorrow, with no explanation given, he would have been there. And they would have been there for him. Lacking a family of his own, he had created a family from strangers. The flavor of his soul had always been tough but loving. However, his strength concealed that love from all but a few.

He was a tall boy, big boned, and fast as a leopard. His coloring left no question about his ethnic origins: it was classically Black Irish, blue black hair, dark blue eyes and white skin that flushed easily. His forehead was broad, his eyes set wide apart under heavy brows, and his open smile was so winning that it was easy—though dangerous—to forget how bright he was.

By senior year he was president of the class, captain of the football team and first in all his classes. He won a full scholarship to Tulane from which he graduated in three years by taking an extra class load, going to summer school every summer, and restricting his sports activity to football. At twenty-three, Patrick Shannon was a graduate of the Harvard Business School and ready to conquer the world.

A week before graduation he had been hired by Nat Temple, the man who had founded Supracorp many decades before. Shannon gave himself ten years to make it to a position close to the top in the corporate structure. He allotted the first three years to absolutely unrelenting work. Pat Shannon was perfectly aware, from visiting his friends, that living *well* took time and money and he would have neither to spare, by his calculations, until he was twenty-six. Although he felt an impatience to enjoy the good things in life, his self-discipline and bred-in-the-bone motivation were strong enough to make him keep to his plan. He never considered marrying money—he had met many of his classmates' sisters who would have provided it—but everything about the idea displeased him. He *had* to do it on his own—that need to prove himself was stronger than any other he had ever experienced, and each victory only led to new challenges which had to be met. In Shannon's life there were no plateaus, no resting places from which to look back and contentedly relish the victory gained, the game won, the achievement completed.

Now, at thirty-eight, he was saturated with success. Nat Temple, the man who had first seen his potential, had retired as president of Supracorp three years before, retaining the title of chairman of the board, leaving Shannon to run a conglomerate that, from the time he was put in charge, started the expansion that had recently doubled its earning per share. His own salary and bonuses were in excess of three quarters of a million dollars a year.

A fair number of the powerful and conservative men among the major Supracorp stockholders were still not at all sure they approved of him. He had his enemies, watchful ones, who resented the firmness with which Nat Temple had backed Shannon and given him his head, who envied him his youth and his achievements, men who didn't like to take chances of any sort. These enemies were quiet for the moment but they were waiting and watching, ready to push Shannon out if he ever gave them the opportunity.

Shannon had acquired all the material things that go with this sort of success: an apartment high up in the

United Nations Plaza, decorated by John Saladino in what he told Shannon was a style of "elegant alienation," a style that Shannon found out—too late—that he didn't enjoy although he admired it in the abstract; memberships in the Century, River and University clubs; the house in East Hampton which he almost never had time to use; and the inevitable divorce from a woman he should have known better than to marry: a socialite and beauty who had one of those dark, sensuous, syrupy, knowing voices which other women dislike and mistrust instantly and for good reason.

There had been no children. If there had been, perhaps there would have been no divorce, for Shannon, although not a religious man, never forgot the loneliness of being brought up without parents. After his brief marriage was over, he permitted himself only a series of second-string girls whom he took with such intense, entire, purely physical thoroughness that it was as if they had been consumed by a brush fire set by a carelessly flung match in late autumn. The finality of falling truly in love, the possible pain of it, was something he avoided with ease. Love, he sensed, was a greater risk than even he cared to take.

Supracorp, with its web of companies—cosmetics, perfumes, foods, magazines, liquors, television stations and real estate—was his baby. His children were the boys of the Police Athletic League, with whom, unknown to anyone in his world, he spent as much of every weekend as he could. With these boys, an observer would have seen uncritical, undemanding, extravagant love pouring from him. To his boys, being with him was like being in a brisk sea breeze on a day of blue sky. He made them aware of life's possibilities, and he tried to give them as much as he could of any knowledge he possessed, whether it was how to hit a ball, how to fly a kite, or how to do long division. The years had not changed his smile; it was still open, still winning, and his eyes were still of that blue which proclaims a victory, but now he had deep vertical lines on either side of his mouth and deep horizontal lines on his broad forehead over which his dark hair always fell no matter how often he pushed it back.

Patrick Shannon had propelled himself right past and through his youth, and he would never be able to recapture a time—not even in memory—that simply hadn't existed for him. He had never been really young. He had never played. He had never had time for irresponsibility or carefree freedom. It was quite enough, he told himself, that he had accumulated success, power, money, information and a small group of friends, without also having reaped a harvest of nostalgia for fun and games.

And what's more, now he could—more or less—ride a goddamned fucking horse.

When Hamilton Short, a shrewd, tough real-estate manipulator, made his first, second and third million he put them in treasury bonds and forgot about them. At forty-two, already paunchy and bald, his tenth million safely behind him, he had little trouble in convincing Topsy Mullins, a timidly luscious eighteen-year-old from an ancient but impoverished Virginia family, to marry him. During the next eight years, as business took the Shorts to Dallas, Miami and Chicago to live, Topsy produced three children, all girls, and Ham produced more millions; by his estimate he was worth twenty-five million, and the real-estate business had never been better.

Topsy had gone to a famous horsy finishing school on the last remnants of her family's money, and there she had met many New York and Long Island girls from rich, social families. She had followed their careers in fashion magazines and society columns with biting envy. She had married for money and all it had brought her was three pregnancies and fleeting acquaintances in three, to her, provincial cities. The only way to really be a part of the fashionable world was to be considered fashionable in New York City—other places didn't exist on Topsy's narrow horizon.

However, she had a clear-eyed idea of just how difficult it was for strangers to be launched in New York life, particularly a stranger who could claim only a few school-girl friendships, long faded, and whose husband was hardly an asset to a dinner party. She resolved to make her assault on New York from her home territory, from Virginia where her family was known and respected. She decided that an estate in the heart of the thousand square miles that make up Northern Virginia's Hunt Country was the answer; it would take the curse off new money. When Ham was informed by Topsy that it was time for them to buy a place in Middleburg, a town of 833 people, lopsidedly, if conveniently, divided into two groups, millionaires and servants, there was more than restlessness in her words. He heard the unmistakable indication that only a considerable, a *very* considerable establishment in Middleburg, would guarantee that Ham Short's marriage would continue to run in the comfortable, well-ordered and convenient way he had learned to take for granted.

At twenty-five, Topsy's early promise had ripened into decided beauty. Seven years of marriage, with only the birth of children to disturb her concentration on herself, had polished her chestnut-haired, hazel-eyed prettiness until it gleamed. The large breasts, wide hips, and tiny waist that had first caught Ham Short's eyes were as appealing as ever. Even if he rarely bothered to appreciate them now, he certainly didn't want any domestic problems. He was not a sensual man, a quick fuck every week or two was all he asked, but he insisted on peace and quiet at home while he worked on more millions. Middleburg or Miami, it made no difference to him, as long as Topsy would stop complaining about their lack of social life.

Fortunately Ham Short continued to increase his millions in the next two years, because the restoration of Fairfax Plantation consumed money as greedily as if it had been a whale swallowing plankton.

Fairfax, a late Colonial mansion, had been built in the 1750s by master craftsmen brought over from England by the first Oliver Fairfax who, like other wealthy Virginians of the time, had a fine taste for architecture and enough knowledge to realize that only in England could he find the workmanship he demanded. Unfortunately, the last Oliver Fairfax had long outlived his family's fortune and when the Shorts bought Fairfax Plantation, it was close to a ruin. But nothing, short of fire, could disguise the glorious wood carving throughout the house, which the legendary William Buckland had fashioned out of clear, mellow white pine and perfectly seasoned walnut and poplar, all of which came from the plantation's own forests, as did the bricks which were baked from clay dug from the broad fields. Buckland's Palladian woodwork, equal to that of any great home in England, had been set off by a collection of Chinese Chippendale, Hepplewhite and Sheraton furniture, covered in reproductions of the richest fabrics of the late Colonial period. The marvels of the interior—Topsy Short's decorator specialized in Instant Museum Quality—were quite overshadowed by the gardens which no amount of neglect could affect, depending as they did on a severely classic plan of slow growing boxwood hedges which had taken a full two hundred and twenty years to reach their current majestic proportions. Topsy Short had to be content with letting her horses graze in the great fields behind the house although she would have preferred to be able to see them from the front rooms of the mansion—as did many of her neighbors.

"Lordy," she would say enviously. "That old Liz Whitney Tippett's horses can just about poke their noses into her drawing room."

"Well, dig up the boxwood," Ham suggested absently.

"What? My landscape architect would kill me. They're historic. There's nothing like them, not even in Upperville or Warrenton or Leesburg. He told me that even Bunny Mellon doesn't have older boxwood," she said, invoking the name of the largely invisible queen of the Hunt Country.

"Then don't dig up the goddamned boxwood."

Ham Short, master of all he surveyed, had more on his mind than hedges. The offer from Supracorp was interesting, highly interesting. If he consented to the marriage of his healthy real-estate company to Supracorp's even healthier two-billion-dollar operation, the stock he would receive would rise to a point where, instead of working on his thirtieth million, he could start thinking in terms of his sixtieth. Not only that, it would get him out from under the day-to-day operation of what was essentially a one-man show. His children were all girls, he had no one to bring into a family business, and it would give him the time to start living the life of the gentleman Topsy had always tried to pretend he was. But on the other hand, did he want to give up control? Wasn't it more satisfying to have his own company and be free to run it as he chose? Why become another acquisition of Supracorp, why become another division head under Patrick Shannon? Did he really want to live like a gentleman and take an interest in the Middleburg Hunt and give an honest damn about horses? Perhaps the coming weekend, with the chance to see Shannon as his guest, would provide the answers to some of the questions he asked himself, as he wavered between selling and not selling. He'd asked Topsy to keep the guest list small for exactly that reason.

"Who's coming this weekend?" Ham asked abruptly.

"The Hemmings and the Stantons from Charlottesville, the Dempseys from Keeneland and Princess Daisy Valensky, to do a sketch of Cindy. That Shannon of yours, of course, and . . . some people from New York." Ham Short knew the first three couples, Horse People all. "What people from New York?" he asked idly.

Eyes wide with a mixture of terrified anticipation and excitement, Topsy answered, "Robin and Vanessa Valarian."

"The dressmaker? Now what the hell do you want with them?" Ham asked the question casually, not noticing his wife's flustered air.

"Oh, Ham, I don't know how I stand it," Topsy wailed plaintively. "You're a disgrace. The Valarians are—oh, how can I make *you* understand—they're the chicest people in New York! They go absolutely *everywhere* and know absolutely *everybody*. I knew Vanessa Valarian a little at school—she was three years ahead of me—I bumped into her last time I went to New York for shopping, and we had a drink together, but I wasn't sure they'd come when I asked them."

"Why not, aren't we good enough for a dressmaker and his wife?" Ham demanded.

"We're not chic, Ham, we're just rich, and not as rich as *really* rich people either!" she said with an accusing note in her voice. "No use your snorting like that . . . you have to be worth over two hundred million to be really rich—I read all the lists—and you know as well as I do that we're just small potatoes compared to—oh, never mind!" She flounced off the chair in which she'd been sitting and started to finger a Chinese Export bowl her decorator had insisted she buy—a steal at twenty-eight hundred dollars.

"Not chic? Well, who the hell said we had to be chic? Who the hell gives a shit? What the hell does it mean anyway—who elected the Valarians to decide?" Now Ham was injured. He was proud of his money and he didn't like being reminded of the fact that, rich as he was, he still couldn't play with the big boys.

"Oh, Ham, honestly! It merely means that they're in—*in*, damn it, the way we'll never be! They're invited to every good party, and they get pages and pages in *Vogue* and *House and Garden* and *Architectural Digest* on their apartment and their table settings—oh, and they fly all over the world to be with people like Cristina Brandolini and Helene Rochas and André Oliver and Fleur Cowles Meyer and Jacqueline Machado-Macedo—people you wouldn't *ever* know! Unless the Valarians are there a party doesn't have cachet!"

"Cachet? Christ, Topsy, you've got another bug up your ass, that's all it is. First we had to have this museum and enough horses for the Charge of the Light Brigade. Now you've finally become best buddies with our neighbors and you still need a stamp of approval from a dressmaker? I don't understand you."

If Ham Short hadn't been so offended he might have realized that there was something a little overdone in Topsy's insistence on the chic of the Valarians . . . something a little overdone in her display of pique.

"Robin Valarian is one of the most famous dress designers in the country," Topsy answered loftily, "and, as for Vanessa, she happens to be considered the most elegant woman in New York."

"I've seen his picture enough to know what he does—if you ask me, he looks like a fruit—full-blown."

"Don't be disgusting, Ham! They've been married almost as long as we have. Men like you always think other men, who don't happen to be interested in merely making money, have to be gay."

"Oh, so now it's 'gay'—I suppose that's the only possible word to use?"

"Yes, as a matter of fact, it is," Topsy retorted, in a voice she decided to make conciliating. This argument was driving her wild with nerves.

As Ham Short's irritation cooled, Topsy found herself replaying, for the thousandth time, the scene in the Valarians' library a few weeks ago in New York. Vanessa had poured her a Dubonnet and flattered Topsy with questions.

"Tell me about your life," she'd asked with unmistakable interest. "What's it like living in Middleburg most of the year? Divine or drear?"

"If I couldn't get up to New York every few weeks I don't think I could stand it," Topsy had admitted. "I'm Virginia born but I think I have New York soul. It's simply too quiet . . . but Ham loves it."

"And what Ham loves, Ham gets?"

"More or less."

Vanessa got up and closed the door of the library. "I think it's a crime that anyone as deliciously pretty as you is wasted in Horse Country," she told Topsy, coming to sit next to her on the loveseat. Topsy blushed in embarrassment and surprise. In school Vanessa had been the leader on whom half the girls in Topsy's class had had a crush—Vanessa, even then, had been sophisticated beyond their teenage dreams.

"Thank you," she murmured, sipping her Dubonnet.

"It's the simple truth. Do you know that way back at school I noticed you? I'll never forget how you looked with all that wonderful red brown hair—it's only a little darker now—and even those frightful uniforms we had to wear couldn't hide the fact that you were going to have a perfect figure. I envy you—I'm so damn skinny—I'd give anything for a few curves. Didn't you ever notice me watching you, young Topsy?"

Topsy could only shake her head in denial.

"Well, you must have had other things on your mind—I used to look at you at meals—just a peek, mind you." Vanessa laughed and casually took one of Topsy's hands in hers, gazing at it as calmly as if she were a fortuneteller. Suddenly she bent and kissed Topsy's palm with a warm, open mouth, laughed, and released the hand as if nothing at all had happened. That had been all, but again and again, from that afternoon until now, Topsy's mind had returned to the scene, wondering what might have happened next, and then telling herself that nothing, absolutely nothing could possibly have happened next—she was just being silly.

"Ham," she said, returning to the present, "let's not fight, please. I'm nervous enough about the weekend without having a fight."

"Okay, honey—I don't know what the whole thing's about anyway, but so long as it makes you happy, that's fine. And, if you want my opinion, those Valarians will be more than enough impressed by the Hemmings and the Stantons and the Dempseys and Patrick Shannon—and what's her name, that princess, so will you, for Christ's sake, just stop wandering around like you're about to break that bowl? Sure, it's insured, but I'd hate to try to collect!"

On mid-Saturday morning all of Topsy Short's house guests assembled at the stables. Topsy supervised the matching of horse to rider and only her lifetime of riding enabled her to fulfill this task with an outward show of calm. She was in the grip of an emotion she avoided examining, but she felt more ill-at-ease, more electrically anticipatory than she had in years. She was staying behind to keep Vanessa Valarian company since Vanessa had announced, at breakfast, with a laugh that was delighted with itself, that she had always been terrified of horses, even at school. She made the confession sound like an asset.

Patrick Shannon was firmly in the saddle of a large black gelding, but he was too intent to take in much of the busy, cheerful scene around him. This was the first time he'd actually been on a horse in the company of riders other than his instructor. He was absorbed in remembering every detail of every lesson he'd taken, blocking out the distraction of the stomping and blowing of the other horses, the maddening way they persisted in getting in each other's way. He tried to keep his lively mount to one side of the milling crowd of horses and riders, hoping that the brute wasn't as nervous as he was, and wondering if it was true that the horse knew how he felt just from his touch on the reins.

Young Cindy Short was mounted on a handsome pony, and Daisy had been allotted a grand chestnut mare who had fetched a healthy forty thousand dollars two years ago at the world famous Keeneland July auction of yearlings. After sharing Cindy's breakfast and spending the early hours of the day with her in the stable, she and Cindy were fast friends. When she rode, Daisy dressed with severe correctness. She braided her hair tightly and then hid it under the regulation protective hat, covered in black velvet, that is to riders what a hardhat is to construction workers. She wore a snood into which she tucked the ends of her braids so that they wouldn't catch on branches.

Ham Short wanted to demonstrate his daughter's equestrian achievements to his guests.

"Cindy," he called, "you go first and we'll follow."

Cindy, who was patient in her familiar role as a show-and-tell child, kicked her pony into a trot and then into a canter. Daisy, who wanted to observe her as she rode, waited until Cindy had had ample time to be admired and then followed the roly-poly figure. Daisy sat her thoroughbred with such beautiful calm that she made a noble and gallant sight in the crisp Virginia morning . . . in spite of the fact that Theseus followed closely behind the heels of her horse with his rolling half-drunken gait.

As Patrick Shannon watched Daisy disappear over a slight rise he had a sudden perception of what riding could be. Whoever that is, he thought, *she's the real thing.* All of his life spent in conquering new worlds had sharpened his eye to the look of those who do effortlessly what it is supremely difficult to do at all. He knew little about ballet but he could always tell a great dancer by the way the hair rose on the back of his neck at the sight of certain, apparently effortless gestures. Daisy's slender, straight back, her perfectly relaxed shoulders and arms, the carelessly confident poise of her head as she rode away, filled him with admiration . . . and bitterness. He was acutely aware of the splendid economy of her movements, movements over which he'd spent the last month sweating and cursing and bleeding. To be able to command a horse, with an imperceptible pressure of the hands and knees and calves, so that the damn fool beast sprang forward, not at a walk, or a trot, or a slow canter, but at a fast canter and no nonsense about it . . . shit, you had to be born to it, he thought, it has to be *given* to you, handed over as just another of the accomplishments people like you are expected to master.

Patrick Shannon never allowed himself to compare his grim and lonely childhood with the lives of the people who lived in the world in which he was now such a potent force, but every once in a while, taken unaware, in a situation he hadn't yet conquered, he would become briefly, but stunningly, conscious of early deprivation; relive in a flash the late and difficult transition from the gauche boy who entered prep school on a scholarship to the man he was today. The others—his friends at St. Anthony's, at Tulane, at Harvard—most of them had had it good, so good—and it showed—perhaps not to them, but to him because he wasn't one of them and never would be.

The ease of it, he said to himself, the momentary bitterness fading, that's the secret. As he ordered himself to relax, Ham Short walked his horse over to Patrick's.

"Do you mind if we don't try to keep up with the others?" Ham asked. "I ride Western—kinda like a rocking chair—never had time to learn English—a bunch of nonsense if you ask me." Patrick looked down at his host, incredibly attired in cowboy boots and chaps, slumped in a Western saddle on a comfortable looking cow pony.

"Whatever you say," he answered. Ham Short wondered

why Shannon was looking so stunned. Didn't a man have a right to ride any way he chose, for Christ's sake?

Vanessa Valarian and Topsy walked back to the house in silence, broken only by Vanessa's vague comments on the weather, the location of the house, the landscape; comments which Topsy barely heard. As they walked up the driveway, Vanessa grasped Topsy by the wrist.

"Show me the house," she demanded in the low, ardent voice that was her chief beauty. She was supple as a piece of silk, so lean and slender that her husband's dresses never looked as right on a professional model as they did on her. She had made the most of looks which depended on absolutely white skin contrasting with the blackness of her hair, which she wore in a pageboy style with straight bangs right down to her eyebrows. This unfashionable Prince Valiant hair style, "signature hair" as a fashion magazine called it, was only one of the marks of personal style which made her unmistakable. Others were the wide, angular jaw, the heavily made-up, almost Oriental eyes, the bright red lipstick on her wide mouth, the big, unabashed grin she wore in every photograph ever published of her. She had curiously beautiful hands, long and slim, as supple and strong as if she were a sculptress or a pianist, yet her nails were always cut short and she wore no rings on those elegant fingers. Vanessa never compromised or changed her looks. She wore her long nose as if it were the mark of royal birth. For this mild, Virginia morning she had chosen a thin, far-from-simple dress of black cashmere, huge gold earrings and eight David Webb bracelets, a costume she had picked deliberately for its incongruence, the way it jarred with her surroundings; an effect she enjoyed creating.

Topsy flutteringly led the way through several excessively fine rooms in which the Hepplewhite hunting boards, the Sheraton barrel chairs and the Sully portraits had been assembled for just such a display. She found herself forgetting which period pieces of furniture belonged to, fumbling over the simplest names, actually trembling at the entrance to each room, not because she had any doubt of its correctness, but because she was so intensely conscious of Vanessa's elegant, dark presence at her side, never touching her, but never as far away as people normally kept from each other. She felt as jittery as she had before her first dance.

"It's enchanting," Vanessa pronounced, "and it suits you . . . it makes New York look terribly raw. But now, my young Topsy, don't you think it's time to show me the upstairs? I'm curious to see your bedroom—the reception rooms of a house are never as revealing as the private rooms, don't you think? Or am I being too nosy? It's just that I've already seen so many marvels that I'm quite ill with envy. Next time that you come to visit us in the city—and I hope it'll be soon—you'll understand."

Topsy caught her breath in leaping joy. Magic words— a promise, a visit!

In Topsy's bedroom Vanessa sat down on the edge of the wide canopied four poster that Topsy had prevailed on her unwilling decorator to swathe in three hundred yards of peach silk.

"And is this the *letto matrimoniale?*" asked Vanessa, indicating the four poster with a languid wave.

"*Letto* . . . oh . . . I see. No, Ham sleeps in his own room. He likes to work late and start telephoning early."

"And does he come to visit his wife in her bed, or does she go to his?" Vanessa continued, imperturbably.

"Why . . . ah . . ."

"Oh, Topsy, what a darling you are . . . you're blushing again, the way you did in New York. Oh, I know, when people tell you that, it only makes you blush more—but I couldn't resist. Sit here . . . I can't talk to you when you're a mile away." Vanessa patted the coverlet, until Topsy, almost unwillingly, sat down next to her. Vanessa took her hand and circled Topsy's palm with one of her talented, Gothic fingers. "I wondered if you were going to invite us . . . after what happened in New York I was worried that you might be afraid of me . . . no? I'm glad . . . so glad. I've been thinking of you everyday . . . thinking that we could so easily become very, very close friends . . . would that please you, young Topsy?" Idly she licked the tip of her forefinger and with a rapid movement touched the wet finger gently to the center of Topsy's outstretched palm. When Topsy gasped at the unmistakably explicit signal but didn't draw back, she raised the hand to her lips and took one of Topsy's fingers in her mouth, sucking on it gently from the base of the finger to the tip of the nail. Topsy moaned. "You like that—don't you? Remember the first time I kissed your hand— remember how surprised you were? And do you still remember what I told you—that I'd had my eye on you years ago?"

Mutely Topsy nodded.

As strong and fast as a man, Vanessa put one arm around Topsy's waist while she bent and brushed her neck with a feathery kiss, just above her collar bone. "Darling, I won't do anything to you that you don't like . . . don't be afraid of me . . . you're not, are you? Good." Swiftly, on stocking feet, Vanessa locked the bedroom door and returned to the bed where Topsy half sat, half lay back with eyes wide and wild with reluctant temptation. "How adorable you are—you still have your shoes on." Vanessa gave her low laugh. "Let's get rid of your shoes, at least . . ." She bent and took off Topsy's shoes. "Close your eyes," Vanessa whispered, "and let me be good to you—you need someone to be good to you, don't you, young one—someone who just wants to make you feel all the things you've always dreamed of feeling but haven't really ever felt . . . oh, yes, I thought so . . . I could tell just by looking at you that you were ready for me." As she spoke she deftly unbuttoned Topsy's blouse and released the hook which held her brassiere together in the front. Topsy had magnificent, soft round breasts, with prominent brown nipples, surprisingly dark on her white, abundant flesh. "Oh, but you're beautiful! You're superb . . . I knew you would be," Vanessa whispered, lightly tracing the outline of Topsy's half open mouth with one dark red fingertip. She glanced carefully at her prey, not wanting to do anything too suddenly. With her warm, agile fingers she traced a line from the girl's throat down under and around each heavy breast, creating a circle of exquisite lightning, but holding herself back from the nipples that she could see were becoming tight and hard. A voluptuary of the most accomplished kind, she was infinitely willing to wait for her pleasures and nothing excited her as much as the initiation of a woman she knew had never experienced the excruciating pleasure she could give her.

"Topsy, this is all for you . . . I don't want anything . . . you don't have to move an inch . . . just lie back and let me look at you . . ." As she unbuttoned the waistband of the woman's skirt and slipped it off in a gentle movement, she sucked again on Topsy's fingers, taking two of them in her wide mouth and fluttering them with her practiced tongue. Topsy shuddered, unable to believe that she was becoming so excited by nothing more than being touched on her breasts and on her fingers. She relaxed when Vanessa told her that nothing was expected of her ... she wouldn't have known what to do. Now Vanessa surrounded each nipple with five adept, caressing, gentle fingers which delicately teased them up into two hard points. Only when Topsy began to sigh, unable to remain silent, did Vanessa finally fasten her mouth on one nipple with luxurious leisure, flicking the point of her tongue over first one hot, hard nubbin and then the other. She spent long, long minutes without ever leaving those wide, brown nipples, pulling on them, bathing them with swift strokes of her entire tongue, until they were stimulated to a point just below pain. Only then did she stretch down her arms and take off the rest of Topsy's clothes.

The girl's eyes were still closed, Vanessa noted as she rapidly took off her own clothes. Good, it was easier that way ... the first time. She cradled Topsy's head in one slender, strong arm and with the other reached down and ran her fingers as lightly as possible, so that their touch was barely perceptible, yet maddeningly arousing, over the delicate swell of her, down to just above the chestnut tangle of thick pubic hair. When Topsy made no indication of protest, Vanessa moved, with the grace she was famous for, and straddled the woman's body, one knee on either side of Topsy's full hips. She sat back on her heels and devoted herself to gliding her fingertips down Topsy's beautiful white thighs and calves all the way to the tip of her rosy toes and then back again, avoiding the pubic curls with absolute discipline. She saw Topsy's hands come to life; one of them reached down and captured one of hers and pulled it toward the mound of Venus that the girl was lifting up toward her. Vanessa freed her hand and whispered, "No, no, you can't have it yet ... you're not ready ..." and she began to caress the soft skin inside of Topsy's thighs, her fingers reaching higher and higher until they were fluttering just at the rim of the pubic tangle. Topsy moaned imploringly and opened her legs. Vanessa saw the slick glisten of wetness on the offered lips. Her own vulva was so heavy and congested that she could scarcely restrain herself from grinding it into the girl, but she held back, crouching low to blow gently on Topsy's thick hairs, parting the curls with her breath, until she could see the girl's swollen clitoris. Then she reached out again with her tongue and, making it into a point, darted and darted it again and again at the tiny organ, sometimes sucking it with her whole mouth, sometimes just licking it with a light. flickering touch.

"*Fuck me*, for God's sake—fuck me!" Topsy muttered, unable to endure any more.

Vanessa knit the three middle fingers of her right hand together. and worked them several inches up between those eager lips. Topsy strained upward frantically, and Vanessa. kneeling, bent again and took the girl's vulva entirely into her hot, avid, wide mouth, sucking rhythmically on the clitoris at the same time that she slid her three fingers firmly in and out of Topsy's vagina, sometimes only an inch or two up, sometimes as far as they could go. Topsy was aware only of the most intense delight; the fingers in her vagina produced a hardness and knobbiness of stimulation that a smooth penis never had, and the sucking, oh, the teasing sucking, was like nothing she had ever believed possible. She felt herself pausing on the edge of orgasm, pausing, pausing and then coming into Vanessa's mouth with a bursting rush and a widening pool of spasms which made her scream in incredulous abandon.

While she was still throbbing and jerking her hips forward, Vanessa threw herself on the other woman, kissing her for the first time on her dry, open mouth, pressing her own vulva, lightly covered with dark hair, into Topsy's curly mound, cupping Topsy's full, round bottom in both her hands and rubbing, relentlessly, until she came quickly into the masterful orgasm she had been holding back for so long.

Minutes, many minutes passed before Topsy sat up, dizzy but still aware of the passage of time. "They'll be back for lunch in ten minutes . . . and Ham'll be calling for me. What must I look like?"

"You look glorious," Vanessa said, slithering quickly into her clothes. "Do you have a garter belt and stockings around somewhere?"

"I bought them once . . . for Ham . . . but they didn't work any great wonders. Why?"

"Would you wear them, for me? Without panties? All day long, all evening, all day tomorrow? So I can look at you and think of just how I could be touching you under your clothes . . . so you can look at me and see me thinking?"

"Oh!"

"Will you?"

"Yes, God, yes!"

As the members of the Shorts' house party gathered for drinks before lunch, Robin Valarian approached his wife and put his arm around her.

"Did you have a good ride, my angel?" she asked him, tilting up her proud nose and widening her Oriental eyes.

"Marvelous—it's really a shame you've become afraid of horses, my poor pet. You used to ride so well. And you, was the hunting good?"

"Superb, quite simply superb."

"I hoped it would be. I almost envy you."

Daisy lunched with Cindy and her sisters in their playroom and then spent the afternoon sketching the little girl on her pony. The younger girls, who were seven and five, equestrians both, watched respectfully for a while and finally, bored, wandered off. After she'd worked until Cindy would pose no longer, Daisy indulged in the great gift the weekends with the Horse People could provide: a solitary ride accompanied only by Theseus. These hours alone, galloping, free, abandoned, mindlessly happy, as if she moved in a wind of vernal delight, were a luxury she could never have afforded otherwise, and she'd become adept at snatching them when she could, without taking time she could have used for work. Reluctantly, in the last afternoon light, she trotted back to the stables and went to her room to bathe and dress for dinner.

It was the thing she liked least about these weekends, she thought, as she carefully put away her riding clothes, the obligatory dinner with the assembled guests, the obligatory conversations, the obligatory princess image her hostess expected from her, *exacted* from her actually. Kiki often wondered why she disliked it so, why she endured it only to help sell her work. "*I* would adore to be a princess," she said, shaking her head at Daisy severely. She'd never been able to explain, not even to Kiki, what she could barely begin to work out for herself, that she felt, in some deep way, like an impostor in the persona of Princess Daisy Valensky, as if she had no right to the title. Granted, titles were out of date in the modern world, except for those few countries still ruled by monarchs, but many people in many other countries still used them without the malaise she felt.

As Daisy lowered herself into her hot bath, she realized, because of the sudden shock of comfort she experienced from the embrace of the water, that she was sad, with a familiar sadness which overcame her from time to time, a sadness against which she battled without understanding its origin. She had periods of depression that she could see coming like the first hint of a sea fog dimming the light, a tendril drawn across the back of her mind that soon turned the furnishings of her life into dismal heaps. In such a mood, if she were home, she would creep under all the blankets she could find, thrust her feet into heavy wool socks and lie shivering for hours, wondering why the future held no delight, trying to imagine a situation, a place, a happening which could tempt her back to reality. She would hold Theseus close, ruffling him over and over, and cuddling him tightly.

Whenever she tried to trap this despairing sadness, lay it bare and examine it, Daisy was immediately caught up in a web of unwelcome questions that no one left alive could answer for her.

What if, for instance, she had two parents like most people? What if her mother, like other women who are separated from their husbands, had managed to explain to Daisy, when she was a child, why they lived hidden in Big Sur, seeing no strangers, having no contact with the outside world? Even if the explanation hadn't made too much sense it might have satisfied her for a while, until she was old enough to understand. What if her father had ever told her *why* he could only spend such a short time with her and had to leave so abruptly, year after year, keeping her in constant fear that he'd never return, in spite of the letters he sent her? What if her mother—that all-too-vague memory of absolute security and love—hadn't gone without a farewell, vanishing into the sea on a sunny afternoon? What if her father had allowed Dani to stay with her instead of imposing a rigorous, hermetic seal of silence on her very existence? And what if Stash hadn't died when she was fifteen; what if he were still alive, protecting her by his very existence? What if Ram had been a real older brother, concerned and kind, someone to whom she could go with her problems, instead of the sick madman only she and Anabel knew he was?

Daisy got out of the tub and started to dress. As she brushed her hair she looked at Kiki's fake emeralds that lay on the dressing table. The necklace and bracelets would be perfection loaded onto the green tweed jacket with its ruffled lapels, but the earrings would be wasted, hidden by her hair. She found some hairpins and twisted them through the great oval pendant drops, rimmed with rhinestones. She was wearing her hair down naturally this evening, after having kept it braided all day, and the gorgeous, heavy, silver-gilt stuff, in which she deftly fastened the earrings, fell in little ripples. Her Schiaparelli trouser suit made her look like a young Robin Hood, a Robin Hood who'd gone all the way to Paris to rob the rich, and, as she finished dressing, she stared at herself in the mirror as firmly as if she were dealing with a skittish horse and said out loud, "Daisy Valensky, it's no good wondering 'what if?' What is—*is!*"

Patrick Shannon recognized Daisy as the girl he'd seen riding that morning only from the set of her head as she entered the drawing room. Otherwise he would have thought she was a new arrival, since he had not seen her at either breakfast or lunch. As she entered the room, in which the other guests were already assembled, a small piece of time seemed to be frozen, a split second in which the hum of conversation hesitated, fragmented and then resumed.

Daisy knew no one in the room, and Topsy guided her around, making introductions. As she approached Patrick, he thought, so that's who she is, he might have guessed. Although he spent no time at all keeping up with celebrity news, like everyone else he had been aware of Daisy's existence. He could vaguely remember the cover of her as a baby in *Life* when he'd been a teenager.

They shook hands with perfunctory smiles, Daisy preoccupied with remembering all the new names—these people were her possible future customers—and Shannon trying to fit her into a slot. He was a man who liked to place new people immediately, get a fix on them, so that he knew where they stood in relation to him. He had already dismissed the Horse People as utterly unimportant in his scheme of things, tagged Vanessa and Robin Valarian as people he would never do business with and become convinced that Ham Short was a man with whom he could work profitably and well—he liked his style. As Daisy turned to be introduced to the Dempseys, he thought, another butterfly, pampered, petted, indulged, flattered and vain. The lesson of his ex-wife had been well learned ... he knew the type.

At dinner his judgment was confirmed as he listened to the conversation between Daisy, who was seated on his right, and Dave Hemming and Charlie Dempsey.

"I'll never forget seeing your father playing in a high goal tournament in Monterey in the thirties," Charlie Dempsey said to Daisy. "I don't remember the exact year but he was playing at three with Eric Pedley from Santa Barbara playing at, Tommy Hitchcock at two and Winston Guest at four—greatest team ever mounted in my opinion."

"Nonsense, Charlie," Dave Hemming interrupted from across the table. "The greatest team ever mounted was Guest, *Cecil Smith,* and Pedley, with Hitchcock at three—with all due respect to Stash."

"I'm sure you're both right," Daisy smiled. "But nobody, not even Cecil Smith, could ride like my father." She had grown accustomed to these conversations in the last few years. Almost every Horse Person over fifty had his own memories of her father, and she liked to hear them discuss him ... it brought him back for a moment, even though they were talking of memories of very long ago, before she'd been born.

While the familiar argument went on, Daisy turned to Shannon.

"Are you a polo aficionado, Mr. Shannon?" she asked politely.

"I don't know a thing about it," he answered.

"That's refreshing."

He thought she was mocking him. "And what do you do, Princess Valensky, when you're not arbitrating arcane disputes about a game that took place forty-five years ago?"

"Oh—this and that. I'm sketching young Cindy this weekend, on her pony."

"For fun?"

"More or less." Daisy considered it necessary at all times to hide the true commercial nature of her presence at these house parties. The fact that she was there to make money she had to have, the fact that she spent the evening carefully and casually finding out if any of her fellow guests had children who might be prospective subjects for her, the fact that she was doing nothing more or less than commission hunting, was best concealed by the mask of the dilettante. Her profession was well served by word of mouth rather than self-advertisement.

"Do you hunt in the neighborhood, Mr. Shannon?"

"Hunt? Here? No." My God, Patrick thought. After one month of riding school how could anyone expect him to be jumping fences?

"Then where *do* you hunt?" Daisy continued, confidently.

"I don't hunt at all," Patrick said shortly.

"But of course you do—or did—no? Oh, then why have you given it up?"

Shannon looked for malice in her eyes and found nothing but the gleam of candlelight on black velvet. The flames, the chrysanthemums on the table, the reflections from the heavy silver and Irish cut glass—all had become accomplices in illuminating her beauty which met and outmatched every brightness in the room. But he thought he heard a sardonic note in her amused interrogation.

"I assure you that I don't hunt, have never hunted and have no intention of ever hunting," he answered her with a coldly reined-in courtesy.

"But . . . your boots . . ." Daisy murmured, confused.

"What about them?" he snapped.

"Nothing," she said hastily.

"No—I insist. What about my boots?" Now he was certain that she was making fun of him.

"Well, only . . . oh, it's not important, really, it's just silly of me to have noticed . . ." Daisy babbled, trying to avoid his eyes.

"The boots?" Patrick asked, implacably.

Now Daisy got angry. If this man was going to treat her like a witness in a murder trial, she'd jolly well speak up.

"Mr. Shannon, your boots are black with brown tops. Only a Servant of the Hunt, that is a Hunt official, like a Whipper-In or the Master of the Hounds or the Master of the Hunt himself is *entitled* to wear boots like that. If you don't hunt, your boots should be one solid color."

"The devil!"

"Someone should have told you," she hastened to add.

"Aren't you saying that it's one of the things which everyone is expected to know?"

"It's really not important," Daisy answered as coolly as possible.

"You mean it's not the 'done thing'?" he said, stingingly, venting his fury at Chuck Byers who had given him the boots without an explanation.

"It's unheard of," she said, her temper rising.

"Then why hasn't anyone else said anything—I've been out riding all day," he accused her in a hard voice.

"They assumed, as I did, that you hunted. It's as simple as that."

"I don't ride well enough for any rational person to imagine that I hunt," he replied furiously.

"Then perhaps they were being tactful, perhaps they guessed that you'd get upset and they didn't want to risk your mighty wrath? Why get angry at me, Mr. Shannon? I didn't sell you those boots." Daisy turned to Charlie Dempsey and started to talk polo to him.

Patrick Shannon was left simmering in the suspicion that all of the people he'd ridden with today must have been curious about his boots and been too polite to question him—and, no doubt, had been laughing at him behind his back.

Shannon did not enjoy feeling like a horse's ass.

16

*T*here was only one private
room in the Valarians' apartment, only one room which
had never been photographed in the course of Robin's
never-ending redecorations, which totally renewed the
look of their Park Avenue duplex every two years. This
was the room in which they spent their rare time together,
in which they indulged in a cherished ritual before dressing to go out or to entertain at home as they did virtually
every night of the week. Each evening at six o'clock Robin
and Vanessa met in their private room which had walls
and floors covered in thick carpeting the color of vicuna
and a domed copper ceiling, from which warm light,
glowing from hidden recesses, spread over the many orchids that grew in hanging baskets. In the center of the
room, which was otherwise entirely empty, was a carpeted
platform on which rested a gigantic oval hot tub—a tub as
large as most ordinary bathrooms—made of black fiber-
glass. Six inches deeper than tubs generally are, it had four
adjustable water jets of brushed chrome that created whirlpools of water that could reach 110 degrees. Naked in the
soothing water, their marvelously taut, superbly kept bodies glimmering, they lay and sipped cold, dry white wine,
gossiping about their days and their doings. There they
reaffirmed the deep bonds which held them together.

Like many married homosexual couples they formed a
stronger, more solid and durable relationship than almost
any of the heterosexual couples they knew. There is no
team so committed to their joint and individual successes
as the homosexual husband happily married to a lesbian
wife, no love match as tight and protective and close-knit.

Together they received immense benefits they could never have obtained outside of marriage, the most important of which was that protection from being single which leads, in the case of any attractive male or female over thirty, to lively speculation about their sexual preferences on the part of almost everybody who meets them. Together they formed that unit, "the married couple," that is far more easily absorbed into social life anywhere than any single homosexual or a homosexual couple of the same sex: they provided their hostesses with that most desirable addition to any party, a perfectly matched pair.

Together they made a traditional, infinitely secure home for each other, in which Robin was free to indulge his talent for creating resplendently baroque surroundings and ever more sumptuous flower arrangements. It was he who found and trained perfect servants, and Vanessa who planned the exquisitely thought-out parties she had used so effectively to promote Robin's career. Finally, since they had no jealousy of each other, as lovers might have, each was free to indulge his sexual tastes with the added pleasure of knowing that the other was eagerly waiting to hear about it, to advise, to assist, to smooth the path, even to entrap, and if necessary, to comfort and console.

Their marriage gave them an entrée into the mainstream of the establishment of society and wealth which would not have been possible on the same level had they remained single. As "the Valarians" they dined at the White House, sailed on the largest yachts, stayed in the most historic English and Irish country houses, an impeccable couple, above scandal, if not entirely above rumor—but who paid attention to rumors in these days?

As "the Valarians" they were forever free of the taint of the homosexual; as a married couple they moved with impunity in the widest world of celebrity, while, in their own inner circle, they were not only recognized as brilliantly successful deceivers, but applauded for their cleverness in finding each other and using each other so well. They had understood the secret, so rarely brought out in its raw and naked state; the fact that among the successful of the world, there is *no gender*—there is only success or lack of success. The only important question is: *are you or are you not one of us?*

Homosexual married couples come in a variety of combinations: the bisexual husband, the kind Robin always called "a Jazz-Tango," who in the first years of marriage occasionally enjoyed his wife and almost always produced astonishingly beautiful children; the true homosexual man and the wife who is terrified of sex of any kind; and the lesbian with the passive, almost neuter husband. The Valarians were of the variety that most certainly has the best stories to tell each other, since Robin was as active sexually as his wife.

Robin Valarian truly loved Vanessa and she truly loved him, both with anxious tenderness. If he had a cold she brought him vitamin C every hour and watched while he swallowed it. If she had a tiring day, he would rub her back for an hour until she purred with relaxation and then he'd go into the kitchen, tell the cook exactly what to put on a tray and bring it in himself, settling her among the cushions on the bed and insisting that she eat. The life they had made together was a living, growing, deeply rooted thing, totally dependent on their joint contributions. Vanessa often quoted Rilke: "The love that consists in this, that two solitudes protect, and border and salute each other."

Beyond love, they were each other's best friends. Robin admired her nerve, her savage pursuit of what she wanted and he was particularly grateful for her role in his career. She had so much style, which leapt out directly from her personality, that she imparted it to his merely fashionable clothes. His abilities as a designer were limited: he knew how to make women look pretty and feminine—he specialized in cocktail and dinner dresses, leaning heavily on the allure of ruffles and the rustle of taffeta, but never in his life had he had an original design idea. Yet, year after year, rich women all over the country bought Robin Valarian's expensive couture clothes. This came about only partly because of the exceptionally friendly way in which he was treated by the fashion press, whose members enjoyed being included in the parties given by this most exclusive of couples. Essentially his clothes sold because Vanessa was so frequently photographed wearing his dresses with her swaggering, devil-be-damned flair, surrounded by people of taste and status, that "a Valarian" had come to mean a safely pretty dress in which an upper-class woman could feel almost as if she were Vanessa Valarian herself, rising to the challenge of being dashingly, ruthlessly, clashingly chic.

Their duplex reflected the strength of their bond. It was not cupidity that made them load every table with precious bibelots, but the nesting instinct gone wild, castle building on a domestic scale. Every object they chose and bought together reaffirmed their commitment, a set of Pyrex mixing bowls as strongly as a costly silver mermaid fashioned by Tony Duquette. There was to them a sacredness about their table linen, their silver and china such as only newlyweds know. Long before it became fashionable for a man to be interested in domestic detail, Robin Valarian prided himself on his abilities as a homemaker. Unlike the goddess of interior design, Sister Parish, whose two watchwords were luxury and discipline, the Valarians believed in luxury *and* luxury. Every one of their down pillows was piped, or tasseled, every lampshade lined in pink silk, every curtain double-lined, looped and caparisoned, every wall rich with at least twelve costly coats of lacquer, when it wasn't covered with rare fabric, every sofa overstuffed and oversized and totally comfortable, so that their guests felt as comforted and cocooned as if they were babies in their cribs, an illusion which caused them to gossip more freely than they ever did in less cushioned settings. The Valarians never gave a party at which at least one reputation was not made and another reputation ruined.

This couple, who defended the fortress of their marriage with the rigorous loyalty of blood brothers, was spared the ambiguous changeable moods of lovers, escaped the predictable limits imposed by monogamy and enjoyed all of the privileges granted to matrimony.

Vanessa Valarian was a subtle and devoted practitioner of the art of doing favors. She had long nourished a private theory that a favor done for the right person at the right time, done without planned motive or direct expectation of reciprocity, would eventually prove to be a useful, even an essential piece of the superb mosaic of her life . . . caviar flung on the waters. The right time was, in her experience, when the person for whom she did the favor had no reason to expect anything of her, when the favor seemed to come straight from good-hearted openhandedness and appreciation of that person's rare qualities. She almost never did favors for anyone who came to her for one; her favors had to appear as unhoped-for and unforgettable. The person for whom she did a favor needed no recommendation aside from Vanessa's keen intuition that told her who was coming up and who was going down, who would make it, who had potential that hadn't been detected, and who wasn't worth bothering with. Like an expert surfer, she was able to detect the big waves before they gathered momentum, able to hop on board before the other women in her world had spotted the swelling and the power.

When Topsy Short had mentioned that Daisy Valensky was sketching Cindy as a sort of trial before Topsy made up her mind about commissioning an oil of all three girls on their ponies, Vanessa felt the tingle of opportunity. She had observed Daisy the evening before at dinner. She had known instantly, as no one else did, that the green Schiaparelli suit was almost forty years old and that the emeralds were false and that the girl was, in some way or another, *vulnerable*. How she could possibly be vulnerable in light of her title, her share of her father's presumably fabulous fortune and her beauty was inexplicable, but Vanessa *knew*.

"Why don't we look at her sketches before she goes back to New York," she suggested.

"Oh, I don't think she'd like it," Topsy answered. "She told me when I asked her to come that they'd just be rough studies, like shorthand notes. She'll send me the finished sketch in a few weeks."

"What does it matter what she likes, young Topsy? Let's have a peek—it might be amusing."

Reluctantly Daisy allowed the two women to see her sketch pad. There were dozens of rapid, bold line drawings but none of them could convey to a nonprofessional what the finished sketch would be like.

Topsy was silent, her disappointment visible on her face, but Vanessa instantly grasped the extent of Daisy's talent.

"You're good—but of course you know that," she said to Daisy. "Topsy, you'd be making the mistake of the year if you don't have Princess Daisy paint all three of your girls. In a few years you'll have to pay twice the price for anything she does—if she even has the time for you."

"Well . . . I'm just not sure—what if Ham doesn't like it?" Topsy looked at Vanessa adoringly. How could she be interested in making decisions about paintings when, under her skirt, she could feel her naked thighs rubbing softly together, aching, trembling for the touch of Vanessa's marvelous hands?

"I can't imagine anything he'd like more, and if you don't do it now—Topsy, pay attention!—you won't have a record of the girls before they start to grow up—they're just at that perfect age. If I were you I wouldn't hesitate for a second. I'd have a really big oil, an heirloom . . . that is," she said, looking at Daisy, "if you have time to take on such a job?"

"I could make time," Daisy said, thinking that she'd paint all night for a month if necessary to get it done before the next bill came from England.

"Well, then, that's settled. I've done you a great favor, Topsy, and I don't want you to forget it. You'll bless me someday."

"Thank you, Mrs. Valarian," Daisy said hastily.

Vanessa spied the hidden relief on Daisy's face. So, she needed money after all. *Curious.*

"Thank me? Topsy's the one who should thank me—she's damn lucky to get you," Vanessa answered with the guileless, great, open smile that accompanied the execution of a promising favor that every instinct told her to grant. Daisy Valensky was now in her debt. "The next time we're in England, I'm going to tell Ram just how talented I think you are. He's a great friend of ours—we're devoted to your brother."

"Thank you, Mrs. Valarian," Daisy said again, automatically. She felt a chill like a stain spreading over her heart.

"What you need, Luke Hammerstein," Kiki announced sweetly, "is someone to wreak havoc with your life."

"That last exhibition just about did it for me," Luke answered as they found a table in The Ballroom.

"I thought you'd like it—how many people have ever seen Quebec manhole-cover rubbings?"

"It was a definite first. I've been curious about them as far back as grade school. And I like the fact that the group who did them is making rubbings from the manhole covers in SoHo to show in Quebec. It's that kind of cultural exchange that may do something to help the uncertain relationship we've always had with Canada."

"Yeah—I worry about Canada a lot."

"Do you?"

"Naturally. There's a tunnel in the heart of downtown Detroit which takes you right into Canada. When my brothers and I were kids we used to pester our father to take us. It sounded so romantic."

"Was it?"

"Of course not—that just proves that you know nothing about Detroit . . . or Canada."

"We can't all get lucky."

"You're making fun of me again," said Kiki, her eyebrows, with their jubilant angles, rising toward her ruffle of hair which was temporarily its natural brown.

"I'm sorry but I can't help it. You're like Beatrice in *Much Ado About Nothing*—remember, she was 'born in a merry hour'?"

"Well, did she get the guy in the end?"

"You never stop, do you?" Luke Hammerstein had been pursued by females since he was twelve, but never had he met one as frank about her intentions as Kiki Kavanaugh. Was she a compendium of every craft and guile known to women, or was she what she presented herself to be, an innocent sensualist out to have a thoroughly good time—with him as a partner? Luke was used to the new breed of women, but Kiki was a Green Beret in the battle of the sexes. It put him off balance, he admitted to himself. He was actually playing hard to get, like a woman was supposed to do—this role-reversal stuff was kind of fun.

"Get me a drink, for God's sake—I'm beat," he said. They were both carrying baskets loaded with the afternoon's purchases.

"Have you ever had hard cider?" Kiki asked. It was her favorite next to the iced Irish Coffee.

"Not yet, but why don't you order it since you're obviously going to anyway."

He looked in mild exasperation at the baskets they'd deposited on the white tiled floor. Kiki had bought, if he remembered correctly, an appliqued apricot satin cover for a hot-water bottle at a store called Harriet Love, a sculpture of a green frog, done entirely in neon tubing at a gallery called Let There Be Neon, two black satin garments, ambiguously called "guest kimonos," two bottles of Soave Bolla and one of Wild Turkey bourbon at a liquor store which had, in its window, a sign announcing WE DO NOT HAVE PINT BOTTLES OF WINE, and a piece of jewelry which made him nervous, an ivory heart with a red stone hanging from it like a drop of blood. Even the jewelry in SoHo had names, he thought—this one was called "They've Been Kicking My Heart Around." And that wasn't counting what she'd bought at Dean and Deluca, the great gourmet grocery store, where overflowing baskets of garlic buds, apples, lemons, black radishes, walnuts and plummy dried yuccas stood decoratively in the doorway and expensive pots and pans hung from the skylight two stories above. There she'd gone wild. Slabs of pâté en croute and duck gallantine, both at over twelve dollars a pound, from a counter on which two dozen different pâtés were displayed; a jar of heather honey from Holland; whipped cream cheese and a Petit St. Marcellin, the small cheese wrapped in chestnut leaves; three different kinds of salami, one from Spain, one from Italy and one from France; a pound of smoked Scotch salmon; a jar of hot okra pickles; a pound of Black Forest Ham; a dozen freshly baked croissants; half of a perfect brie; and, from the baskets of bread which hung all over the store, she'd picked one twisted challah, four bagels and one loaf of dark pumpernickel. Then she'd added a box of Dovedale Butter Shortbread from an English company which had been established in 1707, and several bars of bittersweet chocolate from the Ghirardelli Chocolate Company in San Leandro, California. There was something about the combination of foods she'd bought which struck him as highly suggestive.

Luke had been to SoHo a number of times before, since no advertising man he knew would miss the opportunity to see the big new works that were displayed in the galleries; but mainly he'd stuck to quick visits to 420 Broadway, where the major uptown dealers had their downtown branches: Leo Castelli, Sonnabend and André Emmerich.

Today he'd seen a SoHo he'd overlooked, the SoHo of people who actually lived here, a SoHo in which the Porcelli Brothers displayed fresh honeycomb tripe in the window of their butcher shop; in which a little kid walking a bike had stopped Kiki at a corner and asked, "Miss, could you cross me, please?"; in which a sign proclaiming PERSIAN CAT FOUND was displayed in the window of the M and D Grocery, a shabby, old-fashioned store which nevertheless had a freezer full of expensive Häagen-Dazs ice cream and shelves on which salted nuts shared the space with religious pictures and ten kinds of yogurt; a SoHo where, in the Mandala Workshop, you could buy a symbol representing the Jungian effort to reunify the self, made of hand crochet and stained glass. This SoHo was one of exotic contrasts. J. Volpe, General Machinist, was next door to a gallery which offered prints of "erotic food"; stores selling plumbing supplies and the A and P Cordage Co. existed cheek to jowl with the Jack Gallery with its Erté and Jean Cocteau watercolors.

Kiki looked at Luke shrewdly. He was in SoHo shock ... she knew the signs. She had planned to have dinner at The Ballroom but the enormous mural on the wall opposite their table would only intensify his discomfort, showing as it did, in vivid photo-realist fashion, nineteen of SoHo's most famous artists and citizens, including Larry Rivers and Robert Indiana.

"I know what you need," she told Luke.

"Now what?"

"Chinese food.'"

"By God, you're right! It's the only thing I could eat. How did you know?"

"You're Jewish—it's simple—when Jews go into culture shock the only thing that brings them back is deli or Chinese. We gentiles feel better right away if we just sit around and watch white bread burning."

"Don't you mean toasting?" he asked limply.

"No, burning, like a Yule log. Come on, we'll go to the Oh-Ho-So. It's right across the street."

Since no one had yet taken their order they unceremoniously picked up their baskets, left The Ballroom, crossed the street and staggered into the bar at the Chinese restaurant: a most welcoming bar crowded with worn, green velvet loveseats and chairs of carved wood, no two alike, all pulled up around tables which were made from a clutter of Victorian leftovers and, when the Victoriana failed, battered sewing-machine tables.

In the light of the jukebox, Kiki's umber eyes were shot with sparks of opals, yellow diamonds and glee.

"The gentleman will have a double Wild Turkey on the rocks," she told the waiter, "and I'll have some hard cider. Now let's talk about the other night. Why didn't you want to make love? Were you really too tired?" she asked Luke, with her bawdiest smile.

"Shit—just when you start to coddle me, like a real woman, you turn all aggressive. Wait till after the egg roll, won't you?"

"All I meant was *I* wasn't too tired—and I'd had to handle Theseus all day. So how come? Are you shy ... do you wait till the third date—have you religious scruples?"

"*After* the egg roll," he reminded her mildly. He had the

equilibrium of strength. Luke was fully aware of his forces, so he didn't mind revealing his weaknesses. He'd never met the woman who was a match for him—it was his secret pride. Three older sisters had taught him more about women than he needed to know, he had once liked to say, although he was aware that those had become fighting words in recent years. He saw Kiki sizing him up with the skill of a Monte Carlo croupier, no, make that a pit boss in Vegas. He smiled at her faintly, tauntingly.

"You know what you remind me of?" she said heatedly. "Those crypto-Greek heads in the Met from five hundred B.C.—they all have the same smug, superior, secretive smile—not even the decency to *pretend* to be honest—total conceit that has lasted for three thousand years."

"*After* the egg roll."

"All right—but then—watch out!"

"Do you always warn your intended victims?"

"I try to be fair. Men are, in many ways, more fragile than women."

Luke sighed, looking, giving Kiki the feeling that he was like nothing so much as a whole pile of presents that she was itching to unwrap.

"Okay, we'll talk about other people. Tell me about your mother," Kiki suggested.

"My mother is an arch-conservative. She never redecorates. We still have art deco."

"My mother redecorates every year. We're just getting art deco."

"My mother warned me that if I ever marry a beautiful gentile girl, one day she'll turn out to be just another old *shiksa*—*shiksa* is the only Yiddish word she knows."

"My mother believes that the way to break in a sable coat is to wear it to a Japanese restaurant the first day it comes from the furrier. She orders sukiyaki cooked at the table, and sits in the coat during the whole meal. It takes about a week to air it out, but after that the coat knows that she's the boss. Also I think she's an anti-Semite."

"My mother is such an anti-Semite that when her club started letting in Russian Jews, instead of only German Jews, she left it."

"My mother's worse than that. She took a course in mouth-to-mouth resuscitation in case my father ever got a heart attack and then, when she was in a bank, a man had a heart attack right in front of her and she didn't try to save him because he was so repulsive looking she was afraid of catching whatever he might have had . . . and he died right there in front of her."

"Jesus! Did she really?" Luke said, fascinated. Kiki was winning the mother-game.

"No, but it did happen to her real-estate lady," Kiki admitted.

"My mother doesn't have real-estate ladies," Luke said with a cool smile.

"Don't you ever move? You have to have a real-estate lady to buy a house."

"My mother doesn't believe in moving—it's nouveau. She just has . . ."

"The apartment on Park Avenue and the house in . . . Pound Ridge . . . and the place in Westhampton—no, East Hampton—right?"

"Almost—how'd you get so close?"

"It figured. I think we have the same mother only they don't know it."

"Do you realize," Luke said moodily, "that five times more people buy pet food than buy baby food? Isn't that horrifying?"

"No, dummy. It's because babies grow up and start to eat like people but pets eat pet food all of their lives."

"You're not entirely stupid," Luke said, reluctantly. Most people reacted to the pet-food statistics with dependable indignation.

"Do you want to hold hands?" Kiki asked hopefully.

"Not during lobster Cantonese!" he said scandalized.

"You lack passion," Kiki warned, looking yearningly at his mouth—there was something about a man's mouth, presented between a mustache and a beard, which made it so much more edible looking than if it just sat there on his face surrounded by skin.

"You're just saying that to make me prove to you that I'm not boring. It won't work." Luke applied himself to his lobster with calm relish. Kiki looked at him in dismay. This wasn't going right at all. Most men, in her large experience, had no defenses against a well-mounted, absolutely shameless attack. Bewildered, confused, flattered, they fell for it, and once they'd fallen for the idea they were only a step away from falling for her. Luke made her uneasy . . . she had the feeling that somewhere she'd gotten her act wrong, but she'd started out with him as she had with dozens of others and now the pattern had been set.

Maybe he *was* just hungry. Maybe he *had* just been tired. With Daisy away for the weekend, and the provisions she bought for breakfast and lunch tomorrow, she still had lots of time to work on this unexpectedly stubborn customer. She really *had* to have him.

"Could you please bring us some hot tea," she asked a passing waiter, "and some optimistic fortune cookies?"

The Friday following her weekend in Middlebury, Daisy found the studio unexpectedly peaceful. North had gone off for a week's vacation, the first in over a year, so there was no production meeting scheduled until the middle of the next week. There were myriad details for her to check in the office, but she was pleased when Nick-the-Greek and Wingo Sparks invited her to have lunch with them. Normally she ate lunch at her desk, with a sandwich in one hand and the phone in another.

Once the waiter had brought them their food, Nick said casually, "So how's the job going, kid? You holding up all right? I mean, we all know it isn't easy working for North. Sometimes I get the idea that he doesn't realize what you're worth."

"He's not exactly given to praise, but when he doesn't foam at the mouth, I know I've done a good job," Daisy shrugged.

"So you're willing to settle for that kind of validation?" Wingo asked.

"Why not? Is there something wrong with that?" Daisy wasn't about to complain to her coworkers.

"Lots wrong," said Nick. "It's like being satisfied with crumbs from a rich man's table, *campesina*, and I, Nick-the-Greek, am here to tell you that in no way is it enough."

"What are you trying to start, Nick?" Daisy asked curiously. "You get your commissions and they're hardly crumbs."

"You want to tell her, Wingo?" Nick asked the young cameraman.

"You bet I do. Listen, Daisy, Nick and I have been talking. We both think that we could go into business for ourselves. Nick's the best rep in the city—he knows where all the accounts are who want the North look but don't want to pay North's prices. North thinks of me as just a cameraman, but I can do his stuff, too—lots of guys are director-cameramen. It took me five years to get my cameraman's card—but I could be a director tomorrow just by saying I'm one. And I'm good—"

"How do you know?" Daisy challenged.

"I've been watching him long enough—I'm on to his tricks . . . and face it, how hard is it to direct a commercial?"

"This is what we have in mind," Nick interrupted Wingo. "We want to start our own shop but we want you with us . . . as a partner and producer. You wouldn't have to invest a dime, but you'd get a third share in the profits. Once I'm free of North, I could go out and sell Wingo— I've got a piss pot of prospects lined up. The reason we want you is because you happen to be the best producer anywhere—you work harder, you can talk people into doing anything for you, you watch the money as if it were your own, you double check everything—so, lucky lady, you get a free ride on this deal."

"You and Wingo and I would just up and leave—taking the store with us?" Daisy asked.

"It wouldn't be exactly that," Wingo protested. "North could replace each of us . . . eventually . . . nobody's indispensable."

"Yes, eventually—but meanwhile he'd be crippled for how long? You're talking rip-off, Nick," Daisy said, in growing anger.

"Tough shit," Nick said, carelessly. "This is a rip-off business."

"Nick," Daisy asked, "who gave you your first chance at repping—who took you out of that ad agency and taught you the ropes? Who showed you where to dress and encouraged you to let loose your natural chutzpah and okayed your expense accounts for those first months when you were getting nowhere? North, right? And Wingo, just who the hell hired you on a regular basis instead of using a free-lance cameraman like almost everyone else? How many days a year would you be working if you were merely another free lance? And who was the only person willing to take a chance on a kid who had *just* gotten his card? Most directors go for experience—they don't want to touch a raw kid . . . too much trouble. And how come you think you're such a hot-shot director when all you know is what you've *seen* North do? Don't you understand that you don't know *why* he does it, or *how* he gets his ideas? Perfect proof is that you think it's *easy* to direct a commercial—maybe it is—a bad commercial or even a fair commercial. But a *good* commercial? A commercial you don't absolutely hate when it interrupts your favorite television show? A commercial that doesn't make you want to vomit with the sheer banality of it? A commercial that looks so good you remember it a week later? Or even a month later, when you've seen thousands of others since? What's more, you don't know word one about casting. Alix and I only make a selection of possibilities, North does all the final casting and that's essential to the success of a commercial."

"Shit. Daisy, if you're going to talk about loyalty . . ." Nick interrupted in disgust.

"You're goddamned right I'm talking about loyalty. I remember the time you got drunk and came on so crudely with that gal art director from BBD and O that we lost the job, and I remember the time you were so anxious to get those big beer spots that you gave them a Y and R firm bid without checking with Arnie and we lost money every day we worked, and I remember the time—or rather the times —when North was going crazy on shoots because of client interference and you showed up too late to take them to lunch and get them out of his hair for a few hours, and I remember . . ."

"Shut the fuck up, Daisy," Nick said, looking sick.

"The hell I will— My point is that all those times North got furious, but he *didn't* go looking for another rep—he stuck to you because he had a commitment to you and you're more good than you are bad—but when you're bad, you're *horrid!*"

"But North's so rude to you . . ." Wingo started, defensively.

"That's my problem," she snapped, "and I don't need your sympathy. He's rude because he never works any way but under tension. There isn't a minute that the time pressure isn't getting to him. If somebody can screw up, somebody *will* screw up . . . and he knows it. It's my business to keep the confusion to a minimum. There's nothing personal in his rudeness—I'm an extension of his work and he doesn't need to play Sir Walter Raleigh with me. As a matter of fact, you two are only extensions of his work, too. Nick, if you weren't selling North, you just might have to work for a living. Wingo, if you didn't have North checking each shot before you roll a foot of film, I wonder just what your work would be like? You've both had a good ride on his back. I'm not saying you don't have talent, Wingo—just that you aren't ready to be a director-cameraman yet, and that for you and Nick to get together behind his back and try to steal off with everything he's given you both in terms of learning and experience and confidence—and to try to get me to go with you—that's the lowest kind of ingratitude!"

"Nick," Wingo said nastily, "we've obviously made a big mistake about the princess here . . . she just hasn't got what it takes to go out on her own. Daisy, you won't get a chance like this again."

"Maybe next time somebody will ask me to rob a bank . . . who knows, I could get lucky. Now listen, you two masterminds, I haven't had one bite yet of this lunch you invited me to and I'm not hungry anymore. I'm going back to the studio and work. As far as I'm concerned this perfectly splendid meeting never took place. You didn't ask me about anything and I didn't tell you how I felt. Whatever you decide to do is up to you. I've forgotten the whole thing. Personally I hope we'll be together for a long time. We're not a bad team—*all* of us. Or, on the other hand, if you do leave, good luck! I predict many wonderful days for the two of you shooting the attack of the fifty-foot hemorrhoid. See you later."

As Daisy left, Nick looked at Wingo. "I wish I could say she's a bitch."

Wingo's face was that of a man who had just missed being run over by a bus. "You can't and neither can I. I just wish I could say she was *wrong*."

When Daisy got back to her apartment that night she found Kiki thumbing through an issue of the *SoHo Weekly News*. "Daisy, do you have a date tomorrow night?"

"You know I do—your cousin is coming to town to take me out for dinner."

"Oh, right, I'd forgotten . . . so he hasn't given up on you yet, huh?"

"Henry? I don't think he understands English. I've said no so many times it's boring, but, my God, he's persistent. He's so sweet I don't want to hurt his feelings. I keep telling him he shouldn't see me because it's like cutting off a dog's tail in little pieces—it would be kinder to whack it off with one quick stroke—sorry, Theseus darling—but he won't pay any attention. Why'd you ask?"

"Oh, I just thought we might do something—there's a

tap dance epic at the Performing Garage and a poetry reading at St. Mark's Church and La Mama is doing Brecht for a change and there's Microwave Music at Three Mercer—all kinds of things," Kiki said glumly.

"Christ! What's the matter? Have you taken your temperature? Where does it hurt?" Daisy said, looking at her friend with concern. Kiki was curled up on the couch in an old caftan, surrounded by scripts, letters and magazines.

"Don't be an ass—there's nothing wrong with me—I just thought we should seriously invest in a little cultural enrichment, that's all. I have my theater, even if it is temporarily dark, but *you*, what do you do all day but think about things that are directed at making millions of women have anxiety attacks?" Kiki asked waspishly. "That, plus those Horse People will make you a cultural idiot if you're not careful."

"Let's just stick to the facts," Daisy said, ignoring her words. "You've never gone in for cultural enrichment since Santa Cruz misguidedly gave you a diploma. That means you don't have a date for Friday night for the first time in something like eight years, and you're in a panic. Now that's absurd and you know it. There are a dozen guys you could call who'd jump . . ."

"I don't want *them!*" Kiki said, sounding more confused than adamant.

"Who do you want?"

Kiki remained stubbornly mute.

"Shall we play guessing games? Who is it my Kiki wants? Who did she fill the fridge for last Saturday so that we had to eat pâté and cheese for breakfast all week long to get rid of it, who was unkind enough . . ."

"Oh, stop it, Daisy! You're getting so rotten," Kiki snarled.

"Luke still hasn't called," Daisy said flatly.

"No, he hasn't. I'd like to kill him. How dare he do this to me? I simply don't understand it! Nobody does this to me, nobody!" Kiki's whole little body was huddled and shivering under the caftan as if she were preventing herself from springing forward and pounding her fists on the floor like a baby in a tantrum.

"Nobody but Luke Hammerstein."

"That's right, rub it in," Kiki said bitterly.

"Kiki, come on, I'm sympathetic! But you have to face facts if you want to change them."

"Oh, spare me—Miss Lonely Hearts rides again."

"Do you know somebody else you can talk about it with?"

"Daisy Valensky, you have the makings of a first-class bitch somewhere inside that glorious exterior. You know I don't," Kiki said, seizing Theseus in a despairing embrace.

"I think you're right," Daisy said with a pleased smile. "This is my day for telling it like it is or some such slogan left over from—was it the fifties or the sixties?—never mind . . . but you're not the first person who isn't happy with me today. And guess what—I don't give a shit."

"Oh, be quiet and listen. That son-of-a-bitch has refused my advances, not once but *twice*. How can there be any *possible excuse* for that? Do you think he's impotent? Do you think maybe he has an incurable form of some kind of V.D. and doesn't want to tell me? Do you think . . . oh, God . . . do you think he's in love with somebody? Oh, Jesus . . . I bet *that's* what it is—that's the only thing it could be!" Kiki's hands flew up and covered her mouth as she contemplated this worst of all possibilities.

"If he were, I'd know it. He and North are tight—I'd have picked up something, somehow—that studio is like a commune, gossip like that would have zipped around by now. Kiki, it's simple, and you brought it all on yourself."

The phone rang and Daisy picked it up. "Hi. Oh, hi, Luke, it's Daisy." Kiki lunged for the phone but Daisy backed away holding it firmly on its long cord. "Nope, sorry, she's not here. No idea . . . could be any one of a dozen places . . . I haven't really seen her all week, to tell you the truth, except running in and running out . . . but I'll take a message." Kiki signaled frantically but Daisy made horrible grimaces and ferocious eyes at her while she shook her free hand menacingly back and forth. "All right—I'll ask her to try to call you when she gets a chance. I'll leave it on the top of her other messages . . . I'm beginning to feel like a switchboard. I don't know why Kiki doesn't get a service or something. No, that's all right . . . I don't really mind . . . at least you're a client which is more than I can say for all of the others. Bye, Luke."

"Daisy! How could you?" Kiki cried as soon as she'd hung up.

"That's how you do it!"

"You've got to be joking. That's the oldest game in the book. Nobody does that anymore."

"*Everybody* does that who has the sense she's born with. Too bad you didn't know Anabel better."

"But I've never played hard-to-get in my life," Kiki sputtered, "and I've had more men than anyone I've ever known."

"Men you were not really after. It's easy to get a guy if you genuinely don't want him. I've seen you in operation for years; everything made easy for the poor sucker, and he walks right into your big, beautiful spiderwebs, thinking how he's made a conquest, and before he knows what's happened, he's a goner because right at the *heart* of your whole number is the fact that you simply couldn't care less—you're just doing it for kicks, a slap and a tickle, and he senses this, subconsciously anyway, and *that's* what drives him crazy, not your availability but your essential *unavailability*. I defy you to name just one man you've had whom you didn't give up if someone more attractive came along . . . I defy you to tell me the name of one guy who made you suffer . . . up till now."

"Why should I let a man make me suffer? What's so good about that?" sniffed Kiki rebelliously.

"Nothing. Suffering isn't noble. But the fact that you have steadily refused to put yourself in a position where you might have had to suffer is what I'm talking about. You've always gone in for basically unimportant relationships; good sex, lots of laughs, but not 'meaningful,' if you can overlook that cliché. Sorry, *sorry*, but it's true and you know it, too. Now, along comes a man who could be important to you and you haven't got any idea how to approach him. You're putting on your old act with a new cast and it just isn't working. So try a new script. Luke is smarter than you are, hard as that may be for you to believe. He's got you figured out, he can tell that you're used to having your way with men, and he isn't going to let that happen to him. What else is he doing but playing hard to get with you? He waited five days to call? Well, you're not going to return his call for a week . . . maybe more. And when you do see him again, you're going to be a whole new Kiki."

"It's too late, I've already blown it," Kiki said dismally. "I mean I really let him know I could be had . . . and all that food! I could cut my throat! And, Daisy, I do adore him so . . ."

"First impressions can be changed. You're an actress, aren't you? It's simple—you threw yourself at him because you had nothing better to do *that* particular week. *But,* since then, things have changed. Don't *ever* be specific about what has changed—he'll imagine them. *Now* you're not interested in getting involved. You're cool, restrained and maddeningly off-hand. You can't accept the first two times he asks you out but you leave the door open—you're friendly—in fact, it's as if the two first encounters had just never taken place. But don't overdo it. Be yourself, but *don't come on.* Let him try to figure that one out! I think they call it 'bait and switch.' "

"I think they call it entrapment," Kiki murmured, radiant with admiration. "Daisy—I can do it—I know I can. But what if it doesn't work?"

"Then you'll just have to resign yourself. It's better to know right away than to find out after you've turned yourself inside out for months over the guy. 'Men have died from time to time, and worms have eaten them, but not for love.' "

"Betty Friedan?"

"Shakespeare—*As You Like It.*"

"Oh, what did *he* know. 'Dost thou think, because thou art virtuous, there shall be no more cakes and ale?' "

"I knew you didn't need cultural enrichment."

"I put on *Twelfth Night* last year—don't you remember —on skateboards?"

"Could anyone who had the good luck to be there forget that immortal evening? Listen, I can't stand eating any more of last Saturday's gourmet leftovers. Let's go get a pizza as soon as I've cleaned up a bit. All right?"

"You're on." Kiki was already pacing the room like an oversized elf, holding herself tall, with an elusive, faintly amused, slightly preoccupied expression on her face and her body clearly expressing "touch-me-not." Daisy flung her a fond look and left the living room quietly. When Kiki was getting into a character she liked to be alone. Daisy deliberately took her time washing her hands and suddenly she found herself plummeted from the peaks of the day into another of those strange pockets of sadness she had experienced only a week before, in Middleburg, at the Shorts. She'd been flying high all day today, telling Wingo and Nick-the-Greek what she thought of their sneaky plan and now straightening out Kiki.

But abruptly, face to face with herself, her life seemed,

in a frightening way, to be composed of a patchwork of odd bits and pieces which didn't form anything as substantial as a quilt. Her work at the studio, difficult though it was, didn't have the virtue of continuity; with every new commercial the achievements, the triumphant struggle of the week before were immediately replaced by today's crisis. North's lack of anger was not really a substitute for genuine appreciation, no matter what she'd told the others at lunch. She felt that she was forever playing catch-up on the job, always having to prove herself, over and over. As for her painting: her scramble after commissions was at the whim of capricious patrons who often treated her sketches and watercolors as just one step higher than a professional photographer's studio portrait. And her raggedy excuse for a love life was even more unfulfilling than she'd admitted to Kiki. The reason she could sound so wise on the matter of Kiki's refusal to be vulnerable was because it was a trait she knew all too well, an element that was far more deeply established in her own sensibility than in Kiki's prankster emotions. The idea of spending another evening fending off poor, dear, damp-minded Henry Kavanaugh was dreary. She should never have let him make love to her in the first place. She had never been in love—it was as simple and bare as that, and a constant source of uneasiness and depression, like a low-grade fever which would not go down. She thought of Kiki, practicing being hard-to-get in the other room—that was the one constant in her life, her friendship with that great, good loony. Nothing she could ever do for Kiki would pay her back for all the emotional support and unswerving affection she'd given Daisy in the years since her father had died.

Theseus padded into the bathroom and sensed her mood. He put his front paws on her shoulders, just as he used to do when she was little, and licked her nose. "You lovely lurcher, you," Daisy told him and realized that she was crying. He was licking up her tears. Damn it, Daisy, she told herself, you go around as if you have the answers for the whole world, so just stop feeling sorry for yourself. Enough! You're doing fine . . . just keep on truckin'.

17

"*H*ello, Ham?"

"Yup?"

"It's Pat Shannon—how's it going?"

"Couldn't be better," Ham Short grinned. The one who phones first in the mating dance of companies and corporations has put his cards on the table. And he liked a man who made his own phone calls. Nothing offended him as much as having another man's secretary get him on the line and keep him waiting until she put him through to her boss. He invariably hung up on her, unless, of course, he wanted something.

"How about coming up to New York, whenever it's convenient, and spending the day with me at Supracorp? I'd like you to know more about us."

"How's tomorrow?"

"Fine. We'll send one of the company's Gulfstreams for you."

"The hell you will—I only fly in my own Aero-Commander . . . got it fixed up the way I like it."

"Western?"

"Damn right—the thing's got everything but its own still and an outside crapper."

"A car and driver will be waiting for you. When will you get in?"

"Nine sharp, give or take an hour waiting for landing clearance."

"See you tomorrow. I'm looking forward to it."

"You bet."

Supracorp's New York offices occupied five full floors at 630 Fifth Avenue, where the great bronze statue of Atlas, bearing the globe on his shoulders, guards the enormous doors. Ham Short stepped out of the elevator on the tenth floor to find himself in a world designed by Everett Brown to combine drama with rich spaciousness. The receptionist sat behind a twenty-foot semicircular desk made from glowing white oak which curved in front of a wall of bronze mirrors. On either side of the huge reception room were floor-to-ceiling, free-standing columns of plexiglass and stainless steel in which were displayed examples of Supracorp's products.

Ham gave his name to the receptionist and turned to inspect the columns. Before two minutes had passed, he was gratified and surprised to see Pat Shannon, in shirtsleeves, the knot of his tie off center and the top button of his shirt undone, appear to greet him. They passed through wide corridors carpeted in deep brown, so well lit and humming with invisible energy that Ham felt as if he were on a spaceship. Shannon ushered him through a large room with yellow linen walls in which three women were busily telephoning or typing, each at her own large rosewood desk, and on into his own office. Ham, anticipating an expansion of the refined, subdued, but unembarrassed opulence he had just glimpsed, was astonished to find himself in a room which could have been in a ranch house in Sante Fe. Shannon gestured toward a pair of deeply tufted, pleasantly worn leather chairs and poured Ham a cup of coffee from a large thermos which stood on a low pine table.

"What's this? Shirtsleeves to shirtsleeves in three generations?" Short asked.

The lines on either side of Shannon's mouth deepened in amusement. "Beats the hell out of me how a man can get a day's work done in a jacket. As for the three generations— I'll never know. You're looking at a genuine orphan, Ham."

"Don't look to me for a drop of sympathy. I left home at twelve—always wished I'd been an orphan. Still do— I'm supporting two dozen no-goods back in Arkansas," Ham said, still inspecting the room. The walls were simply painted in a calm, pale gray. It was sparely furnished with a few mellow, not exceptional pieces of pine furniture, and several Navaho rugs were hung on the walls. The door was covered with adobe tile. It was so clearly a room that had been designed by the man who used it, and only for his comfort, that even Ham Short was impressed. This lack of pretension was more meaningful than the most magnificent office would have been. There wasn't even any art—only a few large chunks of quartz and a number of American Indian blankets. Ham, looking through three big, uncurtained windows at a startling view of the spires of St. Patrick's Cathedral directly across the street, thought that this had to be one of the most expensive pieces of office space in the world.

"How much do you know about Supracorp, Ham?" Pat Shannon looked even younger than he had in Middleburg. The informality of his open shirt, the obvious comfort he took in his old chair, the lack of any attempt to disguise his intensity, his focus on Ham Short, the glint of playfulness in his eyes, all made Ham feel as if he were meeting a good friend rather than someone with whom he was merely having an exploratory business discussion. He remembered, looking at Patrick's muscular neck and the big, hearty Irish smile of the man, that he'd been one hell of a linebacker when he'd played for Tulane. Ham Short felt very much at ease.

"Only what I read in *The Wall Street Journal*. Not a tenth of what you fellas must have found out about my little outfit."

"You and your outfit interest us a lot, Ham."

"I gather so. How come you picked on me?" Short was quite as wary as he was flattered.

"Obviously we want to get into shopping malls. We already have a real-estate division and it's healthy and growing. There are many real-estate operations we could be interested in besides yours. But it's Ham Short we want to acquire, as much, and, in fact, more than your property. We admire the way you've built your business, we like your brains, we like your methods, we like the way you operate and we like your results. We need a man like you."

"Don't beat about the bush much, do you?"

"It takes too much time. A lengthy courtship isn't necessary when two people want the same thing. But there's no point in talking specifics unless you're interested as well, and that's why I asked you up to visit—to show you what we're about. If we bought your company, Ham, you'd not only double your net worth within a few years, as one of the largest single stockholders in Supracorp, but you'd be on our board of directors and we'd be able to get the benefit of your thinking in operating all of our various divisions. Hell, Ham, we'd pick your brains like a bunch of vultures. And, of course, you'd continue to run your own show with the advantage of our lines of credit and the profits we're sitting on, ready to invest."

"Reporting to you?" Short said flatly.

"Yes. And I report to the stockholders. I don't believe you and I would have problems getting along."

"Hmmm." Ham Short liked Shannon, but he had never reported to anyone in his life. Still, he had always been intrigued by the activities of the large, varied conglomerates. He felt he was ready to spread his wings over a great deal more space than that covered by mere shopping malls.

"Come on—let's take a walk around." Pat Shannon knew just how bitter a pill he'd just given Short to chew on and he didn't want to leave him too much time to taste it. On the other hand, it had to be said, and the sooner the better. There was only room for one man at the top. He led Ham out of his office, this time stopping briefly to introduce Short to his three secretaries.

"Some of our divisions are based here," Shannon explained as they walked on down the corridor. "Lexington Pharmaceuticals, which was Nat Temple's first baby, has its main office on the next floor up—did you ever hear the story of how this whole company was founded on a cough drop? Nat Temple cooked it up on his mother's wood-burning stove and was the first person to give the Smith Brothers real competition. Now Lexington makes everything from miracle drugs to ... Hi, Jim." Shannon stopped a man passing in the hall. "Ham, this is Jim Golden, one of the vice-presidents of Lexington Pharmaceuticals. Jim, Hamilton Short."

"Mr. Short, it's a pleasure. Pat, how was Paris? When'd you get back?"

"Yesterday. And Paris was as usual—two full days of meetings. Choiseul and O'Hara, our wine and liquor importing division, is based there," he explained to Ham. "For every one taste of the new vintages I must have had a bottle of water. We're looking to buy a big natural source water but the one I liked best wasn't for sale—belongs to the government."

"No jet lag?" Ham asked, with curiosity.

"No, almost none. I have them put all their watches on New York time when I get there and stay on New York time until I leave, so it doesn't hit me. It's a necessity. Yesterday, only hours after I got back, I was the guest speaker at the New York Society of Security Analysts, and last night was the opening of a Broadway musical to which we own the movie rights, and I'd invited a few senators and their wives up from Washington, so I had to be awake."

"But what about meals? Don't your French people get mixed up?"

"They're used to it by now. They don't complain so I assume they don't mind. When I fly to Japan—we have four hundred people in the office there—I do the same thing."

"And they don't complain either?" Ham asked, looking suspicious.

"Not so you'd notice. But I don't stay more than three days at a time—they manage. Now, let's take a look at Troy Communications. It's our entertainment division. The film studio and the television production company are both based on the Coast, of course, but the paperback publishing house is right here, two floors up, and the main offices for our seven radio stations and our TV stations are in this building too. Next year we're thinking of getting into hardcover publishing."

"I thought publishing was strictly a gentleman's business, and a dying one at that," Ham said.

"Not anymore, Ham." Both Shannon and Jim Golden laughed. "If it were, you can be sure Supracorp wouldn't be in it. We've only got one division that's doing badly: Elstree Cosmetics."

"Elstree? The English firm? Seems to me my mother used Elstree."

"That's the problem. It's even more ancient and venerable and respectable than Yardley or Roger et Gallet. Everybody's mother used it, but nobody's *daughter* is using it. We bought them almost two years ago and we haven't been able to turn them around yet. Elstree lost over thirty million last year. I'm going to get involved personally in the new advertising campaign. The whole line is being redesigned—again."

"Pat," Jim Golden said, "I know you're busy, but when you get a chance, would you drop into Dan's office?"

"Problem?"

"Big, big problem."

"Why didn't you call me sooner? Let's do it now," Shannon said impatiently. Walking quickly, he guided Ham and Golden straight past the bank of elevators and took the fire stairs, two at a time, to the floor above. Quickly he threaded his way through the maze of handsome corridors and went straight into the offices of Dan Camden, president of Lexington Pharmaceuticals. Ham Short was fascinated to note that the large office, which had the same view as Shannon's, was furnished in an all but overpowering mixture of jewel-hued damask and eighteenth-century antiques. He felt so strongly that he could have been at home at Fairfax Plantation that he knew the antiques were genuine. Stepping from behind an enormous Chippendale desk, a small, bespectacled man welcomed them with a worried and preoccupied air. Almost immediately he directed their attention to a large white square that lay on top of his desk.

"Pat, this is one of the first completed samples. In my opinion the last layer simply isn't as good as the lab boys thought it was. Six months of testing and they haven't got it right! Now these first five layers here are all right, they perform to specifications perfectly. So far, so good. We could wipe the competition off the map, except that the last and crucial layer doesn't work. Or, let me put it this way, it works, but just not well enough to justify the claims we plan to make."

"Got any water?" Pat asked quietly.

"Right here—I've been working with it all morning." The three men stood dripping water, drop by drop, onto the first layer of the white square. They all watched a large desk clock as, patiently, carefully, with intense concentration, they bent over the desk for long minutes. Ham Short sat down and watched the utter intensity on the faces of each of the three men. Patrick Shannon's gaze never left his task. Ham felt himself dozing off.

"There!" Dan Camden exclaimed at last. Ham sat up with a jerk to see the man pointing an accusing finger at a tiny bead of moisture on the highly polished wood of his desk. "It's at least two or two and a half minutes too soon."

"Shit," Shannon said in a soft voice. "Dan, you assured me only ten days ago that the tests looked good and you know that I went before the stockholders at the meeting last week and told them that we were planning to grab a large chunk of the market with this new product. We're not just looking at three million dollars of lab work that doesn't come up to the mark, and we're not just talking about a well-plotted media campaign to test the market in twenty cities which will now have to be postponed, we're talking about the expectations you let me present to our stockholders, not one of whom will forget them." He spoke quietly and calmly, but the flush which Ham Short noticed on his neck gave away his controlled anger.

"Pat, I'm just as upset about this you are," Camden protested, wiping his glasses in agitation.

"Not really. You only have me to contend with and I'm perfectly capable of understanding how the lab could fuck up—which, as it happens, I do. But I've got those blood-thirsty stockholders to deal with and I relied on *your* advice and *your* documentation. Next time, don't give me a green light until you're absolutely sure. Personally sure. Don't take anyone's word for it."

"The chief chemist . . ."

"Not even the chief witch doctor's. Understood? Now I want those lab people over here from Jersey and in my office at four sharp this afternoon, so make sure they're all present and accounted for, Dan. We'll go into this then. See you later."

He turned away from the president of the giant phar-maceutical company who was, once again, absorbed in the white square on his desk.

"Come on, Ham, we've still got a lot of touring to do."

"What was all that about?" Ham asked, once they were out of earshot of the secretaries working in the outer office. "Some sort of new invention?"

"When it works, and it *has to*, it'll be the softest dis-posable diaper on the market. But it'll never sell if the mother has to change her baby too often. We have to have a minimum of another three minutes of resistance in the outer layer and we can give Pampers a run for their money." Pat's jaw was set in determination as he talked.

"Hmmm," grunted Ham Short.

"Now, let's go up to Troy Communications. I'll give you a quick tour before lunch."

"Sure." Lunch sounded like a good idea and the sooner the better. Later that afternoon Ham had an appointment at his investment banker's and he planned to ask the man what he thought of Shannon . . . personally.

"He's a damn *privateer!*" Reginald Stein said.

"Didn't strike me that way," Ham Short commented.

"Listen, Ham, he's a damned riverboat gambler, or halfway to it. He's too bold, takes too many risks for my taste and I've got too much Supracorp stock not to be worried about him."

"But look at the growth of the corporation," Ham protested.

"I know, I know, you can't fault that, but everybody's growing, Ham. These are fat years for certain kinds of businesses and Supracorp's in a lot of them. What worries me so much is the downside risk, and Ham, you know as well as I do that there is *always* a downside risk. Shannon takes chances he doesn't *have* to take—and I don't like that. He's not involved in safety and I am. And so should you be, my friend." The banker paused. "Ham, just why do you ask?"

"No real reason, Reggie, just curiosity."

By now Ham Short knew for certain that he wasn't going to have anything to do with a business that not only had a downside risk but was a business in which the seepage rate of baby piss was treated as a matter of life or death. He had enough plumbing problems in his life as it was . . . and sewage disposal problems as well—to get involved with dirty diapers. He was too old and he was too rich. He didn't need these complications. Maybe Pat Shannon could live with the shadow of the stockholders hovering over his daily life, but Ham Short didn't intend to ever have to report to anybody. Not even to Topsy.

"And please give me only brown eggs with breakfast tomorrow, Mrs. Gibbons," Ram instructed his housekeeper after dinner late on Friday night at Woodhill Manor.

"Certainly, Sir," the stout, self-respecting lady replied. Queen Elizabeth, too, would eat only brown eggs from a farm in Windsor. Mrs. Gibbons, to her relief, had seen few changes in forty years at Woodhill but she was beginning, albeit reluctantly, to approve of her late master's grandson and heir.

This rare weekend alone in Devon was a necessary respite for Ram. Recuperation and meditation were on his agenda. All winter he had been working particularly hard and staying out much later than was usual for him. His decision to set about a search for a wife had led him to accept invitations to a number of weekends and parties he normally would have refused, but the candidates had to be surveyed before he could make a logical and reasonable choice.

Now, at least, he was able to define what he did *not* want, although he still hadn't found anyone remotely suitable. As he methodically got ready for bed he reviewed the possibilities he had rejected. They included any number of that group known as the "Sloane Rangers"—after fashionable Sloane Square in Chelsea. They were clever young society women who spent their days shopping and having their hair done and trading secrets over lunch at San Lorenzo in Beauchamp Place, a close-knit clique who dressed in an informal uniform of checked or plaid blazers, silk shirts, wool skirts from St. Laurent and highly polished boots. Ram found them highly antipathetic. They knew each other far too well, they told each other far too much, they had, quite simply, been around too long to attract him. And having thoroughly looked over the current debutante crop of last spring's beauties who had just been hatched, he hadn't been charmed by a single one of the worldly herd of Amandas, Samanthas, Alexandras, Arabellas, Tabithas, Melissas, Clarissas, Sabrinas, Victorias and Mirandas, who at only eighteen already "knew everybody." He fell asleep while he was mentally rejecting every girl he had met in the last four months.

The next morning Ram took one of his Purdey shotguns and set out on foot. He intended to inspect his fences, at least symbolically, since nine hundred acres of fields could hardly be covered except by his bailiff and his men. However, Ram liked the idea of walking on his own land.

There was something in the air, even now, as early as the beginning of February, which if it was not quite green, somehow smelled of approaching greenness, but it went unnoticed by Ram, who was thinking of an article he had recently read by Quentin Crewe, who pointed out that if a man had earned 250 pounds a week since the Crucifixion and saved every shilling of it, he still would not be as rich as the Dukes of Westminster or Buccleuch or Earl Cadogan. There were nineteen dukes, thought Ram, who each possessed over ten thousand acres—yes, land was still where the money was in England. But only as long as it wasn't taken away by the government in the form of taxation. Private British wealth might only last out his lifetime—perhaps not as long as that. Ram had foreseen that possibility long ago and invested so heavily in other countries that even if he had to leave England and all he owned, including these ancient acres, he would always be excessively rich.

Did he require a wife to be rich? Not necessarily, thanks to his foresight. Did he require her to be of absolutely impeccable birth? Yes... sheer self-respect demanded that minimum. A virgin? Again yes. It was perhaps, in fact, unquestionably, an old-fashioned notion in these days, but firmly in Ram's mind was a need to find a girl of innocence, someone who hadn't been exposed prematurely to the taint of the London Season, a girl not quite formed, who would adore and admire him. A proper wife.

He turned to look back at Woodhill Manor, a dwelling dating from the Elizabethan period, added onto in the time of Queen Anne, and boasting a new wing of Edwardian origin, which, because of the fairly uniform use of gray limestone and stone-tiled roof, formed a charming harmonious whole. It was not a truly grand house in the tradition of the great English country estates, but it had something new money could not buy: tranquility, grace, timelessness.

He had sensed that same quality—to a much higher degree—on a trip he had recently made to Germany, in connection with investments in a large ball-bearing factory. There, he had been invited to spend the weekend at a Bavarian castle, a *schloss* which had belonged to the family of his hosts since the thirteenth century, in which twenty-two generations had managed to live without interruption in spite of wars, pestilence and other nastiness of history. This Germany, the Germany of the Furstenburgs and the Windisch-Graetzs, the Hohenlohe-Langenbergs, and Hohenzollern-Sigmarigans and von Matternichs, this Germany of Serene Highnesses and Royal Highnesses and Illustrious Highnesses, called to something elemental in Ram. Not only did he appreciate the straightforward, unabashed richness of his hosts, he also approved of the emphasis he found everywhere among the nobility on serious, sensible application to the *business* of life. These were practical, stern, proud people who did not let the antiquity of their names deter them from extracting the maximum from their forests and their vineyards, from expanding their family businesses and investing in foreign countries. As he had sat at lunch with his host and hostess,

Ram had seen, outside on a path on the other side of the lawn, two young girls, perhaps not more than eleven or thirteen, accompanied by a groom, riding past.

"Our daughters," the Prince had said with a casual wave toward the window which did not conceal the pride he took in them, even as he returned to an explanation of why anyone listed in Part One of the *Almanach de Gotha* cannot marry somebody who is not listed in either Part One or Part Two without losing his royal prerogative. This discourse was largely lost on Ram, as, in his mind's eye, he contemplated the momentary vision of the two blonde children as pure and untouched as if they were figures in a tapestry.

Still, he could not look to any young German girl for a wife. It was out of the question, for no matter how perfectly brought up and carefully protected she might be, no matter how flawless her English, how ancient her lineage, how splendid her accomplishments, she would still be foreign. To people like the Fulfords of Great Fulford Devon, and the Crasters of Craster West House, Craster, Northumberland, to others of the great untitled families of England, the Monsons, the Elwes, the Henages, the Dymokes—he, a direct descendant of Rurik, Grand Duke of Novgorod and Kiev, founder of Imperial Russia—he, Prince George Edward Woodhill Valensky, was still something of a foreigner.

Ram shrugged and resumed his walk. He faced without rancor the fact that he felt that his own Englishness was not firmly enough established for him to take a non-English wife. In his own opinion, even Queen Victoria had never quite lived down the stigma of Prince Albert's nationality.

As he cast a last backward thought at the memory of his glimpse of the two young German princesses he realized that he had been wasting his time prospecting in London, evaluating the harvest of young women. Although they told anyone who would ask that they were *not* officially entered in the marriage stakes, although "having" a London Season was now emphatically dismissed as merely a chance to "widen one's circle of friends," Ram was not fooled. A rich husband was even more avidly sought after in tax-poor England today than he had been in England of yesterday. Granted, the time was past when the first thing openly asked about any prospective mate, male or female, was the extent of that person's wealth or expectations.

Such healthy honesty had gone underground since the days, not so long ago at that, when Jane Austen would cite the precise number of pounds of income per year as an absolutely essential part of her description of any of her characters.

Ram had always known the importance of money. There had never been a time he could remember when he was too childish to realize that his father was rich and his mother and her second husband were not. Nor did he believe that other people weren't as involved with money as he was. It was merely that they hid their fascination, as indeed he did, except at work. It was all very fashionable and up-to-date for a girl to protest that the worst thing that could happen to her was to be considered a prominent debutante, that what she really longed for was to become a student of Russian or Chinese history or travel around the world in a sailboat, that all she wanted was to be young and carefree and never think of things like income. Ram knew better. Her career, such as it was, would be abandoned gladly when the proper young man with the proper amount of money came along. That's what they were after, all of them, except for a few rare, odd females who had always been out of step with their world, a world that was certainly dying but nevertheless, as far as the English upper classes were concerned, the best world that had ever been.

As Ram moodily considered the case of certain eighteen-year-old eligible beauties—Jane Bonham Carter, great-granddaughter of Prime Minister Herbert Asquith, who was already ensconced in the study of economics and philosophy at London University; Sabrina Guinness, working for a living and in a frightfully unsuitable way if what Ram heard was true, as a governess for Tatum O'Neal—he suddenly realized that he should be searching in the world of seventeen-year-old girls. Eighteen was just too sophisticated, too headstrong, too stubborn, too self-oriented an age for a wife. By eighteen, a girl was ruined, Ram decided, breaking off a branch from a young oak and inspecting the buds without really seeing them.

Sarah Fane, Sarah Fane? The name swam into his mind, and it took a minute for him to remember that last week over a business lunch, her father, Lord John Fane, had grumbled to him about his daughter. Had he been complaining because she insisted on coming out at Queen Charlotte's Birthday Ball next May or because she had

refused to be presented at the ball? Ram couldn't recall—
he hadn't paid attention—but he did remember that he'd
been surprised that the subject was even raised. It seemed
a short time ago that he had seen her, a child of fourteen,
when he'd gone to spend a weekend in Yorkshire at Lord
John's—it must have been mid-August because they'd been
gathered for the opening of the grouse-shooting season.

Could it have been three years ago? He had a memory
of a tall, shy silent girl with blue, clear eyes and long,
straight blonde hair that kept falling over her face, but
with something of an air about her. She had held herself
with none of the stoop-shouldered attempts at invisibility
one might have expected of an adolescent, but walked
well, her steps firmly planted on the Fane moors as she
followed the shooting party at a discreet distance. Well,
whatever her plans for the London Season, it didn't traditionally start until the Private View at the Royal Academy
on the first Friday in May. Ram decided to investigate
Sarah Fane—the Honorable Sarah Fane, to be exact. She'd
probably prove to be another of many disappointments,
determined to become a photographer's model or a cordon
bleu chef—but she had carried herself well, and by all
calculations she must still be under eighteen. He'd write
himself a memo when he went back to the house. It was
worth looking into. And after all, her grandfather *was* an
earl.

18

"*I* just don't like it, Kiki, can't you understand?" Daisy went to the window and looked out at Prince Street, already busy with tourists from uptown spending this early fall day of 1976 wandering about SoHo. The air was still warm and the potholes of the winter of 1975 were twice the size they had been, and half the size they would be by next spring, but there was no sign that the city intended to repair them. Perhaps, she thought, they were already considered historic landmarks.

"Daisy, look at it this way," Kiki implored her. "You're doing them a favor by wearing his dress to their party—you'll probably be photographed and that's good publicity for Robin Valarian."

"I don't trust the whole thing," Daisy repeated stubbornly.

"The dress? But it's so pretty," Kiki protested.

"No, I admit the dress is nice, even if it's not my style. I mean, you don't think that a wisp of chiffon and feathers like this, stolen practically line for line from St. Laurent's last collection, will still look great in thirty-five years, do you? But that's not what I mean. I get this feeling of spider webs, spun from pure gold—but still webs. You think I'm being paranoid, don't you?" she accused Kiki.

"Maybe a little. In the last year you've got Vanessa to thank for two major commissions, that big oil of the three Short girls and the other oil you did last Christmas of the two Hemmingway boys. She persuaded you to raise your price for watercolors by five hundred dollars, she's insisted on giving you a couple of dresses, she's invited you to a lot of parties—I grant you that. But look at what she's had in return."

"What *has* she had in return? That's precisely why I don't trust her. She is simply not the kind of woman who does nice things for the pure joy of it. I know her better than you do, Kiki, love—tell me what she's getting from me?"

"Ah . . ." Kiki was momentarily wordless.

"Another party guest? You don't really think that's enough, do you?"

"Well—*yes,* if you're a people collector, and she is."

"Come on, Kiki. I'm not all *that* important or that glamorous or that anything."

"You underestimate yourself—will you never stop! Look, you don't do the New York social scene because you're too busy during the week and on weekends you're usually away working at your portraits, so you have a definite *scarcity value*. That means something to Vanessa!" Kiki's eyebrows shot up to their most demonic heights. She thought it only normal and right that the Valarians should be generous to Daisy. It infuriated her that Daisy had never taken advantage of the collateral she possessed merely by being who she was, that she didn't milk her beauty and her title for all they were worth, that she hadn't jumped on board the great American celebrity train that was just waiting for her to ride it. "Daisy, you're not Cinderella, you know, you're legit."

"And you're a romantic—you still believe in fairy tales —no, take that back, you're a terrible cynic who wants me to cash in on an accident of birth. Even Serge Obolensky doesn't use his title anymore."

"Well, he doesn't have to sell portraits to Horse People —and plenty of other Obolenskys are still called prince and princess."

"Kiki, do you think we could stop splitting imperial hairs and get started on figuring out what I'm going to take to Venice? What do you suppose the weather is like in Venice in September?"

"Changeable," Kiki answered authoritatively.

"Luke should take a stick to you."

"He doesn't go in for kinky sex," said Kiki smugly.

"Oh? And just what does he go in for?"

"Hugging and kissing and touching . . . giving pleasure and caressing and . . ."

"Fucking?"

"Really, Daisy, how crude! As a matter of fact . . . since you insist, he definitely goes in for . . . making love," Kiki said, prim as a mid-Victorian clergyman's daughter.

"Mercy, mercy! Aren't you ever so pure now that you've got him . . . you *do* have him, don't you?" Daisy asked with a touch of anxiety.

"I just don't know." Kiki's small, pointed face suddenly looked like that of a baffled kitten. "I did everything you told me. I only accept dates with him every other time he asks—sometimes not even that often—I've worked up a whole fantasy world of other men that's so real I believe in it myself, and I'm more and more in love with that son-of-a-bitch every day. But he *eludes* me!" She pounded her small fists on Theseus who licked her hand. He liked pounding. "Do you think I shouldn't have gone to bed with him . . . was that a mistake?"

"Of course not. The day is over when a girl can get a man by withholding sex. That wasn't my point at all when I told you to be essentially unavailable. 'Essentially' doesn't mean sexually, dumbbell—it means somewhere way down deep. In your soul."

"I think my soul *is* available," Kiki said despondently, "and he knows it. Can you harden your soul the way you harden your heart?"

"Do you have a spiritual adviser?"

"Of course not."

"Perhaps you'd better start looking for one. Now, come on! What do you have that I can borrow?"

Arnie Greene, North's business manager, was unhappy. He'd advised North against taking the Pan Am job. It was a top account, but a Venice location meant that North and Daisy and Wingo would all be out of the studio for almost a week, unable to attend production meetings with other clients during the entire period, a fact that might cause a few days gap in their work schedule when they got back.

"Isn't it going to take more time than it could possibly be worth?" he asked North when Nick-the-Greek first brought in the job and asked him to bid on it.

"Probably," North had answered. "But for some reason or other, I've never been to Venice, and I want to get there before it sinks."

Arnie sighed. If he had his way, North would never shoot on location farther from the office than Central Park. He reluctantly accepted the fact that when a story board called for flocks of pigeons, the Piazza San Marco and gondolas, you couldn't do it in Central Park Lake . . . the pigeons maybe, but not the piazza. With melancholy, he wondered if gondolas were as unpredictable to work with as kids or animals. Well, he'd made damn sure that there was enough padding in the bid to absorb the overtime of even the most incompetent gondolier. Hell, he'd even taken out insurance in case a gondolier *drowned*. Arnie had also taken into account everything he'd always darkly suspected about *La Dolce Vita*, assumed that local technicians, wardrobe and make-up people, all brought in from Rome, would insist on two-hour lunches, counted on problems of crowd control and pigeon shit, figured out what it would cost to transport North, Daisy, Wingo and six models to Venice and back, first class all the way, added in a per diem living cost for all of them at the Gritti Palace which would pay the rent on his apartment for almost a year, made sure that every single item on the five-page list every commercial producer has to submit to the agency was as exact as he and Daisy could estimate, *plus*. They'd done their job. Even if something went wrong and North had trouble, they could handle the extra expenses out of the padding of the bid—standard procedure. Fortunately they weren't financially responsible for the delays caused by weather. If he'd had to worry about the weather he'd have three more ulcers than the two he already had.

"All right, but for Christ's sake, North, don't fall in a canal. The water will give you, at the least, hepatitis."

"Arnie, have I ever fallen into a canal?"

"You just said you'd never been to Venice. And don't eat raw shellfish . . . also causes hepatitis."

"Is it all right to look at the sunsets, or will they give me eyestrain?"

"Nobody appreciates me."

"Not true." North gave Arnie a friendly glance. "But you worry too much."

"Well, something always does go wrong, doesn't it?"

"Sure—if it didn't we might as well be making buttonholes. But you know Daisy will take care of it, whatever it is. That's what we pay her for, isn't it?"

By the time the luggage was retrieved at the Marco Polo Airport and they'd gone through customs and piled everything into a *vaporetto,* the Venetian equivalent of a bus, it was too dark and too late for either Daisy or North to see much of Venice. Wingo and the six models, three male and three female, were due to arrive the following day, but North had decided that he would leave a day early in order to see the sights of Venice undisturbed. Daisy could use that extra day to make a last-minute survey of the locations, check with the local police about crowd control and make sure that the accommodations were ready for the technical crew, wardrobe people, make-up people and hairdressers who were due in from Rome the next afternoon.

Venice was an audible shock, Daisy thought, looking out of the window of her room directly onto the Grand Canal, still hearing the slap of little waves against the side of the *vaporetto*. It didn't matter how much one had read about Venice or how far back in memory one had known that it was built on water, the reality came as a total surprise. It was impossible, she realized, to *imagine* Venice. In spite of the thousands of paintings it had inspired, it had to be experienced to become real, and even as a reality, it seemed improbable, as if she had, like Alice, gone through the looking glass into a land of wonders, a play world, insubstantial, so romantic that it was almost ridiculous, a city that was one vast composition of great art, presumably dying and crumbling for hundreds of years, yet still vital, the inexhaustible subject of so much prose that there was nothing left to be said about it, yet millions of words had not drained one drop of magic from it. What ambitious creatures men were, after all, to have even attempted such a city!

Across the canal, in the middle of the moonlit night, she could plainly see the dome of Santa Maria della Salute, that supreme masterpiece of Venetian Baroque. The fact that it was actually exactly where it should be was somehow miraculous and unexpected. . . . Daisy wouldn't be surprised if it had vanished by morning, nor if it remained standing long after New York and London had been reduced to rubble.

Tomorrow, at 7:00, she had to be up to start work, Daisy realized with a start, turning back to her high-ceilinged room, gay with striped blue-and-white satin walls and pink brocade draperies. That meant five hours sleep at the most. Luckily she had been able to nap a little on the trip over. North had sat in the front aisle seat of the first-class compartment, where he had room to stretch out his legs, and Daisy had taken a vacant seat several rows behind, so that she wouldn't disturb him. She knew that before a shoot as complicated as this one promised to be, he liked to withdraw into himself even more than usual, in preparation for the energy he would be pouring out during the next few days. As she got ready for bed Daisy wondered if, as she had plotted, she was going to be able to return to New York by way of London so that she could see Dani. She hadn't been able to go to Europe at Christmas this year. The two large oils and six watercolors she had done had just covered Danielle's expenses, so Daisy had been forced to choose to make the money rather than to make the trip. It had been too long, oh, really much too long, she thought, since she'd seen either Danielle or Anabel. She had decided not to ask North about taking the extra days off until the shoot was almost over. Then, with London so near, it would be difficult for him to refuse and her ticket could be rewritten at a minimum of expense.

Wearily, Daisy pulled off the ancient jeans, T-shirt and British Army Commando jacket—fifty cents at a church jumble sale in London five years ago—that she'd worn on the plane and hadn't had off since they left New York. She took a shower, a long, languorous shower, very different from the brief "working" shower she was used to at home, which, dictated by the inadequate plumbing, she told Kiki was as much fun as bathing with a Water Pic. Her nightwear was ordered from the Montgomery Ward catalogue, an old-fashioned straight-top vest in pink cotton with a drawstring around the top of the camisole and ribbon straps. Instead of the matching bloomers, Daisy wore purple satin basketball shorts, and her man's dressing gown was from Sulka, a dark-red, figured silk with a shawl collar, still in excellent condition after twenty-five years, even if it swept the floor in a way it had never been intended to. Her mind jumbled with practical considerations and the waiting excitement of Venice, Daisy fell into a light and confused sleep, full of fragmentary dreams.

When her traveling alarm clock went off, she was glad to jump out of bed and run to the window, the dreams disappearing in the promising, water-refracted light of morning. Dazzled, almost paralyzed with wonder, she stared at the view until she shook herself out of her reverie. It was really insane, she thought, to be expected to work here. They should have come a week earlier just to get acclimated to the beauty. But perhaps even a month wouldn't have been enough. Bitterly she envied North his day of sightseeing and promised herself as she dressed rapidly that she'd get everything checked out so efficiently and quickly today that she'd have a few hours, at least, to roam around by herself before the others arrived.

Late that afternoon, when North finally wandered back to the hotel, he found Daisy waiting for him right inside the entrance, curled up in a chair.

"All set?" he asked her.

"Not exactly."

"What d'ya mean? If everything isn't buttoned down, why are you hanging around the lobby? Isn't there something you have to do?"

Daisy stood up, her hands on her hips, her feet apart, her energy restored.

"North, hold it." She put up a hand like a traffic cop. "It seems we have a small problem."

"You and your problems," he said indifferently. "My feet hurt." He started for the desk to get his room key. She followed and tapped him on the shoulder.

"North?"

"Oh, what the hell is it? Honestly, Daisy, isn't it your job to worry about the little things? Oh, all right, tell me . . . there's a permit missing, the gondola's painted the wrong color, one of the models has a pimple? Improvise—how many times have I told you? *Improvise,* Daisy. If I've said it once I've said it a thousand times—you take care of the little things and I'll make it come out all right once I start working."

"Do you think you could get Alitalia to go back to work?"

"Why worry about Alitalia—we're working for Pan Am. Christ, Daisy, you have no sense of proportion," he said, turning away in exasperation.

Behind him she said softly, "None of the other airlines is landing in Italy, North. Sympathy strike." He spun around. "Wingo and the models can't get here."

"So what?" he said in renewed irritation. "Worse things have happened. Haven't you contacted models from Rome? If I can't use the girls I picked I'll use others, and I'll manage without Wingo. Rome is full of cameramen—and beautiful women."

"The trains are on strike too," Daisy said softly.

"Tell them to *drive*, damn it! If they start now they'll be here by tomorrow. If they'd started when you found out about the strike, I bet they could have been here by now," he added accusingly.

"The technicians are out on strike too. No crew, North. There's nobody in Italy to handle the equipment, which, incidentally, is sitting somewhere between Rome and here. No camera, no brutes, no fey lights, no clapboard, no dolly, not even a stopwatch—*nada!* And that's why I didn't book models from Rome."

"All right, very funny, very clever. Didn't it occur to you that we could drive to France or Switzerland and shoot there? Get ready to leave," North snapped.

"Shoot the Piazza San Marco and the pigeons and gondolas in France or Switzerland?" Daisy asked sweetly.

"But, damn it to hell, call New York! You know that the agency can rewrite the story board in an hour if they have to—"

"The strike," said Daisy slowing, lingering delightedly on every word, "has most unfortunately spread to the telephone system and the telegraph system. If some of those birds outside are carrier pigeons . . . Otherwise we're stuck here."

"That's insane! Daisy, you're not trying! Call up and rent a car. We'll take a motorboat to dry land and drive to the nearest border and call New York from there. Let them pick out an alternative location—Pan Am goes everywhere. Why the hell did you have to wait for me to get back to figure out something as simple as that? Why aren't you packed? What's the matter with you—you're slipping badly!"

"The car-rental people are out on strike. So is the gondoliers cooperative, and the *vaporettos* as well," Daisy said, her black eyes so dark that the dance of joy and amusement in the depths of her pupils was almost concealed.

"Shit! Daisy, they can't *do* this to *me!*"

"I'll tell them you said so," Daisy said, "when they've gone back to work."

"It's . . . it's . . . uncivilized!" shouted North, waving his arms around the princely lobby of the hotel which had been the residence of a doge in the sixteenth century.

"Why don't we try to be philosophical, North? It's not as if we can do anything about it," Daisy suggested calmly.

Daisy had been thoroughly enchanted by the events of the day. As each avenue of escape closed, as, finding her phone useless, she went down to the lobby to keep in touch with news of the spreading strikes that the reception desk relayed from the radio, every moment became more pleasurable. She felt something invading her which she had difficulty in recognizing until she finally identified it as a sense of leisure . . . she remembered how leisure felt from college vacations. The charmingly attentive hotel employees, of whom there were two to every one of the hotel's hundred guests, joined in her holiday mood—for tomorrow, who knew, might they not be out on strike too? It was just the right weather for a strike, one of them had pointed out to Daisy. She agreed with him completely. If there was one thing in the world she could have wished for in Venice it would be a few days outside of time. And the hall porter assured her that no guests at the Gritti Palace had ever starved. Even if they had to eat buffet style, the management was prepared. At the worst, the *principessa* might have to make her own bed.

"Philosophical?" North was outraged. Events did not do things to him, he did things to them. "We're locked up here as if this were the Middle Ages and you talk *philosophical?*"

"There is still one way out," Daisy said faintly.

"*What*, for Christ's sake!" he roared.

"We could . . . swim."

North swung around wrathfully and looked at his demented producer. At his gaze Daisy squeaked with suppressed laughter until she sounded like a whistling teapot about to come to a boil.

"Arnie's . . ." she sputtered before she was shaken by great outright howls of mirth, "Arnie's . . . *face!*"

The vision of Arnie Greene's mournful visage prophesying his inevitable hepatitis appeared before North's eyes and his face splintered slowly, reluctantly, but unconditionally, with laughter.

The hall porter and the doorman looked at the two Americans, shaken by spasms of hilarity, and shrugged smilingly at each other. The young *principessa*, the concierge thought, dressed rather unsuitably for the daughter of Prince Stash Valensky, who had been a faithful guest before his death, always coming to Venice for a week or two in September after the polo was over in Deauville. Only this morning she had come downstairs in man's white pants and a striped purple-and-white soccer jersey. But perhaps it was a new fashion?

"You planned this whole thing, didn't you?" North gasped, getting control of himself.

"It wasn't easy," Daisy admitted modestly.

"A whole country shut down so you could get a day off—nothing to it."

"I'm efficient, I grant you, but I couldn't have pulled it off in New York—too many gypsy cabs."

"Have you checked out gypsy gondolas?"

"A boy in a rowboat is the best I could find."

"Where to? I've got to have a drink before the bartenders go on strike." North felt giddy. The combination of a day in Venice with the complete collapse of the support system he took for granted, made him feel like a kid let out of school just before an exam.

"Harry's Bar?" Daisy suggested.

"You mean like tourists?"

"Of course . . . but I have to change first. And you need a bath. I'll meet you down here in an hour. Actually, I think we can walk there—I've got a map."

"I've been walking all day. Tell the rowboat boy to wait."

"Yes, boss." North found himself smiling at Daisy. He supposed there really wasn't anything *specific* he could fault her with . . . at least not until he found out more about this strike for himself.

Back in her room, Daisy hesitated among the dresses she had packed, just in case something came up that she couldn't do in her work clothes. She felt entirely feckless, as weightless as an astronaut. She picked the most elaborate dress she owned, a Vionnet gown from the mid-1920s. Kiki had insisted that she take the bare-armed chemise, skimpier than a slip, cut on the bias from black velvet. It had the deepest possible rounded neckline held up only by shoulder straps of crystal beads. The same beads were embroidered on the velvet in wide, fantastic circles, in a descending oval, so that it looked like a long necklace and the hem hung in two rippling points on either side of Daisy's body, showing a flick of knees in front. It was a dress that must once have caused a major scandal. Black velvet in September? Why not? thought Daisy as she unbraided her hair. The style of the dress indicated a sophisticated hairdo, but she didn't have sophisticated hair, Daisy realized, as the Venetian light tangled in the blonde strands. She lifted it in both hands, extended her arms at full length still holding onto her hair and whirled around and around. What to do, what to do? She wasn't in a chignon mood or in a braid mood—she was in a crystal mood. Finally she parted her hair in the middle, took several yards of silver ribbon she'd saved from a Hallmark commercial and twined it around so that some of the most flighty locks were held back from her face, the rest flowing loose. She flung on the cape of green and silver-shot lamé made in the same period as the dress by a now unknown firm called Cheruit and went down to the lobby, more romantic than any heroine ever painted by Tiepolo or Giovanni Bellini.

North was waiting, ready to leave. Not much of a drinker, he was unusually anxious for a drink. Alcohol was supposed to be a depressant, wasn't it? A depressant might help counteract the dangerously free-floating feeling in the atmosphere tonight. He needed to be brought back to earth, and there was no damn earth here—only the rippling reflections on the canal which made everything tipsy to start with. Where the hell was Daisy? Why was she keeping him waiting? He couldn't remember ever having to wait for Daisy since he'd started employing her.

"Dio! Che bellissima! Bellissima!" the hall porter said behind him.

"Bellissima!" echoed the doorman and the passing waiter and two men lounging about the lobby.

"Well," said North, looking at Daisy. Now he really needed a drink.

"A Mimosa, Signorina, or perhaps a Bellini?" the waiter suggested. North looked around at the long, narrow, famous room.

"Do you make a martini? I mean a *dry* martini?" he asked, dubiously.

"Fifteen to one, Sir. On the rocks?"

"A double. Daisy?"

"What's a Mimosa?" she asked the waiter.

"Champagne and fresh orange juice, Signorina."

"Oh, yes, please." The waiter showed no signs of leaving. He simply stood there looking at Daisy, expressing the most pure admiration with every inch of his wrinkled face.

"We'll have our drinks now," North said flatly, breaking the spell and sending the waiter hurrying off.

"So," North said in a voice which invested the syllable with discovery, mistrust and surprise and belligerence.

"'So'?" asked Daisy with slightly fake innocence. "What does that mean? Do you think just because it looks as if nobody in Venice is worried, there isn't really any strike?"

"*So* this is what you look like when you're not working, and *so* you must be putting on quite an act at the studio, and *so* I really don't know a hell of a lot about you, and *so* this is what you get up as soon as you have a chance."

"So?" Daisy shrugged blithely. "What's wrong with that?"

"That's exactly what I'm trying to figure out. I know there's *something*."

"North, North, go with the flow."

"What the hell is that supposed to mean?"

"I'm not sure, but it sounds just right for this time and this place. How's your martini?"

"Adequate," he said grudgingly. It was the best martini he'd ever had in his life. "How's your orange juice?"

"Pure heaven, absolute bliss, total delight, a dream, a vision, a revelation . . ."

"You mean you'd like another?"

"How could you tell?"

"There was something . . . just a touch . . . almost but not quite a hint . . . an intimation."

"Very good, North," Daisy approved. "When you start with intimations you're getting there."

"Where, getting where?"

"Into the flow."

"I see."

"I thought you would. I've always considered you a fairly quick study," Daisy said airily, whirling her champagne glass between her fingers.

"Calm affrontery—that's your game after hours. Damning with faint praise."

"I think flattery is tacky."

"I'm just surprised that you didn't say that when other people said I was stupid, you defended me."

"Wrong. When other people say you're an absolute shit, I defend you." Daisy smiled angelically.

"Christ! Wait till we get back to the mainland! Waiter, a butterfly net for the lady please, and two more drinks."

"I'm having fun," Daisy announced.

"So am I," said North, startled and newly suspicious.

"Feels odd, doesn't it?"

"Very. But I don't think it will do any permanent damage. Unless we got used to it, of course," North said thoughtfully.

"You mean that fun's fun but real life isn't supposed to be fun, at least not this much?"

"Absolutely. You're not utterly devoid of a sense of values. That's what I tell people when I defend you. They say that Daisy Valensky is nothing but a hard-working drone who never has any fun, and I defend you. I say that for all they know you may have fun sometimes—they shouldn't judge by appearances."

"You really *are* a shit, North," Daisy said, in a lilting voice.

"I *knew* you were shining me on."

"Why don't you fire me?" Daisy suggested.

"I'm too lazy. And anyway I am a shit, sort of. I mean, I'm not your ordinary good-natured slob."

"You're not even an ordinary bad-natured slob."

"No use trying to provoke me . . . you said to be philosophical so I'm being philosophical."

"How long can this last?"

"Go with the flow, Daisy."

"That's my line," Daisy said possessively.

"I'm a creative borrower," North loftily proclaimed.

"Get your own line," Daisy insisted.

"That's stingy. You must be hungry. Should we eat?"

"I didn't have lunch," said Daisy plaintively.

"Why not?"

"I was too busy finding out about the strike." She looked at him virtuously.

"Which strike?" wondered North.

"We *should* eat."

"That's my line," said North. "But I'll let you have it. I'm feeling generous. Where shall we go?"

"We can stay and eat here," Daisy suggested.

"Thank God. I can't get up. Waiter, bring us everything."

"Everything, Signor?"

"Everything." North gestured broadly.

"Certainly, Signor." The waiter appreciated the signor's dilemma. How could he order sensibly in the presence of such glorious, fresh, young beauty? How could he even eat? Still, they must be properly nourished. To begin, naturally the famous *filetto Carpaccio* and then the green *tagliarini gratinati*, the noodles blended so suavely with cream and cheese and after, perhaps the calves liver in tiny strips *alla veneziana* served of course with polenta and for dessert—he would wait to decide on their dessert until after they had started on the liver. Sometimes tourists skipped dessert.

"Thank you so much for a lovely evening," said Daisy in a small, precise voice, outside the door to her room at the Gritti Palace.

"Ah . . . I enjoyed it, too," North answered. "That's the right response, isn't it?" He willed her to look directly at him, to meet his gaze, but she kept her eyes demurely downcast.

"No, you should have said that you hoped you'd see me again and asked if you might telephone when we get back to the city."

"Can I?"

"May I," Daisy corrected him.

"May I come in?" asked North.

"No, you may call me."

"But I said, 'May I come in?'" North repeated.

"Oh, well, yes, in that case do call."

Impatiently, he put one finger under her chin and tipped her head up toward him, but she lowered her lids and continued to avoid his glance. "There's a phone strike—so how can I call you?" North asked.

"True. But you could knock on my door," Daisy said, vamping for time.

"I said, 'May I come in?'" he repeated urgently.

"Why?"

"Just because . . ." His face had lost its sharpness in the dim light of the corridor. His stance retained its swagger, his toughness still proclaimed itself in the set of his shoulders, but the familiar North air of indomitable willfulness, of battle readiness had softened, as if the moonlight had begun to wash it away.

"Oh, well . . . in that case . . . I guess so," Daisy said, opening the door with her key.

"It's only reasonable," he assured her.

"Reasonable?"

"Stop questioning everything I say."

"Stop telling me what to do," Daisy countered.

"Right." North took her in his arms and bent down to her lips. "From now on I'll order you."

"How will I know the difference?" Daisy asked in a panic, leaning away from him.

"You'll figure it out."

"Wait!"

"Why?"

"I'm not sure that this is a good idea."

"I'm the one who has the ideas . . . and this is a natural." He picked her up and carried her to the bed as wide as a barge. "You, Daisy, are the detail person—I'm involved in the larger creative effort." He kissed her, holding her head between both of his hands.

"North?" she said, pushing herself up on the pillows.

"Huh?" he answered, busily coaxing the crystal straps from her shoulders.

"Is this a mistake?"

"I don't think so, but we have to make it to find out . . . oh, oh you never told me you tasted so good."

"You never asked."

"My mistake."

There was awe in his voice as he murmured, "Where have you been hiding all these years?" a note Daisy had never heard from this man whose terse, rapid commands had been the whip that drove her on. He, who had always crackled with combative directions, touched the tips of her breasts as carefully and reverently as an archaeologist, amazed and moved by the discovery of a long buried statue of Venus. His sharp features were blunted by the light reflected from the Grand Canal, and through her half-closed eyes she searched for the harsh and contained fire of the man she knew. But all his hard edges seemed to have melted as he was transformed into a tender, laughing, unknown lover, who covered her with long, sweet, almost thoughtful kisses as he slid his hands down to her waist and took possession of the warm, supple curve where her hips began and pulled her closer to him so that they lay face to face.

"May I?" he murmured, waiting until she nodded before he undressed her and then took off his own clothes and stood looking down at her with a smile of revelation on his lips, his naked body finer than she would have imagined it . . . and now she knew that she *had* imagined it, perhaps since she had first seen him. The turmoil of this sudden knowledge made her pull him down to her and finally dare to kiss his pointed nose and his eyes and his ears and his cheeks, all the surfaces she had watched so anxiously for years, trying to anticipate his orders, always tense with the necessity of keeping up with his frenzied pace, of being ready to supply whatever he needed. Abruptly, in their nakedness, they were equal, and under her lips there was only a warmth and this new, dear proximity. In a rush of prodigious pleasure Daisy thought, but he *likes* me, he approves of me, I'm a human being to him, he must truly care. She opened her arms wide with surprise and flung them around his neck, pressing herself close, as close as possible, trying to keep him there in the compass of her arms so that he wouldn't change back to the North she had known. Little by little she became convinced that this unknown lover would not vanish. As he sensed Daisy gradually yielding up her fears and her hesitations North's caresses became more firm and more insistent. He allowed himself to learn her body an inch at a time and when all protest, all holding back was long past, he parted her willing thighs, but before he entered her, he whispered again, "May I?"

"Yes, yes, yes."

"Still no change?" North asked the hall porter.

"No, Signor, I regret, nothing is happening, but we have learned that these strikes do not end as quickly as they begin. However, they do not occur often, a major strike like this, most positively, I assure you."

"Well, that's show biz," North smiled, his lean body relaxed. "Did you notice where Miss Valensky went? She's not in her room."

"Ah, the *principessa*, yes, she just left, Signor. She said she had to pay a boy who was waiting with a gypsy rowboat. At least that's what I think she said. Perhaps it was a gypsy boy. In any case, I offered to do it for her but she insisted."

"My God!" North's mouth quivered with laughter. "She really had one lined up . . . I should have known."

"Signor?"

"Nothing. I'll go find her." He walked quickly toward the entrance to the hotel and bumped into Daisy who was hurrying back in.

"You weren't trying to escape, were you?" he asked.

"Merely cutting off the last route to civilization."

"I overslept," he told her.

"So I noticed. You're very interesting to watch when

you sleep. You don't look at all the way you do when you're awake."

"How do I look?" he asked, warily.

"It's how you *don't* look—no turbulence, no truculence, no irascibility, no sound and fury, no invulnerability, no . . ."

"You're taking advantage of me," he said, trying to cut her off.

"Oh, I hope so! I've always wanted to—it's been one of my heart's desires. In matters of this sort I find that it's always best to be the first one awake."

"How much do you know about matters of this sort?" he barked.

"I don't know you nearly well enough to tell you," she said airily, smiling at him at the same time with an insolent light in her eyes. He seized her by the scruff of the neck, to the discreet delight of the entire lobby staff, and dragged her over to a window.

"Let me get a look at you, damn you. How can I see into your eyes when they're so black?"

"You can't possibly," she said triumphantly, her dark gold eyebrows forming a straight line. "But as for you, you poor, transparent, red-headed, blue-eyed man, I can look right straight into your brain and out the other side!"

"Bullshit. Nobody looks into my brain."

"Wanna bet?"

"Not before breakfast," he said hastily. "Anyway, haven't you got better things to think about? Do you realize you haven't done any sightseeing yet, outside of Harry's Bar?"

"And the ceiling of Room Fifteen at the Gritti Palace . . . dimly," she added with a reminiscent grin that made him shake her again.

"Let's grab breakfast and go walking."

"I've had breakfast, but I'll watch you eat," Daisy announced graciously.

"Why do I have this strange feeling that you think you're smarter than I am?" North grumbled.

"That's the sort of question you must search your soul to answer." Daisy laughed.

"See, you're doing it again!"

Daisy and North felt as if the fabric of the world had been whisked aside and another, alternative world presented in a sumptuously tarnished cornucopia of unforeseen pleasures, as if, during the march of centuries, Venice had been waiting confidently just for them. They found themselves miraculously stripped of those defensive postures that had passed for character, and turned into wondering children. Everyone, from the shopkeepers to the cats in the narrow *calles,* was an accomplice, locked willingly together into this sea-bound relic, this most sensuous city on earth. Their sense of life, strong, blood-hot and buoyant, had never been so focused on each individual moment as it was in this generously proffered world in which the familiar concepts of time and space and light had all been washed by the patient sorcery of centuries into something better than either of them had ever known.

A dark church, illuminated in an unexpected corner by a masterpiece, a wicker table at a café, an arched bridge over a canal, a barking dog, the rose-orange-lavender façades of faded, still-regal palazzos, the regular tolling of the bells in the Campanile at dusk, a hamburger of Florentine beef, the Viennese waltzes played at Quadri's, or the glimpse of a courtyard garden in which old roses still bloomed in the Campo San Barnaba, all mingled together in one blissful dream as they walked and ate and talked and made love, waking each morning with the fear that the strike might be over, a fear immediately banished by the sight of the Grand Canal on which only private boats and market barges could be seen.

Making love with North had finally taught Daisy what it meant to truly desire a man and be fulfilled physically by him. But, as the nights passed, drugged with pleasure, Daisy realized that in a way she seemed to be unaware of, she was still holding back. That caged *thing* in her heart that begged to be liberated, that thing that craved and yearned to be dissolved, to achieve a release beyond the physical, still held tight, taut and unbending even when they were closest to each other. She ached for it—whatever *it* was—to burst into flame within her, and still it remained solidly locked behind bars of reserve. North, she thought, had yielded up to her his cantankerous, difficult and abrupt exterior and brought forth moments of incandescence, yet, try as she would, Daisy still knew him, as she had always known him, as an opponent, beloved now, but an opponent, even during these days carved out of time.

Was it North's essential nature, his essential apartness that did not yet permit her to sense the full merging with another that she had always sought? She asked herself what it was in him or in her that wouldn't permit her to surrender to absolute intimacy. Just as Daisy had somehow felt an impostor when she was being treated as a princess, she wondered if she and North were, in some way, impostors when they treated each other as lovers? Perhaps, she told herself, it was just too soon, perhaps the leap they had made had been too quick, jumping from a working relationship of many years to becoming lovers after only a few hours of unexpected flirtation.

Daisy was troubled by something indefinable in the new way they acted with each other, something that rang with a note of the illusory, the temporary, something that might be dissipated by a minor incident. As she drifted off to sleep she thought that perhaps it was always this way at first. Perhaps, later, there would be more. But if there were not more, was this enough?

Yet, as one day followed another, Daisy felt herself like a field of flowers on a summer afternoon, buzzing and humming with the busy sound of happiness. She wondered what she and North were creating together. Was it just a few days in another time frame? She had known him so well in his movements of command, and of watchfulness, known his favorite words and catch phrases, his gestures and expressions. Now she knew him as the first man who taught her body true passion. But what did they know of each other on a more profound level, a level of deep and continuous connection? Did he want that knowledge? Did she?

In their conversations there was a hint of expectation, of restless waiting, as during the chatter that precedes the raising of the curtain at the theater. Yet, it was clear to her that the time hadn't come to speak of any of her closely kept secrets ... perhaps it would come tomorrow, or the day after ... or never. Perhaps it should not be something she longed for, perhaps these secrets were meant to stay hidden—she didn't know. She couldn't judge, and present joys prevented her from giving the subject more than a thought or two, before sleeping.

It always seemed, in their private weather, to be either the first best day of spring, that day on which people finally realize that spring really *is* in the air, or else that day just before they say with a disappointed sigh, "Oh, but it's summer already." They were living an idyll trembling on the brink of becoming—Daisy couldn't complete the idea, nor could she share it with North. The fragility, the evanescence of passion had become evident to her almost as soon as she first experienced it.

There were, during that week, an infinite number of harmonies in her beauty. Venice inspired her to meet its fantasy with her own, to finally wear the Norman Hartnell dress designed during the last years of the twenties, a dress that she had never quite dared to put on in New York, a "picture frock" as it had been called, with a pink chiffon bodice under an orchid taffeta surplice above a skirt of pale blue taffeta with a hem thickly bordered with hand-painted flowers. During the day in her sailor pants and rugby shirts, she weighted her wrists with barbaric bracelets, bought for three dollars, but at night her hair was entwined with fresh flowers.

As the sun, constantly reflected from the water, turned North's freckles darker and his blue eyes bluer, it tinted Daisy's warm color with a light copper glaze that contrasted so strongly with her hair that people openly pointed to her in the streets.

Although Daisy and North ate lunch in any convenient trattoria during their daytime rambles, they always had dinner at Harry's Bar, which instantly becomes a club to anyone who has been there twice. There were other tourists, of course, but they were far outnumbered by true Venetians who, since 1931, have stopped by Harry's at least once a day to find out what is new in the world, that, to them, is simply and entirely Venice, Venetians who possessed a cool lacquered elegance which belongs to an ancient race who have learned that everything must be treated as a surface.

One night, a week after they had arrived, Daisy spilled the salt on the pink tablecloth. Both she and North reached for it and simultaneously flung a pinch over their shoulders.

"You realize that's just superstition?" North asked.

"Of course. It's not as if anything bad would happen if we didn't." They both knocked on the wood of their chairs quickly and automatically.

"A pure atavism," North assured her.

"A primitive ritual," Daisy agreed.

"If there isn't any wood around, you're allowed to knock on your head—it counts," he offered. "Or use mine."

"Oh, I know. But you mustn't wait longer than three seconds."

"I walk under ladders," North said, with the air of one who knows more than he tells.

"I never even *think* about broken mirrors," Daisy countered. "Or hats on the bed or whistling in dressing rooms or black cats."

"*Only* salt and wood?" he asked skeptically.

"And wishing on the first star at night. You can wish on the new moon too, but only if you happen to see it over your left shoulder without planning to."

"I didn't know that."

"It's a very important one," Daisy said wisely, tweaking a lock of his red hair. "And you can wish on a plane, too, if you really think it's a star, but only as long as you're in a car moving in the same direction as the plane."

"I'll remember that," North said with rue in his voice, the wistfulness of falling leaves, a sad, autumnal tone he'd never used before.

"What's wrong?" she asked.

"Absolutely nothing. Everything's perfect."

"Yes . . . I know what you mean." Daisy was thoughtful. "It is a problem."

The next morning while they were still asleep, the phone by the bed rang.

"You didn't leave a wake-up call, babe, did you?" North muttered, confusedly, after the phone had rung several times, dragging them both from their dreams.

"No, no," Daisy sighed, reaching with acrid resignation for the insistent phone.

"Don't answer it!" He put his hand tightly over hers.

"North . . . you know what it must mean," Daisy said urgently.

"Leave it! We can have one more day." She listened carefully to his voice, torn between the honest urge to shut out the world and his instant inescapable response to the continuing summons of the phone. Daisy evaluated what she heard and picked up the receiver while she smiled at him with love, regret and understanding, so mingled that they formed one cloud of feeling, so bittersweet that her voice trembled.

"Hello Arnie. No, no, you didn't wake me—I had to get up to answer the phone."

19

$\mathcal{S}$arah Fane, in Ram's considered opinion, was both more and less than he had hoped she would be when he had acted on his decision to investigate her as a candidate for marriage, months ago in the early spring of 1976. She pleased him rather better than he thought she had any right to, since she did not fulfill all his requirements for a wife. True, she had been most carefully brought up and she was accustomed to holding her own in the great world as she had seen it, as a future debutante, in its country hunting-fishing-shooting manifestations. In this he found her irreproachable, neither too sophisticated nor too provincial. Yet, according to Ram's calculations, according to any reasonable analysis of what any woman, much less a young girl, could hope for from the attentions of an excessively eligible bachelor such as he, she should have been prepared to adore him, as Miss Fane, the Honorable Miss Fane, did not. At least not visibly.

She was a flirt. A damned hard, cold, calculating flirt. And she was a beauty, a damned hard, cold, ravishing blonde beauty of the kind that has always been known as the "English Rose," a kind whose unblemished perfection of feature, whose dainty pink-and-white coloring, whose lovely lips and candid eyes, has caused many a man to curse the falseness of the sweet exterior that concealed a temperament and a will worthy of Queen Victoria. Ram wondered how he could ever have suspected that Sarah Fane had intended to skip the Season. She was going to have it *all*, not just Queen Charlotte's Birthday Ball, dressed in her long white gown and long white gloves, but

Royal Ascot and Henley as well. She was invited to every important private dance that would be given from May to July, and there would be six hundred guests at her own dinner dance in July. After the dancing season was over, she had planned to go to Goodwood for Race Week, Cowes for the Regatta, and Dublin for the International Horse Show. When Ram pointed out that Cowes Week and the Dublin Show overlapped by several days, she only smiled beautifully and explained how she intended to attend almost three-quarters of each celebration by leaving the Isle of Wight for Ireland right after the Royal Yacht Squadron's Ball. "It would be a pity to miss Dublin, Ram, now that my parents have finally admitted that I'm old enough to go," she said with a ravishing smile which Ram only wished he could say was too practiced, a smile he had to admit was both innocent and unspoiled. Her prettiness was of the kind which would never slide into mere decorativeness but rather would grow greatly distinguished as she aged—and she even knew *that*.

Sarah Fane's last three years had been spent at the Villa Brillantmont, the Lausanne finishing school which still provides a rapidly vanishing minority of upper-class girls with a polished education, excellent French and friends culled from the richest families around the world. As far as Ram was concerned, its chief function had been to serve as a quarantine that kept Sarah from being overexposed to London.

Brillantmont had confirmed Sarah's opinion that almost all girls fell into two categories: those who wanted to get out of school and find some exciting, glamorous job, and those who wanted only to free themselves of chaperones as soon as possible and enter into a giddy whirl of romantic adventure. Both categories she judged were equally self-deluding. However, she was delighted that they didn't understand, as clearly as she did, that the first step in any future life was the right marriage. For some it could be merely an acceptable marriage, for others a good marriage. For herself she contemplated only the *exceptional* marriage, even taking into account the fact that in any given year only a few exceptional marriages were made. She added up her assets, without false modesty, and decided that she was entitled to the very best.

Sarah Fane despised the relative poverty she saw gradually enveloping the English upper classes. She felt personally offended by the fact that she'd been born into a society that had virtually undergone a bloodless revolution, a socialist society with the name of a monarchy.

But, she reminded herself, there was no point in being petulant. The 1970s wouldn't go away because she found them odious. The trick was to evade them, to escape them, to ensure a life that would come as close as possible to being the life she *should* have led by right.

From Brillantmont, Sarah had closely observed the elaborate cotillion of each London Season as she waited for her year to come. She had concluded that the best marriages were those made during a girl's first year out, while she was still a novelty. The expression "post-deb" actually made her feel a pang of revulsion—could there be anything more bedraggled? *Timing*. Timing was the secret, she thought as she sat at her desk, going over the guest list for her ball. She put down her pen to add up the months. She had the entire spring and summer of 1976, lasting through September if she went north for the great Scottish balls. Then, of course, to London for the Little Season which continued until Christmas. After that came the exodus to country houses. With the coming of the spring of 1977, the focus of the year would change and it would begin to belong to the next crop of girls who would be coming out. So a mere nine or ten months, in reality, were all that existed of the best part of her debutante year.

That increasingly rare and elusive species, the eligible English bachelor, with great wealth and solid background, often waited until they were well into their early forties before they were brought to the altar. Some, too many, never married. No fools they, she thought, tightening her dainty pink lips over her faultless teeth in a momentary grimace. They never went out of style: a man could be sixty-five, ugly, bad tempered and boring and he was still a catch if he had a good position in the world. As for the bachelors who were distinguished chiefly by the fact that they were someone's heir, they wouldn't do for her at all, living, as they did, on overdrafts and expectations. Nor was she attracted by those possessors of ancient names who formed syndicates to open flashy new restaurants or discotheques. The young lord as a saloon keeper struck Sarah Fane as an unacceptable prospect, quite as bad as those who, for financial reasons, became photographers or film producers and pretended it was merely a whimsical lark. In her eyes this substantially diminished their value, even if they enjoyed worldly success. Nor would she be happy as the chatelaine of a great house who had to allow the public to come in and look around, at so much a head, in order to keep the roof in repair. A mug's game, that. Why be a Marchioness if you had to run a roadside attraction?

How did she feel about Ram Valensky, Sarah asked herself, pushing the list aside? Ever since he had invited himself to visit for a weekend, he had shown certain signs of becoming attached, although never quite enough for her to consider him as a declared suitor. He had been one of the great catches of the country for seven or eight years now, and, so far, he had easily resisted capture. He was certainly handsome, in his steely, slim, aristocratic way, with those intelligent gray eyes which looked at her with keen interest yet cool appraisal.

She couldn't help but enjoy seeing herself reflected in all her immaculate prettiness in the expression of measured approbation on his dark, aquiline face. He had just enough grave, quiet distinction; he approached life in a way she shared—he, too, felt a desire to get the best out of what was left to people of their kind. She liked the way he held his shotgun, at a lazily alert angle, neither too tensely nor too casually. He danced adequately for a man who didn't like to dance, and he rode superbly. And he was a great gentleman. Of course he didn't have a sense of humor, but humorless people were easier to deal with in the long run. Sarah Fane had little tolerance or need for humor.

From a purely objective point of view, and Sarah Fane was nothing if not objective, there were a great many things right about Ram. His age was ideal: at thirty-two a man was ready to settle down. From her father's grunts and offhand remarks, she judged that his fortune, the vastness of which was so often the subject of speculation and rumor, must be remarkably solid. Sarah had great respect for her father's money sense, and he was as closely informed as it was possible to be about Ram's financial position since they did a great deal of business together. Her mother was the genealogical expert in the family and she had indicated in her vague but fully conversant way that Valensky, while not an English name, was quite good enough, joined as it was to the Woodhill side of the family. A trifle unorthodox perhaps, but quite sound, and indeed one mustn't be stuffy, especially since his father Stash Valensky had flown with her father during the war. Her mother wouldn't have said anything more approving if she had been discussing the heir to the throne. In fact, she had even been known to sniff at the House of Windsor, when she had a genealogical rampage going. And how fortunate it was that his father was dead. With Ram, one knew exactly where one stood in respect to those death duties which could hang over other eligible prospects indefinitely.

She didn't know about Ram's sensuality, Sarah Fane reflected absently. She had always reserved sensuality for some time in the future. She feared and respected the powers of sensuality, thinking of it as a priceless coin in the game of life which should never be played unless it were the very last coin you spent in order to ensure the future. Sensuality, poorly handled, was clearly responsible for bad marriages. Thank God her sensuality was no problem and never had been. In her opinion, uncontrolled sensuality was for people who couldn't afford luxuries.

Ram Valensky was quite possibly her best shot, Sarah Fane decided. Hers and that of every other girl who was hoping to marry as well as she intended to. But he was far from a sitting duck. He behaved more like an inquisitive, measure-taking eagle. As she thought that, she decided definitely not to ask him to be her escort at Queen Charlotte's Ball. She knew that he expected to be asked, as he had been asked year after year by other hopeful girls. A marvelously guileless expression spread over her pure features and lit her lovely, clear blue eyes as she imagined Ram's reaction to being excluded from the first important event of her year. It was the best idea she'd had all morning, she told herself, and returned to her guest lists with renewed zest.

Reluctantly, in spite of his well-concealed rage, Ram began to respect Sarah Fane. He suspected every move she made, but nothing she did or said ever betrayed the glacier-hard calculation of her maneuvers.

Her manner toward him was admirable. Instead of the melting and preening he had every right to expect from a young and inexperienced girl to whom attention was being paid by a man of his stature and desirability, she presented an unwavering picture of placid, sunny charm. She almost, but not quite, treated him as just a friend of her father's, younger than the others but still not inordinately interesting to her. She thanked him for his flowers on a note of gratitude that indicated precisely that they were far from the only flowers she had received that day, yet her thanks never dipped into the perfunctory. She let him take her to the theater and to restaurants almost as often as he asked, but somehow other couples always joined them so that he was never alone with her. "But Ram, dear, it's always like this during the Season—you know that," she lightly reproached him on the solitary occasion on which he protested that he did not enjoy being part of an eternal crowd. After that, he accepted the flock of young people with whom she was surrounded without any sign of impatience. I know her game, he thought, as she teased some young man with one of her classic smiles or delicious pouts, but he found himself wondering more and more if he really did. Ram decided it was advisable to be seen with other young women: there were many he took out or served as escort to during the months of the Season, treating them with the same, exactly the same, careful, restrained, lordly gallantry as he did Sarah.

The Honorable Sarah Fane was having a splendid Season. All the magazines and newspapers agreed that she was among the most beautiful debutantes of the year and her name was proposed as a possible bride for Prince Charles, despite the fact that he favored her with no more—and no less—notice than he did other young ladies. However, finding brides for Prince Charles was a permanent national pastime. April and May passed and June came, with no change in Sarah's bright, serene attitude, as she continued to float through a series of parties and dances, always faultlessly dressed in clothes chosen to play against her pink-and-white beauty. Rather than the obvious pastels, that were almost mandatory for debs, she leaned toward deep dusty blues and rich emerald greens, severely cut, never too sophisticated gowns above which white shoulders gleamed with a special distinction. She never mentioned to Ram the almost unending parties to which she was invited, unless, as she did occasionally, she asked him to go with her. Her bland reticence was more infuriating than any amount of information would have been. He waited for her to boast and he waited in vain. He waited for her to mention the other girls he saw, and again he waited in vain. She was a formidable adversary, he finally admitted to himself. He would have preferred to have found the proper wife embodied in someone less sure of herself, and yet he was flattered to think that his choice, now that it had been made, was of an exceptional young woman. It began to seem inevitable that, rather than some unformed girl who would have fallen automatically into his hands, he should have picked a girl who knew her own worth and disdained to sell herself cheaply.

Fane Hall was the scene of Sarah's own dance, catered by the venerable firm of Searcy Tansley, a dinner dance under a series of elaborate tents, flung out from all sides of the rosy, Tudor grandeur of the great house. A number of young people had been invited to spend the night at Fane Hall and the other guests, unless they drove back to London, were all to be accommodated at the homes of various neighbors. The entire proceedings were almost as complicated and detailed as in the planning of a coronation, Sarah observed with a merry laugh, as if they had nothing to do with her. Hers was to be the sort of party that was rarely held in the straitened, stingy 1970s, a party that was a comforting throwback to the good old days. The Fanes could afford it, people thought to themselves, and added another layer of respect for Sarah to her already glowing aura.

The date was the first weekend in July, 1976, after all the university and university-entrance exams were over, and it would mark the beginning of the very height of the Season, as all of England's wellborn youths were freed from the prison of academia.

Sarah ruled over her ball in a strapless gown of white silk, tied with satin ribbons below her breasts, at her waist, with more ribbons twice restraining the enormously full skirt, so that it fell in three billowing tiers. She wore her grandmother's tiara on her neat, lovely head; she wore a smile that was as kind and pleased and unaffected for a duke as it was for another debutante; she wore an air of being a living part of a great tradition of aristocracy without stiffness or self-consciousness; she wore her flawless prettiness as if she were so accustomed to it that nothing could ever fade or diminish it. As any debutante is, she was the queen of her own ball, but there was something in the air which tipped her reign over into the realm of the legendary, something that told everyone there that Sarah Fane's ball would go down in the history of great debuts. She reached a summit that night as she danced with more than two hundred men, whirling and whirling with tireless grace, never faltering in her command of the occasion. Ram was able only to capture her for a moment or two and he spent the evening dancing with many other girls, observed favorably by mothers and daughters alike. He was almost tempted, that night, to propose to her, but he held back. On a night of such victory, such self-importance, he estimated that his proposal would not be accorded the total value it should be given. It would be just too much icing on the cake for Sarah Fane . . . he'd let her have the run of her Season. It would do her good to wonder for a few months more why he continued to favor her with his attention and still said nothing.

"Just give me a for-instance," Kiki invited. It was a Sunday morning in Luke's apartment, specifically in Luke's bed, and she really didn't want a for-instance, she wanted Luke to kiss her again. Luke kissed her again.

"For instance," he said, "Christ, you're never as delicious as you are in the morning *before* you've brushed your teeth . . . 'morning mouth,' I *love* it! And then you look at the camera with those big pussycat eyes and that foxy focused sensuality around your nose and lips, and we hear your voice off camera saying, 'What man wants to kiss the smell of mint the minute he wakes up? A little Scope the night before . . . that's *my* secret.' And then I kiss you again, like this, and I say, 'Yum, yum . . . don't you dare get out of bed.' "

"But that's terrific! Why can't you use it?" Kiki asked. "It even makes *me* want to buy Scope so it must be a good idea."

"It's a great idea but it could never get on the air. The sponsor doesn't want animal sexuality, the network won't allow it, the public would be shocked. Also it probably isn't true and we have to worry about truth in advertising."

"Do you mean I should brush my teeth?" Kiki said, worried.

"No, darling idiot, only that not every man may be queer for morning mouth, the way I am." He kissed her again. "You can't claim that Scope works all night long, and if you have two people in bed, one of them must be suffering from acid indigestion or stuffed sinuses and the other should be Florence Nightingale, not a couple of happy lovers who obviously just woke up—America's not ready for that."

"But it's real," Kiki protested.

" 'Real' isn't why we make commercials. If we wanted 'real' we'd do documentaries," he mumbled, kissing her under her arm. "I think I like morning armpit more than even morning mouth."

"Give me another for-instance," Kiki purred.

"There's this one woman and she says, straight to camera, 'I *hate* Howard Cosell!' And then there's another and another until you have the screen split sixteen ways, all types of women all saying, with increasing hysteria, 'I hate Howard Cosell!' And then you hear a voice over—a calm woman's voice saying, 'Monday-Night Football getting to you? Try Bufferin. It won't make *him* shut up, but *you'll* feel better.' "

"Now, what's wrong with that? You're not saying anything that isn't true."

"No, but Howard Cosell just might have grounds for legal action, and the network wouldn't run it during the game which is the only time it could play to maximum effectiveness, and all the Howard Cosell fans would never buy Bufferin again."

"Are there Howard Cosell fans?"

"I've never met one, but it figures," Luke said morosely.

"But what if you hired Howard Cosell to say, 'Try Bufferin—it won't make *me* shut up but *you'll* feel better'?" Kiki wondered. "I bet he'd do it—he's probably dying to be a spokesperson like Don Meredith and Frank what's-his-name."

"Kiki," Luke said, almost sitting up in excitement, "I think we've just stolen the Bufferin account!"

"Come back here," Kiki ordered. "It's Sunday—you can't snatch accounts on Sunday." Luke settled back under the covers and continued his list of dream commercials.

"I've also got a great one for Tampax. You get someone like Katharine Hepburn or Bette Davis, an authority figure with total moxie, and you just shoot her straight, and she's saying something like, 'If women didn't menstruate there wouldn't be any human race at all so why don't we stop being so coy about it and realize what a marvelous thing it is that women have ovaries that release an egg each month and that since they do, it's only sensible to use Tampax when the egg isn't fertilized, because Tampax is comfortable and does the job.' "

"Hmmm," said Kiki.

"Yeah, you see, even *you're* shocked. Women don't have menstrual periods or ovaries or vaginas or any of their equipment on television—except in the soap operas when they're always taking out everything in the hospital—

hysterectomy city—it's the biggest fucking taboo—even if you can discuss it in detail on a soap, you have to use little hints like 'difficult days' in a commercial. We're the last bastion of the Puritan fathers."

"Poor sweetheart—you must be so frustrated."

"Sometimes I am, but generally I just forget what I'd like to do and do what I can as well as possible. It's a living," he grumbled.

Kiki flung her arms around Luke and held him as tightly as she could. "Listen, it's more than just a living, you dope. Don't you ever realize that without advertising there wouldn't be any newspapers or magazines or televisions except whatever the government paid for? Advertising is what supports all that information and entertainment, so don't get all snooty about it. You do a job that has to be done and you do it better than anyone else!"

"I'd forgotten that I was talking to a native-born capitalist," Luke laughed. "I'm so used to girls who put down advertising that it's a pleasure to hear from the delegate from Grosse Pointe."

Kiki, who already had him firmly in her grasp, tried to shake him, but he was too big for her to move satisfactorily, so she contented herself with hissing, "No gratitude. No class. No taste. To even *mention* other girls at a time like this—I'm getting out of bed, Luke Hammerstein, you goat."

"Ah, don't—I'm sorry, I was just kidding, honest."

"I have to pee," she said haughtily.

"How about this? This great-looking girl, beautifully dressed in the height of fashion, says, 'Excuse me, but I really have to pee,' and the other beautiful girl—they're having lunch at La Grenouille—says, 'What toilet paper do you prefer?' and the first one says, 'Lady Scott of course, because even the best people have to pee—so you might as well do it in style.'"

"Brilliant," Kiki sneered, "I think you should be teaching English at Harvard. Your mind is sick, Luke Hammerstein, *sick*."

"Just because I mentioned Grosse Pointe?" he said wickedly.

"Go fuck yourself!" Kiki said angrily.

"Not while you're around."

"I suppose I'm to take that as a compliment?" she huffed.

"Damn right. Now will you go pee and make it

snappy. And don't brush your teeth while you're in there!"
He stretched lazily and happily in bed. There was only
one problem on his mind. Bagels, cream cheese and
smoked salmon first and fucking later, or fucking first
and bagels after? Even Maimonides wouldn't be able to
decide that one.

"What's it all about, Theseus?" Daisy asked her dog,
scratching his ears in a way which he particularly enjoyed.
"Just tell me what's it's all about."

"If I weren't here," said Kiki, "I'd understand your
asking him, but since this great wisewoman is available,
I'm rather offended."

"I thought you were too busy changing your nail polish
to talk."

"One thing has nothing to do with another." Kiki bent
over her hands rapidly, using polish remover on the deep
red, almost brown polish she had been affecting recently.
"How many manicurists are tongue-tied?"

"I've never been to one—how would I know? I thought
maybe they operated in holy silence."

"Wash your own hair, do your own nails—no wonder
you have to ask a dog for advice," Kiki snorted.

"How can I talk to you?" Daisy said reasonably.
"You're so happy and excited that you can't possibly be
intelligent. You see everything through the eyes of true
love, than which there is nothing so distorted ... your
perceptual apparatus is anesthetized, your judgmental
functioning is paralyzed, your free will has been taken
away from you and you're operating on a set of premises
which no one in this world understands but you—at least
Theseus isn't in love."

"Ever since you came back from Venice," Kiki said,
thinking out loud, "—it's November now, so that means
two months ago—you haven't been yourself. My perceptual apparatus, as you see, is as sharp as ever, as long as you
don't ask me about Luke. You're semi-miserable, semi-
demi-tormented, mini-pleased with yourself, major-mini-
yearning of a somewhat sentimental nature toward North.
Why didn't you ask me before you got involved with the
man you work for?"

"There was a phone strike," Daisy reminded her.

"Excuses, excuses. What is the exact status of the
relationship, if I may use such a word about something so
sacred?"

"Shifty," said Daisy.

"A *shifty* relationship? You mean there's something not kosher about it, something sinister?"

"Oh, God, Kiki, you've missed the point again. Shifty like the wind blowing from the east and then blowing from the west, shifty like the mist forming and then dissipating and then coming back, shifty like I don't know which way is up, quicksand-type shifty."

Kiki glanced sharply at Daisy. She had lost weight, Kiki thought, which she certainly didn't need to lose, and her temper had suffered, not that she was ever bitchy, but she was strung very tightly these days, and she spent too much time grooming Theseus and taking him for runs around the neighborhood and too little time with North, in Kiki's opinion.

"Could you be more specific?" Kiki asked, unwrapping a new bottle of pale pink polish and beginning to apply it.

"It's hard to point to any one particular thing. When we got back, I knew that everything had to change. After all, the circumstances in Venice were totally abnormal—I don't think North's had that much time off in his life before. And, of course, I was right—everything piled up afterward and we had to work twice as hard as usual to make up for the week we'd lost, but I understand that—I'm part of it, hell, without me they couldn't have done it. And the working together felt good. He treated me the same as he always had in front of the others—I certainly don't want Nick and Wingo and the rest to be leering at us—and when we were alone he's . . . fun . . . and he wants me physically . . . and he's loving . . . I guess . . ."

"But . . ." Kiki prodded.

"But . . . that's as far as it's gone."

"I don't see how that makes it shifty."

"It's something in the *way* he's loving, something that doesn't firm up, something that isn't going anywhere, something hanging, incomplete, something unconsolidated, something tentative . . ."

"Is it in you or is it in him?" Kiki asked shrewdly. Daisy stopped fluffing up an unfluffable Theseus and considered the question as if it hadn't occurred to her before.

"I think—in both of us, now that you ask," she said slowly, sounding surprised.

"Then you really can't complain. No, I take that back, you *can* complain! If you can't complain to me, what kind of friend am I? So go on, complain!"

Daisy cocked a loving eye at Kiki who, now that she noticed, was looking very strange. Her ruffle of hair was brushed neatly down around her face and even her bangs had been arranged to fall quite calmly across her forehead. Her eyes looked two sizes smaller without the exaggerated make-up she always used on them. She had on just a touch of mascara, and her lipstick matched her nails. Her gypsy quality was minimal, replaced by a subdued, quiet, well-kept, and somehow diminished manner, as she sat there in her underwear waiting for her nails to dry. Which was also strange. Since when had Kiki taken to wearing half-slips and bras?

"Go on. I won't be satisfied, if you don't complain now," Kiki urged again.

"I have this feeling inside . . ."

"Yes? Oh, come on Daisy. I'm good with feelings."

"It's—I keep wondering if there hadn't been that strike, would anything have ever happened? Wasn't it maybe just the circumstances? We'd never even flirted before and I've worked for North for more than four years— If there *was* anything there before Venice I would have known it, wouldn't I? Maybe it's just one of those things?"

"That's not a complaint and that's not a feeling—that's just a quibble. It *did* happen and it's still going on. If he'd been stuck in Venice with someone he didn't care for, nothing would have happened at all—right?"

"I suppose. On the other hand, in that magical atmosphere almost anyone might have looked good to him."

"Daisy! Stop that at once!" Kiki was outraged at her friend. Even after years of experience, she still couldn't believe that anyone so beautiful could poor-mouth herself like Daisy Valensky.

"You're right—I'm doing it again, shit! But there was something just the other day that I can't get out of my mind. We were lying around North's place, we'd just made love and I was lying there, just wanting to be petted and hugged, you know—held—and he moved away, restlessly, and he said in this sort of remote, lazy voice—not bored exactly—well maybe just a little—and he said, 'Daisy, amuse me.' "

"That *asshole!*"

"That's exactly what I thought! I don't plan to see him again, except at work."

The two girls' eyes met, each understanding the other perfectly.

"But what did you say next?" Kiki asked hotly.

"Nothing . . . I felt sick. I just got up and put on my clothes and came right home."

"Why didn't you tell me right away?"

"First I thought I was making too much out of it, being oversensitive or humorless about it—it was just a *little* thing," Daisy said broodingly.

"Yeah, and it's the little things like that you have to pay close attention to—those little things get you where you live and they show you where *he* lives," Kiki said, smearing her polish in agitation. "Making 'too much' out of his talking to you as if you were some sort of amusing convenience? A harem girl, a popsie, a toy doll you can wind up and have it play a funny little tune? No wonder North's been divorced twice—that son-of-a-bitch doesn't know shit about women." Kiki's heart sank for Daisy.

"Listen, not to change the subject, but isn't Luke coming for you in five minutes? You don't even have all your make-up on yet, or even your dress. You'll be late."

Startled, Kiki reached into her closet and came out with a plastic garment bag from Saks. She opened it and deftly slipped into a simple, conservative and expensive dress in creamy off-white flannel with a belt of braided navy and cream-colored leather. She put her stockinged feet into demure navy pumps, closed at the heel and toe, and clasped a modest strand of pearls around her neck. She turned and looked defiantly at Daisy.

"What's *that?*" Daisy said, in disbelief.

"Mollie Parnis," Kiki rapped out.

"You're not ready to go out?" Daisy asked. She'd seen Kiki in every possible variety of costumes, but this one was the most impossible to credit.

"Yes."

"Somebody died? It's a funeral?"

"No."

"It's a girl who's entering a convent and you're invited to watch?"

"No."

"You've been asked to the White House?"

"Not that either."

"A costume party and you're going as a nice girl."

"Close. Luke's taking me out to Pound Ridge . . . to meet his mother," Kiki said with a little grin.

"Praise the Lord!" Daisy shouted, jumping up so excitedly that Theseus, half-asleep, was spilled to the floor.

"And sing hallelujah!" Kiki shrieked, breaking into a triumphant little dance.

"But you can't, you simply *can't* go like that!"

"Why not? It's perfect—his mother is ultraconservative."

"Because you'll tip your hand. Who do you want to impress the most, Luke or his mother? If you dress like that, he'll know you're trying to get his mother's approval and that's *fatal* with a guy as cool and hip as Luke. You've got to look as if this isn't any big deal. Don't disguise yourself as a fiancée before he's even asked you to marry him, for heaven's sake. Oh, dumb, dumb . . . the Grosse Pointe has surfaced. He'll laugh himself sick."

"Oh fuck—you're absolutely right," Kiki wailed. "But what *am* I going to wear? I haven't got anything even vaguely appropriate." She was a study in dismay, plunging clumsily into her closet and throwing one outrageous get-up after another onto the floor in a panic.

"Pants? What about your good black crepe Holly Harp pants?" Daisy asked.

"They're covered with paint. I forgot I had them on and painted scenery in them yesterday."

"The other ones? The wools?"

"They're all at the dry cleaners. Oh, Daisy, why am I such a mess? Why does this always happen to me? He'll be here in a minute," Kiki lamented.

"Just stand still for a second." Daisy surveyed Kiki closely. "All right. Take off those pearls and your bra and your pantyhose and put the dress back on. Good, now put on your wedgies, the ones with the glitz all over and the twelve-inch cork soles. Lucky thing your legs are still tan. Now unbutton the dress to the waist. No, that's too far . . . go up two buttons. Fine—I still see tits, but only a little. Here's a belt . . ."

"Daisy, that's Theseus's collar," Kiki protested.

"Shut up and see if it goes around your waist," Daisy snapped. "Damn, too short, and it would have been perfect. Belt, belt . . ." she muttered, scrabbling through her drawers and finally pulling out a length of bright red chiffon onto which she had stitched a large 1920s diamanté buckle she'd unearthed in a thrift shop. She looked further and came up with a small red silk flower.

The doorbell rang. "Go do your eyes," Daisy ordered. "I'll entertain Luke. Don't hurry it, stay calm, keep a steady hand for God's sake," Daisy fretted, pushing Kiki into the bathroom and closing the door behind her.

Luke darted into the living room spouting greetings to Daisy and Theseus. To Daisy, who was accustomed to his usual absent-minded, dreamily remote manner, he seemed unquestionably nervous. Even his eyelids were too jumpy to be melancholy and he kept tugging at his beard and picking invisible lint off his sleeves.

"Where's Kiki?"

"Just getting ready," Daisy said with dignity.

"I suppose she's got on one of her acid-green body stockings and some sort of Mayan serape?" Luke asked.

"Something like that I imagine."

He turned away and looked out of the window, tapping his foot on the floor and drumming his fingers on the wall. "My mother hates it when I'm late," he remarked.

"She won't be long. What's happening tonight?"

"Sort of a family dinner actually. In fact, my grandmother is going to be there," he said moodily.

"A three-generation dinner, hmm?" Daisy probed.

"Also a couple of aunts and uncles who invited themselves when they heard I was coming with a girl."

"Haven't you ever brought a girl home for dinner before?" she asked, astonished.

"Not since high school." Luke gave Daisy a swift, terrified, feverishly determined glance which told her everything she needed to know.

"Excuse me for a minute, Luke, I'll just go in and see if I can persuade Kiki to hurry up," she said. On the way to the bathroom she stopped in Kiki's closet and retrieved the navy Ferragamo pumps and the navy and cream belt that Kiki had had on before. She looked consideringly at the bra and pantyhose which lay in a heap on the floor. She took the pantyhose and left the bra. No point in going overboard. She opened the bathroom door quietly. Kiki had put her eyes back on. "Take off those atrocious wedgies," said Daisy, busy unclasping the red chiffon belt and retrieving the flower.

"*What?*"

"Change of procedure. Don't ask me to explain. You don't have time. Here's your belt. Were those real pearls?"

"Of course—my mother's."

"Okay, put them back, too. Do up one more button and let me look at you. Here, brush your hair a little so it doesn't look too meek. You'll do—divinely. Here's a heavy sweater you can borrow—you don't own a decent fall coat."

"A white cashmere cardigan? Daisy, that's from before we went to college, it's from when you were a kid in London!"

"Anyone can buy a sweater, but ancient, definitely yellowing cashmere—they'll understand that."

" 'They' who?"

"Never mind. Luke's impatient to get going. No, wait . . . you still need something . . ." Daisy tucked the red silk flower in the belt. She stood back to inspect the effect. "Refined, elegant, expensive, quietly sexy and *patriotic* . . . could they ask for more?"

"I could be Jewish," Kiki said gloomily.

"They can't expect miracles."

" 'They' again—you're making me nervous," Kiki jittered, while she admired herself in the mirror.

"That's all right, too, they'll like it if you're nervous— it's only decent. Get going." Daisy pulled Kiki away from the mirror and pushed her in the direction of the living room. She heard rapid, muffled greetings and then the front door slammed behind Luke and Kiki. Slowly she walked into the empty room. Theseus was standing there with a questioning tilt to his head, one white ear up, the other down.

"You may well wonder what's going on," she told him, with a catch in her voice. "But can you answer this question? Why, oh why, can't I do for myself?"

20

*W*hat the fuck do you mean, the sponsor's coming!" North screamed into the phone. "Luke, you know as well as I do that that's impossible. The campaign's all set—why should he come now? Why should he come *ever?*"

"Listen, North, don't you get angry at me. The last person I want in any meeting is anyone from the account's side of the table, you know that," Luke said heatedly. "But it's unheard of that the man himself should insist on coming. On a small account I could begin to believe it, but the president of Supracorp? He should be a thousand miles above this sort of thing, damn it."

"Who cares if he's above or below—the point is he's taking away our freedom!" North shouted.

"North, you just think you have freedom because that's what you like to believe. Basically ain't none of us got freedom—the money is there for the sponsor to decide how to spend it. He's the one with freedom. All the freedom I have is to suggest clever ways for him to spread it around, and all the freedom you have is to make the commercials the best way you know how."

"Spare me the deep-thinking bullshit. My point is that he's gonna poke around in things he doesn't know fuck-all about and he's gonna think he's smarter than we are and even if he likes what we've got he's gonna change it just for the pleasure of meddling in something that's none of his damn business. The bastard is going slumming! Probably he's already given nervous breakdowns to everyone who works for him, so he's looking for someone new to do in—I know the type."

"You don't know Patrick Shannon."

"Do *you?*"

"No—but I've heard he's tough, rough and smart as hell."

"Perfect," North said bitterly. "Just the kind of trouble I don't want hanging around my production meetings. It's bad enough with just the two of us. More rough, tough and smart is unnecessary."

"Listen, I'm on your side. But I can't tell him he isn't welcome, can I?"

"You could try."

"You try, North. You're the one who's so free."

"I'll see you tomorrow." North hung up the phone and sat thinking about this new development. That an actual real live sponsor, that legendary hangover from the early days of radio and television, should come down from his place on Olympus and attend a commercial production meeting was an atrocity! North knew exactly where sponsors were supposed to be: they were disembodied, invisible entities, probably groups of people rather than one man, who sat somewhere up in the clouds of vast corporations, in enormous boardrooms, overlooking huge views of the Hudson and nodded yes or nodded no to advertising campaigns proposed, prepared and carried out by lesser beings.

They didn't mess with the way the machine worked, they weren't the mechanics who tended the Cadillac, but just the aloof, super-rich passengers. Somehow they managed to convey to the chauffeur the direction they wanted to take, but aside from this they had nothing to do with the running of the car. Or that's the way it should be, by God! All the sponsor had to do was decide if a program "paused" for his message, or was "presented" by him, or was made "possible" by him or merely received a "word" from him.

The idea that the sponsor should choose to reveal himself in the person of Patrick Shannon was monstrous. What abomination could it lead to? Maybe he'd like to deliver the "message" himself like those homemade used-car commercials ... maybe Pat Shannon was another Cal Worthington. So what if the Elstree campaign was going to be a multi-million-dollar media buy—this joker, Shannon, should have the grace to let his highly paid professionals worry about it. It followed that there was no telling how deeply he'd want to be involved. He'd already broken all the rules by proposing to attend the meeting, just when Luke and the Elstree ad boys had finally agreed on a decent campaign. Nobody coming in at this point could spell anything but trouble. Major trouble.

"Daisy," he snapped into the interoffice phone. "Come in here right away." If Shannon was coming to the meeting, North wanted everyone in his organization to be there, too. Daisy'd have to be responsible for that. He had important things to attend to.

Daisy made a last survey of the large conference room. The most irregular meeting that was scheduled to begin in minutes had already caused such consternation and high irascibility that she had decided to make sure that, even if nothing else went smoothly, at least the people who would be gathered together would have enough ashtrays, pencils and carafes of ice water. It was a fortunate decision since somebody had forgotten to put out scratch paper. If people couldn't doodle in preproduction meetings they would quickly take to using their nails on each other, Daisy thought, as she rushed to tell North's secretary to provide piles of fresh white pads.

There was still a minute to spare, and Daisy went to her own office to make a final check before the mirror. All seemed to be in order. She had managed to make herself nearly invisible. Her hair had been gathered ruthlessly into one thick plait that she hid by tucking it into the roomy neck of her white work shirt and letting it hang down her back. Over the shirt she had a deliberately baggy pair of white carpenter's overalls and she had pulled a white canvas sailor hat well down over her forehead so that it effectively hid her eyes. She was satisfied that against the white bricks of the conference room, she would fade into the background.

There had been no possible way for Daisy to avoid being at the meeting, but at least she felt reasonably certain that Patrick Shannon could not possibly spot her as the woman he had met at the Shorts' dinner party in Middleburg, a woman who had, in a way that must have seemed malicious, made him very angry, so angry that she was concerned that her mere presence might add considerably to the high tempers she knew everyone else was bringing to the studio today.

Now the sound of the rising elevator told Daisy that the meeting was about to begin. Luke Hammerstein, accompanied by five of his subordinates, was the first to arrive. Daisy stood to one side as the room started to fill up. North had excused nobody from today's summit conference and Arnie Greene, Nick-the-Greek, Hubie Troy, Wingo Sparks, Daisy's two assistants and Alix Updike were all there. Full-dress parade today, Daisy thought as she saw a perfect place for her to sit—in the lee of Nick, whose peacock figure was clad in a particularly lively glen plaid. Every eye, she judged, would stop at Nick and, wildly wondering, go no farther.

Precisely on time Patrick Shannon entered, followed by five people whom he introduced quickly: Hilly Bijur, president of the Elstree Division of Supracorp, Jared Turner, head of marketing, Candice Bloom, head of publicity for Elstree, Helen Strauss, head of advertising, and Patsy Jacobson, product-line manager.

In the time it took for them to all find chairs, Daisy was able to peek out from her strategic position and briefly study Patrick Shannon, who had seated himself without hesitation at the opposite end of the table from North. It was the first time she had seen North with a man who was clearly his equal. She could feel, even without looking, how Shannon dominated the room. Everyone, no matter how they were placed, seemed to be leaning toward him as if he were a magnet. Perhaps it was the weight of all their ears cocked in his direction that gave her that impression, she thought, restraining a giggle at the absurdity of this whole solemn occasion. Shannon's appearance in the room was so unnecessary that she couldn't believe that Luke and North had taken it all so seriously . . . and with such vehemence. If that pompous man wanted to get the impression that he was doing something "creative" about his company's commercials, why not humor him, she wondered. He was no different from all the other people who employed North. Invariably, on a shoot, they asked to look into the viewfinder of the camera before a take. North always let them go ahead—once—although they didn't know what they were seeing or what it would mean on film, and all they ever did was nod wisely and approve of whatever he had been planning to do in the first place.

Still . . . Shannon *had* entered the room with the firm, possessive step of a ship's captain strolling on his own deck, a ship, Daisy suspected, that would raise a flag bearing a skull and crossbones just as soon as it was safely out to sea. He was a pirate, a rumple-haired, blue-eyed,

Black Irish brigand, improbably disguised as a prince of industry.

The meeting opened as Luke rose to his feet. He was privately, but thoroughly, annoyed at having to recapitulate the story of work that had already been through weeks of discussion, work that had been finalized, but Shannon had phoned him and asked him to fill everyone in on the entire picture at the start of the conference.

In a voice that brought them all to immediate attention, Luke began abruptly. One of the requirements of all the jobs he'd had in the past, which had led to his present position, had been the ability to "talk" a commercial so dramatically that you could see it without pictures.

"Elstree suffers from an image problem. Fuddy-duddy, old-world, your grandma's favorite. We knew that was the trouble going in. Last year another agency took off on a losing basis, using the purity of the ingredients as their main selling point. It didn't work—that's why Elstree changed to our agency. Purity isn't enough in a world in which there are a number of lines of cosmetics making similar claims with as much justification." He paused and checked his audience. They were all listening intently.

"Faded gentility and purity are *out!* We are going to capture today's most lucrative market: the working woman—dynamic, adventurous and *with her own paycheck.*" Luke picked up a large, glossy blow-up of a girl's face and displayed it to the listening crowd. "This is Pat Stephens, the new Elstree girl. The commercials will present her in a number of situations that have never been done before in the cosmetics-fragrance field . . . she'll be doing aerobatics in a small plane, we'll see her weightless, in a pressurized chamber taking training for space flight and racing in the Indy 500 in a special car G.M. is making for us. Pat will always wear some sort of uniform and a helmet. In the last thirteen seconds of each commercial, as she talks Elstree, she'll fling off her helmet and we'll finally see her face, conveying a tremendous impression of vitality and strength —driving, exciting, dashing and above all, *young*—not just the woman of today but also the woman of *tomorrow*."

Daisy contemplated the blow-up as objectively as possible. The girl was splendidly clean-featured, but her sleekly cropped head and screechingly All-American look rendered her devoid of nuance, Daisy thought. Teeth and cheekbones she had in abundance . . . but appeal?

"We intend to sign Pat up for two years so that no one

else will be able to use her," Luke continued. "She'll become the living symbol of the utter now-ness of Elstree. Within months, maybe less, everyone will forget that Elstree has been in business for a hundred years because they'll associate it with Pat Stephens, functioning confidently in the present and on into the future."

He sat down to a round of applause led by Nick, who had received his instructions before the meeting. Then silence fell.

Patrick Shannon nodded in the direction of the people from Supracorp. "Ladies, Hilly, Jared—and the rest of you—first of all I want to apologize for butting in here. I know it's irregular to have this mass meeting with everyone involved but I've no time to go through channels and no time to spare anybody's feelings. As you know, although Mr. Hammerstein and Mr. North may not, I've been away for months, off and on, and I have to leave for Tokyo today." He waited, pausing just long enough to receive the expected nods from the men and women whose positions he was preempting.

"When I got back to the office a few days ago I found this campaign on my desk, ready to go. It was the first time I'd seen a photo of the Elstree girl."

"We were waiting for Danillo to photograph her with her new haircut, and he took longer than expected," Helen Strauss explained quickly.

Shannon slammed his hand down on the huge blow-up. "She looks like a tight end for the Dallas Cowboys." Nervous laughter greeted his remark. Sponsors were entitled to a sense of humor.

"It's not funny, ladies and gentlemen. I'm not joking. She's a good-looking kid, but unfortunately you picked a jock. This campaign can't work." The sound of shock, an absence of breathing or moving, filled the conference room. Shannon continued evenly.

"I'm sure I don't have to emphasize that Elstree lost thirty million dollars last year—it's the talk of the fragrance industry. My competitors dine out on it. I'm going to spend many millions more to turn the company around —launching a new fragrance, new packaging, a new advertising campaign. Big as Supracorp is, Elstree cannot afford to lose any more money because my stockholders will not—I repeat, will not—understand. They have a hell of a lot less patience than I do."

Shannon paused, but no one in the room showed any

inclination toward speech. He picked up the blow-up of Pat Stephens and held it up. "This girl and Mr. Hammerstein's campaign will certainly *change* Elstree's image, but they will not sell, and I repeat the word *sell*, cosmetics or fragrance. I simply don't believe that women will identify themselves with this girl or the situations you plan to put her in. It must have sounded original and fresh when you all decided on it, but do you think it remotely *believable* that this tough cookie would be using blusher and mascara under all those helmets? I'm damn sure that she wouldn't be wearing perfume inside that space capsule or whatever the hell it is." Shannon let the glossy fall to the floor before he went on. "I think that the time has come to return to a romantic sell in fragrance, a classy, feminine sell. The working woman hasn't become any less womanly because she earns money. This tomboy you want to sign for the Elstree girl may well be somebody's fantasy of today's woman, but, sorry gentlemen, she's not mine."

Luke finally had to protest. "Look at the Charlie campaign, Mr. Shannon," he said calmly. "It's been a fabulous success for Revlon and their entire selling point is that girl with her extra-long legs taking huge strides all over the world—clean-cut, not especially pretty, but putting over that to-hell-with-everything-folks-I-can-take-care-of-myself image."

"That's one of my objections, Mr. Hammerstein," Patrick Shannon countered. "Charlie is three years old now—soon that campaign will be dated. And I don't intend to imitate Charlie . . . not even Charlie in the year two thousand." His wide mouth tightened in a way his employees knew well.

"Pat . . ." Helen Strauss began. Advertising, after all, was her responsibility, or, at least, it was *supposed* to be.

"No, Helen, I don't buy this campaign. Not any of it."

"Did you have something else in mind, Mr. Shannon?" North asked with politeness. His face quivered with impatience at the whole windy proceedings, but he knew he wasn't nearly as disturbed as the agency and the Supracorp people. He only had to make the commercials, not create them.

"I don't throw things out unless I have a notion of how to replace them, Mr. North," Shannon said. He took off the jacket of his suit, rolled up his shirt sleeves with deliberation and stretched; a big man thoroughly at ease in a roomful of people who had just seen months of carefully made plans laid waste. Daisy heard Nick-the-Greek whispering, "Shee-it" in admiration. She could almost feel him wondering if he should stop wearing the vests he adored.

"I've done a little homework since I first saw this photo," Shannon continued. "The natural look is still the most important one; the natural-looking blonde is still the model who will sell more than the brunette. I want you to find me a natural blonde and put her in natural situations. I want her to have class, warmth and a kind of glow that seems achievable. I want a real woman, not just the Elstree Girl—but someone who will become known by her own name. If Candy Bergen weren't already committed to work for Shulton and that new fragrance of theirs, I'd say she's the girl for us, but it's too late to get her now."

"You mean you're looking for a celebrity endorsement?" Luke asked, keeping the incredulity out of his voice. It just might be the oldest idea in advertising. They had actually used it in the days of Queen Victoria, for Christ's sake.

"Why the hell not? Remember 'She's engaged, she's lovely, she uses Ponds'? Nothing basic has changed since then, Mr. Hammerstein. Nothing in human nature. I didn't promise to be original—just different." Shannon grinned, with a larky bandit's look in his eyes, that freebooter gleam that told everyone from Supracorp that his mind was made up.

For a few seconds Luke was stunned into silence as he pictured his wonderful girl of the future being watered down into a simpering deb with white satin draped around her privileged shoulders, selling drugstore cold cream to the masses. His voice stayed reasonable but it demanded an effort. "Don't you think that there's a danger in an approach that might be perceived as snobbish—and outmoded?"

"I'm not talking debutantes, Hammerstein—Ponds was merely an example. I'm talking *star*. People still love stars, today more than ever. I want you to make a star or find a star to be the Elstree Girl. Just remember—she *cannot* be one of the boys."

Until this minute, Hilly Bijur had refrained from interrupting, although he was president of Elstree. Let Helen Strauss take the heat. But now he sought to regain the control he had lost by Patrick Shannon's intervention.

"You're on the money about natural blondes," he said to

his boss, overriding Luke who was about to speak. "I managed to sneak a look at the new, top-secret Clairol report that says the trend toward blondes is hotter than ever—not the streaked blonde but the total blonde, the blonder-than-ever blonde."

Luke and North looked at each other in disgust. The meeting was being taken over by report-quoting, image-crazy civilians, and there wasn't a damn thing they could do about it. Nick-the-Greek sat squirming in frustration in his seat. Everybody was putting his two cents in and he hadn't said a word yet. He didn't like being ignored. Since North had insisted that he come to this asshole hassle, he was going to add something to it. In spite of his tailored-to-the-eyeballs exterior, Nick had never abandoned one habit that he'd learned in his childhood in Spanish Harlem. In each of his startling suits there was a special pocket in which he always kept a sharp knife which, had he cared to give it its precise name, was a switchblade. It kept him from feeling nervous. Now he reached for his dangerous security blanket and quietly snapped it open. All this pissant talk about blondes . . . they wanted blonde, they'd get blonde—from Nick-the-Greek.

In one fast movement, he turned his powerful body, snatched off Daisy's sailor cap, pulled her braid out from its hiding place and cut the ribbon which bound it so tightly. Before she could move, using both hands he rapidly unplaited the braid until her masses of hair were firmly held in his hands. Daisy struggled and gasped in disbelief, but he'd moved so quickly that she wasn't even sure of what was happening. Nick stood up, bringing Daisy with him since he had grabbed her by every hair on her head, and said loudly, "This what you mean, Mr. Shannon?" He waved Daisy's hair triumphantly, as if he were raising the flag on Iwo Jima.

"Damn it!" Daisy sputtered. "Nick! Let go! Stop it!"

"What the hell do you think you're doing?" North snapped.

"What's going on?" asked Hilly Bijur, while Wingo Sparks was doubled up in malicious laughter.

"You guys don't know shit from a real blonde, that's all," Nick insisted loudly, without releasing Daisy. "You think they're so easy to find?"

"Nick, put her *down!*" Luke said, crisply cutting through the confusion. Nick looked around with indignant righteousness, but let Daisy loose so that she could regain her seat. She kicked as hard as she could at his ankles, wishing she were wearing pointed shoes instead of sneakers. "You *bugger!*" she hissed at him, looking for her sailor hat without success.

"Excuse me, but could I just see the young lady again?" Patrick Shannon asked as the tumult died down.

"*No!*" said Daisy.

"Mr. Shannon, the young lady is my producer, Daisy Valensky. She works here, she works for me and she happens to be blonde. Could we just go on with this discussion and get something settled before you have to leave for Japan?" North said impatiently.

"I want another look at her, North," Shannon demanded.

"Daisy?" North asked. "Would you mind?"

"Yes, I *would*," she said wrathfully. "Get yourself some other blondes to look at—call the model agencies, leave me alone."

"Daisy, cool it. Take it easy, it's no big deal. Mr. Shannon just wants to *see* you again—a look won't kill you," North insisted in annoyance. Sponsors—all clients when it came to that—were a law unto themselves—idiots one and all—but there were times when you had to humor them.

"See *what*, damn it!" Daisy muttered, trying to make her hair less conspicuous by pushing it behind her ears. She glared at Shannon, her skin flushed as much with fury as embarrassment.

"I remember you," he said flatly.

"How nice," she said, forcing herself to speak with cool politeness. Even in her anger, the incident of their meeting had been enough to warn her that this high-flying, risk-taking, master builder of the world of big business did not take kindly to what he might perceive as an affront.

"She has an unforgettable face," Shannon said to the room at large, in an uninflected voice.

"Very pretty," Hilly Bijur said busily. "Very pretty . . . thank you, Miss . . . ah . . . thank you very much."

"I said," Patrick Shannon repeated quietly, but in a way that brought every one of them to instant attention, "that she has an *unforgettable* face."

"Of course, Pat, you're absolutely right," Hilly Bijur, flurried, hastened to agree. "Now that we know what you have in mind, it won't take Helen more than a day or two to find a dozen girls who are suitable. She'll contact every agency in town, won't you, Helen? Or Luke will be in charge of it . . . or . . ." He floundered and subsided, not entirely sure into whose department casting fell.

"Wait a minute—just wait a minute—she's *also* a princess." Now Shannon spoke rapidly, his face concentrated in sudden excitement.

"You can forget it, Shannon. I've just told you, she works for *me*," North burst out, popping like a dry log on a brisk fire. He had become a bad-tempered redhead, his above-the-battle manner quite abandoned.

"A blonde . . . a face . . . a title," Shannon repeated to himself. "Princess Daisy . . . yes . . . yes . . . I like the sound of that."

"Mr. Shannon, this is not another remake of *A Star Is Born*," North said with escalating asperity.

"She might just do—might do very well," Shannon said, as if he were alone in the room.

"Hey, that's not fair—it was my idea!" Nick-the-Greek exploded harmlessly into preoccupied ears.

"Helen," Shannon directed, "send her to be photographed immediately so that this time we know what we have. She looks like what I want but I won't be sure till I see the actual pictures." He rose, ready to leave the meeting.

Hilly Bijur hastened to join himself to Shannon's point of view before his employer could leave. As Shannon put on his jacket, Bijur spoke quickly. "I like it, Pat, you're absolutely right. Princess Daisy? . . . Didn't North say Daisy Valensky? Valensky? Wait a minute! That means her mother was Francesca Vernon. And for Christ's sake, her father was Stash Valensky—doesn't anyone here remember? Holy shit, but this little lady's going to move merchandise!" He subsided, pleased at a chance to exhibit his memory even as he dissociated himself from the unfortunate ad campaign he had approved.

"Tell them you want a hundred grand a year," Nick whispered to Daisy, who still sat speechless in her chair. "And don't say I never did anything for you . . . plus, you bruised my socks."

"We'll have to change the packaging," worried Jared Turner, obsessed, as usual, by marketing considerations. "Princess Daisy doesn't sound like a modern line."

"It's going to postpone our distribution date by almost a year!" Patsy Jacobson complained. "Meanwhile, what do I tell the stores?" This was a product-line manager's night-mare.

"Could I have some quiet!" North shouted and then stopped as he saw Daisy jump out of her seat and stride rapidly around the table. She stood just behind Luke's art director, who had already lettered in the words "Princess Daisy" with Magic Markers on a piece of paper. She snatched the paper from the table, tore it in four pieces, and jammed them in one of her pockets. "Mr. Shannon," she said in a voice which rang with clear outrage, "I am not for sale! I have absolutely no intention of letting you use my hair or my face or my name to sell your products. How dare you treat me as if you own me? You're crazy, rude and totally insensitive—all of you—and . . . and . . ." Swiftly, she gathered up the battery of Magic Markers the art director had arranged in a neat row and flung them on the marble table where they scattered loudly like small firecrackers. "I suggest that each of you goons take one of these and—stick it where the sun don't shine!" She slammed the door behind her.

"I didn't know Daisy even knew that expression," Arnie Greene marveled.

"She doesn't usually talk that way unless something goes wrong on location," Nick agreed, still aggrieved at the theft of his inspiration.

"She's awfully touchy," brooded Candice Bloom. If she were going to have to work with *that* girl, public relations were not going to be easy.

North sat back, smiling nastily at Shannon. He enjoyed vindication. "I told you that Daisy was just a working girl. She doesn't seem to want to be a model, does she? You'll have to excuse her."

"I have absolutely no intention of excusing her," Shannon answered with confidence. "She'll be the Elstree Girl."

"Daisy's not in the habit of changing her mind. You'd better not count on it," North retorted smugly.

"Oh, but I do," said Shannon. "Hilly, hold all Elstree decisions until I get back from Japan. We're going to get it right this time."

"Daisy's invaluable at my studio, Shannon," North said hotly. "You can't try this."

Patrick Shannon gave North his buccaneer's smile, that big, reckless Irish grin that everyone in Supracorp had learned to watch out for.

"Would you care to bet?"

Just before Christmas of 1976, Ram decided that it was time to get the matter of Sarah Fane settled. She'd had her fill of the Season by now and was not yet engaged to be married, but soon she'd be leaving for a round of country house visits and, just to be on the safe side, he judged it a good idea to arrive at an understanding before she left.

"I want you to dine with me tomorrow," he said on the phone. "But alone, none of your friends coming along."

"But Ram, I'm invited to Lucinda Curzon's little cocktail tomorrow."

"It's one or the other, Sarah," he said in a level voice.

Her sense of timing whispered urgently in her ear. "Since you put it that way, and since I can, after all, go to Lucinda's first, before meeting you, why not?" she said with a tiny hint of delicate reluctance.

"Why not indeed?" he said, admitting to himself that one had to admire her nerve.

They dined the next night at Mark's Club on Charles Street in Mayfair. Behind the tall unmarked door of the thin townhouse which houses Mark's, lie several dining rooms. Ram had reserved a table in the first and largest dining room from which they could see everyone who came and went. He had deliberately not chosen a quieter corner of this supremely exclusive dining club, owned by Mark Birley. Ram preferred to spend the first part of the evening in the richly appointed candle-lit room with its turquoise cut-velvet banquettes and deep terra-cotta walls whimsically covered by realistic Victorian paintings of animals, framed in gold scrollwork, square, oval and round, which almost hid the walls entirely.

Although Sarah had heeded him and arranged for them not to be joined by any of her friends, between them they knew almost everyone who was at Mark's that night, and their dinner was interrupted dozens of times by greetings, something Ram had anticipated. After they had finished their coffee, he asked, "If one more person comes by to tell you that you are the deb of the year, what will you do?"

"I shall howl," she announced, managing to look both fragile and charmingly modest. "I shall get up from my seat and howl until they have to send for the police to take me away."

"Then shall we go to my house for a brandy?" There had been the strain of a balanced, formal minuet tinkling in their ears all evening, a minuet to which they had both been dancing for many months. Abruptly, with Ram's invitation, the music came to a stop. Something wavered, hesitated in the air between them. Sarah's mind jumped to memories of the many beautiful and courted girls she knew he went out with. Whenever she saw him with them he looked as seriously watchful of them as he had ever been of her. She looked at him thoughtfully. If she went to his house with him now, she had no question of what he would expect.

"I'd love a brandy but . . ."

"Does that mean yes or no, my dear Sarah?"

"Well . . . we can't stay here forever . . . so I suppose . . . again, why not?"

"It's an absolutely marvelous house, Ram," she said, after he had shown her the first floor.

"Let me show you the upper floors."

"No, I don't think so," she said sharply, drawing inviolability quickly around her shoulders like an invisible cape.

He smiled somberly. "Are you playing the prude?"

She was stung. "How ridiculous! I'm just tired, Ram. Will you take me home please? It was lovely brandy."

"No, Sarah, darling, I won't take you home. I love you, Sarah."

She stood quietly by the fireplace, watching him, without responding to his words.

"I want to marry you," he continued. Still she was silent. There was, she thought, something inaccessible about his mouth. "Sarah," he repeated, coming close but not touching her. "Will you marry me?"

It had taken him long enough to get to the point, she said to herself. Should she put him off and wait until the next time he asked? No, it was best to cap her Season with the engagement of the year. Next year another debutante would be in the spotlight—but if she were Princess Valensky, what difference would a mere debutante make to her? She curved her perfect lips in her perfect meaningless smile and inclined her perfect head. She didn't move toward him until he leaned down to her.

As he kissed her he sighed, "The first time . . ." She well knew that indeed it was the first time they had kissed like this alone and on the lips. Only occasionally had she given him the smooth skin of her cheeks before, in impersonal public thanks. She had played a hard, long relentless championship game.

He kissed her again and again, with increasing hunger, and the Honorable Sarah Fane couldn't tell whether what she was feeling was excitement because she had achieved her victory and caught Ram Valensky, or whether the excitement was that sensuality she had never had any trouble dismissing.

"Come upstairs with me now, my darling, come with me," he urged against her mouth.

"No . . . Ram, please . . . I can't . . . I never have . . ."

"Of course you haven't, Sarah, my lovely Sarah . . . but you're going to be my wife—it's all right now."

"Ram, no. I couldn't . . . I couldn't *possibly* . . ."

He let her go so abruptly that she teetered slightly and had to catch the mantel. He backed away from her and stood frowning at her with scornful eyes.

"You haven't even said you love me, Sarah . . . did you realize that? Perhaps you don't love me, perhaps you're not yet ready to make up your mind? I've been watching you, my dear—do you think I don't know the kind of flirt you are? Does it amuse you to make a man propose, and then not even give him an answer except a tiny *gracious* nod of your head? I've rather enjoyed seeing you play the innocent coquette, the untouchable and pure aristocrat, every single calculating second of it, everything you do orchestrated to the greatest glory of Sarah Fane." His accusing, sardonic eyes began to frighten her a little, but at the same time, she felt a thrill at seeing Ram lose his composure. Oh, yes, it *was* exciting to be able to do this to a man. She could not prevent a shadow of a complacent smile from touching her mouth. Ram saw it and took a swift, angry step forward and grasped her arm.

"So you *do* think you can make a fool out of me," he said, suddenly furious in a way that took her by surprise. "So that's your little plan, so that's what goes on inside that manipulative, self-centered mind of yours—another conquest for Sarah, another contest you've won—probably you'll be boasting about it tomorrow." His fingers tightened on her arm and the triumph that had been hers a moment ago seemed about to disappear. She knew she had to play her last coin. Still, wasn't it for exactly this moment that she'd guarded it?

"Ram, stop it! You didn't even give me a chance to say I love you. You're not being fair, you're wrong about me . . ."

"Am I? Am I?" he whispered, in a hot, maddened voice,

as if her words had meant nothing to him. "A common tease, that's what you've been all along...a common tease, right out of the schoolroom...." He let go of her arm and stood wrathfully in front of her. Everything she would get if she married Ram Valensky formed one great ball in Sarah's mind, a great golden ball studded with precious jewels. She stretched out her hands to it and to him.

"Upstairs..." she whispered, in a faltering voice. Ram grasped her in strong hands and led her stumbling toward the staircase. He was hurting her arms again, but in her mixture of greed and confusion and dread and excitement, all Sarah could remember was an American friend at school who used to say, "Always pour cement over a bargain." Suddenly Sarah knew exactly what that meant.

Oh, God, why did it take him so long, Sarah Fane wondered in agony. No one had ever told her it would be like this, long and painful—so disgustingly painful—and labored and utterly ignominious. And so silent, so wordless. Where was the romance she had expected, where the pleasure? There was only shame. She was plunged into a revolting dream, the kind that went senselessly on and on, captured under the weight of a man who was so far out of control that there was nothing she could possibly do about it. His hard lips and hard hands never allowed her a second's respite, but all she could hear above her was the sound of his tormented breathing. In her hideous misery she tried again and again to protest but he didn't, *wouldn't* hear her. His breathing grew louder and louder until it seemed to her that it must finally burst into a shout, but then it would start all over again, on a lower note, and rise to another crescendo. His eyes were tightly closed in the low light of the room, but he had his hands in her hair and was pulling at its golden strands until he made her cry out in pain. Oh...oh, now it was surely going to end...no one could gasp and labor like that for long and live. Please, please, let it happen quickly, quickly...

"*Daisy! Daisy!*" Ram screamed into the dimness, "*Daisy, I love you!*"

Finding strength in her violent outrage, Sarah Fane flung herself away from Ram and stood, huddled in a mixture of humiliation, growing rage and incredulous, but certain knowledge, looking at the creature on the bed, a mad, sobbing loathsome creature who had buried his disgraced head in the pillow, a creature she would have to destroy for what he had done to her, done to Sarah Fane.

21

$\mathcal{W}$hen the Valarians had invited Daisy to join them on their chartered yacht in early January of 1977, she had refused. The idea of spending five days cooped up with Robin and Vanessa and their cronies, cruising the Caribbean, sounded like going to a very expensive jail. She could almost hear the worldly, self-important exchanges of gossip and hidden spitefulness, count the never-ending games of backgammon, imagine the cases of white wine and Perrier that would be consumed, estimate the number of changes of costume and jewels that each woman would be making during the day. It was everything she hated, but Vanessa had been relentlessly insistent and Daisy had finally not known how to get out of it without becoming truly offensive. Vanessa had come as close to anger as Daisy had ever seen her.

"I won't take no for an answer again," she'd finally said. "I've invited Topsy and Ham Short—he happens to be a fan of yours, and there will be several other people aboard who have children who need painting—among the other guests—but I don't see why the devil I have to lure you with the possibility of commissions. Really, Daisy, you're making me feel very much as if you've been *using* me. When I say that Robin and I are counting on the pleasure of your company don't you feel that's enough of a reason to accept?"

Remembering what she indeed now owed Vanessa, Daisy had hastily agreed. The studio could get along without her for a few days, in fact her last vacation had been so long ago that she couldn't remember it. Most important of all, she couldn't risk allowing a source of income to disappear, as Vanessa was clearly threatening.

Now, as she sat with Ham and Topsy in their Aero Commander, on the flight to Nassau, where they would all join the yacht the Valarians had chartered for the holidays, transforming it with their own possessions into a floating approximation of their New York apartment, Daisy reflected that it was, after all, a good time to get away. Since that scene when she had rebelled against the idea of becoming the Elstree Girl, she had felt at odds with almost everyone in the studio. North seemed to think that she had gone out of her way to insult an important client, and the atmosphere at work was tense and heavy. As the plane began to descend, Daisy thought that it was no longer anger she felt, nor even genuine annoyance at the way the men from Supracorp had treated her, at the cavalier way in which they had simply assumed that she was a blonde *thing* for them to use to sell products. After all, without her consent they were powerless and they knew it. No, what still made her feel a deep stab of warning, a warning that still reverberated throughout her, was the idea of *becoming* Princess Daisy in that horrifyingly exposed position called the "public eye"; a profound fear of being perceived as a particular personality who was called Princess Daisy and who would be photographed and manipulated to sell Elstree in commercials, in ads and on display counters, until her Princess Daisy-ness would be burned permanently into the consciousness of the consumers of the Western world. So far, in her adult lifetime, she had managed to slip by, to soft pedal, to hide out.

No one at Santa Cruz had ever thought of her as anyone but a girl named Valensky; at North's studio any vague interest anyone might have had in her title or her background had long ago vanished and only occasionally reappeared as a joke. To all her coworkers she was Daisy-the-producer who knew where everyone was supposed to be and when—and why—and raised hell if they didn't perform as expected. Only in the well-guarded enclaves of the Horse People was she Princess Daisy, and there she was protected by their associations with her father, whose name was still well remembered and honored. Horse People were safe.

Patrick Shannon's proposal to make her a public figure, to exploit her as Princess Daisy, touched on a vital nerve—it aroused terrors she had fought in the shadow, year after year, without being able to explain to herself why they had such a hold over her. All she knew was that they planned to tag her, to label her something called *A Princess Daisy*, and if she allowed them to do it, she would be giving up something more precious than the relative anonymity she had preserved for so long. As well as privacy, she would be giving up something Daisy could only think of as *safety*. The public eye was a dangerous place in which to conduct her life—she didn't need to search for any logical explanations to be certain that she was right.

A launch brought Topsy, Ham and Daisy out to the yacht where Vanessa was waiting for them all. After she had had the Shorts shown to their quarters, she led Daisy to a medium-sized stateroom done in yellow-and-white striped canvas. Vanessa's mood was cheerful.

"Everyone's on board now, thank heaven. I'll tell the captain he can get underway as soon as he's ready," she said. "We're all getting some sun on deck—no? Too sleepy? Well, then, drinks in the main saloon at seven o'clock. Good to have you aboard, love bug." Vanessa squeezed Daisy in an impersonal way. Like all accomplished lesbians, she had never in her life committed the mistake of making the slightest sexual gesture toward another woman unless she was convinced that it would be welcomed. Daisy wouldn't have been importuned by Vanessa if they'd been cast away together on a desert island . . . at least not until a month had passed without rescue.

The gently rocking motion of the ship, the escape from New York, the subtle freshening of air in the room as the yacht's distance from the shore grew greater, all combined to make Daisy's nap as relaxing and refreshing as a short voyage in itself. She woke to the reddening light of a tropical sun, a light so pure in its clarity and the intensity that came from its refraction on open, blue water, that it seemed to be actively resisting the approach of twilight. She lay on her bed, a mock four-poster, with the bed clamped to the floor and the curtains firmly anchored to the ceiling, and, in a ruminative mood, decided that she was well off here, away from the city where she would have been alone all week. Kiki was spending two weeks of winter vacation with Luke, at his little place in northern Connecticut. She had looked like an untamed powder puff as she flung clothes into her suitcase with the abandon of one who knows that a possible potential mother-in-law will not be around to observe her. Theseus, impossible on a yacht, had been left for these few days with Daisy's landlady, whom he had grown to accept peevishly.

Daisy showered and dressed, but it was still too early to join the others. Thank heaven they'd all be in their staterooms, intently adjusting their resort dinner clothes, caparisoned for the delectation of each other.

She made her way to the prow of the yacht and stood there alone, blending and losing herself in a breeze that danced with her. The rays of the sun crystallized her hair, turning it into a spun-sugar forest, like some treat from a children's Christmas. The large ship rose and fell comfortingly as it chopped through the water, already many marine miles from the harbor in Nassau. The thought of Patrick Shannon, that presumptuous, impossible man, touched Daisy's mind and she found that it barely annoyed her. She had, after all, shown him that he couldn't command her life, no matter how everyone else deferred to him. And what about North, who, as surely as Shannon, had treated her as if she had no more humanity than a chess piece in his confrontation with the sponsor—a piece of property that belonged to the studio, a parcel he wasn't inclined to part with? Daisy shrugged and smiled. She found that she didn't care about North either. To hell with all of them. Her eyes filled with the sea and the sky, Daisy was at peace.

She stayed on deck until she knew she was unquestionably late for cocktails, and then, as reluctantly as she had done her Maths at Lady Alden's, but knowing that there was no way to avoid them, she went in search of the main saloon. She passed one large room in which crew members were laying tables for dinner. Next to it was an even larger room in which Daisy could see the silhouettes of more than a dozen people. On the opposite side of the yacht, a wall had been opened up with great glass windows, and the gory, blinding pyrotechnics of the sunset backlit the guests so that Daisy couldn't make out their faces. As she pushed open the door, Vanessa materialized out of the glare and took her by the hand, leading her, blinded, into the room. A man's figure walked toward them and Vanessa put Daisy's hand in his, and immediately drifted away.

"Hello, Daisy."

Ram's voice.

She staggered backward. Ram steadied her swiftly, catching her by the arms as he tried to kiss the top of her head, but even as Ram's lips reached for her, she had lunged backward. She was beyond words, beyond screams, beyond any movement except retreat. She stepped back again, turning to run, but as she did so a strong arm grabbed her around her waist. Vanessa, clutching her in a jailer's grip, pressed her forward insistently. The pulse of time, like a power line struck by lightning, dimmed, lurched, flickered until it almost went out and then, as Vanessa's voice began, time began to beat again, but slowly, without assurance. The other guests were watching, not understanding, but suddenly curious and listening. Vanessa's voice, that charmingly ardent voice, was raised to address them all, covering Daisy's silence, distracting attention away from the brute fear in her eyes.

"See, Ram, I told you she'd come," Vanessa said triumphantly. "I've always said family quarrels are utterly silly, haven't I, Robin, darling—and when Ram told us he hadn't even seen his little sister in years I just said to myself, well, that's too ridiculous—just totally absurd. I knew my Daisy would never carry a childish grudge that long, no matter what the spat was about, and Ram certainly has no hard feelings, so we all planned this surprise together, this family reunion, when Robin and I were in London for New Year's Eve. And now, love bug, aren't you pleased that I did? After all, how many brothers does one have in a lifetime? You and Ram are all that's left of the Valenskys, and I promised myself I'd make you friends again. Everybody! Let's all drink to the end of misunderstandings and to all good things—come on, Ham, Topsy, Jim, Sally, the rest of you ... a toast!" Releasing Daisy, she raised her glass and moved toward the others. The hearty clinking of their glasses broke the circle, like an evil enchantment, in which Daisy had been locked in frozen black terror.

"Why?" she hissed under the sound of the toast.

"Just a reunion," Ram answered, his gaze, set and hungry, denying his social smile.

"How? What does that bitch *owe* you?"

"Nothing," he lied easily. Ram had persuaded his partners to loan the Valarians the money to launch an entirely new dress line, priced for the average woman, an expensive undertaking on a large scale.

"I don't believe you!"

"It just doesn't matter what you believe. You're here ... you can hardly run away." His eyes scavenged her face.

He was as quiveringly rapacious as a miser alone in King Solomon's mine. He spoke without knowing what he said and without caring. He didn't have to placate her. She was weak, weaker than she yet knew, and he was strong, and that was all that mattered.

Swiftly Daisy turned to walk away. He put a restraining hand on her arm. She turned back in a frenzy of disgust. Pure contempt flooded her as she looked straight into his avaricious eyes.

"Never, never touch me, Ram. I warn you," she spat at him. Acid black hatred poured from her eyes. She went rigid in a passion of revulsion. Slowly he released her arm, but his eyes refused to let her go. For an instant they stood locked in the intensity of their emotions.

"Daisy! Ram! Dinner's served ... didn't you two hear the steward?" Vanessa gestured toward the general surge in the direction of the next room. Automatically Daisy found herself following the others.

Two round tables had been laid, not in Robin's marine manner, all silver-mounted conch shell, chunks of rare coral and blue and white Chinese Export ware, that he reserved for particularly snowy winter nights in the city, but in his grandest Chinese form. At each place was a round red lacquer tray set with a rare K'ang Hsi plate, inlaid black and silver chopsticks and a single green and white orchid in a black porcelain bud vase. Between the trays were artfully scattered a collection of ancient Oriental weapons, dirks and daggers, mixed fetchingly with eighteenth-century *Famille Noire* cats in various sizes. In the center of each table was a low *Famille Noire* bowl filled with the heads of enormous orange tiger lilies from the pistils of which Robin had carefully cut the dark rust pollen heads that, if touched, left a stain that was almost impossible to remove.

Vanessa had not pushed her audacity so far as to seat Daisy and Ram at the same table. Daisy's dinner partner on her left was Ham Short. Stunned into immobility by shock and growing panic, she found she couldn't begin to eat the first course of ginger-flavored minced squab. Ham attempted to distract her with an account of his own worthless passel of relatives back in Arkansas, but he might as well have been talking to a dead girl, propped up beside her. She sat with her eyes fastened on the bowl of tiger lilies, until Ham, in embarrassment, turned to the woman on his left. When the second course was served,

Daisy made a half-hearted attempt to pick up her chop-sticks, but before her hand touched them she realized that she wouldn't have the coordination to be able to use them, and that even if she could, the taste of any food would make her vomit. Her dinner companions, who had been forced into a general conversation by her silent presence, tacitly agreed to pretend to ignore this fascinating phe-nomenon even as they covertly watched her, storing away all their deliciously scandalized impressions for the stories they'd tell once they got off the yacht. As course after course of exquisite food was presented, prepared by the chef the Valarians had hired for the cruise, who cooked in five different cuisines, Daisy touched nothing and talked to no one. Ham Short, who admired her, dominated the conversation and kept it flowing, so that no one turned to her with any questions. At one point he sought her hand, as it lay still on the table, and squeezed it to show his support. Although she returned a tiny pressure, she didn't remove her unseeing eyes from the tiger lilies.

Vanessa had certainly gone too far tonight, more than one of the women in the room managed to signal delight-edly to another during the endless dinner, which proceed-ed as if Daisy were invisible. Ram, habitual diner-out that he was, presented to them all his normal, handsome, unbendingly correct, indisputably gentlemanly surface. He ate with polite relish and discussed Henry Moore with the lady on his right and the merits of various saddle makers with Topsy, on his left. There was well-concealed malevo-lence as, from time to time, he scanned the room for a split second, searching for his prey like a carrion bird, but no one noticed. To Daisy, the walls of the dining saloon pressed in like those of an echo chamber. The voices of memory, ugly and dangerous, clamored at a distance, sometimes louder, sometimes softer, and the other guests seemed as distant and indistinct as large fish languidly waving their fins behind the wall of an aquarium.

After dinner, Vanessa led the way back to the main saloon. Daisy had been waiting for this moment, and, as soon as Vanessa rose, she flew up from her chair and darted out of the door which led to the deck. Although she moved quickly she felt as if her body were numb and incapacitated, with that helplessness, that slowing down and impairment of all the faculties that appear in a nightmare. She had passed the main saloon, running in the direction of her own stateroom, when Ram caught up with her.

"Stop! We have to talk. It's important!" he shouted, but he didn't try to touch her.

Daisy stopped. It was so impossible that he could imagine that they had anything to say to each other that sheer incredulity overcame her other emotions. She felt safe enough, with a steward in sight, carrying a tray of brandy and glasses, and the door to the main saloon only feet away. She could see people inside, buzzing away like flies in a bottle, but on deck it was quiet and the breeze was warm. She held on to the railing of the yacht with both hands and turned to face Ram, creating a distance between them merely by the way she stood.

"Nothing is important enough for us to discuss, ever again," she said through dry lips.

"Anabel," he said quietly, with vulturine watchfulness, "Anabel."

"Anabel? She has nothing to do with you. Do you ever stop lying? I had a letter from her only a week ago."

"And of course she didn't tell you." Ram was sure of his ground. It wasn't even a question.

Daisy went white and clutched the rail. He knew something she didn't know. She recognized the unmistakable expression of repressed pleasure on his face.

"What about Anabel?" she whispered, as if a whisper could soften his answer.

"She has leukemia."

"I don't believe you!"

"Yes, you do. You know I'm telling the truth."

"Why didn't she tell me? Why should she tell you?" Daisy demanded automatically while the shock of his words went inward, surrounded her heart like an explosion of fragments of pointed glass.

"Because she thought that you have enough problems of your own, supporting your sister. She had to have money for the treatments and she simply didn't want you to know she was in need. She knows you're stretched as far as you can go, so she came to me."

"Oh, dear God, *not* Anabel," Daisy moaned. Anabel, who'd come closer to being a mother to her than anyone, Anabel, the dear friend and counselor and confidante of her youth, Anabel, whose presence in her life warmed it with generous laughing love and still lent it a quality that even today was almost like having a home, Anabel who kept her from feeling utterly orphaned.

"The doctors have told her that with luck and care she can expect to live for many years. It's chronic leukemia, not acute. She's not sixty yet—she can still live the rest of her life in comparative comfort and security but . . . it's a question of money."

"*You* have money!"

"Anabel threw me out of her house ten years ago and told me she never wanted to see or hear from me again. She's never changed that position—except now, to ask for money. I don't feel I have any reason to give her anything unless I choose, *choose* to be generous. Anabel is merely a former mistress of my father's. He left her a sizable estate which, since she declined to take advantage of my advice, she let slip through her fingers. She held on to her Rolls stock as long as you did. I have no sympathy for people who can't take care of their money."

"Anabel was so good to you!" Dasiy almost shouted, but he ignored her words.

"If I should choose to help her it means taking on heavy and unforeseeable expenses for an unknown amount of time—hardly the act of a prudent man. Obviously, she can't keep *La Marée* any longer by taking in paying guests —she won't have the energy. When she sells it she'll have some money, but it won't last long since she has few other sources of income. After that's gone, it's a question of finding a place to live, either a nursing home or an apartment, depending on her physical condition. She'll need help, later if not immediately. And there will be constant doctor bills. It could last ten years, fifteen years— even twenty. There's no way for Anabel to pay for these things . . . the expenses will have to be met as they arise."

Daisy struggled to keep to practicalities while the points of glass pressed deeper into her heart with every word he spoke.

"Why should she sell *La Marée?* You know as well as I do that if Anabel can live for years there is no other place in the world she would be as happy. You have the money to support her without thinking twice about it . . . and she'll have to live somewhere . . . since she's come to you for help, *why* should she be forced to sell? You are going to help, aren't you . . ." Her voice faded as she looked at his face, locked in brooding righteousness.

"I feel no moral obligation at all to become financially

responsible for Anabel. None. However I have a proposal which can solve the problem. I've been disturbed for years by reports from my friends who visit the United States for the hunting that you go about visiting at their hosts' houses trying to drum up commissions for your little paintings. I know, of course, although they don't, why you need the money. The only way I would undertake the support of Anabel for as long as she lives is with the absolute understanding that you give up your shoddy job and your hand-to-mouth sideline of portraits and come back to London."

"You really are insane," Daisy whispered slowly.

"Nonsense. I'm asking nothing in return for what will prove to be many years of heavy expenses except that you live in a way in which an unmarried sister of mine should live, properly and respectably. I'm even prepared to let Anabel keep *La Marée* since you feel so sentimental about it. And naturally I'll take over your sister's support as well."

"I'd be your prisoner!"

"How absurd. Don't be so melodramatic. I simply want you to fill your normal place in society in a country in which society still means something. Your life in New York is disgusting—a vulgar world full of vulgar people. It happens to embarrass me among my friends. I offer you protection and security. I want nothing from you—I have my own life to live." His voice was cool and reasonable, but Daisy saw that his eyes had never ceased their urgent assault on her face and body. Like furtive cat burglars, they snatched and grabbed. Lust lay like a dry powder on his thin, fine lips. She had been in the presence of his madness before and nothing had changed except that this time she knew him for what he was.

"Every word is a lie! You'd be after me again the way you were before—*I smell it on you!* You say my life in New York is disgusting—I say if my father weren't dead, he would have *killed* you and you know it!" Her voice rose dangerously.

"Shut up, shut up! People will hear you!"

"Why should I? So that you won't be embarrassed? Do you think I give a damn . . . do you still think I'd ever let you force me to do anything against my will?"

"Anabel . . ." he began again.

"Blackmail!" she raged at him. "How can you live with the filth you are?" She turned and strode rapidly back in the direction of the main saloon. She opened the door and stood there for a second, panting, open-mouthed, searching for Vanessa. When Daisy saw her, sitting at the backgammon table, she walked straight toward her and put a hurting hand on Vanessa's shoulder.

"I want to talk to you."

"Daisy, love bug, wait till the game's over, hmmm?"

"Now." The pounding, molten emphasis in Daisy's voice summoned Vanessa to her feet. "Outside," Daisy ordered. Vanessa followed, smiling broadly and flittering her hands as several inquiring looks were directed at her.

"Daisy, just what is it—how dare you?"

"Vanessa, tell the captain to turn this boat around and put me ashore."

"That's impossible. Now just calm down . . ."

"You've collected on your debt. Whatever I owed you, I've paid. Vanessa—I'm *warning* you."

Vanessa, experienced, astute Vanessa, didn't have to think twice. The menace, almost out of control, that she saw on Daisy's face could only lead to trouble. And, in Vanessa's brilliantly balanced life, that life of so many delicious but dangerous secrets, risk and consequences had to be eliminated as quickly as possible.

What could Ram *have done* to her, she wondered to herself, as she hurried to the bridge to speak to the captain. Oh, how she'd love to find out.

"What's all this?" Patrick Shannon demanded of his executive secretary as he sat down behind his desk. He had just come back from Tokyo and he expected, as usual, to find the clean desk he'd left. Each of his three secretaries would have compiled dossiers of matters to be attended to, but he hadn't sent for the folders yet.

"Mr. Bijur asked me to put them where you'd see them first thing."

Shannon lifted the six photographs, each of which had a sheet of paper attached to it. "They're all princesses, Mr. Shannon. Mr. Bijur thought you'd like their family trees, too. There are two Belgians, one French and three Germans. He said to tell you that he'd gone over every white princess in the world and these were the only really beautiful ones. Princess Caroline and Princess Yasmin won't return his calls, but he's still trying, through channels."

Shannon roared with laughter as he looked over the photographs.

"Oh God, oh God," he groaned as he laughed, "he must have worked like a son-of-a-bitch—poor Hilly—doesn't he know when I say unforgettable I don't mean merely beautiful? Miss Bridy, will you put me through to Daisy Valensky at North's studio? If she's not there, find out where she is and get her before you try any other calls."

Daisy was standing with her arms akimbo, eying both of her production assistants severely.

"Do you mean to tell me that that grip just walked into Central Park and sawed a limb off a tree without either of you telling him to do it? It couldn't possibly have been his own idea. Don't you creeps realize that there were five people trying to make citizen's arrests following him? We almost had a riot."

"It was just a little branch."

"It isn't as if there were leaves on it."

"We needed it in a hurry—the tree on the street was too puny."

"No excuses," Daisy said. "If it ever, *ever* happens again, you both go back to robbing graves."

"Daisy, phone," one of them said, grateful for the interruption.

"Studio," Daisy answered, as she always did.

"Princess Valensky, this is Patrick Shannon."

"How was Tokyo?" she said in a neutral tone, watching her two assistants slink off as inconspicuously as they could.

"Too far. Listen, I didn't get a chance to apologize to you for the way I talked to you the last time we met."

"Or the first time we met either."

"That's exactly what I was about to say. . . . I feel that somehow we've gotten off to a bad start—all right, two bad starts—and I'd like to do something about it. Is there a chance that I could persuade you to have dinner with me? I promise not to say a word about Elstree. This is not an attempt to get you to change your mind. I wouldn't be that obvious—or devious."

"Just a friendly meal?"

"Right. I don't like leaving the impression that I'm a heavy."

"Would you admit that you're aggressive?" Daisy asked sweetly.

"Aggressive—sure, but not a heavy. Will you be free for dinner sometime this week?"

"I think I might manage dinner," Daisy said.

"What's a good night for you? I haven't made any plans for the rest of the week so you pick the day."

"Tonight," she said without a second's hesitation. There was a moment of blank silence.

"Oh. Of course. Tonight."

"It's the corner of Prince and Greene. The southeast corner, third flight up. I'll expect you at eight o'clock. Ignore the sign that says 'Fierce Guard Dog'—he doesn't bite unless I tell him to . . . as a rule."

Daisy hung up before he had a chance to say goodbye. "Ginger," she said to North's secretary. "If North comes in, tell him I've taken the afternoon off. If he wants to know why, tell him I didn't say. If any of the others need me, tell them to figure it out for themselves. If anyone calls, tell them I can't be found. If anyone asks you what the hell is going on, tell them you don't know."

"It'll be a pleasure," Ginger assured her. "Got a date, huh?"

"Not exactly," said Daisy.

Daisy knew exactly what she was looking for. There has never been a season, in spite of the programmed fluctuations of fashion, in spite of swings in taste from classic to kinky, in which Bill Blass has not quietly made a group of sublime black dresses, the witty, wily discretion of which combines the ultimate in rich-lady good taste with the ultimate in naughty-lady sexiness. Sometimes he does it with net and chiffon, sometimes with lace and silk, mixed with such supreme distillation of the tactile advantages of each fabric that it is impossible to say just where one melts into the other. Daisy finally found the Bill Blass she sought on Bendel's second floor and, on her way out, she stopped at Jerry Miller's first-floor shoe department, Shoe Biz, and bought a pair of thin, high-heeled black silk sandals with tiny rhinestone buckles. A pair of sheer taupe pantyhose were found on another counter and Daisy left the store on West 57th Street having spent just a dollar or two more than three weeks salary.

Recklessly she took a cab home instead of the subway, and, as soon as she'd hung up the dress, she washed her hair in the shower. Even with a powerful blow dryer it took almost an hour to get it all dry, and by the time she finished her arms ached. Theseus, back from his brief stay with the landlady, cowered under a sofa. The only thing in the world he was afraid of was the hideous whine of the blow dryer. Fortunately Kiki was still out of town with Luke. Daisy would not have liked to answer questions about her extraordinary preparations for the evening ahead. She would not have liked inquisitive Kiki to wonder why she was cleaning up the living room, throwing dozens of extraneous objects in closets with abandon, until the room presented a perfectly neat and, in fact, elegant appearance —thanks to Eleanor Kavanaugh's latest shipment of expensive white wicker furniture covered in a flowered Woodson print which cost forty dollars a yard and looked like the surface of a lily pond painted by Monet. She burrowed anxiously into Kiki's chest of drawers until she eventually found the black silk evening bag she had counted on using. Kiki really should take better care of her things, Daisy thought, as, nervously, she started to dress.

At precisely eight o'clock the doorbell rang. As Daisy opened the door the smile on Patrick Shannon's face froze.

Daisy had put herself together tonight with the most meticulous attention to each part of her self-presentation, but she hadn't been able to assess the total and get an objective view of herself. All she was sure of was that she had made a desperate investment in the Blass dress and done her hair in the most classic way she knew. It was a roll of the dice, risking so much money, but the stakes were too high to leave anything to chance. Any one of her jumble-sale costumes, no matter how exquisitely made, might make her look eccentric. She had to look *solidly rich*. It was as simple as that.

How many times had she heard Nick-the-Greek explain that the reason North could charge a higher fee than any other director in the business was because he had more clients than he had time for—all, of course, thanks to Nick's own efforts—and so, not needing the money, he commanded it? If she were to become the Elstree Girl, and now Daisy knew she had to take that job at whatever cost to herself, she had to make it pay enough so that she could take care of both Anabel and Danielle for a long time into the future. She couldn't settle for model fees, not even the thousand dollars a day that certain top models were commanding. It must be more money, much, much more. Against the spiritual threat which emanated like a stench from Ram, money was her only protection. It was the only shield solid enough to trust.

The woman who greeted Shannon was not the fantastic girl he'd met dressed in green sequins and corduroy with fake emeralds pinned in her long hair, nor the disheveled, furious, funny figure in carpenter's overalls, but the most unreasonably beautiful creature he'd ever seen. He literally gaped as he looked at her. The heavy, low braided chignon into which all of Daisy's hair was caught, emphasized the length and molding of her neck, and the proud, high carriage of her head. With her hair pulled back from her face, the particular ripe peach bloom of Daisy's skin, her thick, straight brows over her dark purple, pansy-centered eyes and full, strongly marked mouth, all stood out in the kind of relief which the wonder of her unbound hair would have diminished. Her dress had a halter top of dotted black net which dissolved at the slender, wrapped waist into a swoosh of full, rustling black skirts, and from it her arms and shoulders, quite unornamented by any jewels, rose in simple majesty.

"Aren't you going to come in?" Daisy said, with a gracious smile, which she had sternly prevented from turning into a satisfied grin. Apparently she'd managed to achieve the effect she was trying for, if the test was rendering Pat Shannon unable to function normally. And he was.

Silently he walked into the apartment and stood in the center of the living room.

As gently as if she were talking to a sleepwalker, Daisy asked, "Won't you sit down and have a drink?" Shannon sat.

"Vodka, whiskey, white wine?" Shannon nodded agreement, to all her suggestions, his eyes never leaving her. Rather than disturb his concentration, she poured wine for both of them, brought the drinks and sat down near him. Finally he spoke, automatically saying the first thing that entered his bedazzled mind.

"I like your apartment."

Demurely she answered, "My roommate and I have lived here for four years. It's rather an amusing part of town."

Daisy could tell from the faint tightening of the lines around his mouth that he was aware of how many different kinds of romantic relationships were tucked into the convenient, ubiquitous title of roommate.

"She's Kiki Kavanaugh," Daisy continued, composedly. "Perhaps you know her father—he's president of United Motors? No? She's back home this week," Daisy said. "I was supposed to go, too—Uncle Jerry, Kiki's father, is having a birthday and I'm considered part of the family, but I didn't think it was quite fair to leave the studio. My assistants aren't as dependable as I'd like and I've just been away in Nassau."

"Your work," Shannon asked tentatively, "is it something recent? When we met in Middleburg somebody said that you were a painter . . . at least that was the impression I got."

"Oh, that—it's just my hobby. I love children and I love horses and I love to paint, so sometimes I treat myself to all three of them together," Daisy said with a fine carelessness. "Actually I've worked for North since school—it's so much more amusing to *do* something, don't you think? Otherwise, life tends to become self-indulgent . . . one simply must fight that dreadful tendency to drift. And the studio is the ideal solution. No week is the same as any other, we have new problems, new crises, new solutions and never a second to get bored."

She smiled as complacently as Marie Antoinette discussing her cows while she briefly batted her eyelashes in supplication to Kiki's patron saint, the deity of all those who told lies in a good cause and gave themselves airs and graces.

Shannon looked at her questioningly. "Funny, I've picked up the idea that a job like yours demands a high degree of efficiency and very long, hard hours . . ."

"Oh, of course it does," Daisy drawled. "But *that's* the joy of it . . . it's *such* a challenge! Would you enjoy doing something that wasn't a challenge?" Daisy leaned languidly back against the water-lily pillows in an attitude which persuaded Shannon that long, hard hours must be the inevitable choice of any rich girl with a brain in her head.

"I take it North is a good man to work for?"

"The day he stops being one is the day I'll quit," Daisy said lightly, thinking of North's sardonic snort if he could hear her. "Of course, you mustn't judge by Nick-the-Greek—the one who insisted on displaying my hair—he's a bit of a barbarian, lacks finesse, but I'm fond of him just the same . . . he just got carried away."

"So did you, rather."

"Oh that. I'm well known for my evil temper." She smiled with that particular smile of people who are proud of their defects, because they are themselves so important that no one dares to rebuke them. Actually, Daisy thought, it was North's smile she was borrowing.

There was a scratching at one of the doors of the apartment, followed by the sound of a body hurling itself against the door. Daisy murmured, "Excuse me," and she walked toward the door, her skirts swaying, her back naked almost to the waist under the dotted net. Patrick Shannon followed her with his eyes, marveling.

"Now stop it, Theseus," she called through the door.

"Is that your guard dog? I'd like to meet him, or her, as the case may be." He was intensely curious about everything about this rare creature, Daisy. He imagined her idea of a guard dog would be an overbred Afghan, or a yapping poodle.

"He's nervous with strangers," Daisy warned, but she opened the door.

Theseus appeared, ears perked up like flags, and silently padded into the room with his drunken-sailor gait. Shannon rose at the approach of the big, rough-coated animal, with the mixture of gray, brown and blue hair. Theseus gave Shannon a suspicious, furtive, sideways look and started to sidle past him to his favorite pillow on the floor. As he got closer to the visitor, to Daisy's astonishment, he changed directions, reared up on his hind legs and hurled himself on Shannon in a brazen display of sniffing, licking and searching. Shannon, laughing, started to calm him with a game of tickle, scratch, rough and tumble that left Theseus his slave for life.

"How very strange," Daisy said coldly. "He usually doesn't go near strangers. Are you sure there isn't anything to eat in your pockets?"

"Oh, dogs like me—dogs and children."

"And that, I suppose, is traditionally the sign of a man you can trust?" she asked, leading the dog out of the room with a most unusual firmness of touch of which only Theseus was aware, since it was accomplished with an imperceptible movement of her strong wrist.

"That's what they say," he called after her.

Daisy returned, walking with a dignity that made Shannon think confusedly of throne rooms and crown jewels and the Changing of the Guard. "You haven't touched your drink," she said. "Can I give you something else?"

"Why don't we go on to dinner?" he asked, looking down at his full glass in astonishment. How had it got there? An authentic guard dog. An authentic roommate. What more did she have hidden here? "The car and driver are just downstairs. At least, in this neighborhood, I hope they're still there."

"Oh, it's absolutely safe. The Mafia protects us—half their grandparents still live within blocks—SoHo is the most crime-free area in the city." Airily Daisy had converted her semi-slum street into a whimsically inhabited island paradise.

Le Cirque is the kind of grand and expensive New York restaurant that only certain New Yorkers really understand. It's not about food, as the great restaurants are, and it's not about décor, as so many others are, nor is it about beautiful or chic people. It is a restaurant about power. Only the powerful go there, to test their power by the table they are given and to enjoy their power in the company of other powerful people. Le Cirque is attractive enough, with its obviously costly décor of murals of costumed monkeys painted in a Watteau-Fragonard manner, its heavy linen tablecloths and flattering light coming from clusters of tulip-shaped fixtures. The food is firmly if unimpassionedly French. It could equally well be Spanish or Italian since most of the people who dine there order veal or fish, cooked as plainly as possible—the diet of thinness and ulcers—the diet of power. A visitor to New York might find himself lunching and dining at Le Cirque every day for a week if he were being treated to a display of the power of his hosts. On the other hand, if his hosts were true gourmets or devoted to amusing atmosphere, he might never even hear Le Cirque mentioned.

Daisy had never been there. It was not North's kind of restaurant, since he refused to dress in a suit and tie for any meal unless Nick-the-Greek had finally persuaded him to be pleasant to a big client. Nor had Henry Kavanaugh, Daisy's still languishing suitor, ever thought to take her there. Le Cirque at lunch was chiefly about publishing power, and at dinner it was about corporate power, but it had nothing to do with young-Grosse-Pointe-fortune power.

Tonight, as always, Patrick Shannon had one of the three best tables in the house, the banquettes just to the right of the entrance. Daisy sensed the power in the air as they walked into the restaurant. She glided to her seat perfectly aware that almost all of the people in the room were watching her, although she seemed oblivious to them. Her memories of the heavily power-weighted atmosphere of the Connaught made her impervious to being impressed by a mere restaurant, and no amount of being looked at could intimidate the daughter of Stash Valensky, who had become blithely accustomed to the covert sensation she and her father had made whenever they went out together on those Sunday mornings so many, many years ago.

She looked around with calm approval. "How pleasant," she said in a casual lilt, breathing in the palpable atmosphere, compounded of smug self-satisfaction, of self-confidence, of frankly appraising glances from people who were secure enough not to think it rude to stare, and of the mutual congratulations—just on being there—that were beamed from one table to another until they formed an invisible tent in the scented air. Although Daisy was starving, she ordered with the unmistakable Spartan lightness of someone who is so often confronted by menus, one more elaborate than the next, that food has become almost, but not quite, boring.

Pat Shannon found himself, for the first time in years, at a loss for conversation. Daisy seemed to be utterly comfortable looking idly around the room, without making any attempt to talk to him. Why didn't she chatter, why didn't she flirt, why didn't she try to get him to talk about himself like any other decent, self-respecting woman?

As Daisy sipped her cold cream-of-cucumber soup, Shannon launched into an account of his trip to Tokyo. She asked just the right questions, he thought, but she seemed . . . was it reserved, or bored, or withdrawn? None of those words aptly described the faintly detached, although perfectly polite way in which she somehow indicated that there was perhaps something overly *mercantile* about conglomerate affairs in Japan.

As they were served their filet of sole Véronique, several men Shannon knew passed on their way to the street. They greeted him in a lingeringly hearty way that virtually demanded that he introduce them to Daisy. What the hell, Shannon asked himself, had inspired that ass Harmsworth to kiss her hand—a man who had been born and brought up in the great Midwest, even if he did own half of Chicago? And why did Zellerbach give him that meaningful parting look, as if Shannon had just won the decathlon?

Daisy sat back, not permitting the lure of the soft banquette to caress her shoulders. She sat in a straight-backed way that, although it was not stiff, indicated, by her example, that while others might lean over their plates or loll in their seats, she had been so trained in queenly posture that it was second nature. She blessed the example of an old Grace Kelly movie she'd seen on television a few nights ago.

Shannon turned the conversation to Daisy, asking her where she'd gone to college, but even as she told him the bare details she was gently unenthusiastic about reviving memories of her student days, nor did she find the topic of Ham and Topsy Short, their only mutual friends, particularly spellbinding, a judgment with which Shannon privately agreed. While Daisy thought about and wistfully rejected the idea of ordering cheese—she had made herself refuse dessert because rich women never eat dessert—two couples Shannon knew stopped by their table. The women, Shannon thought in disgust, literally fawned over Daisy. How else could you describe their asking her where she'd found her divine dress and who did her divine hair? People had an atrocious way of demanding information from strangers, he told himself, as Daisy answered their questions with every indication of the mild, automatic pleasure of someone who is accustomed to such admiring questions, consigning her homemade chignon to Suga without a blush.

As the waiter brought his floating island Shannon realized that he was about to burst. His promise not to talk business seemed, retrospectively, absurd. What were they doing here, the most looked-at couple in the room, the focus of curiosity of the whole damn place, if it didn't lead to a reopening of his Elstree proposition? He envisioned a dozen dinners during which, to keep from arousing Daisy's ire, he would allow the Elstree campaign to go down the drain, drop by expensive drop. In a last effort to keep from stirring up her evil temper again, he blurted out a question that had been on his mind since they'd left her apartment for dinner.

"Where did you get your lurcher?"

She turned toward him, black eyes filled with a disquieting gleam, a lively suspicion on her lips. "And just how did you know Theseus was a lurcher?" she demanded.

"Oh, shit!" Shannon groaned.

"How? I called him a guard dog."

"It's Lucy—" he started to sputter with laughter.

"Who's Lucy . . . your clairvoyant? Nobody in this city has ever recognized a lurcher," she said, the light of battle in her eyes.

"Lucy's my lurcher," he confessed.

"Ah-ha—the man dogs and children just naturally trust! So that's what he smelled on you, *eau-de*-lady-lurcher. Why didn't you tell me then?"

"I honestly don't know . . ."

"You don't? I've never met a lurcher owner who didn't ask me, *immediately,* what cross Theseus was."

"What cross is he?"

"Don't try to change the subject."

"I believe I was trying to impress you," Shannon said, his dark blue eyes under their black brows challenging her to a frolic, "but I blew it, didn't I?"

"Not necessarily," Daisy said with her first provocative smile of the evening. She had decided to let him off the hook. He was not a man who would enjoy being embarrassed again. "Since you ask, Theseus is Irish wolfhound crossed with greyhound on one side of the family and deerhound with greyhound on the other, with whippet and sheepdog thrown in. What's Lucy?"

"Brindle greyhound with Alsatian but I'm not positive about the rest—more greyhound certainly. She's a bit of a bastard."

"What lurcher isn't? Do you hunt on foot with her?"

"Lucy'll chase anything that moves, but she's anti-blood sport. She nearly died of fright one day when she killed a rabbit. She must have bumped into it."

"I've had to train poor Theseus to heel—or keep him on a lead—I can't let him hunt—he's the most frustrated lurcher in captivity," Daisy said sadly.

"Perhaps," Shannon said delicately, "they should . . . meet."

"And what," asked Daisy, "would you do with the pups?"

"I'd give you the pick of the litter, of course, and split whatever the rest of them went for." As soon as he said it he felt like a fool. Did one discuss money with this sovereign woman?

"That's generous of you," Daisy said, lifting her eyebrows in a tiny movement of disdain, "but I don't want the responsibility of a pup. You keep the best one and give the money to some charity or other." She was silent for a moment and then added, smiling, "I don't usually meddle in Theseus's romantic life—he manages quite well enough on his own—but since Lucy is a lurcher, too, I think a blind date might be a good idea."

Emboldened by her affability on matters canine, Shannon decided to take the risk of discussing Elstree with this proud and so easily offended creature. The more he looked at the pure felicity of her profile and observed the serene harmony of her gestures, the longer he listened to her low and charming voice, the more convinced he became that she could restore faith in hereditary aristocracy in any land, including Red China, and what was more important, sell important quantities of cosmetics and perfume to American women.

"Daisy," he started and then stopped. Her heart, which had been beating hard at the prospect of having to reopen the Elstree question herself, slowed to a slightly slower pulse. She could tell by the way he'd said her name that he was about to begin negotiations.

"Yes, Shannon?" she said invitingly, and the way she looked at him made him think of a shower of dark falling stars.

"Daisy, I know I promised not to talk about it, but I wish you'd reconsider the matter of doing the Elstree commercials. I promised not to put any pressure on you, but it occurred to me that you might not have thought of it as a challenge—you said you loved challenges when we were talking before—and perhaps if you could put your mind to the question in that light . . ."

"I already have. In fact, I've given it a great deal of serious consideration."

"And? . . ."

"Shannon, if I sign a contract to endorse a Princess Daisy line for Elstree, it would mean the loss of a number of things that are very precious to me: first, and most important of all, my privacy; then my reluctance to trade on my title; and almost certainly my job since I could never do justice to both. I'll have to give up my ability to come and go as I please without anyone looking at me and thinking, Oh, that's Princess Daisy, the Elstree Girl—and I detest being pointed out and stared at. I'd lose all the anonymity I've guarded so carefully for years." Her voice was almost harsh with this accurate picture of the future. "I'd become just another household word—if the campaign worked—and you can't go back from that."

"So it's no," he said.

"It's yes." She didn't wait for him to react. "I want one million dollars and a contract for three years, during which time you can use my face, my name and as much of my genuine blonde hair as you want to sell Elstree in everything from commercials to department stores. But the million dollars has to be paid in three installments, the first third on signing, and the rest to be paid over the next three years, *whether or not* the campaign is successful, whether or not you decide to drop the Princess Daisy line because it isn't selling, whether or not you change advertising agencies again and they want to try something else. Otherwise we don't have a deal."

A million dollars, said Shannon to himself, and I don't even know how she'll photograph.

"Or," said Daisy, "we can forget it."

"We have a deal," he said hastily. "What made you change your mind?"

"Private reasons," Daisy answered, with a small, secret smile and a great wave of terror and triumph lifting her heart.

22

$\mathcal{N}$orth was amused for not quite three minutes. As amused as if a familiar, fluffy pussycat had taken it into its head to snarl at him. Why not let it exhaust itself while he fended it off with a touch of fancy footwork and the casual back of his gloved hand? Less than three minutes into Daisy's patient repetition of her plans he realized she was serious.

"Don't be absurd," he said severely, a frown settling on his face. "You can't do it, you don't know the first thing about modeling or promotion—you'd be rotten at it—the whole business is ridiculous. I thought you had more sense than to make a fool of yourself."

"Shannon doesn't think I'll be a fool," Daisy said sharply. She had enough inner doubts without fighting North's assessment of her value.

"Shannon! That meddling prick! Coming in here and junking a perfectly good campaign, going ape-shit over your gee-whiz hair and your classy look—he's nothing but another businessman-snob who imagines himself a star maker," he sneered.

"I don't want to get into a screaming match about Pat Shannon," Daisy said. "I just want you to realize that I have to leave the studio."

"Something that you haven't the slightest right to do! Who the hell took a chance on you when you came out of that crazy California college desperate for a job—a job I must have twenty applicants for a week?"

"Bootsie Jacobs hired me, as a matter of record."

"Only because I said she could. Do you have any idea of how much time and money it cost me to make you into a commercial producer? Your whole learning process has been at my expense. I don't care if you worked your ass off fourteen hours a day, you got invaluable training and not every director in town would have put up with you—eagerness isn't everything."

"I learned fast. You've had me working hard for five and a half years and even in the beginning I had talent, too," Daisy said defiantly. "Always."

"Talent isn't everything! Lots of people have talent. It's knowing the ropes—and now, now that you're useful, you choose to walk away. How you can do this with any decency is beyond me. I don't think anyone has ever been so ungrateful."

"I repeat, I need to make a lot of money, North."

"Money. *Money*—you know damn well you get paid as much as any other producer in the business."

"Then add a hundred dollars to what I make and you can try to hire Bob Giraldi's producer or Steve Horn's producer or Sally Safir—you've always admired her."

"But Sally's an equal partner with Richard Heimann! Who could afford that?" North cried in highest outrage.

Daisy surveyed him calmly. "Evidently Richard can."

"Is that what you're holding me up for—a piece of the action?"

"Of course not. I'm not holding you up for anything. I'm leaving to make as much money as I possibly can."

North's whole face sweetened into an expression of intimacy that she hadn't seen on his features in weeks.

"Okay—I admit that I can't compete with Elstree. I don't understand why you have to make all that money, but I respect the fact that it must be very important if it's led you to make this bizarre decision. All right—go in good health, Daisy. I wish you luck. But all I want to say is, have you considered what this will do to our relationship?"

"What will it do?" she asked in deceptively mild curiosity.

"Since you insist on leaving, it's got to change things." He looked at her narrowly, radiating all the valuable, disabling charm he knew how to project whenever he chose to.

"What things?" she asked innocently.

"Oh, shit, I loathe this sort of discussion," North flung at her. "It's typically female."

"And you started it. Listen, North, what went on in Venice should have stopped right there, the day the strike ended. You just can't stand inactivity and that's why it happened. It's been over for weeks now and you know it. Stop digging in the ashes. I'm quitting, and you'll manage without me."

"You're goddamned right I will!" He was outraged, this man who had almost never been thwarted and certainly not left. When there was leaving to be done, he did it, on his terms, just as easily as he did the plucking of the fruit when it was ripe. His tame beasts did not roar back at him and they never, ever left the cage without permission. "You're not fucking indispensable," he shouted at her.

"I have no choice."

"The hell you don't!"

Daisy looked at him consideringly. She knew she was right not to tell him her reasons for taking the Elstree offer; the same instinct that had prevented her from talking about herself, except in a superficial way, when they had been together in Venice, still hummed deeply within her. North was too flinty, too harsh, too quick to discard anything that was less than perfect. He was like her father in that, she suddenly realized. Even during the hours of their lovemaking she had seen only minor signs of any change in him. There had been no deeply loving tenderness, no true softening of his taut exactingness, no greater allowance made for human vulnerability. He lacked some gift, some talent for loving and accepting. She would not use information about Anabel or Danielle as emotional blackmail to force him to be forgiving, she could not spread out her personal problems before him in order to bribe him to allow her to accept an opportunity she had every right and every reason to take. She stood still, facing North, patiently, undemandingly, yet so obdurate in all the power and dignity of her beauty, that he used his last ploy.

"I hope you realize that we could have meant a great deal to each other, Daisy. We could have had a wonderful relationship." His voice and expression would have caused ten cobras, a dozen pythons and at least three boa constrictors to lie down and coo.

Daisy listened to him in silence and put on her coat. As she reached the door, she turned back.

"North, if you found yourself stuck on a desert island

with no phone service, you'd have a relationship with a coconut."

"I don't know what to be more excited about," said Kiki, "and I may have a nervous breakdown from indecision." She dallied with Luke's beard and asked, "Did you know your eyes are exactly the color of seedless green grapes?"

"You have problems, lady," Luke agreed. "Tell the doctor about them and I'll make you all well." He settled her more comfortably against his shoulder and pulled the covers up over them.

"Well, on one hand Daisy's going to be rich and famous and be a star in commercials, which is wonderful and thrilling and makes me very happy, and on the other hand my mother is coming to town and she wants to meet your mother and your mother wants to meet my mother, which is terrible and awful and makes me sick to my stomach."

"But it's only natural that they want to meet, poor baby—their children are going to get married. They are going to be *mishpocha* for the rest of their lives, so they're a touch curious about each other. Plus you've been hiding me from your mother long enough."

"What? What are they going to be? It sounds revolting. Oh, God, you never told me about that before!" wailed Kiki indignantly.

"It means, ah, sort of relatives, or maybe relatives by marriage—something like that, I can't be a hundred percent positive. You know my mother has always discouraged the use of a single Yiddish word—puts me at a hell of a disadvantage sometimes . . . maybe I should take lessons? But it's plenty serious, believe me. A *mishpocha* is a *mishpocha* forever!"

"But why do we have to *be* there when they meet? Couldn't we just make a lunch reservation for the two of them at some very nice restaurant and let them introduce themselves to each other?" Kiki suggested, nervousness making her sound like a ten-year-old.

"I'm not too sure about the protocol of getting engaged, but I know that your suggestion is strictly inadmissible. Don't even think about it. God—but it *would* be wonderful to miss it. Eleanor Kavanaugh, the queen of the Grosse Pointe Country Club, and Barbara Hammerstein, the queen of the Harmonie Club, neither of which will admit members of the other's religious persuasion—except as tokens, if at that—*mishpocha!*"

"Please stop saying that word," Kiki pleaded. "There must be some nicer way to put it."

"*Mishpocha* has nothing to do with niceness—it's a condition of life, visited upon you by your children, and if you're lucky it isn't quite as bad as any of Job's afflictions, but you have nothing to say about it—you take it as it comes and moan a lot in private. Try to think of this as an interesting episode in the joyful ongoing relationship between the Christians and the Jews."

"I think it's going to be more like the Six-Day War," Kiki said ominously. "Luke, do you have to . . . I mean, are you planning to? . . ."

"Go on—you can ask me anything," he encouraged her.

"Wear a . . . hat? At the wedding?"

"Good heavens, of course not. Why should I? Unless you think I look good in one. It might be rather chic with my beard, at that. Perhaps a homburg, or maybe a derby. After all, I am piss-elegant, or so they tell me."

"But I thought you *had* to," Kiki said, bewildered.

"Not when you're being married by a judge," Luke laughed. "But, of course, sweetheart, if you'd prefer a rabbi—no? Well then, we could always elope."

"What, and break my mother's heart? I'm the only daughter she has, you unspeakable cad. I've explained why we have to wait till summer for the wedding—there's the trousseau to get together, thousands of engagement parties *and* we have to wait for all my cousins to get out of school, or else someone would miss the wedding."

"God forbid!" sighed Luke with resignation.

"And then I have to have eight bridesmaids and Daisy as my maid of honor and my brothers for ushers—you'll have to dig up six more from somewhere—and now, of course, we can't have the bishop, but I never liked him anyway. Mother's taken the judge part very well, considering that she's been planning my wedding since I was confirmed."

"I doubt that she ever dreamed it would be a triumph for ecumenism," Luke laughed wickedly. "We must all take the broad view," he said as superciliously as possible, wondering where he could find six presentable ushers. He'd be laughed out of the Art Director's Club.

"Oh, fuck you, Luke Hammerstein!"

"Willingly. You just put your little hand right here and sort of slide it up and down . . ."

Two days later, at the stroke of one o'clock, a trembling, neatly dressed Kiki, her lips quivering with fright, guided her majestic and still-beautiful mother through the doors of La Grenouille. She and Luke had picked the most elegant restaurant in New York in the hopes that the atmosphere would soften the two dragon ladies. There would be at least ten minutes worth of conversation on the topic of the flowers on the table, Luke had pointed out, and another twenty in considering the menu. Luke was already seated with his mother, a fine and youthful-looking woman in a definitive hat, a hat that would inform Grosse Pointe exactly who Barbara Fishbach Hammerstein was. Luke and his mother rose at the approach of Kiki and Eleanor Kavanaugh who was standing tall and formidable.

"Mother," both Luke and Kiki said at the same time. Then they stopped and started over. "Mother, this is Luke's mother," Kiki babbled, having forgotten Luke's last name.

Eleanor Kavanaugh extended her hand, peering closely from the near-sighted eyes on which she refused to wear glasses, and then she slowly withdrew her hand, saying questioningly, "Bobbie? Could it possibly be you, Bobbie—Bobbie Fishbach?"

"Oh my God! Ellie! Ellie Williams—I'd know you anywhere—you haven't changed a bit!" cried Barbara Hammerstein in wonder and joy.

"Oh Bobbie!" Kiki's mother threw herself into the arms of Luke's mother, "Bobbie precious! I've always wondered what became of you."

"You never answered my letters," replied Barbara Hammerstein, bursting into tears.

"My parents moved so many times—I never got them. I thought you'd forgotten me."

"Forget my best friend?" Luke's mother said, still weeping. "Never."

"When did all this happen?" Luke asked wildly. "How come you didn't recognize each other's names?"

"It was in Scarsdale—we went all the way through tenth grade together," Eleanor Kavanaugh sniffed emotionally. "Then Grandfather went bankrupt and we had to sell the house and move—and, for heaven's sake, Luke, just never mind. Oh, Bobbie—isn't it wonderful? Now we'll be *mish-pocha!*"

"How do you know *that* word?" asked Mrs. Hammerstein, recoiling.

"I've been practicing it for weeks, Bobbie darling. But let me kiss this son of yours ... after all, he *is* going to be my *aydem*," said Mrs. Kavanaugh, proudly reeling off the newly learned Yiddish word for son-in-law.

"Your *what?*" asked Mrs. Hammerstein.

Patrick Shannon paced the adobe tile floor of his office. It was the day after he had obtained Daisy's agreement to represent Elstree, and he had taken the first possible opportunity to call together the people who would be involved in the new campaign, the same people from Elstree and the agency who had been at the meeting in North's studio.

Shannon seemed to thrive on the necessity to cut through red tape, Luke thought to himself, trying to count the number of essential meetings he was missing at this very moment, back at the agency.

"We haven't got a day to lose," Shannon told them all, looking as determined as an outlaw chieftain who has caught sight of a fully loaded wagon train innocently crossing the prairie. "The cosmetic and fragrance industry does ten billion dollars worth of business every year, and one third of that is done between Thanksgiving and Christmastime. We've got to be in the stores by Thanksgiving this year to even think about breaking even. That gives us just under seven months to launch the line next September."

"It's not enough time, Pat," said Hilly Bijur. "Look at what you're talking about: new packages, new commercials, new print ads, a whole new sales pitch to the buyers ..."

"Hilly, look at what we've got," Pat interrupted him. "We have the basic cosmetics, a complete line. We don't have to change anything about them except the packages, because they're perfect—they just don't sell. Yet. We've got the doors—Elstree is already carried in five thousand class retail outlets. We've got the shipping and the billing and the cost accounting down to a science. It's not as if we have to start up from nothing—all we need are the trimmings, the icing on the cake. For Christ's sake ..."

"Pat ..."

"Now, listen, Hilly, that new fragrance the Elstree chemists came up with last year is a *winner*. It never even had a name—now it's called Princess Daisy and even my dog likes it. As well she should with oil of jasmine at four thousand dollars a pound. All we've got to do is get women to smell the perfume and try the cosmetics—they'll like them—they're good items."

"Pat," Jared Turner, the marketing director, asked, "considering that Elstree lost thirty million last year, what sort of figures have you projected for this year?"

"I'm looking for a volume of one hundred million in retail sales."

Oh, fuck and be damned, Turner thought to himself. Out loud he said reasonably, "But Avon's the biggest cosmetic business in the world and they do a billion. You're talking about ten percent of their business, and we're in the hole as of now."

"One of the things I like about this game is that you can turn it around fast," Shannon answered, pulling some thorns out of one of his cacti in excitement. "Really fast—if you just get the right handle."

"You haven't told us what your ad budget is going to be," Luke broke into the conversation. All this talk about handles meant nothing without the money to back it up.

"The industry average is to spend ten percent for advertising and promotion out of every dollar of retail sales—I'm planning to double that. Based on my estimated volume, we'll allocate twenty million dollars to Princess Daisy perfume and cosmetics."

There goes the ballgame, thought Hilly Bijur. I wonder if Norton Simon, Inc., isn't looking for someone to head up Max Factor for them. It's in trouble, but not as big trouble as Elstree is going to be in.

"Twenty million dollars," Luke said impassively, stroking his beard in a way that had Oscar Pattison and Kirbo Henry, his team of copy writer and art director, looking at each other in glee.

"And one third of it right before Christmas," Shannon added. "That means, of course, that I'm blowing our potential profit for this year, any way you look at it, but I'm thinking in long-range terms. In two years we'll be in good shape, in three years—the sky's the limit."

"But Pat," Turner persisted, with the reckless air of a man refusing a blindfold before a firing squad, "what if you just don't turn Elstree around? We'll lose another fucking fortune!"

"And the stockholders will roast my testicles for breakfast," Shannon said cheerfully. "In a hot chili sauce, over a slow fire, to loud applause."

"We could cut back in packaging," Hilly Bijur said helpfully. "We have a hell of a lot of money invested in last year's packages—maybe they could be used in some way so that they wouldn't be a total loss. . . . Maybe . . ."

"Hilly, we're introducing an absolutely new line—Princess Daisy—no *retreads*." Shannon cut him off. "I thank you for thinking about economy, but this is no time to cut corners. Get your packaging designers together and tell them to go all out, full throttle—it's got to be so classy it makes your hair stand on end. Electrify me! Spend whatever you need, but make sure the packaging reflects Daisy's personality—nothing too modern, nothing space age, no gimmicks."

"Right, Pat," Hilly Bijur said, thinking that, now that Charles Revson was safely dead, it would be a good time to take a shot at a job at Revlon. He'd even take a cut in salary if he had to. "Reflects Daisy's personality"—that girl in the carpenter's pants—where the fuck had he put his Rolaids?

"We've come up with a concept or two," Luke said, "since that last meeting with North. You were talking romance, warmth, glamour and star quality. Now that we've got Daisy to work with, we've been playing around with what Oscar here calls the Romanov approach—Princess Daisy as she would have looked back before the Revolution, dressed in period court costume, wearing the crown jewels or as close to them as we can find outside of a Russian museum . . ."

"Sorry, Luke, but that's too high and mighty for my taste—I want her to be closer to the customer than that," Shannon said instantly.

"I thought you'd feel that way," Luke smiled. He always gave them a plausible bummer to shoot down. He continued smoothly.

"Our next concept is contemporary and I think it taps into every woman's deep and constant desire to be attractive to men, which women's lib doesn't seem to have diminished by one jot or tittle, thank God. We'd film a ballroom full of dancers—or a disco full of dancers—any and all variations on dancing, panning in from above, and then cutting closer and closer to Daisy dancing, hair flying, absolutely radiant, sensually abandoned to the music, the spirit of the dance incarnate. Then . . ."

"Sorry, Luke," Shannon interrupted again, "but I don't buy that either. It might work with just any ordinary model but since we're dealing with a princess we've got to play up every inch of class, it seems to me, and that abandoned sensuality doesn't hit the right note." Shannon frowned. Since all the chairs in his office were taken, except the one behind his desk, which he never used unless he was alone, he was leaning against the wall. He looked like a studious boy, his black hair tumbling over his forehead down to his furrowed brows, his blue eyes concerned, the vertical lines around his wide mouth set in consideration of the problem which, for the moment, had replaced all the other business of Supracorp.

"We have a third concept, which I personally think the most appealing," Luke said without discomfiture. Not only did he have a third but, if need be, he'd come up with a thirtieth. Fifteen percent of twenty million was three million dollars; the advertising agency's commission. Shannon was entitled to a piss-pot full of concept for that.

"Let's have it."

"Daisy is a member of the aristocracy and there are two main ways in which Americans perceive aristocrats, foreign aristocrats, that is. They're either presiding at state functions—boring—or they're having fun because they're rich and go where the fun is. I'd like to send Daisy all over the world, to wherever the aristocracy of various nations gather—St. Moritz, for example, or the Aga Kahn's resort on the Costa Smerelda—and show her mingling with her own kind of man, dressed in whatever the newest outfits are for the particular place we'd be shooting—ski clothes and furs, bathing suits, French dresses and big hats— whatever—she'd be living a dream life, *but* because of who she *really* is, it would be believable. Here we'd tap into every woman's desire to lead a glamorous life . . . she could lead it through Daisy. And by association, when our potential customer uses Elstree, she'd have a little of that glamour rub off on her."

Everyone in the room waited for Shannon to receive this latest idea. Helen Strauss, although she was the advertising director of Elstree, had again realized that this decision was not hers to make. The silence lengthened as Shannon thought.

"Luke, it's a good idea, but it turns me off because I think that the Jet Set, which is really what you're talking about, is perceived as basically worthless—the old, idle rich. If Daisy is constantly shown as a part of that world, she'll be tainted with the same brush. I think you risk creating envy and a woman won't go and buy the products that are being touted by someone we're deliberately giving her every reason to envy. Our consumers, so far a non-existent group, will be drawn from a population in which over half the women work and the other half are house-wives or students. We don't need to sell the idle rich because there aren't enough of them. But I like the idea of presenting Daisy as an aristocrat—that's what Supracorp's buying in her—but in another, more subtle way. I keep visualizing her in England, for some reason, and I'm not absolutely sure why."

"It's because she still has a tiny, almost unnoticeable trace of an English accent—she was brought up in England until she was fifteen," Luke informed him.

"How do you know so much about her?" Patrick asked with a sudden touch of suspicion which surprised him even as he heard it in his voice.

"I'm ... ah ... engaged to her roommate," Luke said sheepishly. Being engaged was as square a thing as original, unconventional Luke Hammerstein had ever done.

"The roommate from Grosse Pointe?"

Luke nodded.

"Kiki Kavanaugh—United Motors? Congratulations, Hammerstein, that's wonderful."

Everyone in the room looked at Luke with new appreciation. Kavanaugh—Detroit—United Motors—well, well! Good for Luke! They'd known he was smart—but not *that* smart.

Luke, annoyed, hurried back to the subject. "You said England, Mr. Shannon?"

"Yes, and castles—I see her with castles in the background, *always castles,* and doing something like galloping up to the entrance—no model alive can ride like that girl, or maybe walking dogs in a garden with a castle behind her ..."

"Corgis—that's the dog the Queen of England always has with her—they're the royal favorites," Candice Bloom said helpfully.

"A lurcher, maybe two," Shannon said in a visionary voice, confusing everybody.

"Eating strawberries and cream on a lawn, with the castle in the background," Oscar Pattison said.

"Good—that's a nice one," Shannon agreed, "yup, outdoors, England, castles—maybe a guy with her—*always* a guy with her—but no male models—real lords, young ones—but a gentle approach, simple things, so long as you have that castle . . . she'll supply all the rest, the glamour and the romance. Every woman would like to be a princess and live in a castle—maybe not for always but certainly once in a lifetime," Shannon said, finally satisfied. "And since she's American they can identify with her—by the time this campaign is ready to go the whole country *should know* that she's an American working girl who also happens to be a princess.

"Candice," he continued, turning to the publicity woman, "you're going to make sure of that. I want the biggest publicity push you've ever worked on for Daisy—a fabulous party to introduce her to the press right before we launch the perfume, and really *lean* on all your contacts for interviews and photos. It's a natural for the press, considering who her parents were and considering that she's pretty much of a mystery girl—but just because it's a natural, I don't want you to wait for them to come to you—be as aggressive as if you had an absolute unknown to work with. Of course we'll get *Women's Wear* and *Vogue* and *Bazaar* and the syndicated columnists, but I want the mass magazines too, *Good House* and the *Journal* and *Cosmo*—you know the drill. But more than anything else, I want *People*. I want a cover on *People* just before Thanksgiving—in fact I'm counting on it."

Candice Bloom merely nodded. She knew how good she was. She could probably deliver just about anything except covers on *Time*, *Newsweek* and *People*. If Daisy were a teenage rock singer, or the star of a weekly comedy sitcom—or a new pope—she could *maybe* get *People*—but what the hell, she had contacts over there she'd been saving for something crucial and it was worth a try, if she wanted to keep her job, and she did. P.R. was pure shit but she liked it—even her analyst didn't know why.

Luke thought that this was the first time he'd created a campaign with a sponsor in on it from the beginning and doing most of the talking, but it seemed to be working. He had heard of a "hands on" top-level manager, and now he understood what that meant. However, Shannon didn't know everything. Luke had a few cards still up his sleeve.

"Mr. Shannon, a major problem here, for Elstree as for any perfume sold in America, is that women tend to treat their perfume as an art object. They buy the bottle or get it as a gift and then they only use it for special occasions or let it sit on their dresser tops unopened—unlike the Europeans, who will wallow in the stuff and then buy more. American women really use the cosmetics, but they act as if perfume were champagne instead of Gallo white wine. We haven't talked yet about the copy line for the Princess Daisy campaign. We're trying to sell *two* things—an entire line of cosmetics, and an entire line of perfume and cologne. I'd like to use only one line in every commercial and on every piece of print advertising, a line which applies as well to the cosmetics as to the perfume—and a line which has the advantage of being one which Daisy can say convincingly, without having to be an actress." Luke rose to his feet. Only a loser presented the copy sitting down. He paused for exactly the right beat and then spoke. "I wear it *every* day—Princess Daisy—by Elstree."

"Perfect!" Shannon said. As soon as the word left his lips, the room was as clamoring with congratulations as it would have been full of silence if Shannon hadn't liked it.

"Simple but eloquent!"

"Easy to remember!"

"Great product identification!"

"Tremendous message! It's better than Western Union!"

Luke smiled modestly. He felt modest. Art it wasn't, but it sure as hell was a living.

Ram walked briskly along Old Bond Street toward his club on St. James Street. He was at least five minutes early for lunch, but he saw no temptation to stroll in the miserable London weather of late February 1977. He passed into the warmth of Whites quickly, swinging his umbrella and greeting a young man he knew who was leaving. The man neither returned his words nor seemed to have seen him. But surely, Ram thought, they had spent several evenings together last fall? Wasn't the fellow one of the group who had hung around Sarah Fane? Or perhaps he just looked like him? In any case, he was a nobody. Ram shrugged and went into one of the lounges to wait for Joe Polkingthorne of *The Financial Times*.

Ram had, in past years, made a habit of lunching with this journalist every three months or so. Although the great newspaper he worked for had correspondents all over the world, Polkingthorne was often sent abroad to write special reports. He had a shrewd flair for sniffing out areas that were ripe for financial development, and his advice had sometimes proven to be rewarding for Ram and his investment trust. Polkingthorne, for his part, thought of Ram as one of the two or three brightest and best informed men in the City, one who would surely become more powerful with each year, and it pleased him to exchange pieces of information and opinion that they both considered, quite rightly, as more valuable than any material gift they might have made each other.

Before Ram could order a drink from one of the stewards, he saw Lord Harry Fane and several other men he knew leaving the lounge on their way to lunch. Ram had not seen Henry Fane since he had stopped showing attention to the man's daughter, almost two months before, but he had prepared himself mentally for the inevitable time when they would resume their business relationship. As Fane came closer, Ram inclined his head at precisely the proper, impersonal, yet friendly angle which would, as no words could, indicate that he, Ram, did not intend to allow any hasty and shallow behavior on the part of Sarah Fane to make any difference to him. He held no foolish grudges.

Harry Fane stopped walking as he saw Ram. He looked at him incredulously and then turned an angry red from his collar to his hairline. The men with him hesitated. Then Lord Harry Fane started to walk again, scowling fiercely, his fists jammed into his pockets, passing by as if Ram were invisible, followed by his friends, none of whom greeted Ram, although they had all known him for years.

Ram sat down in a deep chair and heard his voice calmly requesting a whiskey and water from the steward. This was impossible, he said to himself, even as his body, which knew what had happened, felt as if he had received an all-but-killing blow in the gut. This was not the eighteenth century, his rupture with Sarah Fane was the sort that happened constantly among young men and women busily arranging and rearranging and generally sorting themselves out into couples. While he was telling himself this, Ram knew that there must be something more to explain his having been cut—*cut*, for God's sake, actually cut—by five men in the space of a few minutes. What had happened to destroy the respect that he had always prided himself on so intensely? He had spent an entire lifetime shoring up that respect against any attack, respect that had always been a thousand times more important to him than any amount of affection or good-fellowship.

Even as Ram asked himself this question, he simultaneously acknowledged that it had been over a month—perhaps more—since he had received any invitations, either to dinner or for the weekend. After his return to London, after that accursed trip to Nassau to try to reason with Daisy, he'd been too busy working to worry about his social life. In any case he'd had no desire to see anyone in London, and he had paid only faint attention to the fact that his mail consisted chiefly of bills and that his phone rang only for business calls.

Yet last year at this same time he'd been out six nights a week and refused twice as many invitations as he could accept. He sipped his whiskey and water as he added up the evidence that told him that he was a social outcast. At the very moment that he asked himself what had caused this to happen, he understood, with cold and complete horror, that he would never know.

Sarah Fane could not possibly have told anyone what had actually happened between them without ruining her own reputation. Therefore, she had invented something— some lie that was plausible enough for everyone to believe, some foul, degrading, disgusting lie that he would never hear repeated but that would follow him forever throughout the only world in which he cared to live.

Ram knew the rules and he knew he was finished. He could still work effectively; Sarah Fane's lie would not tarnish his placements of capital all over the world. Her words could not reach the ears of art dealers or the men from whom he bought rare books or custom suit makers or the men who sold him horses or who farmed his land. But, sooner or later, it would come to the attention of everyone who mattered in the world in which he had been one of the most sought-after bachelors in the land.

English society had a way of dealing with people it thrust out from itself; a silent, deadly, irrefutable method that Ram had seen at work before. There was no court of appeals because there was no one to whom an appeal could be addressed, no one to whom a question could be put, no one who would admit to having heard anything. If he had had friends . . . Ram realized that there was no man nor woman among the hundreds of people whose parties he had attended in the last years whom he could consider a close enough friend to go to in this moment. A lawyer? What was there to say? Could he imagine himself complaining that some men with whom he was acquainted had not greeted him? Could he claim damages because he had not been invited to dinner? It was nothing—and it was everything. And the shame could never be brought to light and reduced to the lie that it must be.

Whatever she had told people, this girl who was the reigning debutante of her year, this girl with her hundreds of years of aristocratic English blood, it would go no further than the members of a small group. Ram was free to make a new life among intellectuals, among artists, among businessmen without society connections, among foreigners who lived in London, among people of the theater or among people who cared for politics. He would be barred only from some country houses and certain parties, from shooting with a particular selection of men and from riding with others. He would lose—had lost—only the company of everyone in the world whose respect he valued.

"Well, there you are, Valensky!" Joe Polkingthorne thrust out his hand and Ram shook it as he rose from his chair. "Not going to finish your drink? Well, there's always wine . . . make up for it at lunch, eh?" As Ram found himself feeling *grateful* for the journalist's hearty, easy manner he first realized the full measure of his destruction. When the headwaiter led him to his usual table and informed him, deferentially, of the various specials of the day, when the wine steward waited attentively as he made his choice, when he looked around and realized with relief that the men at the next table were strangers, the great, yawning wound in his middle opened wider. Each attention by a paid servant, each new face cautiously observed, was another door shutting behind him as he walked into the jail in which he would spend the rest of his life.

He listened intently as Polkingthorne discussed South Africa and the impossibility of depending on the gold miners; he launched himself with more vivacity than he had ever displayed into a long account of the most recent doings at Lion Management, he ate avidly and drank more than his share, as he tried to do something to stem the seepage he felt in his center, but it was steady and relentless.

"Well, shit, what's the point of arguing about it ourselves? Let's call up and make sure that Shannon didn't really mean only castles—he was probably thinking of great houses and palaces, too," said Kirbo Henry.

"I wouldn't do that if I were you," Luke answered warningly.

"Damn it, Luke, a real castle, by definition, has to be defensible by a fucking army . . . most of them are in ruins, for Christ's sake—they haven't been built since the feudal times, unless you're going for the fake ones the Victorians built which, in my opinion, look like backlotsville. Take Culzean Castle in Ayrshire—it even has palm trees in the foreground! I mean look at these pictures, will you—Hedingham Castle in Essex and Rochester Castle in Kent—they simply don't look lived in!" he said, handing Luke pictures of the ruins of great square twelfth-century towers, menacing Norman keeps, massive and square.

While Luke shook his head at them, Kirbo produced pictures of Stourhead, that meltingly lovely, enormous Palladian villa which was built during a period which lasted from 1727 to 1840. "I'm sure that's what he had in mind—it's where Kubrick filmed *Barry Lyndon*—it's absolutely gorgeous! Can't we check it out, at least?"

"Shannon said a castle and he meant a castle. Don't show me anything without a tower, a keep, a moat, a drawbridge, battlements, ramparts—some place where you can pour boiling oil down on the enemy, Kirbo. Just stop complaining and get back to the research. There have got to be castles in England that people still live in, or that look that way, because *that's the concept*." Luke dismissed his grumpy art director, who was pissed off, in his opinion, because he hadn't thought up the castle idea himself.

"Gelatinous!" Daisy said rebelliously to Theseus. He looked at her questioningly. She had always talked to him, but this was not within the range of his understanding. "The way the time goes," she continued, "the hurry up and wait . . . it's driving me crazy." Daisy continued to complain to Theseus as she walked around the apartment looking without success for something to put in order, something that might be blessedly in need of mending or straightening or fixing. The months since she had signed the Elstree contract had passed in the most unexpectedly slow manner. Somehow, having made her decision, she had imagined that she would be caught up at once in a whirl of work, but she found out that instead she was a prisoner of Supracorp.

Although they didn't need her on a full-time basis until July when commercials would be shot, they wouldn't let her leave town either, because she was sporadically needed for public-relations opportunities. "I'm sorry," Candice Bloom had said firmly, "but you really *cannot* go to England, not even for just a few days. Leo Lerman's giving me a call about lunch and I'm not sure what day he'll be free, Trudy Owett at the *Journal* wants to see you for a possible fashion layout and I'm waiting to hear from her any minute ... no, Daisy, I want you where I can get my hands on you in five minutes."

During the long, tedious spring and early summer Daisy's days were broken up, from time to time, by consultations and fittings with Bill Blass, who was doing a capsule Princess Daisy wardrobe both for her personal wear in public appearances and for use in store promotions. There were also occasional interviews, most of which had not yet appeared, as well as photographic sessions for the Elstree ads.

She huddled, disconsolate and wistful, in one of the wicker armchairs in the living room and wished that Kiki were there. Although Kiki still nominally shared the apartment with Daisy, in reality she spent most of her time at home, in Grosse Pointe, doing complicated, ritualistic things connected with her wedding. Whenever she was in New York, she stayed at Luke's, flying in and out of the apartment like a demented bee. Daisy felt as abandoned as a dog who had been left alone locked in a car, unexpectedly, with no reason given. She had not been fully aware of her need for Kiki's volatile, insouciant, brazen and consistently confused presence until her friend had disappeared into the busy world of premarital goings-on.

Kiki with monogrammed towels indeed, Daisy thought sadly, as she realized that the towels were only a tiny sign of the difference Kiki's marriage was going to make in her life. "I am suffering from separation anxiety," she announced to Theseus. It started as a joke, but as she said it she heard the catch in her voice. "Fool, silly fool—no, Theseus, not you, *me*," Daisy assured the dog, realizing that behind her feeling of impending loss at the thought of

Kiki's getting married were other losses, ancient losses she could not afford to dwell on, lest she start to weep. She got up briskly and started to get dressed. In a mood like this, the only answer was to take to the streets with Theseus, avoiding butcher shops and other temptations, but, at all costs, getting out of the empty apartment.

As she dressed, Daisy admitted to herself that in spite of her impatience to finally get down to work, healthy consuming work, in spite of her feeling that once the whole Elstree business started, her boredom and restlessness would be cured, she was terrified of that future moment. I'm going to be such a big target, she thought, confusedly, not knowing precisely what she meant. All she was sure of was that she had kept a low profile for all of her adult life in the nebulous hope that it would prevent her from losing any more than she already had. Now, with her face and name soon to be exposed many hundreds of thousands of times in the most public way possible, she felt an almost superstitious fear of the future. Fool, she thought again, but didn't say out loud, to spare the feelings of her dog.

As Daisy roamed SoHo with Theseus, trying to keep busy, Luke found time to telephone North.

"All packed and ready to go?" he asked heartily.

"Fuck off, Luke."

"Thanks, North, but you haven't answered my question."

"I've decided that I decline to be any part of this absurd production. Get yourself another commercial maker."

"No way. Arnie bid on the job, we accepted the bid, and we're counting on you."

"It's not the same job—the conditions have all changed."

"However much money Arnie wants to tack on because we're shooting in England, is going to be all right with the agency—I can guarantee that. But we want a Frederick Gordon North commercial, my boy, we want your verve, your sense of design, your perception of volume and contrast, the nuances of your unique lighting, your inspiration and audacity, your inimitable taste and your technical integrity—or, to put it more bluntly, we won't let you off the hook because Shannon stole Daisy from you."

"That has absolutely *nothing* to do with it!" North shouted.

"Splendid! I'm relieved to hear it, because I admit that I

certainly could have understood it if you were unable to do these commercials because you can't function without Daisy. Since that's not the case, as you've just assured me, you have a commitment to us, and, as one of your old and faithful friends, and occasional major customer, we certainly expect you to honor it. Gee—I'm sure glad to hear there are no hard feelings."

"Shitweasel!"

"Temper, temper." North was still his good pal, Luke thought, but he needed him, or rather Daisy would need North's skill to direct her. Of course, he had no legal hold on North, but sometimes a little arm twisting was in order, especially if you know how to use a man's failings against him—and North's was pride. Or rather, pride was *one* of his failings.

"We're waiting to get permission from the National Trust—they own the castles we're going to use," Luke told North. "I hope your new producer has settled on Daisy's wardrobe and decided who you're bringing to England and who you're going to hire over there and all the other little, petty, niggling details Daisy used to handle with such dispatch."

"You really *are* a first-class prick."

"How many times have I told you that compliments don't affect me? Oh, and by the way, North, will you be my best man? We're having the wedding after the shoot so you can't use that as an excuse. And I think you'll enjoy the ambiance of Grosse Pointe. It's shaping up into a fairly decent little wedding; unpretentious, impudent, almost, but not quite, petulant, and of a promising year."

"I'm not the best-man type," North snapped.

"I quite agree . . . but it happens to be one of the burdens of friendship. Why should you escape? I had to do it twice for you."

"Go shit in your hat, Luke."

"I take it that means you accept? Knew you would."

Now, late in June, Daisy looked forward with a feeling of urgency to the next month when they would all leave for England, where a ten-day shoot was scheduled. Meanwhile, from her position of outsider, she watched in concealed anxiety as Mary-Lou Duke, North's new producer, coped with the job of getting the shoot organized. Daisy had, as a courtesy, offered to show her the ropes at the studio, but her offer had been coldly declined by the woman North had hired away from his closest competitor by dint of paying her one and a half times as much as Daisy had been getting.

Mary-Lou was a woman in her thirties, handsome, almost imposing and placid. Placidity, constant, indestructible, relentless, was her secret weapon. She was as sparkling as lead, as much fun as an empty beer barrel, as humorous as a plain pipe rack—but you could depend on her. While Luke's people were finishing their own preproduction work, she took Daisy on a tour of Seventh Avenue, selecting clothes for the shoot. Mary-Lou hailed the cabs, she held the elevator door open for Daisy, and led the way into the showrooms with Daisy, captive, at her side. Daisy, so used to being the fusser rather than the one fussed over, felt like a cop, accustomed to absolute charge of passing traffic, now reduced to watching a ten-car collision without raising a hand. But she resisted all her impulses to jump in and try to make decisions. She knew damn well, even as Mary-Lou was informing designers of just what she was looking for, that most, if not all, of the clothes they brought back to the studio for North's final approval would be rejected. She kept silent as North, increasingly impatient, sent them back for different clothes on three occasions. After the third time Daisy had to go through a wardrobe parade, and after North had again turned down the clothes, Daisy felt she had to say something. They had only seven days of preproduction time left. She took the new producer aside.

"Mary-Lou—may I make a suggestion?"

"If you feel it's that important," she said reluctantly.

"The reason North doesn't like the riding jackets and the shirts we've been bringing back is that I shouldn't be in a tailored jacket and shirt—I have to be in proper riding clothes from the waist down, but above the waist I should be wearing something dashing and unusual."

"But that wouldn't be *proper*," Mary-Lou said severely.

"No, not at all, but it'd work, for what they want."

"But if people don't ride dressed like that . . ."

"The number of people who'll know the difference will be tiny. It's the general effect that counts—don't you think?"

"If you don't mind breaking the rules . . ." Mary-Lou shrugged. Even her shrug was inexpressive, not an easy thing.

"And for the picnic on the lawn, the trouble is nobody is

doing the right clothes for that this year . . . but I know a place, a special place I've never been able to afford, where we might find just the thing," Daisy said eagerly.

"Daisy, perhaps you'd better just run along and look for clothes without me," Mary-Lou decided. It went against her principles to delegate any authority but she had so many more important things to do.

Mary-Lou didn't care when people insisted on trying to contribute ideas, just as long as they didn't get in the way of her logistics. Ideas were like balloons children play with—let them have their fun being "creative"—logistics were serious business. Her mind was almost entirely occupied with the mechanical details of getting North and company to England, picking up the English technicians, conveying everyone to their locations, housing them, feeding them, and making sure that they had every last piece of equipment they needed. The only thing that bothered her was that the first-class section on British Airways seemed to be heavily booked on the day they were leaving. Now *that* was something she couldn't wait to get her teeth into.

Daisy, released, dashed out to costume herself, not forgetting that she had an appointment with the Elstree make-up people that afternoon. They were taking no chances on untested English make-up artists. A top commercial make-up expert would be part of the troupe that went to England, as would one of the highest paid hairdressers in commercial work. They were each getting fifteen hundred dollars a day plus all expenses for each day they'd be away from New York. "Hardship pay" they called it, although it was difficult to see where the hardship lay in England. However, they would have charged no more to go to the Sahara. Once out of Manhattan, it was "hardship," and let no producer forget it.

Since the make-up expert had her own prized collection of dozens and dozens of hard-to-find, *recherché* types of make-up she had discovered over the years, she was not at all happy about having to use only Elstree products, but truth-in-advertising laws forced her to do so, since Daisy was going to say, "I wear it every day."

"Luckily," she said, looking at Daisy, "you don't need much make-up—I'm not used to this muck."

The Elstree product-line manager flinched. "They're excellent products," Patsy Jacobson said in irritation.

"Yeah—but its not theatrical." The two women glared at each other.

Daisy, who was sitting in front of a mirror, as motionless as a mannequin, was seized by an urge to get into this conversation. Severely she stopped herself. Develop an *attitude,* she told herself. *Be a star!* Don't get into their act. If they're having problems, that's not something I should be worried about at this stage of the game. It'll put them in shock if I turn back into Daisy the Fixer. It'll get resolved faster and better without me and if it winds up being something I don't like, I'll simply tell them to start all over again, until I do like it. If I dare. If I dare? Of course, I'll dare, won't I? After all, I am the star.

She sat quietly, thinking of the check for three hundred and thirty-three thousand dollars, and thirty-three cents, she had received from Supracorp last January when she had signed her contract.

She had written Anabel as soon as she had made the deal with Patrick Shannon at Le Cirque, telling her the news of her riches, telling her she knew of Anabel's illness, telling her not to sell *La Marée* whatever she did, telling her that she, Daisy, could easily meet all of Anabel's expenses, in addition to Danielle's, and that Anabel was not to even think about money but just concentrate on getting better. She never mentioned Ram. Even as Daisy wrote the letter she knew that she wasn't being rash in making these promises before the contract was signed. Whatever kind of man Patrick Shannon was, he wouldn't change his word, once given. She knew that as surely as she knew that Columbus had not circumnavigated the globe.

There had been several other dinners with Shannon in the months between then and now, oddly formal dinners, Daisy thought, to which various members of the Supracorp hierarchy were invited, almost as if she were being presented to them, or them to her. Shannon had been away a great deal, off and on, during the last months, on Supracorp business, and he had not renewed his suggestion about a rendezvous between his lurcher, Lucy, and Theseus. Daisy wondered if perhaps her princess act had been a little too convincing.

At last, it was July, and the shoot had officially begun, although filming would not start for another day.

Daisy was alone in her suite at Claridge's. Somehow, by means she preferred not to discuss, Mary-Lou had contrived to get them all first-class seats on the flight they wanted. Now she and North were conferring with the actors who had been chosen to be with Daisy in each commercial. Shannon's desire to show her with genuine lords had given way to North's absolute refusal to use more than one untried, nonprofessional in the shoot.

As Daisy wandered about her suite, so large that its closets could have been small bedrooms, she thought of all the things she might be doing in London, from riding in Hyde Park to hunting up a jumble sale. She had only a few hours before they all met the English location crew to leave in a procession of cars and equipment-filled trucks for their first location, in Sussex. Not enough time, she fretted, to visit Danielle and be sure to be back in time. But once the shoot was over a few days would belong to her. Then—ah, then she'd see Danielle, and go to visit Anabel.

As she waited, she felt absolutely alien in the city that had been her home for so many years. Who knew who now lived in the pale yellow house on Wilton Row in which she'd grown up? Who had bought Anabel's house in Eaton Square? The only places in which she might perhaps feel a sense of belonging were the stables in the Grosvenor Crescent Mews or at Lady Alden's School, and something kept her from revisiting these old haunts. Restlessly Daisy went down the great flight of stairs to buy some magazines to read in her sitting room, which was large enough for a cocktail party of sixty.

"Magazines, Madame?" the head hall porter said politely. "Oh, we don't *keep* magazines, Madame. However, if you will just tell me what you require, I'll send a lad to get them for you, immediately."

"Oh, never mind, it's perfectly all right." Daisy retreated to her room, furious with herself and furious with a hotel so uncommercial that it didn't even have a magazine stand. She realized why she hadn't gone out anywhere, why she had not chosen to leave the absolutely protective luxury of this monolithic hotel during these last free hours before work started. She was afraid of meeting Ram.

Herstmonceux Castle, in Sussex, had been chosen as the location of the first of three thirty-second commercials.

The soft-rose brick building was surrounded by an exceptionally wide moat which could be crossed only by a long drawbridge, built on a series of graceful arches sunk into the deep waters of the moat. Its builder, Roger de Fiennes, Treasurer of the Household of Henry VI in the mid-fifteenth century, must have had good reason to suspect that someday he might need to defend himself, for he had built a strong and most beautiful fortress, with a gatehouse protected by two powerful octagonal, crenelated towers, above which stood double fighting platforms. This castle had been chosen for the commercial in which Daisy would ride up to the entrance, since Kirbo, when he had finally found pictures of it, had suddenly seen that a gallop across a bridge was more visually interesting than a gallop up just any driveway. North planned on shooting at Herstmonceux first, since it involved horses and would demand less of Daisy's acting ability than the other commercials.

When North had first seen the pictures of the castle, he was disgusted. "That bridge is thirty feet above the surface of the moat, Luke. Even with a barge and a crane, I can't get high enough—it's a helicopter or nothing, for the approach and the gallop, and then as she rides closer and gets off the horse I'll only have the width of the bridge to work on."

"Old Roger didn't want to make it easy for strangers to walk in uninvited," said Luke, unmoved. If there was one thing he never let worry him, it was the technical problems of commercial makers. He had never met a good one who couldn't have humped a camera to the top of the Great Pyramid of Gizeh—all by himself if necessary. They wallowed in stories of technical impossibilities they'd conquered; their magazine, *Millimeter*, was full of harrowing tales of difficulties overcome, and while it was true that nine commercial makers *had* been killed in helicopter accidents, they'd still swim a river crawling with man-eating alligators for the right shot ... or get out of the business. Even as Luke refused to react to North's niggling objections, North himself was thinking that the old bricks of Herstmonceux would look even lovelier through an amber filter and a few smoke bombs set off in the background would make it seem to literally float on the surface of the moat, a trick he thought he might have invented even before David Dee.

As North stood just outside the great portcullis of Herstmonceux that first week in October, with Wingo just inside, riding the camera, watching Daisy, her hair flying like the standard of a great queen, galloping toward him on a huge black horse, followed by a white horse carrying an actor who looked more like a lord than any lord could have, he had to admit that she didn't look like an amateur. She didn't even *sound* like an amateur as she dismounted and spoke her one line, dressed in fawn breeches, black boots, and a soft, open-necked, full-sleeved, billowing white silk blouse such as one of the Three Musketeers might have worn. The changes of expression on North's face, flickering with quick emotions, sometimes crossed by a smile he didn't know was there, the descriptive pantomime gestures of his hands, as if he were engaged in hypnosis or legerdemain, led Daisy through her paces over and over, and still once more, and then again, and yet again, until he was satisfied. She had never, not even in Venice, felt so much closeness between them as during each take. She finally understood his particular genius in its very special manifestation and she knew, finally, why he had married his two best models—she knew already why they had divorced him.

Even before he looked at the rushes in London, less than three hours away by car, North was aware that he had something extraordinarily special on the film; he could tell by the way a chill had run down the back of his neck and upper arms each time Daisy galloped closer to the camera and he anticipated the lyrical moment when she pulled up her huge beast and leapt off, laughing. It had been years since he'd felt that chill, that promise of something inexpressibly *right*.

The mystery that had always engaged him, the deep unsolvable mystery of the human face and its ability to convey emotion—even if it was only an emotion that led the viewer to a certain counter in a supermarket—this mystery was charged with power by Daisy's features on film, North realized, as he watched the rushes. Why had he never even thought to film her before? He resented her excellence only a little less than he was relieved by it.

From Sussex, using cars, planes and trains, with admirable precision, Mary-Lou led the entire company far north, to Peeblesshire, in Scotland, where the castle called Traquair House was located. Totally different from stern

Herstmonceux, it had evolved from a simple stone tower built in the middle of the thirteenth century. By the time of Charles I, the castle itself had grown into a tall, pale gray edifice guarded by a long expanse of delicate iron gates which had been shut by the owners until such a time as a Stuart was again crowned King of England, and, even for Frederick Gordon North, they could not be opened. However, right outside the gates was a flower-dappled meadow in which Daisy, and an actor, were to picnic on strawberries and cream.

Daisy was wearing a dress from Gene London's Gramercy Park Shop made of antique Victorian panels. It had cost four thousand dollars to rework the rare material into a dress that didn't look like a costume, a dress that floated almost transparently from her half-bare shoulders, with wide, long sleeves, like wings. The color of the frail, old ivory lace against her skin was entrancing, and the hairdresser had pulled her hair up and away from her face with a twist of silk ribbons, as green as the color of the meadow, and then let it fall down simply at the back.

"No helicopter here," North decreed, when he saw the Traquair location. "The rotors would blow the grass and flowers flat. There's only one way to get this shot right. Mary-Lou, get me a Hovercraft."

"Who is she, when she's at home?" asked Wingo.

"Mary-Lou," North rapped out. "Hovercraft."

"As large as the ones that cross the English Channel or a smaller version?" she intoned, expressionlessly.

"As small as you can get. Since it rides on a cushion of air, a few feet above the ground, or above the water, as the case may be—are you listening, Wingo, you ignorant lout—it'll look as if we're lighter than air. What I want in this entire scene is the viewpoint of a *butterfly*, not a bird, not a bee, but a dipping, gliding, lazy, fucking butterfly."

"What keeps it up?" Wingo asked suspiciously.

"Keep your eyes open. Maybe you'll find out," North answered.

As Mary-Lou went off, looking quietly pleased with herself, to conjure up a Hovercraft, North said, loudly enough so that Wingo and Daisy could hear him, "Damn that broad."

"North, she's only being efficient," Daisy protested.

"Yeah. But why does she have to be so fucking surreptitious about it?"

"That's not fair. She's just doing her job."

"Daisy, do me a favor, will you? Try not to explain my prejudices to me?"

When Patrick Shannon made a deal, he liked to understand both sides of it. He always knew what he intended to gain, but the other man's motives, the reasons behind his agreement, were more fascinating. Shannon realized that he had no idea why Daisy Valensky, a rich society girl, who worked to keep from being bored, who insisted that she cherished her anonymity, would have consented to the ordeal of becoming the linchpin of an entire company's efforts to put themselves back on the map through exploitation of her personality and persona. "Private reasons," she had said when he'd asked. What private reasons? Why did she want a million dollars during the next three years? It didn't make sense if she was what she was, and he couldn't believe she was not.

For months, these questions occurred to him from time to time as he spent weeks in California, dealing in Supracorp's entertainment division, as he flew back and forth twice to Tokyo and once to France. This gap in his understanding bothered him like a grape skin stuck between his teeth. He suspected that he'd fallen into some sort of trap, that something was going on over which he was not quite in control, but the never ending pressures of running a conglomerate had prevented him from digging into the matter.

He had no trusted second-in-command with whom to discuss this unusual state of affairs, nor was he the kind of man who could speculate with a chosen cohort. At Supracorp, either the employees accepted the fact that, at any time, Shannon might step personally into their domains, or they quit. But they never had to worry about a court favorite screwing things up between themselves and the man at the top. Problems, pressures, tensions, the cat's cradle of thrust and counterthrust of corporate politics were pure joy to Shannon and he had no urge to share them. But he hated operating in an unclear area and, as Patrick Shannon inspected the folder of publicity material Candice Bloom had built up on Daisy, now a respectable pile of photographs and interviews, he decided to fly to England to see what the hell was going on.

As the chauffeur-driven Daimler carried him from Heathrow to Bath, where North and company were staying during the shoot of the final commercial at Berkeley Castle, Shannon realized that he was attaching a unique importance to the Elstree problem. He'd never visited the locations of any of the dozens of commercials which were made yearly for various Supracorp products. He paid people well to do just that. When had this begun, he asked himself. When had Elstree stopped becoming a worrying trouble spot on the conglomerate balance sheet and turned into something almost personal? Damned if he knew. But he'd soon find out. He instructed his chauffeur not to stop at the hotel in Bath, but to continue on to the location.

"Where are the commercials being shot?" he asked the man who sold him his three-shilling ticket in front of the gray stone keep which dated from 1153.

"Beg your pardon, Sir?"

"Americans, with cameras," he said.

"All over the place, Sir."

"No, I mean big cameras—lights—for *television*," he explained impatiently.

"Oh, them, Sir—yes, they'll be in the Bowling Alley, I believe."

"Could you tell me where it is and I'll ..."

"Straight through the Castle, Sir. Here, Mildred, you attend to the tickets. I'll show this gentleman to the Bowling Alley," the man said, glad of a chance to get a glimpse of the goings-on. "Right up these stairs, Sir," he said, as Shannon followed him into the vast pile of stone. "Now here, Sir, you have the room in which Edward the Second was murdered," he said proudly, pausing for effect. "And that hole in the corner goes down to the dungeon!"

"Could we just keep going?" Shannon said, without hiding his impatience. His guide sniffed in surprise. *All* visitors like to linger in the infamous chamber and peep into the dungeon. However he went on, old and walking at his own pace, through a narrow door into the later parts of the huge savage building, leading Shannon as quickly as he could through the Picture Gallery and the Dining Room and the fourteenth-century Kitchen and Buttery—the only way to get to the other side of the Castle.

"Sinks of solid lead, Sir?" he said, hoping for a pause. Patrick Shannon groaned to himself as, silently, he navigated the Buttery, which led to the China Room, and the China Room led to the Housekeeper's Room and eventually to the Great Hall.

"Are we getting nearer?" he finally asked, surveying the unexpected immensity of the Great Hall.

"Ah, well, there's still the Grand Stairs, and the Long Drawing Room and the Morning Room and the Small Drawing Room—we're a bit more than halfway, Sir," said his guide encouragingly, beginning to walk the sixty-two feet of the Great Hall with an air of proud possession, wondering why this strangely uninquisitive visitor didn't want to know more of the history of this most famous of castles that had been and still was inhabited by the very same family that had built it eight hundred years ago. Why, he thought, indignantly, Berkeleys had lived at Berkeley since before the Magna Carta. Twenty-four generations of them.

Since his guide was obviously neither inclined nor able to hurry, Shannon resigned himself to following, feeling at each step a plucking in his chest that refused to go away, a queer, peevish, nervous twanging of some chord of impatient longing. Damnation, why couldn't the man walk faster?

Eventually, they came out on the south front of the Castle and there, below them, Shannon recognized the clutter of cables and equipment he had been waiting so expectantly to see. There it all was at one end of a long rectangle of close-cropped lawn flanked by a tall, creeper-covered wall on one side and great old yews on the other. But no people were visible. "Where are they?" he asked his guide.

"I should expect they're having tea, Sir."

"*Christ!* Oh, sorry—but I'm in a hurry."

"So I gathered, Sir."

"Well, then, where would they be having their tea?" Shannon asked, biting out each syllable politely.

The old man pointed out a charming country house at a little distance, surrounded by trees. "The Berkeley Hunt stables and kennels, Sir. That's where they parked those great lorries of theirs."

Pat wheeled on him. "Then I could have come the way they came?"

"Ah, certainly—but then you would have *missed* the Castle, Sir," the man reproached him.

Shannon left him standing without another word and strode hurriedly down the terraces which would lead to the stables. Below the deserted Bowling Alley lay a lily pond on the other side of which was a stone staircase that he hoped would open out onto the meadows and the trees. He was almost running as he crossed the lawn to the lily pond.

"Are you looking for someone, or just lolling about?"

He spun around. Daisy was sitting on a low stone wall, barefoot, a mug of tea on the grass beside her. She laughed at him with the lavishness of one who knows her beauty is inexhaustible. He stopped and looked at her.

"I was in the neighborhood . . ."

"So you thought you'd drop by," she finished. "Here, have my tea." She held the mug up to him and he took it, automatically sitting down on the wall. "Anyone who makes it through that Castle needs a stimulant—I wish I had some brandy for you."

He drank the entire mug of sweet, still-hot liquid. That strange, unnerving, nagging tugging in his chest had gone, dissolved into a feeling he couldn't identify or name, a feeling which brought with it a rush of pure gladness.

"Your tea's all gone," he said, struggling to repress what he knew would be an idiotic grin.

"Not a hundred yards from us is an entire trailer filled with people completely devoted to brewing tea, day and night, night and day—not to worry," she said.

"Okay—how's it going?"

"Very well. We should be finished by tomorrow. Today I was working with the dogs, walking them on that lawn you just came over—it might have been easier if the story board hadn't specified lurchers."

"Oh, damn—that was my fault."

"I *knew* it was—we had to send them back—too excited—and now we're waiting for some dogs who don't go crazy every time they smell a bird or a rabbit. They almost pulled my arm off. They just wouldn't *listen* to North." She started to laugh again and he joined in. The idea of two skulking, criminal lurchers daring to disobey North's commands struck them both as the most irresistibly agreeable thing they had heard of in their lives.

"Oh . . . oh . . ." Daisy gasped, "nobody else thought it was a joke, let me tell you . . . he kept saying, 'I'll *kill* the person who wrote that story board, *kill*.' But don't worry . . . I didn't tell."

Shannon suddenly stopped laughing. "Your arm . . . is it all right?"

"Of course."

He took her hand and turned it over. The palm was hot,

red and swollen where she'd been gripping the leashes for hours. He stared at it for a moment and then lifted it and pressed her palm gently, remorsefully, to his cheek.

"Forgive me," he muttered.

"It doesn't matter . . . *really*," she said in a low voice. Her other hand reached out and touched his dark hair, lifting the lock which lay on his forehead. He raised his head and looked at her. He kissed her feverish palm. They drew apart, still looking at each other.

"And just what the fuck are *you* doing here?" North demanded in furious surprise, coming around the corner.

23

$\mathcal{F}$ive days later, North and Luke sat wordlessly in North's screening room. They had just finished seeing the rough cut of all three Elstree commercials.

"What can I say?" Luke asked finally, pushing his words through the wall of North's frosty, unfamiliar indifference.

"You'll think of something."

"I don't have to tell you it's the best work you've ever done?"

"Nope."

"I don't have to tell you these will be the best fragrance commercials ever made?"

"Nope."

"Can I just thank you?"

"I consider myself thanked. Could you just stop gushing, Luke? I'd take that as a favor."

"Right! Oh . . . Kiki wanted to ask you if you had any idea when Daisy'll be coming back—she hasn't heard a word."

"No idea."

"Well, I'm going to call Shannon." Luke turned away from the uncomfortable atmosphere his friend had created. "Christ, wait till he sees these!" he said eagerly, picking up the phone and dialing Supracorp's number. He spoke to one of Shannon's secretaries briefly and hung up, disappointed.

"Apparently he's in England on business—his secretary didn't have any idea when he'll be back."

"I could have told you that."

"Huh? Oh. OH! Oh, my God, wait till Kiki hears . . . so

that's what's wrong with you . . . oh, *shit!* I'm sorry, North, that was totally stupid and tactless of me . . ."

"It could not possibly matter less," North said, spitting out each word venomously.

"No, no, of course not. I don't even know what made me say it." Luke was as close to dithering as he'd ever come. "I've got softening of the brain, probably coming down with Chinese flu, everyone in the office has it." Hastily he returned to business. "When will you have an answer print? Until these spots are completely edited and scored I don't want anyone to see them. The whole cosmetic industry is rip-off city."

"Two—two and a half weeks."

"Well, I've got to get back to the shop. Let me know the instant they're ready—okay? The sooner the better—put as many people on it as you have to. They've got to start to run well before Thanksgiving. And North—thank you again. There's no way anyone but you could have pulled it off."

"You can do me a favor, Luke. Next time you want a job done with a fucking amateur, give it to somebody else. I don't need the hassle," North said viciously.

"Right. You've got it. Talk to you soon? Take care of that flu," Luke said, getting out of the room as quickly as possible and ignoring North's roar that Luke was the one who was sick, not him. It just didn't seem like the appropriate time to remind North about being best man at the wedding. And he could hardly call Kiki and tell her how magnificent, how wonderful, how preposterously perfect Daisy had been, and he seriously doubted that North would have appreciated his using the studio phone for that. On second thought, wouldn't Kiki be more interested in the news about Daisy and Shannon in England? Where was the pay phone, damn it?

During the last day of the shoot at Berkeley Castle, Shannon had been unable to stay away. Although he removed himself as far as he could from the scene of the action, he kept edging closer and closer, without realizing it, until a look or a word from one of the crew, or a cable grazing his foot would remind him that he was in their way. He watched, in a trance, as Daisy and an actor walked the length of the Bowling Alley with two well-trained miniature collies, the gray-lavender walls of the great keep visible on their left.

He was in a most peculiar state, Shannon told himself. Most peculiar. It would seem, he thought, trying to analyze himself, that he felt something that could certainly be called a *decided preference* for Daisy. She seemed to be the person he most wanted to be with. All the time. Just why this was so, he didn't yet understand. It wasn't as if she'd *done* anything to make this so. She simply *was*. That was what puzzled him so mightily.

Patrick Shannon had, from the time he was a young man, been able to spot the inner truths of other people the way a stag could sense a doe in the forest. He moved on instinct, intuition and an inner knowledge based on a hundred perceived clues that had proven, time after time, to be reliable and valid. Ambition, talent, fear, goodness, pettiness, honesty—he could sniff them in the air. If he'd been a mystic he would have said he could see them like auras around people's heads. And because he so firmly believed in the accuracy of his senses, he used them. In the corporate power world this ability translated itself directly into action.

But today he felt as if his sense of the realistic had been switched off and his instincts were as unstable as King Arthur's had been when he'd wandered into the charmed circle of Morgan le Fay. What, after all, did he know about Daisy? He discarded as worthless evidence their meeting in Middleburg and the time he'd seen her in North's studio. Dinner at Le Cirque? The laughing girl he'd sat with on the wall yesterday just was not the same grandly reticent woman he'd dined with at Le Cirque nor the pleasant, proper, aloof young princess he'd introduced to the Supracorp division heads from time to time during the last few months. Last night, when everyone had eaten together at the Toad in the Hole in Bath, she'd been very silent, exhausted from the day perhaps, or just quiet. And now, today, she was different again.

Daisy was wearing the same dress she'd worn yesterday, a simple turtleneck dress made from the softest wool woven in shades from pale fawn to rich brown, with rust and bark and berry mixed into a subtle woodland conspiracy. It just brushed her high breasts and was lightly caught by a chain of woven gold at her waist. Daisy called it her Maid Marion dress and wore it with boots of thin, russet leather. Shannon thought it looked like a dress of spicy feathers. Each time she came to the line, "I wear it every day," she pulled the brown velvet ribbon off the one heavy braid which lay over her right shoulder and shook free the silver of her hair. As she did this, time and again, he could think of no other word to express what he saw: she was a star. Everyone there, every single person on the location, had no reason for existence except to record her walking on that centuries-old lawn. Yes, North told her what to do, but he couldn't tell her how to do it—that spirited, natural grace had to come from her. No one could make her up to look so virginal and yet so fruitful. No one could bestow on her that combination of gentle approachability just touched with an air that said, unmistakably, that she was far, very far, from the girl next door.

That afternoon North announced that it was a wrap. The plane back to New York would leave from London the next day at noon. As Mary-Lou dispatched the crew with the crispness of a NASA flight control officer, Patrick Shannon made his way to Daisy's make-up trailer.

"Are you going home tomorrow?" he asked her, his manner as gauche as if he were back in his first year at prep school.

"No, I have business to attend to in London. And then I'm going on to France to visit—family."

"I have business in London, too."

"Ah?"

"But you know the English—you just can't interrupt their weekends. So I'll be staying over till next week. Would you like . . . are you free for dinner tomorrow night? I suppose you're busy? . . ."

"No. I'm free. I'd like to have dinner."

"What time shall I pick you up?"

"Eight-thirty at Claridge's." She'd be back from spending the day with Dani by six-thirty. That would give her two hours in which to get ready. She wondered if they were going to be dining alone or would he produce yet another couple of Supracorp strangers for her to meet.

"Well . . . I'll see you then," Shannon said awkwardly as he backed out of the trailer.

That moment on the wall yesterday, interrupted by that total bastard, North, had left him in a condition he didn't have any reference points to explain. He was buffeted by shivers of crystalline delight, filled with impatient, precarious joy, conscious of an excess of something vital and valuable but yet unidentified that was invading his spirit.

Altogether a most intemperate state to be in, and thoroughly disconcerting. He scarcely knew his own name. Damn, but he was happy!

Usually a reservation at the Connaught for Saturday night has to be made almost a week in advance. But, since Shannon stayed at the Connaught on his frequent business trips to England, he had no trouble getting a table. He had given a lot of thought to the question of where to take Daisy for dinner, and the honeyed hum of the Connaught dining room appealed to him more than the high-priced, hurried atmosphere of London's many fashionable Italian restaurants or the solemn elaborations of its best French restaurants.

Daisy was waiting in the lobby of Claridge's when he arrived, and they spoke only a word or two on the brief drive around the corner. She was emotionally drained by her reunion with her sister. It had been a difficult day, long, and both sad and happy as she saw that Dani had not changed, had remained eerily beautiful and untouched by time, a happy five-year-old in Daisy's body. She felt frail and vulnerable tonight, disconnected, muddled, at once very old and very young.

As the chauffeur stopped the car in front of the familiar entrance with its elaborate glass canopy, Daisy only said, "Oh," so quietly that Shannon didn't hear the note of shock in her voice. She stepped into the lobby in a dream, and walked the familiar route to the restaurant, not stopping as she used to, to inspect every dish on the laden trolleys, but looking straight before her, biting the inside of her lower lip so that it wouldn't tremble as the sounds and smells and light of a never forgotten paradise surrounded her again. As she and Shannon waited to be seated, standing for a moment in the entrance to the room, a headwaiter suddenly stopped taking an order at a table near the door. He looked only once. He left an astonished duke, who was inquiring about the family tree of the *fois gras*, and walked swiftly, much too swiftly for any self-respecting maître d'hôtel, to the door.

"Princess Daisy," he cried in astonished joy and then abandoned all professionalism entirely as he enfolded her in a great bear hug. "Princess Daisy—you're back! Where did you go? Everyone missed you so much—but no one knew what had happened—you disappeared!"

"Oh, darling Monsieur Henri, you're still here! I'm so glad to see you!" Daisy cried, returning his hug with all her might.

"We're all still here—you were the one who left," he said, rebuking her in his surprise, ignoring the fact that all the diners in sight of the door had abandoned their food to watch the unimaginable sight of a Connaught headwaiter hugging a Connaught customer, as if she were a long-lost daughter.

"I didn't want to, Monsieur Henri, but I've been living in America."

"But when you came back to visit? Why did you never come back to see us, Princess Daisy, during all those years and years?" he said reproachfully.

"I haven't been back to England," Daisy lied. "This is my first time home." She couldn't tell him that on her trips to see Danielle she didn't have the money to eat at the Connaught.

Shannon coughed. The maître d'hôtel abruptly re-entered the real world. Within seconds they were seated. He had, without thinking twice, given them the same table Stash Valensky had always requested, central yet private. Shannon looked at Daisy carefully. She was holding back tears, the struggle visible on her face.

"I'm sorry . . . I had no idea," he said. "Does it bother you to stay? Wouldn't you rather go somewhere else?" He took one of her hands and covered it protectively.

Daisy shook her head, and gave him the beginning of a smile. "No, I'll be fine. It's just . . . memories. I'm glad to be back, truly. Some of the happiest moments of my life were spent right here at this table."

"I don't know anything about you!" Shannon burst out. He felt overwhelmed by jealousy of her mysterious past. What a terrible way to start the evening—reunions, memories, tears. What next?

"It isn't fair, is it?" she asked, reading his mind.

"No, it isn't. Every time I see you, you're different, damn it. I just don't know what to make of you. Who the devil are you, anyway?"

"This from the man who's so sure of my identity that he's going to blazon it all over the world? If *you* don't know who I am, how can 'Princess Daisy' exist?"

"You're laughing at me again."

"Do you mind?"

"I like it. Anyway, you're right. 'Princess Daisy' has to

do with Elstree, not you. And I still don't know who you are." Entreaty, as loud as trumpets, shone in his eyes.

"I used to come here with my father, for lunch, almost every Sunday from the time I was about nine until I was fifteen. Then he died and I went to college at Santa Cruz in California. After that I worked in New York for North."

"Except when you were painting pictures for fun on the weekends?"

"For *money*. I painted every single picture for the money," Daisy said gently, "and I worked for North for the money and I'm doing the commercials for the money. If you want to know me, you have to know that." As she heard herself speak, she realized that she had just told Shannon more about herself than she had told any man. Yet she wasn't surprised, nor was she dismayed at what she'd revealed. Perhaps it was the result of her day with Dani, but her emotions were close to the surface tonight and she knew, with a profound, bright certainty, that it was safe to tell this man things she had muffled in shrouds for so long.

"Why do you need the money?"

"To take care of my sister." As she spoke, Daisy felt a wave of relief so strong that it made her give a great shuddering sigh and slump back in her chair, but her hand didn't move from under his.

"Tell me about her," he asked softly.

"She's very, very sweet and good. She's called Danielle. Today, when I saw her, she remembered me perfectly even though it's been several years since I could come to visit her. The teachers there, at her school, told me that she talks about me often—she says, 'Where Day?' and she looks at all the photographs of us together," Daisy said in a dreamy voice.

"How old is she?" Shannon wondered, at sea.

"She's my twin."

Two hours later, dinner finished, they sat still talking over brandy in the restaurant which was now more than half-empty.

"Something went wrong way back in my life," Daisy said. "I've never been able to be sure what it was exactly."

"Was it when your mother died?"

"Nothing was ever right after that. But I think it went

wrong long, long before that, perhaps even when I was born . . . born *first.*"

"You can't remember back to when you were born," Shannon said, startled. "How do you know you were born first?"

Daisy looked at him in astonishment. "Did I say that? Did I really say 'born first'—say it out loud?"

"Whatever it means, you did."

"I didn't realize," she murmured. Since they had started talking, as with the first faint lilt of a waltz played at a distance, she had begun to feel a dancing pace lift her heart. It was as if that stubborn stone she had carried there for so long had begun to dissolve into music.

"Daisy, what are you talking about? Up till now you've made sense, but suddenly you've lost me. I don't understand."

He looked at her in bafflement. She seemed to be talking out of a deeper dream than the one she'd been in when she first told him about Danielle.

"All my life I've been trying to repair the damage, trying to make it unhappen, to solve it, to pay for it somehow, and, of course, it hasn't worked."

"Daisy, explain—what do you *mean?*" he begged. "You're still talking in riddles."

She hesitated. She had broken the taboo her father had placed on any word about Danielle, she'd told Shannon all about the way in which she'd been brought up, about Rolls-Royce and why she had no money, about Anabel's leukemia, about *La Marée*—she'd told him everything except about Ram. She never, never in her life would tell anyone about Ram.

"The only reason Danielle's retarded is because I was born first." Daisy took a deep breath before she continued. "She got less oxygen—I got everything I needed and she didn't. If it hadn't been for me, she would have been perfect."

"Jesus! *You've lived with that all your life!* My God, Daisy, that is the craziest thing I've ever heard! Nobody in the world, *nobody,* no doctor, no thinking person would agree with you. Daisy, you simply *cannot* really believe that."

"Of course I don't believe it logically—but emotionally . . . I've always felt . . . *guilty.* Tell me, Pat, how do you unthink something you *feel?* How do you forget something you heard when you were a little child, something that explained everything you didn't understand, something you couldn't tell a single other person about, something you lived by for so long that *whether it was right or wrong didn't matter,* because it has an inner truth for you that is stronger than any logic?"

"I don't know," he admitted slowly. "I'd give anything to know. Perhaps you have to replace the truth that is wrong with the truth that is right? Does that sound possible? Or am I getting too metaphysical? I'm not used to this sort of problem. I wish I were," he added humbly.

"Come on," she said, mirth changing her face, "the metaphysical Mr. Shannon—if they could only see you in the boardroom now."

"It would make a lot of people happy—Pat Shannon without an answer." He studied the sweeping line from Daisy's forehead to the tip of her straight, fine nose and thought that it had a particular determination he had not properly taken into account before. The furrow between her nose and upper lip was a deliciously shaped shadow, full, suddenly, of lurking laughter.

"I have a sneaky feeling that the waiters, adoring as they are, wouldn't be unhappy if we left now—there's no one here but us," he said.

"You may have to carry me out. I'm exhausted. I can't remember when I've been so tired," Daisy said. "But I feel, oh, I feel . . ."

"Yes?" he asked anxiously.

"Like the crazy title of a song Kiki picked up somewhere—it's called 'The Name of the Place Is I Like It Like That.'"

"I know what you mean. Now listen, I'm taking you back to your hotel so you can sleep. Tomorrow, are you going to see Danielle again?"

She nodded.

"And Monday? Will you be here Monday?" he asked.

"No, Monday I have to go to Honfleur to see Anabel."

"Let me go to France with you," he blurted.

"But you have business in London," she reminded him gravely.

"Did you really believe that?"

"That comes under the heading of leading questions."

"Well, can I come?" he asked again. He had never felt so much at risk.

"I think Anabel would like to meet you," Daisy said slowly. "She's always had an eye for men. Yes, that's a fine idea. And unless you've been to *La Marée,* you can't really understand when I talk about it. But what will Supracorp do without you?"

"Who?"

In the early days of July the ivy which covers *La Marée* begins to turn red in streaks. By the end of the month the entire sprawling *manoir* is hidden by rippling flames of shouting color and the huge-headed dahlias in the garden are in full flaunting bloom, each one of them worthy of a Fauve canvas all to itself.

Anabel was standing at the front door when Daisy and Shannon drove up. As she kissed her, Daisy inspected Anabel carefully for signs of change. There was an expression of resolution on her loving face which had never been there before. Perhaps it was a sign of the price she had paid for acceptance, for knowing the truth. And there was a new and unfamiliar shallowness in the color of her eyes. But her gaze with its supreme pragmatism had not changed, nor had her eternal amusement at life.

"What have we here?" she exclaimed, looking Shannon over. "A distinctly tall and rather gorgeous American? That does make for a pleasant change. Why is his hair so black and his eyes so blue? But, of course, it's Irish blood. I must be getting old not to see that immediately. Daisy, couldn't you find an American who looked like an American—rather blond and bland? I've always heard about them, but I've never seen a specimen. Perhaps they don't exist? Never mind—we'll make do with this nice, big, beautiful one. Come in, children, and have some sherry."

"You're a terrible flirt," said Shannon.

"Nonsense, I've never flirted in my life. I have always been dreadfully misunderstood," Anabel said, with that laugh that had half-seduced every man who heard it. The red of her shiny hair was fading and she had grown thinner but, as she led them through the salon out to the terrace overlooking the sea, it was uncanny to see with what gentle strokes time seemed to have touched *La Marée* and its owner. Daisy's heart leaped as she thought how this place, this haven, at least, could never be taken away from Anabel.

That evening, after dinner, Shannon took himself off to read in one of the balcony window seats above the salon while Daisy and Anabel sat together in the chairs around the dining-room fireplace. On this summer night there was no fire, but the memory of the many holiday fires of childhood still lingered there.

"How do you feel, *really?*" Daisy asked, at last.

"Now? Not really all that much different. The first few months were a bit nasty—drug therapy isn't much fun, but now I only have to see the doctor once a month and I'm over the sticky part. I've lost weight, which I rather like, but my energy is low ... still, I can't complain, darling. It could have been much worse. I promise you I'm telling the truth."

"I know you are." Daisy bit her lip before she spoke again. She didn't want to use Ram's name. "Did you let him know you didn't need him?" she asked.

"The instant I got your letter. I told him that I wouldn't trouble him again, ever, and I told him why, or he'd never have believed me."

"What did you say?" Daisy asked anxiously.

"I simply said that you'd been picked to do some commercials and that you were going to make enough money to take care of both me and Dani."

"And thank God for that," Daisy said, gazing into the fire.

"Yes. Ram is truly evil. I wish I could have helped him, but it was too late when I met him. Yet he was only twelve or so."

"Who was to blame?" Daisy asked.

"I've often wondered. He was always unhappy, always envious, always an outsider, a child of divorce, of course, but that can never be the whole explanation. He was also your father's son and your father was a hard and selfish man. Often he was a cruel man. Perhaps Stash could have helped Ram, but he never even bothered to try."

"You've never said that to me before," Daisy said, astonished.

"You weren't mature enough to hear it ... to hear it and understand it, and know that I still love your father even as I say it. Now I think it important that you know. That day Stash left Danielle at the school, I almost left him, too."

"Why didn't you?"

"Because he needed me to keep him human ... and, as I said, I loved him ... and perhaps, even then, a little bit, I stayed for you. At six you know, you were quite irresistible ... before you grew so old and ugly."

"Flirting again, Anabel. I'll tell Shannon."

"Ah, that Shannon. Since you have finally asked me, I approve. You've begun to show a little sense. I've been worried about you, Daisy, for years. You have a truly incredible talent for staying out of trouble—it wasn't normal. Now, with Shannon—ah, well, I have to admit that I envy you . . ."

"Anabel! I hardly know him!"

"Indeed! Then, if I were only thirty years younger . . . or even twenty . . . you wouldn't have a chance! I'd take him right away from you."

"You would, too, wouldn't you, Anabel? You really would," Daisy marveled. "No sense of fair play at all?"

"Where a man like that is concerned? You must be joking. What does 'fair play' have to do with it? Your British education has given you some very odd notions. No wonder they lost India."

Soon afterward, Anabel declared that she felt tired and she was going to bed. She had given Daisy her old room, the walls still covered in green silk, now faded and even frayed in places, and she had put Shannon in the brown and white room, the most comfortable of her guest rooms, all the way at the other end of the house.

After they'd said their goodnights, Daisy sat on her window seat in the dark and looked out over the spangled estuary of the Seine to the lights of Le Havre. There must be ghosts here, she thought, watching the beloved silhouettes of the three umbrella pines, listening to the rustle of the long-leaved eucalyptus trees, smelling the wood-brown ivied fragrance of the walls of *La Marée*, hearing the occasional lowing of cows from the dairy farms at the bottom of the hill. There *are* ghosts, but tonight I'm free of them, tonight I'm safe from them, tonight nothing can hurt me . . . I could even walk in the woods and feel no fear. Abruptly, she remembered Ram, stretched out in a familiar pose in one of the striped deck chairs, looking at her intently through his half-closed eyes, beckoning to her with a careless, owning hand. No, you have no power over me, mad ghost, Daisy thought, none at all—and you know it.

Shall I walk in the woods, she wondered as she brushed her hair. Sparks of static electricity like a flock of indignant fireflies crackled in the night air. She wandered over to the chest of drawers in which she kept a store of old clothes for her visits to *La Marée*. She was wearing a pair of much-washed cotton pajamas which she'd owned since she was sixteen. The jacket had missing buttons and the pants had shrunk.

Or, Daisy asked herself, shall I go and see if Pat Shannon is quite comfortable in his room? Standing with the hairbrush still clasped in her hand, she thought of how he had looked rushing down the terraces of Berkeley Castle. What urgent errand had brought him there? She remembered how quickly he had brought her back to Claridge's last night, understanding that she was so tired that even an arm around her shoulders would have been a burden to her, of how tactfully he had left her alone to talk with Anabel earlier that evening. And yet I do believe he finds me attractive, she told herself, smiling in the dark, remembering the wordless moment when he had kissed the palm of her hand. Yes, unquestionably attractive. He's almost *too* considerate. Wouldn't it be hospitable to see if he's comfortable? Truly and deeply hospitable? Thoughtfully, Daisy took off her pajamas and searched rapidly in her suitcase for the good-luck present Kiki had given her before she'd left for England. Daisy pulled out of the tissue paper a nightgown such as she'd never owned, a slithery gown the color of apricots, made of two shining pieces of satin held together at the sides only by tiny bows which linked one piece to the other at eight-inch intervals. Daisy dropped it over her head, gasping as the fall of satin touched her naked skin with its coolness. Then she put on the matching robe that closed with a bow at the base of her throat. She considered looking in the mirror to see how she looked, but she didn't want to turn on the light.

Daisy opened her door as silently as a somnambulist, but there was nothing of the sleepwalker about her steps as she walked, on her hospitable mission, quietly, but with eager determination, down the entire length of the house to the door of Pat Shannon's room. She knocked at the door and waited, hardly breathing, for it to open. There was no response. She knocked again, rather louder this time. It was, of course, possible that he was asleep, she thought. But it was also entirely possible that he wasn't comfortable. There was only one way to make sure. Daisy opened the door and saw him, sound asleep in the wide, double bed. She padded silently across the room and knelt on the floor next to his dreaming form, throwing off the long robe as she leaned over him. There was enough moonlight for her to study his face. In sleep the lines on either side of Shannon's mouth softened and their relaxation lent his characteristic expression of purposeful banditry a youthfulness at which Daisy peered tenderly. His hair, always tousled, fell more carelessly than he would have permitted in a waking moment, adding to his unguarded look. He seemed trapped in a savage solitude, Daisy thought, wondering what he was dreaming about. Shannon, so often seen in action, swift, set apart, beyond self-doubt or failure, the powerful conductor of the great conglomerate orchestra, was sleeping the sleep of childhood, his wide mouth vulnerable, somehow beseeching, a look on his face as if he'd lost his way. She pressed her lips softly to his. He slept on. Again she kissed him and still he slept. This is not at all gallant of him, thought Daisy, and kissed him once more. He woke up gasping.

"Oh, the *best* kiss . . ." he mumbled, still half-asleep.

She kissed him again, fleetingly, before he could say more.

"The sweetest kiss . . . give me another . . ."

"You've already had four."

"No, impossible, I don't remember, they don't count," he insisted, finally awake.

"I just came by to see if you were comfortable. Now that I see you are, I'll go back to my room. I'm so sorry I woke you—go back to sleep."

"Oh, Lord, don't! I'm not! It's freezing here and the mattress is lumpy and the bed's too short and too narrow and I need another pillow," he grumbled of Anabel's luxurious guest accommodations, as he adroitly lifted Daisy from the floor where she was still kneeling and tucked her under his covers.

Shannon cradled her in his arms as gently as a cherished child and they nestled quietly, each tentatively experiencing the warmth of the other's body, the sound of the other's breathing and the beating of the other's many pulses—a communication without words, so full of a sense of the extraordinary that neither of them dared to speak. Little by little they sank deeper, and surrendered themselves, with their whole sentient beings, becoming immersed, enlaced in awareness of the life force of the other, until, without voices or motion they had attained a trust that had been waiting to be born.

It seemed a long time before Shannon began to imprint a blizzard of tiny kisses at the point where Daisy's jaw joined her throat, that particularly warm curve, spendthrift with beauty, that he had not allowed himself to realize had haunted him for weeks. Daisy felt fragile and rare to Shannon, as if he'd trapped a young unicorn, some strange, mythological creature. Her hair was the most intense source of light in the room since it reflected the moonlight creeping through the windows, and by its light he saw her eyes, open, rapt and glowing; twin dark stars.

It seemed to him now as if they had never kissed before. The kisses she had awakened him with were so chaste, so tentative that they were only the memory of a kiss. Now he pressed her mouth with a rain of kisses like blazing flowers.

Oh, yes! she thought, opening her lips to him, tumbled and craving and daring. She arched her body toward him, nudging his hands toward her breasts until they were clasped and claimed. It was she, not he, who raised her nightgown over her head in one swift impatient movement and tossed it on the floor. It was she who guided his hands down the length of her body, she who touched him wherever she could reach, as playfully as a dolphin, until he realized that her fragility was strength, and that she wanted him without reserve. He bent to the glorious task, dimly aware that never before had life flowed through him without the static and interferences of thought, never had he been so close to drinking the elemental wine of life. He tasted it on her lips and on her nipples and on her belly, his whole skin drank thirstily of her and when he thrust into her, he knew he had arrived at last at the source, the spring. Now, Daisy lay quietly, invaded, filled, utterly willing. She felt as if she were floating down a clean, clear river with birds singing in green trees on the bank. But there was more; more than this blissful peace and together they quickened, panted, quested as eagerly as two hunts-men after an elusive prey, plunging through the forests of each other until they came at last to their victories, Daisy with a sound that was at least as much a cry of astonish-ment as it was of joy. She had experienced fulfillment before, but never with this excellence, this plenitude.

Afterward, as they lay together, half asleep, but unwill-ing to drift apart into unconsciousness, Daisy farted, in a tiny series of absolutely irrepressible little pops that seemed to her to go on for a minute.

"Termites riveting," observed Shannon lazily. She lunged out from under the covers and almost managed to jump off the bed before his long arms pinned her on the mattress.

"Minuscule termites, midget Rosie the Riveters. You get an E for effort."

"Let me go!" she cried, humiliated.

"Not until you realize that if you fart, you fart—and that's fine . . . farting's part of life."

"Oh, please stop repeating that word!" Daisy begged, more embarrassed than ever.

"You've never lived with a man." He stated this rather than asking.

"What makes you think that?" she said quickly. Of course she hadn't, but at twenty-five, what woman would admit it?

"Because of how you reacted to . . . ah, giving a salute to the queen . . . does that sound better?"

"Yes, much," she murmured, pressing her face into his shoulder. "Is that your idea of a romantic declaration?"

"The circumstances were not of my choosing. I think I can do better."

"Go right ahead."

"Dearest, darling, adorable Daisy, how can I convince you of the profound chivalry and absolute tenderness and devotion which lie in my heart of hearts?"

"You just have." She trembled with laughter. "Now, go to sleep, Shannon, or it will be morning. I'm going back to my room and you'll have to make the best of the terrible lumpy bed."

"But why? Sleep with me. Don't go. You can't leave me here all alone," he protested.

"Yes, I can. Don't ask me why because I don't know." He sat up, watching as she wrapped her robe around her naked body, all shadows and secrets in the moonlight. "Goodnight, sleep tight, and don't let those termites bite," she whispered, kissing him on the lips with the speed of a hummingbird, and was gone.

At breakfast Anabel serenely offered Shannon a choice of five kinds of honey to go on his buttered brioche while she managed simultaneously to watch Daisy, incendiary with joy, yet limpid as dawn and dressed like a ruffian.

"And what are your plans for today, children?" she asked.

"Children?" Shannon grinned at her.

"A generic term," responded Anabel, "for anyone not of my generation."

"You don't have a generation," he assured her.

"And you grow more charming every day."

"We were going to walk into Honfleur to show Shannon the port, but perhaps I should just leave you two alone together," Daisy suggested. "You could spend the time doting on each other."

"No, much as I would like that, there's a long list of things for you two to pick up for dinner. When you're ready to go, it's on the kitchen table. I'm going to cut some flowers," Anabel said tranquilly.

"I'll go get it now—I'm all set," Daisy said.

"Like that?" Shannon asked.

"Naturally." Daisy looked down at her costume. When she woke that morning she had jumped into a pair of jeans with holes in the knees which dated from her freshman year at Santa Cruz, a sleeveless jersey equally as dilapidated, and tennis shoes that had weathered almost a decade. Around her neck she'd slung a moth-eaten navy cardigan which had been part of the detested uniform at Lady Alden's School, worn when the girls had marched into the park to play rounders. She'd made two long, absolutely simple braids which hung down her back, and she wore no make-up at all. "Not chic enough for you?" she asked him with a grin which should have told him that she knew exactly what she was doing and that she had prepared this new metamorphosis of herself just to further enchant and befuddle him. However, she doubted that he was in any fit condition to figure it out—hers were hardly Supracorp tactics.

"I like you like that," Shannon said. "It makes another Princess Daisy for my collection. And quite a different one than the Princess Daisy I saw recently, just last night in fact."

She said nothing but she instantly noted his words. *Another* Princess Daisy? His *collection*? Her grin faded imperceptibly while Anabel's eyes brightened as she watched them. She supposed they thought she couldn't read their words and actions as clearly as if they'd made an announcement. Oh, but it was strange to watch old stories being acted out as if they were fresh and new, and had never happened before. Still, one never knew the endings, only the beginnings were the same.

"I'm trying to count how many people kissed you on both cheeks this morning," Shannon said when they had finally filled their shopping baskets and found a seat at a café looking out onto the arc of the old port with its motley collection of boats bobbing in front of the tall, narrow houses that edged the opposite side of the little harbor. "There was the butcher and the cheese man and the vegetable lady and the fruit man and the fish lady and the mayor and the policeman and the postman—who else?"

"The baker and his wife, the man who sells newspapers, the old fisherman who used to take me out in his boat and the two art-gallery owners."

"But the waiter here only shook hands. Why is he so unfriendly?"

"He's new here—It's been about eight years since he was hired, so I scarcely know him," Daisy answered, drinking her Cinzano.

"This is really home for you?"

"It's as close to a home as I've had since my father was killed. And remember, they watched me grow up, every summer from the time I was a child. Nothing changes here . . . only more tourists."

"You're lucky to have a place like this," he said wistfully.

"And you? What do you have? You complained that you didn't know anything about me. What do I know about you?" She touched his lower lip with one finger, the quirky lip which she found herself looking at so often, that expressive lip which could be thoughtful, humorous, decisive—she didn't doubt it could be disapproving, angry—perhaps even merciless?

"I have a few faint memories of being a little boy with a mother and father who loved each other and loved me very much—we were very poor, I realize now, and we didn't have any family in the mill town where my father worked—at least I don't remember any. He was a mechanic, and I think that he must have been out of work a lot because I remember that he was around the house much of the time—too much." He paused, shook his head and sipped his drink. "When I was five they were both killed in an accident—a streetcar—and I grew up in a Catholic orphanage—I was a miserable kid, suddenly all alone, not understanding anything and too much of a handful for anyone to want to adopt me. It wasn't until I realized that the only way out was working, working much harder than anyone else, getting better marks, being the best at everything, that I changed—and by that time I was too old to be adopted."

"How old was that?"

"Maybe eight—nine. The nuns put up with a hell of a lot from me."

"Do you ever go back?"

"The orphanage is closed now. They ran out of orphans —or maybe they relocated it, but I've lost track completely. I wouldn't want to go back anyway. My real life started when I got a scholarship to St. Anthony's at fourteen."

Daisy listened attentively, almost painfully, trying to extract the secret meaning of his bare recital. Nobody's "real" life could begin at fourteen, she thought, too much of what forms the personality of the adult has happened by then. Perhaps she would never know enough about him to be able to share his childhood as he had shared hers. Perhaps it didn't matter? In any case, they would soon be late for lunch, which would annoy Anabel.

As they walked back, up the steep hill of the Côte de Grace, Shannon was thoughtful. He'd never talked as much about his early years. He sensed that he'd left out something, missed some essential connections. But all he could find to explain himself to Daisy was his favorite quotation from his durable sage.

"Listen—this is the way I feel about life—George Bernard Shaw said it. 'People are always blaming their circumstances for what they are. I don't believe in circumstances. The people who get on in this world are the people who get up and look for the circumstances they want, and if they can't find them, they make them.'" He had stopped walking as he spoke.

"Is that your motto, too?" she asked.

"Yes. What do you think of it?"

"It's almost probably half true . . . which isn't at all bad for a motto," she said. "You might try to give me a kiss . . . there's no one to see us."

He kissed her for a long moment and Daisy felt that she was growing around him as a climbing rose grows around a sturdy arbor.

"Am I a 'circumstance'?" she murmured.

"You are a silly question." He pulled her braids. "I'll race you back."

As the three of them ate dinner Anabel asked, "How long can you stay, Patrick?"

"I'm leaving tomorrow," he said. There was regret in his voice but no touch of indecision.

"But can't you stay just one more day? You've just come," Anabel protested.

"Impossible. I've been out of the office and out of touch for days. The people at Supracorp will think I'm dead. It's never happened before."

"Don't you take vacations?" Anabel asked curiously.

"Not out-of-touch vacations. Not even out-of-touch long weekends. It makes them nervous or it makes me nervous; I'm not really sure which." He laughed, the buccaneer again.

"Daisy, you can stay a while, can't you?" Anabel inquired hopefully.

"No, she can't, Anabel," Shannon said firmly. "She has to get back to New York. There are dozens of things going on—interviews, photographs—my publicity people have been working on stuff that I don't know about yet. Remember, Supracorp has a ton of money tied up in Princess Daisy. The commercials were only the beginning."

Daisy bit the inside of her lip in vexation. She was perfectly aware that she had to return, but she bristled to hear Shannon answering a question Anabel had asked her. But there was a gulf between her responsibility to the corporation and being told by Shannon what she could or could not do. Did he, by any grotesque chance, think that now *he* owned her? Bugger that!

She turned to Anabel, ignoring Shannon's words. "Actually I really have to go back for Kiki's wedding. . . . Nothing Supracorp needs me for is more important."

"Well, thank heaven that wedding's taking place," Anabel said with that slightly condescending appreciation of respectability to which only the most successful of retired courtesans feels entitled. "From what you've written me, and what her poor mother has hinted at, I'd say it comes not a minute too soon."

Daisy giggled wickedly. She had a pretty shrewd idea of Anabel's life history.

Anabel looked at her sharply with the eternal, invaluable complicity of females. Although they were speaking of

Kiki they were both thinking of Shannon. He's a good man, and you deserve this—go to it! Anabel's glance told Daisy. Don't jump to conclusions, Daisy's eyes warned Anabel, as clearly as if she had spoken.

24

*W*hat do you mean I 'tried so hard to get him'? I'd never sink so low," Kiki fulminated.

"Selective memory," Daisy marveled.

"You're the one who forgets. Who was a free agent? Footloose, jaunty, jolly, lighthearted, having the most wonderful time in the best of all possible worlds? ME! You never saw me go out with the same guy for two nights in a row," Kiki swaggered.

"Or in the same bed for more than three months at a time," Daisy replied.

"Oh, that. You know, Daisy, you have a sort of shit-eating grin now that I get a good look at you. And you used to be almost pretty." Kiki hunched her bare shoulders in a way which indicated clearly that she had given up on her friend. Dressed only in a pair of unqualifiedly indecent black lace underpants from Frederick's of Hollywood, she pawed in an idle way through a pile of spidery, suggestive garter belts, some black, some red. Around her neck she had draped a pair of thin black nylon stockings with seams down the back.

"Just answer some questions for me," Daisy said patiently. "Do you actually hate him?"

"I wouldn't go that far," Kiki answered in a disobliging voice. "Hate is too strong a word to use—indifferent might be more like it."

"Does he bore you?"

"Not totally—he just doesn't fascinate me. My God, Daisy, the world is full of men, absolutely crammed with them. Do you realize how many men there are out there?

Each one different, each one with some particular kink or craziness or talent or charm or sweetness that *you'll* never know about because you're too lazy to investigate them? You really lack something—*tempérament* I think they call it in France—it's what makes great amorous women, the legendary lovers—George Sand, Ninon de Lenclos and *me*, damn it, only you won't admit it."

"I'll admit it," Daisy said in a conciliatory voice. "You were really something."

"I still am!" Kiki objected like a bad angel. She shook her head until her hair looked like a ball of tumbling tumbleweed, and her tanned naked breasts quivered in indignation.

"When you make love," Daisy asked, "can you tell him how it feels—you know—tell him that you like this or that, or do it more, or three inches farther to the left—can you tell him things like that just as easily and freely as if he were rubbing your back?"

"Well, naturally," Kiki said in a mean-spirited tone. "But so what?"

"Just asking, just indulging my prurient curiosity."

"Indulge mine—what about Patrick Shannon?" Kiki asked, suddenly fizzing with interest. "Just precisely what is going on with you two?"

"We're getting to know each other," Daisy answered with dignity.

"Oh-ho—so you won't answer the kind of questions you expect me to answer."

"I'll tell you anything you want to know."

"Is he in love with you?" Kiki pounced.

"He's very . . . attentive."

"You mean he hasn't said anything definite, hasn't asked you to marry him?" Kiki put aside her own troubles. She'd been so busy complaining that she just hadn't had time to interrogate Daisy.

"No, and that's the way I prefer it."

"Keeping him at a safe distance, like your other men, is that what's happening?"

"The distance is too narrow to be called safe. There's a confusion—he's so much *there*—I love to watch him dealing with the world, but he's so dominating that it scares me . . . a little anyway. Or maybe a lot. I find myself wondering if he doesn't intend to run everybody and everything, and yet I can tell him almost anything and count on him to understand. Still . . . I'm not absolutely sure that it isn't just another one of his many ways of getting what he wants. I just don't know. Sometimes—it's so right, so *honorable*—and then I'll find myself wondering if he doesn't think of me as just another *acquisition*, like having the Elstree company embodied in one person. One thing is clear—he's totally in love with that whole 'Princess Daisy' *idea*. And I don't like *that* one bit! Oh, shit, I'm mixed up."

"But is he a good lover?" Kiki probed. Daisy blushed. "Hmmm?" hummed Kiki encouragingly. "You promised you'd tell."

"The best—oh—better than that! But that's no reason to get a fix on the future. I'm not ready to even think about making decisions. I don't want to jump into anything prematurely. I want to stay the way I am, and I'm not going to get deeply emotionally involved . . ."

Kiki jumped on her like a hellcat. "But you're the one who's telling me to let myself be corralled, captured, rounded-up and branded and tied up in chains like a galley slave! Daisy Valensky, you have one hell of a nerve! How dare you give me advice when you're not ready to get involved! Of all the revolting clichés!"

"Well," said Daisy mildly, "it's not *my* wedding day, those three hundred people downstairs in your mother's living room aren't waiting to see me get married, I'm not the one with eight bridesmaids and eight ushers, to say nothing of a groom, all dithering around and wondering why you're locked in here with me and when you're coming out."

"It's all his fault!" Kiki cried, her slender body looking as forlorn as if she were a kitten who'd been left out in the wet all night. "That smooth-tongued advertising man, I should never ever have let him talk me into this. Oh, Christ, what a horrible mistake."

"You're the one who's a cliché, darling Kiki. You're just like all the others before they get married, don't you realize?" Daisy asked kindly.

"They're the clichés, I'm the *real thing!*" Kiki stormed. "What *am* I going to do? Is it too late to call it off? No, it's never too late. Who cares what people say? Daisy, look, I won't ask you ever again to do anything for me, but could you just go and find my mother and tell her to call it off? She can handle it, she's good at organizing things. I think she'd take it better coming from you." She looked at Daisy with low cunning.

Daisy shook her head. "Tergiversations. I should have known."

"What the hell are they? Don't change the subject!"

"Repeated changes of attitude or opinion—Kiki, you know perfectly well that your mother would never call it off. And even if she did, would that make you happy? How long would it take for you to change your mind again? Nope. You're going through this if I have to haul you down there myself. But you'd be more comfortable if you put on your wedding dress first."

"You're a cold hard bitch, Daisy Valensky, and I'll never forgive you as long as I live."

"Oh," said Daisy, looking out of the window of Kiki's bedroom, "I just saw Peter Spivak drive up. Here comes the judge! We're practically in business."

"No!" Kiki said frantically. "I *can't!*"

"Do it one day at a time, Kiki. The way AA tells people to give up drinking, just one day at a time. Don't sit around thinking about how you'll feel living with the same man for fifty years—just ask yourself if you could stand being married to Luke until tomorrow morning—or even just till midnight tonight. Could you possibly endure it? Just till midnight?"

"I suppose," Kiki said sulkily.

"Well, that's all you have to do. Tomorrow you can get divorced. Okay?"

"I see right through you—you know I won't want to get divorced tomorrow. *Nobody* ever got divorced the day after she got married. It's unheard of. That whole number is just more of the kind of scheming that got me into this!" Kiki accused her.

"Right, I admit it. But now get dressed! On the double!" Daisy sounded as menacing as if she were talking to Wingo.

Kiki chose a red lace garter belt and put on the black stockings, hooking them carefully into the red satin snaps and straightening the seams with gloomy attention.

"I love your underwear," said Daisy. "It's so suitable."

"Damn it, Daisy, if I have to wear white at least I'll know that what's on underneath isn't Miss Grosse Pointe Virgin of the Year," Kiki said, stepping defiantly into a pair of plain white satin pumps. "Fuck-me stockings without fuck-me shoes," she said sadly. Glaring at Daisy, she opened the closet where her white satin wedding dress was hanging, draped in plastic to keep it spotless.

"I think I'm supposed to be doing that," Daisy said, jumping up. Her chiffon dress was the color of spring grass and her hair was worn in plaited coils over her ears. She had on flat green slippers so she wouldn't tower over Kiki any more than was absolutely necessary. Daisy carefully slipped the wedding dress out of its protective wrappings and unzipped it so that Kiki could put it on. She held it by the shoulders and fluttered it temptingly at Kiki, the way a bullfighter attracts a fighting bull. *"Olé,* anybody?"

"Oh, shit . . . *olé* . . ." said Kiki grudgingly. "As if I had a choice."

"Girls? Girls? Aren't you ready yet?" Eleanor Kavanaugh's nervous voice was heard through the locked door. She'd been completely dressed for over an hour now. The wedding was unquestionably going to be late.

"We're getting there, Aunt Ellie," Daisy answered. Kiki pulled a horrible face but said nothing.

"Can I come in?"

"Ah—we'll be out in a sec," Daisy called.

"Do you need any help, Daisy darling?" she quavered. She couldn't have the vapors, Eleanor Kavanaugh told herself. They would wrinkle her dress.

"How about . . ." Kiki began, but Daisy put her hand over her mouth.

"No, we've got everything we need, Aunt Ellie," Daisy said. "Honestly. Why don't you just go downstairs for a minute."

"I was just going to ask for some Valium," Kiki whispered cantankerously.

"I've *got* Valium."

"You do?"

"Did you think I was going to let Theseus disgrace us?" Both girls looked at the lurcher, sitting calmly and happily on a pillow, with a woven satin basket full of baby's breath, white orchids and freesia tied under his chin, a leash of white velvet around his neck. "He's doped to the eyeballs," Daisy said, proudly.

"A stoned flower dog!"

"Couldn't take a chance."

"Oh, Daisy, darling, you'd do that for me?" Kiki wailed.

"Of course. Now why don't you put on that dress, for me? Hmmm?"

Slowly Kiki allowed Daisy to hook her into the full-skirted dress, the white of the best quality whipping cream, the white of a baked Alaska, the white of a meringue glacé. She finally looked at herself in the full-length mirror and a seraphic smile began to touch her lips. Daisy, encouraged by this sign, asked, "What are you thinking about?"

"All my old lovers. Just think if they could see me now—they'd be *sick* with envy."

"Is that any way for a bride to feel?"

"It's the *only* way ... imagine, getting married if you didn't have any old lovers, what a bizarre idea!"

Jerry Kavanaugh, Kiki's father, in his morning coat and striped pants, now knocked on the door. "Kiki, for heaven's sake, when are you going to be ready? Everyone's waiting. My Lord, Kiki, don't just hang around in there, girl—get moving."

"We're coming right out, Uncle Jerry," Daisy assured him at the top of her voice. "Kiki, let me put on the veil, quickly now, no more kidding around. They're playing your song."

"What song?"

" 'Here Comes the Bride.' "

Kiki paled, kissed Daisy on the cheek and squared her shoulders. "It's all so fucking grown-up!" she murmured plaintively as she walked toward the door and the future.

Candice Bloom was thinking. She stood, as always, with her hands thrust deep into her pockets, leaning slightly backward, her sharp hipbones tilted prominently forward. Candice, who never let anyone call her Candy twice, squeaked with chic and had refused one excellent job in California on the grounds that there was simply nowhere there to shop for shoes. Her assistant, Jenny Antonio, waited patiently for her instructions.

"Call Grossinger's," she said, finally, "and the Concord. Find out the total capacity of their snow-making machines and how long it takes before the stuff will start to melt in mid-September, assuming that we don't have our usual heat wave, which, in itself, would be a miracle. And ask what it costs to rent them. *Tu comprends?* Oh, and get the Parks Department on the phone for me. Something tells me I have to get a permit for this. Where are the proofs for the invitation?"

"What if Grossinger's and the Concord are using their machines themselves? Don't they have skiing practically all year round?" Jenny asked, with the eager and bright-eyed intelligence of her twenty-three years.

Candice looked at her in stupefaction. "Jenny, you don't know much about how Supracorp works yet, do you? We're giving The Great Russian Winter Palace Party of this or any other year, we're taking over the entire Tavern on the Green in Central Park to launch the Princess Daisy line—and that means *snow*—even if we have to *buy* snow-making machines or build them. Just get on the phone and stop asking silly questions. *Vraiment!* I bet you don't even have the answers for me on the troikas?"

"Any carriage drawn by three horses can count as a troika, so we don't have to find actual sleds. Just the carriages and a hell of a lot of horses."

"One problem solved and ten thousand to go," Candice brooded. "When is my meeting with Warner Le Roy to discuss the menu?"

"He wanted to make it tomorrow at lunch, but that's when you and Daisy are having lunch with Leo Lerman for the 'People Are Talking About' column, so I said I'd call back."

"Good. This is really the ultimate crunch," Candice Bloom said with a gloomy relish. "It's all very well to run commercials and print ads—and thank God they're all done—but without P.R. you can forget your enormous impact because you don't get free editorial space, and without free space you might just as well not exist. Now get out that folder again and let's take another look at it. Okay—we have all the fashion magazines and *WWD*, but they had to give us the space—look at the advertising dollars they're getting. And *Cosmo*'s promised us something, also Trudy Owett's spread will run next month in the *Journal*. Here are the clips from AP, UPI, Reuters and the Chicago Trib Syndicate. So far so good. But we haven't heard from the Los Angeles Times Syndicate and I want them. *Merde!* Where did you put my list of columnists? Why hasn't Shirley Eder called back, damn it? Try her in Vegas ... or at the Beverly Hills Hotel. Has Liz Smith confirmed? Only a maybe? The 'Today Show' is still being negative and Mike Douglas and Dinah all want to know what Daisy can talk about. Merv, bless him, said yes—next month sometime. But the others insist on a theme, damn it, and they don't give a shit that she's a gorgeous princess." Candice prowled around her office in disgust. "*Shtick!* They want *shtick* from a princess, a hook, some peg to hang her on—it'd be easier if she were a stand-up comic on roller skates."

"You can't really blame them," Jenny ventured.

"I don't. I know their problems better than mine. But Shannon isn't going to give me brownie points for being turned down for even the best reasons. We've been trying —and not doing badly under the circumstances—to create an instant celebrity. But Daisy's not famous for being famous, like a Gabor, she's not a designer, she's not a major heiress, she's always avoided publicity like the plague—so we had to start from ground zero. Sure, her father was a hot-shot playboy and her mother was a legend in her time, only all that was over twenty years ago and who remembers? Francesca Vernon never made another movie after she married Stash Valensky; she just disappeared." Candice assumed her habitual expression of discouraged optimism as her secretary buzzed her for a phone call.

"Put her through." She put her hand over the mouthpiece and hissed excitedly. "It's Jane, my old, so-called friend from *People*. That bitch has been dodging my calls for practically half a year. *Now* she's decided to call! It's got to be bad news." Both Jenny and Candice waited galvanized.

"Hi, Jane—*pas mal*, and you? Good. Princess Daisy? No, we haven't definitely got a go-ahead from any other news magazine yet but it's all in the works. *Exclusively? Merde!* Jane, I'd give my all to say yes, but I just don't think my boss would agree. After all *Time* and *Newsweek* and *New York*, you should pardon the expression, all have departments she'll fit into perfectly. *A COVER STORY!* Are you sure? No, no, I didn't mean that . . . but it's just that I'd have to promise him and if it didn't work out I'd be looking for a job. *Definitely?* You said definitely? Ah ha. Ah ha. I see. He's absolutely right. I couldn't agree more. Ah ha. Got it. Look, let me check it out with the man and I'll get back to you within a half-hour. A quarter of an hour. Right. Bye."

She put down the phone with the stunned care of one who has just handled an artifact which has been buried for five thousand years, and that proves the existence of another civilization.

"It's *incroyable*," Candice said in a remote voice.

"I don't get it—you pitched them a story—but a *cover?*"

"She said that her boss is tired of having eight out of ten cover stories coming right out of Hollywood or the tube—he thinks the West Coast is trying to take over, in spite of the fact that the editorial department is here. He says *People*'s turning into nothing but a fan magazine. He wants something different, something high-fashion and elegant and New York—and he fell in love with the pictures of Daisy we sent over. Also he had a mad crush on Francesca Vernon when he was young—saw all her movies a dozen times—he says Daisy has her eyes."

"My God," Jenny said slowly.

"Jenny, this is fucking unreal and you may never see it happen twice so don't get big ideas, but now you understand the fatal fascination of public relations. And my analyst had the nerve to hint that I had a Snow White complex—he suspects that in my heart of hearts I'm waiting for my prince to come." She laughed shortly and gleefully. "Well the prince just did! Wait till I tell my doctor that!"

"What'll he say?" Jenny asked curiously.

"Nothing—Good Lord, Jenny, you are an innocent—it's the principle of the thing. It proves my analyst doesn't know *everything*. Oh, shit, if he doesn't know *everything* maybe he doesn't know *anything*." She opened her mouth in a grimace of worry.

"The other day you told me that analysts were only human," Jenny reminded her.

"Jenny, this whole thing is too deep for you. You're not neurotic enough. But you will be. *Je t'assure*. How long has it been since Jane called?"

"About a minute."

"Too soon to call back. I don't want to seem overeager."

"But you said you'd have to check with Shannon, and he's in Tokyo again."

"Check? On a *People* cover? Not while I'm alive! You don't think I need his permission for this?"

"Exactly two minutes," Jenny said helpfully.

"Balls! I may not last. Oh, wow!" Cynical, blasé Candice Bloom did a frenetic Irish jig in the center of her office carpet. She stopped and faced her astonished assistant. "Bet you didn't know the only four magazines you have to stock at any magazine stand in the whole United States—the must magazines?" Without waiting for a reply, she recited the four sacred names. *"Playboy, Penthouse, Cos-*

mo and *People*—as long as you have those four, you can pick and choose from among hundreds of others from *Field and Stream* to *Commentary,* but the big four are the ones that keep a newsstand going. Without them, you're dead. End of second lesson for today. What was your first?"

"If Shannon wants snow, we get snow."

"*Très bien, très bien!* You may make a P.R. person someday. Then you can afford your own analyst."

A week later Daisy hesitated rebelliously outside the ostentatiously discreet studio of Danillo, the world's most celebrated portrait photographer. She held Theseus's leash tightly as she studied the inconspicuous door behind which was a brownstone as narrow as any private house in Manhattan. The door itself was adorned only by a single push button and a small brass plate which bore the initial D.

The emotion with which Daisy faced the door was divided into equal parts of resolution and reluctance. Earlier that morning, as she was getting ready to leave, Kiki had telephoned and offered to take Theseus off her hands while she was sitting for this all-important photograph, but Daisy had refused. She knew perfectly well that clinging to Theseus was a sign of her precariously ambiguous feelings toward the process which would be put into high gear by today's session. She knew how childish it was, and she had also decided that she didn't give a good goddamn. The idea that *People* was actually going to do a cover story on her made the reality of the disappearance of her privacy seem far more palpable than had the making of the commercials, the interviews or posing for the ads. Nothing Candice Bloom had planned for her had quite seemed *real* until this moment, and now everything seemed focused on the inescapability of the next few hours. Yet her obligation to go through with the sitting was stronger than her premonitions, and she pushed firmly on the maliciously unimpressive button.

When the door clicked open, Daisy, closely followed by her dog, ambled into the small and crowded reception room which was already filled with people waiting for her. While they chirped greetings, Daisy surveyed her surroundings. They were remarkable chiefly for the absence of Danillo.

Daisy had expected this. She had overheard too many models gossiping not to know that Danillo would stage his entrance much later in the proceedings.

She felt the glances of sweeping appraisal from Alonzo, the make-up artist, and Robertson, the hairdresser. The two were veterans; they knew when Danillo booked them that they would have to put in at least three hours work on his subject before he started to shoot. His work depended on their talents. He needed them in order to achieve his trademark, the more-perfect-than-life face. His success was not based on his camera technique or communication with his subject or any depth of inspiration. All of his portraits had the same basic quality, an easily identifiable, inhumanly slick veneer, a spurious but convincing imitation of invention that resulted in a faultless, irresistible and dependable surface of resolute, just-short-of-plastic perfection that editors loved. They never worried about the results of a sitting with Danillo, and Alonzo and Robertson, who were paid seventy-five dollars an hour, with a minimum guarantee of five hours of work, were delighted to have been chosen today from his pool of fawning painters and crimpers.

"I won't need either of you," Daisy said, smiling at the two men. "I thought that had been settled."

Robertson glanced swiftly at Alonzo. Who did this one think she was?

Candice Bloom hurriedly intervened.

"Daisy, I told Danillo what you'd said, but he insisted *absolument*." She made a piteous face at Daisy to indicate that the people from *People* were not to be upset by any ructions—the cover story was simply too important. Alonzo tried to lure Daisy into the dressing room.

"Just come in here and sit down, dearie," he said, "and we'll get started. It's a bit late, you know."

"I think not," said Daisy. The magazine researcher, sensing a confrontation, automatically slipped out her pad and pencil.

"Get Danillo, Robbie," the make-up man commanded. "And what kind of nice doggie is that?" he asked Daisy while the hairdresser hurried up a flight of stairs.

"Theseus? You might say that his pedigree is unknown."

"Oh, I'm sure of *that*, dearie. Or should I call you Princess?"

"Daisy will do," she answered briefly. God, how tired she was of that question.

Danillo appeared, annoyed at being interrupted in his real art, that of retouching. The photographer was slender, unobtrusive, with close-cropped blond hair. In one keen quick glance he observed the inescapable power of Daisy's beauty and rejected it. She was a twenty-five-minute job, one of hundreds this year, and the adamant impersonality of the famous man in faded jeans and high-heeled boots had punished the egos of many women who had thought themselves tougher than he. He raised one indifferent, languid eyebrow at the crowd in the reception room. "We'll do it my way," he announced.

But Daisy persisted. Years of making commercials had taught her a great deal about make-up, although she used very little of it.

"I've done my eyes and lips, Danillo, and I never use a base," she insisted. "So why do I have to be made up?"

"Boys, you're running late," Danillo said, not in reply, but as if she hadn't spoken. With Candice Bloom grasping one arm and the senior of the *People* editors clutching at the other, Daisy realized that she was not only outnumbered but that nothing could be more ludicrous than a scuffle. She shook them off and walked into the narrow dressing room where she found a high, backless kitchen stool in front of a long table, behind which ran a mirror. Theseus settled himself on top of the red vinyl couch.

"Danillo, darling," she heard the senior *People* editor say anxiously, "you *are* going straight for the regal quality, aren't you?"

"I thought we were agreed to try for *ancien régime* nostalgia, Marcia," the junior editor said in surprise.

"I have nothing against nostalgia, Francie, so long as it's majestic," Marcia snapped.

"Try some fresh papaya juice," Danillo said and left them abruptly.

Daisy sat still and watched Alonzo deftly cover the warm blush of her skin with a thin, even layer of beige liquid that turned her into the blank page on which he intended to paint his own concept of what she should look like. He covered her face and neck completely. Even her lips lost their own deep rose and were wiped out by beige. Her golden eyebrows disappeared as the coat of base extended from her hairline, where the tiny tendrils of her silver-gilt hair sprang untamed, right down to the base of her throat.

"This gets a bit messy. Don't you want to put on a

robe?" Alonzo asked, pleased at the obliteration he had wrought.

Daisy opened her mouth to speak.

"Don't talk!" he cried warningly. "I haven't got your lips on yet."

Danillo's stylist, Henri, a tawny boy, lounged in the doorway, carrying a King Charles Spaniel in his arms, and surveyed the scene disdainfully. However, he condescended to hand Daisy a terry robe and indicated a bathroom in which she could change. Then he saw Theseus.

"Who brought that *thing* in here?" she heard him ask indignantly. Daisy shook with laughter behind the door at the thought of anyone with intentions of evicting her animal. She hoped he'd try. As she emerged, the King Charles Spaniel, who rejoiced in the name of Yves St. Laurent, was yapping in high-bred protest at Theseus's existence, but a glance at her own dog told Daisy that he was maintaining his ruffian dignity, the saturnine yet convincing composure of a dexterous and unrepentant scoundrel.

"Doesn't anyone want to order *un petit* sandwich?" Candice Bloom asked eagerly. P.R., as she had so often told Jenny Antonio, was *merde*, but today things seemed even more tense than usual. However, there was no situation that couldn't be helped by food. This was lesson number one from the public-relations course Candice aspired to teach at a great university in the far future. Everyone, including the hair stylist and Alonzo, hungrily gave her complicated and detailed orders, and she sent Jenny off to the nearest delicatessen.

Daisy returned to her uncomfortable stool and looked on in resignation as Alonzo began to sculpt shadows on her beige mask with a stick of brown grease.

"Five different psychics told me that I was going to be called to Hollywood this year," he confided to her earnestly, dabbing away. She tried to signal polite curiosity with her looming eyes, the only thing left on her face that still showed any expression, but their very darkness was too intense to convey such pallid emotion.

"Do you know Hollywood? No! Don't talk! Close your eyes." Relieved, Daisy did as she was told, and the small room, crowded with watching people, faded behind her lids as she felt him doing things with brushes of various sizes. She felt hands on her hair and heard the angry admonition, "Get away, Robbie! You can have her when I'm finished and not before. You almost jiggled my arm!"

While the editors and Candice chattered, Daisy reflected on the fact that she had never been looked at the way Danillo had looked at her; not coldly but not warmly, neither approving nor disapproving, but with a simple and absolute lack of interest. He was bored, Danillo was, she decided, and she realized she didn't care. He had sittings like hers as often as twice a day, every day of the week, charging an average of three thousand dollars for the single shot that would be chosen. Even the best plastic surgeon, doing two face lifts a day, didn't make more money than this man. Four babies could be delivered by a Park Avenue gynecologist for one of Danillo's portraits, Daisy thought, trying to ignore the tickling of a brush inside her ear. "You can open now," Alonzo instructed her. Warily, she raised her lids and confronted her image. The beige mask still looked at her, embellished by deep, unfamiliar shadows that had settled on its cheekbones, its neck and its eyelids. "We're only getting started," Alonzo explained to Candice Bloom.

Robertson, the hairdresser, wearing an expression of exaggerated patience, slumped against the wall, his battery of curling irons and hot rollers unpacked in readiness for a job he wouldn't start for at least an hour and a half. Featherbedding. Daisy knew his expression well, from years of dealing with the unnecessary grips and gaffers on whom the union had insisted. She felt sharp, poignant regret for those days, so recently over, those hectic, harried days, so many of which had resulted in thirty or sixty seconds of the finest commercials ever made.

Jenny Antonio came into the dressing room bearing a platter of thick sandwiches which she had unwrapped and arranged in a tempting pile. She put the platter down on the couch and joined Candice and the *People* editors in their inspection of Daisy. Alonzo had started to fill in his new version of Daisy's mouth, and when she tried to say something he wagged a stern finger at her. Five women clustered around while he deftly redesigned Daisy's upper and lower lips to his satisfaction. "Okay," he grunted, "you can talk now."

"I'm afraid it's too late," Daisy said, trying to sound regretful.

"Too late for what?" he asked.

"Lunch," said Daisy.

Seven pairs of eyes looked at the bare sandwich platter. Seven pairs of eyes accused Theseus but no one had seen him move, no one had heard him eat, he was sitting, as ceremoniously uninvolved as Al Pacino during a gangland murder, in the same position he'd been in since he first sat down.

"I fed him before we came, but . . ." Daisy tried to explain.

"My God, he's a monster," breathed Marcia, the senior *People* editor, but the researcher, who had grown to know Theseus while interviewing Daisy, said, "He can't help it."

"How *dare* he?" shrieked Marcia, deprived of her ham and swiss on rye with plenty of mustard and coleslaw.

"I'll tell you when we get back to the office. It's a long story," said the researcher with an informed smile.

"Jenny, *vite, vite!* More sandwiches!" Candice ordered urgently. Lesson number two in her public-relations course would be to never permit a *chien*, no matter to whom it belonged, on any job she was involved in, ever again.

Alonzo stolidly continued his handiwork. Daisy felt as if she'd been sitting on the stool forever, although only two hours had passed. If she'd had Alonzo on a location shoot he'd have been long dead by now, she told herself, with mounting irritation. She would have stabbed him herself with one of the many instruments he was using on her. But it was typical of the anointed necromancers of the glamour business to insist, as Danillo did, on subjecting his subjects to discomfort. For a sitting with Danillo one had to step within his magic circle, pay endless obeisance before this very mirror, showing an essential neediness by putting up with this transfiguring nonsense in order to be assured of the master's imprint.

Jenny returned with a new supply of sandwiches and Daisy was relieved as the room cleared. At length Alonzo decided that he'd done all he could do and he turned her over to Robertson.

She no longer recognized the painted person in the mirror, with the wrong mouth, the wrong brows and the wrong skin, who looked ten years older than she had this morning. The face in the mirror had nothing to do with her, and when Robertson began to build her hair into an elaborate, tall coronet, rather like that of Princess Grace at a Monaco Red Cross gala, Daisy didn't bother to object.

"I have to make a base for the tiara," he told her as his hands deftly reduced her hair to a solid package of complicated swirls and curls.

"Tiara?" she questioned with lips that moved in a strange and disquieting way.

"Henri's borrowed a tiara and pendant earrings and a dog-collar necklace from *À la Vielle Russie*," he told her. "We're going for a real pre-Revolutionary look, kind of Anastasia, you know, the whole Romanov bit."

"I didn't know," said Daisy, "and I wish you hadn't told me."

"Huh?"

"Never mind." Candice Bloom, with her little French phrases, dropped like a tic into every other sentence, had evidently made plans she hadn't seen fit to tell Daisy about. Daisy's visual indigestion was being joined by a feeling of actual nausea at the thought of being turned into a reincarnation of the long dead and pathetic Grand Duchess. But just as she was about to get up and speak to Candice, Henri sauntered in carrying several black velvet boxes. Without a word he clasped the dog collar of emeralds, rubies and diamonds around her neck, and he fastened the matching tiara in her hair.

"You don't have pierced ears!" he whined, accusingly.

"Would you care to try and pierce them?" Daisy asked softly. He backed away from the menace in her eyes.

Danillo's voice could be heard calling impatiently from the studio. He was finally in the mood to work, and if everyone was on schedule he'd be finished with this in less than a half-hour.

"Ready?" asked Robertson.

Daisy took one more look in the mirror. It was hopeless to make any objections. They'd done so much to her that she hadn't the faintest idea of where to start to make it less awful.

She got up gingerly. The stool had cut off the circulation in her legs and she felt stiff and weary. She didn't need to change from the terry robe since she would merely slip it off her shoulders for the head shot. She belted it more securely and turned to look at Theseus.

"Now you stay right here until I get back," she told him. Instead of his usual patient acceptance of her instructions, he stood up on the couch, bared his teeth at her and growled low in his throat, breaking his lurcher's silence. It was unthinkable. Daisy went closer to him and he suddenly cringed away, growling desperate protest all the while.

"Theseus!" she cried. He shivered all over at the sound of Daisy's voice coming from the stranger's face, and when she put out her hand to him, he flinched and refused to sniff it.

"THAT DOES IT!" Daisy said and turned back to the table, plunged her hand deep into a jar of cold cream and smeared it forcefully from one cheek to another. "Take off the jewels, take down my hair and call Alonzo in here to take off the rest of the make-up!" she ordered the hairdresser. Robertson, who could feel the room darkening and whirling around him, had retreated to a corner to get away from this madwoman.

"Alonzo," Daisy called out to the reception room, "I need you."

The make-up man hurried in as she was scrubbing the second handful of cold cream over her chin and forehead.

"Get me some towels," Daisy demanded. "And tell Danillo I'll be out in just a little while. It only takes me about three minutes to do my own make-up if I start with a clean face. Robertson! Hairbrush, please! Oh, for heaven's sake, Alonzo, just put your head between your legs and take a few deep breaths!"

"Could we just go over what we have so far, Warner?" asked Hugo Ralli, the general manager of the Tavern on the Green. Candice Bloom and Warner Le Roy had seen eye to eye so quickly that he wanted to make sure that they hadn't overlooked anything.

The secretary read from her notes. "The Elm Room is to be used for the receiving line. Both the Elm and Rafters rooms will have ten rolling tables circulating from the moment the party starts, with two waiters at each table. The tables will carry three ice sculptures of the Princess Daisy bottle, each three feet tall, one to contain ten pounds of caviar, one to hold a jeroboam of champagne, specified Louis Roederer Cristal, another a bottle of Stolichnaya vodka. The caviar will be served on small plates with whatever trimmings the guest chooses."

"You left out the gypsies," said Candice, adding a touch of lemon juice to the smoked trout she was eating. Warner

Le Roy looked at her kindly from behind the glasses. As always, when he went over a party with someone who was taking over the entire restaurant, he dressed in his most conservative way. Today he had adorned his agreeably liberal girth with red trousers and a gray, red and white plaid jacket. He enjoyed clothes even as subdued as these. He enjoyed boyish, bossy Candice Bloom. He enjoyed owning Maxwell's Plum and the Tavern on the Green. He enjoyed life and life enjoyed him.

"I was just about to get to the gypsies," the secretary said. "During the arrival of the guests there will be a thirty-man gypsy band playing outside on both sides of the front entrance and another thirty gypsies strolling through the Rafters and Elm rooms, not, note *not*, playing loudly, or else they may drown out the introductions to Princess Daisy on the receiving line. There will be eight searchlights placed around the restaurant and an additional fifty parking attendants will be hired to supplement our regular staff because of the troikas. The men must be trained in handling horses."

"What did we finally decide about the buffet?" asked Candice, as she sat, finishing her trout, at a round table under an umbrella on the terrace of the restaurant.

"It's supposed to be set up in the Pavilion Room," the secretary said, consulting her notes.

"I'm not sure about that," Warner Le Roy said. "I think that with six hundred guests we've got to have two separate buffets."

"Agreed," said Walter Rauscher, the banquet manager, who made the fifth member of the lunch party.

The secretary made a note and continued. "During dinner there will be a waltz orchestra playing in the Crystal Room and waltzing will take place both in the Crystal Room and outside under the trees on the terrace. Both gypsy bands will play in the Pavilion Room. The disco band will play in the Terrace Room at the back of the restaurant, starting right after dinner."

"What if it rains?" asked Candice.

"We can put up a tent outside and have radiant heat but I think that so early in September, you don't really have to worry," Warner Le Roy reassured her.

"Warner," Candice said, in as waggish a tone as she'd ever permitted herself. "I'm still not *tout à fait* happy with the caviar. We just say 'caviar' but I'd like to get more precise. I take a personal interest in it."

"If you want to go all the way, I could try to order the golden Iranian, but I doubt that there'd be enough available," he told her. "And most people wouldn't know what it was, anyway."

"What's the next best?" she asked, finishing her trout. Public relations had its moments of compensation. She must remember to tell her analyst.

"The best beluga. No problem getting it. If you want to be reasonably lavish you provide two large scoops for each person, three ounces in all, so that makes one pound for every five people, considering that not everyone likes caviar."

"My orders are to be unreasonably lavish," Candice said with gusto. "How about four ounces per person? And let's figure that everyone wants caviar because I intend to put away two pounds myself and I expect a large doggie bag and a dogsled to take it home in."

"So, six hundred people at four ounces to a person... makes two thousand, four hundred ounces... of course the Russian pound is only fourteen ounces so that makes ...."

"To be on the safe side, Warner, one hundred seventy-five pounds of the best beluga at a hundred and twenty-five dollars a pound, wholesale, and one large doggie bag," Walter Rauscher suggested.

"Done and done," Candice pronounced, her Tootsie Roll brown eyes sparkling with anticipatory greed.

"Shall I go on?" asked the secretary. Candice nodded.

"The buffet will feature whole cold sturgeon and salmon, roast quail, roast wild boar with sautéed apples and lingonberries ..."

"Ah, look, Warner, I just don't know about that wild boar," Candice said. "I know it's Russian, but are you sure?"

"It's sensational. We marinate it for five days and do it in light bread crumbs with a Béarnaise sauce." He waved at the secretary to continue reading the long buffet list. Eventually she came to her last notes.

"The desserts will be served at the table. Mr. Ralli and the head chef will decide on the most appropriate ingredients for a variety of sculptured bombe desserts to be carried in, *en flambé*."

"Not a flaming Princess Daisy bottle," Candice warned.

"Of course not!" Warner said, shocked. "Trust me."

"I do," said Candice wistfully, "but I just don't see why

we can't have icicles on the trees on the terrace. We're going to have snow all around the Tavern, except on the outside dance floor, so *pourquoi* isn't there some sort of real dripless icicle?"

"We could do theatrical icicles, I suppose, or I could put up the winter lights," Warner said thoughtfully.

"Oh, yes! That's it! The winter lights, all white and tiny and twinkling—I remember them from last Christmas, driving by. They were *incroyable!* Let's put them up," Candice said in excitement.

"There's just one problem. They'll have to come down the next day—I don't start winter until just after Thanksgiving."

"What's the problem?"

"There are sixty thousand lights. That's going to cost a lot for labor."

"Mr. Shannon wouldn't like to hear that I decided to draw the line at twinkle lights," the publicity woman told Warner. "Not with fifty thousand dollars worth of man-made snow."

Hugo Ralli coughed. "Did we say *only* candlelight?" he asked, thinking of places that demanded electricity.

"No, we said at least two thousand candles, in silver candelabra—candles everywhere they could possibly be, but electric light in the johns," Candice remembered. "And now, about the flowers, Mr. Ralli, they're terribly important. Millions of daisies. I don't know where you'll find that many in the city, but we've got to have them, no matter what. *C'est indispensable!*"

"I can get them, but they won't make the right effect unless I mix them with white roses and spider chrysanthemums in yellow and white," he insisted.

"Okay, just so long as you find the daisies." Candice turned to Warner Le Roy, grandson of Harry Warner, grand-nephew of Jack Warner, heir to a sense of the spectacular not possessed by any other restaurateur in the world. "Could you just give me a ballpark figure on how much this party is going to cost? Forget the snow and the troikas and the horses."

Warner thought for a minute, remembering the twenty-fifth anniversary party for the Klebergs of the King Ranch in Texas, who had flown 250 people to New York and taken over the restaurant. "Somewhere in the neighborhood of—well, with all the extras and the ice sculpture and all, somewhere in the neighborhood of two hundred thousand—it could go higher, depending on how much caviar you want in your doggie bag."

"Sounds reasonable," Candice said, judiciously, waiting for the next course to be served. Lunch, thank God, had only started.

When he woke from his first restless hours of sleep, Hilly Bijur, president of Elstree, often wondered what had ever lured him into the jungle of the fucking fragrance business. As soon as this question formed in his mind, he had trained himself to try to relax his muscles, grimly starting at the top of his scalp and working down to his toes, and then back up again, not neglecting his clenched teeth, as the hypnotherapist he had gone to for insomnia had taught him, but by the time his ears were relaxed and he started on his forehead, words started to whirl in his mind: Quadrille, Calèche, L'Air du Temps, Arpège, Cristalle, Jontue, Halston—damn Halston—why couldn't he have a French name like the others?—Aliage, Infini, Cabochard, Ecusson ... when he got to Ecusson he usually was able to return his concentration to his forehead and sometimes he got down as far as relaxing his jaw muscles when another set of names would start dancing behind his eyes: first, Dick Johnson, perfume buyer for the Hess chain based in Allentown, Pennsylvania; then Mike Gannaway, merchandise manager at Dayton's in Minneapolis; swiftly followed by Verda Gaines, head of cosmetics at Steinfeld's in Tucson; Karol Kempster, buyer for Henri Bendel; Marjorie Cassell, buyer for Harvey's in Nashville; Melody Grim at Garfinkle's—the list could go on all night, but when Hilly Bijur reached Garfinkle's he gave up trying to work on his muscles, got out of bed and took a sleeping pill that his doctor had guaranteed to be nonaddictive, nonbarbiturate and without evil side effects which might cause it to build up in the body. This remarkable pill had only one drawback, Hilly Bijur reflected, it did not put him to sleep. However, just swallowing a pill made him feel calmer, even if it only acted as a placebo, he assured himself as he crept out of the bedroom so as not to wake his wife. He read a few more pages of Leon Edel's five-volume biography of Henry James. This great scholarly work, detailed, leisurely and undoubtedly good for him, had the virtue of not being a page turner. At about five in the morning, trying hard to think only about James churning out books in London, books Hilly Bijur had never read, he ventured back to bed and usually managed to sleep for several hours before he woke up to another day of the Princess Daisy project.

It was now early September of 1977, almost eight months since preparations had begun for the new line of perfume and cosmetics. The fragrance which Patrick Shannon had named Princess Daisy had actually been seven years in the creation, the work of a man who was considered the greatest "nose" in France. To Hilly Bijur's pragmatic judgment, it smelled good. As far as he was concerned, the world needed only one perfume, Arpège, the scent of the first woman he'd ever laid. Arpège turned him on in the way Youth Dew, his mother-in-law's perfume, turned him off. What, he wondered, if his first real fuck had worn Youth Dew and his mother-in-law used Arpège? Would his tastes be reversed? Did perfume smell like sex or did sex smell like perfume? What would sex smell like without any perfume at all? Better? He thought so—but business was business and if people wanted to describe a perfume as "irrepressible yet romantic" or "spirited yet reserved" or "endearing and joyously feminine" they had as much right as wine freaks. He didn't even give a good goddamn when they started talking about "single-note florals" or "ylang-ylang notes" or "little greenies" or throwing around phrases about a "serious perfume that goes with serious clothes" or the "musk revolution," and he was indifferent to whether a perfume was "created" or "designed," whether a claim was made that a woman didn't just "put on" Chloe, but "entered it" or any equally baroque fragrance-world bullshit.

It was a question of merchandising, that's all it was about, he thought to himself in the shower. Merchandising the sizzle, not the steak. Merchandising the fantasy, not the reality. Merchandising a luxury that had become increasingly a part of American life, a luxury that was sold in discount drugstores and continued to base its advertising on snob appeal.

He remembered, shudderingly, that first sales conference at which he had announced the new Princess Daisy concept to his sales staff, and told them of Shannon's one-hundred-million-dollars' sales expectation for the new line. Six of his top salesmen had resigned on the spot, and the ones who were left made the crew of H.M.S. *Bounty* look like the peaceful and contented seamen of the H.M.S. *Pinafore*. When he boiled it down, Hilly reflected, it simply amounted to the fact that no one was happy about being in on a launch. They'd have been more willing to go along with the old Elstree line, fading quietly into the back of consumers' minds, than to have to hustle their asses trying to get cosmetic buyers to place orders for anything new, no matter how good, no matter how it was going to be backed up by advertising and packaging.

Hilly Bijur, seasoned merchandising man, had not been picked by Shannon as president of Elstree by accident. Within a month, spending freely, he'd cleaned house and built a much stronger group of sales people, who, since they hadn't worked for the old Elstree, had nothing to prevent them from being enthusiastic about the new plans. He'd made the important decisions about how many items to offer in the new cosmetic line, knowing how store buyers detested being asked to order a great variety of stock they weren't sure they would sell. The Princess Daisy cosmetic collection was a full but strictly edited group of products: the essential moisturizing lotion, a cleansing cream, a body lotion, a liquid make-up base in the six most important shades, lipsticks and lip glosses in the basic groups of pinks, reds, raisins and plums, nail lacquer to match, four shades of blusher, four hues of face powder, roll-on mascaras in black and brown, eyeliner in four colors, eye shadow in eight shades (an area in which he congratulated himself on almost unheard-of self-restraint, since over twenty shades were average for most cosmetic companies) and, of course, the soap, the after-bath dusting powder, the spray cologne in three sizes, and finally the perfume, in the half-ounce, the one-ounce size and the two-ounce bottles. As he turned over and over in his mind the array of new products, Hilly Bijur was remembering the words of the voice of his conscience, the very same Dick Johnson of Allentown who woke him up at night.

"Yeah, you would not be exaggerating at all if you were to say we have too many products on the market today—the manufacturers are overdoing it completely." Oh, Dick Johnson of those eleven eastern Pennsylvania cities which shelter a Hess's, Inc., why were you not more like adventuresome Verda Gaines of Tucson who said, "Without new products, there is no progress." Why???

Eleven percent of every dollar cosmetic and fragrance manufacturers spend goes into packaging. It was this fact that made Hilly Bijur erase Dick Johnson from his mind as he plunged into delighted contemplation of the marvelous bottle that had been designed for the perfume. It was inspired, at Daisy's suggestion, by the Easter eggs which Peter Carl Fabergé had made for the Imperial Family —fifty-seven eggs in all, between 1884 and 1917. Now they were scattered in museums all over the world, although some had found their way into private collections. Marjorie Merriweather Post, the great heiress of the General Foods Corporation, had been one of the few private people in the world to possess several of the Imperial eggs, and even in her vast collection of Russian treasures, they were the rarest, most prized objects.

The Princess Daisy bottle was egg shaped, hand-blown crystal, bound from its base to its top with four slender, rippling vermeil ribbons which came together above the stopper to form a bow. It stood on a graceful three-legged vermeil stand surmounted by an oval hoop into which it fit snugly. In a year of ever more modern bottles, at a time dominated by the severity of Halston's packaging and the classicism of Chanel's, the Elstree bottle was jewel-like, unique. It was impossible to see it and not want to lift it from its stand and caress it. After all, Bijur reflected, was the egg not considered nature's most perfect form? *Take that,* Dick Johnson of Allentown! And take the rest of the packaging as well, jars and bottles and cases of deep, brilliant lapis lazuli blue, so highly glazed that they resembled Fabergé enamel itself, each one bearing a single white and gold daisy on a green stem, a highly stylized design which was the trademark for the entire line. They were so fucking *perfect* they could make you fucking cry, Bijur had told Patrick Shannon and, for once, Shannon had agreed without even trying to suggest a single improvement.

Princess Daisy perfume was going to sell at a hundred dollars an ounce. Justified? Bijur thought so. Unlike many perfumes that sold for less, it was made only from natural oils and essences, produced and bottled in France. Of course, it didn't cost anything close to one hundred dollars an ounce to make it or bottle it or merchandise it—my God, he thought, if it fucking did, where would the profit be? When cosmetics and perfumes start selling for anything even *near* the price they cost to produce, it'd be like fucking Russia.

As Hilly Bijur walked briskly down Park Avenue to the Supracorp building, he thought about the Christmas catalogues which major stores all over the country had sent out in August, almost all of them offering Princess Daisy perfume and gift boxes of various combinations of perfume, cologne, soap and bath powder. If they'd missed being in the Saks and Neiman-Marcus catalogues, to say nothing of the dozens of other catalogues in which they had been featured, Shannon's wild dream wouldn't have had a chance of being realized.

The Princess Daisy launch was being coordinated as if it were as important as D-Day. Shit, if you had a sense of perspective, it fucking *was* D-Day, Bijur ruminated. On the one hand there was Candice Bloom taking care of the fluff, building all that media excitement about Daisy herself which would finally flare into an explosion with the publication of the *People* cover story tomorrow, to say nothing of The Russian Winter Palace Ball, the launch party that should make every newsmagazine and newspaper women's page in the country. And Helen Strauss had the advertising well in hand, the commercials, the double trade magazine ads, the four color brochures. Hilly himself was complacent about his shipments of perfume in the New Jersey warehouse. Everything had arrived from France in good time and in good shape. and the salesmen had taken spectacular orders. Even Saks Fifth Avenue, traditionally the one store to get a perfume before anyone in New York had been persuaded to share the launch with Bendel's and Bloomingdale's; the special Princess Daisy capsule collection of fall fashions by Bill Blass was one of the most opulent that consistently elegant designer had ever created, and the clothes had been shipped to major stores across the country to be shown in banks of display windows the week of the launch; the Elstree saleswomen were being given an extra bonus commission on top of their regular commission for the first three months of sales; the samples of Princess Daisy perfume had already arrived in the chosen stores by the tens of thousands, to be distributed with an open hand at special designer "outposts" on the stores' ground floors, and Daisy herself was scheduled to fly from one city to another on a whirlwind tour of thirty major markets during the weeks following the party to make personal appearances at the largest department stores and draw the winning number which would give one of the women at each store who had bought Princess Daisy perfume or cosmetics a gift certificate for a thousand dollars.

So what could go wrong? Christ—almost everything, Hilly Bijur thought, shuddering. In the crazy world of fragrance, who the fuck knew?

"Of course she's unimportant, a totally unimportant miserable little bitch. You don't have to tell me that . . . it only makes it worse, Robin, don't you understand?" Vanessa said furiously. "She was never worthy of our kindness. And no, I do not want a Miltown or a Valium or a sleeping pill, so will you please stop trying to make me take one?"

It was three in the morning and Vanessa had awakened, as she had so often in the last months, in a knotted fury. Although she tried not to disturb him, Robin always seemed to know when she couldn't sleep and woke, loyally prepared to listen as Vanessa poured once again over the rosary of her grievances. It made him sad to look at her. Although her long, slashingly elegant body was unchanged, her mouth was tightened in an unattractive line and her face looked thinner than it ever had, almost gaunt. But no matter how he tried to distract her with plans for vacations, new ideas for redecorating, no matter how often he held her tight and massaged her upper back where the worst of the tension was, she wouldn't forget Daisy and what Daisy had done to her.

"First and foremost, and you have to admit it, Robin, she was *never* properly grateful, not for a second. Oh, she said thank you, but only when it was absolutely necessary, when I persuaded Topsy to let her do the children in oil and when I got her that other commission. But how did she say thank you? As if she were doing *me* a favor! If there is one thing I can't forgive, it's ingratitude—she never had me fooled for a minute. And she owed us so much! How many parties I invited her to was she 'too busy' to come to? Who the hell does she think she is? No one—*no one*—is too busy to come here. Ever!"

"Vanessa, everyone who counts says you give the best parties in New York. What does she matter?" Robin said patiently for the hundredth time.

"That's not the point and you know it. It's her whole attitude! That high-and-mighty 'You can't touch me because I'm special,' and 'You don't impress me no matter what you do'—it's *that* I simply cannot endure. And what about those dresses you gave her? You practically had to force them on her, for Christ's sake—you'd think she preferred to wear those crazy, playacting castoffs of hers."

"She has to wear decent clothes now," Robin said, realizing an instant too late that he could hardly have been more tactless. Vanessa had been filled with wrath on the topic of Daisy ever since the unfortunate yacht incident last winter, but when the news of the Princess Daisy campaign was announced, when personal publicity started to appear about Daisy, when the story of the million-dollar contract was bruited about and, finally, now that she had heard that there was to be a *People* cover story, Vanessa's envious outrage grew until it consumed her.

"I notice she didn't come to you for them," she sneered at her husband spitefully. When he merely shrugged and refused to answer, she sighed and touched his arm tenderly. "Sorry, darling, I didn't mean that the way it sounded. Her taste is so outlandish that of course she wouldn't have the intelligence or the class to wear your things, that's all."

"It's all right," he assured her. "Would you like a little wine? It might make you sleepy." Vanessa shook her head again, sternly.

"Robin, I assure you that I'm indifferent to all those cheap advertising ploys—I'd say let her have her moment in the limelight and who cares—but what I can't forgive, what I'll never be able to forgive, is the way she ruined that yachting party. Don't you have any comprehension of what a fool she made me look? Do you have any understanding of the things people have been saying about us ever since? Yes, *ever* since, even now! Everyone on that boat must have blabbed to every last solitary soul they knew in the whole world. It's been months and months and people haven't stopped baiting me ... 'Vanessa, love, so that little family reunion you planned backfired, did it?' 'Vanessa, I've heard the most fascinating story . . . what *really* happened, darling?' 'Vanessa, why on earth did you have to turn the yacht back—Why did Daisy Valensky sneak off in the middle of the night? What could have caused Ram Valensky to spend the rest of his trip in his cabin ... so rude of him, poor sweet ... do tell ... I'm sure you know more than you're saying ... how *could* they act that way toward you?' Oh, Robin, you just wouldn't believe the rumors—vindictive, mean, stupid, ugly—and all of them making me look like the biggest idiot alive. And it comes from everyone—people I thought were friends—I hardly dare to make a lunch date even now because I know there's going to be this inquisition. Don't you see what she's *done to me,* that pretentious bitch!"

"It was just a nine-day wonder, darling. I'm sure people can't still be talking about it," Robin said, without conviction. He had been the target of many questions himself.

"Bullshit—and you know it. It might have been all right if Ram hadn't acted the way he did. I could have just said that Daisy was seasick or had an allergic attack or something, but he had to go and shut himself up, for God's sake, and not even say goodbye to anybody—that's what really did it, that's what really made people talk. When I think how much trouble I went to for that bastard, talking Daisy into coming with us, I could die. Even if he did finance your new line, nothing entitled him to hold *me* up to ridicule," she raged.

"Vanessa, dearest, please, you're just eating yourself up about this. You can't go on . . . you've got to try and put it behind you."

"I damn well will!" Vanessa pulled herself up from her pillows and wrapped herself in a bathrobe.

"Robin, what time is it in England now?"

"Morning. Why?"

Without answering him she placed the call to London, waiting in their bedroom, that often photographed jungle of Victorian chintz and Edwardian lace, until she had Ram on the line.

"Hello, darling—it's Vanessa! Robin and I were just having a nightcap and suddenly we both realized how frightfully long it's been since we've had news of you. So I thought, why not just pick up a phone? We were so sorry you weren't well on the yacht—in fact we were rather concerned. But of course I understand, I get the most fearful migraines too. No, no, don't apologize. But you're fine now? I'm so glad. Yes, Robin and I are both in the pink. And I suppose you're up to date on all the good news about Daisy? She must have written you . . . such excitement, my dear, you can't imagine. They're making simply the most marvelous fuss about her—isn't it thrilling? To think that she just never seemed to have two dimes to rub together and now a million dollars! That old title of yours is worth something over here after all . . . democracy or no democracy, like the English, we dearly love a lord. Even *People* is doing a cover story on her now and if anything will put her on the map, that will. So you, my darling, had better get used to seeing your little sister simply plastered all over the billboards and magazines and television—even in England—hadn't you? Just imagine, a Valensky *touting* lipsticks and God knows what else. Still, I suppose there are just no lengths she won't go to for Patrick Shannon. What do you mean, what about Patrick Shannon? He's the head of . . . sorry, darling, obviously you know who he is. What I meant was that they're *madly* in love. Everyone in New York is gossiping about them ever since they came back from England together. They've having the most *glorious* affair! It's simply delicious to watch them . . . makes you believe in romance again. But didn't you see them when they were over there together? Oh, I see . . . in the Mideast . . . so you missed the lovebirds. Well now, *there* is where I think Daisy's been particularly clever. *People* covers are all well and good, but Patrick Shannon is the most divine man these old eyes have seen in years. And a man who gets *everything* he has ever wanted. Just yesterday there was an article about Elstree in *The New York Times* and they quoted him as saying that Daisy was 'one of a kind.' Pretty faint praise, considering—but, on the other hand, he was probably just being discreet—the last time I saw them at a restaurant together he could *barely* keep his hands off her. Now don't be old-fashioned, Ram! Daisy's hardly a teenager. She has a perfect right to a dozen lovers . . . but she only wants Shannon it seems, and who could quarrel with that?

"Well, listen sweetie, I won't keep you any longer. Just checking to make sure you were better—old friends shouldn't be out of touch for so long. Robin says to tell you he sends his best. Goodbye, love. See you in the funny papers, as they used to say."

With the first genuinely pleasant look he had seen on her face in months, Vanessa put down the phone very softly. "Robin, perhaps I'll have a little wine after all."

"Feeling better darling?" Robin asked anxiously.

"Infinitely!"

The pain Ram had felt ever since he had crept away from *La Marée*, leaving Daisy bleeding on her bed, had been a pain of such need, of a wanting so great that it lived in a place where no one knew about it but himself, a place so far inside that his sanity was unquestioned because his outward appearance was correct, impeccable. He was to continue to live and function without Daisy because no one else had her. But she had always lived on in his fatally obsessed mind as if she still belonged to him, lived on in a cage of hopeless, endless longing from which he had neither the will nor the desire nor the power to escape, a cage which contained no images but those of Daisy and himself. True, she turned away from him, in the cage, but she did not turn toward anyone else. How could she, since she was his possession?

Ram had not been jealous because there was no one to be jealous of, no actual threat, no embodiment of a third person between him and his fantasies.

Now, with a few insinuating words, chosen with her infallible instinct for weakness and vulnerability, Vanessa had aroused a literally unbearable sense of impotence, of mutilation. There was no place left for Ram to stand, no inner core in which to take refuge from the pain. Jealousy was born, ravening and gibbering, as old and as mad as if it had had a million years in which to reach hideous, unendurable, acid-drenched maturity.

He dressed quickly, and within half an hour after Vanessa's phone call he was at the mews garage in which he kept his Jaguar.

Ram had always known where Danielle was. The directors of the school were accustomed to his occasional phone calls as he checked up to find out if Daisy had been able to continue to pay for Danielle. For years he had waited for the day, the inevitable day on which she would be unable to shoulder the burden and would be forced to come to him for help.

Within twenty minutes Ram was headed out of London, speeding in the direction of Queen Anne's School, by a route that had been clearly mapped out in his mind for many, many years.

25

*O*h, my God, NO!" Candice Bloom screamed. Jenny, her assistant, whirled around. Her boss had turned the color of a Kleenex and on her desk was an advance copy of *People* which had just arrived by messenger, a magazine that would be on every newsstand in America twenty-four hours from now.

Jenny rushed over to Candice's desk, almost afraid to look at the cover. She was sure they'd been bumped for another story ... Candice had been dreading that all along. She'd always said it was too good to be true. But no, there *was* Daisy ... obviously rebellion was one way to inspire Danillo ... it was a marvelous picture. On the side of the cover a copy line, in red, shouted "PRINCESS DAISY: Her life isn't just sweet scents; the strange, secret story of Francesca Vernon and Prince Stash Valensky's daughter." Jenny's hands fumbled as she tried to find the page on which the story appeared.

"Page thirty-four," Candice gasped.

Jenny finally found the double spread with which the cover story began. The entire right-hand page was one huge black-and-white photograph. She stared at it, read the caption and then looked again at the picture. The world was reduced to that page, that photograph, those two girls, two girls with blonde hair and black eyes, two girls with the same faces, two girls with their arms around each other, two smiling girls of about twenty-three, so alike, *so impossibly alike.* The caption read: "Princess Daisy on a recent visit to her identical twin sister, Danielle, in the home for permanently retarded children in which she has been secreted since she was six."

The two women stood frozen, staring, staring, unable to speak, struggling for comprehension of something that just could not be.

Finally, in a white voice, Candice said, "She ... she's a little shorter."

"Her eyes ... they're the same ... but her look is ... vague?" Jenny's words stumbled. She could only absorb the shock detail by detail.

"And her hair, it's just shoulder length and it's not as, not as ... bright ... but it grows in just the same way, exactly the same way." Candice sounded as if she were speaking from another room.

"Her features are different, no, not *different* really, but just not quite as ... clear, not as fine. She looks, oh, younger, as if she doesn't have a sense of humor," Jenny said wonderingly. "But it *is* the same face . . . Daisy's face."

"No!" Candice said. "Not the *same*—you wouldn't look *twice* at her!"

"No, no ... you would *not*." Jenny agreed in horror. "My God, look at that other picture," she said, pointing with a finger that shook. It was a reproduction of the *Life* cover of twenty-five years before ... Stash and Francesca, and the laughing baby on Merlin's back. She read the caption out loud. "No one knew, when Prince and Princess Valensky posed for *Life* that another child had been born to them, a child they hid away from the eyes of the world."

"Jesus God!" Jenny whispered. They both started to read the story, flipping through the five pages, skimming and reading out loud.

'In an exclusive interview with Prince George Edward Woodhill Valensky, half-brother of Princess Daisy, *People* learned of the existence of ... sister ... I.Q. of a four-year-old . . .' My God, Candice, a *four-year-old!*"

Candice stopped Jenny firmly. "Shut up, Jenny—there's more. Listen to this, just listen! 'Prince Valensky violently opposes the commercialization of his ancient family name by his half-sister whose endorsement of a new line of cosmetics he termed "a vulgar and unseemly action." ' That son-of-a-bitch!" She continued reading in a voice that grew progressively louder. " 'In his opinion, if Francesca Vernon had not abandoned his father and kidnapped the twins, they might have had a normal childhood, but by the time his father regained the children, it was too late to help Danielle ... Prince Valensky, seven years older than

Princess Daisy, is a highly respected investment adviser. Bitter toward his sister, who has been paid one million dollars for her endorsement, he said, "She inherited ten million dollars and let it slip through her fingers because she was too foolish to take any advice. She'll go through this money just as quickly." ' "

"My God," said Jenny, "do you think she did?"

"Wait! Here's the worst. 'Daisy Valensky has been called "one of a kind" by Patrick Shannon, the sometimes controversial president of Supracorp'—Jesus, Jenny, 'one of a kind'—'who is betting many millions that her face and name will lend prestige to the line of . . . . Last year Elstree's losses were reported at over thirty million . . . unparalleled media blitz to promote the newest face in the beauty business including . . .' That's it, I can't read one more word." Candice sat down. "Get Mr. Bijur on the intercom, Jenny, and tell him I've got to see him immediately."

In spite of the urgency of Candice's order, both she and Jenny stood for another minute looking at the photograph of Daisy and Danielle. Neither woman could take her eyes off the haunting picture of the twins. They were unable to stop comparing the slight but all-important differences in their faces which made of one a glorious beauty and left the other unformed, unfinished, uninteresting, with a muted little smile, pathos in her big black eyes.

" 'One of a kind,' " Candice murmured. "God—we've had it—by tomorrow this picture will be seen all over the world."

"Do you think *People* knew about this stuff when they decided on the cover story?" Jenny asked.

"No way. They angle stories in a special way, but not as bad as this. I can tell by the way the text reads that it must have come in at the last minute—it's hasty, reads more like a newsmagazine piece than a *People* story."

"But then how could it have happened?" Jenny asked.

"God knows, and I don't care. When something this bad happens, 'how' just doesn't matter any more. Get me Bijur's secretary."

"May I make a suggestion?" Jenny asked.

"What?"

"Fix your eye make-up before you see him. You've been crying."

"So what? So have you. Oh, okay, okay."

Daisy woke late on the morning that Candice and Jenny were reading *People*, and considered her day. At lunch she was going to be interviewed by Jerry Tallmer of the *New York Post* for a feature article, at 2:30 she had another interview with Phyllis Battelle of King Features and at 5:00 a date for drinks and an interview with Lammy Johnstone of Gannett for their national wire service. Candice would be with her at all these interviews, somehow disappearing into the background as Daisy answered questions, yet listening carefully and sometimes stepping lightly into the conversation to amplify a statement or suggest a new line of discussion. Even though that skinny, swaggering, terse young publicity woman was only three years older than Daisy, she managed to convey a faintly maternal feeling; that of an accomplished and socially secure matron introducing her daughter to the ladies who run the debutante cotillion. She was able to gently point to Daisy's qualities in a way that Daisy would never have been able to do for herself.

Nevertheless, as a veteran now of at least a dozen interviews, Daisy realized that each reporter, no matter how pleasant or charming, was looking for an edge, waiting for her to say the one thing she shouldn't say, probing, in a seemingly random and innocent way, for the stray remark that would make news. Just the day before, one of them had actually asked her if she liked the way the new perfume smelled. My God, did he actually think she'd say no? But it was all part of doing his job, she realized—and if she had said no, it would have made a much better story.

She dressed carefully in one of her new things. That was another part of her job. Everytime she was interviewed, she was closely scrutinized; every detail of what she had on went into the reporter's notebook. The *image*, the absolutely essential image was being created day by day, interview by interview, dress by dress, question by question. Perhaps eventually, Daisy thought, she'd get hardened to it, accustomed to the process, but she still had to remind herself of that million dollars before she could get started on the morning metamorphosis. But it went with the job, and, by God, what went with the job, she did. Daisy brightened as she realized that she could save all the new clothes she was being given and then, thirty or forty years from now, bring them out again and really enjoy wearing them. She'd be the most originally dressed sixty-year-old in the world.

She looked at her watch. She just had time to feed Theseus, get him settled on his pillow, and rush down the street to the Café Borgia II for a quick cup of espresso before she had to start uptown for her lunch interview. It had taken her a full hour to dress, put on her make-up and do her hair. This patient triangulation of her obligations to the image had, in the past, taken only seven minutes, or less. Being a princess just took too much time, Daisy thought, as she grabbed her mail without looking at it and hurried out.

At the café on Prince Street, she found an outside table. She sat there and basked in the September sun while her sense of smell leaped in response to the odor of freshly made bread from the bakery across the street. But she wouldn't have anything to eat now. She'd learned it was important to eat heartily at lunch interviews because the excuse of a mouthful of food gave her time to consider her words, before she had to speak. She finished her espresso and ordered another. With Kiki gone, there was very little mail. Why had she brought along this manila envelope? Now she'd have to carry it around all day. She looked at it again. It had been delivered by hand and the name of the researcher from *People* was written on the left corner. In dismay, she thought that she hadn't planned on facing *that* until tomorrow. She supposed they meant to be nice, but an advance copy was the last thing she wanted. However, she might as well get it over with. She opened the envelope and drew out the magazine. A smile of pure delight spread over her face as she saw the cover photograph. She knew she'd been right to take off all that awful make-up. As she read the cover line, her smile stopped. "The strange, secret story? . . ." She turned to the inside pages in a sudden fright, the slippery paper evading her fingers. What editor could have turned the detailed, exhaustive, but resolutely cautious interviews she'd given the researcher into a "strange, secret story," she asked herself as the chill of what she still did not know, except in some part of her brain that had always, always, always, been alert to attack, began to creep over her.

She turned another page.

The cruelty exploded inside her heart and spilled into her entire chest cavity. She screamed and shut the magazine. A waiter approached and she waved him away, covering the copy of *People* with her handbag. A violent burst of pain, like steel knitting needles driving their points into her breasts, made her clasp her hands tightly to them in an incredulous attempt to protect herself. It couldn't continue to hurt like this for long or she wouldn't be able to breathe. A sharp, rippling feeling of breakage and rupture made her pull her head down to her hands as if to doubly protect her heart, yet it would not stop. She felt lacerated, attacked from all sides, by gratuitous evil, utterly exposed to the tearing and crushing of the teeth of nameless beasts.

The waiter came back, an expression of concern on his face. In another second he'd speak. Daisy got up, clutching the magazine and handbag and staggered, with the cautious, clumsy movements of an old woman, to a table inside in the corner of the empty café where she couldn't be seen from the street. Panting with savage pain, streaming with the sweat of utter panic, she hunched over the table and opened the magazine and read the entire article. Then she read it twice again. There were no tears, just as there were no words in her mind. Nothing existed except the article and the need to stop the feeling that she was being cut apart, opened up, her insides torn out. She could not believe that the floor wasn't covered with her blood. Daisy folded the magazine and hid it in her handbag. She wrapped her arms around her body and bowed her head, trying to become as small as possible.

"Another espresso?" the waiter asked softly.

She nodded.

She drank as if it might save her life. Slowly her brain began to work again. The evil fastened at her breast with metallic teeth, but she began to think. She had to get help. There was only one person who could help her. She put some money on the table, walked swiftly to the street and stopped a passing cab.

In Patrick Shannon's office three people sat silently: Shannon, Hilly Bijur and Candice Bloom. Only Candice knew what time it was and that Jerry Tallmer and Daisy were waiting for her at Le Perigord Park. Thank God Tallmer was a gentle, kind man and thank God Daisy knew where to meet him for lunch. They wouldn't miss her.

Bijur was the first to break the silence. "Pat, this doesn't have to be a disaster."

Shannon looked at him without comprehension. He had to find Daisy before she saw this. "Where's Daisy?" he asked urgently.

"Having lunch—she's okay," Candice reassured him.

"Pat, will you just listen! Look, for Christ's sake, just let me read some of this stuff back to you," Hilly insisted. He turned to the second page of the article. " 'Queen Anne's, a well known school for retarded children, is regarded as one of the finest institutions of its kind. The fees are high, averaging twenty-three thousand dollars a year for each child. Mrs. Joan Henderson, head of the school, said that four years after Prince Stash Valensky's death in 1967, Princess Daisy took over the entire financial burden of her sister's support.' And then they quote this Mrs. Henderson, 'It could not have been easy for her,' Mrs. Henderson said, 'since we sometimes had to wait for her checks, but eventually one always came. I don't believe that more than a few days in any week have gone by in the last ten years'—*the last ten fucking years*, Pat—'that Danielle hadn't received a letter containing a drawing or a picture postcard from her sister. Princess Daisy always visited every Sunday while she still lived in England, even though she and Danielle were only six when they were separated.' *Six*—only six, Pat! And, look, here she says, 'The twins are very close in spite of the difference in their intellectual capacities. Danielle certainly understands Daisy better than she understands any of her teachers—indeed, in a long lifetime, I have rarely seen devotion such as Princess Daisy's.' End quote. And then there's the picture of Daisy painting a kid on a pony, and just listen to this caption, 'Daisy's expert portraits paid for her twin's continued residence in the only home she's ever known, while Daisy herself lived in a low-rent SoHo walk-up and held down a full-time job as well.' "

"On the next page, right under the picture of Daisy on a set wearing her baseball jacket and her sailor hat, there's a quote from North. Let me read that one, Mr. Bijur," Candice said eagerly.

" 'Top commercial director, Frederick Gordon North, says that he was very disappointed when Princess Daisy decided to leave her job with him. "She was unquestionably the most creative and hardest working producer any director could hope to have. Everyone who ever worked with her loved her. She has a great talent for this business." When he was asked if he missed her collaboration on such widely admired commercials as those he directs for Dr Pepper, Downy, and Revlon, Mr. North said with a rueful smile, "She can have her old job back any time she wants. I wish her well." ' "

"Mr. Shannon," Candice said, "Daisy's a heroine."

"My point, my point exactly!" Hilly Bijur said in increasing excitement. "Look, Pat, yesterday we had just another pretty face going for us and today we have a candidate for Joan of Arc—she can fucking get the Helen Keller humanitarian award of the year—look at it that way, for Christ's sake."

"But," Candice said with a trace of timidity rarely heard in her, "how do you think Daisy's going to feel about having this all come out? Since she's kept it secret for so long, she couldn't possibly have wanted anyone to know."

"What the fuck does it matter how she *feels!*" Hilly Bijur gloated, fairly jumping up and down with glee. "It's probably the best fucking publicity break anybody ever got in the history of fucking fragrance. Holy shit, it'll make every paper in the country tomorrow. Ha! Just you tell me Candice baby, what Lauren Hutton or what's her name Hemingway or Catherine Deneuve or Candy Bergen have in their private lives that could be one-tenth as fascinating as this? Those stores are going to be mobbed when she makes her personal appearances! Every woman in the country will want to see Daisy with her very own eyes. She can get on Phil Donahue . . . a whole hour! Merv will love her, Mike Douglas, 'The Today Show' . . . maybe even Carson . . . sure, Carson, too . . ."

Patrick Shannon stood up. "Get the hell out of my office, Hilly, and don't come back," he shouted at the president of Elstree in a passion of disgust.

Shannon had told all his three secretaries to go to lunch and he was still sitting, his elbows on the desk, his head in his hands, a copy of *People* open before him, when Daisy silently opened the door of his office. She saw immediately what he was staring at although he slid the magazine into a drawer the instant he realized she was in the room.

"You don't have to hide it," Daisy said, in a voice without color, as if she were apologizing to someone in a dream.

Shannon jumped up from his chair and strode across the

room. He took her in his arms as she stood just inside the door, wearing her fine new dress, with the face of a punished, terrified child. She was so cold, so frighteningly icy that he did nothing but try to warm her, clasping her with all his warmth and strength, kneading her back with his big hands, cuddling her head to his chest, murmuring endearments like a mother. When he touched her hands and felt how frozen they were, he took them and slipped them under his jacket so that the heat of his chest might thaw them. Daisy pressed into him as if he were the only refuge in the world. As he hugged her to him, as she felt his heart beating strongly under her hands, as he stroked her hair and tried to fit her ever more closely to the shelter of his big body, she could feel the shattering pain in her heart becoming less shrill, as if it were being absorbed into him, melting from her coldness into his warmth. The relief was so great that at last she felt tears come to her eyes and, as he kept holding her and stroking her, she thawed even further and was able to sob, great howling sobs that came from her guts, but no matter how violently she shook, Shannon continued to clutch her firmly, taking her grief into himself with a total acceptance that gave her the freedom to hold nothing back. At last, after a long time, her shuddering, open-mouthed sounds became weeping and she finally reached for his handkerchief to try to dry her cheeks.

"Candice said you were having lunch or I'd have come to find you."

"She didn't know. They sent me an advance copy and I got it this morning."

"Daisy, come sit down. There." He nestled her close to him on the couch, one arm protectively around her shoulders. He found another handkerchief in his trousers and mopped gently at her face, but soon gave up the hopeless job and simply took both of her hands in his free one. She sighed deeply and laid the whole weight of her head on his shoulder. They sat there like that, breathing together for many minutes, before Daisy broke the silence.

"It was Ram." Her voice was unemphatic and flat, without emotion.

"Ram?"

"My half-brother. He was the one person I didn't tell you about."

"I don't understand. Why didn't you tell me about him?

Why should you hate him so much? Why did he do this to you?"

"He must have gone to the school and taken the picture," Daisy said, not answering his questions. "It was on the wall of Dani's bedroom. And then he told them those terrible lies about my mother. They must be lies if Ram told them. And I'll never know the truth—I'll never, *never* know it—everybody who might know is dead. Even Anabel said my father would never talk about it."

"But *why* would your brother want to hurt you?" Shannon persisted. "What was his motive? He says it's commercialization of the family name—but I can't buy that, it's not enough of a reason, not in this day and age."

Daisy gently disengaged herself from Shannon and pulled herself back on the couch so that they were sitting six inches apart. She clasped her hands tightly together and looked straight into his eyes.

"When I was a little girl, I loved him best next to my father. And then, when my father died and I was fifteen, Ram was the only one left. That summer . . . that summer . . ." She shook her head with impatience at her own cowardice and went resolutely on. "There was a week that summer after my father died when we were lovers. The first time he raped me. And he had to rape me the last time, too. But the other times in between, I—I didn't try hard enough to stop him. I let him. I didn't tell Anabel. I wanted someone to love me so badly . . . but that's no excuse."

"The hell it isn't!" Shannon said, taking her interlaced fingers in both his hands, and trying to pull her toward him.

"No, let me tell you the rest," Daisy said, holding herself away stiffly. "Ever since, ever since I got away from him I've refused to answer his letters. Finally, I wouldn't even read his letters—that's why my money was all lost I think. Of course, I could never ask him for a penny. But then, finally, when Anabel got cancer, Ram knew I couldn't manage it by myself anymore. Last Christmas I was trapped into seeing him. He said he'd take care of everyone, Anabel and Danielle, too— In exchange, he just wanted me to move back to England. But I know Ram and I knew enough to be afraid. That's why I took your offer, to be safe from him. This—this story—it's his way of having his revenge. He doesn't hate me, Pat, he loves me in his own way, he wants me the way he used to, he's never stopped wanting me."

"Daisy, he's a monster, a madman! That happened when you were *fifteen?*"

Daisy nodded.

"Didn't you tell anybody? Couldn't anybody *do* anything?"

"I finally told Anabel—when it was all over—and she found a way to send me far away from him. And now you know. Nobody else. I've never told anyone else, not even Kiki. I was too ashamed."

"I'm going to kill him," Shannon said quietly.

"But what good would that do?" Daisy dismissed his threat. The damage had been done. Done and done. She reached into her handbag for the copy of *People* and opened it to the photograph of herself and Danielle. "I wonder if Dani ever noticed that this picture is gone? It was her favorite, because we looked the most alike in it," Daisy said in sad wonderment. "She probably didn't notice. Oh, I hope she didn't."

Shannon reached for the magazine and put it behind him. "Daisy, don't think about it anymore."

"Don't think about it! You're crazy! My God, that's *all* they're going to want to know about now. I know how they'll slide into it, ever so tactfully—'How did you feel about that piece in *People,* tell us more about your sister, how well does she talk, what exactly do the two of you find to say to each other, what does it feel like to have an identical twin who can't, can't'—oh, they'll find the way to ask, they'll find a way to accuse me of keeping her a secret because I was ashamed of her instead of the real reason ... and Pat, I just don't know anymore. Oh, God, Pat, those questions, it'll be like having fingers tearing at my face, it'll be like being naked to everybody. Can't you hear them too? You don't think they're going to pretend they don't know, do you?"

"It doesn't matter what anyone would like to ask you," Shannon said. "Nothing would make me put you through more publicity. Candice will cancel all your interviews and all the store appearances. You'll never have to talk to anyone from the press again for the rest of your life."

"But the *launch,* the whole campaign? Pat, you can't do that."

"Don't worry about details. It's all going to go as

scheduled except for your personal participation. Just leave it up to me."

"Pat, Pat, why are you doing this? I've been in advertising too long not to know what difference it's going to make. You can't fool me."

"Daisy, you know how to make commercials, but you're not an expert on Supracorp's business." He took her in his arms again and kissed her lips. "I am, and I say you are *not* going to do it."

"Why are you being so good to me?" she asked as relief began to creep over her.

"Would one reason be enough?" He kissed her again and she nodded in acquiescence. "I love you, I'm in love with you, I love you absolutely and completely. Three reasons, and I could go on and on . . . but they'd all be variations on the same theme. I love you. I think I forgot to tell you that at *La Marée*. That was a serious omission, and I'm going to spend a lot of time making up for it." He wanted desperately to ask her if she loved him, but he didn't think it was fair. She was too open, too raw, too wounded. She'd feel gratitude and she'd say yes and if she didn't really love him, she would never tell him. He felt tingles as if from a million injections of love. He was tatooed for life. He could wait.

"It was a bloodbath," Luke said, dropping wearily into a chair. "And that's just for openers." Kiki gave him the martini she had just made, her only domestic skill, and watched like a mother wolf to make sure he drank up every last medicinal drop. That's what wives were for.

"I called Daisy," she said when he'd drained the glass. "She knew already, she'd seen it. I'm having lunch with her tomorrow."

"Christ! What kind of shape is she in?"

"Weird, didn't want me to come down to be with her tonight. Kind of strange, far-away, detached, terribly tired."

"Maybe we should both go down anyway."

"No, I'm convinced that she wants to be alone. She just didn't want to go into it anymore."

"I've been talking for the last six hours—I have a faint notion of how she feels. Could you give me another of those splendid martinis, sweetheart? Did you know that a theory exists that it doesn't hurt if you put a tiny drop of vermouth in it?"

"Oh." Kiki's father, as his last piece of paternal advice, had told her that the secret of a dry martini was just to pour straight gin of an excellent quality. That way you couldn't possibly go wrong.

"Tell me what happened," Kiki said.

"When I got back from lunch, there was a message to get my body over to Supracorp right away. Hilly Bijur was there, in Shannon's office, and Candice Bloom and her assistant and a dozen other people from Elstree. Shannon told all of us that Daisy was going to be left absolutely alone from now on, that no one was going to bother her, and then he just simply dropped the bomb—no Princess Daisy line, no launch, no commercials, no nothing. Zip! Finished! Over! Like it had never happened. Everything—every fucking thing."

"*But why?*" Kiki cried in astonishment. "Can't they go on without Daisy in person for goodness sakes?"

"He's right, Kiki. The launch wouldn't get off the ground and the stores wouldn't promote the stuff the way they've planned to and there are a half-dozen other perfumes being launched this month which were going to mean stiff competition for attention, no matter what. Without Daisy, we've got only some print ads and commercials which we could keep running for a while, but after that—nothing. *Bubkis.* See, the whole thing is based on *her,* on Daisy, her name, her face, and most of all, her personality. If Charlie lost that girl, they could replace her because the perfume isn't called by her name and most people don't even know who she is—just another pair of pants. If Lauren Hutton lost all her front teeth, instead of having that famous little space there, Revlon would find another girl or buy her new teeth. With Estée Lauder, it's not so much Karen Graham as it is Skrebenski's fantastic photographs that's the trademark. With Halston and Adolfo, Oscar de la Renta and Calvin Klein you've got four big-name designers, already enormously established, famous guys, all of whom are going to do store promotions like crazy, with their new fragrances—with Daisy we only had the romance of Daisy herself to *build* on. No, honeybunch, Shannon knows that it's time to cut his losses. No matter how much Supracorp has spent on the Princess Daisy line now—something like forty million—it's better to lose that much than to pour in more millions and end up losing them too. We spent all afternoon canceling what could still be canceled. But just money isn't the biggest part of the loss anyway—not for Shannon."

"I guess it's just a lucky thing that Supracorp's such a big business," Kiki said, testing the waters.

"No business is so big that they can overlook this sort of disaster. Not when they have stockholders. Shannon's going to be eyeball-high in serious shit. He could perfectly well have held Daisy to her contract. However, he made the decision not to. Don't worry about Daisy though—according to her contract, she still gets paid. Worry about Shannon. Oh, baby, worry about them both."

"I am!" Kiki breathed.

"Yeah. Listen, should I console you or should you console me, since Daisy won't let us console her?"

Kiki sat in his lap, tickling her nose on the tip of his beard. "That sounds like six of one and half a dozen of another."

"Let's try it and find out. Those old sayings usually have some truth to them."

26

$\mathcal{T}$he following morning, shortly after *People* appeared on the newsstands, Joseph Willowby and Reginald Stein, two major stockholders in Supracorp and both members of the nine-man board of directors, telephoned Patrick Shannon's executive secretary and demanded an immediate meeting. They arrived within ten minutes, flushed with a combination of anger and triumph. Shannon had finally given them the ammunition they'd been waiting for.

"What do you intend to do about this mess?" boomed Willowby, brandishing a copy of *People*.

"I warned you a year ago that the best thing to do with Elstree was to sell it, but no, as usual, Patrick Shannon had one of his off-the-wall strokes of genius and he had to have it his way," Reginald Stein said in tones of vindictive satisfaction.

"Sit down, fellas. I'll tell you what I'm going to do," Shannon said cheerfully.

They sat down and he told them. When he'd finished, Willowby said in fury, "In other words, Elstree is a total loss for the third year in a row? And you call that a way to run a business? We'll have lost almost a hundred million on that one pet division of yours—Shannon's baby. Of course, you realize what this has done to our over-all profit picture?"

Shannon nodded calmly. There was no point in interrupting Willowby. And he also happened to be correct.

"To say nothing of our stock," Stein chimed in bitterly. "It went up in anticipation of this new move and all the excitement you spent so much money to create, but by the time the exchange closes today I don't even want to think about how far down it'll be. And when the news gets out that we're closing down the whole Princess Daisy operation—shit, Shannon, would you like to bet on how many points Supracorp will drop? Would you? How many points, Shannon?" he roared.

"I don't know, Reg, but this move isn't something I'm prepared to negotiate with you. I've told you what I intend to do. I made the decision and I'm standing by it."

"You cocky bastard, don't count on that!" shouted Willowby. "I'm going to call a special meeting of the board, Shannon, and throw your ass out of Supracorp if it's the last thing I do. I've had it with your so-called independence and high-rolling and flying by the seat of your pants. We'll get someone in here who doesn't throw away millions of dollars on a lousy whim. If you hadn't let the Valensky girl off the hook we could probably salvage this fuck-up—in part, anyway. It's your own fault and I'm going to nail you on it. You've made one high-handed decision too many, Shannon!"

"Call a meeting by all means," Shannon said. "I'm perfectly prepared to sit down with the board at any time. But now, gentlemen, if you'll excuse me? We do have seven other divisions and I've a number of matters to attend to."

After the two fuming men had left his office, Patrick Shannon sat and thought for a few minutes. Several other members of the board had leanings toward caution and conservatism quite as strong as those of Joe and Reg. He'd had constant trouble with their group in the few, short, exhilarating years during which he'd been head of Supracorp. They didn't know him well enough yet to be entirely convinced of his basic soundness, but as long as he'd been making money for them they'd been prepared to put up with him, little as they liked it. Supracorp was perfectly strong enough to withstand the Elstree problem in the long run, and they knew it as well as he did, but this was the best opportunity Joe and Reg and their gang had yet had, or probably would ever have in the future, to get rid of him. Yesterday, when he'd made the decision to protect Daisy from all the exposure necessary to ensure the success of the launch, it hadn't been a business decision. As a business decision it stank, Shannon admitted to himself. He'd taken losses before, but never for reasons he could control. He'd risked failure before, but never, *never* for anyone else. But he wasn't going to win at the expense of Daisy, not while he had a choice left. And without a choice he wouldn't want his job anyway. A good thing too, since it was entirely possible that he would be voted out of Supracorp.

"So . . . fuck *that* noise!" Shannon said out loud, grinning, and went back to work.

In North's studio the copy of *People* had been passed from one person to another all morning. A Planter's Peanut spot was being shot on a closed set while a football star did fifty-four consecutive takes which involved actually eating two nuts and delivering four lines on the virtue of "freshly roasted flavor," while simultaneously opening a fresh can and holding it up to the camera. This feat of hand-to-eye-to-mouth coordination had prevented anyone from exchanging their reactions until the lunch break. Wingo, Arnie Greene, Nick-the-Greek and North finally had a chance to meet over sandwiches in North's office with the door closed behind them.

"I should never have gotten her into this shitpot," Nick said, with an air of great gloom. "It's all my fault."

"Typical," Wingo said waspishly. "You'd take credit for everything, including pogroms, floods and stuffing ballot boxes."

Nick mournfully fingered his switchblade. "Be fair, Wingo, it all started with her hair, and that *was* my fault. Say, remember how cute and mad she was the day we tried to get her to join us in the new production company?"

"Nick," Wingo hissed, "could we be spared your reminiscences?"

"What are you talking about, Nick?" North asked, suddenly interested.

"Ah, balls, I couldn't care less if you know," Nick said. "Wingo and I were thinking of going out on our own if we could get Daisy as our producer, but she straightened us out good; loyalty, what we owed you and all that bullcrap, horse turds and eighteen other kinds of buffalo droppings. Wish you'd heard her."

"I don't want to be just a cameraman forever, North," Wingo said defensively. "I can direct—even if Daisy didn't think so."

"How long ago did this happen?" North demanded.

"Maybe a year, maybe more, and there was nothing cute about her that day," Wingo answered. "She was as angry as I've ever seen her, even worse than the time the Cinemobile people got lost in Arizona and we wasted the whole day sitting broiling under a tent like a bunch of fucking Bedouins."

"Nah," said Nick, "I think she was angrier the time that chimp she located down in Mexico took a piece of luggage into his cave and just played with it for six hours, instead of trying to tear it apart so we could show how tough it was. Remember the things she said to try and make it come out?"

"None of you ever heard Daisy really upset," said Arnie miserably. "Because you weren't there the day she found out that the caterer had charged us for ten pounds of smoked salmon on a shoot for Oscar Mayer where we only served the sponsor's products. Now *that* was angry! We'll never find another producer like her again."

"Listen, why don't you guys get out of my office?" North bit out the words. "If I want to go to a wake, I know a couple of Irish funeral parlors—at least the ethnic quality would be pure."

"Shove it, North," Wingo said. "You're more upset than any of us. You think you can kid us?" North looked at him and fell silent.

"I never realized why she worked so hard," Arnie said, compulsively turning to the pages of the *People* story again. "No wonder she didn't seem to have much of a private life. That poor kid."

"Listen," North said, "I want this whole subject dropped, permanently and forever. None of us really knew Daisy and none of us really understands her now, even with that magazine piece, so will you all just shut the fuck up about it and go back to work? And that's not a suggestion."

He watched the three men file out of his office and locked his door behind them. Systematically, methodically and quietly, he then proceeded to demolish a new Cooke zoom lens, a twenty-five-thousand-dollar piece of equipment that had just arrived from England. He didn't know any other way to mourn, he didn't even know he was mourning, and he certainly didn't admit for whom he was mourning, but never again in his life did Frederick Gordon North visit Venice.

Vanessa Valarian called Robin at his showroom the minute she read *People*.

"Send someone downstairs to buy you a copy and I'll meet you in a half-hour for lunch. I can't possibly wait till tonight to talk about it. Oh, Robin, darling, it's so thrilling!"

As soon as they were settled on their banquette at La Côte Basque, without preamble, Vanessa fixed Robin with her eyes. "Now, listen, sweetheart, the main thing to remember is that we knew her *when*. We were her very first friends, her first sponsors, the first people who held out a hand to her without knowing a single thing about how or why she had to struggle, that brave, wonderful little darling."

"We helped her first, before anybody cared," Robin repeated.

"Because," Vanessa went on, paying no attention to him, "we sensed a rare spirit in her, a beauty of spirit that others had overlooked. And we always knew that there was something marvelously worthwhile about her—her sensitivity, Robin, her enchantingly modest reluctance to accept gifts or invitations because she couldn't reciprocate —*as if we cared!*—but, thank God, we were able to help her with commissions and clothes—I don't know if she would have managed without us."

"It wouldn't have been possible, darling," Robin assured her. "I'm sure everyone who knows us will realize that."

"I can hardly wait for the Winter Palace party—she'll be so happy to see a few familiar faces in the mob—I feel so *protective* of her, Robin. Almost maternal. And now I'll be able to tell everyone about what *really* happened on the yacht—all those people who've been hounding me with their nasty questions—and vicious insinuations. At last I'll be free to reveal the truth without betraying Daisy."

"What *did* really happen, Vanessa?"

"Never mind about the details, dearest. I'll think of something."

It was a dreary, wet morning at Woodhill Manor, ugly weather for early September, which usually was fine in England. Ram, sitting down to breakfast, could think of nothing but the fact that, allowing for the difference in time zones, the issue of *People* with Daisy on the cover would be appearing on American newsstands by the time he ate lunch that same day. He contemplated, with a lack of interest, those choice brown eggs, boiled for exactly three and a half minutes, that faced him on the table. He rang for the manservant who attended his breakfast.

"Why are there no gooseberry preserves, Thompson?"

"I'll inquire, Sir." He returned within seconds. "The grocer had promised them for yesterday but he didn't deliver because his van broke down. The cook regrets the problem, Sir."

"All right, Thompson. It's not important." As Ram sat motionless in the dining room of his gracious dwelling, one of the most peaceful in all of plenteous, gentle Devon, he wondered how many people in the neighboring market town would eventually read that issue of the magazine. It was easily available in London, of course, with scarcely a day's difference in time. And in Paris, Rome, Madrid . . . within a week it would be everywhere. Leaving his breakfast untouched, Ram rose from the table and rang again. "I'm going out, Thompson. Tell the cook to make sure the grocer delivers today. If he can't, go into town and pick up the order yourself."

As Ram walked, carrying his shotgun, across his ancestral acres, as he opened the gates of fences and wandered across the meadows, he thought about the pictures and the interview he had given the correspondent for *People*. It would be an enormous story. It would destroy her. She would never recover from it. He had made sure of that.

And so her picture was going to be used on the cover? Was it indeed? Ram stared out across the wet fields, imagining her face, imagining it smashed, crushed, broken, punctured, blood running from her nostrils, from her ears, from her eyes. From moment to moment he was able to sustain himself with these images but then he would see her again and again as she had been on the night of the *Quatorze Juillet*, see her as she danced in her white lace dress, flying mirthfully from arm to arm, ardent and innocent, eyes alight with discovery and jubilation, hair flying, tangled . . . laughing, laughing, dancing—dancing with everyone but him . . . the night on which he had finally acknowledged that she must be his or he would die.

He didn't come back for lunch on that rainy day, nor did he return for tea. Mrs. Gibbons, the housekeeper, began to fret about her employer, who was always so gratifyingly precise in his habits.

"It's ever so windy out," she complained to Sally, the

housemaid, "and not a day to go out shooting, not at all. There won't be any birds about. I thought so when I saw him leave the house, but of course it wasn't up to me to say anything."

"Gentlemen have to have their sport," the housemaid replied, philosophically.

"It's pneumonia weather, that's what it is, and cook had such a lovely bit of steak for his lunch," Mrs. Gibbons grumbled.

"Someone's knocking at the pantry door," Sally announced to the housekeeper, who had become increasingly deaf during her long years of service to the Woodhill family. "I'll go."

"Tell whoever it is to wipe his feet before he comes into the kitchen."

The housemaid's screams penetrated Mrs. Gibbons's deafness, penetrated into the most distant corners of Woodhill Manor, penetrated into the wing that had been built during the reign of Elizabeth I, into the wing that had been added in the days of Queen Anne, into the wing of Edwardian vintage. Every room in the time-blessed, lovely old house echoed for minutes with the screams of the woman who had opened the door to the farmers carrying Ram's body, his head half shot away, but washed so clean of blood, because of the hours during which the rain had fallen on his dead body, that they could see the half of the brain that remained.

That evening, when they sat huddled together over a glass of brandy, after the local mortician's men had finally taken the body away, Sally, her eyes red, said in bewildered tones, "Why aren't gentlemen more careful, Mrs. Gibbons? I never do like it, never, when I see someone walk out with a loaded gun, no, not ever, no matter how good a shot he is. I don't care for the sporting life. Poor Prince Valensky."

"There'll be another Woodhill to take his place as soon as the lawyers get on the job, Sally. I wonder who it will be?" said Mrs. Gibbons, comfortingly. "Time will tell, I suppose. It always has."

No one studied the cover photograph of Daisy more thoroughly than the Honorable Sarah Fane. No one read the article more carefully, almost memorizing each word, than the Honorable Sarah Fane.

As she held the magazine up to her mirror and compared herself to the cover picture, an expression of pleasure and finally gratification dawned on her features, the features of that exquisite English rose that takes hundreds of years to breed.

She's a very, very good type—if one likes that type, thought Sarah Fane. Actually, one could hardly ask for anything more lovely. It could be considered to have been a compliment, a rather strange compliment . . . and one she could never repeat . . . nor forget . . . but nevertheless . . . yes, definitely a compliment.

She threw the magazine into a wastepaper basket and continued dressing. She was so punctual that she was able to linger a bit, admiring her thirty-two-carat engagement ring, far, far too big to be vulgar, thinking of the marvelous life that stretched in front of her as the future wife of the richest oil man in Houston. He was rich beyond comprehension, beyond passion. Nothing in the entire world would ever be out of her reach. His mother's family came from Springfield, Illinois, and it included two vice-presidents of the United States, one great senator and one signer of the Declaration of Independence. He had a pioneering robber baron as a paternal great-grandfather, a combination which, in America, melded neatly into the equivalent of royalty. Sarah Fane had always sworn to herself that anything was better than being an unmarried post-deb but there was no way to deny—although only to herself—that she had mismanaged her year. Still she'd made the best of it before it was over. Life in Houston, where she would, of course, reign as queen, was by all accounts remarkably civilized. They would travel a great deal. And he did worship her, she reminded herself. His worship was so palpable that she could smell it on her hair, feel it swirl around her like smoke burned before an idol. His worship created an image of herself which even she could not wish to be more faultless. And, whatever the future held, he would do exceptionally well as a first husband.

Daisy slept the deep sleep of complete emotional exhaustion. She woke early the next morning, filled with a profound, dream-induced joy. All specific memory of her dreams faded except for one fragment, a single glimpse, one bright image of running rapturously through a vast, flowered field, hand in hand with Danielle, who could run as lightly and as rapidly as Daisy herself. That was all there was to it. Daisy lay bathed in a transport of happiness so phosphorescent, so tangible that she did not dare move for fear of losing this vision, this completely mysterious visitation. Had it ever happened? Had they ever run so together? How old could they have been? She had no memory of such an experience, but she felt, deeply, that it must have occurred—or, if it had never happened, it had *now* happened in such a vivid dream that it had become a memory more real than reality. It was part of her existence, crystallized forever in light and color and the sensation of running—she and Danielle had run together during that night and they had both been happy. So happy. Together and equal.

The rapture of the dream lasted, the glorious vision persisted, even as the phone started to ring and Daisy realized she had to get out of the apartment in a hurry. She dressed quickly in jeans, sandals and a thin navy cotton turtleneck. She pulled all her hair tightly around her head and secured it firmly and impatiently. Then she wrapped a large navy and red scarf over her hair so that not a strand of it showed. She found the biggest pair of sunglasses she owned and, when she put them on and glanced in the mirror, she was satisfied that no one would recognize her. It was just past nine now and the phone kept ringing eight or nine times, then stopped and then started again.

Daisy put Theseus on his leash and hurried out, away from the phone, away from any contact with anyone who might be trying to reach her. She took a cab through the morning traffic from SoHo all the way up Park Avenue, then went west, crossing the park at 72nd Street. When the driver was near the Sheep Meadow, she got out, paid him and let Theseus loose to frolic. Around her swirled the other dog-walkers, the children playing with Frisbees, the perpetual volleyball games, the young couples necking on blankets under the sun of the morning, as settled in as if they had been there all night. Daisy sat cross-legged on the dubious grass and watched the towers of the city circle around her.

After a few minutes Daisy was aware of a feeling rising like a tide from her toes to the roots of her hair, a feeling she was unfamiliar with and couldn't identify although she knew it was important. She tried to capture its essence, but it wasn't until she had watched Theseus running loose and wild, ranging from one end of the vast field to another with the bounding energy of a dog who usually has to be kept under stern control, that she began to understand. *She felt free.* She felt as if a great clutter of debris of the past had been swept away, debris as caked in mud and sediment as objects brought up by a diver from a sunken ship, debris that had enchained her. It had demanded so much of her attention, that heavy, mucky load. She had needed to dismantle the past before she could dive into the sea of the future and, in one stroke, Ram had unfettered her, no matter how brutally, from a lifetime in which she'd been bound and gagged by irrational taboos, fears, secrets. She had been led out of the labyrinth, led, by cruel surprise, out into the fresh, clean air by an act that was meant to annihilate her. Again she saw Ram lying in the deck chair at *La Marée,* beckoning, always beckoning, and this time she began to forgive him and, in forgiving him, she made her first step toward forgetting him.

A grimy little boy stumbled over Daisy's legs and fell, crying, into her lap. She comforted him until his mother arrived, in no particular hurry, to collect him. Another baby hung in a sling on the woman's back. Daisy gave the child up without reluctance and returned to her thoughts.

In London she had asked Shannon how she could unthink her feelings of guilt for Dani's condition, just because mere logic told her it wasn't her fault. He had answered that perhaps it was necessary to replace a truth that is wrong with one that is right. But what if there was a third way? *What if she simply had to let it go?* It was not her problem to portion out blame. Why should she be limited forever by whatever it was her father and mother had done to each other—and to her and to Dani?

Ram's assertion that Dani might have had a normal childhood was disproved by dozens of memories Daisy had of the time in Big Sur, of the differences she had seen between herself and Dani from the earliest days she could remember. Her dream of running in a field of flowers—she knew now that it had never happened. Dani had never been able to run like that. But Ram's falsehoods had been printed and no amount of later retraction or clarification would ever change the public's idea of the truth. *But what did it matter?* Everyone concerned was dead now, and she was the only person left who cared. And it was all too long ago. Ram's series of ancient recriminations made Daisy realize how much she, too, had been caught up in the fatal net of the past.

Abruptly Daisy found herself in the line of fire between four leaping, shouting Frisbee players. She sat quietly while they threw the plastic disk harmlessly over her head. In a few minutes, their game moved to one side and their exhortations to each other faded, as her thoughts turned to feelings she had tried to cope with so often during her life, the feelings of being an impostor, not Princess Daisy, not someone with a right to that title. Suddenly it seemed so clear that she gasped. She hadn't been Princess Daisy because Dani had not been Princess Danielle. All the while that Danielle had been hidden away from everybody, the thought of her, closer than any sister could be, had always been carried within her. Her knowledge that Dani was doomed to never grow up had prevented her from really living her own life. She had always held back from taking happiness as her due, she had not felt *entitled* to enjoy to the fullest whatever joy had come her way. But now! Now she and Dani were rejoined. There in *People* she stood with her arm around the twin who had been taken away from her so long ago. Their separation was over. Their immemorial kinship had been avowed, once and for all. And now Daisy could admit that Dani was happy in her own way and that nothing that Daisy did *not* have would make Dani any happier. She couldn't solve the past. It was impossible. It had always been impossible.

And in the dream, in the dream . . . they had both been happy.

Theseus came loping up, a pigeon held gently in his mouth, and deposited the struggling bird in her lap. It was unharmed and indignant and Daisy, knowing the fearless gangster ways of New York pigeons, watched without surprise as it merely walked away with hasty dignity.

"No, Theseus. Naughty dog." Oh, why not, she thought, let him catch another if he can. It's not as if he ever kills them. "Go on, run, Theseus, run as much as you like. Good dog."

What was it she had always thought she wanted? The freedom to become herself? Well, by God, she'd become herself, willy-nilly, in full color and black and white and hundreds of words of text. In spite of Ram's inaccuracies, her double life, with the tiptoeing around the Horse People to make the money to keep Dani in Queen Anne's was now common knowledge. And so what? She'd never sold a portrait of which she was ashamed. And what difference did it make that she'd taken the Elstree contract to buy her freedom from Ram? She had the right to dispose of herself any way she chose, just as any other woman did. She didn't have to worry about the Valensky name—she *was* the Valensky name and she could do with it what she liked. What a pompous, stuffy fool Ram had sounded. Daisy knew exactly who she was and she knew why it was worth a million dollars to Supracorp to obtain the rights to an image that could be photographed and interviewed, an image that was a potentially profitable approximation of someone called Princess Daisy. But, since she was clear about the difference between the two, what harm was there in it? The people she cared about knew the difference: Kiki, Luke, Anabel—even Wingo and Nick-the-Greek. And North. To be fair, North had known the difference. Maybe that was what had made him so angry at her.

And Patrick Shannon. Daisy carefully inspected the shabby turf of the Sheep Meadow before she lay back on it. Patrick Shannon. Patrick Shannon. He loved her. He didn't love the *idea* of "Princess Daisy"—he loved Daisy. She had been so agonized yesterday that his words hadn't really hit her with their full impact, but now, as she lay staring up at the sky over Central Park, her heart, to which entirely too much had happened in the last twenty-four hours, leapt around like an unleashed lurcher surrounded by pheasants. How much of her fine new courage, Daisy wondered, how much of this feeling of glorious freedom, how much of her new wisdom, how much of this unmistakable intuition of permanent change, came from the knowledge that Patrick Shannon loved her? How much of it came from the realization that she loved him, as she had never loved a man before or ever would again?

Daisy jumped up. *That* was one more question that definitely didn't need answering. To hell with weighing, measuring, examining, testing, holding back, calculating, protecting herself, always protecting. Over! She looked at her watch.

There was still a half-hour before she had to meet Kiki at the zoo. She whistled for Theseus and dodged another Frisbee. As she bent down to attach his leash, she almost snarled her hair in the catch. Daisy straightened up in surprise. What had happened to her scarf? She pivoted and spotted it lying where she had been sitting and thinking. Evidently ... apparently, unless you believe in ghosts who go around untying scarves and undoing hair, she must have done it herself. Daisy laughed in joy and reached into her shoulder bag for the little brush she carried there. She brushed out her silver-gilt hair, brushed and brushed it until it streamed down her back like a cape and danced in the wind like a thousand bright butterflies. She looked in her compact mirror and used a dab of powder on her nose and some pink gloss on her lips. She dropped her sunglasses into her bag, tucked in her pullover and threaded the scarf through the loops of her jeans and tied it with a huge bow in the front.

Daisy and Theseus strolled leisurely toward the zoo, both of them, the proud dog and the proud princess, holding their heads high. As she approached the zoo, the crowd began to grow thicker. The fine fall weather had brought out half of New York; not just the nannies and children and out-of-work and the elderly. As Daisy approached a bench, two middle-aged women who were sitting there, passing a copy of *People* back and forth, spotted her.

"Oh, look! It's just got to be her!" one of the women said to the other.

"I think—yes, you're right. Oh, I don't believe it, Sophie. I just don't believe it."

"I'm going to get her autograph," the first woman said excitedly.

"Oh, no, you wouldn't dare, oh, Sophie, don't."

"Just watch me." The woman snatched the magazine away from her friend and walked up to Daisy.

"Excuse me, but you're Princess Daisy, aren't you?" she asked.

Daisy stopped. So it was starting. She hadn't thought it would be so soon. She smiled at the woman.

"Yes, I am."

"Could I have your autograph—would you mind?"

"Oh, it's—it's okay—it's fine—but I don't have anything to write with."

"Here, here's a pen." Daisy took it and started to write her name on the cover.

"Oh, no," the woman protested, taking the magazine and turning to the photograph of Daisy and Danielle. "Here's where I want it. And could you write to Sophie Franklin? That's spelled S-o-p-h-i-e F-r-a-n-k-l-i-n," she added helpfully.

Daisy looked at the big black-and-white photo. Two girls, together, both smiling, both happy. She wrote quickly, gave the magazine back to the woman and walked on.

"Oh, look, just look what she wrote," Sophie Franklin said delightedly to her friend. "See—it says 'With best wishes to Sophie Franklin from Princess Daisy and Princess Danielle Valensky. Well! And you didn't want me to ask her!"

Kiki was sitting grimly at a table outside the zoo cafeteria clutching an extra chair and snapping at people who tried to sit down and share the table with her as was the zoo custom.

"Are you keeping that chair for anyone, lady?"

"Daisy!"

"I'm sorry—am I late?" Daisy laughed, taking the chair.

"No—I got here early—but ... my God, Daisy, you look gorgeous!"

"So, what else is new?"

"Daisy!"

"Kiki, do you think we could eliminate these exclamations of 'Daisy' every other sentence? I know I'm Daisy, you know I'm Daisy, we both know I'm Daisy, so why make such a point of it?"

"Daisy!"

"Really, Kiki, you're not getting the point again."

"You're goddamned right I'm not," Kiki said. "I was thinking of myself as a Saint Bernard dog or a knight in shining armor, or at least a friend in need, and what do I find but a blooming, downright glowing ... no, more like delirious ... what's come over you?"

"I've come over me."

"That makes no sense at all."

"Well it does to me and that's what counts. Poor darling Kiki, you must have been so worried. I'm sorry I gave you such a bad time."

"Me? I've had a wonderful time compared to everyone else involved in this shindy. Luke came home absolutely wrung out last night. And the whole media department spent the afternoon on the phones canceling the network commercials and the print ads—whatever wasn't too late to be stopped ..."

"*Wait a minute!* The only things Pat said he was going

to cancel were my interviews and the store appearances and maybe the party! What are you talking about?" Daisy asked in alarm.

"Oh, Christ. Maybe I shouldn't have told you . . . I just don't know . . . they had a meeting yesterday afternoon at Supracorp and Shannon told them he was going to give up the entire Princess Daisy line. Luke agrees with him that without you the whole thing just wouldn't work. Shannon decided to cut his losses before they spent any more money than they already have. Luke said it's got to be at least something like forty million down the drain what with one thing and another in the last eight months. He says they'll probably try to sell Elstree—*if* it's worth anything now."

"But Kiki, I am going to do the publicity and the stores. I'm going to do everything—everything I said I would."

"Daisy!" Kiki groaned. She wished her friend would be more consistent. All these changes were confusing, even to someone as poised as she.

"God, Kiki, where's the phone? What if it's too late?" Daisy said in a sudden frenzy of realization.

"They can cancel the cancellations!" Kiki shouted at Daisy, who was running rapidly into the cafeteria. "Don't worry!" She sat down and looked at Theseus. "Don't ask me why, kiddo," she told him, "but I'm going to get you eight hotdogs. No? Ten? Oh, all right then, I'll make it a dozen. We both know you're spoiled, so why fool around?"

In the phone booth Daisy fumbled frantically in her change purse. It bulged with infuriating pennies and un-usable half dollars. No dimes. Finally she dredged out two quarters. She dialed Supracorp, got a wrong number and listened, appalled, as the first quarter dropped. The second time she dialed with the care of a scientist dealing with a dangerous bacteria culture.

"Mr. Shannon's office," trilled one of his secretaries after Daisy had been put through by the switchboard.

"Please, may I speak to him?" she asked, breathing so fast that she could hardly speak.

"I'm sorry, Mr. Shannon is in conference and he partic-ularly asked not to be disturbed," the secretary said with the self-satisfied pleasure of the shoe clerk who tells you he has nothing at all in your size. "Would you like to leave a message?"

Daisy took a deep breath and found a voice of ringing

metal. "This is Princess Daisy Valensky and I want to speak to Mr. Shannon immediately," she commanded.

"Just one minute, please."

"I'm in a pay phone, I've run out of change and if you don't put him on in two seconds, I'm going to ..." Daisy realized she was talking to dead air. The secretary had put her on hold.

"Daisy?" Shannon said, with tense concern.

"Pat, is it too late?"

"Too late for what? Are you all right?"

"Yes," she said quickly. "I'm fine. But is it too late to put the Elstree thing back together, everything, the whole campaign, me included, media, stores, everything—is it too late to go back to yesterday where everything was before I saw you?"

"Wait a minute, how do you know what's been going on?"

"Kiki told me, but that's not important. Pat, Pat, it's too complicated to explain on the phone but I've ... oh, I've come into my own *self* is the best way I can say it ... it's ..."

The operator's voice intoned, "Five cents for the next five minutes, please."

"Daisy, where are you?" Shannon shouted.

"Will you take five pennies, operator?" Daisy asked pleadingly.

"Daisy, what's the number there for Christ's sake?"

"Oh, Pat, just listen, I could have been one of quintuplets and I'd still be me, I could cut off all my hair or dye it black, I could never paint or ride again, or I could learn Speedwriting or sky diving, or I could become an interior decorator or a movie star or a bookbinder, and *I'd still be me,*" she exalted.

"Where the hell are you calling from?"

"The zoo. Pat, Pat, don't you see? I'm the person you know, just her—or is it just she?—never mind, but I'm no one else, I'm me, Daisy Valensky, from the inside out, all the way through down to rock bottom and I like it, it feels good for the first time, really good, and *real,* Pat, real, as if I deserve it, the good of it and the bad of it—oh, I keep forgetting—it's not too late to go back to the plans for the Princess Daisy business, is it, to cancel the cancellations?"

"Hell, no, of course not, but Daisy, where are ..."

His voice was cut off and the shrill of a nonfunctioning telephone replaced it.

Daisy looked in astonishment at the box on the wall. She, the utterly efficient organizer of a thousand complicated location shoots, had failed to follow the basic technique required of the lowliest production assistant: when calling from a public booth, give your number and wait to be called back. She hung up the phone and went to borrow some change from Kiki. She hadn't finished talking to Patrick Shannon, not by a long shot.

If a person lives in Manhattan long enough he gets to accept the fact that there are perhaps only a dozen perfect days in any given year; days during which New York City regains that sea-girt light that once was responsible for so much of the magic; days on which a breeze sweeps the city but does not blow so hard that it creates whirlpools of filth on the pavement; days on which it is possible to remember and understand that the city was once a pastoral island, surrounded by swift rivers; days on which the eye is able to see clear across town from the Hudson River to the East River; days during which New Yorkers congratulate themselves on sticking it out during the rest of the year. It was on the night of such a day that The Russian Winter Palace Ball took place. An unexpected calm descended on the detail-burdened spirit of Candice Bloom as she woke up that morning, looked out of the window and sniffed the air. She knew immediately that there would be no last-minute illness in the ranks of Warner Le Roy's four hundred and fifty employees at the Tavern on the Green; no single one of the six hundred guests, carefully culled from the upper reaches of every segment of New York's overlapping worlds of society, the arts and power, would fail to appear; there would be no problem with the ice sculptures melting before they could be displayed; none of the horses hitched to the troikas would bolt and run off with their precious passengers; the night would be mild, the stars would be clearly visible in the plum-colored New York sky and there would be no need to put up a tent on the outside terrace of the restaurant, that, only yesterday, had been planted with seven hundred pots of tall daisy bushes flown in from California. No moon, but who needed a moon with two thousand candles and sixty thousand twinkle lights? In every bone of her lanky and skimpily fleshed frame she knew that Friday, September 16, 1977, was going to be her lucky day.

Daisy woke up early on that same morning with a moment of confusion before she realized that last night she had gotten into bed with Patrick Shannon and never left it. This was the first time she'd spent a whole night in his apartment and she blamed it entirely on Lucy, Shannon's lurcher, who, after first flirting and then spurning Theseus's affections for an absurdly long time—at one point tucking her tail resolutely between her legs and biting him on the nose—had finally, capriciously, changed her mind just as Daisy was about to take a crestfallen but still willing Theseus home to his own pillow. Lucy was not an easy customer, Daisy thought sleepily, but if there was ever to be a chance to breed true lurcher puppies so that she could give one to Kiki, she would have to put up with the bitch. She fell asleep again for a few minutes and woke up in Shannon's arms. Oh, but this was something outside of the realm of past experience, this emotion of deep, sure gladness. From head to toe, her body was dancing with joy and welcome. There was a lack of any barrier between their two skins and their two minds and their two hearts, as, intertwined, they seemed to lie in a pool of golden light, pure, gay and penetrating, even though the sun itself had not yet entered the room. Daisy felt as if she were at the very center of the earth, like the pit of a great fruit, and at the same time she felt as if the two of them were flying together at the rim of the world, on the outer edge of experience.

"Is this bliss?" she whispered to him.

"This is love," he whispered back and when she reached up to put her arms around his neck, he felt the tears of happiness on her cheeks.

The snow-making machines had started on the bridle path where it coiled past the entrance to the park at 59th Street. They had spread a thick carpet of snow, one hundred feet wide, all the way to the Tavern at 67th Street. There the bridle path passes directly in front of the terrace of the restaurant and the snow makers continued to cover the path until the terrace was out of their sight. Then they doubled back and covered the entrance court of the Tavern and the street leading out to Central Park West, so that the guests, whether they came by limousine or by troika, all crossed into winter. From as far as Florida, Maine and Texas, Jenny Antonio had located thirty troikas and had them trucked to New York, but even she hadn't been able to get enough for all six hundred guests. Troikas are in short supply in the United States and, in spite of the dictionary-assured fact that any carriage drawn by three horses could be reasonably called a troika, Candice had insisted on picking only those that looked foreign, if not absolutely Russian. "I don't intend this to look like a *nouveau* version of 'Wagon Train,' " she told Jenny with asperity.

The Parks Department had given Supracorp permission to gather the troikas, their drivers and horses together and erect a temporary platform from which they would pick up their passengers and depart. Joseph Papp's chief set designer had been inspired by Supracorp's money to develop a healthy capitalistic outlook. The result was a daisy-bowered, latticed pavilion which managed to suggest what the Kremlin might look like if anyone with taste could get hold of it. Huge flags, in Princess Daisy lapis lazuli blue, with the stylized single daisy embroidered on them, blew from every corner of the pavilion, which was bathed in the footlights and spotlights, cunningly concealed in trees. All thirty of the troika drivers had been outfitted by a theatrical costumer in authentic greatcoats and three-cornered hats, some in red, some in green and still others in blue.

That night, as dusk fell, Candice Bloom and Jenny first took their hired limousine to the Tavern on the Green, where they made a final inspection of the arrangements, lingering a minute to watch the ten ice sculptors who were just finishing their work. The press photographers were already gathered at the entrance to the restaurant. Candice decided that she had hired more gypsy violinists than anyone needed, so she delegated a group of them to trudge down ten blocks to the pavilion where they could fiddle for the specially honored guests who had been invited to assemble there and arrive by troika.

As dozens of waiters started to light the two thousand candles in their silver candelabra, Candice and Jenny climbed back into their long, black car and were delivered to the empty pavilion. A few minutes remained before Daisy and Shannon were supposed to arrive so that they could be driven to the restaurant before the first guests were due. Candice, quivering with nerves, bent over her immaculate, thoughtful, quite possibly perfect list, a creation of the Art of Public Relations which, she now insisted, deserved its own graduate school.

Troika One: Princess Daisy and Patrick Shannon.
Troika Two: Mayor Koch, Governor Carey, Anne Ford and Bess Myerson.
Troika Three: Sinatra, Johnny Carson, Sulzberger and Grace Mirabella of *Vogue*.
Troika Four: John Fairchild, Woody Allen, Helen Gurley Brown, David Brown and Rona Barrett.
Troika Five: Streisand, Peters, Barbara Walters . . .

Something disturbed her in her devout contemplation, some movement that should not yet be there in that bright, waiting, flower-filled pavilion. No, Candice thought, no, that simply could not be Theseus. He was NOT ON HER LIST. Big, hairy and, for once, horribly frisky rather than sly, the terrifying beast bounded into the pavilion, hanging his head in a sinister manner and looking at her in a leering fashion that obviously preceded some sort of attack. Candice was frozen in bewitched abhorrence. The dreadful animal sidled up to Candice, nuzzling her crotch in a yearning way that, had she but known it, was a serious compliment. She shivered in outrage.

"He likes you," Daisy said.

It was only then that Candice realized that Theseus was firmly attached to a leash of silver sequined ribbons into which a bunch of daisies had been threaded. She was saved from whimpering out loud. Still not daring to raise her eyes, she quavered pitifully, "Daisy, exactly what breed of *chien* is that, for God's sake?"

"A noble lurcher," Daisy answered, settling the question forever.

As Daisy advanced, all the lights in the room broke into millions of sticks of splintering brilliance as they were reflected by her dress. It was paved with silver sequins and, at the narrow waist, bands of gold and bronze sequins had been woven into trompe l'oeil ribbons. The same bands formed a great bow at the high neck and defined a wide hem. The dress was a concentration of matchless theatricality such as no one had dared to wear in the last fifty years—a once-in-a-lifetime gown, fit only to be given to a museum after tonight.

Daisy and Patrick Shannon, with Theseus between them, crossed the pavilion and stepped outside where a silver-lacquered, flower-filled troika waited for them. The muscular driver looked at the three of them kindly.

"Let me know when you're ready and then sit back and brace yourselves," he announced.

"Please," said Daisy, "give me the reins. You can get down and drive the next troika."

"But you can't drive this thing, Miss," the man replied, shocked.

"If I can't," she laughed, "then there's no such thing as heredity."

"It's at your own risk," he warned her.

"Perhaps . . . but that's not going to stop me."

Recognizing defeat, the driver jumped out, muttering to himself.

Princess Daisy Valensky rose, in one fluid, untroubled motion, and placing her weight equally and firmly on both feet, her arms extended, gathered in the six reins with a movement that made the night sing. At her touch the three white horses quieted, gentled down, waiting. Shannon and Theseus both sat easily, looking up at her. She was strong, pliant, serene, joyous, mistress and servant of the moment.

"Well?" she asked questioningly to Shannon, "how do you feel about 'Tallyho'?"

"I sort of prefer, 'Lafayette, we are here,' " he answered.

"But why not *en avant?*" Daisy asked, prolonging the delight.

"Perhaps even a simple giddy-up would do," he replied, feeling an instant's worth of pity for all the men in the world who were not Patrick Shannon.

The silver bells of the horses jingled sweetly in the night and, with one effortless gesture of authority, so flawless, so decisive that she needed no words of command, Daisy started the three white horses at a gallop, racing the troika over the snow toward the lights she knew were beckoning in the distance.

Judith Krantz
&
Princess Daisy

Faced with the challenge of what to write after the fabulous success of her first novel, SCRUPLES, Mrs. Krantz searched for her next subject. As she tells it, the idea of writing about "an American princess" occurred to her about two years ago, after the press began to publicize the adventures of Grace Kelly's daughter Princess Caroline of Monaco, and Princess Yasmin (daughter of the Aga Khan and Rita Hayworth). But Mrs. Krantz emphasizes that PRINCESS DAISY is not a roman à clef, "the characters all come straight from my imagination."

For the first half of the two years she spent on the novel, she researched St. Petersburg aristocracy, tuberculosis cures in Switzerland, polo, and lurchers—the exotic type of hunting dog that Daisy owns. Since the Princess turns into a working girl and produces TV commercials, Mrs. Krantz spent a month on location—a world she knew as the daughter of an ad agency owner. She relates, "my mother says the first word I knew was 'orange juice,' the second was 'client.'"

She adds, "I could never write about a woman who didn't work. I couldn't feel emotionally involved." Since her graduation from Wellesley College she has "never had a day when I didn't have to face a deadline. It was understood in our house that when a girl grows up, she gets a job."

After her research, the author worked six days a week at her typewriter, becoming so well acquainted with the character of Daisy that, "I came to feel Daisy was a real person." Mrs. Krantz also believes PRINCESS DAISY will attract a much wider audience than did SCRUPLES. She states, "Daisy is a more well-rounded and lovable character than Billy Ikehorn. She's steadfast, loyal, hardworking—and not a rich woman."

Golden Hill

SHIRLEY LORD

Set on the exotic island paradise of Trinidad, *Golden Hill* tells the story of three families whose destinies interweave to shape the history of the island. It is a passionate story of love and hate, lust and greed, malice and envy in which the members of the three families struggle and clash violently against the background of the depression, World War II, and the island's fight for independence.

"*Golden Hill* is indeed golden and glorious. I don't know when I've enjoyed a novel as much. It is insanely romantic and at the same time historically fascinating. It is as sensuous as a Caribbean night and the characters are memorable"

David Brown, co-producer of *Jaws*

0 552 12346 3   £2.50

CORGI BOOKS

The Debutantes

June Flaum Singer

They are the golden girls. A quartet of blue-blooded beauties whose names and faces fill the society pages. Poor little rich girls whose glamorous exploits make international headlines – but whose tortured private lives are the hidden price of fame:

Chrissy, survivor of a notorious custody battle between her mother and her grandmother, with a fatal weakness for all the wrong men . . .

Maeve, daughter of the celebrated Padraic, and Daddy's little girl in every sense . . .

Sara, whose father could hide his Jewish origins from the world, but couldn't hide his taste for lechery from his blackmailing daughter . . .

Marlena, Sara's poor cousin from the South, swept into a world of affluence she couldn't quite handle . . .

0 552 12118 5 £1.95

CORGI BOOKS

JUDITH KRANTZ
MISTRAL'S DAUGHTER

Maggy, Teddy and Fauve – they were three generations of
magnificent red-haired beauties born to scandal, bred to
success, bound to a single extraordinary man – Julien
Mistral, the painter, the genius, the lover whose passions
had seared them all.

From the '20s Paris of Chanel, Colette, Picasso and
Matisse to New York's sizzling new modelling agencies of
the '50s, to the model wars of the '70s, *Mistral's Daughter*
captures the explosive glamour of life at the top of the
worlds of art and high fashion. Judith Krantz has given
us a glittering international tale as unforgettable as
Scruples, as spellbinding as *Princess Daisy*.

0 552 12392 7   £2.95

CORGI BOOKS

Helen VanSlyke

SISTERS AND STRANGERS

Three sisters return home to celebrate their parents' Golden Wedding Anniversary. Thirty years have passed since they were together.

Alice pines to find the son she has not seen since he was born. . .

Frances returns home famous, sophisticated, rich — and jaded. . .

Barbara has wasted her youth as the mistress of a famous congressman. Will he reject her to avoid a scandal?

Within days, the lives of all the sisters will change dramatically. . .

0 552 11321 2   £1.95

CORGI BOOKS

A SELECTED LIST OF NOVELS
FROM CORGI BOOKS

WHILE EVERY EFFORT IS MADE TO KEEP PRICES LOW, IT IS SOME-TIMES NECESSARY TO INCREASE PRICES AT SHORT NOTICE. CORGI BOOKS RESERVE THE RIGHT TO SHOW NEW RETAIL PRICES ON COVERS WHICH MAY DIFFER FROM THOSE PREVIOUSLY ADVERTISED IN THE TEXT OR ELSEWHERE.

THE PRICES SHOWN BELOW WERE CORRECT AT THE TIME OF GOING TO PRESS (AUGUST '84).

All these books are available at your book shop or newsagent, or can be ordered direct from the publisher. Just tick the titles you want and fill in the form below.

CORGI BOOKS, Cash Sales Department, P.O. Box 11, Falmouth, Cornwall.

Please send cheque or postal order, no currency.

Please allow cost of book(s) plus the following for postage and packing:

U.K. Customers—Allow 45p for the first book, 20p for the second book and 14p for each additional book ordered, to a maximum charge of £1.63.

B.F.P.O. and Eire—Allow 45p for the first book, 20p for the second book plus 14p per copy for the next seven books, thereafter 8p per book.

Overseas Customers—Allow 75p for the first book and 21p per copy for each additional book.

NAME (Block Letters) ....

ADDRESS ....

....